the Moroccan Empire Series

MELISSA ADDEY

The Moroccan Empire Series

Published by Letterpress Publishing

Cover and Formatting: Streetlight Graphics

Map of the Almoravid empire by Maria Gandolfo

www.melissaaddey.com

Kindle: 978-1-910940-73-0
Epub: 978-1-910940-75-4
Paperback: 978-1-910940-74-7
Wide Distribution Paperback: 978-1-910940-76-1

Table of Contents

The Cup 1

A String of Silver Beads 85

None Such as She 277

Do Not Awaken Love 481

Interview with Melissa Addey 679

Current and forthcoming books include: 688

Biography 689

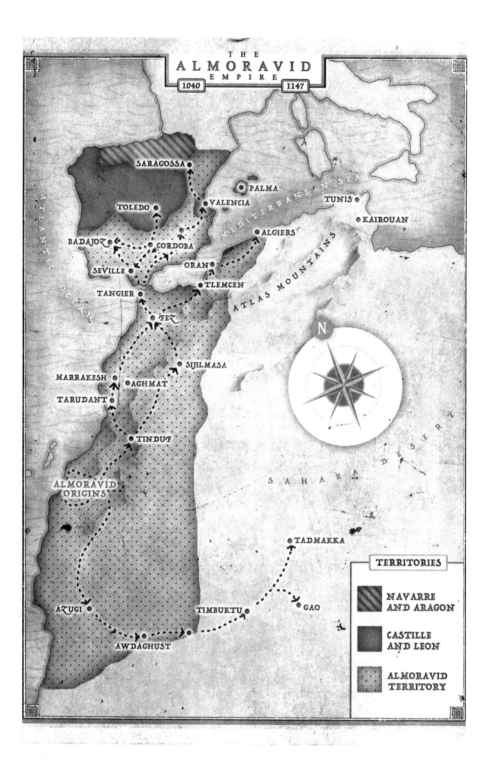

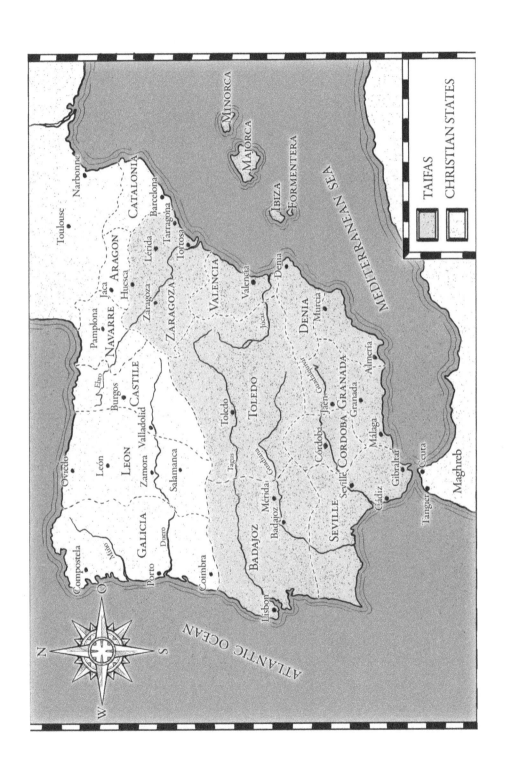

MELISSA ADDEY

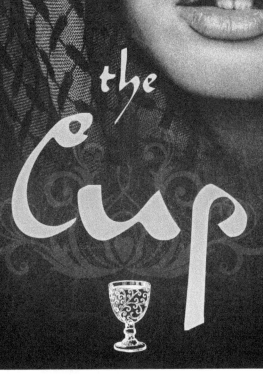

the

Cup

The Cup

For Ben

Black Feathers

They were so bright, these feathers. So bright. She loved the birds, perhaps they were easier for her to love than her husband, her daughter. The birds made her smile, a rare sight. Their chirrups and songs lightened our heavy house.

I wander the rooms, returning again and again to their cages. They could not escape their fate and perhaps neither can I. Now their feathers are black with the force of the fire and when I touch them they crumble beneath my fingertips, ashes falling to meet the ashes on the floor.

I did not mean for this to happen. I was a child with powers too great for a child when this began. I am not even sure when all this began, whether it was one moment or another.

My father was a trader of slaves when I was given the cup. That is as much of a beginning as I can be sure of.

The city of Kairouan, Tunisia

c. 1020

The Slave Woman

SLAVES SHOULD NOT BE SOLD in the hottest part of the day, they tremble on the block or sometimes faint away and no-one will buy a slave who shows signs of weakness. Besides, the customers grow weary of standing in the heat themselves and are unlikely to buy, growing ill-tempered and tight fisted. The heat today is reaching its zenith and my father is anxious to finish his work for the day and retire for food and drink.

"A fine man! Broad shoulders, calloused hands. Long legs. A good worker sir, he will serve you well."

There is a pause while my father watches his customer's face as he inspects the slave. Standing by his side I murmur something and my father pretends to give me water to drink, the better to hear me.

"He is afraid," I say, speaking directly into my father's ear. "A slave beat him once."

My father does not change expression, nor ask how I know. He pats me on the head before speaking loudly. "Be off with you, stop pestering me now, Hela. I have business to attend to." I move away and become wholly engrossed with a doll, a ragged little thing I have very little interest in. My father's camel whooshes in my ear and I slap its hairy face and stinking breath away from me.

My father turns back to his customer. "Of course, one must be careful with such an ox of a man that he has also a good temperament," he says. "One cannot be too careful." Without warning, he cuffs the slave's head. The unexpected blow causes him to stagger. He regains his stance looking a little bewildered but shows no sign of anger. I watch the customer's face relax in relief and know that my father has made a sale.

He makes many more sales that morning. A slave girl of unusual good looks to a man filled with lust, a giant of a slave to a man convinced his enemies are trying to kill him, a rounded slave woman suckling a child to a household where the mother needs a wet-nurse. Each time a slave is brought to the block I find some way to draw my father's attention to the person in the crowd most likely to pay a high price.

I feel them. I feel their desires, their needs, I feel their fears and hopes. I sense what they feel when they gaze at my father's wares, the silent men and women whose lives hang in the balance, their destinies chosen by me, a child barely ten years' old.

I feel the slaves as well, if they have feelings. Some of them do not. Their feelings have been buried somewhere so deep I cannot touch them, cannot penetrate beyond the numbness that fills the space where they should be. Sometimes I will feel their shriveled hopes and fulfil them if I can, a frightened and broken woman going to a lonely old mistress rather than a hard master. But I am a child and mostly I think of my father's profits and the little gifts he will give me if I choose well for him. When a customer pays more than a slave is worth because of their own desires, then my father will nod to me and I know that I will be rewarded. Perhaps with a fine leather belt, a sweetmeat, once even a kitten of my own. My father says that when I am a grown woman I should marry a slave trader myself, for I will undoubtedly bring him much success in his business. To my mother, when she enquires, he tells her in good humour that I am no trouble to him at all, that I may play nearby when the slave auctions are held and she smiles, thinking him a kindly man for indulging his little daughter's fondness for being near him. She does remind him, though, that as a girl, my place is with my mother and that one day soon I must learn her trade.

My mother is a quiet woman, a skilled woman. A wise woman. Her rooms are silent and cool, nothing like the heat and noise of the slave market. Neat jars line the walls, her pestles and mortars below them, ranked by size and use. Some may be used for more than one purpose, others are set far back and used for only one ingredient, for even their taint could be dangerous.

It is mostly other women who come to my mother. They enter hesitantly, greet her with respect and a little fear, whisper their needs. Sometimes my mother nods and bids them return another time for what they seek and they will disappear. Sometimes, if she can make what they ask for quickly, she will tell them they may wait. They do so, squatting by the door, as far away from her as they can manage. They watch her with hope as she chooses and grinds, mixes and pours. They look about them with awe at the myriad containers and most of all at the books.

My mother can read, a rare skill for a woman. She reads slowly, one arm cradling the heavy tomes, one finger tracing the words. Sometimes I see her struggle to mouth a new name. She spends time looking at the illustrations, nodding to herself at the uses for leaves, stems, roots, flowers and berries, seeds. She can write too, in a careful hand, each stroke laborious. She is careful because her little jars must not be confused one with another.

Sometimes I watch her when she is grinding herbs, but it seems dull work and I flit away soon enough, back to the noise and smells of the market.

Now there is only one slave left to sell. My father pursed his lips when he saw her and muttered under his breath. She is twisted, one shoulder higher than the other. Her body is scrawny, no tempting curves here to sate a man's desire. The few clothes she wears are mere scraps and at her waist she carries some kind of pouched bag, badly made from reddish leather. Where the other slaves stood still and silent behind the block, awaiting their turn to stand on it, their eyes cast down, the woman sits hunched up on the ground, her head twisting this way and that. Occasionally I hear words coming from her but she hails from the Dark Kingdom and I do not understand her. My father glances at me when he sees me looking at her and I shrug. I cannot feel her own desires and so I must think of who might want her, must spot them in the crowd and feel their need for her.

But when she mounts the block there is nothing in the crowd, already fast-dwindling. The woman limps when she walks, not a small limp but a strange, whole-body lurching. She would barely be able to carry water without it spilling. She may not sell at all and if she does not my father will be angry, he has no use for slaves who do not make him money. She stands for a moment and then sinks to a low crouch, my father cuffs her but she will not stand again.

My father tries to entice the crowd forwards. "She's strong enough," he says. "I've had bigger, stronger women die on the journey here, but I never heard a whimper from her. She may be a cripple but that won't stop her working. Might stop her running off though, eh?" he smiles.

The crowd begins to drift away. My father names a price for her but only receives shaking heads as a reply.

I look about me and spot one of the tannery-masters. I tug at my father's robe and he nods, climbs down from the block where he has been standing and joins the master, speaks smilingly with him. Anyone who works in the tanneries is likely to die soon enough, their skin scarred and burnt by the foul vats of stinking mess they use to soften and dye animal skins. It's a hard life, carrying heavy pails of bird droppings, water, lime and ash, your back bent beneath the burning heat of the sun, your legs trembling from the endless stamping down of the skins in the skin-stripping liquid. The tannery master buys plenty of slaves at a knock-down price: the old, the crippled, the mute or stupid and uses up what is left of their broken lives. My father does not usually sell much to them, for he prefers a better quality of stock but on this occasion he has been let down and he is not about to waste much time on such an unlikely proposition. I see the negotiations going on between them while closer to us the crowd has dispersed entirely.

I'm growing hungry and my father could be a while. If I set off now I will be home ahead of him to warn our household to prepare a meal. My mouth waters at the thought of fresh hot flatbreads dipped into *lablabi*, a thick soup of chickpeas and garlic, or perhaps wrapped around slices of spiced sausage. Maybe my mother will have made sweet *samsa*, nuts and pastry flavoured with rosewater syrup. If she has it is probably still cooling, made for the evening meal but I might beg some from her while it is still warm. I stand up.

"Girl."

I turn, surprised. The old cripple has spoken in my own language. "You can speak?"

She shakes her head. "Little." Her voice croaks, as though she has not spoken for a long time or is desperate for water. Either is possible.

I shrug. "You'll learn. You don't need many words at the tanneries."

She makes a slow gesture, a beckoning.

I step closer to her. I am not wary. My father is close by and what harm can she do me?

She is scrabbling about in the red pouch, searching for something among her meagre belongings. At last she pulls something from its depths and holds it out to me. It is a cup made of a dark carved wood, the carvings rough and not very clear, for the cup looks to have been used for many years, so that what were once sharply etched images are now almost smoothed away by the touch of many hands. It has been stained red at some time, but again the redness has been worn away, leaving it mottled here and there.

I look at her without touching the cup. "Your new master will give you water when you reach your home," I tell her, miming drinking and pointing to the tannery master, who is now nodding agreement with my father.

But she becomes agitated, perhaps realising she does not have a lot of time left before her new master will claim her. She thrusts the cup towards me and I reach out and take it, one finger brushing her skin as I do so.

The jolt knocks me to the ground. I lie there, clutching the cup to me, rage and an unholy power flowing through me as though I am possessed by a djinn. Above me the woman lurches to her feet and looks down on me over her twisted shoulder. Her eyes fix on mine and I whimper and wriggle away from her, but I do not let go of the cup. I have never sensed such feelings from a slave, nor even from any free-born man or woman. I have felt the uncontrolled rage of small children, stamping their feet at some perceived outrage, I have felt the power emanating from desert warriors but this... this is a rage that would make a grown man kneel in fear, a power that would topple kings. How can a crippled slave woman possess either? I stare up at her and she points at the cup.

"Yours," she rasps and then she smiles. It is a crippled smile, like her body, a lopsided thing that does not offer comfort.

I have spent the rest of my life wondering about her smile at that moment, whether she saw my abilities and meant to give me a gift or whether the cup was a curse on me for sending her to the tanneries.

I am still not sure.

My father rejoins us and does not notice anything amiss. I am upright again and the cup has disappeared into my own bag, a cheerful thing of yellow leather, a previous gift for my services. The slave woman is led away and although I watch her every step she never once looks back as she follows her new master across the square and into the dark souk beyond.

The next time I accompany my father I do not tell him anything useful, nor the time after that. I am wary of the slaves now, I do not trust the numbness that is in them. I am afraid of what they may do to me if I send them towards a bleak destiny and there are not many destinies I could choose that would not be bleak in one way or another. And so I am silent until finally he tells my mother, not unkindly, that it is time I learnt her trade, he cannot have a half-grown girl loitering near the slave block, it is not proper at my age. I must learn her trade and then I will be married.

My Mother's Rooms

EVEN MY MOTHER IS STARTLED by how fast I learn her skills. I learn to read at a pace that astonishes her and yet it is her jars that help me. I have only to unstopper one, to smell its contents and look at the label, the shapes marked there coming to mean that smell so that even now, I can read a word and at once inhale its scent from the empty air. My mother teaches me to read as she does everything: with a slow care but when she sees how fast I outstrip her, how I do not need to trace each stroke to know its sound, she allows me to touch her precious books and soon enough it becomes my task to read aloud to her.

She only has to tell me once the properties and uses of a plant and I remember it. She tests me over and over again, uncertain whether I have been lucky in my guesses, whether perhaps I have cheated her in some way but eventually she accepts that my memory does not lie. It takes her a while, however, to notice my other skills.

"Why did you give her that?" I ask.

My mother looks up. Her patient has left us, clutching a small pot to her. "The swelling may be helped by the application."

"But she is dying," I say, with all the hard truth of a child's tongue.

My mother gazes at me for a long time. "Why do you say that?"

"She smells sick," I say.

My mother's eyes narrow. "Smells?"

I nod, shrugging. Surely my mother can smell what I smelt? "It made me feel ill," I say. "It was like honey mixed with rotting meat."

My mother does not reply. But after each patient visits her, she looks to me and asks, "What did they smell of?"

Sometimes they smell of the food they have been cooking, or of the black olive soap from the hammams, sometimes of the rose perfume that Kairouan is famous for. Sometimes I smell the strange smell again. But I smell other things. I smell fear, happiness, despair. I smell anger, need, desire. Each has its own smell and sometimes it is so strong I cannot stand it and have to open the windows in my mother's room. When I do this she watches me and then she speaks with more care to her visitors, asks them more questions, until, often, they tell her what I had already scented in the air: their fear of a husband's fists or his belt, their desire for a person forbidden to them, their desperate need for a child to hold in their arms. They come for minor ailments, but they soon confess to greater wounds.

"You have been given a gift," says my mother, and she does not say it with smiling praise for her little daughter, she says it with the respect due to a fellow healer and perhaps a little fear at how easily her own skills fade beside me. Perhaps she expects me to show some pride, even arrogance at how easily I learn her skills, but when she says 'gift' I think only of the slave woman's cup, hidden in my room and I fall silent and bow my head.

Now a little room is set aside for me beside my mother's and here I am made to grind down roots and leaves, to preserve berries and flower petals. I take my place beside my mother when her patients visit and listen to their whispered confessions or groaning complaints. My mother will look to me, to see what I suggest, and I will stand before the tiny jars and choose one and another and my mother will nod, perhaps point to a third, or shake her head a little and suggest another choice. But she does not often have to correct me, as time goes by.

We visit the souk together and wander its narrow mazelike streets to find the stallholders who keep the items we need. Fenugreek, to make a woman's breasts swell with milk. Argan oil to make blood flow within the body more freely, black cumin to father a child. Sometimes we go to meet traders who are newly arrived in one of Kairouan's many caravanserai. They bring fresh supplies of ingredients but also powerful amulets and living plants for my mother's herb garden, which I learn to tend. The courtyard of our home is stacked everywhere with pots of plants that the slave girls are not permitted to touch, for some can bring death. Only my mother and I may care for them.

When I am free of tasks, I pore over my mother's books. She has only three, but they are huge and beautiful and she treasures them. Sometimes I take up her reed pen and try to draw what I see, the shapes of leaves, the petals curved like so, the tiny roots like hairs, creeping across the page. My mother nods at my efforts and allows me more paper, even though it is costly, as well as ink, although I have to make my own supplies, from the burnt-up wool and horns of sheep.

She allows me to sit in her place, to hear her patients' stories and they look startled at such a young girl taking on her mother's work so soon, but she only says, "She has a great talent, greater than mine," and they hurry to agree, hoping that perhaps there is healing in my hands.

When the first headache comes, I think I am going to die. The pain is so great that I cannot stand. I stagger to my room and fall onto my bed, my mother following me.

"My head," I say, and I can hardly speak above a whisper.

My mother makes the room dark, gives me the correct herbs, holds cooling cloths to my head and murmurs words of prayer. But the pain goes on so long I begin to weep. It feels as though a giant has a hold of my head and is slowly trying to pull it apart, as my father can split a ripe pomegranate in two with his bare hands.

The pain goes on and on. I try to sleep but it is impossible. At last there is a faint lessening and I cry again, from relief.

It is my mother, older and wiser than I, who notices the pattern after a while.

"Do the women's pains enter you, Hela?" she asks.

"When they are afraid I feel the fear," I tell her.

"And all their other feelings?"

I nod.

My mother sighs. "Too much for one body, to sense the feelings of a hundred others," she says. From that day she tells me to sit further away from the patients and I do not touch them if I can help it. The windows are kept open, no matter the weather. Slowly, the headaches lessen.

I grow taller than my mother. The years pass and my body forms into a woman. I am not beautiful. There is a stockiness about me, not the kind of womanly curves that other girls my age are beginning to flaunt, but a wide-shouldered solidity, like a working beast. My eyes are large but somewhat hooded rather than wide. My hair is good enough, long and dark, but I twist it up and wrap a cloth about it when I work and so its lustre is rarely seen.

At fifteen, I begin to build up my own tools and ingredients in my small work room. My mother allows me to go and purchase ingredients alone. When I walk the streets of Kairouan's souks, the traders nod and smile to me, each trying to court my attention, for if my mother and I purchase from them they can boast of having us as customers. Sometimes I stop to examine their wares, to sniff roots and touch leaves, but mostly I walk onwards, to the trader from whom my mother has been buying ingredients since before I was born. He is an affable man, rotund in body and offers a pleasant smile when he spots me.

"Ah Hela," he calls out. "I have freshly-picked caper buds if you have need of them for stomach pains."

I nod, looking over the contents of his stall. Ginger, rosemary, saltbush, ruta, pomegranates, cinnamon, cloves and many other ingredients are neatly laid out. I smell a few items and look up to see Moez, the trader's young son, hovering.

"*As-Salaam-Alaikum*, peace be unto you," he says, stumbling a little over his words, though he must say them a hundred times a day.

"*Wa-Alaikum-Salaam*, and unto you be peace," I say, my mind elsewhere. "I need anise and lemon balm, if you have them."

Moez hurries to serve me and I notice his fingers trembling. I meet his gaze and see him blush and half-smile to myself. It is always a little pleasing to a young girl to be desired, though shy Moez is not quite what I dream of when I dream of marriage, he is a little too young and awkward to make much of an impact on me. Still, I smile and nod as I depart, leaving him beaming.

One day I take the now-dusty red cup from where I had left it years ago in an old chest, clean it and place it on a shelf above me. I am not sure why, but it seems to me to be something connected to healing. I wonder if the slave woman was a healer herself and knew that it was my destiny. I do not use it at once. I tell myself it has no special properties and indeed five years ago is a long time now, long enough for me to question whether what I remember of my encounter with the slave woman was true at all. But still, I do not use it. It is only on a day when I am very busy, when the slave girls have not yet cleared away the many bowls and bottles I have been using that a young woman comes to see me. She says that my mother is busy and there are several women waiting but that she is willing to be treated by me, if I have time. She needs to be back home soon, her husband does not know she has come here.

I nod and she sits in front of me. Hesitantly, she confesses that she has been unable to have children, even though she is of fertile stock and young. She is afraid that her husband, whom she loves, will turn away his gaze and bring home another wife if she cannot bear him a child.

It is a common enough complaint and I have barely finished listening to her when I am already collecting the right jars and bottles to mix her a draught which she must take each day. It does not always work but occasionally a woman bears a child after she has seen us and so they all come. My mother shakes her head when we are alone and says that only Allah can grant a child. Still, I grind the ingredients, mix up the concoction until it has the right consistency and bottle most of it. The first draught, she must take now. I look about me for a cup but the only one to hand is the carved cup. I hesitate for a moment but, feeling her questioning gaze, I take it and pour the drink into the cup before passing it to her.

As our hands touch the woman gasps. The cup rocks, neither of us willing to hold it alone until I slowly release my grip and the woman holds it, her eyes wide.

"What did you do?" she asks. "I saw a baby in my arms, I heard it cry and knew it was mine."

I shake my head. "I do not know," I say truthfully. "It must be that your desire for a child is very strong." I improvise. "Drink," I add.

The woman nods and quickly drinks every drop, clutching at the cup as though she is afraid that the brew's efficacy will go if she hesitates.

When she has gone I turn the cup over in my hands and wonder at what has happened. I wash it with care and replace it on the shelf. I do not use it again. I have so many others, I excuse myself.

But the young woman is back when less than two moons have passed and she brings me more silver than I have ever been paid.

"I am with child," she says. "My husband sent you this. He says he is the happiest man in Kairouan. He smiles all day."

I take the silver and murmur something in reply, I am not sure what.

"It was the red cup, wasn't it?" she says, looking eagerly up at it on the shelf, where it has sat unused since her first visit. "It has a special power, does it not?"

I do not look at the cup behind me. "The herbs will have done you good," I say.

She nods and thanks me again and goes away but she has a busy mouth, for now one and then another woman asks if I will use 'the red cup' when I treat them. If I try to dissuade them, saying that one cup is much like another, they insist that they must drink from the cup.

And strange things happen when they do.

Often as I hand them the cup something passes between us, a shock as though a power jumps from one to the other, a pale copy of the jolt I felt from the slave woman so long ago.

One woman recovers even though my mother shook her head when she saw how ill she was and I had already smelt the smell of death upon her.

A child who had not spoken before speaks.

Woman upon woman finds herself with child when they had lost hope. My mother asks me what I give them and I shake my head and say that I give them what we have always given them. My mother frowns and says she has never known it to work so well. She asks about the red cup and I mumble something about it coming from the Dark Kingdom. My mother turns it in her hands but does not seem to feel anything when she does and shrugs, saying that it is my own healing abilities that the women are benefiting from and that their nonsense about a cup is only superstition. To which I do not reply.

By the time I am seventeen I have amassed a sum of silver that would mark me as rich, for a healer. Women give me their jewellery, their husbands send coins, as many as they can spare, for my name is now known across the city of Kairouan. Now it is my mother who grinds ingredients for me, who washes the pots and cups, the pestles and mortars, who tidies the workrooms. I am too busy, there is a never-ending line of people who wait, squatting on the stairs leading to my consulting room. And always, always, I must use the red cup or face their disappointment.

The Boy with the Red Lips

*I*T IS HIS LIPS I notice first. They are full and so red that the first time I see him I believe he has been hurt, that his lips are bleeding and that he is standing in my room to be healed. But it is his mother, a woman named Safa, that he has accompanied here. She is the wife of a copper merchant in the city. She wants some minor cure, for a cough or some such and I mix what is needed without knowing what I am doing, my hands moving alone from years of practice. When I let her sip from the cup she shudders. She rises to leave but I stop her, my hand on her richly decorated robes.

"You must come every day," I say. I can see she is wealthy, she will not baulk at the price.

"Is it worse than a cough, *Lalla*?" asks the woman fearfully, using the term of respect I have heard more and more often over the years.

"N-no," I say. "But I am giving you a new remedy. It must only be taken here, under my supervision. It is very efficacious," I add quickly. "You will be well very soon."

She leaves me murmuring thanks, which I do not hear. Every part of me is focused on her son, on his red lips.

Each day she comes and each day I see something else in him. His red lips give way to the darkness of his eyes, to his black curls, the golden-brown of his skin, the ripple of the muscles of his forearm when it emerges from beneath his robes to help his mother up. I do not know what I give his mother but when I see that she is indeed getting better I grow desperate. When she is well she will no longer come to me and nor will her son. He is strong and healthy. I may never see him again.

"A woman has asked for a love potion," I tell my mother, standing behind her while she cooks our dinner.

My mother laughs. "There is no such thing. Love comes when it wishes."

My mother has never believed in such things although plenty of other healers offer love philtres and other, perhaps darker concoctions for those whose feelings have run away with them. Magic is part of most healers' work throughout the Maghreb and beyond, but my mother has always trusted only in her knowledge of plants, in the leaves and berries and roots. She says magic is not her place to know.

"But one could excite the pulses or quicken the heart," I say, thinking of my own heart and how it pounds when he stands near me.

My mother shakes her head. "It is not the same thing."

"Or excite the male member…" I say. I do not blush to say this as I should. I have spoken of such things many times. My face is pale with concentration.

My mother shrugs. "That is between a husband and wife," she says. "Does her husband have such difficulties?"

"I – I did not ask," I manage.

My mother makes a face that shows she does not think very highly of me if I have not even asked such a simple question. "Tell her she must give you more information," she says and goes back to the cooking.

It is night and I do not sleep. I have not slept well for many days, since I first saw the shape of his lips, their blood-red curves. At last I get up from my bed and I make my way to the healing rooms. I open the shutters and a full moon lights the room so that I do not even light the lantern that I meant to use. The night air is cool and my half-naked body shivers.

I place a hand on one jar and then another. I smell their properties without removing the stoppers. I think what each will do when it enters the body, what they might do when mixed together. I do not take down the jars, only touch each one while in my mind the boy appears, his eyes lit up with desire, with love for me.

The next day before his mother arrives I make up her medicine and have it ready in a small bottle of its own. Then I take down the cup. I think of what it does, for I have had time to watch its work, these past years. I have come to believe that it intensifies the desire of the person who drinks from it, that whatever I mix takes on added power from their need for a child or a cure. The greater their desire, the more the cup makes powerful my own skills as a healer.

Now I turn the cup in my hands. I have never mixed anything inside the cup, I only pour into it what has already been made. What if I were to mix the potion I have in mind within the cup itself? Will it add to its power? Will my own desire affect the drink I make? I have never added my own desires to the cup, it has been my patients who have added theirs. Will my love, my lust, pass from me to him when he presses his lips against it and drinks?

As I mix together quantities from each bottle that I touched in the dark of moonlight last night I allow myself to think of him, to unleash the desire I feel for him into my fingers as I stir. At last, as I hear footsteps on the stairs leading to my room, I press my own lips against the cup. When I set it down, my hands shake.

Safa settles herself on the floor opposite me while her son gazes, bored, out of the window. I cannot help but admire his silhouette with the light behind him, each part of his profile outlined as though for my gaze alone.

Safa is all smiles. "I feel healthy again, *Lalla*," she tells me. "You are gifted."

"I am glad you are better," I manage. "I will give you one final draught and then you will be entirely well. But – but before you go I thought that perhaps your son should also drink a preventative. I would not want your cough to spread to other members of your household."

Safa looks a little surprised, glancing over her shoulder at her son. "Faheem? He is strong as an ox, but if you think it best…"

Faheem, I think. I had not known his name until now. *Faheem*. "Yes," I say, trying to keep my voice clear and firm. "He should have a mixture I have prepared. I am certain it will be good for him. One cannot be too careful."

Safa nods, "Of course. Drink this," she orders her son, waving towards the cup, which I am holding out.

Faheem steps forwards and takes the cup from me. One slender fingertip brushes mine and I rock back, placing my hands on the floor where no-one can see them shaking. The wave of desire I felt as we touched frightens me. It is what I feel for him but magnified so greatly that I want to snatch the cup back from him. It is too much, I think. Too much for one body to stand. But it is too late for me to countermand my own orders. His red lips press against where my own lips were moments ago and instead of a girl's foolish pleasure at the thought of it I feel my face draining of colour with fear. I take back the cup, wash it, fill it with Safa's innocuous mixture, watch her drink it. I do not hear her thanks, nor do I see Faheem's face as they leave, for I dare not raise my eyes.

If I had known that I would not see him again alive, perhaps I would have raised my eyes and looked once more at those red lips, perhaps I would have summoned every part of my boldness and traced them with one fingertip, the better to recall them when it was already too late to save him.

I hear nothing. Late at night I lie awake and wonder what I expect to hear. That Faheem has asked for my hand in marriage? His family is well off, the copper pots they make can be found in half the households of Kairouan. Would they even wish for such an alliance? Is he, even now, begging his father to relent and allow marriage to a healer? I hear him reminding them that I am not some purveyor of whispers and nonsense, mixtures of who knows what. I can read and write, I am known as the best healer in the city. My father is a slave trader, we have a comfortable home.

But days go by and I hear nothing. The moon wanes and rises full again and I hear nothing. I cannot bring myself to ask questions. I am silent. I do my work.

And then Safa arrives. Alone. Her face is drawn, she looks older than the last time I saw her, only a month ago.

"*Lalla*," she sighs, settling in front of me. "I have need of your skills."

I try to swallow. "Ask and I will do all I can," I say, my voice croaking with a sudden dryness.

"My daughter Djalila refuses to be married. She will not eat. She grows thinner by the day and nothing we have done helps. After what has happened to us, my husband is distraught. He cannot lose another child."

I feel a terrible coldness settle on me. "What – what happened to your family?"

She looks at me wide-eyed. "You did not hear?"

I shake my head.

"My son Faheem, whom you saw when I came here before, he – he died."

I force my lips to move. "Died?"

She nods and her eyes fill. I wait while tears trickle down her face and she wipes them away. "He said his heart pounded, that his hands shook and his lips burnt. He died in less than a day. We thought it was a fever. I would have come to you, *Lalla,* for your healing hands but it was so quick."

My heart pounded for him, my hands shook at his red lips. Dark red wood against which I pressed my mouth. I take her hands, murmur the words that should be said, offering my condolences, meaningless words of comfort. I look into her eyes for blame and see nothing. Why should she suspect me, the best healer in Kairouan? Her only regret lies in not rushing for my aid.

I tell her that I am busy today but that tomorrow I will come to her house, meet with her daughter Djalila who refuses to leave her rooms. I embrace her, watch her wipe away more tears and escort her from my rooms back to a waiting servant who will accompany her home.

All of that day I mix and pour, speak words I no longer recall, watch as one mouth after another presses against the redness of the cup and when evening comes I make my excuses to my mother, tell her I do not feel like eating, retreat to my room.

The moon is bright again. I try to sleep but it wakes me again and again or maybe it is the dreams I do not have. I long for nightmares to punish me, to frighten me and yet there is nothing, only falling darkness when I sleep and the moon's too-bright gaze when I awake. At last I rise and make my way back to the healing rooms. I stand, naked and alone, staring at the red cup. When I throw it as hard as I can against the wall I expect to see it crack in two but it only falls to the floor, unharmed, its mottled red colour lit by moonshine. I am afraid to touch it again.

Djalila

I KNOW THE PUNISHMENT FOR MURDER of course. I should pay *diyah*, blood money, to the family of Faheem and beg for their forgiveness, although they may refuse and ask instead for my death in recompense for their loss. If they grant me forgiveness then I should complete my atonement by undertaking to free a slave, feeding sixty poor people and keeping sixty fasts.

It does not seem enough. How can any of that be enough for taking Faheem's innocent life? How can my reckless desire be atoned for with mere fasting and feeding the poor? The silver I have amassed from my healing over the years would be enough to pay the *diyah*, but how can silver pay for the last breath leaving Faheem's red lips?

It is not enough. None of this would be enough, even if I were to confess – and who would believe me, a great healer of Kairouan, if I said that my desire for Faheem had made his heart pound until it broke? No, they would not believe me and my sin would go unpunished.

And so as the dawn call to prayer rings out across the city, I kneel to Allah and I make a vow. I will make amends for what I have done in my own way. I will serve Faheem's family until the day I die and still, in my own heart, it will not be enough. I am cold with certainty and purpose. I claim no reward, I make no bargain, for who am I to bargain? I state only my decision, I do not ask that it is enough to expiate my sin.

My mother shakes her head. "Forever? You are only eighteen. You have your whole life before you. Don't be ridiculous."

I continue packing my clothes into a carved wooden chest. "As long as the girl needs me, I will serve her."

"But why?"

"Because I owe a debt."

My mother comes close to me, peers into my face. "What debt can you possibly have?"

I shake my head. "I cannot speak of it."

My mother begs my father to speak with me and he does, but our conversation goes round in circles, with him reminding me that as an eighteen-year old respected healer I surely owe no debt to anyone and what of my own life, my own future marriage?

To which I only reply that I cannot explain.

My mother tries weeping and for one brief moment I think my father is going to try his fists on me but at last they give up, agreeing between themselves that perhaps once I have helped this sick girl and she recovers (as surely she will in my care), I will put aside this nonsense and return home. To which I do not respond, only embrace my mother and father and ask for their blessing, which they reluctantly give.

The next morning I walk through the streets while the dawn call to prayer echoes around me, the hood of my robe pulled up over my head. Behind me come two slaves, carrying the chest that holds all my possessions, such as they are. My silver I have already given to the poor, keeping only a few coins for myself.

Within a high wall sits the door into Safa's home. I do not call for a servant, I push the door with the palm of my hand and it opens onto the large courtyard of the house, a tinkling fountain surrounded by an elaborate tiled floor set all about with ornately carved and painted doors. This family has money. A servant carrying water pauses at the sight of me: an unexpected visitor at a too-early hour when half the family are still abed.

"Your mistress, Safa, sent for me," I tell her. "I am to see the daughter of the house, Djalila. Where is she?"

The girl hesitates but the fact that I have two slaves with me, my steady stare and the use of the family's names seems to convince her that I should be obeyed. "Her rooms are through there," she tells me. "Upstairs. The green door."

I dismiss the slaves, telling them to leave the chest in the courtyard. They begin to bid me farewell but I am already walking up the cold stone steps where I find a green-painted door. Again I do not wait to announce myself nor to be invited to enter. I open the door and approach the bed on which a girl lies sleeping.

I pause. The same red lips as her brother. Her hair as beautiful, but far longer. The same honey-gold skin. For several moments I stand over her and watch her breath rise and fall. At last I sit by her and turn over her wrist, let my fingertips rest on her pulse. Her eyes open in an instant.

"Who are you?" she demands, snatching her arm away from me and sitting up, gathering her sleeping robes about her in a flurry of movement.

I sit still and look her over. Her arms are mostly bare and they are thinner than I have seen on street children or poorly-treated slaves. Her neck is scrawny, her cheekbones stick out too much, giving her the look of a hungry cat.

"Who are you and what are you doing in my room?" she yells at me.

"I am a healer," I say. "My name is Hela."

"I don't need a healer," she says. "Get out."

"You look ill," I say.

"My brother is dead!" she spits at me.

I swallow and steady my voice. It takes me a moment. "I know," I say. "I would have done anything to save him if I had known of his illness. Now I am here to help you."

"Did you know him?"

If she had asked me before he died I would have said yes. Yes, I knew him. I knew every tiny detail of his face, of his scent. He was all I thought of, of course I knew him. Now I know better. I shake my head. "I only saw him from a distance," I say. "You look like him," I cannot help adding. I do not say *your red lips*, but I think it.

Slowly she sits down on the other side of the bed from me. "He was my hero," she says. "My protector. Now I am all alone." Her eyes brim over with tears.

"You have your mother," I say. "Your father."

The tears stop abruptly. She sits very straight. "Get out," she says. "You know nothing of my life."

"It is not a happy life," I say.

She startles. "How do you know?"

I shrug. "You are half starved. You are grieving." I reach out and touch her lightly on her bare arm and feel a wave of fear course through me. "You are afraid."

She is defiant. "Of what?"

I shake my head. "I don't know. Only you know who or what you are afraid of. I feel the fear, I do not know the cause. For now."

"And if you did know, you would save me?" she spits.

"Yes," I say.

She half-laughs, a bitter sound. "You wouldn't know where to start."

I stand up.

"Where are you going?"

"Downstairs."

"Don't leave me," she says and then looks down as though the words had escaped without her permission.

"I will be staying here," I tell her.

"For how long?" she challenges me.

"Forever, if I am needed," I say.

When I find Safa I tell her that I will be living in this house and serving her daughter until she is well. I do not tell her of my vow. One thing at a time, I think. When she exclaims at my plan I fix her with my most commanding stare and tell her that I will not leave this place until her daughter is well again. She, flustered, orders the servants that I am to be obeyed as though I were their mistress before blessing me and weeping. Unmoved, I leave her. Her blessings are meaningless, for she would be cursing me if she knew the truth. I return to Djalila's room.

"Get dressed," I tell her.

"I don't want to," she says, still muffled by her blankets.

"Rise," I say.

Something in my voice makes her struggle to a sitting position.

"I have told the slaves to bring hot water," I tell her. "Now you will wash."

"Leave the room," she says.

I shake my head.

"I will not undress in front of you," she says.

I stand, waiting.

Slowly, reluctantly, she strips off her sleeping robe and stands before me. She does not meet my eyes.

She is well formed enough, apart from her unnatural thinness. But her hair is lank and uncombed and she stands hunched, protecting herself from some unseen enemy. Near her shoulders and on the upper part of her thighs are bruises.

I kneel before my chest. I had the slaves bring it to the small room adjacent to Djalila's. I open the lid and have to take a deep breath. My mother has placed the red cup on top of the contents, perhaps believing that I would wish to have it and that I had left it behind by mistake. Carefully, I remove it and set it aside. I take out a small jar of ointment and smear it onto each bruise.

"Don't you want to know how I got them?" Djalila demands and I hear her voice tremble with the longing to tell me.

"You will tell me when you wish to," I say.

"I cannot," she says quickly.

"Then I will not ask you," I say. "You will tell me when you wish to."

She stands uncertain, then washes herself in silence, dresses in a robe too large for her.

"That does not fit you," I tell her. "I doubt it fitted you even when you were not this thin."

"I like my robes large," she says.

I look into her dark eyes and see fear there.

She says that she eats only in her own rooms but I make her follow me to the rooftop terrace, where a bright awning billows in the breeze and soft cushions are laid out for our comfort. Servants bring food and I watch while Djalila drinks tea but only picks at the freshly-cooked flatbreads until they are shredded into tiny crumbs, none of which have entered her mouth. I offer her a sorghum porridge and then boiled eggs but although she makes a great show of stirring the porridge and adding honey to it and then peeling the eggs, still none of the food is eaten. Her mother arrives while we are eating and fusses and frets until I ask her to leave us, which she does, looking back over her shoulder as though I am about to make a miracle happen.

We sit in silence for a while. I eat, for the food is good and I am hungry. My mind is mulling over what I have seen so far but as yet I have not understood why Djalila should be so thin, so fearful. I am drinking tea when I feel a wave of terror rise from her as a shadow falls over us. I look up.

"So you are the healer," says the man standing before us.

"I am," I say.

"I am Djalila's father," he says.

I stay silent but in my mind something settles into still certainty.

"I am grateful for your concern," he says. "But it will not be necessary for you to stay here. My daughter is well enough. It is her mother who thinks there is something wrong with her."

I do not look at him, only sip my tea. When I set down the cup I speak. "I will be here as long as she has need of me," I tell him.

"You will leave this house at once."

I stand in one fluid movement and step towards him. We are so close I can smell his breath. He towers over me but I do not break my gaze. "I will not," I tell him.

He raises his hand. "You will leave my house, you interfering bitch," he says.

"Do you wish me to explain to your wife why your daughter is like this?" I ask him. "Because I know."

His hand stops, mid-air. "You – " he begins but he does not finish. He looks at Djalila and then back at me. His hand drops to his side.

I gesture to Djalila without looking at her. "We will return to your room," I tell her.

She gets up quickly and scurries away from us both down the stairs. I look her father in the eyes. "If you wish to lay hands on some girl," I tell him, "go lie with a street woman who at least will be paid for her troubles. Do not touch your own daughter, you piece of filth."

He stands in silence as I leave the roof terrace and from that day onwards I barely see him. If we enter a room, he will quickly find some excuse why he must leave. In this way I am free to try and heal Djalila.

Day by day I entice her to eat. A little mouthful here, a scrap there. I make my way to the kitchen where I tell the cook to serve fat-streaked meat and dainty pastries soaked in honey and oil. Each mouthful she eats must be worth five. The cook has known Djalila since she was a child, she sets to with a will, making her favourite meals and adding richness to them. She serves them up in the tiny portions that are all Djalila will tolerate. She is my ally.

Slowly, slowly, Djalila recovers some flesh on her too-evident bones. I doubt she will ever attain rounded curves, but at least she does not look half-starved.

"You must marry," I tell her, when I see her smile for the first time in the three months that I have been her handmaiden.

Her face goes pale. "I do not want to marry!"

"You need to leave this house," I tell her. "You need to be the mistress of your own home or you will be forever looking over your shoulder, afraid your father is about to enter the room."

"He would not dare touch me now you are here," she tells me.

I shake my head. "Even if he never touches you again," I say, "why would you want to live under the same roof as him? If you had a good man you would be happy and free."

She looks afraid. "How would I know he would be a good man?"

"I will find one," I promise her. "But you need to leave this house."

I tell her mother that Djalila should be married and Safa, encouraged by Djalila's small improvements, calls on the matchmakers of the city to make it known that her daughter is ready for a husband. There is no shortage of offers for the family is well-off and Djalila is beautiful. Various suitors call on the family and with each of them I allow one fingertip to brush them as they pass me, I watch them as they meet with Djalila, who sits quiet and reserved in her still too-big robes.

Some are too passionate, too stricken with desire for her when they see her. Their lust is too great, they will frighten her, remind her of the suffering she has undergone. Others are too old, too much like her father and I can see for myself that she shrinks under their gaze. Some are very young and although a few fall in love with her I shake my head. Djalila needs a man who can be patient, who can woo her and bring her back to this world, who can bring her joy without demanding anything from her.

The man I choose for Djalila is named Ibrahim. He is the eldest son of one of the best carpet makers and traders in the city, a good and even match. Ibrahim himself is young, still in his twenties and although I can see his admiration for Djalila when he sets eyes on her, there is a softness, a sweetness to him that bodes well. He speaks to her of simple things – of the spring flowers opening up around the city and of his family, of his mother's fondness for cooking and his father's rounded belly and Djalila even smiles a little, she watches him when he leaves. When we are alone I nod and Djalila, still uncertain, nods back.

I visit his family's workshops without announcing myself, claiming that my unnamed mistress needs a new carpet for her rooms. Kairouan is renowned throughout the trading routes for its carpets. Ibrahim's family make some of the very best that the city can boast.

The workshop I visit is a chattering place, where the women who knot the carpets gossip amongst themselves. The looms sit before them, threaded in white. Bright balls of thread sit above their heads, trailing their colours down towards the women whose hands knot over and over again in quick movements. Each has a little knife to cut off a colour when she has no further use for it and reaches for another, barely glancing at the pattern as the carpets grow under their fingers, one thread, one knot, at a time. It is delicate work suited to women and those who work here are grateful to have secured such an occupation, prized work undertaken in a clean bright space. Not for them the dust of the potteries for women who paint the designs of pots, nor the close stench of the tanneries for the women whose families work in the leather trade. Their ears do not ring to the heavy beating of copper pots like the workers in Djalila's family business. Here the women can talk while they work and their surroundings are perfumed with roses, for Ibrahim's family believe in scenting the air so that their sought-after carpets will perfume the houses of their customers. I run my hand over the fine wares, feigning interest in their patterns while I watch Ibrahim's family members as they go about their business. His father relies on his children's labour now, contenting himself with sitting in a corner of the workshop, sipping mint tea and jovially teasing them.

"Look at your youngest brother, Ibrahim, there's a way to sell a carpet to a woman, all sweet words and sidelong glances!"

Ibrahim laughs out loud. "He's nothing but a scoundrel and you'd better find him a wife, Father, before one of those ladies claims him for her own!"

Ibrahim's two sisters, as yet unmarried, look up from their work. They are elevated above the women who weave, for each has been taught how to design carpets and they sit musing over future creations, adding a swirl here or a flower there to satisfy their demanding eyes.

They giggle at the exchange and call to a servant to go and buy sweets from a nearby stall. "We can't be working on empty bellies!"

"You work on honey, nuts and pastries," reprimands their father with a grin. "And then turn your noses up at good home cooked food."

"Honey makes the carpets prettier," returns the elder daughter with a smirk, passing a few sweetmeats to the working women.

Something loosens inside me. These are good people. They enjoy life and they relish one another's company. I am changing Djalila's life for the better. She will grow healthy in my care and perhaps her happiness will atone a little for Faheem's lost life. Perhaps she will be happy with a kind and gentle husband and slowly, slowly, I will be set free of the guilt that weighs me down so greatly that when I think of it I can barely lift one foot in front of the other.

Djalila's father catches me on the stairs.

"I forbid this marriage," he hisses at me.

"On what grounds?" I ask him.

He does not answer.

"If you wish to forbid the marriage," I say, "you had better announce your reasons for it before the whole family. And wait for me to have my say."

He stands silently in the shadows as I walk away and no more is said.

Meanwhile her mother is delighted and in no time all manner of fine silks are flowing into the house and Djalila, for once, must wear robes that are more suited to her slender form. When I see her dressed in a blue that rivals the sea, her long dark hair brushed loose as she tries on the golden headdress she will wear, there is a moment when I have to look away from her beauty, which reminds me too much of Faheem.

She is resplendent on her wedding day. The bridal headdress shines atop her magnificent black hair, her large dark eyes are a little wary but also filled with something resembling hope. Her father's face is a thundercloud but I curse him in my mind. The ceremony begins and she looks down in modesty but a little flush of colour rises on her cheeks and I follow her to Ibrahim's new home with relief. His parents have other sons and their families who live with them and so he has set up a home of his own close by to them where his bride will reign as mistress all alone, un-subjected to her in-laws, a rare freedom. I have chosen well.

The house is large. The courtyard is filled with flowers, a fountain splashes. A tree brings added shade within the cool of the tiled space. Above our heads stretch two more floors, glimpsed by balconies and carved plasterwork. The doors are thick wood, painted and carved to a high standard. This is a wealthy house, equal to or better than Djalila's old home. She has done well to secure such a husband.

A woman awaits us, large-breasted, wide-hipped, an air of authority. Slaves stand behind her, other servants peek at us from the entrance to the kitchen.

"I am Hayfa," she tells Djalila. "Your cook, mistress."

Djalila says nothing.

"I am Hela," I tell Hayfa. "I am your mistress' handmaiden and I will command in her place. My mistress does not like to be troubled with household matters."

I can see Hayfa wants to contest this statement. Who has ever heard of a handmaiden commanding in her mistress' place, unless that mistress is old or ill? She frowns but I keep my eyes on her and after a moment she drops her gaze.

"Very well," she mutters. "As my mistress desires."

"How many servants are there?" I ask.

"Four," she says. "And the slaves, of course." Clearly she does not think slaves are worth counting.

I nod. "Where are my mistress' rooms?" I ask.

Hayfa glances warily at Djalila, who has stood in silence throughout all of this. "I will take you," she says.

The servants and slaves watch us as we make our way up the stairs, no doubt wondering what their new mistress is like, sizing me up and speculating on my excessive power.

There are two rooms for Djalila, a bedroom and a larger room in which she may spend her days if she wishes for privacy. I hope that I will be able to entice her out of them. They are well appointed, there is nothing missing that a woman could wish for. Beautiful carpets and hangings, of course, as one might expect. The scent of roses throughout the house. Great carved chests of sweet-smelling wood await our possessions, which the slaves are now carrying up to us.

Hayfa shows us other parts of the house. There is a study where Ibrahim can keep track of his wares and sales, where the precious paper patterns are stored for safekeeping. On the shelves there are many books, perhaps more than twenty, great tomes made with skill.

"Your master reads?" I ask Hayfa. I am surprised. The richer merchants of the city can read well enough and certainly they know their numbers, to manage their accounts and supplies, but I know of none that read for pleasure.

"He wanted to be a scholar," says Hayfa. "But his father commanded he should take over the carpet business, being the eldest son. Still, he insisted on having books in his home." She looks at them with a mixture of pride and uneasiness, as though they are wild animals that might bite her. "He has scholars from the university to eat with him sometimes," she adds, her tone suggesting that this is a very odd pastime but that she is aware that it somehow makes her master important. "They talk all night."

I lift one down from the shelf.

"Don't touch them!" says Hayfa. "Master's orders are that no-one is to touch them."

I open the book. "*The Book of Fixed Stars*," I read. "It speaks of astronomy, the study of the heavens."

Hayfa stares at me, dumbfounded. "You can read?"

I nod, still turning the pages. I am impressed that Ibrahim has continued his interest in such things despite his father's attempts to turn him to a different path.

After this exchange I see that Hayfa treats me with greater respect although she never does get over her wariness of me. I do not gossip with her, I am no ordinary servant, I have too much power for her to relax in my company. She keeps to her realm and I keep to mine: she does as I tell her but speaks about me behind my back to the other servants as though I am some strange creature.

Djalila is shaking.

"He is a gentle man," I repeat. I have been saying this all day. "He will be kind to you," I add, hoping that this is true. "He will not force you. You must trust me."

She says nothing.

I apply rose perfume to her skin, brush out her long hair, undress her and place the bedcovers around her.

There is a soft knock at the door and Djalila clutches at me, her eyes wide.

"I have to go now," I say, trying to prise her fingers off my arm.

"Don't leave me," she whispers and I feel pity for her but what can I do? I cannot tell Ibrahim her history, nor can I refuse him entrance to his bride's bedchamber on their wedding night. As it is I have arranged for there not to be a crowd gathered about the place, cheering and making lewd comments. I pull my arm away and stand up, open the door to Ibrahim.

"My mistress is a little shy," I murmur to him. "You will be patient with her, master?"

He smiles as though I am a fussing old woman. "You may leave us now, Hela," he says and I bow my head and leave the room.

I wait and I listen. I hear Ibrahim speaking softly with her. I cannot make out what he is saying, yet he sounds very tender. There is little response from Djalila, I strain to hear her voice but am not sure she is answering him. I kneel and pray to Allah for this night to be successful, for Djalila to see that all can be well in the bedchamber.

Instead I hear a few little cries of fear and pain before there is silence and then Ibrahim's footsteps warn me to hide myself. I see him leave her room, his brow furrowed, walking swiftly to his own rooms.

Inside Djalila weeps.

"Did he..." I ask.

She shakes her head.

"He tried?"

She nods.

My shoulders slump. "He was gentle?" I ask.

She nods, miserable.

I sigh. "Then it will get better," I say firmly, though I am doubtful. "You will grow accustomed to him, he is gentle as I promised, he will not force you. You must only grow your courage a little, Djalila."

She sobs and I have to spend half the night comforting her. At breakfast Ibrahim is kind, he speaks softly with her, he offers her warm bread with honey and she takes it from him and tries to smile. I see his face lighten a little, no doubt he thinks the matter will soon be resolved.

But the nights pass and the shadows under my eyes grow dark from listening to one failed attempt after another and every night I praise Allah that Ibrahim has not forced himself upon her, as by now many men would have done. I beg for Ibrahim to have a little more patience. Meanwhile I try to build up Djalila's confidence and happiness in her new home.

I try to tempt her out into the streets. She is a married woman now, not a child, she need not cower in her rooms. Kairouan is a great city, a rich city. Sitting on the trading routes, it is home to people from across the Maghreb, for one day or a lifetime. I try to entice her out on the great market days, when thousands of people come from far and wide to buy and sell. I take her through the souks and suggest she might want to buy fine cloth to have robes made, sweetmeats, jewellery. Ibrahim is a generous husband, she can buy whatever she wishes for. But the jostling of the crowds, the blood running in the streets from the hundreds of animals slaughtered, the noise and smells make her shudder and beg to return to our peaceful courtyard, to the safety of her rooms.

I take her into the quieter countryside surrounding the city, where she can see the rich fields swaying with grain, the silvered leaves of ancient olive trees, the fat sheep whose wool supplies her husband with the means to weave the finest carpets of Kairouan. We watch as, before dawn, pickers bend to pluck rose petals before the heat takes their fragrance. They will make the rose oil that perfumes the women of the city and makes men tremble with desire. I try their wares and buy them for the house and workshop, but Djalila says the smell is too much and she turns away, stares at the rising sun's pale rays and the mists floating in the valleys.

We visit the reservoirs outside the city walls that bring water to the city. These great pools protect us from droughts and allow the fine households of the city to have playing fountains even in the great heat of summer. The pools are a deep green colour, dark as the depths of the water. Ibrahim tries to take Djalila there but she does not like the chatter and noise around her, the attention of other people. So I take her there during the daytimes when only street children play near them, splashing each other and laughing. She watches them as though she would like to join them and once or twice I splash her on purpose, to see if I can make her laugh, if she will forget herself and become the child she left behind but she cannot, she only shrinks from me and begs me not to do it again and so I desist and we sit in silence until I take her home again.

At last I think that perhaps she could gain confidence through faith, for some women find great solace in it. Kairouan is a holy city. The water from the Bi'r Barouta well is holy, for a river supposedly flows between here and Mecca. If you drink enough of it you are exempted from a visit to Mecca, so I take Djalila to the well, that she can drink and feel blessed. We stand by the blindfolded camel who trudges round and round to pull up the water. We drink the fresh cold water from little cups and I tell Djalila that she is a lucky woman to live in such a holy place. She sips from the cup and nods, silent and meek as a cowed child. I take her to pray at the towering mosque with its myriad ancient columns, but she is uncomfortable with crowds and prefers to pray in her own rooms. I do not know what she asks Allah for, what desires she has, for even to me she is closed.

I try to encourage her in meeting other young wives with whom she might pass the time. But on the few occasions when such a woman seems friendly, a neighbour, the wife of a fellow tradesman, Djalila shrinks from them, stays silent as though displeased and I see them falter in their speech, their smiles fade and they do not invite her back to their homes, do not return to visit ours.

At last I speak with her. "Ibrahim is a kind man," I tell her. "But the moon has waned twice since you were married and he will lose patience. You must succumb to him, you must be his wife in more than name, Djalila, or he may force himself upon you or even put you aside."

Her eyes well up.

"I know you are scared," I say to her. "I will ask him not to visit you often. But if you can give him some children you will secure your place as his wife and then he might even be persuaded to go elsewhere for his pleasures. Please, Djalila."

"Watch over me," she begs.

I gape at her. "I cannot watch you while you are with your husband," I say.

"I need you there," she says. "I feel safe when you are by my side."

I stand in the shadows where I will not be seen. My heart beats hard for I will be surely be turned out if Ibrahim catches me and yet Djalila asks this service of me and so I must obey, to try and secure her happiness. I try not to look but still I catch glimpses, of Ibrahim's body as he strips off his robes and his limbs intertwine with hers.

I cannot fault his patience. He offers gentle caresses and soft words, he uses his lips to touch her skin and his hands smooth her dark hair where it lies tumbled on the pillow. When he enters her he is not rough and his arms hold her with tenderness, though her hands stay clenched throughout and her eyes stay fixed on me over Ibrahim's muscled shoulders.

And so Ibrahim leaves her room with a smile rather than a frown, though it is I who has to hold her while she cries afterwards.

"You might come to enjoy it," I suggest, thinking of his soft words, his lips on her skin. But she only shakes her head in misery.

The next day Ibrahim gives her a magnificent necklace and places it smilingly about her neck, but she hides her face.

I follow him as he goes to his rooms. "I am sorry my mistress is not more willing," I say. "She is very timid. I ask on her behalf that you do not visit her too often, but I will tell you the days when she is most likely to conceive a child."

He is not best pleased, this I can see. But perhaps he believes that the matter will improve over time. "Very well," he says, his good humour lost as he turns away.

And so his visits to her rooms grow fewer and I need only watch their twisting shapes in the flickering light of lanterns for a few days in each month, sometimes casting my eyes down, sometimes drawn helplessly to watch. Djalila still shrinks from his touch but at least she does what is expected of her.

She has other duties. Ibrahim is firm on few things, but on this he is certain. "Your place is by my side when we entertain guests," he tells Djalila. "As my mother sits by my father's side. You must dress well, you must smile. A trader who buys carpets must think of luxury when he buys from us, of beauty and perfume, of comfort and generosity. Our carpets are not just the knots that make them but the reputation that goes before them."

And so Djalila dresses with care and descends to entertain guests. She twitches beforehand, she trembles but I stand in the room where she can see me and she learns to do this one thing well. She speaks little but she smiles and she stays by Ibrahim's side, no matter how late the evening wears on, no matter how dull the talk. Guests to the house notice her beauty. Her silence they take for the appropriate demureness of a woman from a good family and they praise her for it. They buy in large quantities from Ibrahim because of the quality of his hospitality and in turn Ibrahim smiles on Djalila, comforted that in this duty, at least, his wife is accomplished and a credit to him. On the nights when Ibrahim does not need to entertain traders he entertains his own choice of guests, philosophers and men of the law, holy men and they talk for many hours. On these nights Djalila is excused early and it is only I who stand in the shadows or squat outside the door, the better to learn from these men. The months pass and at last, at last, Djalila retches and turns pale. I place my hand on her and feel a new life beginning.

Ibrahim

ALL NIGHT I PACE WHILE the midwife attends to Djalila. Below, in the courtyard, Ibrahim matches my paces, step for step. He, perhaps, longs for a boy: I pray only that no harm comes to Djalila. Every cry she makes pierces me and I berate the midwife more than once.

"Give her something for the pain!" I shout at her at last, when Djalila's screams grow so loud that they rock the household.

The midwife is an old hag who has done her work for a great deal longer than I have been alive and she almost laughs at me.

"She is well enough," she says complacently. "The pain is normal."

"Make her stop screaming," I say through gritted teeth.

"You used to be a healer," she says. "You give her something."

I shake my head. "I do not use my skills," I say.

"Why not?" she asks, her eyes sharp and bright on me.

"Mind your own business," I tell her. "Make her stop screaming."

"She'll stop when the baby comes," she says.

I curse her and walk away, to another room, but Djalila shrieks for me not to leave her and so, reluctantly, I return to her side, to feel wave after wave of fear, Djalila's pain coursing through me so strongly that I nearly scream myself.

Time passes so slowly that I think there must be some trick being played on me. Surely the sun should rise, where is the dawn call to prayer? And still the night goes on.

At last Djalila's screams change and the midwife bestirs herself.

"The baby will come now," she says with certainty and she makes Djalila kneel on the bed.

When the tiny slippery body emerges the midwife barely holds it before passing it to me, wrapped in a cloth. I hold the mewling, wriggling, still-wet body in my hands and stare down at it.

"Boy or girl?" asks the midwife.

I pull the cloth a little to one side. "Girl," I say.

"Ah well, she is alive at least and has a strong cry," sniffs the midwife. "It will be a boy next time, if Allah wills it."

I offer the baby to Djalila but she is too weary. She holds the baby for only a moment and then passes her back to me and closes her eyes.

"Keep a watch on her," says the midwife. "Any sign of a fever, send for me. And make the baby suckle."

"How?" I ask but she is already gone.

Ibrahim stands outside the door, hovering tentatively. I give him the baby and he holds her as though she might break. He gazes down on the little body in delight.

"What will you name her?" I ask.

"Zaynab," he says, as though he has had this name ready for a long time. "Flower of the desert. She is a little flower." His voice is unsteady with tenderness.

I cannot help smiling at him and he returns the smile.

"I am sorry she is not a son," I offer politely.

He shrugs. "It is only the first child," he says, cheerful with relief. "There will be more and Allah will grant us a son."

I nod and take back Zaynab. Her fists ball up and she wails.

"I think she needs feeding," I say helplessly.

Ibrahim nods and backs away, leaving me alone with the baby and the sleeping Djalila.

Awkwardly I try to make the baby suckle but she does not seem to understand what to do. Gently I wake Djalila to help me, although since neither of us know how to encourage her, there is not much improvement.

"I am too tired," says Djalila, her eyes closing again.

She sleeps for a long time, during which the baby sleeps a little but mostly wails. When I try to wake Djalila again, her skin feels hot and in a panic I send a slave running for the midwife.

The woman shakes her head when she sees the sweat forming on Djalila's skin. "You had better find a wet-nurse for the child," she says bluntly.

"And Djalila? What should we do for her?"

She shakes her head. "Once there's a fever they rarely recover," she says.

I feel a coldness sink into me. "I cannot lose another," I say in a whisper. "I swore."

"What did you say?" says the old woman.

"Nothing," I say.

I send a servant to find a wet nurse for Zaynab and leave her in the arms of the midwife, who sits by Djalila's panting, shaking side. I make my way to my room and kneel down to open the chest I have rarely opened since I first went to serve Djalila's family. Slowly I lift the lid and remove the cloth that covers the contents.

The red cup lies there, its dull surface seeming like something broken or dead. I touch it, wondering if it still has powers. I feel nothing.

I set to work. I mix herbs to cool a fever, herbs to strengthen, herbs to make a womb healthy. I am so frantic I forget half of what I know. Even while I choose one herb and then another I know that I do not believe that any of the ingredients I am using will offer a cure: I know that what I truly believe is that the cure will come from the cup itself, that it hardly matters what I put into it. While I mix the medicine I pour all of my prayers into it, my hope that it will cure Djalila, that she will not die. If she dies then I will have failed in serving her, I will be guilty once more of allowing harm to come to Faheem's family.

I am not gentle with Djalila. She coughs and splutters and moans but I slip my fingers between her teeth and hold her mouth open as though she were an animal, pouring the liquid down her throat while a good portion of it dribbles down her sweating chin and stains her blankets. The midwife watches me with interest.

"I thought you said you did not use your skills," she says.

"Be quiet," I tell her. "Look after the child, you've already half-killed her mother."

"Not my fault," she tells me. "I told you, once the fever starts a woman is as good as dead, whatever you're giving her."

I don't answer her. I sit on Djalila's bed, wiping the sweat off her clammy skin. I am so focused on her that I am only dimly conscious of a wet-nurse arriving, a plump woman who has the baby suckling in moments. The silence, after her constant cries, should be a relief but all it means is that I can hear Djalila's panting breath more loudly.

I had thought the previous night long, but the day passes in a haze of exhaustion. Again and again I feel my head jerk upright. Again and again I force the brew I have made down Djalila and when the distant calls to prayer can be heard I kneel to beg for help and think that I will fall asleep even as I touch my head to the ground. By nightfall the wet-nurse has been comfortably installed in the house and the midwife, shaking her head, has left us.

I sleep. I cannot stay awake. My body slumps by Djalila's side, the cup still in my hand, the last dregs of the drink leaking onto the cold floor. I dream of Faheem, see his red lips and hear a baby crying, see the heaving bodies of Ibrahim and Djalila and her red-rimmed eyes afterwards. When I awake there is a thin pale light and my legs have lost all feeling. I am stiff with cold and for a moment I forget why I am here and what I have been doing. The room is silent and wearily I turn my head to look at Djalila, expecting her to be lifeless, for I cannot hear her panting.

Her skin is pale but no longer clammy. She is asleep, not dead. I have to touch her breast and feel her heartbeat before I am certain and I lift the sheets to see if there is blood but there is only a little. She is not dead, nor even dying.

I pick up the cup and walk slowly back to my own room. Along the way I catch sight of a slave girl.

"Take food and clean water for bathing to your mistress," I tell her. "Tell the master she is safe. And make sure the wet-nurse is well fed."

"Praise be to Allah," says the girl. "Shall I bring you food and water also?"

"I am going to sleep," I tell her.

I sleep for a day and a night and a day again. When I awake I wash the cup before I wash myself, then I wrap it in a soft cloth and lock it away again. I wash the stink of sweat and fear from my body and dress before descending to eat.

"Praise be to Allah, Djalila has recovered," says Ibrahim. "And I gather it was down to your care."

I shake my head. I do not want to talk about the red cup nor what was in it. "I did nothing," I say.

"The midwife said otherwise," says Ibrahim earnestly. "And I thank you for what you did, whatever it was. Djalila will be able to bear more children, thanks to you."

"No!" I say loudly and Ibrahim looks shocked at my outburst.

"No what?" he asks.

"She is not to have another child," I tell him. "Not soon, not ever."

"But..." he begins.

"No," I tell him and my voice is cold. "She must not have another child. I saved her once, I cannot do it again."

Ibrahim looks at me in disbelief. "What do you suggest?" he asks. "Another wife to share my bed and bring me sons?"

I shake my head. "Djalila would be crushed," I tell him.

"So what do you suggest?" he asks me.

"Take me," I say and I know as I say them that these words have been waiting all this time in my mouth, that as the months have passed I have been wooed by Ibrahim without either of us knowing it. That something in me has taken his learning, his soft words and the sight of his flesh pressed against Djalila's and fashioned them into my own desire. "Take me."

He refuses at first. Whether out of repugnance for me or love for Djalila, I do not know. But time goes by and I see him watching me. I see him look my way when Djalila goes to her bedchamber and I know he can only wait so long before his desires bring him to me.

I visit baby Zaynab in her nursery from time to time. She learns to crawl, exploring the world around her, her chubby hands grasping at whatever she can reach, wondering at what she finds. Her black hair fuzzes around her face, framing huge dark eyes and honey skin, along with tiny red lips, which close around anything she can get into her mouth before her wetnurse stops her. She beams when she sees anyone, expecting only love.

I dare not love her. I fear all my passions, how they grow out of nothing into such desires that they threaten those around me. And so when I wish to clasp her in my arms and stroke her soft black curls, when I want to hide my face behind my hands and then playfully show myself to her again to make her laugh I do not. Instead I retreat, turn my face away when she smiles at me and return to Djalila's rooms. Ibrahim does not spend much time with Zaynab, perhaps he thinks it is a woman's task, perhaps she reminds him of the sons he will not have. Djalila, despite my urgings, does not visit Zaynab much. Perhaps she reminds her of her own shortcomings as a wife. And so Zaynab grows, clutching at chests and beds until she takes her own unsteady steps surrounded only by servants, unaided by those people who should offer her love, her own parents and myself, each of us too tightly wrapped in our own fears and desires.

More than a year passes before a night comes when the heat is too great for anyone in the city to sleep. Djalila tosses and turns in the room next to me and I hear Zaynab wail more than once, her nursemaid shushing her with some old lullaby and a fan. The maids splash one another with water as darkness falls and then retreat to their own room, giggling between themselves at the names of this boy or that, their empty imaginations running riot.

I hear Ibrahim's footsteps come up the stairs and pause, first outside Djalila's room and then outside of mine. I hold my breath for a moment and hear the thudding of my heart before his footsteps turn away. I hear him climb the stairs to the roof terrace, perhaps the only place where the night air might bring the hope of coolness.

I rise, then, and follow the echo of his steps. When I reach the rooftop he is standing with his hands on the perimeter wall, looking out over the night city. Here and there lanterns flicker, above us stars cover the sky in a pale glow.

"I have treated her with kindness," he says without turning.

"Yes," I say.

"I have not forced myself upon her."

"No," I say.

"I have made her mistress of her own home and all has been done to her satisfaction, to her command. She has but to say the word and she is obeyed. She has everything a woman may desire."

"Yes," I say.

"But she is not happy. She will not lie with me of her own desire. I have only one child by her and now no hope of any others."

"No," I say.

He is silent for a moment and far away we hear carts rattling through the streets, the clip-clop of hooves going by in the alleyways outside, traders readying themselves for the dawn.

"Have I done something wrong?" he asks.

"No," I say.

"I need more than Yes and No," he says. "I need to know what is wrong."

"She is damaged," I tell him.

"By what?"

"Things that happened to her as a child," I say. "I cannot tell you of them."

"And she will never recover, is that it? I chose a wife who had a hidden flaw in her, one that I could not see beneath her beauty and now there is no way to heal her?"

"If I knew a way I would do it," I say.

He is silent again and I step forward, take up a place beside him, look out at what he can see, the dark rooftops and the stars above.

"I am at fault," I say and the words come fast because it is a relief to me not to hold them in. "I chose you as her husband."

"What?"

"She had many suitors. I chose you."

"Who were you to choose?"

"Her handmaiden," I say. "Her companion. I made her as well as I could and I thought she should marry. I thought if she found a kind man, a man who would help her to be happy, if she had a house of her own and could be its mistress, that it would heal her."

"Why me?"

"You were a good man," I say. "I saw it in you. I – I felt it in you. When I met you I felt your kindness, your patience. She would not have to live with elder members of a family, she could have the freedom of being her own mistress at once. And – and you did not just lust after her, you cared for her."

"How do you know?"

"I saw it in your eyes," I say. "And the day of the gift giving. You brought all the traditional things – the sheep, the fruits, the jewellery – but you brought her flowers as well, the ones she wore in her hair the first time you ever saw her. And so I knew you had thought of her."

He shrugs. "I thought we would be happy together," he says. "Now it seems that will never be possible."

"It is my fault," I say. "I have made you miserable even though I meant for the two of you to be happy."

"Why do you serve her?" he asks.

"I hurt her family a long time ago," I say. "I swore to serve them until I die."

He shakes his head. "That sound like a child's promise."

"Perhaps it was," I say. "But I made a vow and I will keep it."

"And what do you propose I do now?" he asks.

I swallow and keep my eyes on the stars. "Lie with me," I half-whisper into the darkness.

"And Djalila?"

"She will not know," I say. "I will never tell her."

"And in this way you seek to make us both happy?"

"Yes," I say.

"And will you be happy?" he asks.

Yes, I think. *Yes.* "I will be content," I say and even as I speak his arms are around me.

I keep my promise. Djalila may wonder a little at Ibrahim's no longer coming to her rooms, but the relief she feels stops her from enquiring further. She grows a little happier. She still stays mostly in her own rooms but she allows me to open up the shutters more often, she lets the sun touch her skin, sometimes she will even watch people go by outside her windows. She sends me to buy songbirds in the souk and they fill her rooms with a semblance of life that has been missing until now, their chirps and bright feathers even make her smile a little. By day I manage the household while Ibrahim is in the workshops, Zaynab toddles about the courtyard garden and Djalila, perhaps, begins to heal a little. Once or twice a month she may even call for Zaynab and spend a little time with her, though she is awkward in the child's presence, unable to think what to say or do. I try to encourage her, buying little sweets for her to give the child or suggesting that she encourages Zaynab to play with the birds but Djalila is so stilted in making such offers that Zaynab senses her discomfort and grows awkward herself, shrinking away from possible caresses and eventually retreating behind her nursemaid's legs. Yet when Ibrahim's sisters come they squeeze her and ignore her shrieks, poking her till she giggles, stuffing her mouth with dripping honey cakes and she submits to their round-bellied, double-chinned embraces, feigning a desire to escape but returning to them over and over again as she runs about the house.

I visit Zaynab in her nursery sometimes. The nursemaid I have chosen for her, Myriam, is a plump young woman, full of chatter, the opposite of Djalila and indeed myself. She feeds Zaynab plentifully, she occasionally hugs her for no reason, she berates her for many small reasons, loudly and without malice so that Zaynab pays little attention. She is almost four now, a real little girl rather than a waddling baby. Her hair is dark and curly, her lips are red, her skin is honeyed perfection. She runs about the house, noisy and curious. Often I will see her dark eyes peeping from behind a hanging or a door and I try to smile at her but she flits away, frightened. I know the servants tell tales about me, casting me as the all-powerful handmaiden to their unstable mistress.

By night I make my way to the rooftop. I hold Ibrahim to me and revel in a man's desire, feel his lips on my skin and look up into the thousand thousand stars that shine above me. On moonlit nights I watch the play of our limbs as our skins shine in the darkness and I feel love begin to grow in me. I attempt to keep it at bay. I keep my mind only on my own pleasure, I do not think how to please him, I hold back from caressing him when he lies spent by my side. I do not speak, I do not whisper such words as come to mind when we are together. I do not let him speak either, for I am afraid of what he would say and of my own response. I do not allow his lips to touch mine, for to kiss seems too close to love. Each day I drink the herbs that will stop a child from growing in my womb, even though it tastes bitter to me.

But I am not able to hold back my feelings. A year comes and goes and then another. And I find myself thinking of Ibrahim, I find myself waiting for his return from the workshops. I order meals that will please him. I wear robes that will be soft on his hands when he undresses me. I smooth my skin with oils for his pleasure. The night comes when his lips brush against mine and I do not turn my face away. And I grow afraid. I drink the bitter herbs and they taste sweet in my mouth. I am afraid of what the cup may do, how it might turn the bitterness to something else and allow a child to grow because I wish for it even while I drink the herbs that guard against it. I stop using the cup for myself but even when I use another cup, still I wonder if my own desires will turn against me.

"Marry me," says Ibrahim one night as the stars begin to shine above us.

Something in me twists. In one moment I think of marriage to Ibrahim. Of happiness, of a child perhaps. Of being free to love. To love Ibrahim, to love Zaynab. But I see Djalila's face, her red lips.

"I cannot," I say.

"Do not be so hasty," he says. "Think of it again."

I bow my head in silence.

I do not sleep that night. Ibrahim sleeps and I lie by his side and watch him.

I think of my vow and wonder whether I have atoned sufficiently. After all, I think, I rescued Djalila from her father. She has the kindest of husbands, a child, a good household. What would change in her life? Better that I be her co-wife than who-knows-who, some younger, more beautiful woman to break her heart. Perhaps we could grow closer, be as sisters. The sky grows pale as dawn approaches and my heart lightens. I think that perhaps this offer from Ibrahim is a sign from Allah, an acknowledgement that I have tried to fulfill my vow and that I am released from its bonds. I look down at Ibrahim and smile. When he wakes I will tell him that I will be his wife.

Screams suddenly echo throughout the house, followed by running footsteps from every part of the building and then Hayfa's voice overlays the screams with shouts for help. She calls my name.

"Hela! *Hela!*"

I run down the stairs, half-dressed, my robes in disarray, my hair tumbling about my shoulders, not yet bound up for the day. In the house's courtyard garden are gathered all the servants and slaves, so that I cannot see what is going on but as I approach Hayfa shoves them away.

"Get out of the way. Let her through!"

The youngest member of Hayfa's team, a slave boy, is hurt. He is barely ten, a scrawny dark-skinned thing my father would have turned his nose up at, but lively enough. He runs errands for Hayfa in the souk, taking bread to the ovens or carrying heavy loads home for her through the twisting turning paths of the souk. Now he lies just inside the courtyard's door, one leg at an impossible angle, blood seeping from it, bruises already forming. I catch a glimpse of white bone against his black skin, more sickening for the contrast.

"What happened?" I ask.

"We were buying pastries. A cart crushed him. The donkey was frightened by something, it went careering into him. His body was flung against a wall so hard he did not reply when I spoke to him," says Hayfa, her face pale. "The wheel trapped his leg under it."

I look down at the boy. Even as I do so he closes his eyes and his whole body shakes, only the whites of his eyes showing as his mouth opens and saliva flows down his chin. One of the servant girls cries out that he is cursed and Hayfa slaps her so hard she falls to the ground. The others draw back. At the back of the group I catch a glimpse of Ibrahim and Djalila, drawn by the commotion.

"Help him," says Hayfa to me.

"I cannot," I say.

She looks at me as though I have spat in her face. "I said help him," she tells me. "He is losing his wits and his leg is broken. How can you stand there and do nothing when you have healing skills?"

"What do you know of what I can do?" I ask.

"You saved the mistress," says Hayfa.

"That was luck," I say.

"It was the red cup," says Hayfa with stubborn certainty.

I feel a thud in my belly as though she has punched me. "What did you say?" I ask.

The slave boy shakes under our hands.

"I asked about you around Kairouan," says Hayfa. "You were the great healer. You used a magical red cup."

I kneel down. "Put your hands here," I tell her. "Do not let his thigh move."

"You – "

"Do it," I say and she does what I tell her to do.

Bone grates on bone and one of the servant girls faints behind us. My eyes are closed but I feel the bone as it turns, meets its rightful place and I grip his leg and tell the servants to bring cloths, so that I can wrap it tightly. I use splints to hold the leg in place and tell Hayfa that I have done all I can.

"He must drink from the cup," she says.

"I no longer use it," I say.

"He must drink from it," she insists.

I make a meaningless drink, something that will bring strength and I give it to Hayfa. "Hold it to his lips," I say. I know that her desire to help him, transmitted through the cup, will do more than whatever I have mixed together.

She holds it as though it is a sacred vessel and ensures he drinks every drop.

"If you want him to live he will have to stay in your kitchen without moving for more than two months," I say. "He will not be able to run errands for you."

"He never did much anyway," she scoffs, her relief masked as disdain. "I daresay I can keep an eye on him."

"He will always limp," I warn her.

"What's a limp?" she says, defensive. "Half of Kairouan limps with one malady or another."

I stand up and walk away, past Djalila. Ibrahim follows me back to the rooftop. When we reach the terrace I turn to him.

"I cannot," I say.

"Why?"

I think of my dawn smile, of my foolish belief that I was released from my vow. It was not a release, it was a test and I failed it. The slave boy's accident is my warning. I have not been faithful to the vow I made.

I say what I should have said long ago. "I cannot marry you, Ibrahim. And I can no longer lie with you."

"If you cannot and Djalila will not," he says, and I can hear hurt as well as a growing anger in his voice, "then what do you suggest?"

"Take another wife," I say quickly, before I can unsay the words.

"You said before that Djalila – "

"Leave her to me," I say.

"Very well," he says, looking down at the ground. "I will find another wife. And may Allah help me choose better than I did the first time."

"I will choose a wife for you," I say.

"No," he says.

"A young wife," I say, words tumbling from me. "A healthy wife, a wife who will be good to you, kind to Zaynab. Who will not be afraid of Djalila's ways."

"If such a woman exists," he snorts and turns away.

I stand alone on the rooftop and hold my robes closer against a chill only I can feel. How will it be to have another woman here, a woman who will share Ibrahim's bed? How will I bear it? How will Djalila react? I shake my head. I cannot ask myself such questions. I have hurt too many lives already. I have been warned. I must try harder. I will find a good woman to heal this household.

Imen

I TOUCH IMEN MORE THAN ONCE to be certain, doubting myself. I am
so used to the beats of Ibrahim's frustration and my own wretched guilt,
to Zaynab's pitiful cravings for a love that is not given, to the pulse of
Djalila's endless secret fears, that to touch someone and feel only happiness,
only innocent joy in life, is startling to me. I return to her again and again,
drawn to feel her gentleness. I pull up the hood of a heavy robe over my face
and walk the streets of the souk to find her and when I do I let one finger
brush against her and find once again her light heartbeats, bright and full of
certainty in the goodness of her life. When I walk on I hope that perhaps her
light will enter my darkness and take away the bitterness within me.

She is not from a very great family but they are good people, no-one can
say anything against them when I listen for gossip. Ibrahim's sisters beam
when I murmur to them of a possible match.

Ibrahim is wary, as well he might be. He does not trust me. "I must see her
for myself," he says.

I watch him leave the house for a visit to her father's house and want to
call him back, want to lean from the rooftop that was our secret place and
cry out his name, but I bite my lips and clench my fists instead and know
that I must not.

He cannot help smiling at the thought of her when he tells me that he has
asked for her hand. He tries to hide it from me but I can see that her sweet
face and gentle demeanour have awakened hope in him. I lower my eyes and
murmur that I am glad, that I will see to it that all will be done to please
her in this house.

"I must tell Djalila," he says.

"No," I say too quickly. "I will do it."

He shakes his head, stubborn in his knowledge of what is right. "No," he says. "It must come from me."

There is silence from her room when he emerges and I pause for a moment as I pass him. "Did she cry?" I ask.

He shakes his head and walks away.

I take a breath and then enter.

Djalila sits with a bird in her hand. It pecks lightly at the grain she holds for it and she gazes at it as though it is all she can see.

"Did he tell you?" she asks without looking at me. "Or did you already know?"

"There is no shame," I say. "You are his first wife and you have given him a child."

"A girl," she says.

"A healthy child," I say. "And you nearly died in doing so. The new wife will bear more children but she will never be the first wife. You will have all due honours. You are not set aside."

"Go," says Djalila.

I hesitate. I have never known Djalila to dismiss me in all these years, since the very first day I came to her. Usually she asks where I am going when I leave her rooms, as though to keep me with her always. She does not even like it when I am gone too long in the souks.

"Go," says Djalila, her voice sunken to a whisper.

I go. I do not know what to do with myself. I make my way to the kitchen where the servants all stop speaking as soon as they see me. I inform Hayfa, while the others pretend to get on with chores, that her master will be taking a new wife. That she is to be shown all due courtesy but that Djalila is still his first wife and that she must be treated with honour. I designate rooms that are to be set aside for Imen and order them cleaned and prepared for her arrival. I tell Hayfa that Ibrahim will send new hangings and carpets for her but that any other comforts are in Hayfa's hands and that she has Ibrahim's permission to purchase whatever is necessary to ensure a warm welcome for Imen when she joins us. I warn Zaynab's nursemaid, Myriam, of the impending changes but I cannot bring myself to tell the child myself. She will find out soon enough and I can only hope that it is a welcome surprise for her once she meets Imen. Meanwhile Djalila keeps away from me, she dismisses me from her presence without reason, she asks for other members of the household to serve her and I wander the rooms like a lost child, searching for peace and finding none.

The engagement rituals must be enacted. The house lies in readiness, the whole family has fine new robes. From today Imen will be promised to Ibrahim and her arrival here will be measured in days.

"I will serve her myself," I tell the slave girl whom Djalila has asked for, a mute who only nods and shrinks away from me.

I make my way into the room and stop in horror. Djalila stands naked, her back to me. In her hands she holds a thin strip of leather, which she brings down suddenly across her thighs, the whip-crack making me startle. At my gasp she turns to face me. Red weals are spread across her arms and legs, her belly. There is even one on her neck.

"What are you doing?" I ask, my voice strangled.

"It takes away the pain," she says.

"What pain?"

"*What* pain?" she says, half-laughing in a way I find more frightening than the red marks across her body. "The pain of this day. Of being set aside for a younger, more beautiful woman. Of being a failed wife."

I step closer, hold out my hand for the leather strip, which she clutches to her. "You cannot do this," I tell her. "You must attend the engagement and you cannot be seen with these marks." I begin to dress her as though everything is normal, although my hands are shaking. I lift up the elaborately decorated robes I have chosen, the heavy jewellery, there to give her confidence but which now must also hide the marks on her body. Slowly I pull the leather from her hands and let it fall to the floor.

"I cannot bear it," she says and tears flow down her cheeks. "Make it stop, Hela. Make it stop."

"It is too late for that now," I say. "If he has another wife you will not need to have him in your bed. You will always be the first wife, you can continue as mistress of the house. Imen will provide sons for Ibrahim…" I have to stop for a moment, for my own voice is trembling too much to speak clearly, "…and all will be well."

"You are shaking," she tells me.

I hear bleating from the courtyard and know that the servants are standing ready with the traditional engagement gifts, which Ibrahim must take to Imen's family. A live sheep and a large jewellery box. Dried fruits and the engagement cake.

"We have to go," I tell Djalila. I pull up the robe on her shoulder so that the red mark there cannot be seen.

"Why are you shaking?" she asks.

"They will be waiting. We need to go." I tell her.

I try not to look at Ibrahim. He is so handsome, dressed in his finest robes. I clench my hands into fists and call too loudly for Myriam to hurry up, where is Zaynab?

Myriam is flustered, she leads down Zaynab, dressed in new robes. Zaynab looks fearful and confused. I want to embrace her, to promise that all will be well but how can I know that, much less promise it to a child?

"We are come to ask if you will give your daughter to be married to Ibrahim an-Nafzawi!"

The crowd cheers and I feel Djalila's grip tighten on mine. Somewhere behind us, Zaynab is being buffeted by the crowd, too small to see what is going on. I want to pick her up and leave this place but instead I stay by Djalila as the ceremony goes ahead and blessings are read over the bowed heads of Imen and Ibrahim. It is too late now, too late.

Standing at Ibrahim's side, Imen is tiny. I am not sure she is much taller than ten-year-old Zaynab and her feet and hands are smaller. She has a little waist but plump cheeks and a rounded behind which speak, one day, of a woman who will grow pleasantly fat on good food. She reminds me of Ibrahim's sisters, their good-natured greed for sweets and gossip, their generous embraces and dimples. Djalila's face is a mask-smile set in stone and yet Imen smiles, smiles at everyone and everything until even Ibrahim's lips have to curve to meet her happiness.

I cannot keep away, do not keep away. I let myself into Ibrahim's bedroom and hear him take her, hear her little cries and his deep groans as he thrusts within her, watch his hands grip her soft flesh and his lips close around her dark nipples. I see her eyes close and her mouth open to receive him, see her own hands grasp him and pull him more tightly to her, as though she cannot get enough of him. I hear their loving whispers one to another and I want to block up my ears so that I may not hear what hurts me.

In the mornings he orders warm breads and sweet honey and feeds her from his own fingers until her kisses drive him to desire. They are insatiable the two of them: she, shown what it is to desire for the first time in her life, he, finding for the first time a woman who openly desires him, who begs for more, who gasps and cries out at his touch, who does not hold back from his need for her, who loves him even as he loves her. Their nights torment me, their days apart when he must work torment the two of them. Imen spends her days in a sun-shined daze of exhausted, contented lust while Djalila retreats ever more from what she does not understand, from what she is only able to resent.

Imen is kind to Zaynab and in return Zaynab, who has never known true kindness, emerges like a flower from a bud. She stops running wild with the street children of Kairouan and instead spends time at home. Her face shines when she is with Imen, she draws closer and closer to her until she will lay her head in Imen's lap as the lazy afternoons drag on and kiss her cheek each morning. She chatters to Imen as though she were her friend, asks her endless questions and listens to the answers as though Imen were the fount of all wisdom. I hear her sing sometimes, her usually quiet voice set free by love.

Even the servants change. They cannot wait to please their new mistress. They do not wait to be commanded, instead they hurry to serve her, to receive her gentle smiles and soft words of thanks. The house seems to become merry. New planters of flowers are brought into the courtyard, a larger fountain is built. The table is laid with new dishes, made to please Imen's appetite. I see changes in the bedrooms, where decorative flourishes are ordered by Ibrahim: more beautiful rugs from his workshops, finer blankets with brighter colours, new carvings and paintings commissioned for the doors and ceilings.

Only Djalila stays locked in her cold world, her fearful place. I think perhaps she could be made to love Imen but she is afraid. She fears Imen's openness as others would fear the sun shining in their eyes – a dazzling light too far away from her own capabilities. She cannot see a way to bridge so great a distance and so she hides away. And perhaps somewhere inside she loved Ibrahim and something in her warmed to his gaze, his touch, but she had locked herself away so tightly she did not know how to open up to him and now she sees she has missed her chance.

It does not take long before Imen finds out something of my past.

"The servants say you are a great healer," she says.

I almost drop the cup of water I am holding. "Who told you that?"

"All of them," smiles Imen.

I shake my head. "I do not practice now," I tell her. "That was a long time ago."

She looks surprised. "You are not that old," she giggles. "Why do you no longer use your skills?"

"I found a new way to serve," I say to her.

"I thought you might give me something," she says, confidingly. "Something to bring me a child."

"A child?"

She laughs. "Why so surprised? Of course, a child. For Ibrahim, he would be so happy."

"You are young," I stumble over my words. "You – you will not need anyone's help to conceive a child."

"A little help never hurt," she smiles at me.

I offer her the red cup at arm's length. I try not to think, nor feel, while I mix what will bring a child. Let her own desire work on it, not my own.

I see her with Zaynab, giggling over the antics of a cat, peering over the rooftops while they munch on sweet pastries and drink fresh juices. I see Zaynab's little heart open up to this, the first person to show her real love and kindness, day after day. It makes my heart sting. I love you too, I want to say to her, I love you, but I am afraid to let it show, I am afraid of what I do to those around me. I swallow and look away when I see them happy together. I wish I could join them, hold Zaynab's warm little body and hug her to me, laugh with Imen over nonsense, relish the warm sun on my skin in the company of people who have some faith in life. Instead I lower my eyes and return to the silence of Djalila's rooms where I continue to shield her from a world that means her no harm but which she has designated her enemy.

It is dark when I hear her retch. I listen again but I do not need to hear that sound a second time. I turn my face to the wall, pull the blanket over my face and weep.

Imen's belly swells in the sun, a ripening that foretells happiness for her, for Ibrahim, even for Zaynab who is enchanted with the idea of a sibling. I see the growing curve beneath her robes and look away, conscious only of a gathering storm. There is a darkness growing even as the light comes, its equal and opposite shadow. I know that Djalila is unhappy, the red weals on her skin emerge with ever greater regularity and not all my pleading will turn her from what gives her relief. Meanwhile Imen drinks daily from the red cup and beams at me, certain that it is I who have helped her fall with child.

It is night when I hear a scraping sound from Djalila's rooms. I make my way to her in the shadows, my feet stepping according to memory rather than sight. I reach out one hand and push at the door, remain in the doorway while I watch her.

She kneels in the pool of light cast by a lantern. Her arms are red with weals from wrist to armpit. One hand works frantically, grinding a substance, the other holds the red cup still.

"The cup is mine," I tell her.

"I have need of it," she says.

"For yourself?"

She keeps grinding.

"You do not know what it does," I tell her. "You cannot use it."

"You put a child in her belly," she tells me, her words emerging in little pants.

"Ibrahim put a child in her belly, whether you wish to hear it or not," I say.

She shakes her head but does not stop grinding. A drop of sweat trickles down her face but she does not wipe it away.

For the second time in my life I throw the cup. Even while it is in the air I pray for it to break, but it does not. Its dark wood is too sturdy, the hard sound it makes as it hits the tiled floor echoes around us and I leave the room so that I do not have to hear Djalila's sobs, nor stifle my own.

But I should have taken the cup and cast it in the sea, thrown it into the desert's sands, buried it in some dark place.

I waken to Hayfa's rough grasp on my shoulder, my whole body shaking under her desperation.

"What," I begin but she has half-pulled me to my feet before I am ready to stand. I stagger.

"The master calls for you," she says.

"It is still dark," I protest.

"The young mistress is bleeding," pants Hayfa.

I run.

I try. I try the cup, but my fear is so great when I set it to Imen's lips that I think all she receives from me is more fear to add to her own. I try to change her position while all around me the whole household kneels in silent prayer. In the silence I watch her life leave and know that Ibrahim's son goes with her.

Darkness falls over our house. Ibrahim's arms are empty. Djalila's heart has been shown to be broken past repair. I dare not love. And Zaynab is growing, growing ever more like her mother in beauty, but without a mother's love.

And five long years pass.

Yusuf

*I*F DJALILA ATTENDED MORE TO what goes on in her own household she would have seen her fifteen-year-old daughter fall in love. No-one with eyes could miss it once it happened, though none of us saw what sparked it. Something happened between them, something none of us saw.

The household is accustomed to receiving guests. A merchant of fine carpets must welcome many men to his home, offer them good food and drink, speak with them on various matters. They must feel cared for in luxurious surroundings and then they will associate that care with the wares they are shown. They will see the beautiful carpets and believe that if they were laid in their own homes they would receive such care, enjoy such luxury always. Djalila's presence only enhances such thoughts. Perhaps, think the men, if their own home were filled with such carpets their own wives would be as beautiful. They are fools to be swayed by so little but traders have always had their ways of making fools of men.

Yusuf is good looking, with black curls and dark eyes, his arms wiry with strength. I hear more than one slave girl sigh at the sight of him on that first night, but Zaynab does not join us for dinner and so when she descends the next morning, her skin rose-blushed and dressed in finery more suited to a celebration than the family table her father looks bemused. I watch her face. She does not look at Yusuf but every part of her being is focused on him, she looks away so hard she might as well raise her eyes and gaze on him without shame. She must have glimpsed him last night but I cannot think when.

His name is Yusuf bin Ali, the chief of the Wurika and Aylana tribes, whose boundaries come close to the great city of Aghmat, far to the west from here. His home is a *ksar*, a fortified city built by desert-dwellers. It is for himself that he comes to buy carpets, but he is a loyal and trusted vassal of King

Luqut, the amir of Aghmat and so if he should like Ibrahim's carpets it may well be that we can expect patronage from the amir also.

There are gatherings, some for business, others for pleasure, and Yusuf is our guest at all of them. Some of the evenings are of interest, at others I have to listen to interminable debates about whether or not our rulers are likely to switch their allegiance to Baghdad and what the consequences of that might be. I watch Djalila's face but she is too experienced at these events by now, she keeps her face calm and pleasant, smiles when anyone addresses her and otherwise is silent. I try to stifle my yawns when they speak of politics and hope that one of the scholars will speak of something more interesting.

At first I think it is only Zaynab who feels anything for him, a young girl a little too admiring of a handsome older man. But Yusuf stays more nights than he had originally planned and I see that he does not turn his head when she enters a room, he seems otherwise engaged. I see his nostrils flare when she walks past him and although he does not watch her go he breathes in her scent as she passes and his eyes close for a brief second. He lusts for her, he cannot help himself. He is too conscious of the curve of her body, the sway of her walk. At one gathering I find myself standing briefly between them. I feel the heat rising between their bodies and words as yet unspoken forming in their mouths, waiting to be heard. But there is something else there too, a kind of helpless tenderness from him for a girl caught in her first love. Somehow they have spoken, he has found out what she feels for him. It does not take long before Yusuf asks a question, a feeling-out of whether Zaynab's hand might be granted.

Ibrahim dismisses the idea. "He has a wife already," he says.

"Zaynab is in love with him," I say.

Ibrahim turns his face away. "We do not always get what we want," he says and my heart sinks at the bitterness in his voice, a bitterness he never had before and for which I hold myself responsible.

"Zaynab could love and be loved," I say. "At least one of us could."

He meets my gaze then and I see that his eyes shine with unshed tears. "So be it," he says. "At least one of us should know what that feels like."

I wait until Yusuf leaves the dining room and heads to bed and I intercept him on the stairs.

"I would speak with you of Zaynab," I say and I watch his face, see his colour change a little, his eyes narrow on my face.

"You are her mother's handmaiden," he says. He does not say *what right have you to speak of Zaynab's marriage*, but I see it in his eyes.

"I am her mother's voice," I say.

He looks me over and does not reply, but he waits to hear what I have to say.

"Did you speak with Zaynab before you spoke with her father?" I ask and I am close enough that I feel the rush of tenderness when he thinks of speaking with her. It is not quite love, no. It is something more than simple lust, though. There is a tightness in him when he thinks of her. I almost want to reach out and touch him, to feel what he feels better, to bring it into focus so that I can name it.

"I have spoken with her," he admits.

"She wants to marry you?"

He only nods. Again the rush, the emotion when he thinks of whatever she said. She has made her feelings for him known, that much I can be sure of. Perhaps he found her charming and no more and then she said something. Few men could feel nothing at all if a beautiful young girl confessed her love for them. And Zaynab is burning up for him, she would have confessed it passionately, unable to hold herself back and in so doing she has secured this feeling for herself, not quite love but close enough that he considers marriage to her.

"You already have a wife though," I say and suddenly his feelings change to something so dark that I step back. "You have a wife?" I repeat but this time I am questioning him. From the darkness I have just felt I would not be surprised if he had murdered her.

"She is not a well woman," he says and his voice is heavy, his shoulders drop. "She became unwell after the birth of our son. She was sunk in sadness, nothing we could do would pull her back."

I nod. I have seen such women. "She did not recover?" I ask. Usually they do, although with some it may take a long time.

He shakes his head. "We have five sons," he says. "And none has brought her joy."

"She should not birth more children," I say.

"I know," he says. "I no longer lie with her."

I nod. It is becoming clearer to me. He has a wife in name only. A wife sunken in sadness, a wife he may not lie with. He is alone. And here is Zaynab, beautiful as her mother, full of passion and desire, who offers up her love for him like a rare and precious fruit to be plucked at will. What man could resist? For a moment I think of lovely Imen, so trusting in love and then I put the thought away.

"You will be good to her," I say. It is not a question.

"I would protect her with my life," he says and I nod and walk away.

"She should be told," says Djalila stubbornly.

"Let her find out," I tell her. "What use to burden her with such knowledge?"

"And when she sees the other wife? Then what?"

I shake my head. "There is something wrong with the other wife. She barely stirs from her room. Zaynab will have Yusuf to herself."

"It is not nothing to live with another wife," says Djalila. "What would you know of it? It eats away at your soul."

"Plenty of women manage it," I tell her sharply. "It is time you grew up, Djalila. How much pain do you intend to bring to Ibrahim's life?"

Her face goes pale. I curse myself for my lack of control. She will whip herself again and it will be me who has to tend the weals, coax her back to something approaching normality. I follow her, snapping at servants along the way who have done nothing to deserve my anger. In my prayers I think of Zaynab and I feel some relief. Yes, there is another wife but she is ailing in some way. Zaynab loves Yusuf so greatly that her love will draw him towards her, as it has already done. What man can resist such devotion, such passion? He is already filled with tenderness for her and she is too beautiful not to be desired. It is a short step from tenderness and desire to love, she will make him her own eventually. At least I have made one person in this family happy and I feel a little of my burden lift.

The wedding is rushed. Yusuf needs to return to his people. Djalila shuts herself up in her rooms and appears only when necessary. Ibrahim leaves everything to me. And so my memory of those days is of a whirlwind of rituals and robes, of the golden headdress atop Zaynab's flowing hair, of an endless train of camels ready to leave this place. Above all of Zaynab's ecstasy, her happiness so great that the whole house feels it, reels back from its shining force.

In the end it is only Ibrahim who is brave enough to tell the truth, when there is no longer a choice to be made. I see him speak to Zaynab as he bids her farewell and watch her face grow pale. It is too late, she is lifted into the saddle of her camel and when she turn to look back at us, her still-childish face asking an unspoken question, each of us looks away until she is lost to our sight.

In the darkness of the house that night I kneel and beg Allah to care for Zaynab. I have nothing to offer in return, only the misery of this household in return for her happiness.

Kairouan

*P*ERHAPS WE GROW USED TO darkness, to loss.
Ibrahim takes his pleasures elsewhere, I do not enquire where and he does not tell me. Djalila I manage as best I can and sometimes her best is good enough for something close to happiness to be felt in the household. The servants know themselves to be lucky, for they are underused, and so they care for the three of us well and manage their own affairs behind closed doors. No doubt they are growing lazy, but I do not care.

Often I walk in the souks, sometimes to seek out traders of medicinal herbs and speak with them. I do not often buy their goods, for I use only a few, but they still respect me and ask for my advice on quality and freshness, on the best uses and care in preserving their goods and it soothes me to speak of healing.

Sometimes I pass by the house that used to be my childhood home. My parents have both gone now, my father died suddenly with a pain in his heart and my grieving mother followed not long after. I had seen little of them, over the years. They never failed to ask me when I would return home and I always replied that my vow was not yet complete. I saw their sad confusion at the turn my life had taken but could not think how to explain what had happened, it seemed too long ago now.

More often I only wander the streets, watch children at play and women gossiping, men bartering. I inhale their lives as others might inhale a perfume, relishing their light-heartedness, their small concerns and greater joys. I am thirty-five, unmarried, still promised to a vow I made when I was only eighteen. I do not seek to escape that vow but I sometimes wonder what my life would have been without it. But I put it away from me, for what other options do I have now? Instead I try to find peace in the life of Kairouan, in its daily rhythms and the changing seasons: sunlight, a cool breeze, the welcome rain after the hot months. I listen to the conversations around me, allowing them to flow over me without attending greatly to what they say. As predicted, our Amir, Al-Muizz, has shifted allegiance from the Fatimids, in part perhaps because of their excessive tributary demands of one million gold dinars a year. Now he has sworn a new allegiance to the Abbasids of Baghdad.

"The Caliph is enraged," says one man.

"What can he do?" asks another.

"Don't speak too lightly," warns the first. "If he were to send the Bedouin tribes here in revenge?"

I wander on. Kairouan is a rich and powerful city, it can withstand almost anything. I do not want to hear of the squabbles of one king and another, I walk here to listen to happier topics. I make my way towards the central square, where a storyteller is surrounded by an eager crowd of men and boys. Women rarely stop to listen but I like his stories of old myths and legends, stories of princesses and djinns. I move closer.

"Then the lady Zaynab's vision came true and her husband Yusuf gave her up!"

There are many Yusufs. There are many Zaynabs. But my breath comes a little faster.

"The King of Aghmat heard of Zaynab's vision and he commanded his vassal Yusuf to give up his bride, that he might be the most powerful man in all of the Maghreb."

My hands are clenched. Aghmat is close to Yusuf's territory. Yusuf is the King of Aghmat's vassal. What is this I am hearing?

I walk into the circle and the storyteller stops, confounded. "I am telling a tale, woman," he berates me. "Be off with you."

I face him, paying no attention to the grumblings around me. "These are yours," I tell him, slipping silver coins into his hand. "Follow me to somewhere quiet and repeat the story you were just telling."

Afterwards I sit, my head aching. How is this possible? He told me that Zaynab had some kind of vision. She claimed that she would be the wife of the most powerful man in the Mahgreb. This in itself is strange enough. Zaynab does not have such powers, I would have felt them in her. What, then, has really occurred? I do not know and there is no way to find out. What happened next then, is that King Luqut of Aghmat decided that her vision was interesting enough that he wanted her for his own bride. He commanded Yusuf to give her up and Yusuf – I curse him in my mind for this – gave her up as ordered. What did he think he was doing? What of his vows to protect her with his life? Zaynab, barely sixteen, married for only one year to Yusuf, is now the queen of Aghmat, torn away from a man whom she loved with a passion so hot it burned me to feel it. The storyteller tells me she screamed when Yusuf told her what was to happen. I wish this was only his embellishment but I fear it is true.

I walk the streets again but now my mind is swirling. I do not see what is around me but my feet know me better than I know myself.

"Hela."

"Moez."

I stand still, in front of him. I do not look at the contents of his stall, do not speak of this and that, do not smile. Perhaps this strangeness in me gives him courage to say what he has waited all this time to say.

"I do not have hundreds of camels," he says. "I have only five, for you know that what I carry is light and small. I am not a rich man, for I serve only certain customers, those whose skills are such that they know what to ask me for."

I say nothing. A brown camel, tethered close by, whooshes in my ear and I stroke its velvet nose without looking at it, my thoughts elsewhere.

"But I am not a poor man," says Moez. "I can offer you a comfortable home, a chance to practice your healing skills."

He waits for me to answer but I stay silent, gazing at him as though I cannot hear what he is saying.

He looks down and I see some colour in his cheeks before he raises his gaze to mine again. "And – and a man who cares for you," he says. "I think of you often, Hela, with tenderness." He swallows a little. "With love," he adds, his voice grown thick.

He did not need to say this. I have felt it for a long time, perhaps for years, unfurling in him slowly, a kindliness, a friendship, then something more, a waiting for me, a nervous excitement when he sees me approaching. He has been slow to recognise his own emotions, slow to name them for what they are. And I think, perhaps I could love this man, perhaps his slowness would slow my own passions, would lead me to a gentler love that I need not fear the consequences of, that I could relax into, knowing comfort rather than anxiety. Perhaps my vow to Allah was nonsense after all, the frightened prayer of a young girl too foolish to accept Faheem's death as His will, proud enough to claim it as her own doing. And the slave boy – it was an accident, nothing more. Why have I bound myself to misery when I could find happiness? Zaynab's story is her own to fashion, Ibrahim and

Djalila's stories are also their own. Perhaps all is only the will of Allah and I have no great powers to be fearful of.

I stand silent before Moez and then I hold out my hand to him and he takes it in his own. We stand for a moment.

"Will you come with me on my next journey?" he asks. "It is a trading journey, away from Kairouan, but my mother lives in the countryside now and I would ask for her blessing before we marry."

"Yes," I say.

"We will be away for a month," he says.

"Yes," I say.

"We must leave at dawn tomorrow," he says and I only nod before I walk away, my heart thumping even though I try to quiet it.

"Away where?" asks Ibrahim.

"With a trader, to look at new healing herbs," I say. I am not ready to tell Ibrahim, I do not have the words.

"A month?" says Djalila and I see her hands begin to clench and unclench. I know that the leather strip is not far from her mind, even though it has been a long time since she has used it.

"I will return," I say, but I do not tell her that I intend to marry Moez, that this journey is in part to receive his mother's blessing for our union.

Hayfa nods, uncertain. "Who is to give orders?" she asks.

"Djalila," I say. In my new hope for the future I think that perhaps I have cocooned Djalila too much. Perhaps if I had not been here all these years she would have had to build her own relationship with Ibrahim rather than through me. Perhaps she would have had to give orders to Hayfa, like every wealthy woman who runs a large household. Perhaps in my absence she will find her voice to order what she wants and maybe she will grow up at last. I have kept her a child and she is no child, she is the same age as I am. Maybe this journey will be a new beginning for us all. There is no reason why she and Ibrahim cannot find some small kind of happiness together that goes beyond the careful courtesy they each employ with one another.

I leave at dawn, taking little with me. A few silver coins, a couple of changes of clothes. Moez has promised me a camel to ride on. Djalila weeps in her room but I bid her a brisk farewell as though she were smiling and I nod to Hayfa, who stands silent in the doorway of her kitchen to watch me go. Ibrahim has already left a little while before me and I am glad of it, there is no need for elaborate farewells when I will return soon enough. There will be enough of all that when I leave this house for good.

I have never been free. I was a child when I left my parents' house. Since then I have been bound by an oath that has made me progressively more unhappy. Now I sit on the warm back of a good-natured nut-brown camel and feel the breeze and the sun on my face. Ahead, Moez rides his own camel, a strong beast taller than my own, a pale sandy colour. Occasionally he looks back at me and when he does I smile and his face lightens with joy. There is little noise about us, the soft pad-pad of the camels' steps, the rustle of tree leaves and birdsong. Occasionally a farmer in his fields or a fellow merchant heading to Kairouan will call out a greeting.

In the hottest part of the day we rest for a while under an olive tree and Moez offers me meat and bread, dates and almonds, fresh water. I think that in all the years in Ibrahim's house, where food is plentiful and elaborate, I have not eaten as well as this. I chuckle a little at the thought of Hayfa's face were I to tell her such a thing, she would take offence when her cooking is some of the best in Kairouan, her dainty sweetmeats and well-seasoned dishes of meat being dismissed for such simple fare.

"What makes you laugh?" asks Moez.

"I have been foolish," I tell him. "I have waited too long to live my own life."

He does not laugh. He only nods. "I waited too long to speak with you," he says.

I shake my head. "I would not have heard your words before," I tell him. "You spoke when I could hear you."

We are silent for a while, the cool shade of the tree above us providing respite from the worst heat of the day. After a while Moez lays his head in my lap and I stroke his hair.

We go no further than this. Sometimes it is my head in his lap, sometimes his in mine. We do not kiss, we only enjoy the quietness of our closeness. I have not known this before, this trust and gentleness. When the day comes to meet Moez's mother, I kneel willingly before her to ask for a blessing and my smile is so broad that she laughs at me and tells Moez that he has waited too long to marry such a merry woman.

We stay away longer than the month I promised. I do not want to leave this place, this tiny village, hidden in the fold of a valley, protected by the mountains all around us. Perhaps Kairouan's noise and smell, its boldness and greatness, has lost its magic for me. I picture myself living here instead, a healer using only what herbs come to hand, of service to those who need my help, the red cup left behind in Ibrahim's house, to grow dusty without use.

"We could stay here," I say tentatively to Moez.

"You would not be bored?" he asks.

I shake my head.

He smiles. "I might have to travel away from you, to trade, from time to time," he says.

"You would return to me," I say.

"I would," he says and it is a solemn promise.

We will have to return to Kairouan, of course, to make our farewells, to gather our belongings, to plan a new life together.

"But not yet," I beg and he smiles.

It is a trader who brings the news that Kairouan has been attacked. He escaped the worst of it and fled here, to his family's home village. Half his face is mottled with bruises.

"Attacked?" I ask. "What do you mean, attacked?"

"The Zirids shifted allegiance to Baghdad," he begins.

"That happened months ago," I say.

"The Fatimids' Caliph sent the Bedouin tribes to humble Kairouan."

"Humble it?" I think of the vastness of the city, of its power and wealth and cannot imagine what could humble it.

"They targeted the traders, the souks, the marketplace, for they are what makes Kairouan rich. There were hundreds, perhaps thousands of horsemen, each armed with long lances and sharp daggers. The fine leathers of the tanneries were slashed with knives, the carpets were burnt, the copper pots thrown into the furnaces to lose their beaten shapes and return them to a molten, useless mass."

"Did no-one fight them?" I ask, outraged.

"Those who tried were killed. They were without mercy. Women hid in fear of their honour and their lives, even children were not safe. When night fell the city lay in darkness, all of us cowering in our homes, too afraid to light lanterns in case it drew unwanted attention."

The man takes a shuddering breath and the villagers, gathered around, breath with him.

"And then?" I prompt him.

"We believed the destruction to be complete. They had killed so many, ruined so many livelihoods. Surely it was enough for the Caliph. But in the darkest part of the night certain parts of the city were set alight and many houses burnt to the ground. The smoke choked most of the inhabitants in their sleep."

I feel the fear rising from him even as he speaks, can smell the stink of it even before tears begin to roll down his face. My own fear is so strong I am not even sure the smell of it is not coming from me, from my own body.

"The streets were filled with wailing and screams. Children wandered lost and afraid, animals bleated and brayed. In the shadows men turned on one another and fought, unsure if they were breaking the bones of a stranger or their neighbour, too afraid to pause to find out. By the dawn half the city was on fire and the warriors rode through the streets again, killing anyone they saw. Those who could, escaped the city. Some managed to make their way to a mosque and claim sanctuary, although I do not know if it will be granted once they leave its sacred space."

His family lead the man away to rest, his shoulders heaving.

Moez sits down beside me and puts his arm about my waist. "I cannot believe this has happened," he murmurs. "We will wait before we go there, until it is safe to do so. And we will return here, to live simply, as we planned."

But I am shaking my head. "This is my fault," I say, my face white, my hands cold.

Moez frowns. "What do you mean?"

"I broke my vow," I whisper. "I made a vow to Allah when I was eighteen to atone for a sinful deed and I broke it. I was selfish, thinking only of my own happiness. And He has shown me his displeasure."

Moez turns me to look at him. "Are you mad, Hela?" he asks. "You think breaking a vow you made when you were hardly more than a child has led to the destruction of Kairouan?"

I look into his eyes, his worried gaze. "Yes," I say.

At first he utterly refuses my request to return to Kairouan. "It is not safe, Hela, do you not understand this?" he asks, his usual soft voice rising almost to a shout at my stubborn insistence.

I kneel before his mother. "I ask for your forgiveness," I say. "I am unworthy to be your son's wife. I must go."

"We must not be so proud as to believe that we are the only person of importance to Allah," she says softly. "Hela, I do not know what your vow was, but this destruction – it is our rulers' making, not yours."

I bow my head to her, then rise and leave her home. "I will walk if you will not come with me," I tell Moez.

He does not allow that, of course. We make our way back to Kairouan with only two camels, passing day by day the places where we were once happy. We eat but I do not taste it, we sleep but I toss and turn, then wake when it is still night and beg Moez to continue our journey even in the darkness.

At first we see nothing out of the ordinary, after all we are many days' travel from Kairouan. But when only two days separate us from the city we see the blackened fields where crops and even ancient olive trees have been burnt. We see the city in the distance, smoke plumes still rising from it. We meet more and more people heading away from the city walls, their belongings bundled on carts and camels, mules and donkeys, even on their backs if they have no other means. Their faces are drawn in fear and they do not stop to talk, to tell us more than we already know. We gather only that the warriors of the Banu Hilal and Banu Sulaym tribes still roam the streets, the sharp clatter of their horses' hooves the only bold sound left in a city that cowers and creeps, that huddles in fear.

We leave the camels outside the city walls and make our way in through one of the minor gates. We walk the silent streets, the smell of rotting flesh and smoke thick in our nostrils. I hear Moez retch behind me when we pass a corpse but my eyes are fixed straight ahead. We take care to stick to the side streets and even so we see the invaders pass by a few times, their white robes bright in the sun's glare, their faces fierce. We cower against the walls but they do not care about us, we are too abject to be worthy of their attention now that the city is on its knees before them.

Ibrahim's workshops have been burnt to the ground, the wooden doors gone, with only metal hinges to show where they should hang. I walk through them, my feet sinking in ashes as little scraps of burnt paper patterns and wool float past on the wind.

"Why are we here?" asks Moez.

Because I am afraid to go to the house, I think. *Because people may have escaped from their place of work, but from their own house? Because I am a coward.* I do not speak, only walk away from the workshops and towards home.

The street is silent and the door that leads to Ibrahim's house is gone, fallen into ash.

Moez grips my arm. "Enough," he says. "I ask you not to enter."

I turn to face him and I do not even need to speak.

He steps back from me. "I will be waiting," he says. "Where my shop was, if it is still there – and even if it is not. I will wait for however long it takes."

I do not answer him. I hear his footsteps fade away before I enter the courtyard, where there was once a fountain and a garden.

I do not run or scream. I walk one slow step at a time, as though if I move faster I will not see the full horror of what is before me. I do not scream, I whisper, as though I am afraid of receiving an answer. I breathe in the smell of smoke and I choke out the names of the servants. No-one replies. I stand in silence outside Ibrahim's room and it takes me a long time to raise my hand and push against the charred wood.

I do not enter the room, do not kneel by the side of what I see there, the shape of what used to be a man. I look and then I close my eyes and know that I will never again close my eyes without seeing what I have seen here.

I walk through Djalila's rooms. The metal birdcages sway in the breeze that comes when I open the door and ashes drift in low clouds across the floor with each step that I take. I pause by one cage to touch the black feathers that were once bright yellow and the tiny outstretched wingtip crumbles to nothing. I stand by Djalila's bed and address the wall.

"I failed you."

There is no answer, no sound in this dead house except my own voice.

"I killed your brother because I loved him too much," I tell her, as though she can hear me. "I killed him and then I tried to save you, to atone for what I did to him. I thought if I made you happy again that I would be forgiven. Instead I only made more unhappiness."

The wall is silent but I cannot lower my gaze.

"I made a good man unhappy with my arrogance in thinking I could heal you," I say. "I stole your husband without your knowledge because I desired him and lied to myself about what I was doing." The words come in retches, as though I am vomiting up their poison after all these years of suffering in silence. "I killed a young girl and her unborn child because I could not foresee your bitterness at her innocence. I let your daughter grow up without a mother's touch."

I close my eyes and feel the tears seep out from under my eyelids. "I do not know how to make amends," I say. "I do not know how."

I shelter in the ruins for three days and nights, during which time I do not sleep or eat. I drink a little water, when I remember to, from the last dregs of the courtyard pool, dirty with ashes, which should taste bitter in my mouth but I cannot seem to taste anything. I walk from one room to another, each unrecognisable and then I walk them again and then again, as though I might miraculously find a room that is unharmed. I touch scraps of fabric: blankets, hangings, carpets and each falls to pieces between my fingertips leaving only blackness on my skin. Sometimes I sit and allow the sun to shine on me through the broken window shutters until even its distant heat burns my skin. I try to think but really there is nothing in my mind. I cannot summon up the energy to cry or be angry, not even with myself. Occasionally I close my eyes and something like sleep comes to me although it is not a true sleep but rather a darkness which shows me what I have lost and I quickly re-open my eyes that I may not be tormented.

By the third day something like thoughts return to me. I take things from different parts of the house and collect them in what was once Ibrahim's study. I find coins and some unburnt clothes that only smell of smoke, a water bag.

There is a part of me that thinks: I am free now. Those to whom I owed a debt are all dead and the cup that cursed me is gone, burnt to ashes, all the power it had lost. I am free of its draw, its call on me. I can leave Kairouan and return to the mountains with Moez, live as I dreamt of living. But the ashes on my face when I look in Djalila's mirror tell me otherwise, they show me my only possible future.

Zaynab.

I will serve her if she will let me. I will try to make her happy as atonement for her dead uncle, her dead parents, the love she was never given as a child. I have nothing to offer, but I will serve her as she commands.

I kneel for the dawn prayer and rise, collect up my things and slip out of the garden. I will not go to Moez, for I will only cause him more hurt and he would follow me, would try to help me when I must do this alone.

"Hela! *Hela!*"

I turn and see a boy running towards me, a dirty cloth in one hand. The rising sun behind him makes me squint but as he reaches me I see it is the slave boy I once saved, grown almost to a man. Now he stands before me, panting from his run.

"This is for you," he tells me, holding out the cloth.

I take it and unwrap what lies within its folds. My hands are quicker than my mind, they let the cup fall, as though even my fingers are trying to rid me of it, to let it break into a thousand splinters.

But the boy is too quick for me and he catches the cup even as it falls from my grasp. "I saved it from the fire for you," he tells me solemnly. "So that you can save others as you saved me."

Zaynab

*T*HE JOURNEY WEST AND THEN south to Aghmat is a torture to me. My feet blister from the distances I walk. Few people will give a lift to a woman dressed in rags with a vacant face, who smells of smoke. I frighten them. I have a little money to pay for simple food when I find vendors along the way, but not enough for a place to rest my head when the nights fall, so I sleep in fields or ditches by the side of the road. I see the moon grow fat and thin again and my pace slows, for my feet bleed. I could stop somewhere to let them heal but I am afraid that my money will run out. I stick to the main roads, where caravans of traders pass me by with indifference, but their very presence keeps me safe from bandits and allows me to know that I am travelling in the right direction. A few times a trader allows me to sit on one of their carts or on an under-loaded camel and I bless them in a voice that comes out as a croak, I speak so little. They nod warily at the blessing but I can see that my presence makes them uncomfortable and they are glad when they can leave me behind again. When they ask where I am headed I tell them that I am going to Aghmat, to serve the queen there and they raise their eyebrows at the idea of a crone like myself serving Queen Zaynab, famed for her beauty and for the prophecy that her husband will one day command all of the Maghreb.

Aghmat is a famous city, one that grows with every year that passes. It is a stronghold, a shining jewel along the trade routes. It is one of the first stops when traders return over the treacherous mountains from the desert tribes or the Dark Kingdom in the south. It is their last stop to take on water and food before attempting the desert when they bring goods from the far-off lands in the north, across the sea. Caravans of more than a hundred camels are a matter of course here, carrying salt, gold, silver, the finest cloth – not only wool and linen but silks and those which have been embroidered or woven with golden threads. Delicate glass, sturdy metal, carved wood. As I draw closer I am joined by local farmers and traders on the path to the city walls, bearing oranges, sugar cane, little cakes and pastries, live animals for slaughter. Their baskets and carts make me feel faint with hunger. What food I have eaten along the journey has been the cheapest I could buy: stale bread, scraps of vegetables, worm-eaten fruits. No meat, no sweets. My belly has not been full for a long time. As I enter the city I pass many food stalls but I have no money. I must find Zaynab.

At last the gates of the palace rise up above me. I rest for a moment, tears of relief rising up in me.

The guards are unimpressed when I ask for entry.

"You most certainly cannot see the queen," says one, "Be off with you."

"She knows my name," I tell him. "She will reward you for allowing me into her presence."

"I doubt it," says the other one.

I scrabble through my dirty bag and hold out the cup. "Give this to Zaynab and tell her that Hela is here to serve her," I tell the first guard.

"Fuck off," says the guard and he shoves my shoulder so hard that I fall to the ground.

I look up at him and begin to mumble something. It is only the names of plants, of medicines from far away, but he goes pale, for he thinks I am cursing him.

"All right, all right, crone," he says, blustering but afraid. "Give it here."

I have to shuffle into the throne room, for my feet hurt so badly I cannot bear to lift them up and set them down.

She is here. Beautiful beyond words, lovelier than Djalila but somehow just as sad. She looks at me in fear, perhaps because of the news I bring, perhaps because of my appearance. And she feared me anyway, as a child, she could not see that those about her were scarred from love, she only saw that there was no love given to her and so she sought it elsewhere. And her attempt failed somehow, Yusuf has given her to his king, a man broad in the chest and dressed with magnificence but with something about him that I do not like the feel of.

"You will live here, in the palace," decrees Luqut, once I have told him all I know of Zaynab's loss.

"I beg to live quietly in the city," I ask. "But I will willingly serve the

Queen." I do not want to be too close to this man, to the darkness that hangs over Zaynab, whatever it is.

Luqut shrugs. "As you wish," he says. "A place will be found for you." He calls over an official, speaks briefly with him, nods.

I wait for Zaynab to speak but she says nothing, she only looks at me with her black eyes.

"You will attend Zaynab this evening," decrees Luqut. He indicates a senior-looking official. "Meanwhile you will follow him to your new home."

I shuffle after him. He walks too fast for my blistered feet but we do not go far from the palace. Just outside its walls is a tiny street, almost hidden.

The official stops outside a blue-painted door. He does not bother to show me in, only indicates it with his chin. "Belongs to the king, he says you are to have it now." He hands me a small pouch, which chinks.

I wait for him to enter the house before me but he is already striding away.

The door is small, old, the blue paint thick in its cracks and crevices, as though it has been painted many times. I push against it and it opens with a shudder.

It is a strange little house. There is dust everywhere and no sign of furniture, as though it has been stripped bare at some point in the past. There are only two rooms, each one a little crooked, the walls not smooth. But it has beautiful tiles on the floor and someone has added carved plasterwork to the uneven ceiling, as though the person who lived here before me was both poor and esteemed. There is a tight staircase, which I follow, its walls rough clay, not even painted, but when I reach the top I find myself standing on a small rooftop terrace. It is empty save for a tattered cloth still clinging to two lopsided wooden poles, the remnants of an awning. I could walk the length and breadth of the space in only five steps either way. I stand for a few moments, looking about me at the rooftops around me. Many are taller than mine of course, I cannot see very far across the city. I retrace my steps back to the dark rooms below and place my small bundle on the floor. I look in the small pouch. The money Luqut has given me is generous. I shuffle my way into the bright light of the afternoon to seek out what items I will have need of here. I find a street boy who I pay well to be my guide in this new place and to carry my purchases: a full water jug, cooking utensils and a small brush for sweeping away the dust, blankets, a fresh robe, a bag in which I can carry my belongings, sandals, a cloth to wrap up my hair. I make arrangements with local tradesmen to make me a simple bed, to deliver a large storage jar for water, firewood, to come and make a new awning on my tiny rooftop. I buy food from the street vendors near the blue house and sit on the doorstep to eat, the boy wolfing his portion down in moments.

"Here," I tell him, passing him another coin. "Buy sweet pastries."

He is gone and back in moments and we eat our fill, honey dripping onto our chins, our fingers sticky. My belly aches with fullness, a pain I am grateful for. I pour a little water on both our hands and we drink it, cold and refreshing. The boy's last task is to take me to the hammam, where I bid him farewell, though I am sure he will loiter about my new home on a regular basis now that he knows me as a potential source of both food and coin.

I stand in the blue doorway. My body is cleaner than it has been for a very long time. My hair is wrapped in a cloth, my robe and shoes are stiff with newness. My feet still hurt but I put a healing balm on them and wrapped them in clean cloths, they will mend. The bag I carry contains a few ingredients I chose from the market and the cup. I did not hesitate to take it with me. It was returned to me at the moment when I accepted my fate, it is a sign. I begin my walk to the palace, for darkness is beginning to fall.

When I arrive Zaynab is surrounded by other servants.

"You may all go," I say.

They look to her for confirmation and she hesitates before nodding. They leave the room looking back over their shoulders. Who am I, to arrive in the morning and become their queen's chosen handmaiden by the evening? I do not pay attention to them. I am used to being regarded with suspicion. Instead I look at Zaynab.

"Why did you come here?" she asks. It is the first time I have heard her voice since she left her parents' home.

"Kairouan burnt to the ground," I say.

"You could have gone anywhere," she says.

"I owe your family a debt," I say.

"What debt?" she asks.

I shake my head. "Should I prepare you for the King?" I ask.

I feel the darkness well up in her. "He will prepare me himself," she says and walks away, into another room. I follow her.

The edges of this room are dark. Only the centre gleams in the light of lanterns, their red-gold light shining on polished metal, on the surface of well-worn leather, on the silken ripples of Zaynab's long hair. I look at what is laid out here and when Zaynab turns I meet her gaze in silence. Then I hear footsteps and move behind a wall hanging. She watches me hide and says nothing, only turns to face Luqut as he enters the room.

He orders her to undress and she does so, her robes slipping to the ground. He touches her where he has touched her before, admiring his handiwork, the damage he has done to her skin, rubbing a thumb over each bruise and scar as though it brings him pleasure even now. His large hand grips her throat and forces her chin upwards while his other hand bears down on her shoulder. She sinks to her knees before him.

She does not speak when she is spoken to, she does not beg for mercy when he selects his tools. She is strong, she bears what he does to her longer than I would have thought possible before she cries out and when she does I think, *you will die for this, Luqut.*

He leaves her on the floor afterwards, her body crumpled as though she had fallen from some great height. I wait until his footsteps are far away and then I blow out all the lanterns except one and I tend to her in its dimness. She does not weep, she does not speak, only looks at me when I help her to stand.

"I am here now," I say.

I can see that it is not enough, that she does not trust me, does not believe that my being here can bring about any change in her circumstances. I do not try to convince her. I go over his work with my own, covering each bruise with simple unguents. Now that I am here I will need to make my own, they will be better than the ones I bought in the market. When I am done, I lead her to bed and cover her body with blankets. I ask her a few questions although I am fairly sure of the answers already. I see her eyes well up and think, she is still a child. Married twice, a queen and still a child. I wait for a moment.

"I heard about your vision. Every ambitious man in the Maghreb wanted you for a wife when they heard about it."

I see tears trickling but she does not answer.

"Do you often have visions?"

She does not answer. I already knew it was a lie. I wait in silence for a moment and then I leave her. I pass the servants, the guards. Evidently my name is already known, for no-one bars my way nor questions who I am.

Darkness

I make my way up the rough stairs and reach the roof terrace. I lean my hands on the wall and look out into the darkness, lit here and there with lanterns, before I sit on the bare floor. I take out the cup from my bag and set it before me. And I make a new vow. I may have failed before in what I tried to do but I did not know what I was capable of, I shied away in fear from what was possible. Now I will not hold back from the cup's power. Zaynab's so-called vision may have been the foolish prank of a child crying out for love without knowing the power of what she did but I will make it come true. I have lost everything, there is nothing left to lose.

There will be none such as she, no woman of such beauty or power. Men will lust for her, women will fear her and none will dare harm or stand against her, for I will be at her side. I have been timid and fearful of the powers that I can wield but no longer.

No longer.

Historical notes

Although the settings are as accurate as I could make them at a distance of over a thousand years, Hela herself is an entirely fictional character. While writing my Moroccan trilogy I became fascinated by Hela's backstory. She began as an almost-silent yet powerful woman in the shadows of Zaynab's life and so I ended up writing a prequel novella on Hela's early years.

Zaynab is a real historical character, from Kairouan, Tunisia, a city known for its very fine carpets and rose perfume. Her father was named Ibrahim and she married four times in the course of her life (beginning with Yusuf and then Luqut, the King of Aghmat), eventually becoming the wife of the most powerful man in the Maghreb (North Africa), who created the Almoravid empire, stretching across Morocco and Spain. This apparently fulfilled a vision she had. I tell her story in *None Such as She*, a full-length novel. Her two rivals in love feature in *A String of Silver Beads* and *Do Not Awaken Love*.

After having been a very wealthy and powerful city, Kairouan was attacked in 1057 and more or less ruined for political and religious reasons, although the attacks may have taken place over a longer period. It never really recovered its former importance.

Medicine at this time in the West would have been quite basic but the Islamic world had some very advanced medicinal knowledge and books. Paper was in use.

MELISSA ADDEY

a

String

of

Silver Beads

A String of Silver Beads

Dedicated to Abderrahim El Makkouri, the storyteller in Marrakech.

A glimpse of an older world.

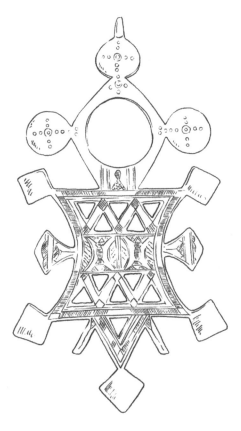

The people of North Africa loosely called Berbers (preferred contemporary name, Amazigh) belong to many tribes and have various names for themselves, including Tuareg. They are known for their blue indigo-dyed robes and beautiful silver jewellery. Women wear the majority of this jewellery and it is highly symbolic, indicating family and tribal ties, marriage status and many other aspects of the wearer's life.

Amongst these peoples it is traditionally the men, not women, who veil their faces.

Marrakech, Morocco, c.1074

A WOMAN'S JEWELS ARE HER LIFE. *I can look at any one of my kinswomen and know her life by the jewels she wears, by their metals, stones, colours, symbols, patterns. I can see her loves and heartbreaks, her children and her family ties. I see all of her while others might see only trinkets bought in the hot jostling souks.*

I sit alone on the tiled floor and look over all my jewellery laid out before me.

I am a woman of the Tuareg people. We are not bound to any one leader to tell us how to live our lives. We are free to wander the desert with our flocks, to move along the trade routes with spices, fruits, nuts, gold and skins. We are free to stay in our villages and care for our crops and beasts. We are many: different, changeable, but all free.

I must choose my path now.

My hands shake. My eyes blur. Across this floor is laid my life, in silver, gold, amber, carnelian, every colour and every symbol that has marked the tale of my days. I begin. I wear only a simple robe. There is no time for fussing over colours and textures to please the eye. I lift each item of jewellery from the floor, in the order in which it came to me. Slowly, I put on each piece, my hands struggling with the clasps.

Watch, now, as I lift up each jewel, for it will tell you my story.

Maghreb (North Africa), c.1067

Tchirot – A Man's Amulet

M Y CAMEL THIYYA CAN FEEL the growing excitement around us. Foregoing her usual stance of elegant boredom she shifts back and forth on the spot, even ignoring a tasty clump of foxtail grass nearby. My knees grip the carved wood of my light racing saddle, the red leather trim slick with my sweat. My face is veiled but my bare feet, resting on Thiyya's long neck, give my nerves away, my toes curling into her short white fur.

"Kella! Not again!" The hissed exclamation below startles me and Thiyya's head jerks up, but I steady her. Looking down at my eldest brother's appalled face, I can't help but laugh.

"Sister – "

His voice is too loud. I lean down towards him. "Shh! You'll give me away."

"Tell me why I should not!"

I tighten the veil to make sure my face is well hidden but he can still hear my laughter when I answer. "Because the rest of our brothers have already wagered on my success." I look across at my youngest brother who is smirking at my eldest brother's outrage. "A dagger as the prize, wasn't it? Very fine. I saw it earlier on that young lout's belt. It will look most grand on you, I'm sure. When I win."

My eldest brother sighs and absent-mindedly pats Thiyya when she nuzzles him.

"Don't sigh like that. Haven't I won you many fine things with my riding skills over these past few years? Where's the harm in that?"

"Would you care to ask our father the same question?"

I shrug. My voice comes out sulky. "I don't see why only men can race."

He walks alongside the camel as we make our way towards the other riders. He gives me his new lecture, the one he has learnt from our father. He never used to be so priggish but having recently been wed he feels he is a grown man and must give guidance to us, his younger siblings. Especially me. "Because, sister. Just because. It is not seemly. Women ride camels for great occasions. A wedding perhaps. And when they do, they have a woman's saddle. They do not ride here, there and everywhere for all to gawp at. And they do not *race* camels."

"But I am the best rider. Five brothers and not one of you can beat me in a race! You have to admit that."

"I didn't question your riding ability. I questioned its propriety."

"Oh, who cares for propriety? I'm dressed like a boy all the time. I ride camels all the time. I might as well enjoy winning the races. Now move away, before the other riders wonder what you're doing escorting me to the starting line. They'll think I'm not much of a man if I have to be accompanied everywhere!"

"And you are such a great man, I suppose?"

I giggle. "Oh, yes. I make a fine young man!"

He raises his hands in despair and turns away.

I call after him, my voice wavering a little now that I'm to be left alone. "Won't you wish me luck?"

He turns back. "I thought you were such a great rider you'd have no need of luck!"

I nudge Thiyya closer so that I can reach out and touch his shoulder. "Everyone needs luck."

My eldest brother is a good-hearted man and cannot stay cross with me for long. He reaches up and puts one broad hand over my smaller one. "May Allah keep the wind from rising and may your camel's feet fly. May you win a great race, my *brother*."

I grin. "Thank you. You may go now."

My brother waves over his shoulder as he walks back to join the gathering crowds.

A big market draws people from a wide area and impromptu festivals spring up. The people come for the food, the trading, the songs and stories and of course for the races, which inevitably take place when the younger men want to show off their camels and their prowess in riding.

For the last few years, ever since I've been tall enough to pass for a young man in my all-encompassing indigo blue robes, I've been entering the camel races at these events and winning more and more often. Now, at seventeen, I am an excellent rider. My camel is a beautiful white beast with blue eyes, a great rarity and a prized gift from my over-generous father. I trained her myself, starting when she was only a baby. I would stand beside her issuing commands, while she peered at me in astonishment through long-lashed blue eyes, wondering who this child-master was. It took a few years, for a camel's training cannot be rushed, but now I have a magnificent beast as my mount, who half-believes she is my sister. I named her Thiyya, 'beautiful', and no-one can argue with my choice of name. I am forever being offered two, three, or even, on a memorable occasion, five camels if I will trade Thiyya for plainer and less speedy animals, but I always refuse. My brothers occasionally race her but she does not try as hard for them as she does for me.

From my high perch I scan the crowds, anxious to avoid my father. My shoulders relax when I fail to spot him. He must be conducting business somewhere. There are traders who buy and sell only one kind of merchandise, such as salt or slaves, skins or jewellery. Their lives are dull to my eyes, always travelling back and forth from the same places, then trading on to the smaller traders such as us. Our family's camels carry delicate perfumes and small packets of herbs or spices, precious metals and stones; some already transformed into glorious pieces rich with patterns and colours, some left unworked for local jewellers who are glad of new materials. There are skins and furs, as well as fine cloths and rugs that are laid flat and then rolled up tightly to keep them smooth and safe from fading in the sun's powerful rays. As we journey we add fresher items to our stock – oranges, dates, nuts – less costly but always desirable. We visit the great trading posts and then go out amongst the little towns, the tiny villages, even to the nomad camps of the desert. We move from dunes to cities and see all manner of people. We are welcomed by all, for we bring news and excitement as well as goods from the greatest city to the most isolated desert tent.

The heat increases and the crowd grows thicker, bodies pressed tightly together. The other camels sidle back and forth, some straining at their bridles, the odd one or two suddenly leaping forward into a run before the race has begun, their owners having to force them back to the start. I wipe the sweat from under my eyes and shift my position to achieve a better balance. There will be no such opportunity once the race has begun. I look about me, waiting for the signal to begin. The men in the crowd are laying last-minute bets, the younger women are giggling over certain names: the riders with the best camels, the best saddles, the best eyes… my eyes fix on the race master, a burly man currently shoving a camel away who has come too close to him, overstepping its mark.

He shouts and for one brief instant the crowd is silent. Then his arm waves and I kick my legs hard into Thiyya's sides. Her neck has already lengthened and now her usual swaying gait becomes a jolting run and then a smooth gallop.

The crowd roars as we leave them behind us. The older women clap and cheer on their sons and laugh at their husbands' wild yells, occasionally grabbing at a younger child and warning them to keep out of the way – the camels will be turning back in moments and they might find themselves trampled by a whirl of long, strong legs. A painful way to end your life, for sure.

I feel as though I am flying, like the desert spirits of the old times. Thiyya's neck reaches out ahead of her as though yearning for even greater speed. Though the dust rises all around the riders we are too far ahead of the pack for it to reach us, faster than the very wind, faster than the swirls of sand.

"On! On!" I shout at Thiyya, though she does not need my command. I shout again and again, a wordless scream of joy and hunger for the win.

Some of the best camels are gaining on us now, for a few improve in a longer race. I look over my shoulder and Thiyya can feel me tense, for she strains forward with her long neck, wanting to be further ahead. But the halfway point has come and I pull hard to make her wheel about, her long legs almost caught up in themselves. As soon as we turn the choking sand surrounds us. I can barely see, can barely gasp for air, even though the cloth pulled tight across my mouth protects me from the worst of it. I do not know how Thiyya can still breathe but she thunders on, the shadowy shapes of the slowest camels passing us in the cloud as we head back towards the screaming crowd. I look back once and see only the blue robes of the other riders, floating above the camel-coloured clouds of sand like some strange vision in the heat of the day.

The screams grow louder and louder until they are all about me and I raise my arm and punch the air. I am the winner. My breath comes hard in my throat and I look down on all the uplifted faces surrounding me, the hands slapping at my legs in praise and feel my face stretched in a hidden grin.

Shouted praises and boasts are all about me. In the crowd, possessions and sometimes even coins trade hands as bets are won and lost. Backs are thumped and hands clasped. The younger boys and older girls gaze adoringly up at me.

I remain on Thiyya, acknowledging comments and praise with a wave before turning her away from the crowd. I cannot let my identity be known and so I never linger once a race is won. Let the glory go to the second and third places, the riders who wish to boast and brag. I want only the wild freedom of the ride, the fierce joy of winning. That, I can best savour alone.

I spot my eldest brother who rolls his eyes at me and comes closer, pulling at my bridle. "Do you have to win *every* time, Kella?" he mutters. "It draws attention to you."

I laugh down at him. "To race without winning is not to race at all!" I say, my voice still elated. He shakes his head, but lets me go.

I make my way to our camp, set up on the outskirts. Here, among the one hundred or more camels of our caravan, I leap down from Thiyya and put on my sandals. I give her water and caress her, croon to her before I leave her to rest. Then I make my way into the main tent, pulling at my headdress as I do so, loosening its folds, then flinging it to one side.

Inside it is dark and cool. I reach for a cup and dip it into the water jar, greedily gulping down the cold water.

"Daughter."

I freeze, then carefully replace the wooden cup before I turn round, my face composing itself into an unworried smile. "Father. I thought you were speaking with the salt trader."

"I was. Then I went to see the camel races."

"Who won?" I try to keep my voice light as I seat myself on the foot of the low bed and kick off my sandals again, feigning a lack of interest while my heart thuds in my chest.

"I believe you did. On Thiyya. No-one else here has a white camel with blue eyes."

"One of my brothers – " I try but my father's eyes tell me not to bother. My shoulders slump.

My father settles himself at the head of the bed and sighs. He looks older than usual. "I know you are a good rider, daughter. And I turn my face away when you race against your brothers. You work hard, after all, and what is a little fun between siblings? In the desert no-one but our family and the slaves will see you. Amongst others you have always passed well enough for a boy."

I seize on this, my only excuse. "No-one here knows I am a girl. Everyone thinks I am your youngest son. No-one would suspect."

"You think not? When your hands are still so slender and your voice so light? No. I believe the time is coming very soon when I will have to return you to the main camp, to live with your aunt."

I feel as though I have received a blow to the stomach. I twist round to face him, appalled. "Aunt Tizemt?"

He laughs. "You need not look so upset. Your aunt is a good woman and she has the heart of a lion. She will teach you to be a fine woman."

"It is her voice that is like a lion," I spit.

"No need to sulk. She is a kind woman beneath her roars. I will not have my daughter dishonoured. You will no longer race."

"But – "

"No buts. No more racing. You will remain disguised as a boy until I can take you back to your aunt. If you are very, very well behaved I may keep you with me a little longer. You are a good trader, after all, I will be sorry to lose your skills in the markets. I believe you secured us a bargain with the salt trader, he was as meek as a lamb when I saw him just now. We will have a camel's load of salt to trade at the next market."

I jump up, my mind racing to find a reason to stay that he will accept. "You cannot send me back to the main camp! I am a trader. I travel with you – with my brothers! What would I do at the camp?"

My father smiles. "Get married?"

"*Married*?"

He laughs at my horrified face. "Have you never thought of that possibility? Your eldest brother is married, two of your other brothers are already betrothed. Did you not consider it might be your turn soon? What, no young man caught your eye yet? No-one beaten you at camel racing?"

I snatch up the swathes of indigo cloth that make up my headdress and glare at him through the narrow eye slit as I wrap it tightly about my face. "No-one beats me at camel racing. And I am not getting married. I am staying with you, with the caravan. I am a trader. Now I am going to the salt trader. He promised me more than a camel's load of salt for that price."

"Your mother would have wanted you happily married," says my father sadly.

I walk so fast to the salt trader's encampment that I am breathing heavily by the time I reach it. The great slabs of salt lashed to saddles are piled up around his main tent, then surrounded by the prickly thorn bush branches placed to discourage every camel for miles around from sneaking up to get a free lick of salt. Camels will do anything for salt. The trader comes out to greet me, warily offering tea and a place in the shade to do business when he sees my glare. My only chance to escape being sent back to my aunt is surely to trade and to trade well. My father cannot send me away if I make myself valuable to him as a great trader.

The moon grows full and wanes twice over and still there is no mention of my Aunt Tizemt. I begin to hope that my good trading efforts have made my father forget his threats. I stay away from the camel races.

We reach an important centre on the caravan routes. A mayhem of a souk. Stretched out over a vast area and yet still crowded.

Its camel souk is beyond compare, and it is here that frantic bids are commonly made for the lovely blue-eyed, white-furred Thiyya, a rarity even here among thousands of camels. She picks her way daintily through the crowds, enjoying the caresses, soft words and sometimes handfuls of fruits that come her way. Seated comfortably on her back, above the crowd, I laugh and joke with all those who make offers for her.

"I'll trade you three fine camels for her," says one, gesturing to what look like three ancient crones, wizened dun-brown, spitting this way and that.

I laugh. "I'd need a hundred of those for this one," I tell him. "One of those will fall over dead before I can even get them to stand up."

"I'll trade you my wife," says one man dourly and there's a shout of laughter.

"I'm sure my camel's prettier than your wife," I tease him.

"She is," he says mournfully and wanders off into the crowd.

More serious offers are made but I shake my head and with a gentle nudge from my feet Thiyya moves on. Grunts and roars are all around us, from baby camels, untrained camels and wise veteran camels. Almost-black camels rub haunches with the rare pure whites, golden sand camels with date-brown camels. Sweet cajoling, shrugged shoulders and moral outrage make up the bulk of the bartering, which may go on for days and is a sport in itself. On the busiest days, of course, there will be camel races and the traders' sons boast of their skills in advance, some louder than other, safe in the knowledge that their fathers plan to move on before the next race and their airy boasts will not have to be made flesh.

Everything is traded here. Some merchants are free to roam and do not have to barter, for they are about to go to the dark south. There they will expend all their energies and all their trade goods to return with precious gold for princes and dark-skinned slaves. They will make their fortunes or die alone in the blistering sun, far away from their loved ones and any merciful shade, on the long, long routes where bandits may steal their goods and their lives. Others have already come from those lands and their relief at having come thus far makes them bold and free with their words. They eat and drink more than others and enjoy the company of their friends, while trading good-natured insults with their competitors.

They reserve their sweet words for certain women who make it their business to attend all such gatherings, whose faces are pretty and whose clothes hint at the goods for sale underneath the shining threads and tinkling bangles. As a young child I thought their lives delightful, for they wore pretty clothes and ate sweet foods all day and laughed a great deal. As I've grown older I've heard comments, here and there, from my brothers and the traders I frequent, and now I am all too aware of what they trade in. The women toss their long dark hair and call out in many different tongues, for they have learnt that a few words in a man's own language can tempt him to take a second look as he walks by, especially if his wife is far away and he is homesick. The women sit in comfort in highly decorated open-sided tents on soft cushions and play with their jewellery, gifts from many men. They drink fresh water and suck on oranges in the heat of the day. They offer honeyed drinks, dried fruits and promises of other sweet things to the men who stray a little too close to their warm rugs and the soft lanterns that will be lit when night comes.

"Come, my handsome friend," they call out as I pass. "Will you not take some – ah – *refreshment* with me?" and they giggle.

I make a mock bow in their direction and try to keep my voice low. "Ah, ladies, if only I could," I call back. "But I must trade or go hungry."

"Surely you are hungry for more than food?" they call.

I laugh and walk on.

The older merchants are known friends by now and often sit with the women during the day, telling lewd jokes, relishing the shrieks of laughter as the younger traders relish the shrieks of feigned delight in closed tents a little way off.

This is my world and I swagger through it in my man's robes, my heart light. My relief at being reprieved and able to stay on the trading routes makes it seem as though I see all of this life anew. My eyes, the only part of my face visible, dart in all directions, taking in every colour, shape and size. I stop sometimes; a quick rub of my fingers establishing quality without a word. The old traders know me and nod without trying to woo me with sweet words. They know their quality will bring me back later when there is serious bargaining to be done. The newer ones offer teas, dates, sweet cakes dripping with honey, a soft seat in the shade, a cool drink of water, the finest goods in the souk – in the world, even! To these my quickly disappearing soles are an instant dismissal.

Oh how I love these moments! Surrounded by the world and all it has to offer, my every sense assailed with wonders. Knowing my own skills, the respect I command for my knowledge and my skills in bargaining, knowing that somewhere here are all the marvellous things that will soon be hoisted onto our camels.

My first stop is the slave souk. I need a new slave; a strong man, for one of our slaves has grown old and weak. He carries out the smaller tasks now, but he is no longer fit for the heavier work. I wait at the back of the crowd while the slave trader calls his wares. We are old friends and he knows that I will spot quality for myself, so he addresses the rest of his audience.

"A little boy here – you may think him small but I assure you he is strong already and can only grow stronger. My wisest clients know it is worth buying them young!"

The boy can hardly be more than ten, although his scrawny body makes me wonder if he is even younger. He stands still and miserable in the heat, till someone pokes him and nods grudgingly at a price that changes hands.

Spices float through the air from the cooking fires where fat spits, sizzles and drips. I am hungry. The slaves for sale stand, heads down in the sun, hoping to be sold quickly to someone who will find it in their heart to offer them water and some shade. Their teeth are examined, their eyelids pulled down and their arms squeezed. The tall and broad ones go quickly;

the thinner or scrawnier ones must wait longer in the heat, along with the ill-favoured women who do not quickly catch someone's eye. Sometimes one faints, only to be slapped back to their feet by an irate merchant. I am impatient at waiting while the slight men and the unprepossessing women are offered for sale. But I have been promised that there is one worth waiting for. We are in need of a strong male slave and his time has finally come.

"You will not see a finer man! From the Dark Kingdom, the land of gold! See his height and his shoulders. He can carry as much as a camel and his legs are like those of a fine racing stallion – see their elegance, ladies!" This last is directed towards two women passing by. They take a startled second look and then hurry on, giggling.

I lean against a scrap of a tree, which gives me a little shade, to watch. The slave is very tall; he would tower over me if we were to stand side by side. He is wearing only a loincloth and I look over his body, assessing it for strength and endurance while shaking my head at the foolishness of putting any man in this sun with no protection, whatever his colour. A few customers prod at him, one even punches him in the stomach to assess either his peaceable nature or the strength of his muscles, but he stays silent and unmoving, head up in the hot sun. He will faint for sure, however big and strong he is. Often the big ones go down first. The trader is a fool to risk damaging his goods like that. A fainting slave can forget being sold for the day; it makes them seem weak and prone to illness, no matter their height and breadth.

The trader has almost finished the bidding. A good price is being offered for the man, but I make a small gesture and the trader notes it at once.

"Come, come, step forward. That is your new master and you had better behave for he is one of my best customers. Move!"

The slave slowly steps down from the raised platform and makes his way to me. I nod to him and turn away, expecting him to follow. After a few steps I realise he has not done so and turn back. The slave is standing looking back at the platform, where the trader has brought on a woman.

"This one is fit for a caliph's harem! A joy, a beauty. See how smooth her skin is, how dark like the precious woods of her land. Her face is very fine – lift your face up, girl! – see! Now, what man would not wish to have such a face by his side in the morning? And such breasts!" He pulls at her simple robe, exposing a breast and tweaks her nipple, while eyeing up his audience to spot interest. If he can make a buyer desire the woman as a companion for his bed, he will get a better price for her than as a mere slave for domestic chores. "You, sir?"

The bidding starts but my eyes are drawn to my new acquisition. He is looking at the slave girl with an expression of abject misery and she is looking back at him instead of at her bidders, as the trader points out sharply, jerking her roughly back to face towards the crowd. Slow, silent tears fall down her face and although she obediently faces the bidders, her eyes slide sideways to catch a last glimpse of the man I have just bought.

I have no need for unnecessary slaves. Women especially are of less use to us than the men, for they cannot carry such heavy loads. I click my fingers at the slave to get his attention and prepare to tell him sharply to come along with me. But there is something about the woman's silence, about the tears that never stop falling. I hesitate and then reluctantly raise a hand. The trader blinks at me, puzzled.

"The pretty slave is sold to the gentleman, it seems," he says. There are some protests but he waves them away and pushes the woman towards me. She stumbles down the steps, almost shaking with relief. She tries a few words of gratitude, although she struggles with our language. I wave her away. It must be the heat, I cannot imagine what else it could be, nor why, in a fit of sunstroke, I have seen fit to buy a female slave only because of a few tears. But it is too late now, the trader will not take her back.

"Follow," I say. I turn away from them and make my way back to our tent, hardly caring whether they are following me or not. I curse under my breath. What was I thinking, to buy a female slave? It is exactly the sort of foolish decision that will have my father sending me home, camel racing or no camel racing.

Back at the tents of our caravan I wave them towards the water jar and they both drink gratefully and then turn to face me.

I take a seat and drink from a water cup. I look them over and then speak slowly, hoping they will understand. "Names?"

This much at least they know.

"Ekon." This from the man, who has a soft voice for such a large frame.

I look at the woman. She is nothing special; I hope she will be useful but she is hardly worth what I paid for her. I have to lean forward as she all but whispers her name.

"Adeola."

I nod, turning the names over in my mind. Slaves often come from the

Dark Kingdom, very far away in the south. Still, the names sit strangely on our tongues.

"You will be part of our caravan. We are traders. We have other slaves. Some of them come from your own country. You can speak together. Join them now." I point towards two of our older slaves who have been with us for many years and have been watching with great curiosity while their hands keep moving, churning milk to make butter, shaking the goatskin bags back and forth to a smooth rhythm.

Adeola turns obediently to join the others. Ekon stands still and then approaches me. I draw back a little and put my hand to my belt where I keep a sharp dagger. He is very tall and I have a quick moment of fear. What if he attacks me? Some slaves do. I have heard of such madness, when for one brief moment a slave finds their own dignity again and the anger that comes with it.

But Ekon ignores my gesture and comes still closer. Then in one smooth movement, he kneels before me and touches his face to the ground, first one cheek, then the other. He looks up and I see tears in his eyes. He does not speak but rises slowly to his feet, looking down on me again for a moment. His dark lips still have a few grains of golden sand stuck to them from the floor but he does not brush them away. He turns slowly and joins the others who have been watching, breathless.

I feel my own breath release, although I hadn't realised I was holding it.

My trading is good in the days that follow. My father raises his eyes at the slave woman's presence but cannot fault my other purchases. While I negotiate my way from the first glass of tea to the last honeyed cake, my parcels, packages and heaps of skins grow ever larger and our caravan prepares for the next journey.

The camels rest, licking salt and enjoying the luxury of sitting slowly chewing the cud rather than the constant walking under heavy loads. They drink water daily and enjoy passing treats given by children, graciously permitting them to play at riding them in return.

The slaves milk goats and churn butter as well as making cheese. They kill the male kids. There is time to roll finely ground grains of barley to make buttery soft couscous, to prepare mouth-watering marinades of goat's milk and spices that bring tenderness and subtlety to the meats. Time to slice oranges and serve them with cinnamon and rosewater rather than quickly munching them and spitting out the bitter skins between one day's journey and the next. Cracked wooden spoons and metal pots are replaced. The new carvings and patterns are appraised and give added pleasure to the dishes.

We eat well and invite many guests to our fire, other traders and sometimes their families. Among them is Winitran, an old trader I have known since my brothers and I were little children. He is a kindly man and an excellent jeweller, although his eyes are growing tired and he no longer does the finer work. Yet we make sure to trade with him whenever we pass by here.

"You'll be back at the usual time next year?" he asks my father.

"Of course," says my father. He thinks for a moment. "Although perhaps my youngest will soon join our village rather than continuing to trade. My sister is growing older and so he may be a help to her." He is careful, always, not to use my name; not to let slip that I am a girl.

I sit bolt upright, seething. I've traded well and yet my father is still talking of sending me back to Aunt Tizemt! I scowl but under my veil no-one can see me. I hope that by next year, when we are due back here, he will have forgotten. It's a long way off. I might still change his mind.

Winitran turns to his attention to me as the others talk of trading. "I have something for you," he says. "Something to remember me by." From his robes he pulls out a little leather pouch and shakes out its contents into his hand.

It's a *tchirot*, a man's silver amulet. A simple silver square, intricately engraved, hanging below a small scroll-shaped silver box. Between the two is a hinge, allowing the two parts of the pendant to move back and forth independently.

Winitran holds it out to me. "It contains the sand from the entrance to my house and my blessing for your own journey, that you may always find your way safely home."

I bow my head, keeping my voice low as I answer. I'm fond of the old man and he's been good to me over the years. But I wish he didn't feel the need to say goodbye to me as though he will never see me again. "My thanks for the amulet. And for your blessings."

Winitran lays his hand gently on my arm. "Blessings, daughter," he says very softly, so that none of the other guests can hear him.

I pull my arm back quickly. "How did you know? No-one ever guesses."

Winitran chuckles. "I am an old man and have seen many things. But I should tell you that a *tchirot* is a man's jewel, you know, not a woman's."

"I know. May I keep it anyway?"

Winitran smiles. "Of course. I think you may be more of a man than many young men who think themselves most manly." He pats my arm and then turns back to the others, joining in their laughter and talk while I finger the *tchirot*. I can't help feeling a little pride in his praise of me.

We prepare to move on. The tent must be taken down and made into bundles that can be quickly and easily pulled from a camel to reassemble into a living space wherever we might be. The slaves curse under their breath when old straps will not come undone but work fast and soon the tent crumples to the ground, sections already being taken away. The camels are loaded up and stand blinking haughtily, shuffling from one leg to the other, pushing out their stomachs as the men tighten their saddles. A quick poke to the belly and they blow out, disgusted at the failure of their cunning plan as the straps are pulled tighter. The lead camel, my father's, is a very dark brown female of great docility when dealing with her master and utter viciousness when approached in any way by anyone else. She values her place in the lead, however, as it enables her to ever-so-subtly adjust her position when walking and reach out her thick lips for the leaves of passing poplars and willows. My father allows her to get away with it when he is in a good mood. When he is not he corrects her direction and she rolls her eyes back at him and glowers at the titbit passing her by.

Each camel receives its due – a saddle and then a range of burdens are meted out. The lucky ones get a single rider; perhaps an inexperienced slave, easy to fool into allowing it a stop or a nibble of passing food. The less lucky ones get heavier people; the strong male slaves, or piles of trading goods and the party's cooking pots and provisions. They droop their heads and try to look hard done by but their efforts are in vain as more goods come their way. At last they give up all pretence of delicacy and stand, blowing their warm breath into the cold air, bored and sulky by turns.

A new city and its souk. One known for its camel races.

The young men boast and show off their saddles; some new and some old but polished so hard that their colours shine, almost reflecting their owners in the wood and leather. The riders introduce their camels as they might a well-favoured bride, boasting of her beauty, her good breeding and wondrous abilities. Meanwhile they pour scorn on their rivals' beasts, pointing out bucked, yellowed and missing teeth, straggly coats, an old saddle that will be bound to break under any strain.

"I don't care for your camel's knees," one says, winking at his friends while shaking his head in sadness at his rivals' grave misfortune. "Too knobbly, as you can see. Not like my camel's – now she's a beauty!"

One camel is given particular care, although mostly in secret. Thiyya grunts as I examine her pads and brush her coat. She sighs when the old worn tack is exchanged for new, stiffer reins and a halter that rubs her face a little at first. She groans when the straps of the saddle pull her stomach in a little tighter. But she makes contented sounds when she is offered a little more salt than the others, a few handfuls of dates and even some whey left over from the cheesemaking. I whisper endearments and praise into her soft ears for her long legs, her speed, her strength. Thiyya blinks her spidery white eyelashes and takes all such praise as her due.

It is months since I have raced and I can bear it no longer. I have avoided all the races in minor souks and trading cities, turned my face away, allowed my brothers to ride Thiyya without a murmur. But this race... this is the one where the champions compete, where the very best stretch their mounts and themselves to the limit; where just last year Thiyya came second by only a muzzle-length and I know that she could win. If I could just spur her on a little more, just the length of her neck and we would win. I can taste the glory of it. Not the prizes or bets, for I have never cared about them. But the elation, the thunder of feet followed by the fierce joyful moment of triumph. Briefly, I consider riding a different camel, to hide my intentions from my father, but I know in my heart that Thiyya will make me a winner, that none of our other camels can win.

I beg my youngest brother to aid me.

"But if our father – " he begins.

I shake my head. "No, no. You will stand close to me all the time in the crowd. When I mount Thiyya, who will know for sure which of us did so? And when I win – "

"*When* you win?"

"*When* I win," I say firmly. "When I win you must be at my side again, as soon as you are able. Then I will slip down and you can take Thiyya's reins. Parade around, show her off, make a fuss, strut a little. People will forget which of us exactly they saw. And with any luck father will only see you. I will be back in our tent, well-behaved and irreproachable."

"Kella…"

"Please," I beg him. "Please."

"Very well," he says. "But if this goes wrong it falls on your head."

"How can it go wrong?" I ask.

The early evening grows cooler as the crowds gather for the race. Those riding arrive with their camels walking proudly behind them. The spectators fight over good positions, some little boys even attempting to watch from palm trees for a better view; their elders laugh at them as their grip begins to falter before the last of the riders has even arrived.

My father is safely in another part of the city; I saw him set off with my own eyes before I crept out of our tent, my younger brother already well ahead of me, leading Thiyya by the reins to the race track. I arrive just before the race begins. Envious looks are cast.

"Azrur's two youngest sons. They are excellent riders and win often. I would not bet against them if I were you!"

"They've been working hard this week though, out every day and half the night trading. Maybe they are a little weary by now. Might be worth a small wager against one of them."

"Don't say I didn't warn you – I've lost a dagger and a belt because of them!"

The crowd jostle, excited as the race grows nearer. Children are hoisted onto shoulders. The women begin their ululation, the shrill trilling echoing out across the dunes, making the younger camels sidestep, ears pricked. The more experienced camels tense. Soon they will be racing and they are keen. After days of good feeding and drinking they are rested and full of strength. They want to run, to feel the heat of the other camels all around them, the sand and wind in their ears, their riders' feet and voice urging them on.

I squat down to take off my shoes. I prefer to ride barefoot. My brother crouches beside me, the better to maintain our deception.

"Are you riding in the race?" An eager little boy is standing behind me. He tugs at my veil, tightly wrapped about my head, hoping for my attention.

"Let go," I snap, feeling the veil loosen.

He makes a face at me and retreats. I fumble with the veil, trying to tighten it again. It is difficult to do; it takes several moments each day to wrap it about my head as a turban and then tuck in the last part as a veil around my face. To adjust it here, in a crowd, is taking too long and I cannot simply remove it and start again.

"Mount," hisses my brother. "The signal will come at any moment."

Quickly I mount Thiyya and move her into the starting place, alongside the orders.

A hush falls. Our eyes look for nothing but the signal and when it comes there is a slow pounding, growing faster and faster. The crowd yells and once again the riders' blue robes float as though we are spirits of the air.

I am lost in the moment, in the rise and fall, the air clear around me as we pass the other riders. I have missed this. The freedom of the wind rushing past my face, the strength and power of Thiyya. A raw scream rises from my lungs as we pass the leading camel. I look back to see the narrowed eyes of its rider, angry at being passed already, well before the halfway mark. I hear the *crack* of his whip but there is nothing he can do. I am flying. Thiyya turns as though she is dancing, twirling, and now I face all my competitors, their heads lowered against the rising sand and the taste of defeat. I am already looking for the finish line, somewhere ahead of me in the whirling sand. Now I hear the ground shaking as the other riders head back, still comfortably behind me but drawing closer and I turn for a brief moment to see them, shimmering blue shapes against the gold of sand and camels. Looking ahead again I see the crowd trying to draw back as we reach them although there is nowhere for them to draw back to. Their screams of excitement are mixed with fear, yet no-one would miss this moment. I raise my arm in triumph when suddenly something blue flutters before my eyes and my whole headwrap falls, falls even as I try to catch it but Thiyya is still running and my clutching is too late, I hear the gasps before it has even fallen to the ground.

For I might be dressed in a man's blue robes, and have cropped hair. But I am no man. The winner of the camel race is a young woman! People jostle forward to take a better look, children ask excited questions of their unhearing parents and the runners-up begin to hurl insults, made more fierce by their shame at having just been beaten by a woman.

I look desperately this way and that, Thiyya's head jerking up nervously at all the excitement and at my shaking hands on the reins. I try to use part of my robes to cover my exposed face and then my head drops as I try to shield it from the gaze of hundreds of people, all staring at me in aghast amazement.

The reins are suddenly pulled from my hands, the leather burning my palms. The crowd falls back around my father as he tugs at Thiyya, who follows meekly as though she feels his anger and fears its redirection towards herself.

People begin to follow as he leads Thiyya back to our tent, but the look he throws at them makes them fall back. They rejoin their friends to gossip and speculate.

"Was it always her then? On that white camel?"

"Must have been."

"It's a disgrace. A girl! Racing!"

When they catch sight of my brothers in the crowd they surround them, asking questions, some outraged, some teasing.

"What kind of man lets his sister ride in the camel races?"

"So – any more beautiful young women under those veils, eh? Perhaps your father has six daughters, not six sons as we were led to believe!"

My five brothers push past in silence, their eyes cast down.

I stand sobbing outside our tent. Thiyya noses me, her moist huffing breath meant as a comfort. All around us is chaos as the slaves hurry about, dismantling our tent, packing up the caravan. They've been given no warning and everything is in disorder.

My eldest brother steps towards me, his face concerned. "Sister –" he begins.

I wave him frantically away, still crying. "Father says I'm not to speak to any of you. He says I'm a disgrace." My shoulders shake uncontrollably before I burst out again. "I didn't mean to unveil! It got caught and came off, I tied it badly and it was loose from the race! He is so angry! He says we are going back to the village, right now. He says I will be left with Aunt Tizemt and never trade again!"

"Where is he?" My youngest brother's voice trembles. He hates angry scenes. He holds out a length of cloth so that I can veil my face again.

I shake my head. "In the tent. He won't let me veil my face again. He said I am a woman and I'd better get used to dressing like one!"

We stand helplessly around the tent. The slaves lower their eyes and speak between themselves in tiny whispers while they hurry to get the camels loaded up. My brothers try to avoid looking at my face with its cropped hair, my skin sun-darkened around the eyes and pale everywhere else.

Our father strides out of the main tent. Behind him the slaves rush to dismantle it, the last item standing.

My father gestures for our riding camels to be brought forward and then yells: "Kneel!"

The camels can feel anger and each of them sinks without protest to their knees. My brothers and father mount, the slaves behind them just managing to prepare the last camel in time before taking their places.

I stand by Thiyya, tears trickling down my exposed face. I feel like a fool. I have lost my freedom and for what? For a race? I look at my father. His eyes tell me there will be no reprieve, no way back.

"Get on Thiyya at once." His voice is tight with anger.

"Father – "

"At once!"

I climb onto Thiyya's back and sit, waiting awkwardly, clasping my waterbag as though it is some magic charm against my current disgrace, not daring to give the command to rise myself.

"Rise!"

More than one hundred camels stand in unison, ready for the long journey home.

Celebra – A Woman's Necklace

*T*HE WATER IN MY GOATSKIN bag is unpleasantly warm and tastes of
goat. We have been travelling since dawn today but now the sun's
heat is beginning to seep into us. We should stop and seek shade but
we are very close to the camp now, so we press on.

My eyes are fixed on my father's silent back, up ahead of me. His camel,
the colour of dried dates, is particularly good at mirroring her master's
moods and at this moment she is walking with her head held very high and
a majestically haughty look to her slowly swaying hindquarters. Neither of
them wants to listen to my repeated pleas to turn back.

I drink again, grimacing.

The camp seems smaller than my memories of it. It's been a few years since
our last visit.

The children playing at the top of the dunes spot us from a distance
and run to escort us with whoops of excitement and endless questions. My
younger brothers smile at them and lift a few of the smaller ones up to join
them on their saddles. These lucky ones cling on tightly and make faces at
their lowly comrades. As we approach the camp's mud walls the men and
women come to greet us with wide smiles as soon as they recognise us,
exclaiming over how much older we are, pretending mock-horror over my
man's robes.

Aunt Tizemt is waiting, hands on her hips, trying to hide a smile. "I
suppose this is one of your brief visits, brother?"

My father grins as he jumps down from his camel. "Sister, you will love
me more than ever. My daughter is coming to live with you at long last. I
do listen to you, you see?" They embrace. When my father steps aside Aunt
Tizemt is engulfed beneath a mass of blue robes as my brothers reach her.

When she emerges, ruffled but smiling, she makes her way to me. I'm still mounted on my camel. I set my jaw. I have been forced to come here, I will not pretend good humour.

Aunt Tizemt looks around as though confused. "My brother said he had a daughter, but I see he is mistaken – he has a sixth son! What do men know, eh?" She smiles and holds up a hand to me. "Take that look off your face, anyone would think you liked being a man!"

I ignore her hand. "I do."

"And you don't want to come and live with your Aunt Tizemt? When she is a poor old thing with all her own children married off and her husband dead so many years and no-one left to keep her company?"

"I want to trade. I'm a good trader." I lift my chin and look upwards to keep my tears from falling.

My aunt lowers her offered hand. Her voice has lost its humour. "You think a woman's skills are not as important? Not as hard to learn?"

"I didn't say that."

"No need. Your voice said it." Aunt Tizemt turns and walks away. No backward glances or coaxing. My aunt is a fearsome woman.

My father comes towards me. I stiffen, waiting for the order to dismount, but instead he stands in front of Thiyya and strokes her nose without looking at me, as though thinking.

Thiyya is impatient. The other camels are free of their burdens, why is she made to stand here in the heat with a slumped, angry rider who keeps pulling sharply at the reins if she stretches out her nose towards the other camels, who are being fed and watered? She drops briskly to her knees, nearly causing me to fall off at the sudden and unexpected movement, thrown fully forwards and then back. Despite my angry urgings, Thiyya sits, uncaring, on the ground and rises again only when I dismount, muttering rude words under my breath and threatening her with a dire fate involving tasty herbs, rock salt and a very hot fire.

My father is trying not to laugh which only makes me more angry. I stand, head down, wanting to walk away but knowing that I am already in enough trouble.

At last I feel his hand on my arm. "Come and sit with me in the shade," he says.

I follow him reluctantly to the first tent which the slaves have managed to erect. There is fresh water and I drink it greedily, relishing its clean taste, devoid of goat.

When I look up my father is holding out a small pouch of soft yellow leather. "Open it."

It's heavy for its size. I pull open the leather strings that hold it shut and cautiously tip the contents into my hand. It's a necklace. A simple thread of small black beads, with a pendant almost the size of my palm made up of five silver rectangles, with pointed ends, which between them create a deep v-shape at the base of the pendant. Each silver strip is intricately engraved with tiny symbols.

I look up, confused, to find that my father is slowly unwrapping the veil round his face. He sighs comfortably as the cool air takes away some of the heat in his cheeks, stained blue in places from the indigo dye of his robes. He closes his eyes and leans back on the cushions for a few moments.

When he opens his eyes again he gives me a weary smile. "There was once a trading caravan in the Tenere desert, between Bilma and Agadez. In the blinding heat and on an unfamiliar trade route, they lost their way."

I frown. "Father – "

"They wandered in the desert, growing ever more tired and thirsty. They were close to death, even their camels' knees trembling with the heat, when suddenly before them appeared a young woman of great beauty, wearing a magnificent necklace with many engravings."

I sit back on the cushions opposite him, unsure where this story is going. This does not seem like an appropriate time and place to be telling old tales.

My father smiles and continues. "The beautiful young woman showed them to a well nearby. The men hurried to drink and then gave water to their camels. When they were sated, they turned to thank the woman, but she had disappeared. When they reached Agadez, the men told their amazing story of how they had been saved from certain death by a beautiful young woman. An old jeweller, hearing their story, set to and made a necklace that matched the men's description of the young woman's ornament. Upon it he carved symbols of stars and dunes, trails and tents. He called it 'celebra'. This necklace carries memories of the trade routes through the desert and night travel guided only by the stars above."

I sit in silence, a cold certainty in my belly, and wait for what I know is coming.

"The necklace is yours. You are a beautiful girl and it is a fine piece of jewellery. But I chose it because it speaks of the trade routes – it will be a memory for you of all the days you have spent in the caravan. The trading, the desert, the goods we have bought and sold, the nights following the trails of the stars. You cannot continue on the trade routes with your brothers and me. I have been foolish and kept you too long by my side because I love you dearly." He pauses. "And for your mother's memory," he adds with a sigh. "But now it is time for you to stay here in the main camp. You will live with your Aunt Tizemt for a time. You will learn new skills from her. You will become a woman, as you should, instead of playing at being a man. Your time on the trade routes is ended."

I look down at the heavy silver pendant and feel the first tears falling, hot and shameful on my cheeks. I try to speak, clutching the *celebra* tightly in my hand as though about to throw it back at him, but manage only a swallowed sob, an ugly gulping noise that makes my tears fall faster.

My father rises slowly to his feet and silently puts his arms about me. My muffled voice produces more gulped noises, intended as flat refusals. He waits. When my sobs begin to slow, he speaks and his voice is kind but firm.

"Your Aunt Tizemt is a very kind woman – for all her loud voice and louder opinions. She will teach you many, many new things, and you will come to enjoy them and be proud of all you will have to show your brothers and me when we come to see you. And perhaps you would like to marry soon." He pauses to allow me to attempt another muffled refusal. "I am sure you will have more choice than you will know what to do with. And I am also sure that you will choose wisely, for having lived for so long with men you know what we are like better than any woman." I can hear him smile. "So, may I see your face again? If it is not too red and ugly after all that crying?"

My father's caravan stays only three days, enough time to share stories and gifts, for saddles and tents to be mended and all the goods to be sorted and re-loaded correctly. My father agrees to leave Thiyya with me, but only after I wept at the thought of losing her.

"No racing," he reminds me. "Thiyya will have to get used to a different life, just as you will."

Thiyya snorts in disgust when she is used to collect water but I cannot let her travel far away from me.

The slaves gather round to bid me farewell. Some of them have known me since I was a little girl and they stroke my face and murmur endearments. Adeola weeps and Ekon stands silent, his sad face echoing my own, but he puts out one large hand and pats my shoulder before my father approaches and the slaves move away, ready to mount.

"We will visit, daughter. We will return in a few months, have no fear."

I stand before him, silent and pale, unable and unwilling to speak.

"Now then." My father's voice becomes overly brisk. "Where are all those sons of mine? Come and bid farewell to your sister."

They are upon me in moments, a swirl of blue robes and five sets of arms hugging me from all directions. Jokes, laughter, my cheeks pinched and my shoulders pulled this way and that before suddenly, they are all on their camels. I stand alone, cold without their surrounding bodies, their smiling faces now far away on the camels high above me. I manage a trembling smile, my cheeks stretching unnaturally, then I wave and wave and wave.

As soon as they are too far for waving I run in the opposite direction, beyond the camp, where I fall to the ground and beat the sand with my fists, my mouth open in a silent scream of rage and unhappiness, my heart racing and my mind a huge black cloud of disappointment.

"It's not *that* bad being a woman, you know. My sisters and mother seem to enjoy their lives."

I look up, spitting sand out of my mouth and see a young man squatting beside me. His eyes are warm and merry.

"Go away."

"Not very friendly, are you?"

I spit out more sand in his direction, hoping some of it will land on him. "Who are you?"

"Amalu. I was a baby when your father left the village and began trading."

"So was I."

"I know. We are the same age. My mother suckled you when your mother died. She said I was a fat enough baby to be able to share some of my milk."

I sniff disdainfully. "You look skinny enough to me."

He pretends to be insulted. "Skinny? Look at my arms! Are they not mighty?"

I shrug but have to hide a smile. "I have seen mightier."

He laughs out loud and makes himself comfortable. "I am sure you have. Tell me."

Talking seems to help a little. We sit together for more than an hour and I tell him stories of the trading routes. He makes a good audience, widening his eyes, shaking his head in disbelief and begging for more whenever I draw breath. By the time my aunt finds me I am sitting upright and laughing.

Aunt Tizemt is not laughing as we enter her tent, my new home.

"Sitting around while still dressed in a man's robes, giggling with some boy you have never met! It's a good thing your father brought you to me. I can see you have never learnt how to behave like a woman. Take off those robes at once. I have poured some water in that bowl. Here is a cloth. Clean yourself and then dress in a more becoming manner." She throws down a cloth and marches out of the tent, closing the flaps behind her. The sound of her grinding stone outside is fierce.

I am alone. And unused to it. On the trade routes there were always people. Slaves, my brothers, other traders, even my quiet father. Here there is no-one but me in the tent, and the camp outside is small and peaceful, not like the hot swarming cities I have been used to. Slowly I take off my robes and begin to wash. My thick black hair has begun to grow out. Now, for the first time in my life that I can recall, it is past my shoulders. I try to tie it back, catching my hands in it and finally succeeding in making it into a tangled knot at the base of my neck.

Once clean I look around. There are some clothes lying on the bed but I am unsure of whether they are the right ones. They look gaudy after my plain blue robes. A long red cloth and a smaller orange cloth, all decorated with little silver discs here and there. A couple of brooches, designed to hold the fabrics together in a becoming way when wrapped around the body. A multi-coloured shawl for my shoulders and a wrap for my hair, although my face will remain uncovered now that I am to be dressed as a woman. The wrap is woven in reds, oranges, yellows and covered with symbols and patterns. A pair of simple leather slippers are the only things that look familiar so I put them on and then stand, uncertain. How to fold the cloth correctly to make my woman's clothes? Oh, for a simple blue robe, dropped over my head in moments and then tied at the waist!

My aunt must have heard the silence that fell after the slow washing sounds had stopped. She appears inside the tent.

"Why are you not dressed? Do you intend to wear only shoes? You'll find a husband a lot quicker like that but I am not sure he's the sort of husband you'd like to have."

She looks me over approvingly as I stand naked before her, as though inspecting a goat for sale. Only seventeen, I have a slender body the colour of golden sand, except for my forearms and feet, the skin around my eyes and a small part of my neck, all burnt walnut-brown from the sun. My tangled hair has already fallen out of its badly-made knot and although it is not smooth, it is at least thick, dark and glossy. My breasts are small but shapely and I have a wiry strength that can be seen in my thighs, belly and arms as I shift nervously from one leg to the other and attempt to cover myself from her unrelenting gaze with my hands.

"I didn't know what to wear."

"What's wrong with the clothes I've laid out for you?"

"They're very…" I falter.

"Very?"

"Bright."

"And your blue robes are not? Bright enough, I think. Now put those clothes on."

I stumble over the clothes until my aunt has to step in to pin them correctly. The wrap for my head is worse.

"Let's start by combing your hair. You look like a wild thing. I can see your hair is new to you – did you keep it cut short before?"

"Yes."

"Well it will grow longer and you had better get used to it. It will be very fine once it has grown to a good length; your mother always had good hair. Come here. The knots in this! It will hurt but you will just have to bear it. It will be a lesson to you to brush it every day." She drags a wooden comb through the tangled mass, taking no notice of the way my head jerks back with every stroke and disregarding my yelps of pain. By the time she has finished the comb has a broken tooth and my tangles have become soft dark waves.

"Better," says my aunt. "Now for your headdress." In a few quick twists she wraps up all my hair, piling up the bright fabric into a high turban. A few folds hang down at the sides and back, but my face, still darker round the eyes than the rest of my face, is fully visible.

"There! You look like a beautiful young woman instead of a skulking boy. And lift your head up. I know you are not accustomed to having your face on display but you must get used to it. Now then, you are properly dressed and your hair is brushed. Do you have any jewellery?"

I nod, my scalp still smarting from her attentions. "I have a *celebra*," I say, clasping the heavy necklace round my neck. Aunt Tizemt gives an approving nod. "And my *tchirot.*" I pull out my square silver amulet from the old jeweller Winitran.

My aunt frowns. "A *tchirot* is a man's jewel."

I close a hand over it protectively. "It is mine and I will wear it."

She shrugs. "As you wish. You do not have a lot of jewellery. That will change when you have a husband. If you are lucky he will bring you many gifts, as your father did for your mother. He spoilt her. He was a good husband, though," she adds, grudgingly giving him his due. "You would be lucky to find such a man."

"I am not sure I want a husband."

"What, you with all your giggling with strange young men? Huh. I will see you married within one month at that pace."

"Is that what I am here for? To be married off?"

"Now, now, no need to get angry. You are here to learn some women's skills, for your father tells me you have not learnt them from anyone."

"I have plenty of skills."

"Really? Can you use herbs for healing as well as cooking? Can you spin? Weave? Sew? Do you know where to find the wild grains and how to make a milk porridge? Cheese? Butter? Or did your slaves do all the work? Can you sing? Dance? Play music?"

"No…"

"Can you read and write the *tinfinagh* alphabet? I would wager that your father and brothers have not taught you. The boys learn it but they do not pass it on, it falls to us women to do that. No, niece, you must admit to being ignorant of many things. It will be my job to teach you. And if you meet a young man that pleases you before I am finished – well, you will have to learn even quicker, for no man will want a woman who can trade but not cook." She gives a rare smile at my dejected face. "Come, it is not so bad. We will sit together and we will talk as we work. I will tell you about your mother and your father when they were children. We can gossip and you will meet girls your own age and find out that it can be fun being a woman. It is not all work."

"It sounds like it is."

"Well, for now you are right. I have a bowl of grains out there and they will not grind themselves. You will learn to grind the grain and roll it to make couscous while I make you some more clothes, for you have nothing but your old blue robes and what you have on. A good thing your father left me with a generous quantity of new cloth for you from his stores. Come."

The women's skills are every bit as dull as I had feared. What skill is there in the washing of sweaty greasy sheep's wool in the little water available, hauled one laborious bucket at a time? The dyeing, staining my hands a multitude of colours. My arms ache with the endless carding, using the big wooden combs studded with metal spikes to make the wool soft and ready for spinning. The spinning! Never-ending fruitless attempts to make the spindle twirl without stopping, one hand holding the distaff, the other frantically pulling at the wool, trying to produce a regular, even thread. And after all that work, the tedium of weaving! Back and forth, back and forth and the cloth growing barely at all. Hours of work for no visible reward. What skills are these? Where is the quick banter, the knowledgeable eye cast over goods, seeing the quality at a single glance, sweeping aside the unimaginative engravings, the shoddy dyes, the badly cut stones. Reaching out for the sparkling gemstones, the soft bright leather, the fine clay pots and when the bartering is done, the pride of the war waged and won. And the greater prizes. The shining bars of salt. The gleam of gold. The rippling muscles under black skin. These were my skills and now they are deemed worthless.

The days come and go. My mind feels slow and dull, its once fast-moving spirit searching across the dunes to find the trade routes and the caravan that has left me here. I wonder about my mother. Did she wish to travel as well or did she stay in the camp willingly? Did she feel her spirit grow heavy with each child that kept her tied to the camp or did she enjoy this life? I cannot find the pleasure in it.

Sometimes when I sit gazing at the dunes, having escaped my aunt's many chores for a moment, Amalu finds me and we talk.

"Enough, enough!" he cries, as five children chase him across the dunes to where I am sitting. "I have no breath left!"

They fall on him as he reaches me, climb all over him while he laughs and succumbs to their insistence that he play the camel and allow them to ride on his back.

"I beg you to save me," he gasps and I cannot help laughing.

"I am afraid not," I say. "If you are a camel then you must endure your burden in life. Otherwise I will have to sell you off for meat."

"Alas, have pity on a poor exhausted camel," he says, lying on the ground. The children thump him and yell that he must continue but he will not and at last they leave him be, tempted by rolling down the sand dunes towards the encampment.

"I think you are safe now," I suggest.

He sits up with exaggerated caution, then re-adjusts his wrap, which has almost revealed most of his smiling face. "I am truly exhausted."

"They are not even yours," I tease. "What will you do when you have children of your own to contend with all day?"

"Ah well," he says, easing himself onto one elbow at my feet. "I will have a wonderful wife who will save me from them."

"Will you, indeed?" I ask.

"Yes," he says confidently, his eyes on mine. "Now tell me what you are doing up here all alone."

I shrug.

"Ah come now, Kella," he says. "I know you miss the trading life. But are you so unhappy here?"

I smile a little. "Not when you make me laugh. But I do miss it."

"Tell me about the trading life," he says. "I would like to be a trader myself one day."

"What do you want to know?"

"Tell me about the jewellers, the leatherworkers, the carvers," he says. He has already learnt that I need little prompting. Just the names of the craftsmen will have me talking for hours.

I gaze across the dunes. "The jewellers have steady hands. They can tell so many stories on a tiny circlet of silver. They spend hours turning over gemstones to find the perfect matches of size and colour for a string of beads or a pair of earrings. You can ask them for magic amulets and they will whisper prayers over jewels for fertility, for luck, for wealth. Some of them roll up tiny scraps of parchment containing verses of the Qur'an, prayers and blessings that will be kept close to the skin within a tiny box of silver."

Amalu nods, touching his own silver amulet, dangling from his neck.

I sit up a little straighter, gesture at my yellow leather slippers. "The leatherworkers buy whole dyed hides from the tanneries and sit in the shade of their tents with all manner of colours spread out before them. The pure whites fetch the highest price. The mixtures used to make them can rip the skin off a man's hands at the tanneries. The yellows are dyed with the stamens of the crocus flower. Aunt Tizemt only needs a tiny pinch of saffron for a meat stew, but a lot more is required for a full hide. They cut out small pieces for shoes and use the bigger pieces for saddles."

I pause for a moment, thinking of the races in which I used to take part.

Amalu sees my face lose its brightness and interrupts my thoughts. "The carvers – you forget to tell me about them."

I nod, distracted from my regretful thoughts by his enthusiasm. "The carvers work precious woods but also ivory. They make such wonders – the tiniest shapes, the most delicate markings. One false move and the work would be ruined."

"No spoons and cups, then?"

I smile. "Those too and in far greater quantity. They are not treated with such care. I used to buy so many replacements just for our own family and everywhere we went we could always sell such goods."

Amalu's eyes are bright. "I will go to all the places you have been," he says. "And see such things for myself."

I want to say *take me with you*, but that would be too forward. Already I know there are whispers about us in the camp, but although Amalu looks at me with loving eyes I am unsure of my own feelings. Still, he is a friend to me and I feel the need for someone who will let me speak of my trading days.

"Kella! Kella!"

I roll my eyes. "Aunt Tizemt is looking for me again."

"I will hide you behind a bush," offers Amalu mischievously. "And tell her you have run away."

I shake my head. "Your life would not be worth living when she found you out," I tell him and together we make our way back to the camp.

Back and forth, back and forth. Buckets from the well, thread on the loom, this grindstone, crushing the wild grains gathered one by one. I refocus my eyes from the horizon and catch sight of Aunt Tizemt, who has paused in her weaving and is looking over her shoulder at me. She smiles encouragingly. Waving her hand at the bowl of grains by my side that are yet to be ground, she begins a story.

"There were once some children lost in the desert. They were hungry and could find nothing to eat. They were surrounded by vile-tasting beetles, beautiful but poisonous oleander bushes, and sand. Sand everywhere, rocks and sand."

I break in impatiently, rudely interrupting her story, which I have heard once too often. "Then one small boy caught sight of a column of ants. Back and forth, they scurried, back and forth, each ant carrying but one grain on its back. The children took the grains of the sand from the ants, one by one, and so they were saved from starvation until they were found." I gesture angrily towards the bowl of grains. "You can tell all the stories you like, Aunt, but there is nothing interesting about the gathering or the grinding of grains. In the great souks I could buy my couscous ready ground and rolled by slaves. Street vendors made great basins of hot milk porridge to be eaten by those who had coins. I traded. I was quick, I knew the gemstones, the quality of skins. I chose the strongest slaves, the finest jewellery, the softest leather shoes. I spent my days seeing all there was to see, bartering for goods from all over the world. I felt the weight of cold gold in my hands and felt its softness against my teeth. I threw coins to the street vendors and they served me fresh bread and roasted meats, cool drinks and sweets to please the tongue and eye. I did not stoop to collect one grain at a time, nor did my hands chafe with the distaff. My hands were tough because of the reins of my camel, the bundles of goods I lifted to the pack animals. I was better than this."

Aunt Tizemt is unmoved by my outburst. She keeps weaving, her broad back firm and upright. She speaks without turning round. "You think you have seen everything the world can offer. I think you have not. You think too highly of yourself."

"What have I not seen? I have seen more than you!"

I cannot goad her. She keeps her back turned and her voice is calm.

"Have you seen a child come slithering out of its mother's womb, covered in blood and slippery to the touch? Have you heard its first cry and seen the joy in its mother's eyes and the pride in its father's? Have you caught a dead child in your hands and seen its shriveled body fall limply without breath to the floor? Have you seen the tears of its mother and the cold hurt of its father? Have you seen the man of your dreams and heard him whisper your name? Have you stood naked before a man and seen his face turn to yours? Have you held a man in your arms and loved him throughout the night? Have you held your dying father and wept your heart away as he leaves you alone and unprotected in this world? Have you held your first child in your arms and prayed that every one of your days would be so happy?" She turns, smiling, to face me. "I think not. I think you have seen a great deal and lived very little. I think you have been so busy seeing everything that you have not experienced the moment when every grain you grind is food for your child and brings warmth to your heart. I think your eyes have been so filled with the wonders made by man that you have not seen the glory of the sunset and sunrise, the rise and fall of the dunes, the tiny ant and the mighty wind. You have seen everything and nothing at all. That will change. But sometimes you must be very, very bored before you can see something wonderful that is right in front of you." She gets to her feet, hands on the base of her back, stretching out her cramped muscles after many hours at the loom. "Now finish those grains. A child of ten would have finished them by now and I need them for our evening meal. Tomorrow I will take you to Tanemghurt."

"Remember to call her *Lalla*," says my aunt in a whisper as we make our way to her tent, which is large and well situated, for she is held in great esteem.

Tanemghurt is our camp's healer and wise woman. There is not a child here who was not born into her hands, as were most of the adults. Tanemghurt has lived longer than anyone can recall.

I roll my eyes. I am hardly in need of lessons on basic manners, of course I would use a term of respect for Tanemghurt. "Why am I going to her at all?" I ask ungraciously.

"She will teach you the uses of herbs," says Aunt Tizemt.

I bite back my rejoinder: that I have seen more herbs and spices on my travels than Tanemghurt can ever have seen, since she has spent her whole life here, in a tent in the middle of the desert.

The tent flap draw back suddenly and Tanemghurt stands before us. Her face is a wrinkled mass of lines, but she stands erect, taller than I am by a good hand's breadth.

"Tizemt," she says to my aunt, nodding her head as though to an equal.

"*Lalla*," says my aunt. "This is Kella."

Tanemghurt turns her dark eyes on me and says nothing.

"*Lalla*," I say.

She holds the tent flap aside. "Enter."

I hesitate, then step inside, the flaps closing behind me on my aunt.

Tanemghurt's tent is very different from my aunt's and I look around it with interest. I have not seen her tent inside, for few people are invited into it unless they have an ailment, and often Tanemghurt will choose to take her herbs and spells to the sick person's tent. It seems larger than most for it is family-sized, but Tanemghurt has never had either children or a husband, so it is for her alone. The space that would have been set aside for her husband's possessions is full of her little pouches and her mixing and measuring bowls, stacked by size and sometimes by colour. She has spoons of every size, not just the big ones for stirring and the smaller ones for eating, but tiny ones for measuring small doses of the powerful herbs she uses. Some are stained strange colours and some, I see, are kept apart from others. They hang on small loops of string sewn onto the wall. Below them and facing the wall is a large seat, something like a saddle but made for her to sit on, for Tanemghurt is now very old and she finds it hard to sit or squat low on the ground as the rest of us do. The large seat has a small ledge on it where she can rest her mixing bowls or mortar and pestle when she prepares her medicines. All around this seat are pots, many containing water, some containing strange substances that I cannot identify. The tent smells of herbs and perfumes.

"Do you miss the trading life?"

I turn towards Tanemghurt. No-one has ever asked this except for Amalu and the question brings a sudden sting to my eyes. She stands, watching me.

I swallow. "I have no choice," I say.

She lowers herself cautiously onto her seat, one bony arm supporting herself as she does so. "There is always a choice," she says.

"What is my choice?" I ask, my tone disrespectful enough that Aunt Tizemt would cuff my head for it.

She smiles. "That is not for me to say. It is for you to make."

"What would you do in my place?" I ask, my voice still too sharp.

"I would be honoured to learn women's skills from a woman as accomplished as your aunt," says Tanemghurt, unperturbed.

I stay silent.

"So," says Tanemghurt. "You wish me to teach you about the uses of herbs?"

I nearly say I want no such thing, but even I know that would be going too far. "Yes, *Lalla*," I say.

And so she teaches me the herbs to drink when I wish to bear a child as well as those to avoid bringing life to the womb. She shows me how to deliver a child, should I ever be called upon to do so. She tests me on my knowledge of the *tinfinagh* alphabet, which only women pass on. She has me recite large tracts of our legends, our songs, the right ways to live. I stay in her tent for many days, leaving only to relieve myself. At night she shows me the stars and nods with approval when I can name the constellations and know how to navigate by them.

"We are done," she announces one day.

I look at her.

"You may go," she says, as though we have only been conversing a few moments.

I stand, awkward. "Thank you," I manage, unsure of what else to say.

She nods. I turn towards the door of the tent.

"Kella."

I turn back to her. "Yes, *Lalla*?"

"Treasure your aunt. She has more to teach than I."

"I have learnt what she had to teach," I say, a little confused. "She said I should come to you."

Tanemghurt looks at me. "Skills are not the only thing to learn," she says. "Your aunt is both fierce and full of love. She lost her husband and yet still she has a great love within her, no matter what her life brings. Perhaps you still have something to learn."

I try to think what to say in return but Tanemghurt has turned away, looking through her herbs. I am dismissed.

I resent her words at first. But as the days come and go and the moon grows and wanes over and over again, I begin to take some small pride in my new life and the skills I am learning. I grow accustomed to my new clothes and even sew myself some new ones, adding decorative panels to the red and orange lengths of cloth I wear, learning to tie my headdresses more elaborately and without help. The blue dye fades from my skin, the rest of my face grows brown and I begin to lose my former long, swaggering strides and take on a slower walk, my hips gently swaying.

"Keep walking like that and your friend Amalu will be falling off his camel when you go by. Perhaps a crack to the skull will bring his mind back," jokes Aunt Tizemt. But she is proud of me and my new skills, developed under her tutelage.

I can cook a good meal now, for I have always had a fine palate for spices and herbs. I know the quality of spices from my time trading.

"Well, at least you learnt something useful in all those years," my aunt teases when she sees how well I judge quality and quantity, allowing the subtle and strong tastes to emerge, scenting and spicing the food I make – the milk porridge sweetened with cinnamon, the kid meat rubbed with cumin. I make fresh-smelling herbal teas, steeped mint for the evenings after a heavy meal, ground almonds for a sweet milk, a dipping sauce of rich argan oil and honey to scoop up with fresh flat breads cooked on a hot stone over the coals of the fire. My aunt has seen how Amalu watches me walk by, follows my newly-graceful walk with his eyes, then licks his lips when he smells the good food I make.

"Men love soft hips but they love good food even more," she says and laughs.

But still I miss my freedom. Traders pass by sometimes. I sit with an arm around Thiyya's neck and watch them with envy when they leave, their camels swaying them onwards to other places, other worlds from here. I wonder whether Amalu, if he does become a trader, would take me with him and my cheeks grow a little flushed at the thought, though I am still unsure whether it is Amalu or the trading that brings colour to them.

He does not wait long to make his move. "*Lalla?*"

My aunt looks up from her work. "What do you want, Amalu?"

"May your niece accompany me to the *ahal?*"

Aunt Tizemt stops her work on the stretched-out goatskin. She is rubbing it with a thick butter to soften it. She sits back on her heels and considers the young man. Nearby, I sit very upright, pretending all innocence. My hands keep moving, carding thick matted wool into soft clouds that drift down onto the carpet where I sit. My ears, meanwhile, strain to catch every word that passes between them.

"How many are going?"

"Perhaps a dozen of us."

"She has never been before. I doubt she would know what to do."

"There are other girls there, *Lalla*. They can show her."

"I'm sure. Show her how to dance and sing and show off in front of you boys."

"I will take good care of her."

My aunt laughs. "You will spend all your time making up poems in her honour and insults for all the other boys to make her think better of you and worse of them. I know your reputation as a fine crafter of words."

He waits, casting quick looks at me from under his dark lashes.

Aunt Tizemt relents. "Oh, very well then. She has to have some fun. I admit she has worked hard and learnt a great deal in a short time. Perhaps she had better learn some new skills from young people instead of a grumpy old woman like me."

"Yes, *Lalla*."

"Yes, what? I *am* a grumpy old woman?"

He shakes his head at having fallen into her trap and makes his escape, winking at me as he flees. Aunt Tizemt laughs to herself and turns her attention back to the skin. After a few moments' work she speaks to me over her shoulder.

"Tonight you may go to the *ahal*. It is in the small oasis half an hour from here. Nothing there but oleanders and palm trees, but I am told the oleander flowers are out at the moment – every colour you can imagine. Don't drink the water there though, the oleander poison may have tainted the water. Take a waterbag. And you can take my *amzad* with you if you wish. About time you learnt to play it. I have too many other things to be teaching you. Someone else can be your teacher."

I want to know more. "I have never been to the *ahal*. What happens there?"

Tizemt sighs. "You *have* missed out. I spent all my evenings there when I was a young girl. I was a very fine dancer. I know you think I have thick ankles and wide hips, but my sturdy ankles kept me dancing long after the other girls had tired – and then the boys had only me left to look at." She chuckles to herself, remembering her youth. "The *ahal* is a place close to the main camp, chosen for its charm, where young men and young women can meet, talk, joke. The boys will make up all sorts of insults for each other and recite love poems to you girls. You girls will play music, sing, dance. About time you learnt to dance as well. Can you sing? I have never heard you sing at your work."

I make a disbelieving face. "What is there to sing about?"

She reaches over and slaps at my ankles. "Stubborn girl. Well, you will start learning tonight. That Amalu cannot wait to recite his love poems to you after all your chattering about your travels around half the world. And the girls will show you how to dance and play the *amzad*."

I hurry inside the tent and come out holding the single-stringed instrument. "How do you play it?"

She waves me away. "Go, go. Better to learn such things from your friends than your elderly relatives. I could not repeat the bawdy songs without making you blush." She grins and returns to her goatskin, growing soft under her strong hands.

The oasis is beautiful in the light of the setting sun. The heat of the day gives way to the welcome cool of the evening. The palms are very tall but some of the boys risk the climb to pluck fresh ripe dates, pale gold in colour, crisply juicy within. The oleander flowers range from palest white to dark purples. The light makes the surrounding sands glow and the well's water is fresh and sweet, with none of the promised taint of oleander poison detectable.

We sit, seven girls and five boys, eating the sweet dates and drinking the fresh water. Amalu begins a soft beat on a small drum and a boisterous girl named Tanamart begins a comedy dance; a small palm tree her solid and dependable, if uninspired, dance partner. We laugh and cheer her on. Tanamart winks and holds out her hands to me. "Come now! The newest member of our *ahal*! You must learn to dance. Come and dance with me."

I demur, embarrassed, but am coaxed to my feet and hand in hand with Tanamart I learn my first dance steps, how to move my hands and sway my hips. The sand is warm under my bare feet and the cool air caresses my arms as I move them. I am conscious of Amalu's smiling face and the beat of his drum that guides my steps.

The rest of the evening is spent teaching me more steps, with much laughter over my very poor attempt at playing my aunt's instrument and applauding of the boys' poems, which range from romantic to insulting depending on their intended recipient. Amalu is quieter than usual, his friends teasing him for shyness in front of his lady-love but he only smiles and spends his time improvising rhythms on the drum for the others to dance or recite to.

It grows late and cold. Slowly we begin to depart. Amalu holds down his hand from his seat on his sand-coloured camel. "Will you ride back with me?"

I hesitate but the other girls nudge me forward, giggling. I smile and hold out my hand to be helped up onto the camel. He pulls me up to sit behind him. I try to settle myself. I have not ridden behind anyone since I was a tiny child behind my father. It feels strange not to hold the camel's reins, not to see where we are going. Instead I hesitantly put my arms about Amalu's waist and feel his warm hand cover mine.

The others clap and laugh. "We will accompany you home," calls out Tanamart.

"You will do no such thing," retorts Amalu and he spurs on the camel so that we quickly outstrip them. It is a strange feeling to be on the back of a camel galloping without having control over it and I hold Amalu more tightly.

Once we are comfortably ahead of the others he slackens the reins and allows his camel to walk. We are all alone in the darkness and for a few moments I rest my head against his back and hear his heart beating, feel our bodies slowly rock together with the pace of the camel.

He peers round at me. "Have you nothing to say to me?"

"What would you like me to say?"

He sighs. "I would like you to say that your heart beats faster when you are close to me. That you like to ride together like this. That you would ride with me always."

My heart beats a little faster. "Would you be a trader?"

"I would."

"And I would travel with you?"

He laughs. "You would be here, in the camp. With our children."

I am silent.

"I would come home often," he assures me. "I would not be able to stay away from you for long. You are too lovely."

I stay quiet and still.

He speaks again, more cautiously. "Would you not like that? Do you not favour me? I hoped you might look kindly on me."

When I speak my voice is low. "I loved the trade routes and our life there. But most women must stay at home and weave and bear children." I stop, for my voice is wavering.

"And you would not be happy to do so?" asks Amalu.

My voice is so low I am not sure he can hear me. "I want to travel the trade routes again."

"Alone?"

My face is growing warm. "With a husband and my children," I say. "I would be happy to travel alongside a husband, to trade together."

Amalu is quiet. "It is not a life for a woman," he says at last. "Women stay in the camp. Would you not be content, if you were my bride?"

I am silent. I feel the warmth of his back, think of his gentle way of speaking, of his good nature. I try to weigh what I feel for him against the desire to travel again, to trade. To be free. I was a trader once, but I am uncertain about this trade. I am not sure if it is weighted in my favour.

Amalu speaks again, very soft and low, his head tilted back towards me. "Will you be my bride, Kella?"

My heart is full but I do not answer. I am distracted by the sight of the main camp. The fires should be burning low, families finishing their evening meals and beginning to think about sleep. But as we approach there is the sound of music, of people talking and laughing. The fires are burning brightly and there is a smell of roasting meat. The children are awake and excited. As soon as they catch sight of us they run shrieking in our direction.

"They're here! They're here!"

Amalu looks up, startled. "Who is here?"

"Kella's father and brothers! And they have such news!"

I let go of Amalu's waist and slide quickly down from the camel, running towards the camp, leaving him alone.

My father looks up with a warm smile as I run towards him. My five noisy brothers whoop and leap up to hug me, before delivering me to my father's side by the fire. All the camp is gathered to hear the news and see them after many months' absence.

My father hugs me tightly and then leans back to get a good look at me. He speaks over my head to my aunt, who is beaming. "Tizemt, I congratulate you. I see a grown woman, not the half-man I brought you! She is most beautiful and I am sure most accomplished. Can she weave? Sew? Cook?"

"All of that and much more besides." My aunt is proud.

"I am in your debt, sister."

I interrupt, tugging at his arm like a child. "They said you have news."

My father nods. "I have, exciting news. Sit by me and I will tell you everything."

The camp makes itself comfortable, the older children as keen to hear the whole story as the adults. The smaller children sit in their parent's laps but doze, the words meaningless to them. My father waits until everyone is ready and then begins.

"Ten years ago the Almoravid army captured the city of Sijilmasa in the north from the Zanata tribe, and then went on to sack the trading city in the oasis of Awdaghast, in the south. In this way they controlled the two ends of one of the great trade roads. But when a few years later they tried to cross the High Atlas to fight the Barghawata tribe and take control of a wider part of the country, their leader Abdallah was killed and the Almoravids were forced to retreat. His general and second-in command, Abu-Bakr bin Umar, took over the leadership. Now Abu Bakr is ready to attempt the crossing of the High Atlas again. His army is far larger and stronger than it was before. They have had a few years to build up their strength and develop their plans. His cousin is Yusuf bin Tashfin, and he is now the second-in-command. A very strong and pious man, so they say – I have spoken more with Abu Bakr but have seen Yusuf also. Together they lead the army. I have met Abu Bakr over the years through my trading, and now they have asked me to help them plan their attack, as I have been to many of the trading cities across the High Atlas. They want to take Taroundannt and then the merchant city of Aghmat, which is very rich. Abu Bakr, Yusuf and some of their men will come here tomorrow, and we will talk. There may be young men from our camp who wish to join their army – many men from local tribes have joined them. My own sons wish to go but they cannot be spared for now – perhaps later on they may join Abu Bakr and his men. Also," he winks at Aunt Tizemt, "I do not believe my sons have the discipline to train and pray so hard whilst eating only meat, water and fruit as the Almoravids do – I think they are too fond of their aunt's good cooking."

My aunt laughs. "I will feed up your boys while they are here. They will be able to taste their sister's fine cooking, too. Tomorrow we will have a feast to honour our visitors when they arrive here. For now, it is very late and time for everyone to get some sleep."

The camp disperses, although I can hear everyone talking long into the night, excited and curious about the news. The young men are probably dreaming of glory, their mothers hoping to persuade them to stay safely at home.

I wake at dawn, nudged into sleepy consciousness by Aunt Tizemt. We creep out of the tent, past my brothers and father sleeping just outside the tent. Wrapped in thick blankets they are indistinguishable from one another.

The goats are milked and herded away from the main camp for pasturing by the slaves before the men wake. They rub the sleep from their eyes and drink hot tea and eat handfuls of fresh dates with bread from the night before. The boys tease me when they see their breakfast. "What, no fresh breads with honey and butter? No soft porridge? No fine meats and stews cooked to perfection? We were promised fine cooking from our oh-so-grown-up sister!"

I laugh and chase them away. "Go and fill the water bags and pots. We are planning a great feast for tonight. This morning you eat leftovers. It will whet your appetite for later."

My youngest brother makes a despairing face. "I am still a growing boy! I cannot survive on such meager fare!"

"Still growing?" I poke at him with my wool carders as I tidy the tent, looping up the sides to let the cool air flow through. The sharp metal spikes make him squawk and leap out of my way. "I think you are only growing fatter, brother, not taller! Now go with the others, I need plenty of water! When you return there are goat kids to be slaughtered so that I can begin to marinate the meat."

When I step outside Amalu is waiting.

"Kella – "

"I cannot talk now, Amalu," I say. "Aunt Tizemt will have plenty to say if she catches me loitering."

"I asked you a question," he says. He is rarely so serious.

"I know," I say.

"And?"

"And I cannot think on it when I am being pulled every which way by work," I tell him. "I need to think carefully before I answer you."

"Do you?"

"Yes," I say.

He nods, his eyes a little sad. "Very well," he says. "When there is a quiet moment, think on what I asked you."

I nod, serious enough that he seems satisfied.

It is not until the afternoon that one of the children comes running to tell my father that our visitors have been spotted. A party of twenty men, all on horseback, "And such horses! Not like ours but grey stallions, their legs so fine and such fast racers!" They are followed by another sixty men variously mounted on camels and horses.

The men gather to welcome the guests. The children peep from behind tents and the women cluster a little further back as they approach. Abu Bakr, at their head, is a stocky man with a broad smile. He slips quickly down from his horse and steps forward to take my father's hands and exchange greetings. Next to dismount is his general.

"Yusuf bin Tashfin," murmurs my aunt, always well informed. "They say he has an even greater vision for the future than Abu Bakr. The whole of the Maghreb united under one rule, a mighty empire."

I watch. Suddenly the camp feels small and dull. I had thought I had grown somewhat used to my life here, but these visitors, bold on their fine steeds with grand visions for the future, about to travel far away from our little camp, have made me envious already. Something in me I thought had been tamed is tugging to be set free.

Chachat — An Engagement Necklace

I AM DRAWN TO YUSUF. ABU BAKR is gruff but pleasant. He seems like a practical general rather than a visionary leader. That role, oddly, seems to belong to his second-in-command.

Yusuf's voluminous black robes, turban and veil hide his body and most of his face, but his forearms, where they are visible, ripple with strength. He has a sharp face, all angles. A long straight nose, high cheekbones and a pronounced browline. His eyebrows are thick and well defined. I find out that he is forty-eight years old but I think that he could pass for a much younger man for his skin is still smooth, his hair dark and his body upright and powerful. He has arrived on a very fine silver-grey horse, which he rides easily, poised and confident on his saddle. Although the fineness of his horse should demand an elaborately decorated saddle, his is entirely plain, made of simple brown leather. It is good quality, my trader's eye tells me that, but it is plainer than a slave's saddle.

When he dismounts to greet the men of our camp he walks briskly. He is of no great height but the other men straighten as he approaches as though attempting to reach a physical height demanded by his presence.

The men gather in one of the larger tents and my aunt and I serve tea. The other men drink and eat, but I see that Yusuf has his tea unsweetened and does not touch the sweet sticky dates we offer.

"Someone needs to stay here with the men and look after them," says my aunt, looking about for a likely candidate. "Make sure they have water and food if they ask for it."

"I will do it," I say before she has even finished speaking. I cannot be stuck over some fire, poking at the coals and seasoning stews when there are people here talking of wars, of trading routes, of great new possibilities. I want to be close to them, to hear what they have to say, to taste my old life, even second-hand.

Aunt Tizemt huffs. "I have enough to do without losing you as a helper."

"But they are our honoured guests," I say desperately. "We cannot leave just anyone to look after them."

"Oh, very well," she says and hurries away, chivvying her other helpers.

I try to be discreet, to keep myself to one side. I speak or move only when someone needs something. I do not want to be dismissed, for one of them to say that they will manage by themselves. I want to hear their plans, about the challenging adventure that lies before them.

They talk until it grows dark, my father sharing information about routes, cities, the terrain that he knows well on the other side of the mountains. Abu Bakr and Yusuf talk about their plans: how many men, how many horses and camels, the weapons they have amassed, their battle tactics. Yusuf is respectful towards Abu Bakr, but not deferential. He speaks when required and falls silent when he has nothing of value to add. His words are measured and certain. He speaks without pause or hesitation. When he is silent he listens with great care to those who speak, considering their words one by one, nodding slightly when an important point is made. He does not become distracted, even when the talks continue for some time. Other men in the group look around with natural curiosity at the camp or smile at the children who peek shyly at them from the folds of the tent, overawed by their weapons. Yusuf seems to notice nothing except the people with whom he is speaking.

Abu Bakr pulls out maps and they all pore over them, tracing possible routes across the mountains. Sources of water are important, along with an understanding of which tribes they may encounter along the way, whether they may show resistance or could be encouraged to join the army.

As cousins, Abu Bakr and Yusuf seem to have an easiness between them, occasionally filling in the words of the other one, comfortable with taking over from one another when necessary. Their military time together must have given them a deep understanding of one another's strengths and weaknesses and the ability to work together closely without needing to question the other's decisions. Yusuf speaks of the army's training, their strict discipline. He wants to try new formations, better strategies. Abu Bakr, for now, wants to talk about routes and recruitment, hence this meeting with my father, whose local knowledge, both of tribes nearby who might be persuaded to join the army and of the possibilities for attack once they crossed the mountains, is invaluable to them. Yusuf's face lights up when my father talks of a possible route through the mountains that would hide much of their progress as they make their way closer to the point of attack.

But my own interest comes when they stop talking of fighting formations and instead Yusuf begins to talk with enthusiasm of what will come after.

"We will command the trading routes. We will create a new city, a great city from which we will control the whole of the Maghreb. We will be better able to protect the traders, in return for their taxes. The trade will benefit all. There will be great souks, larger than those in place now. We can trade further and in greater quantities than before, for we will be the central point between the countries of the north, across the sea via Al-Andalus, and all of the Dark Kingdom in the south. It will be a great new time."

I edge closer. I think of what it would be to have all of the Maghreb under one ruler, to encourage trade from distant countries. The souks would grow and flourish. And a new city! A gathering point of the greatest traders, where north and south would meet and trade. I can feel the excitement growing in me of the trading possibilities, of what could be done. The longing I thought I had buried for the trade routes rises up in me so sharply it is all I can do not throw myself on my knees and beg Yusuf to take me with him there and then.

I feel a sharp dig in the ribs and Aunt Tizemt hisses in my ear. "When you've finished staring, I need your help. They are fine by themselves."

"They might need me," I begin.

"They are wrapped up in their plans," says my aunt. "They don't even know you exist. Come on."

I follow, reluctantly, looking back over my shoulder. "But I…" my voice trails off as my aunt laughs. "What?"

"I think you were staring at the Commander's general. A very fine man, I'll grant you that. But a little old for you, isn't he?"

I feel heat rising through me and know my cheeks are flushed. How to explain it is not the man I am interested in, it is his vision for the Maghreb? Aunt Tizemt will only laugh even more. And perhaps I have to admit that there is something about this man, so fierce-looking but so eloquent, so driven for a life of adventure, that does draw me a little to him. I grab at the dough that has been rising in an earthenware dish nearby and begin to knead it. Aunt Tizemt laughs even more when she sees how violently I press and pound it.

"They say you should knead bread when you are angry. Perhaps you should knead it when you are in love as well. All that new-found passion has to go somewhere." She looks over at the men in the tent, heads bowed over their maps and plans. "Especially when the object of your affections

is oblivious to you. Too busy thinking of fighting and glory. Typical man."
She bustles off, carrying a whole goat kid's carcass high in one hand, a bowl
of spiced yoghurt in the other for marinating. Her voice can be heard as
she makes her way across the camp, exhorting any men, women, slaves or
children who cross her path to work harder – build up fires, bring water, cut
up more meat, grind the grains finer. My aunt can turn a whole camp into
her own personal army when she needs to.

By evening a magnificent feast has been prepared. There is meat in
abundance, marinated, spiced, baked, roasted and cooked in rich stews.
There are soft warm flat breads, bowls with dips and flavoured oils, butters,
cheeses and then fresh fruits and little cakes, soaked in honey and dripping
with spiced sweetness. There are olives, figs and dates in great bowls to be
passed from hand to hand.

The children are half-mad with hunger, their mothers having denied
them anything but simple foods. Perhaps a little congealed porridge, a few
dates, scraps of meat and stale bread for the lucky ones. All day long they
have smelt glorious foods being prepared, tantalizingly faint at first, then
growing stronger as the sun fades. They have been kept busy fetching and
carrying, chopping and pounding, shelling and mixing. Any straying fingers
have earned them a quick slap, knocking their hands away from temptation.
Now that satisfaction and satiety lie only moments away they grow shrill and
restless with no chores left to steady them, hopping from one leg to another,
begging their mothers and more especially their fathers to say blessings over
the food and let them eat.

At last the food is served and the children watch in agony while the
guests are offered the choicest morsels. While Abu Bakr and most of his men
give thanks and eat heartily, praising the fineness of the food, the wide-eyed
children see to their disbelief that Yusuf bin Tashfin, although he also gives
thanks, hardly eats at all. He accepts a piece of plain roast meat, a small
hunk of bread, and a handful of dried figs. The other food he waves away
politely but firmly, or passes it swiftly to the next person. He eats slowly and
with apparent enjoyment, but finishes long before everyone else, for he eats
far less than the other men.

I find myself almost angry. "Why did I bother to learn all those cooking
skills you said were so important?" I hiss to Aunt Tizemt, as we sit side by

side, eating the good food, which tastes like dust to me after a day of endless cooking. I feel strangely awake and feverish.

She frowns. "What are you talking about? Look how much everyone is enjoying the food we have prepared. Look at your brothers – I believe they have become camels after living with them so long – it doesn't seem possible that a mere man could eat so much in one sitting." She chuckles and reaches out for another cake. My aunt loves the little spiced honey-soaked cakes and considers no feast complete without them.

"Well, he has barely touched the food."

She raises her eyebrows. "*He?*"

"The second-in command."

"What, you don't know his name yet?"

"Yusuf bin Tashfin." It comes out too quickly because I have whispered it to myself all day.

Aunt Tizemt grins as she takes another bite and speaks with her mouth full. "Oh, so you are offended because Yusuf does not cram his belly like your brothers?"

I shrug, embarrassed. "Perhaps there is something wrong with the food."

"I do not think so – look at everyone else here, eating until they groan. He is known for being a very disciplined man. He follows a very strict diet, so they say."

"What else do they say?"

My aunt smiles. "There is not much to say. He does not care for filling his belly with rich foods and drink. He drinks water and eats but little. He prays to God. He plans for a country united and obedient to the will of God. This is his mission, his dream."

As the night draws on there is dancing and singing, much discussion of the visitors' plans as well as general gossip. The children begin to sit by their parents rather than chase around.

The old storyteller Aghbalu makes his way slowly to the main fire where the meat was roasted. By now the flames are dying down a little but the children, seeing him make his way there, revive and dash about to gather up more firewood. They like the flames to be high when he tells his stories, for then his gnarled old body and his sun-faded robes take on movement and make his stories come alive as his arms wave and his feet take on some old-remembered nimbleness as he plays every part – handsome young men, terrible djinns, beautiful maidens and their fearsome mothers.

Now the flames rise higher and the children shelter by their parents, who lie back on their elbows or squat comfortably to hear the story. Suggestions are shouted out.

"The moon lady!"

"No, no, the terrible djinn of the desert!"

"Aghbalu! The courting of the camel-girl!"

Aghbalu smiles and claps his hands loudly. There is silence. "Some of us are too old to need to be reminded of our origins." He points at my father and nods at the roars of laughter as my father good-humouredly bends his strong lithe body and imitates the shufflings of an old man.

"Some are too young." He points at a baby, asleep in the golden firelight and the women coo.

"But these ones," says Aghbalu, and he points at the young men of our tribe who have chosen to join Abu Bakr's Almoravids. "These ones must be told once again a great and wondrous story so that they will not forget where they have journeyed from, however far they travel on their mission."

The crowd waits. Aghbalu smiles. He knows how to build up the tension. He claps his hands again. "Tonight, I tell the story of Tin Hinan and the goatherd."

There is a murmur of approval and the crowd makes itself comfortable.

Aghbalu waits a moment and then gradually sinks to his knees on the sand. He stretches out his arms and looks into the distance of the night.

"What do I, a poor goatherd boy, see? What is this sight that comes towards me? It seems to me that I see two camels approaching but this surely cannot be, for there is no-one who lives nearby but my own poor family and none of us has such fine camels. One is very pale, indeed as it comes closer I believe it is white."

There are nods. A white camel like my own Thiyya is a sought-after rarity.

Aghbalu peers far away. "The camels are coming ever closer. And what do I see on these two camels? Two women. All alone in this great desert, far away from anywhere. Their long robes move in the breeze. One is a small woman, strong and wiry. She is a fierce one, a fighter for sure, loyal and kind. She wears robes of black with much embroidery. Her camel is a fine beast, sturdy like her. They could go a long way without succour."

More nods. But everyone is waiting for the description of the other woman.

"Closer they come to me and still closer. My goats are restless and curious. Some scatter but I do not chase after them. I am too curious about this mirage. Is it a many-headed desert djinn, come to claim me for its own? Should I run? But I cannot bring myself to run for I have never seen such a woman as this one who leads. Her camel is white, and it has blue eyes. Such a rare camel! Such a camel would be fit for a princess. I look slowly further up and I see long red robes of great fineness, and then…"

In the firelight he slowly stands and in doing so transforms into a tall and wondrously beautiful woman, graceful and queenly in her bearing, her robes shifting shades of red in the flames. Her face is handsome, framed with long dark hair and high cheekbones. Aghbalu's voice grows higher and stronger as he bends his head graciously towards a small boy sitting by his father.

"Who are you, child?"

Under the gaze of the entire camp only one answer can come from the boy. "I – I am a poor goatherd, lady."

The lady-Aghbalu nods slowly. "And where do I find myself, goatherd?"

The answer is on every person's lips. "You are near the Oasis of Abalessa, lady."

"Is it far?"

"No, lady, but one more day's journey. My family gathers dates from the palms that grow there and our flocks drink from the waters. But there is no one who lives there."

"Then it will do very well. And you and your family may always come and gather dates from the oasis and bring your flocks to water. Thank you, child."

The lady bends her head again and turns away. But the goatherd cannot resist asking a question.

"Lady?"

Her profile comes back into view before she continues her journey.

"What is your name, lady?"

The camp waits for the great name to be spoken.

"My name is Tin Hinan."

The camp settles back, satisfied. The boy hugs his father in delight at having been part of history.

Aghbalu allows him a majestic smile before he gently squats back to the ground, somehow losing the woman's shape as he does so and taking back his own form. "Yes, she was Tin Hinan. A tall woman, of great beauty and strength. She was a noble woman. She set out from the Oasis of Tafilet and went across the desert with her faithful servant, Takama. The country they travelled across was empty but when they came to the Oasis of Abalessa Tin Hinan established herself there. She had a daughter, Kella," he nods in my direction, acknowledging the importance of the name I was given at birth, "from whom came the noble tribe of Kel Rela. Takama had two daughters – from one descended the tribe of Ihadanaren, from the other the tribes of Dag Rali and Ait Loaien. Tin Hinan gave the oases of Silet and Ennedid to the two daughters of Takama, and their descendants have them still today." Aghbalu pauses. "She died a great queen, and when she was buried she was placed on a bed of leather and adorned with her finest robes. On her right arm she wore seven bracelets of silver. On her left, she wore seven bracelets of gold. Beside her were laid fine drinking vessels. Many songs were sung for her and many stories are told of our great Queen Tin Hinan, the mother of all our tribes. This story is but one: the day when Tin Hinan heard tell of the Oasis of Abalessa from a poor goatherd boy."

Whistles and applause break out, along with shouts of praise, before the camp begins to disperse, bellies and minds replete. The younger children are taken to the tents, a few adults still linger, talking amongst themselves. Here and there some of the young women are still dancing but they are growing tired. I see Yusuf turn away from the sight of them, devout even in this. He is sat near my father and now they begin to talk together. I edge closer to them, walking softly and slowly, hoping not to be noticed.

"Kella."

"Amalu," I say, one eye still on my father and Yusuf.

"I came to your tent but could not find you," he begins.

"I am very tired," I say, moving back a little.

"I wanted to give you something," he says.

The men nod between themselves. I wonder what they are speaking of, if I can find out more about Yusuf's plans for the Maghreb.

"Kella?"

I drag my attention back to Amalu. "What is it?" I ask, impatient.

"Nothing," he says and walks away.

I feel bad for a moment but now my chance has come. I manage to step closer to where my father sits and sink to the ground behind him. My heart beats so fast and loud inside me that I think everyone nearby must hear it, but the men are oblivious to me and continue to talk amongst themselves. I have to steady my breathing to stop the pounding in my ears when Yusuf speaks, his voice clear and slow.

"Your help has been invaluable. The information you have given us will make our journey smoother and our chances of success greater. We have trespassed too long on your hospitality and our mission must begin. We will leave tomorrow."

My father nods. "Yusuf, Abu Bakr, I thank you for your faith and trust in me. I am but a humble man and if I have helped your mission, then I am glad. It is my duty before God to help you in your mission. I will ask Allah to bless you in my prayers."

I stand, legs shaking. I sway for a moment and then walk slowly towards my tent. They are leaving. The excitement that has surrounded their visit will go, everything will return to how it was: the daily monotony of rolling couscous, spinning, weaving and whatever other tasks and skills Aunt Tizemt can conjure up. I can hardly bear the thought of it. While Yusuf and his army will travel across the whole of the Maghreb, creating new cities and forging a new empire, I will stay here forever, eventually married to a man who will expect me to be happy caring for his children and no more. My eyes well up at the idea.

"Kella?"

Amalu is standing outside the tent.

"Go away," I say sharply.

"What is wrong?"

I face him. "Will you take me on the trade routes with you?"

"What?"

"Answer me."

He frowns. "Kella – "

I push past him, closing the tent flaps behind me.

"Kella!" calls Amalu outside.

"Leave me be!" I shout back. I fall down on the bed fully clothed and lie still and silent, unable to cry or move.

I am listless the next day. Aunt Tizemt chides me several times for foolish mistakes. I burn the milk porridge and refuse point-blank to serve the men, leaving the task to my aunt while I sit carding and spinning wool. She is appalled at the poor quality of my spinning.

"Anyone looking at that would think it was the first day that you had picked up a tuft of wool! What sort of poor rug will that make?" She tuts and walks away, muttering about young girls and their flighty, sulky ways.

I pay no attention to her comments. Yusuf has just walked past me. I leave my spinning to one side and follow him. He walks a little way outside the camp and then kneels to say his prayers. From behind one of the outer tents I catch a glimpse of his face as he lifts it up to the heavens. His expression is not fierce nor solemn, but calm and full of trust in God. As he prostrates himself his body is graceful and pliant, not sternly upright as he holds himself the rest of the time. He seems at ease with Allah – he offers his prayers as a small child might offer a humble gift to a loving parent, confident in a kindly response. It is a different side to him. I thought Amalu might relent and take me with him when he becomes a trader, if I married him, but he has refused more than once. Now my thoughts turn towards Yusuf. I wonder if I could marry such a man, if he would have me. If I married him, I think, I could travel with him, however dangerous the journey or the battles I would not be afraid.

I would be in the army's camp and taste freedom again. Would my father give permission for such a marriage? How could I draw Yusuf's attention to me as a possible bride? But he is engaged in a holy war, he is hardly about to stop and get married while his army amasses. I duck out of sight as he stands and return to the darkness of my aunt's tent, where I fling myself down on the bed and weep in rage and despair.

After a while, when my cushions are wet with tears, I turn onto my back and stare up at the ceiling. As I do so my hair, which has tumbled out of my headdress, catches in something that has been under my head while I wept. I had not felt it then, for it was only small and my feelings are too overwhelming. But now this thing, whatever it is, is tangled up in my locks of hair. With some mutterings under my breath and much fumbling, I eventually untangle it and sit up to look at it.

I drop it immediately and have to bend to pick it up from the rugs on the floor. I hold it up again. It is a very simple necklace, alternating tiny black beads with beads in the form of hollow silver tubes. At regular intervals there dangle small silver triangles, each with delicate engravings.

My first instinct was correct. It is a *chachat*, an engagement necklace.

I let it drop into my lap and then fall back on the bed, the tears slowly coming again. A *chachat*. It is from Amalu, of course. He must have sneaked into the tent when no-one was looking and laid it here on my bed so that I would find it. He asked me to be his bride and I never answered him, what with the excitement of my father returning and then all the preparations for the last few days, attending to our unexpected guests. Despite my snapping at him he smiled at me more than once and gestured helplessly at all the work we are all burdened with. There has been no time to talk. But now our guests are about to leave and the camp will grow quiet. Amalu must think the time is right to broach the subject again.

I sigh heavily and roll onto my side, one arm lifted to dangle the *chachat* in front of me. It is pretty. Amalu is a good man. He is friendly, caring and my own age. He will not let me trade alongside him, but there is no man who will let me do that. Why am I foolishly supposing that I might find one? Certainly pinning my hopes on an older man who may well be about to get killed is even more foolish than begging Amalu to take me trading.

Slowly I sit up and move my hair to one side, then fasten the necklace round my neck. Amalu is a good match for me. My family will be happy. I will go and find him and tell him.

But Amalu is nowhere to be found. Keeping the necklace hidden until I can speak with him I walk all over the camp but cannot see him anywhere. Meanwhile Abu Bakr's men are amassing, ready to leave. I steadfastly ignore them, turning away from the crowd of men, horses and camels, saddles being lifted into place and harnesses tightened. There are perhaps one hundred men in all. My chance to leave has gone. Yusuf would have to stay in the camp a great deal longer if I were to somehow woo him. Not that I have any idea how to do such a thing and anyway, he is devoted to his mission. He is not interested in a woman.

Not a woman.

I run.

My two youngest brothers are nowhere to be seen. No doubt they are bidding farewell to the soldiers. I know they have asked my father more than once if they may join the army, but he has refused. He needs their skills on the trade routes and he is afraid for their safety. Their tent is empty.

I do not waste time by undressing. I take one of my brother's blue robes and pull it on as quickly as possible. My hair wrap has to come off, for it is too bulky to hide beneath a face veil. I hide it in a large chest. I fasten a belt, take a dagger and my youngest brother's sword, pull at my veil to be certain that my face cannot be seen. If Yusuf bin Tashfin is not interested in taking a wife then I will join his army. Many young men of our camp and others of our tribe have joined him in the past few days. I will not be noticed.

Thiyya watches me as I saddle one of our sand-coloured camels.

"I am sorry," I tell her. "You are too noticeable. My father will take one look and know who is riding you."

She huffs and turns her face away when I try to stroke her, insulted.

"I will send for you one day," I tell her, a lump in my throat. "I cannot stay here."

I join the crowd of men and make sure to keep my distance from my father and brothers, whom I can see a little way off. Instead I mount the camel and join those who are ready to depart. I watch as Abu Bakr and Yusuf bid farewell to my father and other important men and bless the people of the camp for their help and support. Once they mount their horses the signal to move comes quickly. I make sure to be away from the officers, taking up a position within the crowd where I will ride side by side with the men who accompanied Yusuf here and will not know the young men of my camp. I do not speak to those around me and look only ahead, my veil tight around my eyes, my heart hammering in my chest.

We travel through the night to avoid the heat of the day and as the moon rises my heartbeats slow a little. We are moving ever further from the camp. It is many days' journey to the main army encampment and once we arrive there will be many hundreds, even thousands, of men, making it far easier to take my place among them unnoticed. For now I must only stay quiet and be noticed as little as possible. We will travel by night, sleep by day, thus aiding my disguise. I am a little afraid of what will happen when I am expected to train to fight and then join an army. But the thrill of being on a camel again, riding freely towards adventure is too great a pull. With every pace away from the camp my spirits rise. Beneath my veil my mouth is stretched in a grin.

There are no tents. The men wrap themselves in blankets and sleep on the sand under some scraggly trees, hoping to benefit from a little shade when the sun rises. My blanket smells of my brothers and suddenly I am afraid. I should have left them a message so that they know I am safe, for they will be searching for me if I am not seen tomorrow morning at the very latest. They may even have spotted my absence in the evening. How keen-eyed will my brothers be, how quickly will my father see what has been taken and understand what I have done? They will come after me for sure. But I am too tired. The dawn will be here soon and I must sleep; it will be harder to do so once the sun rises and we will ride on come the cool of the early evening.

I wake with a start as the man near me pokes me with his foot.

"Commander says we must be on our way," he says. I put my hand to my face to make sure it is hidden but I am safe. I struggle to my feet and roll up my blanket, kneeling to fasten the strap holding it in place.

"You."

I look up over my shoulder. A man stands behind me.

"Yes?"

"The General asks for you."

I swallow. "The General? What for?"

"How would I know? Don't keep him waiting."

I stand, stumbling over my blanket and then follow the man's pointed finger towards a solitary figure some way away from the men. Yusuf. I hesitate but I have no choice. I make my way over to him. He is sitting calmly, one knee pulled up, his hands wrapped around it while he gazes across the dunes. When I reach him I stop at a distance and wait for him to notice me. I hope he will not ask me to come any nearer to him.

"Come closer," he says, without turning his head.

Reluctantly, I take a few steps forward.

He doesn't move for a moment, then slowly turns his head and looks up at me. His black eyes stay fixed on me for an unnervingly long time. I try to stand like a man, head up, feet planted a little apart, my shoulders thrust back. Still he says nothing.

"Sir," I say, keeping my voice as deep as I can. "You asked to see me."

"Indeed," he says. "Take off your veil."

I swallow. "Sir?"

"Remove your veil," he says.

I try to bluster my way out of it. "It is not seemly…" I begin.

His shoulders shake a little and I see laughter in his eyes. "Not seemly for a man," he says. "Remove your veil."

My shoulders drop. I remove the veil as well as my whole headdress, letting the cloth drop to the ground. My hair tumbles down my back and the wind blows it into my face. I don't move.

Yusuf looks away from me, back across the dunes, nods to himself. "What is a young woman doing amongst my men?" he asks, as though to himself.

"How did you know?"

He looks back at me. "I know every one of my men," he says, his eyes serious. "We have an army of many thousands and I make it my business to know every one of them. They fight by my side, they would die for me. I should at least know their names, their faces, how they move. Do you not think?"

I say nothing.

"Well, you had better tie your hair up again," he says. "And then fetch your camel."

"I won't go home," I say. "I won't go back to the camp."

"No," he agrees. "I thought you might say that. I will take you there myself."

"What?"

"I will accompany you," he says. "Your honour is in my hands. I would not allow any other man to escort an unmarried woman back to her father and explain what she was doing out in the desert with a hundred men, none of them her own family."

"Please," I begin, but he has already stood up and is walking back to the men. He speaks with Abu Bakr, before turning to wait for me.

Horribly aware of a hundred pairs of eyes on me, I use the veil to wrap my hair up into a woman's headdress and walk back to Yusuf, my face flushed with humiliation and anger. I wait for the men to speak, for lewd comments or outrage, but they stand silent under Yusuf's gaze.

Abu Bakr looks me over. "Yusuf will accompany you home," he says. "With an escort. We will ride on to the garrison. Goodbye, Kella. I hope your return will be a comfort to your father."

I wonder that he even knows my name. I stand and watch as Yusuf and Abu Bakr embrace one another and then most of the men ride away. We are left with a dozen men, Yusuf and myself. All of us will be riding camels; Yusuf's fine grey stallion has been sent on ahead.

"Kneel," says Yusuf.

The camels kneel and the men mount their steeds.

I stand unmoving.

Yusuf looks at me. "You are in the middle of the desert, Kella," he says, his voice utterly calm. "You cannot hope to survive alone, even if I left you the camel. Mount." He slaps my camel on the rump and it kneels obediently.

As slowly as I dare, I mount the camel.

"Rise," he orders.

The men riding behind us occasionally talk to one another but their voices are low. Yusuf and I ride side by side as though we are friends but we are silent for a long time. When he does speak, I startle.

"Why did you run away?"

I don't answer; I don't know how to. Where to start and how to explain?

"Were you badly treated by your family?" He sounds concerned. "Beaten?"

"No," I say quickly.

"Promised in marriage to someone you dislike?"

"No," I say. I wonder what Amalu is doing now, whether he has joined in the search for me or thinks that he is well rid of such an ungrateful woman.

He looks amused. "I don't suppose you actually want to fight?"

"N-no," I confess.

"So why are you, a young woman *not* ill-treated by her family and with no desire to fight, running away with an army, dressed as a man? I think you owe me some sort of explanation, since you are wasting my time."

"I used to travel with my brothers and my father when he traded," I say slowly.

"Not a life for a woman, perhaps," he comments. "Not very safe."

"I was dressed as a boy," I say.

"Dressed as a boy?" he asks. I am not sure if he sounds disapproving or just surprised.

"Yes," I say.

He raises his eyebrows.

"I was a good trader," I say defensively. "And an excellent camel racer."

Now he laughs out loud. "You rode in camel races?"

"Yes," I say. "And I won," I can't help adding.

"I see," he says. Suddenly he brings down a whip on his camel, who begins to run. "Race me, then," he calls back to me.

I gape at him but the sight of his back ahead of me brings out my stubborn side. If he wishes to make fun of me, he will find out for himself what I am made of. I do not have Thiyya, more's the pity, but these camels have been chosen for warriors and already I can feel my own mount's power gathering beneath me. I urge it on, lean forward and note exultantly that we are already gaining on Yusuf a little.

He is an excellent rider and I do not manage to beat him. But I am very close to him, only a few strides separate us when he finally reins in his camel.

He is bent over laughing. His men are still a way off, they have not raced with us. "Truly a descendant of Tin Hinan herself," he says, his eyes amused.

I can't help but smile.

"Ah, a happy face at last," he says.

I frown.

"And gone again," he notes. He waits for his men to join us, looks me over. "You miss your trading days so badly?"

"Yes," I say and then swallow, so that I will not cry. I do not want to cry in front of him when he has seen me race well.

"And you thought – what? That you would run away in my army and then slip away unnoticed in some city, set up by yourself as a trader?"

I shake my head. "I don't know," I say. "Time was running out, you were leaving and I had no time for plans."

"Why run away with us? You could have waited."

"You had such a vision for the future," I say and then feel myself blushing, heat traveling up my neck into my cheeks. I sound as though I am flattering him.

"Vision?"

"For after the war is over," I say. "When you win."

"If Allah wills it," he reminds me.

I nod. "If He wills it," I repeat. "But you spoke of the whole of the Maghreb united under one rule. That great cities could flourish, that after the battles would come building: mosques, souks, caravanserai, bath-houses. That the trade routes would be made greater than ever before and traders could travel further and bring back wonders from all parts of the world. That the people would live in peace."

His head on one side, he watches me. "Go on."

"I – I would want to help make that happen," I say. "To plan which routes could be made safer and faster, in return for taxes. To show where cities could best grow because of their position on the trade trails. To build caravanserai large enough for many traders and their beasts to rest. There is so much that could be done."

His men have reached us. Yusuf only nods at what I have said and then falls silent. I turn over what else I could say but all of it sounds foolish in the silence and so we travel back to the camp without speaking again.

My father's eyes are grim. I am afraid to dismount for fear he will drag me back to the tent by my hair, he looks so angry. Instead I sit very quietly and wait.

"I humbly beg your pardon," begins Yusuf. "I have behaved very ill towards you, sir. I must speak with you."

My father looks as confused as I feel. What is Yusuf apologising for?

"In private?" asks Yusuf politely, dismounting.

My father walks away with Yusuf, looking back once over his shoulder at me, frowning.

They are gone some time. Half the camp has gathered to watch. Their silence is unnerving. Aunt Tizemt's lips are pressed so tightly together they have disappeared into a thin line. I look down. If Aunt Tizemt is not roaring then things are very bad. Behind her stands Tanemghurt, who looks amused. I dare not smile back at her. I look away and spot Amalu. His face is pale with suppressed rage, his hands in fists by his side. I have never seen good-natured Amalu look like this. I look back down at my reins.

"Kella."

My father and Yusuf have returned. My father still seems confused but no longer angry. I risk meeting his gaze. He blinks a couple of times, as though he does not quite believe what he is about to say.

"Kella, I understand from Yusuf that he desires to marry you."

I gape. I look to Yusuf, who raises his eyebrows at me, his eyes quite serious.

"Yusuf has apologised for the dishonour risked by allowing you to run away with him but tells me it was only because of your great love for one another. He has now formally asked for your hand and if you are content, the wedding will be arranged with all due haste. After which you may accompany your husband on his onward journey to fulfill his great mission."

I look at my father and then at Yusuf again. There is utter silence all around me. I dare not look at Amalu. Aunt Tizemt's mouth is open.

"Is this true? You wish to marry Yusuf?" repeats my father.

I think of my freedom. I am being offered my freedom if I will marry a man with whom I have only spoken today. I am being offered a chance to leave the camp as a married woman and to follow my husband on a great adventure.

"Yes," I say and my voice comes out so quietly and huskily that I have to say it again. "Yes. I wish to marry Yusuf." It comes out too loud this time.

My father nods, still baffled by all that has happened. "Very well," he says and walks away. The rest of the camp scatters to make ready for the riders and no doubt to gossip amongst themselves. Tanemghurt says something quietly to Aunt Tizemt, who stares at me one more time and then follows. I look towards where Amalu was standing but he is already walking away, towards the dunes, no doubt to be alone as I did on the day my father left me here.

The riders dismount and begin to set up camp. Yusuf walks over to me and holds up his hand to help me down from the camel. I do so ungracefully, half-twisting my ankle. When I have recovered myself I look around. My father is out of sight. I turn to Yusuf. He seems serene, as though he has done nothing worthy of note.

"Why?" I say, blurting out the word.

He looks down at me and chuckles at the expression on my face. "Are you unwilling after all?"

"No," I say, feeling the heat in my cheeks rise again.

"Very well," he says with satisfaction, looking ahead again.

"But *why?*" I ask again.

He looks at me again, his eyes grown serious. He pauses, as though collecting his thoughts. "For many years now I have been set on my path by Allah. I have a mission to undertake and I swore to stop for nothing and no one. But when I made my promise I thought of warriors and armies seeking to cut down my body, of unbelievers seeking to cast doubts in my mind. I did not think a young woman would stand in my path and make me pause in my journey. Abu Bakr thinks only of battles. But I think of what the war will achieve. I want to create a land of peace and prosperity, of holiness and righteousness. And this is not done only through war. It is done through building and prayer, through treaties and trading. And then I hear my own thoughts spoken aloud by a young woman, a woman bold enough to ride away from her family, hidden within an army." He thinks for a moment. "I think Allah has sent you to me for some purpose. You will be at my side, you will help me create an empire when the battles are won." He lowers his voice until it is barely a whisper, we are so close he could touch me. "Perhaps you will be the mother of a son who will continue my work when I am gone."

If I am breathless it is surely only because Yusuf's face is only a hand's breadth away, his lips close enough to touch mine.

Houmeyni — Wedding Necklace

Aunt Tizemt is on the warpath. "What kind of wedding can be adequately prepared for in so short a time? Allah, give this poor humble woman strength to carry out your will!"

Yusuf has insisted to my father that we must be married with all speed for his mission cannot wait, and yet he will not leave me behind. So there is much to do in a very short time, and Yusuf's insistence on speed has thrown the camp into turmoil.

Children flee before Aunt Tizemt as she stamps across the camp, each of them knowing that to be caught will mean hours of tedious work as she commandeers everyone who crosses her path to help her prepare for the wedding. Already the young men have been sent off on the best camels in every direction, to invite kin from neighbouring tribes to attend. Relatives that no-one has seen for many years will be on their way shortly, much food and drink must be prepared. The older children are set to gathering thorn bush branches to make temporary enclosures for any animals that the guests might have with them. The work is difficult and painful, for the bushes have to be sought out and then branches cut with sharp axes, while fighting off the vicious thorns that stick out in every direction. No-one can escape without painful red scratches, which my aunt dismisses airily, and they sting for hours afterwards as a reminder to each child to avoid her in future. The younger children have to build up heaps of dried camel dung, which burns well and is a good substitute for hard-to-find wood in a landscape where trees are a rarity and only bushes and shrubs offer sufficient opportunity for fuel. The camel dung, at least, has no thorns.

For those children who have successfully escaped my aunt's eagle eye, Aghbalu the storyteller is a focal point. He sits in the shade and rehearses his stories for the bridal feast, finding himself surrounded by an eager audience of small upturned faces, which have the disconcerting habit of disappearing suddenly before his very eyes like a many-bodied djinn whenever Aunt Tizemt's heavy tread can be heard approaching.

The older women are preparing their stocks of spices and discussing recipes for the wedding feast, counting how many mouths they will have to feed. The younger women and the craftsmen are set to preparing items for my future. I will no longer use my aunt's cooking pots and musical instruments, her waterbags and rugs. I will have my own possessions.

"And you need your own tent, of course," says my aunt. "I had thought we would have more time before you found a husband. But the time is upon us now and we must prepare everything quickly. Come with me."

I follow obediently, glad to be let off the weaving of a huge rug that will cover the floor of my tent. The other girls wink at me behind her back as I walk by, miming exhaustion and other, ruder, signals that, thankfully, my aunt does not catch. I suppress my giggles and bend to follow her into the cool darkness of the tent.

Inside it is hard to see after the glare of the sun. I narrow my eyes as my aunt searches for something and then sits on the bed.

"Sit."

I sit by her and watch as a large triangle of thick rough cloth, embroidered with once bold but now faded red and yellow symbols is unfolded on the bed between us. I look up questioningly at my aunt.

"Do you know what this is?"

"No."

"It is a piece of your mother's tent. I cut it out after her death, before you all left the camp to trade when you were still a baby." She smoothes the fabric with her hands.

"The tent and everything in it belongs to the woman. When she marries, her husband comes to her tent. If he divorces her, he will leave her tent." She gestures towards the camp outside. "Everyone is preparing your goods – your bowls and spoons, your rugs, blankets and waterbags, even your musical instruments. Your saddles and your husband's weapons will also be kept in the tent. Your brothers and father are preparing you a marriage bed. But you must have a tent to house all of your goods and your family. It is traditional, when you marry, for your mother to cut a piece from her tent and for that piece to form part of your own tent. When your mother died and your father decided to take you far away, I cut a piece of the tent to keep against the day when you would be married. Now that day is coming, and this is the piece of your mother's tent around which we will make your own tent. Every slave in the camp will be working on it to make it in time for the ceremony."

I reach out a hand and touch the strong yellow cloth that once sheltered my mother, father and brothers, and which will now provide shelter for Yusuf and myself. Tears spring to my eyes as I trace the symbols for protection and fertility. Aunt Tizemt smiles and places her rough warm hand over mine.

"Your mother was a most kind and loving woman. She loved your father and was loved by him. She bore six children, five of them sons. She was blessed by Allah before she left this world. You will also be blessed with sons, I am sure. Your husband-to-be must love you deeply. You drew his eye even while he was set on the path of his holy mission. He loves you enough to stop in his path – even though he has insisted that you must be married quickly so that he can continue along that path. You are a Tuareg woman, a free woman. He seems happy to give you much freedom, a rare thing amongst some men today. I hope your marriage will be most happy. May Allah bless you."

I throw my arms around my aunt, the closest thing to a mother I have ever known. She responds with a strong warm hug and then becomes brisk and business-like again.

"There are forty slaves who will be working on this tent. The men are finding strong poles. The women are sewing the cloth and skins together to make the coverings. I will be overseeing the embroideries. I would like them to match your mother's tent." She smoothes the triangle of cloth again and stands. "We have a lot to do in only a few days. Yusuf is an impatient man. Come."

With so many slaves working on it, the tent quickly takes shape. With Aunt Tizemt's urgings, oaths and threats about what will happen to anyone who slows down its progress, it is finished the day before the wedding.

Now it can be erected. A wide, flat sandy area near to the main camp has been chosen for the festivities, and the children have been charged with clearing the space; removing more of the dreaded thorn bushes, keeping the animals away and removing any particularly sharp rocks. The relatives, as they arrive, are shown places to set up their tents by the main camp, close to the area set aside for the marriage.

Within this space is now heaped up a mound of sand, packed down firmly until it resembles a large cushion, wide enough for two people to sit side by side. Over this my new tent is loosely erected, but it is not put up properly, for that will come later when it takes up its permanent location within the camp. The poles are not firmly planted, so that the cloth and skin folds sag and make a small dark enclosure barely big enough for two instead of a wide airy space made to contain a family. I try to peek at the tent but am shooed away by Aunt Tizemt and the other women, who hustle me back to the main camp.

"You have to be prepared! What will your bridegroom think of you if he sees you in that state?"

I have to laugh. I am dressed in my plainest clothes and am unwashed. My hair has not been combed for days as I have toiled away at all the tasks that my aunt has decreed must be done in a short time. Now, the night before my wedding, I am to be pampered.

I am taken to Tanemghurt's tent. She appears in the doorway and looks me over. I stand before her, suddenly conscious of the rank odour of my sweat and the dirt which seems ingrained in my very skin.

"You should be in your mother's tent, of course. She would have prepared you for your wedding. But you were born into my hands and so I have taken on her role at this time."

I step inside. The tent is heavily scented with two perfumes. One is incense, which Tanemghurt has just lit and which has now begun to smoke as its flame dies out. The other is henna powder, which Tanemghurt will later mix with a little hot water to make a paste to decorate my hands, feet and face. She sets the bowl aside and gestures brusquely.

"Take off your clothes."

I obey, looking around for somewhere to put them as I remove each item. Tanemghurt holds out her hand and I deposit the old worn clothes with her. She flings them casually but accurately into a corner of the tent, where they make a neat and insignificant pile.

Once I am naked Tanemghurt sits in her wooden seat and looks me over. I stand silently under her gaze, feeling like a slave at market, fearing to be found lacking in some way. I have grown in all directions since returning to the camp. I am a little taller, my hair now reaches down to my waist, while my breasts and hips have grown rounder, first with my aunt's and now my own good cooking to fatten me up. My calloused skin has grown smoother now that my aunt has shown me how rubbing butter and oils into the skin makes it glow like the warm sands as the sun falls. Still, at this moment I am sweaty and dirty from days of working with no time for washing and I feel unfit to be a beautiful bride.

Tanemghurt finishes her inspection of me without either condoning or condemning my current state. She calls out, startling me, and one of her slave girls appears, carrying hot water from the fire outside. She pours it into a great basin on the floor, then brings more until the basin and three more large pots are full. Tanemghurt tells her to keep the fire going and more water heating, and then stands. She makes her way to the basin and then slowly kneels, her knees letting out a loud cracking noise that alarms me. I try to help her but she gestures impatiently at me and I step back, rebuffed.

She picks up a cloth, wets it in the hot water and begins to pat my body with it. I nearly cry out, for the water is almost boiling. Tanemghurt, however, seems able to immerse the cloth without flinching, her hands hardened after many years. She ignores my whimpers and wets me thoroughly all over, by which time my body is flushed pink.

When I think she has finished she takes a small cloth, woven with rough wool. Aunt Tizemt would scold me for producing such coarse work, but I quickly realise its purpose. Tanemghurt dips it in the burning water and begins to rub me ferociously all over, using small circles, working her way up from my feet. I stand first on one leg and then the other as she scrubs viciously at the soles of my feet, then works her way up without pause except to dip the cloth back into the water. I look down, whimpering quietly, and see my skin being scraped off me in little rolls, layer upon layer. I protest weakly but Tanemghurt has suddenly and conveniently become deaf. Only when every part of me has been scrubbed and I am scarlet from head to toe does she gesture to me to kneel and dips the cloth yet again. She kneels opposite me and pushes back my hair. I close my eyes and steel myself for the assault on my face, the skin so much more tender than the rest of my body, but when the cloth touches my face it is pleasantly warm rather than burning hot and the strokes are suddenly soft as a caress as she gently wipes each part of my face.

This unexpected gentleness lasts as long as it takes to finish my face and then Tanemghurt gets back to her work with a vengeance. My head is all but submerged under water in her largest pot, filled with hot water. I feel as if I might be cooked and briefly wonder what spice she might serve my head with, letting out a hysterical giggle at the thought which is instantly stopped as hot water enters both my nose and mouth. Having dunked me, she begins to rub a thick paste into my hair while I try to get my breath back. The paste smells of herbs and rose petals and she seems determined that it should penetrate my very skull. I grit my teeth and wait for this torture to be over, for there is no arguing with Tanemghurt. Certainly, I muse to myself as my head is violently jerked about under her strong hands, I will never be so clean again, no, not even if I spent whole days in the *hammams*, the great steam baths of the cities.

"Has your aunt instructed you on what happens between a man and a woman?" asks Tanemghurt matter-of-factly.

"Oh yes," I say quickly, seeking to sound mature enough to be a wife although in truth I have not received any instruction on this topic. Aunt Tizemt probably thought there was plenty of time for such things.

Tanemghurt only raises her eyebrows without challenging me.

At last she seems to have finished with me, for I can think of no other part of me that can be cleaned. She has even cleaned my ears with a small stick carved with a curve at the end and has removed not just a few but all of my bodily hairs. I tried not to shriek when she did this but I could hear small children outside, giggling between themselves and know that my howls of pain have most certainly been heard by others.

But I still have the thick paste in my hair and my body is covered with stray plucked hairs and little rolls of grimy skin which is an entirely different colour from my new skin, as though I am a serpent and my skin has been shed to bake in the sun, leaving me with a new glossy set of scales. How am I to remove all of this debris? I think perhaps I could immerse sections of myself into the large pot of water – my head, an arm, a leg, although how to manage my torso is beyond me. But Tanemghurt has bolder ideas. "Go outside," she commands as though I were not entirely naked and there was not a whole camp of people outside, including my father, brothers and future husband, all nearby. I do not move.

"Are you deaf?"

"*Lalla*, I am not going outside naked!" I exclaim.

She laughs as though she had expected me to say this and thinks I am a simpleton. "No-one will see you. Outside. Now." Her tone does not invite refusal. She yanks back the flaps that covered the entrance to the tent and draws back to let me see what she has done.

Outside stand many slave girls in a circle. Between them they hold up bright, fluttering lengths of cloth, making a new tent with no roof, outside. If I step out of the tent now, no-one will see me. I step out cautiously, noticing too late that Tanemghurt has remained in the tent, then gasp as out of nowhere more slave girls appear on the other side of the bright cloths and each pours, in rapid succession, a big pot of cold water over my head. I stand, shaking and choking out some of the water I have accidentally breathed in when I gasped in surprise. Before I can even raise my hands to my face to wipe the water away, Tanemghurt is by my side and has wrapped me tightly in a large cloth. She is shaking with laughter, her few teeth exposed and the wrinkles of her face so creased I can barely see her eyes. She quickly pulls me back inside the tent as the slave girls, smiling at my shocked face, lower the cloths and go about their business as though what had just happened is a daily occurrence.

Back inside the tent, Tanemghurt has lost her fierceness. She seats me, still wrapped in my cloth, on the bed and then kneels before me and begins to rub warm perfumed oil over every part of my body.

"Did you like the waterfall?" she asks, smiling.

I wriggle my toes in her hands and relax as the warmth creeps back into my body, inhaling the smell of roses that fills the tent. "I have never seen such a thing before, *Lalla*," I say honestly.

She chuckles, pleased with her work. "It is hard to bathe out here – water has to be carried so far, and we cannot build the great steam baths of the cities. But I have heard tell of them, how the skin is steamed so that the old skin will fall away and open up to receive softening oils, how great buckets of water are thrown over the women who go there. It is a gift I make, for brides of our camp. Our brides are the cleanest and most perfumed of all the tribes. I have had women come and beg me to do this for them from tribes far, far away!" She is proud of her reputation as a wise woman, one who can manage not only the hard things, like a childbirth gone wrong, but also the joyful things of life, such as the honour of preparing a bride for her husband. Tonight I will sleep in her tent and tomorrow she will send me out as a bride to my husband, for the first day of celebrations.

All day long the guests have been arriving. They are offered hot tea and all manner of good things to eat. They set up their tents and settle down to the best part of a wedding – the gossiping, the catching up with family and friends and enjoying good food and drink. In the afternoon the young men race their camels while the women ululate and praise them with shrill cheers and songs. From Tanemghurt's tent, as I sit still, waiting for the henna to dry, I smile when I think about my camel racing days.

"What are you smiling at?" asks Tanemghurt.

I shake my head. "I used to race camels," I confess. "I pretended to be one of my brothers but it was always me. I won so many races," I add a little wistfully.

I think that Tanemghurt will frown, or tell me that it is high time I set aside such nonsense, but to my surprise she chuckles and then pulls at my foot. With her henna stick she quickly draws a tiny camel on my ankle, hidden from all but there for me and me alone. I look down and smile at its shape.

"Thank you," I say.

She smiles. "We all have our memories," she says.

I am unrecognisable. My hair is brushed and perfumed with rosewater, then draped with many loops of silver circlets, which cover all but every strand. I wear my *tchirot* under my new, brightly coloured wraps made of the finest cloths my aunt can find at such short notice, helped by my father's stores of trading goods. My *celebra* and an engagement *chachat* from Yusuf are round my neck. I have more new jewellery from Yusuf. He has sent the traditional set of wedding gifts to Tanemghurt's tent. I wear a pair of large earrings, multiple pendants, then another necklace with a cross pendant. The final item is a headpiece, which is added to my already crowded head. It is a triangular carnelian stone jutting out of a square of silver, which adds height and elegance to my already elaborate hair. I feel weighted down with silver and stones, but my aunt and Tanemghurt only nod at each other with satisfaction when they look at me. My hands, face and feet are marked with henna paste. I had to sit still for a very long time watching as it dried crustily, like scabs on a wound on my newly washed and oiled skin. But it was worth it, for the patterns are very pleasing to the eye. The whirlwind of the past few days is settling and I am about to marry Yusuf. What at first felt like some strange dream is now becoming real. I am a bride and I am about to be married.

As darkness falls, there is music, singing and dancing. Somewhere on the other side of the camp Yusuf is in another tent, heavily veiled as I will be when I finally emerge.

At last, the women come to fetch me. It is almost midnight, and they are very merry as they encircle me and we begin to walk slowly to my newly-made tent, erected outside the camp over the pile of packed sand that will serve as our seat for a few hours.

We arrive together, the men leading Yusuf, the women leading me, and we are shown into our tiny, misshapen tent. There is only room for the two of us, each swathed in our layers of robes, mine strewn with jewellery, his plain as ever. Outside our tent everyone sings and dances, the drums wild and the singing rippling over their persistent pulse. Even if we had spoken in the darkness, we would not hear one another. Under our many robes Yusuf reaches for my hand. It is a strange feeling, to clasp hands with a man I barely know. I have not yet grown used to it when they come back to return us to our own tents, Yusuf holding a sword and I a knife, for iron is lucky at a wedding.

As we slowly make our way back to our separate tents, behind us my new tent is being pulled down, the mound of sand left in place, to be gradually dispersed across the vast desert by the slow winds of time.

It is almost dawn, but I have time to sleep while the men properly erect my tent. I will not join Yusuf there until later today. At first I cannot sleep, my head too full of the songs and rhythms and the touch of Yusuf's hand. But Tanemghurt bends over me to hold a cup of sweet warm milk to my lips and soon I am asleep, my body a loose heap of twisted cloth and silver.

It is late morning when I open my eyes again, prodded awake by Tanemghurt and my aunt, who stand over me, smiling.

"Yusuf has already gone to your tent," says Tanemghurt.

Aunt Tizemt chimes in. "They are finishing the camel rides in front of the tent. It will be time for you to join him soon. Come, sit up and sip some tea. Not too much. Remember, once you are in the tent you cannot leave till nightfall, not even to relieve yourself."

I sit up and drink a little mint tea to freshen my mouth. The women are gathering again. This time we walk within the camp to my new tent. It is beautiful now that it is fully erected and bathed by the sun's rays. The embroideries shine out and I put up one hand to touch the old worn triangle that belonged to my mother's tent, before I enter.

All my new possessions have been laid out and the tent is now a real home. Rugs cover the floor and cushions are scattered everywhere, inviting comfort. At the centre is my marriage bed, again spread with blankets woven with bright symbols for fertility and good luck. Seated on the bed is Yusuf.

I pause in the doorway. Here I am alone with a man I barely know, a man I chose to marry in a fit of boldness, challenged by him to accept in front of my whole family and encampment. I chose him – why? For a moment I feel panic rising in me. Why did I not spend more time with Amalu, perhaps persuade him to take me trading with him? Why did I think I could marry this stranger and follow him on a terrifying mission to conquer the Maghreb, a mission which has failed once before? If he dies and then I am left alone or worse, taken as a captive and...

Yusuf is watching me. "Will you sit by me, Kella?" he asks gently.

I swallow and step forward, then almost trip and land ungracefully by his side.

He laughs as I struggle to regain my composure. "Your eagerness to be near me bodes well for our marriage bed, I think."

I blush and try to smile, my heart thudding as I think of our 'marriage bed'. How easily he says the words! Does he have no doubts? He is far older than I, does he not think I am a foolish girl who knows nothing and will now be a burden to him? Does he not have any regrets as to his hastily-made choice of a bride – and indeed to marry at all?

The tent folds at the entrance are still open, for now all the guests will dance and sing in front of our dwelling to wish us well and give us their blessings. We have many hours yet before we will close the tent door and be alone. I try to make myself a little more comfortable on the bed. Yusuf offers me additional cushions, which I accept. When I have stopped nervously adjusting my position he reaches out and takes my hand in his, then turns his face back towards the guests, now engaged in good-natured jesting.

I sit still, watching the dancers and singers while trying to grow used to the sensation of holding hands with him. I try to think of something to say but I cannot think of anything and he seems happy in silence, so after a while I stop trying.

At last, as dusk falls, the guests begin to leave. I am certain that all of Allah's ninety-nine names have been invoked as each of them finds a new way to bless us and wish us well. Then they say their goodbyes to one another. The tents are folded down and loaded onto camels before people begin to drift away in every direction from our camp.

By the time it is fully dark the hubbub around our tent has subsided and Tanemghurt comes and shuts all the sides so that we can be alone. "Do not forget," she says as she leaves us, "You are to stay in this tent for seven days and seven nights. You may leave only to relieve yourselves, and that only at night. I will bring you food each day."

We have been given bowls with soft dates and herbed olives, roasted meats, fresh flat breads and dipping sauces to eat with them. There are two large waterbags propped up by the tent.

I clear my throat, as though about to say something and Yusuf looks at me questioningly. I shake my head, feeling myself blush against my will. I have never felt so useless. Surely a new bride should be more comfortable in her new husband's company?

Yusuf interrupts my train of thought by reaching for something in his robes. It makes a clinking sound as he pulls it out and I look to see what it is. He holds it out to me in the flickering light of the fire.

"My gift to you on our wedding day."

It is a *houmeyni.* A leather thong, with a large silver articulated pendant, carved all over with tiny symbols and shapes. A traditional wedding gift, given by grooms to their brides. He should have given it to me at the ceremony earlier, but I am glad he has chosen this moment for it seems more intimate and is a more important gift than the many other items of jewellery he had sent to me in Tanemghurt's tent before the wedding and which I have worn all day. The *houmeyni* is associated with courtship, with moonlit encounters, with romance and even those sexual encounters that sometimes take place before a wedding. I lift off all my other items of jewellery, letting each fall onto the carpet at our feet and allow him to place the necklace round my neck.

When he has done so he sinks to his knees before me and begins to unfasten my clothes. I stand very still, looking down on him nervously, but he takes his time, his fingers do not stumble over the clasps and ties which hold my many layers of finery together. As he undoes each item he places it to one side without looking to see how it falls, never taking his eyes from my gradually exposed body, my outlines slowly becoming clearer in the half-light. When I am naked he sits back on his heels but rather than look at my body his eyes come upwards to my face and when they meet my blushing gaze he smiles. He reaches up to my waist and back, carefully lowering me down to the soft carpets and the furs that have been strewn there, in which he lays me down and covers me. Then he rises to his feet and begins to undress himself.

I am entirely naked except for my *houmeyni* necklace, the silver cold on my skin. I tremble. Not from cold, for I am wrapped in fine blankets and even have furs which feel soft as they shimmer against my bare skin with every tremor. I am trembling because I know very little of what will happen next. I wish earnestly that Tanemghurt had challenged my airy claim to know what goes on between a man and a woman. My erotic instruction comes down to everything I have seen animals do, none of which seems very romantic or alluring; matter of fact information from Aunt Tizemt, which mostly consisted of her view that we are not much better than animals; and hints from girls of my own age and the women of pleasure from the souks, which were nothing but a mass of unlikely-sounding fantasies. None of this is what I need now. I lie silent as Yusuf undresses and I see all of him for the first time.

His skin is very smooth and also very pale, something like a fine golden sand rather than the dark brown of his forearms and feet, for it is always sheltered from the sun under his heavy robes. I shrink back a little in my furs, for it now becomes evident to me for the first time that I have married a warrior. Every part of his body is a weapon. His muscles are large and well-defined and I have no doubt at all that any man facing him on the field of battle would think twice before approaching him. He undresses quickly and efficiently, like a soldier stripping down armour, and as he does so I watch as his muscles ripple and play in the flickering light and shadows. Last of all he unwraps his veil, so that I can see his face. His expression is kind and calm and although I am still nervous, he is gentle with me as he begins to touch me and after a little while I cease to tremble.

Our days are spent in the colourful tent in the camp, where we can hear passers-by and the giggles of the children as they try to peek in at us. Unlike his usual fierce bearing and passionate commitment to his cause, I find that Yusuf can also be humorous. He will suddenly grab at the children's questing fingers and cause high pitched shrieks of surprise, at which he roars with laughter. The tent grows hot in the heat of the day and we laze in each other's arms, sleeping and waking. We play games when we are awake, with pebbles or bones and rough marks in the sand of the floor. We try to cheat and demand forfeits when we catch each other out.

We eat together. Tanemghurt's food is surprisingly good, for I have never seen her cook with the other women. She has her own work, and it is not cooking and caring for children, weaving, or any of the other skills women possess. Her skills are valued highly enough that she has more offers of food, cloth or utensils than she will ever need, from those who have received her healing in the past and know that the day will come when they will need to call on her again. So I have never seen her cook. But all the food brought to us now comes from her hands. She uses herbs and spices better than anyone I know. Her sweet cakes are soaked in honey and then coloured with spices to make them pleasing to the eye as well as the mouth. Her stews warm the heart as well as the body and some of the drinks she leaves for us do more than warm the heart. We feed each other with our fingers, sometimes giving each other the very best morsels, sometimes playing little tricks on each other, such as when I feed him fine cakes which he says are too rich for him, or when he chooses a particularly spicy morsel for me and laughs when I flush with the heat of it.

We pray. As each of the five prayers of the day come and go I grow to care for him more, for his prayers are more sincere than any I have heard before. Many of the tribesmen that I know pray rarely and some still cling to the old ways. Amongst the tribes there are those who are very pious, but even they seem to pray by rote, as if by command. But Yusuf prays with every part of his heart and soul. His eyes are lit as if from within with a soft and gentle light, a true flame of faith. When his body sways, so too does his voice as he murmurs his prayers. At these moments I am certain that my choice was the right one. This is a man who will achieve great things and I wish to be by his side when he does so. I am afraid of the battles yet to come but I know that if he is successful afterwards there will be a time of peace when I can prove my worth.

In the darkness we wrap thick blankets round us and sit outside, braving the cold to gaze at the stars and talk. I hear of his childhood, his friends, his parents and siblings. I hear of how he and his cousin Abu Bakr began by playing at war as children and are now engaged in a true war. Abu Bakr is a dedicated leader, but Yusuf has a vision that Abu Bakr sometimes struggles to comprehend.

"He is a great commander," says Yusuf, as we sit eating dates and bread and gazing at the stars. "He cares for his men. He trains them to be the best that they can be, not only their bodies like any commander, but their minds also. He reads the Qur'an with them daily, he asks them about their families, their hopes for the future. Their prayers are his prayers. He is a good man." He shakes his head as though at an unsettling thought, then repeats his words. "A good man. I would hope to always serve under him. But he may not wish to continue as the commander."

I know nothing of the politics of commanding and armies. I know only that Yusuf's body is warm next to mine and that his voice is soft and soothing, even now, when he is serious. "Why would he not be the commander?"

Yusuf shrugs. "Sometimes he looks at me in wonder when I speak of all of this country united under Allah, under one commander. I think perhaps he does not think it is possible. That the tribes are too many and will not swear allegiance to one commander. That there will always be fighting and squabbling. He knows the tribes well, he speaks easily with them. I do not have that gift. The heads of each tribe always speak more easily with Abu Bakr than with me." He raises his head and his voice grows a little stronger. "But I have something he does not have. I look into the future and I see a great land, united under Allah, with one commander. It could be done. We could do it. But we must keep that vision before our very eyes."

I yawn a little. It is very late. "I am sure you will succeed, husband." I say, warmly. It is the truth. I cannot imagine him wanting something and not succeeding in getting it. Men from all the tribes are willing to join him in his holy war. He can accomplish anything.

He hears me yawn and chuckles. "My poor sleepy wife. Am I boring you with talk of war again? I am sorry. But you are married to a warrior, I am afraid. You will hear much more of war before you are an old woman."

"Old woman?" I feign indignance. "How long do you intend this war to last?"

So our seven days and nights pass, and on the morning of the eighth day we say the dawn prayers together and leave our tent as husband and wife.

Trik — Bridle Ornaments

*T*RADITION DICTATES THAT WE SHOULD now live in my own camp for at least a year before leaving to go to my new husband's camp. But tradition cannot be obeyed. Yusuf is anxious to get back to Abu Bakr and the army of men, who are only waiting for our wedding rituals to be completed before they can begin their first great challenge: crossing the High Atlas mountains. It will be an exhausting journey, but the men have been well trained and are strong. They will fare better than most travellers who attempt to cross the steep and rocky mountain paths, where a simple misstep can result in immediate death. Their strength and stamina will be tested however and once over the Atlas mountains they may be called on to fight at any moment. This will prove a harsh test for men who have only just scaled a mountain range and come safely down the other side, carrying heavy weapons and leading their mounts.

Yusuf suggests to me that I should stay at the camp and he will send for me later on.

"I did not marry you to stay at home!"

He laughs out loud at my appalled face. "I would keep you safe," he says.

"I did not run away with your men in disguise because I valued my safety," I say.

He nods. "Very well. I should not allow it, but I know it is not in your nature to stay here. If I refuse to take you, no doubt I will find you at my side in the heat of battle, wielding a sword."

I have to laugh. "You would indeed," I tell him with mock fierceness.

"It is agreed then," he says. "Tell your slaves to pack your belongings."

I have to decide what to take with me. Thiyya, of course. I must have my tent and its contents in order to provide us with a home. My father says I need slaves to accompany me, but I am reluctant to take too many with me. At last we agree that I will have only two. I can have more later when we are more settled and know where we will be based. My father offers me two young slaves, hardworking and healthy as a gift, and I agree gladly.

But that evening, as I oversee the cooking, the slave woman Adeola comes to me and asks me to come to one side, by my tent. Here I find her man Ekon. When he sees me arrive he kneels before me, as does Adeola.

"What is the meaning of this?" I ask. "Do you have a boon to ask of me?"

They nod, and Adeola speaks, for she has learnt more of our tongue than her man, although her words are still slow and careful. "We want… be your slaves."

I frown. "You are already my family's slaves."

They shake their heads together. "We be *your* slaves, your father's… gift. We go with you when you leave with husband." They both look at me earnestly, waiting for my reply.

"Are you not well treated here that you wish to leave?"

Again they shake their heads. Adeola tries to explain herself more clearly. "You bought us. We would have been…" she struggles for the word.

"Separated." I give her the word and she nods. I am moved by their loyalty to me for an action from what feels like a long time ago, something which I had chosen to do on the spur of the moment, yet which has meant so much to their lives. Now they want to come with me, to serve me themselves, out of this devotion. I try to dissuade them.

"There will be long travels over rough ground, through the mountains. There will be much work, for I will have only two slaves, perhaps for a long time. It will be hard. And we will be part of an army. There may be danger."

They look up at me and then Ekon speaks. I am unaccustomed to hear his voice, for he is a quiet man. "We are not afraid. We work hard. We come." It is not a request, it is a simple fact. I hear the finality of his tone and smile at them both. I know that I could not have two more loyal slaves with me. My father will understand my reasons for taking them.

"Then you had better plan what you will take with you. You will each ride a camel and you will have one camel for your tent and your possessions. We leave in a few days."

Too soon everything is ready. The camels are saddled and most are piled high with my belongings. Yusuf's men are already mounted, as are my two slaves. Only Yusuf's camel and Thiyya stand without riders, each slowly chewing and enjoying their last few moments of freedom as Yusuf and I make our farewells. Tanemghurt says little, giving me a few spices and herbs, then touches my cheek and smiles before walking slowly back to her own tent, with no superfluous tears or words. I notice that she moves a little more slowly than usual and wonder how much longer she will walk in this world.

The children cluster around, full of questions for Yusuf. They cannot wait for the day when they too can be bold warriors and they fight amongst each other now to stand closer to him, touching his weapons with awe.

Aunt Tizemt pours out a string of instructions for my future life as a married woman, everything that is to come and which she will be unable to tell me when the time comes. Foods to please a man's upset stomach, how to bathe a baby, the proper way to dress my hair now that I am married, how to address the grandfather of my children, what gifts to give to my mother in law, should I ever meet her. The list goes on and on, and becomes more broken and confused as she begins to cry, an unheard-of weakness from my fearsome aunt. She is devastated to be losing me now. Only the day before I confided to her that I have not bled, and that perhaps I am carrying Yusuf's child, which made her very happy until she remembered that I was about to leave her and go away and that she is unlikely to see any child of mine for a very long time, if ever. I cannot put together the words to thank her for all she has done for me. Instead I embrace her tightly and bury my face in her shoulder. She smells of all her womanly skills – wool, good food and woodsmoke. I inhale her scent and force back the tears that sting my eyes.

My father speaks mostly with Yusuf, but when he turns to me there are tears standing in his eyes and his voice is a little hoarse as he gives me his blessing and promises he will see me very soon.

It is time to get into the saddle. For the first time in my life I will ride on a woman's saddle, a giant throne of twisted cloth laid over the leather and wooden harness. I will sit in this like some great queen, my feet resting on Thiyya's neck straight ahead of me. Thiyya screws up her nose at the ungainly weight, so different from the racing saddles she has been used to. It will be more comfortable for me for long journeys, but it feels strange to sit there so lazily, as though I am not in full command of my own mount, and the saddle rules out any racing across the dunes for my balance will not be as good; the saddle sways more than the ones I am used to.

Thiyya is made to kneel. I climb into my new seat. As she rises to her feet the saddle sways perilously and I can do nothing but cling to the arms of my throne and hope for the best.

Now my brothers gather round me. Each of them brings out from behind his back a *trik*, a small silver ornament for Thiyya's harness. They attach these to the harness and reins and tears spill from my eyes as I see that each of them bears a letter denoting my brother's names amongst the other symbols etched on them. The symbols are for fertility, long life, good luck and many other blessings. When they are all attached I shake the reins and the *triks* tinkle softly together. My brothers are delighted.

"Ah, see sister, you will not miss us now, for listen to all that noise – it will be as if we are by your side at all times."

"That noise is as the sound of a flower bending in the breeze compared to the noise you boys make," I retort, laughing through my tears.

The camels shift beneath us, made impatient by all these drawn-out farewells. I look at the crowd of men whom I am about to join, Adeola and I the only women. I frown when I catch sight of Amalu, mounted and armed. I guide Thiyya towards him.

"What are you doing?"

"Joining the Almoravid army," he says, looking ahead, away from me.

I move Thiyya so that I am almost face-to-face with him. "Joining the army? Have you gone mad? You never wanted to be a warrior."

"I wanted you," he says.

I lower my voice. "I am married," I remind him.

"And it will go wrong," he says.

"Are you cursing my marriage?" I ask, offended.

He shakes his head.

"Well then?"

"You do not know this man," he says. "All you wanted was your freedom."

He is uncomfortably near the truth but I fight back anyway. "He and I see what the future could be," I say.

"And I will be there when it goes wrong," he says.

"It will not go wrong," I say, angry now.

He turns his face away.

"Amalu!"

He looks back at me. "You do not know what love is yet," he says more quietly. "When you do, I will be waiting."

"And if I never come to you?"

"Then I will be happy for you," he says. "Because I love you."

"You could die," I warn him.

Amalu shrugs. "We all of us will die one day," he says. "Better to die for love than cowardice."

I want to say something else, but while I try to think how to dissuade him Yusuf rides up to us.

"Are you ready?" he asks me.

I nod.

He makes a gesture with his arm and the men fall in behind us, Amalu swept into the crowd where I can no longer see him. Instead I look back to my family, to their waving arms and try not to let sudden tears fall.

Our journey will take us first to the garrison basecamp where the men are being trained, in the foothills of the Atlas Mountains, ready to cross the mountains and begin their planned conquest.

We move off, twisting back to wave at all the people of the camp, gathered to bid us farewell. My brothers, father and aunt wave to us until we are out of sight.

I did not know then that I would never see any of them again.

We travel for many days and I am now sure that I am carrying Yusuf's child, although I do not tell him yet, for it is still very early. But my bleeding should have come many days ago, and it is not yet here. I hold my secret to me as I sway along on Thiyya's back, and I walk gently when I am set down. I am not entirely certain how I feel about a child. I meant to be free, to be a right hand to Yusuf, to help him build a peaceful future and I am nervous that a baby will mean that I am kept back, for my safety and that of our child, that I will be kept out of decision-making. But I comfort myself that Yusuf married me because he liked my vision for the future, that he wanted a child. And I think that perhaps a child coming so quickly is a blessing from Allah on our marriage and mission, that it points the way to a time of peace and plenty. I will have a baby. Yusuf will leave me reluctantly and only for a short while and then he will send for me. I will join him with a healthy infant in my arms and we will have our own little family. I hum as we ride and Yusuf teases me for singing lullabies and asks whether I think he is a little child that needs to be sung to in order to travel quietly. I only laugh back at him and try to sing other songs, although the lullabies return to me day after day.

And so we travel onwards. I have only rare moments alone with Yusuf and I begin to realise the reality of his life, which now is my own. He comes to my tent, but often it is so late that I have fallen asleep, and I wake for dawn prayers to find he has already left the tent and gone to pray, or is training or making plans with some of his men, earnestly discussing tactics, weapons or which animals will make better mounts in the heat of battle. The camels allow the rider to see far but provide an all-too-easy target for the enemy to cut down mid-battle. The swift horses can come closer to the foot soldiers in the enemy's ranks, allowing the rider to strike them from a vantage point. But their swift hooves can also slip at a crucial moment and a tumble would be fatal.

Occasionally I catch sight of Amalu but he never speaks to me. Sometimes I catch him looking my way but when I face him he turns his gaze away and will not meet my eye.

I also hear about the cities they plan to attack. The most important will be Aghmat, a rich trading city, well-guarded by walls and mercenaries as well as the amir's own guards. It is a fine city, with a busy souk through which many treasures pass from trader to trader, hot bath houses that all can visit and water brought by canals to the very heart of the city itself. Aghmat has become the capital of the Sous region under the leadership of the Idrisids. The amir of the city now is the leader of the Maghrawa tribe. Luqut al-Maghrawi is a noble man, so they say, and a fierce warrior. It will be a challenge to take Aghmat, for the amir and his men will defend it to the death and the Maghrawa are not to be taken lightly. But it must be done if the army is to take the region and stand a chance of continuing their progress throughout the rest of the country, heading north. The Almoravids's holy war will come to a stumbling halt if they cannot take key cities, and Aghmat is the first of these that they will encounter. To take Aghmat will be to send a strong message to all the tribes that here is a force to be reckoned with, that a new era is coming.

I hear their words in the still heat of the day or blown to me on the cooling wind of the evenings. Talk of weapons, mounts, men, training, the cities they hope to take easily, those that are better fortified. Sometimes I listen intently, desirous of knowing everything about what the future holds for my husband and therefore for me also, as though knowing every detail will make their plans successful.

Often, though, I turn my head away and watch the soft sand sinking under the camels' feet, see horned vipers slide away at our approach, or fat green lizards clinging to rocks. I close my eyes to enjoy what little breeze blows across my face. I still cannot believe that I have left the camp, that I am journeying again. The sense of freedom it brings me is a joyous thing, my mouth stretches into a smile without my even realising.

Sometimes I seek Yusuf out, looking for a glimpse of his rarely-seen humour and mischievous side, which he shows only when we are alone. Travelling with the men he has been serious again, intent on the plans for the future and the many things to be done at the main camp before they will be ready to face their first real battles. Abu Bakr will be impatient for his arrival, for together they are a formidable pair, their strengths complementing one another. Together they will be able to make plans, to see that all is ready, to encourage the men before the real hardships began. Their training will have prepared them for war, of course, strengthening their muscles and bringing bravery to their hearts, but no training can truly take the place of war. No man who has not fought against a man who wishes him dead can say that he is ready for a battle. Most of the men until now will have fought only each other, where the weapons are handled with caution and no real harm will come to them.

I catch sight of Amalu one day and hurry towards him. "Amalu."

"Kella," he says without emotion.

"I wish you would return home," I tell him. "I am afraid for you."

"You doubt I can fight?"

I sigh. "I do not doubt your manliness, Amalu. I doubt your desire to be a soldier."

"That is no longer your concern," he says and walks away.

I sit with Yusuf one evening, sharing a few dates together, away from the others so that we can be alone. We talk of small things only; the jackals we heard the night before and whether they will be bold enough to approach again tonight, the shapes of clouds, our camels' demeanour. But after a while the talk drifts to his plans, as it always does. He wants to have drummers with him when they go into battle, as their strong rhythm will not only give courage to his own men and unite them but bring fear to their opponents, for only a confident army can have drums beating for them in the thick of battle. He describes the heat of a battle, how they will keep tight formations, no falling back, nor even advancing, allowing the enemy to come to them and then realize their error when they find out how strong the army is, how well-trained its men and beasts, how they can be caught up in the fervour of drums and be merciless in their fighting, leading inevitably to success.

I grip Yusuf's arm, unable to keep my fears to myself. "What if you are not successful? What if your men fail, and you are driven back?"

He strokes my hair. "It is a risk that we must take," he says simply. "We cannot succeed if we do not fight. God is with us, I feel His hand upon us and we cannot fail if it is His will."

I cannot let it rest so simply. "And if it is not His will?"

He smiles sadly at my anxious face. "Then we will die."

"You cannot die!" My voice grows louder and Yusuf puts one finger gently against my lips. I push his hand away and go on, unthinking. "How can I raise a child with no father?"

He looks closely at me. "What?"

I shake my head and lower my eyes. "Nothing. I only meant..." I am suddenly crushed into a breathtaking hug.

"You are with child!"

I cannot deny his hope. I lower my eyes, suddenly shy. "I believe I have your child within me," I say softly.

His face is full of great joy, and he holds me very tenderly. We had been about to sleep, but now he is wide awake. "He will be called Ali," he says firmly. "He will be a brave and noble warrior, and he will follow me to war in God's name."

I shake my head. "There will be no need for war when he is grown. For his father will have won all the wars there are to win. My son will live in peace, caring for his father's people and building a new country."

Yusuf likes this idea. "Yes," he says eagerly, pulling me close to him as we settle into our blankets to sleep. "He will build a great mosque, to honour God. He will ensure that the people of our land live by His word and that they are fairly treated. There will be no unlawful taxes, there will be great cities built and all will be done to praise His name." He continues to talk in this vein, while I fall asleep, happy in his arms, the murmurings of my son's great future still being whispered in my sleeping ears.

From then on Yusuf worries about my health, insisting that we travel only in the cool of the days and that I should sleep well at night, thus making our journey much longer, for we had been riding for many more hours each day than Yusuf will now allow. The men grumble a little, in a good-natured way, about men becoming fathers for the first time and how they turn into old hens, fussing and clucking and wasting time over a healthy young woman who has been riding every day with no ill effects so far. I agree with them and try to convince Yusuf to let me continue as before, for I feel well and happy, but he will have none of it. So we travel only in the cool, and each day he ensures that I am delicately placed in my saddle and that I am well rested before we ride out each day. The long hot days are spent in the shade, which means that we have to find places of shelter or erect my tent, which wastes a great deal of time for it is large and not meant to be moved quite so frequently. Ekon and Adeola erect and dismantle it almost every day, and they work hard, but they do not complain. Adeola smiles at me and points at my still-flat belly and imitates how I will soon look, with a great round stomach like a giant melon, staggering along under the weight of my huge son, which makes me laugh until I see Amalu's expression, his eyes full of pain.

In the heat of the day we sit, the men sometimes playing games with pebbles and bones, or praying with Yusuf. Sometimes they will train, although the fierce heat is not conducive to this and they drink so much water that the water bags need refilling over and over again. We always fill them whenever we have the chance to do so and when we make camp a few of the men will go and find water, for they know all the sources along our route, having travelled it once already.

In these quiet moments I sit with Adeola and spin wool, or embroider cloth for clothes. We cannot chatter to each other as she does not know enough words, but she can make herself understood through gestures and mimicry, and her speaking begins to improve. Ekon is quiet, but he watches over us with interest and smiles sometimes when we laugh. He takes our small flock of goats to find pasture when there is some to find, and milks them with great speed and skill, bringing the milk to us to cook with or sometimes for Adeola to churn by shaking it in a goatskin bag. Our progress is certainly far slower than before, but we enjoy the journey more and it gives me time with Yusuf before I have to relinquish him to his mission.

When he has finished praying or training or talking with his men, he will come and sit with me, and Adeola will move away a little so that we may sit close to one another.

He pats my belly. "My son," he says. "Do you hear me?"

I laugh and make a tiny voice. "I hear you, Father," I say.

"Are you well, son?"

"I am well," I reply. "My mother's womb is a fine dwelling place."

Yusuf chuckles and begins to talk of his great plans for this unborn child while I lie back on my elbows in the shade of my hastily-erected tent and listen lazily, warmed by more than by the sun.

The garrison camp is like nothing I could have ever dreamt of. No matter where I turn my eyes there are soldiers. Some are our own people, some paler, from the land across the sea to the north, Al-Andalus. Some are black-skinned from the kingdoms in the south. All are fearsome to my eyes.

Not to Yusuf's eyes, for they are like water to a dying man in the desert to him.

"At last we are here," he says when he sees the camp and I hear the smile in his voice.

We are surrounded in moments, his men chanting out his name, seeking to touch his shoulder or take his hand as he passes each of them.

"My cousin, we have missed you," says Abu Bakr and they embrace as though they had thought never to see one another again.

"My wife," Yusuf says, bringing me forward. "I believe you remember her," he adds mischievously.

"You are welcome here, Kella," says Abu Bakr. "You must have made quite an impression on Yusuf. No man could have stopped him in his mission and yet his gaze fell on you."

The men tease Yusuf for his long absence but are kind to me, their smiles and nods courteous and welcoming. In their eagerness to welcome me and show their devotion to their general our camels are quickly unloaded by many hands and my tent is erected in a quiet spot where I will be out of sight should I wish not to be seen. Ekon and Adeola's smaller tent is pitched alongside mine. They have nothing to do but seek out water and turn our tents back into homes; Adeola beating the sand from the rugs and blankets and learning where to fetch water while Ekon finds places to graze our sheep and goats. That night I eat alone for Yusuf has much to do, but I sleep well.

The next day I walk around the garrison. I have never seen such a sight, a whole army gathered in one place, ready for battle.

I cannot count how many men there are, but they are many, many hundreds. To see them pray together is awe-inspiring, rows upon rows of strong men on their knees to their God, praising His name together.

They eat sparingly: camel or goat's meat, milk, dried fruits. I smile when I see how they eat, for Yusuf likes to eat like this and now I see why. Their diet is simple, but they are brothers and they share the hardships of their life for the greater glory of God. They dress in plain woollen robes and simple shoes. They are of many skin colours and of all sizes, tall, short, thin or large, but all are heavily muscled and all are ready to fight to the death.

I watch some of the training, and am struck by the formations they use. They move seamlessly into tight, closed ranks, with foot soldiers at the front, then the mounted soldiers behind them. Most ride camels, for they are better mounts in the desert, but Yusuf has plans for more horses once they reach the other side of the Atlas mountains. The ground there is harder underfoot and horses are faster, able to turn more easily and quickly. For now, though, there are hundreds of camels, and they are mostly bad-tempered and fast. Yusuf warns me to be careful of them, and I walk cautiously when I approach them, for they can bite or kick. Unlike most camels chosen for riding, they are male camels, and they are less docile than females like my own Thiyya. They fight amongst themselves, too, and sometimes the men have to beat them with sticks to break them apart from one another when they are enraged. I keep Thiyya well away, for she is of great interest to them all.

The closed ranks of the army are unlike any soldiers I have seen or heard tell of. I thought armies used loose, long lines, which allow for greater flexibility in battle. I mention this to Yusuf but he explains to me that those long lines allow the enemy to attack one part, cutting men off from their fellow soldiers and leaving them to be slaughtered alone. The Qur'an itself, Yusuf tells me, says that fighting should instead be done in these closed ranks, so that all the men are protected by their fellow soldiers. He has studied closely how that might work, training his men for many months until they have mastered the technique. He believes that this way of fighting will serve them best.

The training is an amazing sight. They practice daily with javelins, daggers and swords. They have great shields covered with strong hides, many made of ostrich or antelope, some of other beasts; all thick, heavy and very strong, protecting the men from the deadly weapons of their enemies. They have drummers, who beat a strong rhythm for the men to move to, but

Yusuf wants even more drummers in the future. He talks often of how the army might be made stronger, larger, better. I cannot imagine it. It seems so vast to me already.

I see Amalu joining the men in their training, wielding a vicious-looking sword. I feel guilty. He wanted a peaceful trading life and now he is learning to be a warrior. He looks fierce but I am afraid it is only his anger at my marrying Yusuf instead of choosing him. I feel responsible for him being here and my heart sinks at the idea that he may be harmed in battle, even killed. It will be my fault if anything bad happens to him.

There is a camel fight one night, and I hear the shouts of the men and the hard thumps of blows delivered to break up the camels. Yusuf goes out to investigate and when he returns he tells me all is well and holds me softly in his arms as I drift back to sleep.

There are meetings among the leaders, made up of great men from the Sanhaja confederation of tribes – the Lamtuna, the Musaffa, the Djudalla. These tribes have all contributed their men, weapons, and their support to Abu Bakr. He presides over these meetings, his gruff good-natured manner easing any tensions and his firm belief in their success comforting any nervous doubters. Meanwhile Yusuf will slip away from these meetings when they grow dull and endless, and come back to his men, training alongside them, urging them on, eating and praying with them. They love him; he is their general. While they respect and obey Abu Bakr in all things, still they turn to Yusuf for their inspiration and to find their courage.

I take to watching the men training, for they are an awe-inspiring sight. No-one can fail to be inspired by their courage and fierce faces, they make me truly believe this great war may be a triumph, no matter what happened in the past.

One morning my path is blocked by a group of camels. I skirt around them but as I watch the men training I forget about them and do not notice when they move closer. One sniffs at my hair and I, startled, turn and cry out, which makes the beast panic. In a moment all is chaos. The group begins to fight, biting and roaring at each other, and I, seeking to escape that frightening place, suddenly receive a kick in the belly and find myself lying on the ground, crying out with pain. I hear men come running and

Adeola's shrieks. I hear a howl of rage from Yusuf's voice though I barely recognise his voice, for I have never heard him truly angry. I lie very still and clasp my belly. When I open my eyes for one brief moment I see a glint of metal before a spray of red blood appears on my sleeve. I hear a dying groan from the camel who kicked me as Yusuf slits its throat. I close my eyes and am lifted tenderly by strong hands and taken to my tent.

Inside Adeola, her face tight with worry, sits with me. She tries to feed me broth and sweet dates, but I turn my face away.

"All be well," she says, over and over again, as though it is a charm. "All be well."

But my belly cramps. I slip a hand beneath the blankets and pull it back covered in blood. Adeola repeats her charm faster and faster, but even she has to admit defeat when she sees the blood trickling steadily down my legs. Her eyes fill with tears as I begin to sob. When she has done all she can for me she dispatches Ekon to Yusuf and then sits with me, her small calloused hand tightly clutching mine.

Adeola never leaves my side but it takes three days before Yusuf comes to me. I grow sad – and then angry – at his absence from me, but Adeola whispers in her broken way that Yusuf has been beside himself, that he ranted and raved about our loss and that even his strongest and most-trusted men dared not approach him. He spent the past three days sat alone, not eating or drinking, until Abu Bakr went to him and spoke softly.

Now he comes to me, his face full of misery. I know he killed the camel to try and assuage some of our grief, so I take his hands and thank him for it, although one camel or another means nothing to me, for I have lost my baby and nothing else matters. Then I hold Yusuf while he sobs. I had not thought I wanted a baby so much, after all it would have curtailed the freedom I craved, but now that it is gone I am crushed. Is it an ill omen? Will Yusuf think he should not have married me at all, that this is a punishment for delaying his mission?

"It is Allah's will and we do not question His will," says Yusuf, although his eyes say otherwise. "We will be blessed again if He looks on us with favour. In the meantime, it is my fault that you were hurt."

I open my mouth to argue but he gestures that I should be quiet so curtly that I stay silent. I know from his voice that I have no say in this matter. He is my husband and he has made a decision.

"I will not argue this with you, Kella," he says. "I should not have kept you here at all," he says. "An army is no place for a woman. In a few days we will leave this place to begin our journey across the mountains. I will leave behind only a small base camp. You will remain here and I will send for you when we have crossed the mountains and secured a safe city for you to come to."

I weep, for I do not want to leave Yusuf. How to explain that such an accident could have happened anywhere? That if he leaves he may never return, never send for me at all? But I have no choice. I spend time recovering, during which I am forbidden to leave my tent, although Yusuf comes to me often. The men are sorrowful, for behind their mighty shields and their great muscles are kind hearts and they mourn their general's loss of a son.

One tent after another is packed away. The weapons are sharpened and repaired. The great garrison is now nothing but a small base camp made up of a couple of dozen older men and their slaves, a few wives. The men left behind are grumpy at being left out of the adventure and excitement ahead, however dangerous it may be. When I come out of my tent and see what is to be left I am horrified. It is a tiny, dull camp, I would have been better off staying with Aunt Tizemt.

The night before they leave, Yusuf takes my hand and leads me away from the camp, lifts me onto a camel with him and rides a little way off, far enough that we can no longer see or hear the men. In the still-warm sand Yusuf lets the camel wander off a little way in search of tasty shrubs and we sit together watching the dying sun. Yusuf has brought some water, dates and flat stale bread, but it feels good to eat together, alone, without being surrounded by an army of fighting men. Although we have no fine food or a comfortable tent and furs, sitting together in the bare sand has about it a tenderness that I will miss.

I am afraid for Yusuf, of course. Tomorrow he will leave me and go to fight his holy war. Holy or not, I am afraid. The last time the Almoravids tried to cross the High Atlas their leader was killed and they were forced to retreat back to the desert. Now I try to speak of my fears to Yusuf, but he hushes me.

"Now is not the time to talk of fear, my jewel." He puts one arm around

my shoulders as we sit and turns his head to smile comfortingly at me. "What
will be will be. We are but Allah's servants and we win or lose according to
His wisdom." He sees me begin to object and kisses me gently to stop the
words in my mouth. Then he searches in his robes.

"I have a gift for you."

I cannot help smiling. "What is it?"

"Close your eyes and tell me."

I close my eyes and feel something cold and hard in my hands, dangling
from above. It is jewellery, I can tell, and my smile broadens. "You have
given me so many jewels, what more is there to give?"

He laughs. "A woman can never have too many jewels nor kind words,
so a wise man once told me."

I laugh again and give up guessing, opening my eyes. "A *khomeissa*!"

The thick silver pendant is a triangle with an additional part below
which has five parts to it, making it akin to the 'Hand of Fatima', giving
the wearer protection against the evil eye. I slip it round my neck, feeling
happy that Yusuf's protective gift will be with me even when he leaves me
the next day.

He smiles mischievously. "I hear that women will rather go naked than
without a *khomeissa*, is that true?"

I laugh. "Perhaps."

"A good thing I gave you it, then. I would not have you be naked when
I am not there to enjoy it!"

We lie together under the stars and later tears come to me again for my
lost child, but Yusuf holds me close and whispers kind words. Eventually I
fall asleep in his arms and wake in the pale cold dawn to join him in prayer.
Afterwards we sit together for a little while on our last day together, perhaps
forever.

"You will join me soon," he promises. "Very soon."

"When?" I ask, wanting an answer that I know cannot be given. Who
knows what the future holds? They may all be killed, driven back to the
desert like their leader was ten years earlier. Or they may sweep victorious
throughout the Maghreb, praising the word of God as they go. Only Allah
knows, and He will reveal His plans when the time is right and not before.

Yusuf does not try to give me the answer I want to hear, only the answer
that is true. "When it is safe for you to be by my side I will call you to me,"
he says simply. "I would give my own life willingly, but I will not risk yours."

He strokes my hair and face and looks at me for a long moment before he wraps his veil around his face and disappears beneath it. Only his eyes show, hiding the man I know and becoming once more a warrior and leader of men. I know I will not see his face again for a long time and I fight to not let my tears fall. I want him to remember my smile and to miss it so badly that he will call me to him quickly, danger or no danger.

I wrap my arms around him as we stand and hold him close to me, enjoying his warmth against me.

"Perhaps I am with child again," I say hopefully. "I was with child so quickly after we were married, perhaps when you call me to you I will bring you a child!"

Yusuf smiles tenderly at me. It is unlikely, and we both know it, but he nods, ready to believe in my tentative hopes for happiness. "When I send word for you I shall say to my men, 'Bring my beautiful jewel to me. And her little gemstone must come with her also, for he must meet his great rock-father at last.'"

I giggle at his make-believe family of rocks and embrace him again. Then we ride slowly back to the camp together.

I stand and watch Yusuf and his men as they leave the camp. I try to speak with Amalu, to tell him to be careful, but he does not ride close enough to me, whether on purpose or not I do not know. I wait to wave, but neither he nor Yusuf look back. Slowly their shapes disappear into the shimmering heat.

Assaru Ouanafer – A Veil Key

I LOOK AROUND ME THROUGH A haze of tears.

The garrison camp is now smaller than my own. A wave of disappointment sweeps over me. I could have stayed at home. I could have been with Aunt Tizemt, who for all her roars is a kitten underneath. We could have spent the days together as equals rather than teacher and pupil. We could have cooked and woven together, sharing recipes and patterns, stories, jokes and gossip. I could have learnt skills from Tanemghurt, for she was always willing to teach, and understood the healing powers of plants. I would have been surrounded by my own people, my own kin. I wonder whether I should take my slaves and head back there now, but it is a long journey and Yusuf's men have been ordered to protect me here.

My mind offers up ever darker thoughts for me to consider. What if Yusuf is already tired of me and has chosen in his kindness not to humiliate me by divorcing me but simply to hide me away here?

As my spirits drop I feel a warm, calloused hand on my shoulder. Ekon is standing behind me, with Adeola at his side.

"We are here," he says and my tears fall at his kindness.

When Yusuf first left I hoped that he had left my womb filled again, for I know that he wants a son, and I also wish for a child of his; a part of him to keep by me until we can meet again. I have happy moments when I imagine him sending for me, and my longed-for arrival carrying his own son. I close my eyes and see his smile and his surprise, imagine our loving joy at being together again and our pride in the first of our many children. I want a child that he can love and raise, who will take his name and follow in his footsteps. But the moon grows bright and then dark and I have to resign myself to my fate – I will not be a mother until I see Yusuf again. There are two women in the camp whose bellies swell as the months pass by and I watch them with a fascinated envy.

Time passes quickly when every day is the same. Sometimes I cannot believe how long it has been since I last saw Yusuf. At first I am certain I will be sent for at any moment, but as the months pass my excitement becomes dull acceptance. It takes time but slowly we begin to settle into a daily routine. I take the opportunity to practice new styles of weaving from Adeola, which I enjoy. I share my own designs with her. We cook together and she learns from me as I do from her. Sometimes the other wives and slave women join us and we make enough to feed all of the camp, we eat together and have some sense of kinship, for we are all bound to this place until we are told otherwise.

Here there is much easier access to water than at my own camp. When the rains come we even go into the rocky outcrops at the foot of the mountains and bath in the ice-cold water that falls over the rocks. It sweeps away the dirt and leaves us gasping with cold but our hearts racing with life. There are a few tiny villages close to us but they regard the camp with fear, having seen the size of the army that set out from here. They avoid us where possible, only occasionally trading with us, knowing we will buy what spare food they can grow.

The first news we hear about the army is that they have crossed the High Atlas. We hear little more than this, but I know that it will have been hard. So many men, so many animals, difficult and rocky roads in the mountains, the planning of battles yet to come whilst perhaps being attacked by local tribes who oppose their plans.

It is a long time before we hear of their progress again. I have nights when I toss and turn as though tormented by a thousand djinns. I know that unless they have some decisive victories and secure cities of importance, they will struggle and may well be wiped out.

I pray often and when I do my very heart is in my words and thoughts as I long to hear more news and to hear that Yusuf is safe. My days are mostly passed weaving, for I am skilled at this now and my work will one day adorn a new home. I sew tiny disks of silver onto my work and watch it glitter in the sunlight. When I am not weaving I talk with Adeola, or we sometimes play games together such as chess, moving our carved pieces across the board even as the army must be moving onwards.

One baby and then another is born and although I hold them and exclaim over their soft hair and tiny hands, although I gift their mothers blankets I have woven myself, I cannot help but wish that I, too, had a child.

At last we hear that they have captured Taroundannt in the south and, having left good men to hold it, are now heading north, towards the rich merchant city of Aghmat. That city's wealth could provide them with the riches they will need to feed so many men and animals, and send a message to all that these are not men to be trifled with. But the last time the Almoravid army attempted this it failed and was wiped out. We will not be sent for until Yusuf is certain he has a secure stronghold. Reluctantly, the men begin to make simple stone houses to protect us come the winter, for we cannot be sure that we will be sent for before then and here, so close to the mountains, the weather will be harsh.

I sit with Adeola. All my thoughts are on Aghmat and the army slowly approaching it. I can talk of nothing else, even when I try my words return to the same place.

"It is a trading city. I was there in the old days with my brothers and father. It is a city full of rich merchants and they will not wish to see it taken and sacked, all their profits going to some conquering army on a holy mission. They will pay for mercenaries to fight them if they think it will save their livelihoods."

She keeps her silence and lets me talk, nodding from time to time but not seeking to ally my fears, for she knows they are real.

I think back to the gossip I heard in my trading days as we passed through that city. "The Amir of Aghmat is Luqut al-Maghrawi. He is a great fighter and the richest man in all of Aghmat, which must make him one of the richest men in all the land. His queen is a woman called Zaynab, daughter of a merchant from Kairouan. They say there is none so beautiful. She told Luqut he would be a very great man, for it was foretold that she would marry the man who would rule all of the Maghreb." My voice trails off as I consider the implications of this prophecy. If the prophecy is true and Zaynab is married to the Amir of Aghmat, then he would be the man to rule all of the country.

Adeola sees where my thoughts were taking me and interrupts them. "Not everyone sees truly," she says gently. "Many prophecies are not understood. We cannot know our fates until they are revealed."

I bow my head but cannot control myself. "They say she is a sorceress!

She could use magic against them in some way, to protect her own city and her husband the Amir!"

Adeola shakes her head and leaves me to my own turbulent and dark imaginings, which torment me by day and leave me sleepless at night. As time goes by, I grow to know every constellation of stars as though they were the creases of my own hand. I spend many nights wrapped in blankets sitting outside my tent at night when the camp is asleep, gazing upwards and praying for the army's success and Yusuf's safety.

When the news comes I am jubilant, but we are all shocked at the magnitude of their success.

Aghmat lies in ruins. The city has been taken and summarily sacked; all its riches plundered to support the holy army which has swept across it like the wrath of Allah and left it in tatters. A once rich city now humbled. The Amir is dead, his beautiful queen Zaynab has been taken in marriage by Abu Bakr. I try but cannot image the sturdy, earthy and friendly old Abu Bakr married to a beautiful young sorceress.

The decision has been taken to leave Aghmat in its ruined state and found a new city, which will be the base for the army as they carry out their holy war throughout the rest of the country and beyond. Abu Bakr has chosen a place, a little more to the North of Aghmat, close to the Wadi Tensift, providing them with ample water resources close by. Many men and animals will need a lot of water, and the thick snows of the Atlas mountains will provide the foundling city with water forever. Now the army will set up camp, a rough garrison, while the men regroup and their leaders make new plans.

Abu Bakr will take his new wife with him, forcing her to leave the comforts of her luxurious palace to live in a tent amongst soldiers and beasts.

I wonder about her. How must she feel now? Her husband and king is dead; she is now little better than a captured slave, to be taken to the bed of the Commander of a conquering army. She will have to lie in the arms of the man who has killed her husband. I feel sorry for her.

"No need to feel sorry for Queen Zaynab," says the man who brings us more news not long after. "She is a witch, that woman. Beautiful, but dangerous. They say she talks with djinns and can see visions."

"But still," I protest. "Her husband has been killed and she is taken as a wife by the man who killed him. She has lost her love, her power…"

He laughs. "Queen Zaynab lost no time in making herself agreeable, I can assure you. She claimed that the prophecy that she would marry the man who would rule all of the country is coming true at last, that Abu Bakr is the man foretold, that she was meant for him from the very beginning, no matter that she was married to Luqut and another before him. She offered him all her wealth to aid his holy war."

I frown. "Surely all her wealth was at his disposal already? He sacked Aghmat – all its riches were his to take."

He shakes his head. "It is said that she had a great personal wealth, hidden where no-one knew of it. She went to Abu Bakr and promised him all her wealth to fulfil his destiny. She blindfolded him, then took him alone to a secret underground cave, where she took away his blindfold and lit a candle in the darkness. She showed him the greatest treasure ever known. Gold and pearls, rubies and silver – all his, her gift to him. 'All this is yours', she told him, then she tied the blindfold round his eyes again and led him away from that place." The man subsides, satisfied with the grandeur of his tale.

I narrow my eyes. "So he never knew where that place was and yet the treasure within it is his?"

The man frowns as he follows my logic, then laughs. "Just like a woman! Promises, promises, and then you must go with her in darkness that you may be tricked into believing the treasure is yours when it stays always within her gift to give!" He winks at Ekon who smiles and shakes his head. Then the messenger goes to be given food and beer by the camp slaves, who are keen to hear all the gory details of the battle, and of the legendary beauty of the Commander's new wife.

It is enough for me to know that Yusuf is safe and that his holy mission is smiled upon from the heavens. Truly his war is just, for he is being given great success. I smile a little over Zaynab, who has turned a shameful conquering into a triumph for herself and bound Abu Bakr to her with promises. She is indeed a clever woman, as rumour has it. One day, I think, I would like to meet this woman. No doubt I will for one day, God willing, I will rejoin Yusuf, and we two women will be companions while our husbands fight side by side.

The winter snows come and we huddle in our tiny houses, cramped and impatient, although we know we could not travel in this weather even if word came to join the army.

Spring flowers bloom and the snows retreat. Almost a year has passed and still I am not summoned. I grow resentful, as do the men of the camp, who mutter amongst themselves, disconsolate at being left out of the glory. I think of traveling to Yusuf before I am called for. I know a larger army is amassing and that the new garrison city is beginning to take shape, albeit with tents rather than fine buildings as yet, for the men's strength must be used for fighting, not building. Each time a rare messenger comes to me I grow excited and then am told, once again, that the time is not yet.

"But soon," each messenger assures me. "Soon."

The heat of the summer beats down on us and we grow sullen. Occasionally the men will fight one another, when quarrels break out brought on by too little to do. I pray that we will be sent for before the late autumn rains come, bringing perilous landslides from the mountains above us and forcing us back indoors after a summer spent in tents. Surely the summons must come soon.

Then news comes that there are rebel tribes in the south. They must be fully conquered and made to swear allegiance, or they will prove a grave danger when the army moves north. Abu Bakr himself decides to head up the men sent to fight in the south. He is leaving command of the whole army to Yusuf. Overnight, Yusuf becomes Commander in all but name. The new garrison city is entirely in his hands. I am proud, but fearful. Abu Bakr could be away for a long time, and other tribes might see Yusuf as only the second-in-command and seize the opportunity to attack. But my fears are laid to rest.

"Your husband's reputation is fearsome," a messenger assures me. "No-one sees him as a lowly second-in-command, to be attacked when the Commander is away – he is seen as Abu Bakr's equal and indeed as his successor."

Winter comes again and this time I do not hope for spring and new messengers, only resign myself. I wonder whether I should return to my home camp but I am afraid of looking like an abandoned wife, left behind not because of safety but because her husband no longer cares for her, barely recalls her name. I walk in the foothills of the mountains sometimes, a thick robe clutched about me, the silence all around me only echoing the emptiness of my life here.

I dream of Yusuf at night sometimes, but as time goes by my dreams grow hazy. I see his hands, his robes, feel his warm body beside me and look for him when I wake, but his face has grown less and less clear in my mind. I have not seen my husband for almost two years, after knowing him for only a few months. I think of Amalu and wonder whether I was nothing but a fool to turn him down. The life I rejected now seems like a more pleasant one than the life I am living. If I had married him I would have children by now, I would live and work alongside my aunt. Amalu and my father and brothers would trade, but visit often and tell me tales of their journeys. Here there is nothing, only an empty waiting. The only pleasure spring brings is that we move back into our tents, which smell sweeter than the tiny stone shelters we must call home. The babies born after Yusuf left take their first steps and I shake my head when Adeola assures me that surely he will send for me this summer. I think sadly that he would not have waited so long if my child had lived. If I had birthed a son, he would old enough to run into his father's arms by now.

It is barely dawn and the ground beneath me is shaking. I wake confused and stumble from my tent, looking about me in the half-light, before shrinking back.

Bearing down on me at great speed are six camels, their riders' robes swirling. They stop only a few steps away in a cloud of dust. A tall figure leaps down from the lead camel and strides forwards. I put a hand to the dagger I keep in my robes before suddenly recognising the man.

"Amalu? Amalu!"

He stands in front of me, his eyes bright with pleasure. I can just see the top of a new scar, which must curve across his cheek before coming close to his left eye.

"Kella," he says and the warmth in his voice makes me so happy that I embrace him. He returns the embrace gently before stepping back from me.

"You are safe," I say happily. "And – and all is well?" I add, suddenly fearful.

"All is well," he reassures me.

"Tell me everything," I beg. "But first – oh you have ridden so hard. Let me prepare refreshments." I call for Adeola and she, all smiles, begins to make tea. The other men go to meet old comrades, while Amalu squats down by the fire.

"We have ridden for so long," he says. "The mountain passes slowed us down or we would have reached you sooner. I have been commanded to pack up the base camp."

I stare at him. "Pack it up?"

He laughs at my face. "Did you want to stay here forever?"

"Then am I – has Yusuf?"

"Yusuf has sent for you," he says, his voice flat.

I give him tea, bread and roasted goat meat. "Tell me more," I say.

He sips the tea. "Abu Bakr's new city is called Murakush. It is still more of a camp than a city, a garrison camp at that, full of soldiers and weapons, but some of the soldiers' families are beginning to join them now. The army will not set out again for a while; we have need of more men. They will need to be trained and we must be fortified. The living conditions are rough."

"I do not care," I say quickly.

He looks at me for a moment and then speaks softly, so that no-one may hear him. "Are you certain that you wish to be with Yusuf, Kella? If it is freedom you want I will travel with you wherever you wish to go."

"He is my husband," I say.

"You barely know him," says Amalu. "I have spent more time with him than you have."

"He is my husband," I say stubbornly. "My place is with him. Besides, now that the war is over we will begin to build the vision he has of the future. Together."

"The war is not yet over," says Amalu.

"It will be soon," I say. "When can we leave?"

"I must pack up the camp," he says.

"Do it quickly!" I say smiling but he lowers his gaze and stares into the fire for a long time.

I have never prepared for travel so fast. I throw my possessions together, in my excitement paying little care to proper packing until Adeola and Ekon come to me gently, take everything out of my hands and set to packing themselves, smiling and speaking softly to one another. Their care and skill mean that everything is packed as it should be in very little time. Within three days I am ready to leave, adding my six camels to the escorts – three which carry my possessions, two for the slaves and of course Thiyya.

Meanwhile, Amalu marshalls the men. They are eager to leave, to join their comrades and partake in their success. Everyone hurries about their work, excited and smiling. The camp is dismantled, the camels and horses are loaded. There will be an advance party of myself and Amalu with an escort as well as Adeola and Ekon. Then will come the main group, who will travel a little slower than us, for there is livestock to herd as we travel. The little stone shelters we built stand empty, no doubt the villagers will use them once they are certain we have gone.

Amalu comes to me as I approach Thiyya, sitting sedately chewing the cud and waiting for me to mount her. I smile at him and then impulsively turn and hug him fiercely. "I am so glad you are safe, Amalu. I am sorry that my marriage hurt you. But I am so happy! Be happy for me."

His smile is full of a strange sadness. "I will never forget how happy you are now," he says. "I hope you will find happiness in Murakush."

"Of course I will, Amalu," I say. "Yusuf is waiting for me!"

He holds out his hand. On it is a silver shape, an elaborately shaped *assaru ouanafer,* a veil 'key' or fastener. I look closer and see that it is etched with the Tinfinagh's alphabet letter *ezza,* the symbol of our people. My eyes fill with tears. To have this with me is of great comfort as I ride to my new life. I embrace Amalu again and he holds me for a moment longer than he should. When he releases me I see tears in his eyes.

"Come now, Amalu," I say, teasing him a little. "You are not bidding me farewell. We ride together!"

He nods and gives the order to mount. I look behind me at the deserted camp. The only signs of our time here are the dusty outlines where the tents were pitched and the circles where our fires used to burn.

My escort of six men treat me with great deference as we journey towards the garrison camp and I enjoy the feeling of importance. I am the wife of the second in command of a great and victorious army. I think happily that soon I may even be with child again and that the men will be happy for their leader. It will take us almost a month to reach the garrison camp, for the men have strict instructions that we are not to hurry but to travel with the greatest of care for me. We are a small group and often a merry one.

We must cross the Atlas Mountains, and this takes up much of our journey. There are a few trade routes, of course, but they are tiny tracks amongst the towering and precarious rocky slopes. One wrong step and lives could be lost. The only way is to travel slowly and carefully. We meet few people.

Once across that great barrier we begin to see the landscape change before us. We see more plants, even sometimes a crooked little tree. More rain falls in this part of the world, so the closer we come to the camp, the better the grazing for our camels is and the easier it becomes to find good water sources, cold and fresh, sourced as it is from the very heights of the mountains. There are more trees, these unbent, fruit trees and olives. The travelling becomes a little faster, although we do not push ourselves too hard. We enjoy the bright green of the land before the heat of the full summer burns it yellow. The almond trees have already blossomed, now they are full of tender green leaves and the first soft fuzzy buds, which will become the good sweet nuts. The camels are happy with all the new food that they find. I enjoy travelling again, seeing new faces and landscapes, reveling in the luxury of buying our food from villages that we pass rather than cooking and doing other women's tasks. I will reach Yusuf well rested and ready to work alongside him to achieve our shared vision.

"Wait till you see the camp!" says one of the younger men, too full of excitement to contain himself as we draw closer to our final destination. We are but a few days away from Murakush now, and although we have eaten and slept well during our travels, we are looking forward to our arrival.

"You have never seen such an army gathered in one place! Hundreds upon hundreds of men. Camels, horses. More weapons than you can imagine. So many people! Not just the men, but many of their families, slaves, even children. The General Yusuf has great plans. He wants to gather an even greater army. He says we will look back and laugh when we think of how we are now. He says we will have a mighty army of slaves, fighting men from the Dark Kingdom. Already he has secured the trade routes so he can gather taxes from the merchants to allow him to pay for a larger army. We will go north, he says, but for now we must strengthen ourselves. The men are building trenches and walls to fortify the new garrison city. Yusuf wants a great mosque to be built in the very centre, to honour Allah. But for now we all pray together in the space that he has allocated to the building. Yusuf prays among us and we praise His greatness in all we have accomplished so far and all there is yet to accomplish."

I smile to myself at his enthusiasm. "Murakush," I say, turning the new name over in my mouth. "It is near the old trading city of Aghmat, is it not?"

He nods. "It is. The army took Aghmat and sacked the city. The king was killed in battle and Abu Bakr took the queen of Aghmat to be his wife." He falls silent without adding further details.

I know all of this, of course, but here is a man who will know more details. "Her name is Zaynab, is it not?"

He nods again but does not elaborate, despite his earlier eagerness to talk. I decide to coax more information from him.

"Is she as beautiful as they say?"

He looks uncomfortable but does not disagree.

I smile mischievously, thinking that perhaps he has some feelings himself for the legendary queen of Aghmat, now wife to his Commander. A great beauty will be much admired by soldiers, men far from their own wives, or not even married yet.

"Is the marriage a happy one? Are the lady Zaynab and the Commander well suited?"

He mumbles something. I catch Amalu frowning at him.

I lean forward on Thiyya to catch his words. "What did you say?"

He repeats what he had said and this time I hear him. "They are divorced."

I frown. "Divorced? Already? They have been married less than two years. What happened? Were they so ill-suited?"

The young man looks at the others for help but they are all staring straight ahead as though seeking something on the horizon. He lowers his head and seems to take his courage in both hands.

"The Commander Abu Bakr went into the desert to fight with the rebel tribes. Before he went he decided the lady Zaynab was unaccustomed to a rough life in the desert and that he should set her free as he might be away a long time. He divorced her."

"And now she is alone?"

He takes a deep breath and squares his shoulders. "The Commander gave her in marriage to his second in command, along with the command of the army and the new city of Murakush. When her waiting period is over she may marry him." He takes another deep breath and emphasises his final words with a stubborn nod of his head. "It has been agreed."

I cannot believe I have heard him correctly. Thiyya slows as I let her reins loose and then stops, looking around with interest at the closest trees to see what leaves might be good to eat. The men stop their own beasts and gather around me as I sit slackly on Thiyya's back. I feel the heat sap my strength. After some moments of silence I turn to Amalu. I speak and my voice is hoarse.

"Zaynab is to marry *my husband* Yusuf?"

His silence confirms it.

I grasp at the only part of what has been said that still gives me hope. "He said that she must finish her period of waiting before she can marry again. When was the divorce?"

Amalu clears his throat. "The first month."

I count and recount, but there is only one answer. "She can marry him this month?"

Again silence. Although Thiyya is standing still, I feel that I may fall. "When this month?"

At our present speed we will not get there before the ceremony.

"What were you thinking?" I shout at Amalu. The camels startle.

He says nothing. The men wait.

"Why didn't you tell me? Why did you let us travel so slowly?"

Amalu meets my gaze. His eyes are as angry as mine. "What did it matter whether I told you or not? Yusuf had already decided. Perhaps you should be angry with him for taking a new wife without even consulting you, without even summoning you to his side until now. It was safe enough many months ago for you to join us. He has all but forgotten you in his lust for another woman!"

The men look away as we stare at each other, locked in rage.

"We need to get to Murakush before the wedding," I say without looking at him. "We will ride hard."

"Kella – " begins Amalu.

"Ride," I say.

We ride day and night from then on, stopping only to fill the waterbags. I eat nothing and the men eat as we ride. There is no more banter, no more stories of Yusuf, of the army, of the future. The men are almost asleep on their mounts, Adeola and Ekon's faces are grey with worry but my eyes are kept open with pain and fear. I cannot think properly. I can only ride and pray that I will reach the camp and speak with Yusuf before the marriage takes place.

We see the camp in the far off distance at dawn on the day of Yusuf and

Zaynab's wedding. We ride as fast as we can through the burning heat of that day, but the camels are tired after the last few days and cannot be persuaded to run, ignoring my desperate urgings.

"We will not get there in time," says Amalu. His voice is pleading. "Kella, rest. You are exhausted. It is too late to stop the wedding. Sleep and we will arrive tomorrow when you are strong."

I turn my face away so he cannot see my tears falling and urge Thiyya forwards.

We reach the camp as the sun sets.

Tenfuk – Pendant to Celebrate a Birth

BLAZING TORCHES LIGHT UP THE camp. Songs are being sung and as we approach I can smell a feast – rich roasting meats, good stews, perfumed drinks and the small sweet cakes that Aunt Tizemt so loves.

My aunt seems very far away to me now.

I have never seen so large a camp in one place. The army has expanded beyond my imagining. No doubt all the slaves of the cities they have taken have been pressed into service as soldiers. And perhaps many free-born men have seen that Abu Bakr's army is a force to be reckoned with and have decided to pledge their allegiance to the winning side. Not to mention the many mercenaries who will have seen that there might be spoils of war to be had with this new army, which has such grand plans for the future.

Now many of the men have been joined by their families, or have taken women from the conquered cities as their brides, just as their leader has. There are women cooking. Some are wives, cooking and caring for children, speaking with their men, handsome women, sure of their status and sturdy with years of hard work, women from many tribes but all from the same country.

Other women are there for a different purpose. They are beautiful, of every colouring. One I see even has hair like saffron, her skin very fair and her cheeks as pink as fresh figs. They wear bright clothes and tease the men. They have no need to cook and care for children, leaving them free to wander amongst the tents and chatter amongst themselves. Abu Bakr's men may have been trained as holy warriors, but few would turn away from a beautiful woman. Besides, now there are new men among the army, men who may swear their allegiance to Abu Bakr and profess to worship Allah as required but who are loath to turn away from the pleasures to be had in this world, no matter what the holy book may say on the subject.

There are slave women also of course, their faces visible here and there as they scurry about amongst the tents bringing water, wood, heavy bundles, basins, bags. The slave men herd animals about, cursing in their own tongues, their muscles shiny with sweat, carrying even larger burdens than their womenfolk.

There are tents as far as I can see, of all shapes, sizes and colours, some small and misshapen, faded and greying, kept together more through prayer than good cloth and poles. Some are lavish, elaborate, small palaces amongst the chaos. Animals are everywhere, camels of every colour and size, fine warhorses, old nags, sturdy mules and little donkeys. We pass goats and their kids, sheep and even cattle, for this part of the country has more green fodder to feed them.

Weapons are everywhere. This is no ordinary camp, it is a garrison, and there are signs of warfare wherever I look. Some wounded men groan from their tents as healers seek to remedy their wounds, some of which will not heal or will take a long time to do so. I see missing limbs and terrible wounds to the face and stomach. Fine warhorses are being cared for, brushed and fed and watered, saddles being mended and armour being diligently repaired.

There is food in vast quantities. Great baskets of bread and cooking pots of mouth-watering stews are being carried towards a brightly lit space at the centre of the camp. One day no doubt it will be the great square of the city, but for now it is only a big space with no tents, the ground firmly packed down with the passing of many feet. Huge fires have been lit and whole animals are being roasted over the hot coals, the fat spitting and hissing and throwing up little sparks in the flames. Around the edges are laid out rugs where people can sit and a crowd is already beginning to gather, drawn by the good smells and the chance to sit and gossip before the feast begins.

There are storytellers. Wherever there are a few people gathered and a tale to tell there will be storytellers, and here they are already weaving the army's past two years into legend. The ingredients are all there for the taking – a holy army on a mission from God Himself, a respected leader and his fearsome second-in-command who now leads the army while its founder tames the rebel tribes who dare to challenge their holy cause. A pillaged city. A beautiful queen taken as a bride by first one man and then another. A growing army of fearsome warriors and their glorious future. The crowd listens entranced and people whoop and cheer when their own names are mentioned in the legends being woven by firelight.

Amalu and I have reached this main square, if it can be called that, without anyone taking notice of us amongst the crowd. We have left the loaded camels, the other men of the escort and Ekon and Adeola on the outskirts of the camp, the better to proceed through it unencumbered.

I walk through the crowded spaces as though in a dream, while Amalu brusquely moves people aside, clearing a path for me as he walks ahead. I see everything and yet nothing stays with me. My mind holds but one thought: that if I can speak with Yusuf he can tell me that there has been some mistake, that he has not married Zaynab at all, nor had ever intended to. And yet all around me there are celebrations. A feast is being prepared for everyone to share and I know that the great weight in my belly is there because the marriage ceremony has already been held and now it is about to be celebrated by all the camp. This is why there is so much food, why the storytellers are gathered to tell this latest part of the legend, and why the children shriek and giggle with anticipation of sweetmeats to come. The women of pleasure ply their perfumed trade through the cluttered tents in anticipation of a busy night to come, for a feast will stir a man's senses. A man who sees his leader marry a beautiful woman will turn his own mind to the pleasures that may be his for a few coins or even trinkets, depending on the woman he chooses.

We circumnavigate the edge of the square and as we head towards a large black tent I tug at Amalu's robes.

"Is that Yusuf's tent?"

He nods and I feel my heart race. Now I will see my husband again and he will embrace me. He will brush away my fears. I put my hand to my heart as though to still its wild rhythm.

We reach the tent, which is more than the height of a man and entirely made of thick black cloth and leather. Amalu stops.

The tent is not decorated in any way; unusual for such a large tent belonging to a person of importance, but then Yusuf has always liked things to be plain, he has little interest in material possessions. The flaps are all closed, which is strange when the night is still warm.

Amalu steps a little closer to the tent and calls out. "My lady?"

Even as he speaks I grab his arm. "I do not want to see the lady Zaynab,'" I hiss under my breath. "Take me to Yusuf!"

Amalu flinches as my nails dig into his bare flesh. He turns to look at me and his eyes are full of pity. "Zaynab receives all visitors when they first enter the camp," he says simply. "Those are my orders. They are the orders given to everyone. No-one may see Yusuf or anyone else until she has seen them."

I see from his face that he is telling the truth and that there is no way to escape this meeting. How has Zaynab taken so much power to herself so quickly? I let go of his arm and take a deep breath as I hear the tent folds being opened. I look down at the bare earth, seeking strength.

Perfume scents the air and envelopes me, a heady mix that I cannot identify, but which tells of great riches, sweet beauty and something else, something dark and dangerous.

Slowly I raise my eyes and see Zaynab for the first time, and something in me grows cold.

She stands in the opening of the tent, ignoring Amalu, looking directly at me. She is tall, and dressed all in black flowing robes, which cover every part of her but her hands and head. She wears no jewellery, not even a belt to encircle her waist and draw attention to her form, making her look almost like a man, were she not so beautiful.

Her eyes are large, and so dark they seem black. The fires of the square dance in them as she gazes at me without blinking. Her hair is very long, falling past her waist, entirely straight and again, unadorned. No head wrap covers it.

Her mouth is wide and her lips are full. Her nose is long and straight, and her cheekbones rise high on her face. Her skin is a honeyed bronze, and although she uses no colourings nor has any tattoos to decorate her face I see the smoothness of her skin. By the way it glows I know that somewhere in the tent behind her is a casket, and that in that casket are the finest oils and powders to make her skin beautiful without any further adornment.

Her clothes seem entirely plain, something a slave might be forced to wear, but I have travelled and traded. I know fine silk when I see it. I also know how hard it is to make any cloth truly black, for the dyes are difficult to come by and it takes a lot of dye to make so much silk so black, like the darkness between the stars when the moon is gone. Her robes, appearing so austere to the ignorant gaze, are in fact the finest silk that money can buy. Only a great noblewoman with many riches has the gold coins necessary to have such a silk used for her everyday robes. Her shoes are likewise slippers of black leather, again without adornment but the stitching of them and the quality of leather tells me in one glance everything I need to know. When I traded I would have paid the very highest price for such leather, and counted myself lucky to have found it at all. I would have struggled to find a good enough craftsman to work it so finely and yet so simply, their only ornament being his skill.

We stand still for a moment, and then slowly, she smiles and I know at once that the beauty I have seen until now is nothing. Zaynab could have had any man she desires, for when she smiles she is the most beautiful woman I have ever seen.

"Sister."

It is all she says, but in the dripping honey of her lips, I hear the scorpion's sting quiver a warning.

I take a breath and extend my hands in greeting. I know a great deal about Zaynab just from looking at her, and I know already that she holds more power in this camp than my husband. How she has come by that power I am not sure, but I know she has it and that from this moment on my life is in her hands.

"Sister," I say and the word is like poison to me.

Zaynab's smile widens, and she takes my hands in hers. They are smooth but strong, slender and well-made.

"I am so glad you have come," she says, and I know she is lying. "It is hard being the only noblewoman here. But now I have you by my side, we will be sisters to one another." She pauses. "Now that I, too, am Yusuf's wife."

I want to strike my husband's name from her wide smiling lips. Instead I force myself to ask what I so desperately need to know.

"Where is..." I stumble over the word, "*our* husband?"

She waves Amalu away without so much as glancing at him. "Ensure my sister's belongings are brought safely to her," she says, "and place her tent close to mine, that we may easily visit one another. Clear those tents away," she adds, lifting her chin to indicate a group of tents on the other side of the square. "She shall have that space, so that we may see each other as soon as we rise each day."

She smiles at me again, a smile of great sweetness which takes no account of the families she has just displaced with that tiny gesture, who had a good position in the camp and will now be relegated to the outskirts, where people go to relieve themselves and the animals are kept.

Amalu hesitates but when he sees that I am silent he does as he is told. I stand before Zaynab in my travel-stained robes and wish that I could sleep and forget all of this, that I could wake to find that all this has been only a djinn tormenting me with evil dreams.

But Zaynab has other plans for me. "Yusuf is in a meeting with his officers. He will join us soon for the feast. We were married earlier but of course his mission must come before his new wife." Her smile grows broader. "I am so sorry you did not arrive this morning," she adds, "for I would have wanted you by my side when I married Yusuf, and to have had your blessing. But I am glad you are here for the feast we will be holding tonight to celebrate the wedding. I will tell my handmaiden Hela to prepare you, for of course you are weary with your long travels."

I try to object, but within moments she has swept me inside her tent and is calling for her slaves, leaving me alone for a moment.

The inside of her tent is like none I have ever seen. It is very plain, with very few colours. Almost everything is dark or sand-coloured. No bright dyes enliven the rugs that cover the floor. Prayer mats are ostentatiously visible in one part of the tent. There are two great chests in the other part, more suited, I guess, to her apartments in Aghmat than to a tent in the middle of a plain. They are made of pale plain wood, with simple geometric carvings, and probably contain her clothes and personal possessions. There are no instruments, no embroidery, no jewels on display. Like her clothes, everything is of the finest quality, but very plain.

The only exception is her bed.

It is huge and stands in the centre of the tent, drawing the eye to it immediately, for in that cool, dark, plain interior it sparkles and glows like a jewel.

It is bigger than any bed I have ever seen and is made of a dark wood, almost black. Every part of it that can be seen, even the legs, is carved. There are fruits and flowers but also the figures of men and women. I step a little closer and gasp. The figures are entwined with one another, showing acts of love in intricate detail, such that they would bring blushes to the cheeks of any woman and make the heart of any man beat faster. Covering the bed are soft blankets, some woven so finely that they seem almost transparent. These are of every colour from darkest red to palest yellow, decorated with silver discs in the manner of our people and with silken cushions to lean on. It is a bed for sweet pleasures, for whispers and moans, a bed that promises a beautiful and fertile woman's touch and nights of wild passion. Any man looking at it would want nothing more than to lie on it and to hold Zaynab in his arms.

I stand alone for a moment in the darkness before the great bed. Then the entranceway is pulled back and Zaynab enters with an older woman, who directs two slave girls to place steaming copper basins of water on the floor to one side. Zaynab turns her smile on me again.

"I know you are tired, sister, and your tent will not be ready for some time. Allow Hela to prepare you for the feast tonight. I have sent a slave to fetch your clothes. I must go and oversee the preparations for the feast, but I will return very soon." She sweeps from the tent leaving me no time to protest.

The slave girls leave. I hear Adeola's voice outside and turn towards the entrance but it seems she has been kept from me. One of Zaynab's slave girls comes back in with fresh clothes for me and a casket containing my jewellery, then disappears again.

I feel a touch on my shoulder and turn to the older woman.

She has large dark eyes, somewhat hooded. Her hair is hidden beneath a grey wrap, her clothes are also plain and dark. She has a stocky frame and her hands are square, nothing like the long elegant fingers of Zaynab. I wait for her to address me, expecting her to use some term of respect, but instead she stands very close to me and stretches out one hand, which she lays on my bare forearm. She does not move her hand, only keeps her eyes fixed on mine.

I shrug my arm away. "You are Zaynab's handmaiden?" I say, not because I care but to remind her of her place.

"My name is Hela," she says. Her voice is deeper than most women's, her speech almost too slow, as though she is speaking from somewhere far away.

"I can look after myself," I say, unwilling to be stripped naked by this woman who I do not know. "Or my slave Adeola can be sent for."

She shakes her head. She is already unbuckling my fasteners. My clothes slip to the floor. Too tired to stop her, I simply stand and allow Hela to undress me and wash me, comb my hair and then begin to dress me again. When she has finished my jewellery feels so heavy around my arms and neck that I feel I cannot move.

I sit on the great bed, alone and silent, as though stunned by a blow.

I am too late to stop the marriage. My husband, as is his right, has taken another wife. I am no longer his only jewel, for now his time must be split between Zaynab and I equally, according to the Holy Qur'an. Tonight, on our first night together after two years, he will not come to my tent, for tonight is Zaynab's wedding night, and he must favour her. No man would do otherwise. Tonight, in a strange camp far from my home and family, I am about to attend a marriage feast for my husband and his new wife. I will sleep alone in my tent while she welcomes him to this bed. I feel drained, unable to move.

Hela offers me tea. I sip it slowly, my shoulders slumped. I feel only a great sadness, a hopelessness I do not know how to rid myself of. Hela squats low in a corner of the tent, her dark eyes fixed on me in a way I find unsettling. I look away from her but am still conscious of being observed.

I am interrupted by Zaynab, who rejoins me in the tent. I am conscious of how different we look, standing side by side. I am smaller than her, perhaps ten years younger, dressed in colourful clothes and loaded down with beautiful jewellery. By rights, I should draw the more favourable glances. But Zaynab's beauty, her imposing height and the extreme simplicity of her clothes draws the eye immediately, making me look almost foolish beside her, like a love-struck girl dressing to impress young men rather than the acknowledged wife of a great commander. I feel uncomfortable in my clothes and make a gesture as though to remove some of my jewellery, but Zaynab puts out her long slim hand to stop me.

"I have a gift for you, sister, a gift of welcome. I had it made for you when I knew that you would soon join us here."

She turns away and lifts the lid of one of her great carved chests. I catch a glimpse of many bottles, jars, measuring spoons and pestles, pouches, small decorated boxes.

She closes the lid and comes back to me. In her hands she holds a glorious *tenfuk*, a woman's pendant. It is large, hung from a string of onyx beads. The sharp triangle of metal holds within it an arrow-shaped carnelian. The pendant is a suitable gift for the birth of a daughter, or could even be given to a pregnant woman as a wish for a daughter, with its connotations of sunrise, of life and birth.

I have lost my first child and am not yet carrying another life. Tonight my husband will take another woman as his wife. It is a breathtakingly malicious gift, loaded with calculated hatred. My hands tremble as I take it from her and put it round my neck. There is no other choice available to me. I cannot refuse her gift.

Zaynab is all smiles as we leave the tent. "I rejoice that you can share in my happiness tonight, sister," she says, as we walk towards the centre of the square and people fall back to let us past. "Yusuf will rejoice also, for I know he wanted you here with us."

I let her words wash over me. I feel helpless, swept along in the crowd towards a husband I no longer know.

My meeting with Yusuf might as well be a meeting with a stranger. He comes into the square and is greeted with cheers, many blessings and congratulations as a new husband. He is also the recipient of ribald jokes and teasing by some of his men, which he waves away good-naturedly. When he sees me he smiles and embraces me.

"My dear wife," he says. "You are welcome here."

I swallow. "Husband," I say, the word sticking in my throat. "I am glad to be by your side again."

"It must feel strange to you to join me here on my wedding day to a second wife," he says. "I am sorry I could not speak with you of it before. I hope you understand that this marriage is important for our mission's success."

I want to argue with him but I do not even know where to begin. "Yes, husband," I reply, cursing myself for my meekness. What else can I say? The marriage is already complete, all I will do is cause enmity with Zaynab.

His expression lightens. "The wedding feast is being served," he says. "You will sit by me."

He treats me with nothing but honour and kindness throughout the feast that follows. He inquires after my health, the journey I have made to reach him, my time in the garrison without him. He feeds me choice morsels from the dishes brought to him.

But his eyes stay on Zaynab.

She does nothing to draw his attention. She sits modestly by his side, accepts food from the servers and from Yusuf when he chooses to offer her food from his own dish. She keeps her eyes downcast, a soft smile on her lips and her back straight. Her calm and graceful demeanour make her the very model of a good wife. She praises Allah every time she opens her mouth, which is not often, and smiles at me as much as she smiles at her new husband. She pours his drinks before I can and sends the best dishes to me first. Yusuf speaks to me as a beloved sister, while he looks at Zaynab with a hunger in his eyes I have not seen before. I cannot escape the sinking feeling that he is already lost to me.

The feast over, there is dancing, singing, storytelling. At last it is time for the bride and groom to retire. I stand trembling and watch them go to Zaynab's tent, surrounded by people singing, offering blessings and lewd advice. I feel a soft touch on my arm and turn to see Adeola, the combination of her dark skin and clothes making her barely visible.

"I bring drink," she says in her halting way.

I wave her away. "I do not want to drink."

She shakes her head and tries again. "To sleep."

I frown. "Sleep?"

She nods earnestly and summons all of her vocabulary to make her meaning plain. "Drink. To sleep deeply. Not to hear." She makes a small gesture towards Zaynab's tent, looming within the darkness of the emptying square.

I feel the tears fall hot and fast on my face and nod. I would give anything, drink anything, if it will make me sleep so deeply that I will not hear one single murmur from Zaynab's tent as she spends her first night with my husband, barely a stone's throw from my own tent, foolishly decorated with colourful embroidery promising good luck and happiness and children to its miserable owner. I follow Adeola slowly back into my tent, which she and Ekon have arranged as though I had never left my aunt's camp. I sit on the bed and Adeola undresses me with the care of a mother for her child. When she has finished and has pulled the blankets around me, Ekon brings in a small bowl cupped in his hands. It steams and has a pleasing scent. I do not know what is in it. I drink it without questioning, seeking oblivion.

Oblivion comes, but not before I hear the first moans from Zaynab's tent, leaving my body rigid with despair before I sink into darkness.

When I wake my jaw is so tightly clenched that I fear my teeth will shatter when I open my mouth, but it is daylight and that first terrible night is over. This camp is now my home.

The camp is like a city of tents. Aghmat may still have a few people who live there, but it lost its soul along with its riches. Those who wish to be rich and powerful in the future have seen that this new army is a force to be reckoned with and their best chance is to align themselves to it. The once bustling souks of Aghmat have grown small. More and more people come to the first souks held outside the camp, which are growing rapidly. Craftsmen begin to set up their own little tents and do their work close by the camp, for the camp holds more customers for their wares. The herds of goats and sheep kept nearby grow larger and the first few stone and mud buildings begin to be constructed, small and humble for now, but more will soon be built and they will grow larger in due course. Ramparts will be needed soon, for no important city can afford to be without them and the garrison-camp of Murakush will soon be an important city. It will form the base for the army when they move further north to such cities as Fes, part of Yusuf's plans for the future.

I see little of him. He is busy with his plans for the army. Men must be trained, horses purchased as their steeds. New weapons must be forged, plans drawn up. Negotiations must be made with important men, tribal leaders sought out to create the alliances that will support the army when the time comes to move north. He is a figure that I see only at a distance. At first I wait eagerly for Yusuf to come to me. I have resigned myself to my situation. Our religion allows Yusuf to have more than one wife, however much that pains me. That same religion states that he must treat Zaynab and myself as equals, giving us the same privileges and care. I think that at least I am here at last, in what will one day become a bustling city. If I can speak with Yusuf, spend time with him, remind him of our plans together I may be given a role to play. Perhaps I can manage the traders who wish to set up permanent stalls here. Once I try to speak with him.

"The army must need many provisions," I say. "I could manage the traders who supply you with the traveling food, the weapons..."

Yusuf pats my arm. "Zaynab manages all such things," he says, still walking towards his destination.

I follow him. "I want to be useful to you," I persist.

He pauses for a moment and gives me a quick embrace, such as one might give to a beloved but nagging child. "I must go to the council," he tells me. "You have everything you need?"

"Yes," I say, "But I..."

"Good," he says and is gone.

I stand still, watching him stride away, angry with myself for not telling him that I am unhappy, that I am bored, for not reminding him of our plans, the way we used to talk together. But what is there to say? Zaynab all but rules Murakech, she is its queen. Everything that is done here is done under her command and her voice is respected in council.

Days pass when I do not see Yusuf at all, then I will see his dark robes pass in the distance, always surrounded by other men, always earnestly discussing something. Sometimes I see him at prayers, but he is too far away to speak with before or afterwards. Often he prays alone or only with his men. I am a married woman without a husband. I am treated with courtesy but mostly left alone. Aside from Adeola and Ekon I know no-one except Zaynab, and I avoid her as much as I can. She is too busy overseeing the camp, for nothing escapes her hawk-like eyes. She chooses where the craftsmen may ply their trade, what food will be prepared, where the herdsmen may take their animals. There is nothing she does not know.

I wonder how Amalu fares but I can hardly go visiting him alone, it would not be right for a married woman to do so.

At first I believe that Yusuf is so busy that he has time for neither of his wives. When night after night he does not come to me, I believe that he does not go to Zaynab either. Every night Adeola cooks good food. I sleep deeply and dreamlessly and hope that he may come the next day, or the day after.

One night, though, I have no appetite, for I have idly eaten too many dates while I sit at my loom. When Adeola serves my food, I only pick at it. She looks worried but I reassure her that I am well, although this does not seem to give her much comfort.

Later on I understand why. It takes me a long time to sleep that night, far longer than it usually does. As I lie in my tent I hear the sound I least wish to hear, soft moans coming from Zaynab's tent. Disbelieving, I creep out.

The camp is quiet and dark, for it is very late. I come closer to the large dark tent and hear, unmistakably, the sounds of lovemaking and Yusuf's own voice as he groans with pleasure. My legs shake and my breath seems to be stopped in my throat as I hear him cry out and then speak Zaynab's name softly and her golden laughter answer him. I return to my tent in a daze and find within it Adeola, her head bowed, a cup of the steaming drink from my first night in the camp in her hand. I looked at her and then comprehend her earlier concern.

"The food you make for me each night..." I begin, feeling my way towards the truth, which I do not want to touch.

Adeola shrinks back a little. "To sleep," she says, looking at me in fear. "Not to hear."

I nod wearily. "Every night?"

She lowers her eyes, as though even to look at me is to add to my suffering. "Yes," she says softly.

I take the drink from her and drink it in large greedy gulps. It burns my tongue and throat but I do not stop until it is all gone. I let it fall to the floor with a clang and wave her away. She bends to pick it up and then leaves me alone to the coming gentle darkness.

After that I know the truth. I do not torment myself with it. I eat all the food that Adeola brings me each night, taking large portions so that whatever herbs she is using to make me sleep will be sure to take effect. I eat well and sleep well. My eyes grow bright, my skin grows polished, my curves grow more rounded and the men of the camp watch me pass with more interest. Adeola watches me and says nothing, but one day she comes to me when the sun is high and without speaking begins to undress me, then bathes me and perfumes my skin. She pulls out my finest clothes and dresses me, adorning me with all my jewellery, taking especial care to leave aside Zaynab's *tenfuk* pendant and to ensure all of the jewellery Yusuf has given me can be seen.

"What are you doing, Adeola?" I ask her.

She smiles and shakes her head.

I let her have her way, for the days are long and often dull and my mind needs distraction from its old paths worn bare with my pacing.

By the time she has brushed my hair and hennaed my hands and feet it is growing dusk. She leaves me sitting there in all my splendour, laughing at myself for allowing a slave to treat me as though I am her plaything. Outside I can hear her putting the final touches to the cooking she started this morning. I smell the good smells and lie back on the cushions of my bed, trying to enjoy the simple joys of being cared for by such a devoted slave. Briefly I think of the old garrison camp and regret leaving it. There I was a married woman, respected in my own right and cared for. Here I feel like a child's forgotten toy, discarded for sweetmeats.

"I hope I do not disturb you, wife?"

I sit up, shocked. In the doorway is Yusuf. I have not seen him close to for so long that I stare at him as though he is a stranger.

He smiles. "May I enter?"

I spring to my feet and throw my arms around him, pulling him into the tent. He chuckles, a deep rumble in his chest, making me weak with relief that at last I have him to myself.

Adeola comes and pours water over our hands before bringing in heaping platters of good food; well made but not too elegantly prepared, for everyone knows that Yusuf prefers his food to be simple.

Yusuf smiles at her. "Your slaves are very devoted to you," he says as he takes his first mouthfuls of food. "Your other slave... Aykron?"

"Ekon," I say.

"Ekon, yes. He came to me today and said you had asked that I join you tonight to eat. I told him I was busy, but he was very insistent. He said that you would be very unhappy if I did not come to you." He laughs, taking more food. "So here I am."

I doubt it was so easy. I know that Ekon must have planned his moment and his words carefully, perhaps for many days, for he is a mere slave and cannot insist that Yusuf bin Tashfin, general of a great army, should come to me simply because he, Ekon, has asked him to. I keep my eyes lowered for a moment so that Yusuf will not see the tears welling up as I think of Ekon and Adeola's faithful attempts to make me happy again.

I say nothing. I have a night alone with Yusuf, and I hope that in spending time together he may remember our previous happiness and plans for the future and that over time I may take back at least my own share of my husband. I try to tell myself that he spent much time alone, and that he then spent time with Zaynab for many months, longer than he had even known me, in fact. Perhaps it is to be expected that she comes foremost to his mind rather than a wife whom he has not seen for so long, who has not shared these important past months with him. Tonight I will try to be a loving wife, and we will rediscover the tenderness and partnership between us and then the future will not be so hard for me, for I will do my best to accept Zaynab, even as she must accept me as Yusuf's first wife.

As we eat I speak at first of daily things, the grazing of the many herds of goats and sheep that keep the camp supplied, the training of the horses that takes place every day on the plain, the storytellers, the craftsmen, the souks. I seek to make him feel at ease, to enjoy the meal and our time together, to make him laugh.

I succeed, and after the meal, when Adeola has brought water to wash our hands, we lie propped on cushions on my bed, our faces closer together and talk a little of our time apart and of the time we had spent together when we had been first married, which makes him smile.

"Your face when your father told you I wished to marry you," he chuckles. "I thought you would fall off your camel."

"What kind of man proposes marriage after one camel ride together?" I retort.

"Ah, but you had already joined my men and ridden a great distance with us, you had proven yourself," he says.

I am happy to talk of the time when we first met. I do not press him to talk of the time since then, of the battles, the fear, the killing. Nor do we talk of the future, of the battles yet to come, the difficulties of leading such a large army. Abu Bakr's absence weighs heavily on him, for they have worked well together and been of comfort and support to one another. He talks of these things every day, carries them in his heart and in his prayers. I want him to leave all of that outside my tent and to have only kindness and good memories with me. A place to rest his body, but also his heart and mind.

We have lain together for a while when at last Yusuf takes me into his arms and begins to stroke and undress me. His movements are unhurried and gentle, as I remember from the past, and I close my eyes, my own hands reaching out to him.

We are interrupted. A sweet voice calls from outside. In a moment Zaynab stands in the doorway of my tent, Adeola visible behind, attempting to stop her from entering. Zaynab ignores her. In her hands she has a red wooden cup, which she holds out towards us. I shrink back, pulling my clothes around me.

Yusuf frowns. "What are you doing here, Zaynab?"

Zaynab's smile falters. "I brought this for you both to share. It is a recipe taught me by my mother," she lowers her long lashes almost coyly, "for loving nights. I wanted to offer my sister a gesture of my love for her." She looks up again towards me, her face gentle, hopeful. "I know it is not easy to welcome a new sister as a wife to your own husband, but you have been so gracious, so kind to me." She gestures uncomfortably. "But I am interrupting, I am so sorry. It was not my intention." She holds the cup out awkwardly, almost pleadingly.

I glance at Yusuf. He has lost his frown and is smiling, pleased, no doubt, that his wives are getting on so well, without much of the trouble that can often happen for a man caught between jealous wives.

I have no choice. I hold out my hands for the cup, my clothes slipping as I do so. Zaynab modestly lowers her eyes so as not to see my nakedness, places the cup in my hands and bows her head to both of us as she backs out of the tent. "May Allah bless your bed," she says softly as she goes.

I sit back on the bed trying not to spill the cup, which is full to the very brim with a perfumed drink. It smells of rose petals and honey, with other spices and herbs, which I cannot readily identify. I look at it doubtfully, unsure that I want to drink any peace offering from Zaynab. I do not fully trust her. I take a very small sip, barely wetting my lips, and look at Yusuf.

He smiles and takes the cup from me, then drains it in a few easy gulps. "It is a good drink," he says. "Zaynab often makes it for me. She will not tell me what it contains, for she says it is her handmaid's secret."

I make an effort to smile and draw Yusuf back onto the cushions, for I am not about to spoil our night together turning over Zaynab's strange actions in my mind. She has done nothing but bring a drink to her husband and speak peaceably to me. I lay my hand upon Yusuf and feel him stir in response.

In the morning he is gone, and I lie alone in the cold air of early dawn. The call to prayer goes out but I lie still, unmoving or heeding. My God has shown me no mercy, I cannot shape my mouth to praise His name.

I am bruised inside and out. There are shadows on every part of me, growing darker as the day grows lighter. My thighs ache and my innermost parts are torn and bleeding. Strands of my hair lie on the bed and my scalp hurts where they have been pulled out in a frenzy. My bed is in disarray and I lie half uncovered, too shaken to warm myself, too hurt to move, too ashamed to call for Adeola.

She comes without my calling, her small dark hands reaching out to my body before drawing back in fear. She stands still for a moment and when she sees me look away and slow tears begin to trickle down my face she calls out to Ekon in her own tongue, commanding him to do many things. I can hear him outside, bringing water, lighting the fire and making it blaze to heat the water, a pause and then his return from milking, the milk being heated with honey and herbs all to her instructions. Occasionally he calls out a question and she answers, supplying him with further instructions or his large hand will appear through the flaps holding something she has asked for and she will take it swiftly and ask him for other things and the flaps close again, his hand disappearing at her behest.

I lie still while she strips the bed and brings warm water, washes me and bandages me where she can. I wince as she rubs soothing salves on my bruises and scratches. I groan when she makes me get up and stand for a moment so that she can make up my bed with clean sheets and soft blankets.

She moves quickly, and I sink back onto my bed and feel her strong arms lift my head and shoulders and place me back down gently onto the cushions, which cradle me. All the while, when she is not calling to Ekon, she sings to me, little snatches of half-finished songs made for children. Her gentle soothing kindness makes my tears fall faster. She wipes them away and then brings the warm milk, sweetened with honey and spices, soft breads and little pieces of tender meat. I do not want to eat, but she treats me like a child and like a child I obey and eat some mouthfuls until she is satisfied. After that she brings the drink that makes me sleep, and I grasp the cup with both hands and drink eagerly, for I want to fall into darkness and escape those hours of the night that I have just endured.

After that night I no longer pray for Yusuf to join me. My bruises slowly fade and I am still afraid. The gentleness I had known from our early days of marriage was there at first, but something in the drink Zaynab brought changed him. His desire was insatiable, a raging fire within him that sought ever more extreme ways of being quenched. My body was sorely tested by that one night, I do not think I can bear such treatment again. Now I know why he visits Zaynab's tent and never comes to mine. Every night he is given that drink and spends the hours of darkness with her. He is a strong man, or his body could not bear the strain and so Zaynab binds him to her, for she seems to have the strength to hold his fire in her hands and quench it. Whether she is burnt by it herself I do not know or care. She has stolen my husband, taken his tenderness and kindness and turned a gentle beast into a roaring lion that can be tamed only by those foolish enough to risk their lives. I am too cowardly to risk mine, or my child's. That one night has brought life in my belly but another night like it might well take it away again. So I turn inwards, stay out of sight, and Yusuf goes to Zaynab while life grows inside me. I know that when I tell him he will be gentle with me, but I also know that if he is offered that drink again within my own tent I must find some way to avoid him drinking it.

Time passes and yet I do not share my secret, for I want my baby to be strong within me before Zaynab knows of it, for I know she will be angry. If I give Yusuf a child when she has not yet done so I will be favoured and I can see that Zaynab is not a woman who will accept such a state of affairs.

But Zaynab's eyes are everywhere. She sees everything, she hears everything. She sees the day when I emerge from my tent in the morning and sway before Adeola grasps my elbow and takes me back inside. She hears when I retch. It takes only those two signs and Zaynab comes to see me.

"Sister!" she cries, entering my tent unasked and unwelcomed. "I have barely seen you these past weeks. You are not unwell? The camp life here is very harsh for a woman of refinement."

I want to laugh. I, refined? I lived as a boy for sixteen years, traded all over the country, have always lived in a tent. It is she who has lived her life before here as a queen of a rich merchant city, being pampered and perfumed, with many slaves and servants to do her bidding. I say nothing, but Zaynab knows what she is about.

"I have decided to give you my own handmaiden Hela and take away those two you have, for evidently they are not taking good enough care of you," she goes on happily. "My own servants are well trained and will make your life here so much more comfortable."

I sit up. "I would prefer to keep my own," I say, barely remembering to be polite in how I address her. "They are very loyal and they have taken the greatest care of me."

Zaynab waves her hand dismissively. "They are quite young," she says. "Slaves improve with good training and I have trained many slaves. I have already brought you Hela and two slaves whom she will command. I have sent yours to my tent. I do this for your benefit, sister," she adds kindly, taking my hands in hers.

I am trapped. Zaynab has completed the change without even allowing me to say goodbye to Adeola and Ekon, whose loyalty and kindness to me will now be rewarded with Zaynab's no doubt harsh training. I begin to weep, for I cannot see how my situation will ever improve. It seems to me that I am at this woman's mercy, alone and friendless.

Zaynab is not at all distressed by my tears. She sits and holds my hands gently and then calls for Hela.

She enters bringing a hot broth with small pieces of good lamb in it. She hands this to Zaynab, who holds it to my lips in a kindly manner. I taste it and it is good, if a little strong with parsley. I can taste nothing in it that might do me harm, so I drink it and eat the pieces of lamb under Zaynab's watchful gaze, then sit alone as she departs, all my fighting spirit gone.

She leaves me with Hela and two additional slaves. One is a scrawny girl whom I soon discover is mute. The other is a male slave, who has a permanent cough. He is strong enough but lazy and insolent. All three of them watch me whenever they are near, and I have no doubt that they are spying on me for Zaynab.

Hela cooks all my meals. Her food is good but always heavy with parsley. Despite my reprimands, she continues to add that herb to everything I eat in copious quantities.

I dislike Hela. Her face seems to have no expression to it, she watches me with her large dark eyes in a way I find disconcerting.

"What are you thinking?" I ask her one day, when she has stared at me too long, even for her.

"Whether you are happy," she says.

"I would have thought everyone knows I am not," I say, not bothering to lie.

"You could divorce Yusuf," she says, as though suggesting I might take a stroll around the camp.

"Divorce him?" I repeat in horror.

"You will never be happy here," she says.

"How dare you speak to me like that?" I ask her. "You are only a handmaiden."

She says nothing but she does not drop her gaze, nor apologise.

I try to go about my work and ignore her but at last I turn back to her. If this is a time for honesty then I will have honesty. "Why would you suggest I divorce my husband?" I ask.

"Some women can live with another wife," she says. "Zaynab cannot."

"Why?" I ask.

She shakes her head. "Too long a story," she says.

"Tell me it," I challenge her, but she only shakes her head again.

"It would not help you," she says. "You would be better off divorced."

"I have no intention of divorcing Yusuf," I tell her, but I am shaking.

I wake in pain. At first, half asleep, I think I have a belly-ache, but then a horrible fear steals through me. I put a hand on my belly and feel a cramp run through it, just as wetness trickles over my thighs and I know without doubt that if there had been a child in my womb, there is a child no longer.

I lie still, not through any vain hope that I might save my baby by so doing, but out of a great numbness.

This is the second child I have lost. Perhaps I am barren. Perhaps I have not been granted my mother's fertile womb. Without a child I can never again hope for Yusuf's tenderness, for Zaynab will always be on hand to make him take that drink to unleash his drugged lust on me. No doubt, no matter how rough he is, eventually Zaynab will have a child in her womb. Then I will be a barren and unloved wife, useless and fit only to be set aside.

I lie still until dawn, as the cramps eat at my belly and the blood flows down my thighs. When I do not come out, Hela comes in and when she sees what is wrong she brings washing water and clean blankets and clothes. I let her wash and dress me, give me rags to staunch the flow, remake the bed. Then I lie down and ask for food, for I feel weak.

She brings me a good stew of lamb with apricots. For once there is no parsley in it. I say as much.

She frowns and turns away. "No need for that now," she says.

I turn her words over in my mind as I doze through much of that day, feeling the blood that should have been a child trickling out of me. When the cool of evening comes I leave my tent and walk through the camp, my plain robes and covered head shielding me from passers-by. I head to the outskirts of the camp, where there is a stall, which I have seen before, selling fresh herbs. It belongs to a Christian slave woman who grows many herbs in a small field near the camp, working the soil alone and carrying water to the plants each day. Everyone in the camp uses her mint for tea and her other fresh herbs for cooking. They say she knows all the properties of plants and that many can be used for healing as well as food.

She is of normal height, but stands a little twisted and limps when she walks. She is older than Zaynab, I suppose, although it is hard to tell. Her face is scarred. Her skin is fair compared to mine, but her thick dark hair and deep brown eyes make her seem one of us, although I have heard that she comes from Al-Andalus, the land north of our own across the sea. Her hair is tucked back oddly in a white cloth, not wrapped high up like our own, but perhaps that is how it is worn in her country. She speaks our tongue well enough, but with an accent.

I ask her for parsley. She takes up a large bunch.

I shake my head. "More."

She adds another bunch and then another before I nod.

A shadow falls over her face and she indicates the huge bunch I am now holding, ignoring my hand outstretched with payment. Her voice is clear although her accent is heavy. "Do not eat too much."

I raise my eyebrows as my heart begins to thud. "Why not?" I ask, waiting for her to say what I know already, what I knew as soon as Hela spoke and yet what I cannot bear to believe until I am told it to my face.

"Parsley can take away life from within the womb," she says simply.

I leave her standing at her stall, watching me as I walk away, the vivid green leaves fallen from my hand to be trampled into the dust by passers-by.

Tiraout — festive pectoral necklace

NOW I KNOW THAT I cannot trust Zaynab. I was wary of her before and jealous too, but now I understand that she will stop at nothing to ensure that my status with Yusuf will be lower than hers. I have heard it whispered that she was a concubine to a minor vassal before she became queen of Aghmat. She showed no remorse when her husband the king died, only sought to become Abu Bakr's wife as quickly as possible. When her status might have been in question as Abu Bakr left the camp to go south, she somehow obtained a divorce and married Yusuf, perhaps thinking that his life was in less danger than Abu Bakr's, who would be in direct combat while Yusuf trained the troops and made plans for the future. This is a woman who is more ambitious than most men. And she is fulfilling her ambitions in the only way open to her: through marriage.

I do not care about Zaynab's ambitions. I am not interested in marrying higher and higher.

But I want a child. I want the child that was taken from me by a quick blow of a camel's leg. I want the child that I lost through eating what I thought was an innocent flavoursome herb but which was turned into an evil brew by a crone who works for an ambitious sorceress. Just as Zaynab will stop at nothing to hold her status as the wife of more and more important men, so I grow stubborn. I will do whatever it takes to feel life stir within me again. When I have a child I will live quietly. Zaynab can have Yusuf every night. She can sit by his side in council. She can follow her own dreams and leave me alone with my baby. My child will be a symbol of the vision we shared: of what the Maghreb could be one day, when the blood has been shed and the battles are over. A son for Yusuf will be the beginning of a peaceful era. When he sees his son he will be reminded of how we were together and our plans for the future.

I brace myself. I buy healing salves and drink herbal teas to encourage life within me. I buy them from the herb seller and when she sees what I ask for she adds other herbs.

"For a child," she says and I nod without replying. The kindness in her eyes threatens to undo me and I must be strong.

I order fine foods to be made and eat heartily. I buy new clothes and polish my jewellery. I obtain a sweet perfume and use it on the intimate parts of my body. I wash with fine rose-scented soaps and sit and brush my hair until it gleams. Then I send for Yusuf.

He comes to me and I am kind. When Zaynab inevitably sends her drink for him, I let him drink it with a smile and then lie back and let him have his way with my body, although it hurts me and I long for his old gentleness. The next day I use the salves. I make sure to eat well, drink and eat my fertile herbs. I pray.

Again and again, whenever my body is strong enough, I send for Yusuf. Sometimes I manage to avoid him taking the drink, or manage to spill a part of it. Then he is gentler and I know some pleasure. But drink or no drink, bruises or no bruises, I call him back to me. I want one thing from Yusuf, and then I will be satisfied and trouble Zaynab no more.

He still spends more nights with her, but I do not care about that. I need time for my bruises to fade between our nights, to eat and regain my strength.

I summon up my courage and dismiss Hela. "You may leave me," I tell her. "I will not have a witch like you serve me."

She looks at me for a long moment. "You should keep me by your side," she says. "I know that you hate me but I did not use magic on you, I took life when it was still early. There are worse ways to lose a child."

"Are you threatening me?" I ask her, feeling my legs tremble although I try to sound strong.

She shakes her head. "I stood between the two of you," she says. "You should be grateful Zaynab did not have her way."

"I don't believe you," I say. "I believe you are a witch who works for a serpent."

She does not answer, only gathers together a small bag of her possessions and commands the two slaves to leave.

"Why do you work for her, Hela?" I ask. "What possible hold does she have over you that you would take a child's life to make her happy?"

She pauses in the doorway, without looking back. "You would not understand," she says, her face hidden.

I send word to Zaynab that I demand the return of Adeola and Ekon and they come back to me that very day. I embrace Adeola tightly and Ekon kisses my hand, holding my fingers in his large palm, all of us relieved at being back together.

I stand a little taller now, dress with care and wear my fine jewellery when I leave my tent. I go about my days with light feet and a smile on my lips. I sing when I weave or when I embroider cloth, laying out the symbols and shapes my Aunt Tizemt taught me, although my time with her seems so very long ago.

Sometimes I walk through the camp and sit where I can see the herb seller. I see her answer the anxious questions of those who are unwell and her calm responses, her instructions of how to prepare a herbal tea or tincture, how many days they must eat or drink a herb to cure their ills. She is precise, her voice quiet but firm. Sometimes her eyes will flicker towards me and she will meet my gaze for a moment. I do not know what she thinks when she sees me watching her. She cannot know that I find comfort in her presence even if I do not speak with her. I think of Hela, using herbs against me rather than to cure those who have need of healing and I vow she will not come near me again. Whatever her reasons, she has chosen to serve a woman who does not baulk at demanding the life of an unborn child and neither of them is to be trusted. The sight of the herb seller reminds me that not all those with power or skills are evil, she makes me feel protected.

Zaynab leaves me alone for a time, perhaps lulled into a feeling of safety by the fact that Yusuf still goes more often to her tent than he comes to mine. Besides this, she is widely acknowledged as his right hand. Her days are spent in council with Yusuf and his leaders, for she is a clever woman and has contacts in many of the important cities to the north, which are important to Yusuf's plans for the future. I wish a little that I could be a part of those meetings, for Yusuf to see me as an important strategist too, but I have to admit that although I traded for years, I do not have the knowledge of the noble families that Zaynab can offer. She has been queen of Aghmat, and can advise on the loyalties, strengths and weaknesses of many high-ranking tribal leaders across the land.

When she emerges from these meetings she is drained. I see it in her beautiful face when I catch a glimpse of her as she passes, but she hides it well, retiring to her tent for a few hours and then emerging fresh and calm, despite the stream of visitors she has received during that time.

She is visited constantly by people wanting orders. Zaynab holds court from inside her great dark tent. It is she who specifies how many and which men should stand guard, where new tents should be erected, what foods are to be prepared when there are big feasts. She directs all the daily life of the camp. There are those who do grumble, although quietly, that lady Zaynab has too much power in the camp. But Yusuf does not deny her power nor does he ever countermand her orders. In truth, he has no interest in such day-to-day arrangements, and is probably glad that Zaynab has taken such work off his shoulders. He is too busy training his men and planning for the future. Sometimes important leaders of tribes visit him, and then his council will sit long into the night.

Meanwhile I carry out my plan, and one morning when I open the tent flaps I take a deep breath of the good stew Adeola is making and nearly vomit up all of the milk porridge I have just eaten. Hastily I retreat into my tent and drink water, then lie on my bed and loudly berate Adeola for having made bad food the night before, which has made me feel ill, all the while making a face at her which she understands. I get up as soon as I can and walk about the camp until I feel better.

From then on I cherish my secret and am careful to protect it from the camp. I feel better this time, for after a few days I do not feel so sick when I smell food, only deeply desire fresh milk, which I drink in large quantities, refusing much other food under the pretext that it is too hot to eat much. I see Hela watching me from Zaynab's tent, but there is little she can report, for I keep my distance from her and so I escape her notice for a long time. But not long enough for my liking.

Zaynab sends a message to ask me to dine with herself and Yusuf in her tent. This is an unusual request and one that makes me suspicious. However, I dress well, order Adeola to prepare fine cakes as a gift for Zaynab, and arrive as the sky grows dusky. Flaming torches light up her tent, with smoking lamps inside. A space has been made for a sumptuous meal, where Zaynab is waiting. Yusuf joins us and Hela pours water for us to wash our hands. As we eat we exchange meaningless pleasantries. The food is good and plentiful. There is a silence after we have washed our hands again. It is broken by Zaynab, who reaches out and touched Yusuf's hand. He looks up at her and she smiles. It is the smile of a virtuous and beloved wife. I brace myself for whatever is to come.

"Dearest husband," begins Zaynab. "I have been blessed." I feel a lead weight sink in my belly. Zaynab turns her eyes slightly towards me and a smile curves her beautiful lips. Yusuf only raises his eyebrows and smiles, waiting for her to finish.

"I am with child," she says. "Allah has answered my prayers. Blessed is His kindness to this unworthy woman."

I shake my head as Yusuf embraces Zaynab, and then smile widely for his benefit and embrace Zaynab myself. I can contain my secret no longer, so desperate am I to strike back at her.

"You are twice blessed, husband," I say brightly, and feel Zaynab's hate flow towards me as she hears my next words. "I am also with child, blessed is Allah."

Yusuf, of course, is delighted, and once again we all embrace. As Zaynab leans towards me, her glorious smile struggling to stay on her face, I whisper in her small perfect ear.

"My son will be born before yours."

Then I lean back and smile warmly at her. Shortly after this I make my excuses and leave them alone.

I wait for Zaynab's retaliation. I keep a dagger by my side, for the threat I now pose to her is so great that I think she may well abandon all her subtlety and simply attack me herself, or worse, send an assassin to do away with me. The nights seem very dark and cold to me; any small noises make me wake with a start and then lie awake for many hours until my eyes close without my knowledge or consent.

I wait. And wait. Then I hear the rumours flying around the camp. Abu Bakr is on his way back from the south. He will arrive in a few days. I can sleep again. Zaynab has a far greater threat coming towards her than I, and I know she will have to work harder than she has ever done before to preserve her own status. Although Abu Bakr has been away a long time, and although he gave Zaynab in marriage to Yusuf and left him in charge of the army and the new garrison city of Murakush, he is still Commander of the Almoravids. It is his name that appears on the gold dirham coins that are cast, not Yusuf's. Yusuf might seem to have greater power at his command, but he is Abu Bakr's subordinate. He is also tied to Abu Bakr by blood, being his younger cousin.

If Abu Bakr is truly returning, there are only two options. Yusuf can either accept him back as commander and obey his orders, thus reducing his own status, or he can challenge Abu Bakr for leadership.

The camp is in turmoil. All the men have sworn loyalty to Abu Bakr. But they love Yusuf. He is their general. He is their true leader, the man who prays, fasts, eats and trains beside them. He is the man they look to in battle. The men mutter in corners, for and against. They do not want to see Yusuf lose leadership, but to challenge Abu Bakr could well be disastrous, perhaps leading to splitting into factions, the unnecessary loss of much-needed men, the possibility of their mission failing when it has only just begun. For Zaynab, there is danger too. If Yusuf is demoted, she will lose her status, something I cannot imagine her accepting. But if Yusuf makes a bid for leadership of the Almoravids and fails, Abu Bakr might have Yusuf killed for daring to challenge him, making Zaynab a widow once more and vulnerable. She is Yusuf's right hand, she may well be considered to have been behind this challenge and might even face death herself.

I risk making myself visible to Zaynab, knowing she has more pressing concerns than her jealousy for me. I wander the camp, listening to all sides. There are rumours of ambushes, of formal challenges. There are those who shrug their shoulders and say that Yusuf will have to swallow his pride and accept that he will no longer be the leader of the troops, that he will be a general again, not a commander.

But although I listen to the people of the camp, be they high or low, I watch only Zaynab. I have learnt by now through my own experience and rumours that she is the mistress of such situations, that she can and will bend any situation to her own advantage. If Zaynab looks happy, things are going well for her, no matter how the wind blows or who may fall to make way for her.

She looks terrible.

Her skin is pale and her immaculately plain dark robes grow dusty and stained by sweat under the arms, despite the weather beginning to cool as summer ends. Her thick glossy hair has grown dull and wispy. She grows thinner than before, so that her hands are bony and her face is gaunt. Her eyes are as bright as ever, but they are disturbing to look at, shining like the last embers in a dying fire, a fevered patient about to leave this world. If she had a mother alive, that mother would make her rest, would feed her good foods and soothing drinks, and would bath and care for her, protecting the tiny life within her. I myself rest and eat well and am careful not to over-exert myself, but I see that Zaynab does none of this. The whole camp hears her retching in the mornings, sees her paleness and weakness when she walks, but no-one can stop her.

She sits in council every day, can be seen in Yusuf's company at all hours of the day and night, their dark heads close together, their voices low. Slaves bring food and take it away again barely touched. Yusuf eats as simply as ever and Zaynab cannot stomach anything but a little unleavened bread. The smell of yeast has her on her feet and running to vomit again and again. Perhaps I should feel sorry for her, but like the rest of the camp I mostly feel curiosity. How can she keep going like this? And what will happen when our Commander, Abu Bakr bin 'Umar returns?

We wait.

Despite all the guards it is of course the children, with their keen eyesight and their games on the plain outside the camp, who spot them first. They come running with news that a sizeable number of men are making their way towards the camp. That they are Abu Bakr's men is quickly ascertained, but as they draw ever closer it becomes clearer that Abu Bakr is not among them.

Many of us, especially the women and children, have spent the morning on the outskirts of the camp, leaning on the low mud walls that are slowly growing in and around the camp or sitting on the dusty ground watching their steady progress towards us. We have not been watching Yusuf and Zaynab, nor seen their preparations. As the men draw closer all of us begin to look amongst the crowds to see where they are. Yusuf will surely have to come forward to greet the men and inquire after the Commander, his cousin? And Zaynab should be at his side. But they are nowhere to be seen. A good smell of roasting meats begins to fill the air and I, along with most of the crowd, follow our noses back to the main square, then catch our breath as we see the scene before us.

The square has been cleared, fires have been built and slaves are bustling back and forth, cooking great quantities of food. On a hastily-built raised platform covered with fine rugs sits Yusuf, with Zaynab by his side. Although plainly dressed as ever, both wear clean fresh clothes, and Zaynab suddenly looks as though she has drunk some magic elixir of youth. Her cheeks are tinged with pink, her lips are full and red, her hair glistens as though it is made of precious metals. They sit in comfort, surrounded by coloured cushions, the very picture of a king and queen even though the camp is not a fine city. They look powerful, healthy, at ease. They look like rulers.

Behind the platform stand many of Yusuf's warriors. They are fully dressed for battle, and make an imposing spectacle, like a king's royal guard. Many are the black warriors from the south, whom Yusuf favours for his own protection. Very tall and dark, their faces gleam in the sun. All the men chosen have fearsome battle scars and their bodies are hardened. No-one entering this square could think that reclaiming leadership would be easy, nor think lightly about challenging Yusuf for the command of these men who stand by his side.

We stand, amazed, then scatter amongst the crowd as Abu Bakr's men enter the square behind us.

These men have fought side by side with Yusuf before following Abu Bakr to the south, and it is clear from their faces that they are taken aback by what has happened since they left. When they left Murakush it was a glorified version of their own garrison in the desert – tents of all shapes and sizes, none very fine, scattered here and there. Food was scarce and simple. It was a training camp, not a fledgling city.

It has changed. The tents are larger, better made, laid out in a more pleasing formation, with more space between them to pass by. There are the beginnings of real buildings; small mud-brick walls being worked on here and there, a few small edifices already completed. The square is larger. There are regular markets, craftsmen ply their trade. There are more women and children, older and younger men. It is no longer a training camp. It is a new city and it is growing rapidly.

It is clear that Yusuf has recruited many new men and that they obey him as their commander. The powerbase has shifted. There are many more fighting men in evidence; not only the new black warriors, but also other men of our own lands, from important tribes beginning to align themselves to this new rule.

This larger army and new city has rulers. Yusuf is clearly the commander here, no matter where Abu Bakr might be at this moment. Sat in a position of influence by his side, Zaynab is an imposing consort; a powerful and beautiful woman. The men will remember the prophecy that Zaynab would marry the man who would rule all of the land, and as they look at Yusuf sitting above them they cannot help but wonder if he is indeed that man. The reins of power are held in different hands from those they had thought, the wind changing the shape of the dunes before their very eyes.

There is a long pause, a silence while everyone waits for the first move to be made. Yusuf waits long enough to make everyone uncomfortable, then rises to his feet. At his side, Zaynab rises also, her dark silken robes fluttering in the breeze. Together they come to the front of the platform, where Yusuf holds out his hands to the men.

"In the name of Allah, I welcome you back to Murakush, my brave and noble warriors." His voice is calm and hospitable, his use of a possessive word to refer to the men smoothly uttered. "Come eat with us, my brothers, for you must be tired and hungry." He claps his hands and the slaves spring into action, fetching jugs of scented water to wash the hands of the guests.

The officers ascend the platform where they are warmly embraced by Yusuf while Zaynab turns her dazzling smile on them. The common soldiers gather near to the platform. Water is poured, then generous amounts of food are served to all. I am helped up to the platform, to take my place near Yusuf. The food is richer than the men have been used to, fighting rebel tribes in the desert and scrubland of the hot south, and they fall upon it, enjoying the rest and comfort so long denied them. The rest of us eat less hungrily, still amazed at the spectacle Yusuf and Zaynab have created and wondering at what will happen next.

The feast over, Yusuf entertains the officers in Zaynab's tent, which I avoid. I am uneasy about what exactly Zaynab's plans are, for I detect her hand in all of this, her smiling face hiding some secret plan. I see the men emerge later on, each one carrying noble gifts that Yusuf has showered on them. Even the common men are given golden coins. I wonder whether these gifts can so easily sway the men's loyalty, but they are a small part of the greater impact that the homecoming is having on them. These men have been away from loved ones, fighting and living hard. Now they return to a place of nobility and riches, of bountifulness and kind words. They are dazed, impressed, keen to be part of all that they had seen.

It becomes clear that Abu Bakr has sent these men on as a reconnaissance so that he may know how the land lies. He himself, with a smaller number of men, is now based in Aghmat, which when he left had still been of some importance. Anyone can now see that it is as nothing compared to the authority of Murakush. He will have seen for himself how things have changed since he has been away.

Not all of his men ride back to him. Only a handful of those who were sent out return to him and these are messengers. They are charged with telling him to meet with Yusuf on an appointed date, at a place between Aghmat and Murakush.

They ride out at dawn. Yusuf rides ahead, Zaynab at his side. Behind them follow a party of people of importance. I have been granted a place in this group, not by Yusuf's side. The black warriors come immediately behind the officers and tribal leaders, now Yusuf's vassals and partners. Then come all of his men, in their full battle dress.

The place chosen for the meeting is an open plain, a good place to spot any troops approaching, but with nowhere to hide. A small shelter has been set up to shield the negotiators from the heat of the day, and as we approach we see that Abu Bakr has already arrived and set up a very small camp with his remaining men. He sits under a shelter, a little older and grayer but still the stocky kindly-looking man that I remember. His eyes take in the sight before him as we slowly come to a halt.

There are not just hundreds, but several thousand men gathered behind Yusuf, in tight fighting formations. A personal guard has formed around Yusuf and Zaynab, made up entirely of the black warriors, their height adding to their imposing battlewear.

On either side of Yusuf and slightly forward are guards who carry great chests. These guards stop as we all draw to a halt, then gently put down their precious burden and step back, lifting the lids as they do so, displaying a fantastic array of gifts. There are jewels, rolls of fine cloths, skins, gold, weapons, rich robes, fruits and much more, heaped up in glittering mounds.

There is a long silence. Yusuf should of course dismount and greet Abu Bakr, as Commander, his own cousin, his brother in arms. It is offensive not to do so, but still he waits. Yusuf on a magnificent stallion with his queen by his side, Abu Bakr sitting on the ground on a plain rug beneath a simple shelter. It is a great show of strength and power, riches and importance, a challenge without a challenge needing to be spoken out loud.

Abu Bakr is not a stupid man. He knows Yusuf well, but he also knows Zaynab and what a formidable opponent she can be, perhaps of greater value than any army. No doubt he sees her hand in this. Besides, he is getting older. Perhaps he does not relish the idea of commanding a greater and still greater army, of taking them across all of our land and beyond, fighting, always fighting. He does not have the ambitions of Yusuf, nor certainly those of Zaynab.

I see his broad gruff face sag slightly, a weariness stealing over him. Then he straightens his back and his head comes up. He smiles at Yusuf and his words come smoothly, for he has surely rehearsed them since he has learned of Yusuf's change in status. His eyes are kind and his tone carries with it a sense of inevitability, as though he has waited all of his life for this very moment.

"Will you join me, cousin?"

Yusuf waits a moment, while the men tighten their grips on their weapons. Then he dismounts and slowly makes his way to the shelter, where he sits down. They look at each other for a long moment before Abu Bakr speaks again, finishing what he has no choice but to say. "My cousin Yusuf. My true brother before God. There can be no man more worthy than you to command this army of holy warriors and to undertake a holy war in the name of Allah."

There is a palpable release of tension as he speaks. The men's hands relax on their weapons and I see Yusuf's shoulders loosen. I see Zaynab nod, a small confidant gesture.

Abu Bakr continues. "I am a simple man, one who loves the desert, home of our families and seat of our power. I wish to return there with a small force of my own men. There we will continue our work, fighting back the rebel tribes and securing the trade routes for our own needs. Brother, I ask you to assume command in my name, and I will return to the desert quickly, for this is no longer my place."

After that all goes as smoothly as Zaynab no doubt planned it. A document is drawn up to transfer power. Abu Bakr will retain his nominal power as Commander; but Yusuf is now officially the head of the army, the cities conquered so far and their mission in the future. Witnesses and the tribal leaders watch while all is agreed and at the end of it all the two men embrace and set off back to their respective futures. I look back over my shoulder and see Abu Bakr's small group slowly making their way across the vast plain, never to see Murakush again.

The army comes back to the camp victorious. Abu Bakr's name will be inscribed on gold coins until the day he dies, but the true Commander is now Yusuf. The army is his to command, Zaynab is his undisputed wife. Murakush will remain under his rule, and Abu Bakr, his own leader and once-loved cousin, will retreat into obscurity.

I feel a grudging respect for Zaynab. She is no pampered queen consort, she is Yusuf's right hand. It is her skill that has brought this negotiation to a peaceful conclusion and heaped greatness on Yusuf. My own plans for the trading routes seem simple in comparison with a woman who can think so vastly, so strategically. The never-ending battles and negotiations for power tire me even to think of. I wonder if the wars will ever end, but feel my baby stir within me and promise him that one day there will be peace.

As we reach the square I shake my head. She has done it again. On the raised platform, food being prepared below her, lies Zaynab. How she has managed to dismount, rid herself of her outer robes so fast and appear to have been here all along I do not know. Perhaps she is truly a sorceress, able to fly like a bird, appear in one place and then another in the blink of an eye.

I am helped up onto the platform and Yusuf gives both Zaynab and I *tiraout* necklaces, heavy pectoral pendants, one large triangle with two smaller ones dangling beneath it, appropriate to this festive occasion. Certainly she has earned hers a hundred times over.

Zaynab lies back on silken cushions, a beautiful woman, her smile warm towards all, but dazzling for Yusuf. While I quietly take up a place towards the back of the platform, he takes her in his arms before the whole camp. She lowers her eyes and waves him to a place beside her, then orders the food to be served. As she does so, she makes a tiny gesture, smoothing her silk robes across her belly, where there is now a small but unmistakable curve. The camp roars its approval. Danger has been averted. They have a clear line of command. There has been no violence, no ugly scenes. Yusuf is now their ruler, with the beautiful Zaynab by his side, and now all the camp knows she is expecting his child. There is food, drink and the promise of a great future to come. People eat, dance, laugh, tell stories and sing.

I watch all of this for a little while, then slip away to my own tent. I sit on my bed and gently rub my own belly, sing an old lullaby to my tiny child. I pray that he will be born safely into this dangerous life, where victory and defeat walk on the blade of a dagger, one twist of the handle turning the fate of many in one direction or another with no notice. Into a world where the new commander of a great army is forever in debt to the woman who has made him so.

Issaran — Celebration Necklace

*T*HE ALMOND TREES COME INTO blossom as our two bellies swell. Zaynab's seems larger, for her voluminous and loosely worn robes add to its size. My own robes, shaped to my body with brooches and a belt, make my belly seem a little smaller, although I am sure that I am due a full month before her, a secret only she and I share. While I begin to feel better, Zaynab seems to continue with her sickness, day after day. I do not know how she can stand it.

The camp is happy and busy. Now that Yusuf has official command of the army, he is ready to swell its ranks beyond all imagining. A strong army will allow him to move swiftly as he goes north, making battles both brief and victorious.

Two thousand black slaves are added to the troops, fighting men, who quickly learn the fighting style required by Yusuf. The men train day and night on the plains near Murakush. From Al-Andalusia he brings two hundred and fifty men to whom he gives horses. These form his own personal guard, reflecting his new importance.

All of this costs money, of course. He levies a tax on the Jews living within his own jurisdiction. Besides this he also has taxes from the traders who journey the trading routes, as his men take more and more control of such stretches of land and can offer protection.

The size of the main army now allows him to send out small parts of it to the surrounding areas, under the command of men close to him. These go to different tribal areas and either negotiate alliances or conquer them. The choice is theirs. Many choose to recognise Yusuf's authority without engaging in debilitating battles.

In this way Yusuf gains the region of Salé where the tribes submit quickly, not wishing to take on the might of the new army, of which by now all have heard. Yusuf's position is very strong. If a tribe wishes to fight the smaller army sent out to them, they know that a victory for them will only result in a far larger army being dispatched to finish them off. Those tribes who submit, however, will come under Yusuf's protection, which is worth their allegiance.

The first real assault on the north comes when an army is sent to the city of Meknes. It is close to Fes, which has always been an important target in Yusuf's plan. The amir of Meknes, Al-Khayr bin Khazar az-Zanati, is offered mercy if he will surrender without fighting. Although his people react with anger and suggest he fight back and dispel not just the army but Yusuf and all his men and their mission from the land, the amir is a clever man who can see that this is a growing impossibility. Yusuf is simply becoming too strong and winning over too many allies. Instead he settles for negotiation, offering to take his own key people and decamp to a new settlement, leaving the city free for occupation by the army, who enter it peacefully. The fallen amir visits us in Murakush, where Yusuf greets him with great honour and kindness and gives him permission to remain in the region of Meknes for the rest of his life.

Meknes is an important victory for Yusuf. It is hardly any distance from Fes, and now he turns his attention to fortifying the army in Meknes so that in due course he can order them to take Fes. His territory is growing almost daily.

Yusuf does not head up these armies himself, for he prefers to remain in Murakush and develop not only the city but control his conquests, setting up administrative centres in each of his conquered areas. They will report back to him, collect taxes and recruit more men. He still oversees the training of new recruits, of primary importance in developing a coherent army.

Now Murakush begins to develop like a real city. An outer wall is built with high ramparts patrolled by soldiers. More and more buildings spring up, their apricot-coloured mud walls glowing in the first and last rays of the spring sun, shining in the full heat of the day. No longer is it a chaotic sprawl of tents, a garrison for soldiers. Now come the first houses for the generals and their families, for the officers. There are the first buildings for administration.

Huge water tanks are dug so that the city can have water brought to it more easily, for baths and irrigation. Gardens are built to supply food to the ever-growing population. Already many palms are beginning to grow in a great grove outside the city walls and it is jokingly said that they come from all the dates that the soldiers ate when they first came here after sacking Aghmat, that where the soldiers spat the stones, palms sprung up.

The first quarters begin to develop; a few buildings, little streets between them, the first communal ovens built, one for each quarter. They begin to have everything that a real city would have – the steamy hammams where all can become clean, small shops selling basic necessities for when the souk is not open. Qur'anic schools begin to teach, informal at first, but growing larger. Many of the men recently recruited into the army have no understanding of Islam, and Yusuf insists that they should be taught as well as the many children who now make the city noisy with laughter. The souk grows ever larger as the city's population grows and becomes more demanding. Now there is need for jewellery, for perfumes, for baskets, pots, carved wood, cloth, rugs, good leather and shoes. There is demand for more and better food; some luxury after the early days of camp life when the food was simple. Now the people have a taste for sweet treats, for fruits, fish and seafood from the coast, more herbs and spices. The herb seller seems to have stopped plying her trade, leaving it to the local farmers and traders who have set up permanent stalls. I no longer see her in her usual place.

Metalworkers join the weapon-makers, beating out not just swords and daggers, but great brass and copper dishes, trays and jugs to satisfy the families now expanding their kitchens and the amount of food they must provide. Their part of the city is hurtful to the ears; the great hammers rising and falling, children accidentally scattering brass dishes as they run past and the shouts of the craftsmen at the small disappearing legs.

Now other craftsmen come, their skills suddenly in demand as the builders complete their work. Expert carvers begin their work on the plasterwork inside the houses of the more important people. Tiny intricate designs are worked ceaselessly into wall after wall, elaborate twirls and curls, stylised calligraphy. Never-ending geometric repetitions are shaped, the white dust from the work covering the men until they look like beings from the other world.

The painters sit over wooden panels for doors and ceilings, chests and balconies, painting in vivid colours what the plasterworkers carve in pure white. More flowers, leaves, great arches and circles, squares, triangles. Greens and oranges, gold and blue; the panels slowly transform into works of art and are then lifted into place with much effort and curses. The metalworkers bring their crafts to the woodworkers, their hinges, heavy door-knockers and locks sliding neatly into place.

In the streets clothes grow more elaborate. Brighter colours adorn the women, finer fabrics float around their new owners, shoes are made of softer and brighter leather. Even the weapons carried become more elaborate; no longer strictly utilitarian, they grow elegant scabbards and fine scrollwork on their handles.

There is a prayer hall. It is not nearly large enough, but it is a real building, and that satisfies Yusuf for now. He wants a great mosque, but that will have to come later. For now there is at least a space where people can come together in prayer.

The tileworkers labour over tiny pieces of colour, fitting one after another, each only a tiny part of no importance, but as we pass by them each day their patterns unfold, stretch out, each tiny piece now a part of something larger and more beautiful.

There are still tents on the outer parts of the city where the more lowly live, where the foot soldiers and the cavalry sleep. There are tents of traders for the souks, and there are tents here and there between the buildings, but the city is changing fast. Slaves work daily under builders and surveyors, their bodies and clothes marked with splattered mud indicating the nature of their work even after they have finished, exhausted, for the day.

The petals fall from the almonds and the sun grows hotter. As Yusuf's wives, of course, we now have our own separate dwellings, for although Zaynab and I never waver in our public politeness towards one another, even Yusuf seems to sense that all is not as it seems and when the time came to build him a house, he ordered two. One is larger, for Yusuf spends most of his time there and Zaynab has her own rooms within the building. It has bigger rooms for entertaining, for this is where important guests will come. For all his love of simplicity, even Yusuf knows that an amir such as he now is must offer his guests a certain elegance in hospitality, and so there is a great room in which guests can be received. It is simpler than it would have been had it belonged to a man who loved luxury, but still it is decorated and his courtyard is full of flowers. There are rooms where guests can sleep, as well as kitchens large enough for his growing retinue of slaves and servants.

My own house is nearby, but I am grateful that it is mine alone, despite it being smaller and less grand. Strictly speaking I could complain, could demand all that Zaynab has, for the Holy book would give me justice. But I crave my own space, my own little kingdom rather than to be always under Zaynab's watchful eye. Yusuf offers me more servants, more slaves, but I refuse and keep only Adeola and Ekon with me, for they are all I need and the only people I trust. I do not trust Zaynab not to pay off someone to spy on me in my own home. It is small with a pretty roof terrace, which I fill with flowers in tubs and a great basin of water, which ripples in the breeze. An elegant city house should have fountains but we are not so elegant yet. Inside, the rooms are cool; dark in the heat and brightness of the day, and there I rest, surrounded by my own possessions. I see little of Yusuf, although he visits me occasionally, bringing me fruits and asking after my health. I do not try to make him stay longer than he wishes and he has much to do. We are kind and courteous, but there is little intimacy left between us now. He is wrapped up in his new-found power to take his mission forward, I am wrapped up in my pregnancy and Zaynab stands between us.

My own rooms are simple. I keep the decorations plain, the carved white plasterwork and vibrant rugs enough for my liking without filling the rooms with fine objects. I am used to tents, not living in buildings, and it seems strange to me at first. I feel shut away from the elements. Inside my rooms the breeze cannot come at night for heavy drapes are hung over the windows, and the heat of the sun is kept away by the thick mud walls and wooden shutters. I wonder how Yusuf fares. He was raised as I was. I laugh to myself when I hear that he often sleeps in the courtyard of his fine house.

I eat, sleep and watch the world go by. I marvel at the city and how it grows daily, keeping pace with my own belly. It is a quiet time for me; alone but not lonely in my own little world, while all around me great plans take shape around the growing army, city and Yusuf's power.

My child kicks within me and sometimes a little foot presses against the tight skin of my belly. I rub my fingers against the bump and smile when it is quickly retracted. Soon I will have my babe in my arms and will be able to play with it. I think of stroking its silken hair, of a tiny hand clutching mine.

Yusuf visits me, offering me a box. I take out a beautiful necklace of silver and amber, an *issaran* pendant traditionally worn for a great celebration, perhaps held at the full moon, when the great circle of amber held within the silver will reflect the beauty of that celestial orb.

"For you," smiles Yusuf. "And this is for our child, when he comes."

He pulls out a string of silver beads, each one a thick tubular shape. I smile. These are *ismana,* 'long bones' beads, given to a child to promise good health and that their bones should grow long, leading to a tall child. He shows me how each one has been marked by the jeweler with my own name and Yusuf's.

"When you first see your son he will be wearing them," I promise.

Yusuf pats my heavy belly. "It cannot be long now," he says.

I awake to a strange sensation, which fades as I stir. I think I have been dreaming and lie half asleep as the pale dawn lights my room, thinking to sleep again, for I was restless and slept badly in the night, my body uncomfortable whichever way I lay. Then a slow return of that feeling takes hold of me; a squeezing and tightening in my belly and suddenly I am wide awake, for I know my baby is on its way.

I tell Adeola what is happening and warn her that no-one must know. She has Ekon close the heavy shutters of the house and hang blankets in front of each window, the better to muffle any sounds.

My pains come slowly, building all through the day. I walk up and down in my rooms, restless and in growing pain. I am certain that my baby will be born at any moment, but still time goes by and nothing happens. I want to cry out with pain but I must be silent and so I clench my fists and teeth and try to stay silent.

"You need a midwife," says Adeola.

I shake my head. There is no-one I trust.

But as the pain goes on and on I grow afraid. How will I know if something is wrong?

"Fetch the Andalusian woman, the herb seller," I say at last to Adeola. I know that she has healing knowledge and I have need of someone as calm as she has always seemed to me.

Adeola slips out of the house and returns some time later with the woman.

She looks about her as though curious and when she sees me she looks shocked. "Why do you not have a midwife with you?" she asks.

"There is no-one I trust." I tell her, panting between the pains. "Zaynab..." I do not finish the sentence but the woman nods as though I have said more.

"What is your name?" I ask her.

She hesitates. "Isabella," she says, as though the name is both familiar and strange to her. I do not know if she is lying to me but I do not really care, I only need a name by which I can call her.

"Your child comes too soon." she says before she examines me. Everyone believes that Zaynab will be delivered of her child before me, so she must be worried that I am birthing too early.

I shake my head, awash in a wave of pain.

She frowns and comes closer, giving me her hands to hold, which I do gratefully, drawing on her steady calmness, her air of being unworried by anything. I badly needed her reassurance. As the wave dies away she sits down with me.

"Not early?"

I shake my head again.

She thinks for a moment. "Zaynab..." she begins.

I shake my head again.

She looks at me, eyebrows raised, then nods to herself. "So."

After that she questions me no more. She examines me and I look hopefully at her.

"I think it will be born very soon," I say. "I have been in pain for a long time."

She looks at me kindly. "You have not yet felt pain," she says matter-of-factly. "And your baby will not be born for a long time yet."

I gaze at her with horror and disbelief. She smiles and pats me on the shoulder as I bend over again with pain.

She is right. The hours go by until they are nothing but a blur, the waves by now not even separate, only coming again and again till I cannot distinguish between one and the next.

At last there comes a most terrible moment when I believe I will be ripped in two. All about me goes dark and then at last I feel some relief. The pain brings me back to the light and I hear a small cry.

Isabella busies herself, then comes to my side, where I have fallen back on my bed in exhaustion. In her arms she holds a tiny form, which she hands to me.

"A son," she says.

I hold the strange tiny creature in my arms. He is wet and slippery, and I fear I will drop him. He is still partly blue as well as an angry red. I think of how the indigo robes stains the men of our tribe blue and leads to all who meet them calling them the Blue Men and I laugh so hard that I think I will never stop. I am drunk with happiness for at last I hold my own child, a son for Yusuf. I remember his choice of a name for a son, and now I whisper to the tiny creature who nuzzles my breast impatiently, uninterested in my fits of laughter which make him bounce up and down on my belly. He makes grumbling sounds and I try to help him, although it takes Isabella's help to show us both how he should drink.

"You shall be called Ali," I say to him. "As your father wished. You are his first son, and you will be much loved."

I am interrupted by Isabella who has brought me a strong golden broth made by Adeola under her direction, as well as two raw eggs, the traditional food given to a new mother. She sweeps aside my refusal of her horrible concoction, insisting that I must have something to help me regain my strength. She holds Ali while I reluctantly swallow the raw eggs, which I do not like at all. Under her stern gaze I finish them and then hold my arms out for my son. She shakes her head and hands me the bowl containing the broth, in which I can taste garlic, saffron, thyme and mint, along with pepper in such large quantities that I cough and splutter.

I wipe my streaming eyes as I finish and then set the bowl aside and look up. Isabella and Adeola have disappeared with Ali and before me stands Zaynab. I feel myself cringe at the sight of her.

"You have a son?" she asks, looking this way and that.

I thank Allah that Isabella has already taken Ali somewhere else, away from Zaynab's cold eyes, for I do not trust her not to dash him on the floor if she could lay her hands on him. I stay silent.

"It is my own children who will follow Yusuf," she says and there is a note of desperation in her voice that almost makes me pity her.

"Why do you hate me so much, Zaynab?" I ask. "I am nothing compared to you, yet you hate me and pursue me. You seek to do me harm at every possible opportunity. I have done nothing to you."

She looks away, around the room, still searching for a glimpse of my son. "I am always second," she says, almost to herself.

"What do you mean?" I ask. "You are Yusuf's right hand, you are a queen."

She shakes her head impatiently, as though I cannot see something obvious. "You may have a son," she tells me. "But I will have many more. And if I can do your son harm, I will do it and I will not hold back. Every time I see that life grows in your womb I will find a way to take it from you. Before or after it is born, while I still live each one of your children will die."

Her words are not only horrifying, they sound as though she has repeated them over and over to herself, they sound like a charm, a spell.

"Get out," I say, trying to sound strong, although inside I feel as though I am about to faint. I feel like a tiny bird, watching in horror as a snake eats its young, unable to protect them.

Zaynab leaves, still twisting her head this way and that. When she has gone I call out and Adeola comes in, clutching a newly-wrapped Ali to her chest.

"Where is Isabella?" I ask.

"Gone," says Adeola. "She slipped away but it is well, I have your son here."

I reach out and take back Ali, then hold him to my breast. I look down at him and my tears begin to fall on his head.

"What is wrong?" asks Adeola. "Do not think of Zaynab's words."

"She will find a way to bring harm to him," I say, sobbing now. "You heard her. She will do it."

Adeola's face is worried. "Tell Yusuf?" she says.

"He will not believe me, Adeola," I say. "Yusuf loves Zaynab, she is his right hand. He barely remembers why he once married me."

Adeola doesn't answer. There is not much she can say.

"Go and sleep," I tell her.

"You who should sleep," she says.

"I will, I will," I reassure her.

Reluctantly, she leaves the room, making me promise that I will call for her if I need anything.

I have lost track of time but the streets are very dark. I walk quickly, my shoulders hunched around my tiny son, the hooded robe Adeola uses when she goes shopping in the marketplaces covering every part of me and shielding my face.

I know where Isabella lives; a part of town where the foot soldiers and their families live, not a wealthy area. I find the house I had pointed out to me once when I enquired: plain red mud walls with no decorative moulding, a heavy wooden door. I knock softly, not wanting to draw attention.

She is surprised to see me. "Is the baby ill?" she asks. "Do you bleed?"

I shake my head. "May I enter?" I ask.

She steps back, allowing me to pass by her into the courtyard of the house. It is tiny, only a couple of dim lanterns illuminate the space and I can see a doorway into the house.

The room she ushers me into is extraordinarily plain. There is no carved plasterwork, no paint. The walls are white, the floor is plain gray tiles. There is a table and a chair. Nothing else. The only decoration in the room is a large wooden cross, hung on the wall. I stare at it for a moment, already half-regretting my plan.

"Kella?"

My attention is caught by the table. On it is a stack of good paper marked with fine calligraphy, although it is not our own script. It must be Isabella's work, for writing implements and inks lie to hand. Few people can read and write, especially such fine script. This is the work of a scribe or a religious clerk. I am confused by this room, it feels as though there are clues as to who Isabella is and I yet do not understand them. All I know of her is her calmness, her abilities with herbs, that she is a very educated woman and yet also a slave. I turn to face her, frowning.

"Why are you here?" she asks.

I swallow. "I want you to take my son."

She gazes at me for a long time. "Why?"

"Zaynab... threatened him."

"You could go to your husband."

I shake my head.

She does not argue the point and I wonder what she knows of Zaynab.

"Will you take him?" I ask and I can already feel my tears welling at the thought of her agreeing.

I see her make a tiny movement towards me, as though about to take Ali. "For how long?"

"Forever," I say.

She steps back. "Forever? Where will you be?"

I shake my head. "I do not know," I say. "I may have to leave this place to ensure Ali is safe. But I cannot visit him, cannot see him again or Zaynab will know I am his mother."

"She came to your house."

"She did not see him," I say. "I will say he is dead." Even the thought of him dying brings a wave of nausea. I hold him more tightly and he stirs in my arms, lets out a tiny cry but then settles again.

"And his father?"

I swallow again. "He will know him when he is old enough."

"How?"

I fumble in my robes and pull out the *ismana*, the string of silver beads marked with my name and Yusuf's. "His father gave me this for our child. He will recognise it when he sees it. You must keep it safe and give it to Ali when he is old enough to make himself known, when he is a man."

She stands silently.

"Will you take him?" I ask again.

"I must pray," she says abruptly. She turns away from me and kneels below her cross.

I watch her. I have never seen a Christian at prayer before. Her hands are clasped together, her head is bowed. She stays silent and still for a long time before she opens her eyes and looks up at the cross. She makes a movement with one hand echoing its shape across her face and shoulders, then rises and turns back to me. Her face is very calm, but her voice shakes a little when she speaks, at the enormity of what she is about to do.

"I will take him," she says. "I will keep him safe until he is grown to be a man and I will bear witness to your husband that he is your child and his."

She holds out her arms, her hands open to receive Ali.

I try to move, try to hold him out to her but my whole body convulses in sobs. I rock him in my arms, my face buried against his skin, trying to smell him, feel him, kiss him for the last time. Isabella watches me with a vast pity in her eyes. When she sees that I cannot let him go she reaches out and takes him from me very gently, her hands cradling him. My fingertips stay in contact with him until the last moment and when my arms fall back empty by my sides I let out a low moan of pain, tears falling so fast down my face that I cannot even see. Ali begins to cry and at once my hands reach out for him but Isabella shakes her head.

"You must go now," she says. "Or you will be found out."

I look at the back of Ali's head, at the tiny tuft of black hair, which is all I can see of him. I back away from Isabella and then turn. I walk through the darkness of her tiny courtyard and pull the door behind me, its heavy thud echoing inside me over and over again as I run through the dark streets back to my own home.

When I arrive Adeola is waiting. "Where is Ali?" she asks, seeing my empty arms.

I shake my head. "He is dead, Adeola."

She gasps, stares at me in horror.

I lay one hand on her and look into her face, tears streaming down my own. "You must say he is dead," I tell her. "You must take a wrapped body and have it buried."

She nods quickly, hurries away from me while I walk unseeing to my own bed. When I lie down I weep as though I will weep forever.

It is light when Yusuf comes. Behind him is Zaynab. The two of them look down on me where I lie weeping on my bed.

Zaynab's face takes on a mask of sorrow and she kneels, embraces me, her black robes stifling me, their silk slipping across my mouth and nose like sliding snakes, making my skin tense with disgust and fear. "My poor sister. Your newborn son was weak and now he has been taken from you. It is the will of Allah. We must not question His decisions." She looks up at Yusuf. "Our son will be born soon," she says, as though to comfort him. "You will have an heir, to mend your heart."

Yusuf nods. "You may leave us now," he says and Zaynab, unwilling but unable to refuse, goes out of the room.

Yusuf kneels by my side. His own eyes fill with tears and gently he strokes my disheveled hair.

For a moment I think of telling him the truth. He is a good man, a kind man. I will explain how things are between me and Zaynab, beg him to keep Ali and me away from her, to let us live in peace. But I do not trust Zaynab. I do not trust that there will be no mysterious accidents, no illnesses. Ali is more precious to me than Yusuf's feelings.

"I named him Ali," I say, and then stop, for my sobs are choking me. I close my eyes against the new swelling of pain at speaking his name and when I open them again I see that Yusuf, too, is weeping.

We sit together, embracing, weeping, for a long time. It is almost nightfall when Yusuf rises and I am left alone again.

In the days that follow, Adeola and Ekon treat me as though I am their own child. They wash me and comb my hair, they dress me in fresh robes each day. They hold sweet orange juice to my lips, make me eat rich meat stews and drink broth to give me strength. They bring fresh fruits and the little honey cakes Aunt Tizemt loves. One of them sits by my side day and night, they hear my sobs in silence.

Zaynab is safely delivered of a son. They name him Abu Tahir al-Mu'izz, and the city rejoices that Yusuf has an heir at last. Yusuf holds a great feast. Zaynab is showered with gifts and praise. Her son is said to be strong and healthy; a fine boy who will one day be a great warrior like his father. Those around me lower their voices when they see me coming and tiptoe about. I do not attend the feasts for the boy, only weep at my loss, sleep and weep again.

Amalu comes to me. He kneels before me and his eyes are serious.

"Come away from here, Kella," he says. "There is nothing good left here for you. Come with me. We will trade together, as you once asked me to. I was a fool to refuse you. I have cursed myself every day since, for we would have been happy together and I would have saved you all of this pain."

I look into his dark eyes and I almost speak the truth, for I trust Amalu, but I am too deep in my loss to imagine the life he offers. Instead I shake my head in silence and he kisses my hand and leaves. Later I look down at my hand and imagine what it would be to live a life filled with love and tenderness rather than this unending pain.

Tiseguin — Ring with Container

ES. THE WORD SWEEPS THROUGH the city. At long last, Yusuf is ready to attack Fes.

Fes is a twin city. Long ago, one city was built on one side of the river, then another on the opposite bank. One city is inhabited by the descendants of refugees from Cordoba in Al-Andalus; the other by Kairouanis, from Tunisia. The walls of the two cities are so close to one another that, to an outside observer, they appear as one city, but they are still in fact two cities, each with their own customs. It is known that neither of the two amirs who govern the two parts of the city will peaceably surrender as did the rulers of Meknes. There will have to be a siege.

Yusuf places the command of much of the army under a relative of his, Yahya bin Wasinu, and preparations for the siege begin. There are troops already at Meknes who are well placed to go to Fes and begin the siege. But more troops will be needed before they can begin. Every day new men are recruited and more soldiers set out on the journey to reach Meknes, where they will be welcomed and provisioned to then make their way on towards Fes.

Yusuf wants both parts of Fes to fall to his men, for he has in mind to destroy the wall which separates the two parts of the city, thus making it into one single, larger, city. Fes has been his dream for a long time, for with Fes as his base in the north and Murakush in the south, he can plan future campaigns to the north and the east of our land, as well as further into the south, with Abu Bakr's help.

The stately dinners with leaders of tribes and cities are all but stopped, for Yusuf, always the warrior, only ever undertook them because he knows that negotiation and good relations with his new subjects is important. Now that there is a battle to be fought he sweeps all such events to one side. The servants of his household are idle without the great feasts to prepare or the guests to care for. Their master spends much time in training or poring over plans with his generals. They calculate the number of people in Fes, how much food they may have within the walls, how best to attack when the time comes and the greatest threats to their own men. Having two amirs each with their own soldiers will complicate matters. They sit up talking all night and train men most of the day. When I see Yusuf he is always in a hurry, always surrounded by generals and of course his own personal guard who now go everywhere with him.

As for Zaynab, she has a child to care for but she leaves him with nursemaids and is always by Yusuf's side. While the men train she returns briefly to her own quarters where she will beat anyone who has allowed any harm, real or imagined, to come to her son. She inspects him as though he were a prized object rather than her own flesh and blood, then goes to the outskirts of the city to watch the training, taking up a place in the shade and keeping her eyes narrowed against the sun. Her dark eyes miss nothing. Later she will speak with Yusuf about men who held back, who have not shown courage, strength or stamina. Those men will find themselves withdrawn from the troops riding towards Fes and made to train even harder until Zaynab's lips stop speaking their name. Sometimes I see her in the distance and wonder at her. She does not hold her child and cover him with kisses as I yearn to do with my son. Her eyes light up when she sees him, but the light in them is cold and hard, the eyes of a good trader when they spot a precious gem that they may use to make their fortune.

She uses a gem to attack me.

I come to my rooms one night as the siege of Fes begins and find on my bed a small casket. Inside is a *tiseguin*, a large ring of silver topped off with a very small box, the lid to which is fastened by a tiny chain. The lid of this box is made of carnelian, a stone known for its protective powers. It is customary to fill such a box with kohl for the eyes or with perfume, so that a woman may have her favourite beautifiers carried with her wherever she goes. I am puzzled by the gift and a little suspicious.

"Where did this come from?" I ask Adeola.

"A guard delivered it. He said it was from Yusuf for you."

I open the tiny box and find it to contain a sweet perfume, very light and fresh. It smells of flowers and fresh air and salt, such as one might smell close to the sea. I smile to myself and rub the perfume where my pulse beats.

I wear the ring proudly, hoping to see Yusuf soon and have him smile at my delight in his gift.

The first day of the siege must be terrifying for the people of Fes. They have heard of the great army, of course, but few have seen its full might, for until now Yusuf has never had the need to use all of it at one time. Many cities and tribal leaders have simply surrendered when he has so demanded, seeking to avoid his wrath. Those now looking out from the ramparts of Fes can see thousands upon thousands approaching them, their ranks tight and steady, the men approaching without hesitation, their great shields held high, their weapons glinting in the sun.

My head feels light and my feet seem to float. I feel free. All my fears of Zaynab suddenly seem foolish. What harm can she do me, after all? I am alive and healthy. My son is also alive, even if I cannot hold him. Zaynab is fallible, she will not always win our battles.

I dress in my best, wear my jewellery and apply more of Yusuf's perfume. When evening comes I sit by his side during the meal, laughing and joking, telling old stories from my days as a trader, when I was dressed as a boy. I tell of all the scrapes I got into, the lies I told my father about my camel racing, the tricks I played on my oldest and most serious brother. Yusuf looks surprised but pleased at my lightness of spirit and I make sure that he can see the ring he has given me. When the drums are played I clap my hands and tap my feet. I smile at Zaynab and she smiles back at me, her hands keeping my rhythm.

The drums are never silent; day or night their pulse beats, the inhabitants of Fes unable to sleep so that even their soldiers begin to feel fatigue without even fighting. Babies cry, children whimper, the men and women begin to feel a real fear.

I awake feeling strange. The colours of my rooms seem very bright and I think perhaps that I have slept late, for the rays of sunlight at the window hurt my eyes and make my rugs seem too bright. I wear plainer clothes that day for none of my usual reds and oranges seem right. I take some comfort and pleasure in my new perfume, which smells so fresh.

Yusuf's army never comes forward when the enemy retreats, to avoid a false retreat, allowing the enemy to suddenly turn on them when they follow. But neither do they fall back, staying always together, always facing the enemy. The soldiers of Fes must come forward to be killed or escape back to the safety of the city walls to remain under siege while their water supplies and food dwindle and the people grow ever more fearful.

I cannot stop thinking of Fes. I see our soldiers, blood running outside the walls of a great city, limbs and heads rolling helplessly away from their owners. The weapons gleam so brightly that I shield my eyes even when they are tightly closed. I rub the perfume into my skin and breath it deeply, hoping to wash away the smell of blood in my nostrils, the sound of drums and steel on steel, hurting my ears in my silent room.

There are camels, allowing our men to fight the foot soldiers from a great height, cutting off their heads with one quick stroke of a sword. There are horses, who change direction at great speed, avoiding the enemy's weapons and allowing the riders to chase after those who seek to escape their fate. The great shields, tanned with ostrich eggs and camels' milk, are like iron, protecting the men from any weapon wielded by the soldiers of Fes, such that their attempts to protect their city seem foolish.

I lie on my bed and moan, thinking I hear the men scream as they plunge to their death from the ramparts, the terrified howls of women and children as they see their fathers, brothers, husbands die. I smell the perfume but it does not seem to take away the sound, no matter how much of it I put on. The little box is almost empty and I want to ask Yusuf to bring me more of it, so that its sweet fresh smell might bring me comfort.

Still the siege continues. More lives are lost while the two amirs hide from the conquering army, coming closer every day as their own armies shrink.

I rub on the last of the perfume, feel the room seem to float about me. I think of my life, which seems full of bright colours and sensations.

My childhood, the thick dark indigo of the robes that my father, brothers and I had worn and the pure soft white of Thiyya. The gold of oranges and the orange of gold, the pink rose buds of rich perfumes, the yellow of lion skins, their once-fearsome manes soft to the touch. The choking dust and the blinding sand. The heat and the endless journeys, the flickering warmth of fires and the good smell of roasting kid.

My Aunt Tizemt. Her warm hard hugs, the sweetness of her cakes dripping with honey, her roars when she was angry and her grumbles when she was happy. The waterfall of gaspingly cold water as Tanemghurt prepared me for my wedding night.

Yusuf's warm hands slipping over my body, his hardness melding with my softness, his sudden unexpected laughter and his smell, of horses and leather. His smile, his face at prayer.

My two lost children, the red red blood creeping down my thighs and the sinking pain of helplessness.

My third child gone from me when I had only held him, smelt him, fed him once.

Zaynab. The blackness of her eyes clothes tent deeds.

Darkness.

It is dawn when I stagger to Zaynab's rooms. My heart seems to beat loudly in my chest and I falter, hesitating at each step or uneven surface in the tight streets, for every time I put my foot down it does not seem to touch the floor. I sway as I walk. People draw away from me, whispering. *The amir's wife, swaying as though drunk, her eyes rolling back or even closing as she walks, clutching at anything close to her hand as she tries to take a few more steps to her husband's house.* Some of Yusuf's servants see me. The guards hurry forward and take me inside, away from prying eyes, calling for Yusuf. But I stop them, asking instead to be taken to Zaynab's rooms.

Two of the guards almost have to carry me up the tight stairs to Zaynab's own bedroom. Once there, they sit me down on a thick rug piled high with cushions, facing her great bed. They bring water and food, which they offer me, perhaps thinking my faintness is through fasting. I refuse and ask instead that they bring Zaynab to me at once. They look doubtful but obey me.

I wait and look around me. Zaynab has recreated her great tent here. The walls are white now, the plasterwork intricately carved with the names of Allah, with passages from the Holy Book. The floor is a thousand thousand tiny chips of tiles, making up a simple geometric pattern. There are great wooden chests against the walls but they are unpainted, or painted only with the simplest of flowers. Their wood, however, is precious. Cedar, ebony and citrus wood are used as inlays. The room is austere at first glance, dazzlingly complex and costly when looked at again. Her great bed is the same. It still smells of power and sex, of ambition and lust. It is glorious and frightening. I cannot keep my eyes away from it.

I smell her before I see her or hear her, that strange perfume she wears wafting towards me as she comes up the stairs. I hear the soft rustling of her silk robes, the gentle tread of her fine leather slippers on the steps. I close my eyes and wait, a wave of fear washing over me. When I open my eyes again my fingers are crushing a silken pillow and Zaynab is seated on her bed opposite me, looking down on me with interest, as though I am a rare specimen of some strange beast from foreign lands, brought here for her amusement.

She sits on the edge of the bed, her feet tucked neatly under her long lean thighs, her black robes draped becomingly all around her. Her slippers lie to one side, discarded. Her hands lie loosely in her lap and she leans forward, her elbows resting on her knees. We gaze at each other until I moisten my dry mouth and speak.

"What have you given me, Zaynab?" I ask.

She looks at me in silence.

I go on. "I thought the perfume was from Yusuf, but now I know it was from you. It does strange things to me, I see visions of terrible things and I hear things I do not wish to hear. My feet stumble and I feel that I might fly like a great bird if I were only to leap from my window. I talk and talk, telling all that is in my heart, no matter who is listening. I feel light, and then the colours grow so bright they hurt my eyes until I grow afraid."

She gazes at me silently as though I speak a foreign tongue. Then she frowns, straightening up as though she has much to do. She speaks briskly.

"You are stronger than I thought," she says. "I thought if you rubbed it in day after day, thinking to please your husband – " she allows herself a quick smile " – that you would surely die. But you seem to be stronger than that. The man who sold it to me showed me what only a few drops would do to an animal." She smiles. "It was unpleasant, but quick."

I shake my head. "Why do you hate me so much, Zaynab?" I ask in despair. "I have not tried to fight you. I want only to help my husband succeed in his mission, to bear him children, to build a great country. Yet you treat me as your greatest enemy. What more can I give you? You have taken my husband. You have taken my children – one from my womb, one from my arms – "

Her eyes narrow to slits and she closes the space between us with a single leap. I see a cloud of black silk flying through the air and draw back with a shriek. Her hand comes quickly across my mouth to silence me. When she is sure I will be quiet she withdraws it and brings her face close to mine.

"*Taken* your second child?"

I gasp. "He is dead."

She shakes her head. "You said I took him. He is *alive*?"

I shake my head slowly, terrified. Zaynab stands, looking down on me, then reseats herself on her bed as though she has all the time in the world. She smiles, a loving, kind smile.

"He *is* alive. That is why you stopped your grieving so soon. Where is he? Your *son*. Ali. Where is he? He is alive somewhere in this city. Not with you, I know that."

I tighten my lips.

"No matter," she says, still smiling. "I will find him. I know what a son of Yusuf looks like, for I have my own. Soon he will be Yusuf's only child."

I whimper, unable to stop the sound.

Zaynab relaxes. "So. I need to find your son. Then I will simply... watch you. I have spies everywhere. I will know when your womb is filled, and I will kill all your children, one by one, whether in your womb or in your arms. I will not trust my servants again, not even Hela; I will do it myself. In time everyone will know that you are barren and that your children do not live long. Who would want such a wife? What ill-luck. Yusuf will set you aside, or perhaps being such a pious man he will simply send you away, to live alone in one of his many cities. Who knows?"

"Why?" I ask.

She shrugs. "You are a threat to me," she says. "You diminish my own status. I will be Yusuf's only wife."

I hold out my hands to her. "Why did you even let me come here?" I ask. "Yusuf sent for me. You could have arranged it so that I never received the message, so that I was killed by bandits. Why let me come?"

"I thought you were old and barren," she says as though it was obvious.

I frown. "What made you think that?"

"Yusuf said you had lost a child in the first months of your marriage. I thought you had lost it naturally. It was only later that he told me about the camel. I thought you were much older than you are. I thought you would come here, a poor simple desert woman, withered and barren. That you would be no kind of competition to me." She gestures at me. "Then you arrived. Ten years younger than me. Beautiful. Innocent to the point of foolishness. Dressed in your bright robes, your shining silver. His first wife. He spoke of you with tenderness, your trading skills, your vision matching his for the future of this land. Your womb filled with life so quickly, so easily."

I rise, unsteady on my feet and look down on her. "I am leaving, Zaynab.

You have tried to poison me. No doubt you will try again. What do you want – my life in exchange for my son's?"

She smiles. "I might consider such a bargain," she says.

My son is alive. Zaynab knows this now and I know that she will not stop until she has found and killed him, this time with her own bare hands.

If I were dead, Zaynab might let my son live. She might believe that with my death his identity will be lost. If I am gone, who can name him as Yusuf's heir? And who can prove it if his mother cannot vouch for his paternity?

I shake my head as the darkness comes closer. I have to think.

I could take Zaynab's poison in a larger dose and surely die. Then she might spare my son.

That evening Yusuf calls me to him. Zaynab sits by his side and I try to avoid her gaze, keeping my eyes fixed on him alone.

"When Fes falls, as it will shortly," he begins, "there will be a time of rebuilding, of making it into a great city. But we have many men, and it will not take long. One of the buildings that I will order to be constructed will be a great palace where I will take up residence in due course, for there will be many campaigns in the north. I must be able to be closer to my generals when they set out to conquer new lands."

I steal a quick glace at Zaynab. She rules Murakush with an iron grasp. Will she take kindly to moving to a new city?

Yusuf continues. "It is my wish that when I move to Fes my two wives will accompany me. You will both live within the palace, for I wish all of my family to be together under one roof. In this way we can share meals together and welcome guests together. You will of course have your own rooms within the palace," he adds. "Zaynab has requested that you and she have your rooms close to one another, for she believes that as sisters you will draw on one another's strength and love to become used to a new city."

I feel my heart sink. I am certain that I have escaped many of Zaynab's plots and schemes on a day-to-day basis by living in a different building, and even so she has managed to do me more damage than I would have thought possible. What could she do to me if we were under the same roof, her servants preparing my food? How much easier it will be for her to poison me, to blame an unlucky slave perhaps, who might be killed for having dared to harm me, while Zaynab looks on and weeps false tears for her 'sister'. I shudder inside but keep a smile on my face as I answer Yusuf.

"I will be glad to be closer to you, husband," I say gently and it would be the truth if Zaynab were not part of the bargain. As it is I know now that my days are numbered. Living in Murakush or living in Fes will make no difference. Zaynab will not be satisfied until I die.

Or disappear.

The next day I send gifts to my family. I spend many hours in the souk, wandering from stall to stall, even in the heat of the day when many retire to their homes for food and prayer. I wander on, making good use of my trader's eye. I hold my family in my heart as I walk from one trader to the next. For my brothers I buy fine saddles, each with different colours woven into them, as well as tiny trinkets and toys for their children who will no doubt be numerous by now, although I know I will never see them.

For my father I buy a fine sword, the best that can be found in a city supporting a great army. It is the finest I have ever seen and indeed the maker does not even want to sell it to me, for he hopes an officer or even Yusuf himself will desire it. He has no interest in selling it to an unknown woman, even one as wealthy as I obviously am, with gold coins already held in the palm of my hand while I bargain. But I disclose my identity to him, leading him to believe the sword might find its way to my husband's hand. Then he grows eager and even gives me a fine scabbard for it.

My aunt I heap with gifts. Everything I see that I think may please her I buy. Brass bowls, copper jugs, wooden spoons make their way into the hands of slaves who walk wearily behind me, wondering at my sudden desire for purchases, for I am known for my simple house and belongings. I choose pots made from clay, a rarity for Aunt Tizemt for our earth is not suitable for the potters' wheel. I buy cloth and jewellery, powdered henna and tiny silver discs for her weaving. I laugh to think of her grumblings as she unpacks my gifts, her mutterings that I must have more money than I know what to do with and all the while her good strong hands admiring what her mouth cannot bring itself to say, that I have good taste and that the things I have sent her are useful and beautiful. They will colour her life a little brighter.

I even send a gift for Tanemghurt, though I do not know whether she is still alive. In a tiny pot I place precious rose perfume such as might adorn a bride, paying many coins for it, for it has come from far away and is the finest of its kind. I buy it hoping she still lives and may use it one day on another innocent young bride such as I was before I learnt some cruel lessons regarding marriage. I think of the cold waterfall for her astonished brides and her secret pride in such rituals, the creations of her own imagination. I hold the tiny pot in my hands, think of her wrinkled old face and struggle to stem my tears.

While I wander through the souk with my slaves running back and forth behind me, some taking my new purchases back to the house, others coming to take their place and carry my new items as I walk on, I hear a baby gurgle. I look up at once, for I always hope that I might catch a glimpse, however brief, of Ali in the streets, held by Isabella. My breasts dripped milk for days after losing him and even now, so much later on, they still seemed to ache when I hear a child cry.

It takes me a moment to locate the child, but when I do I feel my heart, so eager to reach out, suddenly pull up short. The baby is Zaynab's boy Abu, only a little younger than Ali. I steer clear of him whenever I can, for his sweet smiling face hurts my heart and his chubby little hands hurt my very soul. Now he is just ahead of me, held as ever by his nursemaid. He smiles over her shoulder at me. She is oblivious of me, striding along as best she can carrying a heavy baby, jostled by the many people who walk along the tight streets.

I gaze at his tiny jolly face and sigh. Certainly I could plot against Zaynab's child as she has done against mine, but I cannot bring myself to harm a baby, nor to wish any bad fate upon him. He is only a baby and knows nothing of his father and mother, nor of me and my secret child who is, after all, his brother. He smiles broadly and reaches out his tiny fingers. I hold out my own hand, unable to resist his enthusiasm and happiness. His fingers grab mine for a brief moment before he is pulled away as his nursemaid finds a gap in the crowd.

I watch him disappear, his bright eyes still fixed on mine, then turn back to the craftsman with a heavy heart. He has been bargaining all this time and appears to have haggled me into a ridiculous price, so I clear my mind. I think of my father and brothers, trading their way across the dunes and begin to barter in earnest.

That night I supervise the packing of all the gifts I have bought and wave goodbye to the men and the camels as they set out on the long journey to my old camp. I wish I might lead them there, but know that for now my fate holds me captive in Murakush, for the news we have been awaiting has finally come.

Fes has fallen.

Taneghelt — The Key of Love

THE SIEGE IS SUCCESSFUL ON the eighth day, when the army breaks through the defences of Fes and crushes the twin cities beneath its might. Buildings are sacked for riches and some even destroyed with brute strength or fire. The inhabitants pay a high price for their stubborn defence. Bodies lie slaughtered in the streets, while the two kings, who were proud enough to refuse to surrender, are now forced to beg for mercy at the feet of Yusuf's general Yahya bin Wasinu. He in turn makes them wait, grovelling, spending each day in fear of their lives, while he sends word back to Yusuf to ask for his clemency. Yusuf gives it, allowing the two toppled kings to live where they may choose. They slink out of their conquered fortresses like beaten dogs, taking those few who are still loyal to them to a new life of lowly status.

Those people who have not lost their lives have a choice – to leave the city with or without their kings, or to stay and swear allegiance to their new ruler. Some leave, unable to bear a new ruler, some to seek their now-demolished fortunes again. Those who remain must accept the changes now ordered by their new unseen amir, Yusuf, far away in Murakush. The wall between the two parts of the city comes tumbling down, men of the city itself conscripted to do the back-breaking work alongside the army's muscular soldiers. Rich merchants cut their hands to ribbons handling heavy tools and curse in whispers over their blisters at night.

Once the wall is down the people have to live day by day, side by side with those who have been strangers to them, now suddenly become neighbours in the rubble.

The city begins to change shape. Now it is truly one great city rather than two placed side-by-side. New people come to it from all over the land, and every day more men join the army, which numbers many different nations within its ranks.

Yusuf has ordered that building must begin as soon as the rubble is cleared away. Mosques are to be built, baths, water canals, mills. The city will be transformed, ready to take its place as one of Yusuf's most important cities in his plans for future conquests.

He has also ordered the creation of the palace he promised. It will be a fortified castle, its ramparts high above the city offering a lookout post where his guards can spot any attackers stupid enough to try and take Fes from Yusuf's army. The rooms will be bigger and more beautiful than those in Murakush. Craftsmen will be called from far and wide to design complex tiled floors, to carve the plaster into swirling gardens of leaves and flowers, and to fill every room with fine rugs and cushions, low tables of scented wood, brass and copper dishes engraved with every possible shining design. It will be a very different life from the one Yusuf and I once knew in the desert, where our only homes were our tents and our meals were plain. Now foods will be brought to us from far away, great banquets will be held, growing ever more formal. Our clothes will become more and more costly, our servants and slaves multiplying day by day. Zaynab's great bed will take up residence in her rooms and we will all live in the palace together, her eyes everywhere, my life in danger.

Murakush is in ecstasy. The army has triumphed yet again, and now Yusuf rules over cities both north and south. His army is huge and each city taken is another part of the greater plan.

There is feasting the night that word reaches us about the success of the army. Torches burn brightly, lighting up the city's growing fineness. Good food and drink are made and eaten, the storytellers fill the squares and people gather to listen to the latest tales spun around Yusuf and his holy mission, his handsome baby son, a new city conquered, two new kings subjugated to Yusuf's mercy. Fes is described to those who have never seen it, its great riches now part of the wealth that Yusuf can command, the wall of division between its people felled at his orders. My husband is becoming the stuff of legend, his conquests something from a fairytale, peopled with extraordinary heroes and princesses. Zaynab, of course, has her own legends, and they grow greater by the day. I have even heard the story of my own younger days when I entered the camel race and my veil fell from my face, showing that a young girl had beaten the men at a camel race. I shake my head when I hear these stories, for I am described as more beautiful and daring than I truly was. No longer a silly headstrong girl who risked her father's wrath in order to please herself and make fun of proud young traders and their sons. Now I am a stunning beauty who defied her father, beat off princes and warriors to claim a great prize and who amazed all when her fine robes unveiled her true loveliness, drawing the eye of Yusuf bin Tashfin himself.

I sit at a window where I can overlook the streets and watch the feasting, listen to the stories being told, the dances and songs that accompany them as the night draws on. Children gradually fall asleep and are carried back to their homes, while the men and women continue celebrating. I see a few men and women who should not be in one another's company, for the night hides much. I hear rumours passed from mouth to ear. One of these makes my heart beat faster.

Two women stand in the street below me. One I recognise, a slave woman in Zaynab's household, who washes her clothes and makes her bed. The other I do not know, a slave from another household no doubt, the two perhaps friends.

"She has not bled this month," says Zaynab's woman.

"By many days?" asks the other.

I lean further out of my window, wondering whether they can truly be speaking of Zaynab or whether they speak only of a slave girl or servant who has been a little too friendly with the soldiers.

"Enough," says Zaynab's woman, nodding knowledgably. "She looked faint today, pale. Like she was with the last one. She will give the Commander another child for sure."

I sit back and breath deeply. Zaynab, who somehow managed not to give her three previous husbands any children, seems fertile after all; her first son not a stroke of luck but perhaps the first of many.

"Praise be to Allah," says the other, although there is not much praise in her voice. Zaynab is not a favourite in her household, for she is harsh with her punishments and entirely lacking in praise. She works her servants and slaves hard, thinking nothing of having them whipped or starved if they displease her in even a small way. Her fertility is not a source of pride to them as it might have been with a more beloved mistress.

They continue talking as they walk slowly back to their own beds, while I allow the night air to cool my hot cheeks and slow my heart.

The next morning I go to the stables where all the camels of Yusuf's own household are kept. I find Thiyya. I have not seen her since I first came to

Murakush, but she is healthy and well-cared for. I thank Allah Zaynab has never known she is precious to me or no doubt she would have found a way to harm her. Thiyya recognises me but makes a great show of ignoring me until I offer her the dried figs I have brought. She immediately fights off the other camels and flutters her long white lashes at me, daintily picking each fruit from my hand, then greedily nuzzling me for more when she has eaten them all. I pat her gently and smooth her fur. I look around the stables but cannot see any racing saddles that would fit her. There are large men's saddles or dainty women's saddles, neither of which are what I like to use with her. I stroke Thiyya's small ears while she tosses her head. She has never liked to have her ears touched. I pat her forehead and leave her.

I am walking back through the streets when a little slave boy runs up to me.

"Lady, I have a message for you from a man."

"What man?" I ask.

He shrugs. "I do not know, lady. He asked me to find you." He pulls out a little pouch. "He said to tell you that a veil sometimes allows you to see more clearly."

He looks at me as though to see if this makes sense to me. I shrug and give him a coin for his trouble. I let him go with my thanks and go up to my bedroom, calling for cool water to be brought to me. When Ekon has left the room I open the pouch.

Amalu has sent me another veil key, one that matches the first one he gave me when Yusuf summoned me.

I sit and look at the little silver fastener for a long time, thinking about the time he had given its twin to me. I was so full of innocent excitement and pleasure, a free and happy woman on her way to see her husband after too long apart. Before I had met Zaynab, before I had lost two more children by her hand. Now I feel like a prisoner, my innocence crumpled and dirtied by all I have experienced.

Amalu knew me before, when my man's blue veil covered my face, allowing my shaded eyes to see clearly in the blinding desert sun.

I see clearly now the path I wish to travel and I begin to take the steps to lead me there.

I leave my room and spend the afternoon in the souk, at the saddle-maker's stall. I make him show me all of his stock, rejecting all the heavy men's battle saddles and all the ornate women's saddles, forcing him to find me the light racing saddles that young men favour. He is mystified by my demands, muttering to himself as he fails to make me take an interest in the more appropriate women's saddles, extolling their softness and comfort. I laugh and wave them away, examining the racing saddles for their quality and workmanship. I find one that reminds me of my days as a trader, one that I think will fit Thiyya well. I pay him more than the saddle is worth, throwing gold coins at him with no attempt to bargain him down, leaving him blessing Allah while looking somewhat bewildered. I give the saddle to a passing slave boy and pay him to take it back to my house, which he does, walking slowly, dwarfed under its weight.

More than once I take up my outer robe with its heavy hood and take a pace towards the door, before turning back. At last I take a coarse cloth and use it to cover my head so that no-one will know me. I slip out of my home and take the smallest streets I can find until I reach Isabella's house, looking behind me more than once in case I am being followed. I hesitate again, my hand held up to knock. At last my knuckles strike against the wood, but there is no answer. I swallow, then open the door myself and step inside her courtyard. I have not been here in daylight. It is very small but pretty, full of herbs and flowering plants. I think to call her name but the silence around me tells me she is not here. I push at the door to her house and enter the room I remember from the night when I gave up my son.

It is still sparse, as I recalled it. The large cross still looms over the small room, but now there are signs of its new inhabitant. I see a bowl of water in which are soaking cloths to keep a baby clean.

The other item lies on the floor, discarded by its tiny owner, perhaps in a fit of temper. It is a little rattle, such as are given to small babies to please them when they cry. They delight in the sound that the beads make when they are shaken. This rattle is made of ivory, a rare and precious substance to be used for a careless baby's toy. I kneel and take it in my hand. I touch its fine smooth surface and then bring it to my lips and kiss every part of it, hoping that when my son next holds it to his rosebud mouth he may feel his mother's kiss touch his lips.

I wipe away my tears, which have begun to fall, and then leave that house. I could walk up the stairs and see every room, could even wait for their return from wherever they have gone, but it is enough for me to have stood in my son's home, to see where he lives each day and to leave a kiss for him. I am not certain that I could see my son, perhaps even hold him again, then walk away for a second time.

I close the door softly behind me and when I have walked three streets away I take off the coarse cloth and give it to a beggar girl, who blesses my name as I walk home.

Now that I have made my farewell to my son I seek out Amalu's home. Yusuf's men no longer live in the barracks formed from tents. I make enquiries on a morning when the army has left early for the plain outside Murakush, where they will practice manoeuvers all day. I find his house tucked down a side street, its plain orange-painted door unlocked. I push at it and enter a small courtyard, modest in size and bereft of comforts: no fountains or flowering plants here. His few rooms are also plain: a simple bed and blankets, a worn prayer mat along with some weapons, perhaps not needed for today's practice. No decoration, no cooking utensils save a water jar and dipper, a cup. I think sadly of all he has given up to be close to me. He, who was always at the centre of a group – playing with the camp's children, playing the drums in the oasis, talking with friends, eating with his family – now lives in this silent house, fights faceless in Yusuf's army and eats alone, perhaps something bought from a stallholder and eaten quickly without the pleasure of company.

I return to my own rooms and call for Adeola and Ekon.

"I have a task for you," I say and tell them what I want of them, leaving them with a generous purse of money.

I visit the hammam where I allow myself to be soaked and scrubbed until I feel newborn. When I return to Amalu's rooms I wear a very simple pale robe and none of my jewellery, but my hair is soft and shining, falling down my back like a great waterfall. My hands and feet and face are marked with henna, in beautiful patterns and the symbols of my people. My body is clean, my skin is soft and hairless. I smell of fine perfumes and the roses from the soap that cleaned my hair. My eyes are outlined with kohl.

I push open the orange door and look about me in awe. The courtyard has been filled with flowering plants and hung all about with lanterns in many colours. A great basin of water ripples in the breeze and sends tiny flower petals scudding across its surface.

"Food will be brought at the appointed hour," says Adeola.

She shows me to a room where a tub of water, cloths and a clean robe await Amalu's return. She gestures to the stairs, scattered with yet more flower petals and I follow her to his bedroom, now lined with wall hangings and fine carpets, his bed draped in soft sheets and colourful blankets. Bright strips of cloth hang at the windows, billowing as though we were back in a tent. More lanterns are hung here, while platters of fresh fruits and little cakes have been placed on two small tables.

We return to the courtyard, where Ekon waits for us. I take a deep breath and feel my eyes fill at what I am about to do.

"I did not know why I bought you, Adeola. I thought it was the heat, that I was foolish to be sentimental. Now I know better. The two of you have been far more than slaves, bound to obey my orders. You have proven yourselves friends to me when I needed you most. There is no way in which I could thank you for what you have done but to give you your freedom, and I do it now."

They stare at me.

I half-laugh, although I can feel tears falling. "You are free," I say. "I have already had documents drawn up, your freedom will be made known and I have left money for you. But I tell you now that you are free. You are no longer my slaves."

Adeola meets my gaze and her own eyes fill with tears. She embraces me and I clasp her tightly to me, our muffled sobs and laughter joining together. When I release her I look to Ekon, who has been watching us, his face solemn. Now he steps forwards until he is almost touching me. I hold out both hands to him but instead he kneels before me.

"You do not have to kneel," I say. "You are no longer a slave."

But Adeola shakes her head. "It is the way of our people," she half-whispers, her eyes still shining with tears as she watches him.

Slowly Ekon bows forward until his head almost touches the ground at my feet. He presses first one cheek and then the other against the cool tiles of the courtyard and I think of the golden sand that clung to his lips when he thanked me in this same way for the purchase of Adeola. When he rises I bow my head to him before I am suddenly embraced, enveloped in his crushing arms, my face buried in his chest which shakes with the violence of his sobs; the years of enslavement he has endured in silence now being released from this most reserved of men.

It takes a while before we are all composed, little bursts of laughter and more tears coming from us as we speak together.

"You must go," I say at last. "Amalu will return soon."

We embrace again and they leave me alone in the courtyard, where I wipe my eyes and try to see myself in the basin of water. Certainly I am not as elegant as I was, the kohl lining my eyes has been somewhat marred by all the tears I have shed but then what I have to say to Amalu is greater than such petty matters.

I find myself a little nervous. I have prepared what I will say to Amalu but what if it is his turn to reject me? I have not been kind to him, I think, yet he has shown me nothing but devotion and care. What if he laughs at my proposition or sends me away? I pace through the tiny courtyard, arrange and then rearrange the flowers to my liking although none of them look right. What looked beautiful when I first saw it now seems too much, a foolish show of affection come too late.

"Kella?"

I spin round, my hands dirty with earth, my face flushed with the effort of lifting a heavy flowerpot. Amalu stands in the doorway of the courtyard, staring at me. For a moment I say nothing, flustered. I had meant to be calm, elegant, clear in what I have to say to him. Instead I am aware that I am sweating from my efforts, my hair is disheveled and my kohl is smeared from the tears I wept earlier.

"Kella?" says Amalu again, coming closer. "What are you doing here? Is something wrong?"

I can't help it. I laugh. "I'm sorry," I gasp. "I meant everything to be perfect and instead..." I gesture helplessly at myself.

Amalu frowns. "What was to be perfect?"

I brush the dirt off my hands and step close to him. "I made a mistake a long time ago," I say. "I mistook freedom for love." Fumbling in my robe I pull out a tiny necklace, black and silver beads intertwined, tiny dangling strips of engraved silver.

Amalu's eyes narrow. "That is a *chachat*," he says.

"It is the engagement necklace you gave me," I say.

"You kept it?"

I nod. "Now I return it to you, Amalu."

His face falls. "No need," he says gruffly, pushing my hand away.

"I have not finished," I say. "You always were impatient."

He waits.

"I return it to you and ask whether you would offer it to me again," I say. My voice wavers.

"I am not sure of your meaning," says Amalu but I see his eyes and the hope that is within them.

"I would marry you," I say. "If you will go away with me from this place."

"Where to?"

"To trade together," I say. "I would like to travel far to the north and east, beyond Al-Andalus, perhaps across the great trade routes to where silk comes from."

"And what is stopping you?"

"You are," I say. "I do not want to go alone. I want to go with you by my side."

"Is it the trading or me you want?" he asks.

"Both," I say honestly.

He laughs a little.

I hold up the tiny necklace again. "It is for you to say," I tell him. "I made the wrong decision. Now I wish to set it right."

"You are married," he says.

I shake my head. "I did not marry for love," I say. "I married for freedom."

"And you have not found it?"

"I am imprisoned," I say. "I would have been better off staying with Aunt Tizemt forever."

He laughs and for a moment his eyes shine with unshed tears.

I wait while he looks down at the *chachat* in his hands. Then slowly he raises his arms and puts it about my neck. I step forward into the circle of his arms as he fastens it and when he is done I lift my face to his and gently unwind the dusty wrap from his face. Veiled, he looks a fierce warrior, unveiled I see a young man, most of his face pale except for the dark brown strip of the sun's heat across his eyes and the scar that crosses his cheek. He looks at me, his whole face serious.

"You could kiss me," I say. "I am your betrothed."

He puts his hands on either side of my face and kisses me so gently I lean forward, wanting more of him, more.

He washes and puts on a clean robe. Food is brought to us by a stallholder as arranged. We sit and feed one another as though we have not eaten for days, lips brushing against fingertips and slowly we begin to speak, not of anything of importance, only the goodness of the food and the colours of the petals all about us, the heat of the day and the cool water we drink. When we have eaten we wash and Amalu takes my hand in his.

"You are my betrothed?" he asks me.

"I am," I say and he leads me to his room.

I am unsure of how we will be together, but my robes fall to the floor and I am not shy, it is as though Amalu and I have been in one another's arms many times before. He is tender to me but our desire grows until our kisses and caresses are fierce and yet still full of love. There is none of the fear I felt when Yusuf drank Zaynab's brew. Instead, we laugh even between passionate kisses, we hold each other tightly even while murmuring endearments, we collapse exhausted even while reaching out for one another again. Afterwards we lie together, the room growing dark as we share the moments we had thought lost.

"I have a secret," I say.

He waits.

"I have a child," I begin. "A son. Yusuf's son."

Amalu props himself up on one elbow, frowning. "But they said... Where?"

"I gave out that he was dead," I say. "But he is not. I gave him to the herb seller."

"From Al-Andalus? The Christian slave woman?"

I nod.

"Why?"

"She was kind," I say. "There was a calm about her. I saw her house, she is no common slave. And I had no-one else to turn to."

"You should have told me. I would have taken him away. I would have taken both of you. He will come with us now."

I shake my head. "He must stay here."

Amalu stares at me. "You wish to leave your son behind?"

I feel tears well up. "No," I say. "It breaks my heart."

"Then bring him."

"I cannot take him away from the only mother he has ever known," I say and the tears begin to fall. "I cannot do that. And besides, he is Yusuf's son."

"Yusuf does not even know he exists."

"He will one day," I say. "I left a sign for him. One day he will know that Ali is his son and he will claim him as his own, as his heir. And then there will be peace."

"Peace?"

"All this endless warfare," I say. "It is not what we had planned."

"We?"

I stroke his face. "Yusuf and I were united by a vision of what the Maghreb might one day be," I say. "Not by love. There was some tenderness between us, but what we saw together was a time when all of the Maghreb would be united and peaceful. When trade could flourish, when great cities could spring up."

He shakes his head. "You expect all this from a babe?"

"When he is grown to be a man and Yusuf makes him his heir," I say, "he will bring peace and prosperity. There will be no more need for war."

Amalu sighs. "There always seems to be a need for war," he says. "I am tired of it."

"We will go away," I say. "You and I. We will travel the trade routes, we will go far to the north and the east, beyond the sea. It will be a great adventure. And we will be together."

"And you will never see your son again?"

I press my head against his chest and let my tears fall. "I will trust in Allah to protect him," I say and feel Amalu's arms embrace me.

We doze for a little while and then Amalu stirs. We light the lanterns, then drink cool water and eat some of the fruit I brought, feeding one another fresh orange dates and tiny red pomegranate seeds, their colours like gems scattered across our bed as we drop them and laugh at one another for our clumsiness. I marvel at the lightness between us, the simplicity of happiness.

"Tell me a story," he says idly.

"A story?"

"Yes. It is dusk and dusk is when the storytellers come to the squares and the people gather to hear a magical tale," he says, biting into a late fig, its delicate pink insides and green-purple skins splitting under his hands.

I shake my head. Then I rise from the bed and stand before him entirely naked. I begin to clap my hands loudly.

He laughs. "What are you doing?"

I point to him. "I will dance for you if you will play for me."

Amalu chuckles and makes himself more comfortable on the cushions. He takes up a little drum from the corner of the room, and begins to beat out a slow rhythm. "Here is your music. Begin, oh most wondrous dancer."

I stand still for a moment, the soft breeze caressing my body. I let my feet begin to move, following the slow beat. My hips undulate and I let my head fall back, my hair whispering from side to side across my back. My hands come up my body, the fingers forming shapes as I dance, a smile growing on my face and on his.

I dance for a long time, the beat growing faster until I can no longer keep pace with it. I fall onto the bed, exhausted, sweat running down my body. Amalu laughs and pats away the drops with a blanket, then pulls me close to him and holds me in his arms again.

"Your turn," I command.

He looks at me in feigned horror. "You want me to dance?"

I nod firmly. "Oh, yes."

He mimicks my movements until I am almost choking with laughter. When he returns to me we laugh together until we subside into weak giggles.

"Sing to me," I suggest.

"I sing like the vultures," he says, making a raucous sound.

"You can tell me a story, then. You must find a way to amuse me after I have danced for you."

"I thought you were amused a moment ago," he says, poking at my belly until I wriggle away. "You could barely breathe for laughing."

"Tell me a story," I insist.

"As you command."

I lie soft in his arms and lose myself in his warm voice.

"There was once a noble young man who loved a princess. She loved him in return and they wished to marry, but her father, the leader of the tribe, was stubborn and thought no suitor was good enough for his daughter. Many men sought the princess's hand, but her father turned them all away. When the suitors attempted to visit the princess by night, her father, a fierce old warrior, devised an extraordinary system of twenty-one locks throughout his palace. Each lock was made by a different locksmith so that there should be no one key that would open all the doors. No one could now reach the princess in her rooms without opening the twenty-one doors and locks that led there."

I open my eyes and look up at Amalu. He smiles and gently closes my eyes again with one fingertip before continuing his story.

"The princess and her young lover were determined that they should be together, and the noble young man was also very clever, and so he went to a silver smith who was his friend and begged him to help them. The smith thought for a long time, and at last he took the two syllables of the word for love: 'ta' and 'ra' and made a shape in poured silver which combined the male and female shapes and the two syllables of the word 'love', making a cross with a circle, a perfect symbol of love. This he gave to the young man, who asked what it should be called. The smith replied '*taneghelt*', meaning melted liquid, for it was in this way that he had made the jewel. The young man paid him well and thanked him profusely, then took the silver piece to the palace wherein his beloved lived.

That night, the young man approached the first door. He touched the lock with the silver jewel and the lock at once melted and the door opened before him. In this way, each of the twenty-one locks opened and when the king came to rouse his daughter the next morning, he found her in the arms of the young man. Astonished at the daring and tenacity of the couple, the father at last gave his blessing to their union."

I smile without opening my eyes. "Was there only one of these magical keys?" I ask, knowing the answer but wanting him to tell me it anyway. His voice is low and tender and I bask in hearing him talk like this, as though we have all the time in the world to spend together, with nothing to worry or threaten us.

"Today there are twenty-one forms of the key, just as there were once twenty-one locks, for different jewellers designed *taneghelt* pendants to their own pleasing. Lovers give these jewels to show that they have the key to one another's hearts."

"And do I have the key to your heart?" I ask him, for I can see that he is hiding something in his hand.

He smiles at my guess. "You know me too well," he says, and gives me a *taneghelt,* slipping it into my hand from his, still warm from his body. I hold it gently in my palm.

"How did you come to have it?"

He shakes his head. "I have had it ever since you came to Murakush. I thought one day to give it to you, to let you know that you still had the key to my heart, though I did not have yours."

I touch the *chachat.* "You had my heart all along," I say. "It was I who did not know you had it."

"I must go now," he tells me. "I must prepare for our departure."

"I will come with you," I say.

He shakes his head. "Sleep," he says. "You will have need of all your strength, for we will have to travel fast to get as far away from here as possible before your absence is noted. Yusuf will not take kindly to his wife running away with one of his soldiers."

"He barely remembers who I am," I say.

"He will remember when you run away," says Amalu. "He will send men after us."

I shake my head. "I doubt it," I say. "Zaynab will be glad I am gone. She will find a way to persuade him not to follow me."

"Not to bring back his own wife?"

"Zaynab always gets her way," I say wearily. "She will be delighted if I leave."

"I wish I was as certain as you are," says Amalu. "Either way, I would like to get far away from here before anyone finds out you are gone."

I nod.

"Sleep, then meet with me. Do you need a camel?"

"I have Thiyya," I say. "She is in the stables, I will find her."

He smiles. "An old friend to accompany you on a new adventure."

I nod and he kisses me very gently on the forehead before leaving. When he is gone I lie back down on the bed and allow relief to wash over me. I will be gone from here soon, I think. I will not have to live in fear. I will travel the trading routes as I once did, with Amalu by my side, knowing that my son is safe. I feel sleep coming and I do not struggle against it, only let its soft embrace comfort me.

I wake to a bitter taste, a wetness on my chin and neck. When I open my eyes Hela is hovering over me, holding a carved wooden cup. I throw out one arm, shoving her away from me and she clutches at the cup to stop what is left of the liquid within it from overflowing, then crouches in a corner of the room, her eyes fixed on me.

I spit the taste from my mouth, a dark bitterness that will not leave me.

"What have you given me?" I ask her but she does not answer.

I grab at the water jar and rinse my mouth again and again, spitting the water onto the floor at her feet. She does not move, only watches me.

"How did you find me?" I ask.

"You were watched," she says. "Zaynab found you growing too free.

Wandering about the souk buying all manner of things, your face no longer sad. She set a watch on you and when they reported back to me I came to find you."

"Why do you serve Zaynab?" I ask. "What possible reason do you have to carry out such dark deeds on her behalf? What hold does she have over you?"

I do not expect her to answer but she half-closes her eyes as though my question wearies her. "It is too long a story," she says.

"Did she threaten you? Did she do something to you?"

"I did something to her," says Hela, her voice almost sing-song. "I did something that can never be forgiven."

"What was it?"

She shakes her head. "Too long a story," she says. "Too long. So long."

I stride across the room and grab at the cup. Startled by the suddenness of my movement, she lets go of it. I pour the liquid on the floor and she holds out her hand. She does not look at the liquid, only at the now-empty cup, as though it is precious.

"Give it back to me."

I draw my arm back and throw the cup at the wall. There is a cracking sound as it hits and when it falls it is in two pieces. I hear a low moan and turn to look at Hela. She is rocking on her heels, her whole body curled up, only her eyes showing, staring at the cup as though seeing something terrible.

"I have a son," I tell her. "He is Yusuf's firstborn son. One day he will make himself known and all your evildoing will have been for nothing."

Hela is not listening to me. She crawls across the room as though I am not there, her robes brushing against my feet, still moaning, a low painful sound. When she reaches the cup she picks up one half in each hand and looks at them, her body still rocking.

"What is the cup to you?" I ask, unnerved. "I threw away what was in it."

She does not answer. She stays crouched against the wall.

I feel faint. "What was in the cup, Hela?" I ask.

She shakes her head. "It does not matter what was in it," she says, her voice husky. "It never matters what is in it."

"Am I going to die?" I ask her. I can feel my heart thudding and I am not sure whether it is from fear or her potion, whatever it was.

She shakes her head. "You broke the cup."

"You put some of the mixture in my mouth while I slept," I persist. "Was it enough to kill me?"

"You broke the cup," she repeats, as though her mouth cannot form any other words.

Her voice and eyes frighten me more than the bitterness in my mouth. Slowly I edge out of the room, expecting her to leap at me, to attack me somehow but she does nothing and I leave her there, still rocking back and forth, her body hunched around the broken cup.

Back in my own rooms I put on a plain robe. A wave of nausea washes over me and I wonder whether I am poisoned, whether Hela's potion was strong enough to kill me or whether I spat it out fast enough. Or perhaps it is only my own fear. I touch Amalu's *taneghelt* and open my casket of jewellery. Even though I should hurry, I cannot help but linger over the contents. I lift up each piece and adorn myself, one by one. Only one piece is missing, the *ismana* long bones.

I think of my little son. All he has left of me is my love.

And a string of silver beads.

Marrakech, Morocco, c.1074

*Y*OU HAVE SEEN EACH OF *my jewels as I have adorned myself. Now you know my journey and how I came to be here.*

The city is quiet. It is dark and only a few torches flicker, making me freeze for a moment when I think I see a person in the shadows, but then all is still and I move again. A drunken guard is snoring. I can smell the orange blossom through the darkness even as I falter beneath the weight of my saddle. One of my jewels slips and falls from my neck but I cannot stop to pick it up. It tinkles as it falls to the ground, but no-one hears me. Zaynab would hear me if she were here, but if she saw me she would say nothing. She would not call for the guards to stop me. Perhaps when I am gone she will be set free from the jealousy that cripples her life.

Outside the camp the camels sigh and make their low groans when they see me. They toss their heads – the day is done, their work is finished, they seem to say – why trouble them now? Can I not sleep like their masters? Only my own camel, my Thiyya, whitest of camels with her strange blue eyes, makes no sound but stares at me coolly as I approach. It is a long time since she was used and she rolls wearily upright, then stands to allow me to fasten the saddle straps. She twitches her head when I put on her head harness but the small silver sounds of the dangling triks *seems to soothe her. I finish my preparations and lean against her for a moment, feeling faint. She looks at me scornfully when I do not climb swiftly up her side as I used to and sinks to the ground again with a soft impatient huff.*

I turn Thiyya to the north and let her walk at her own pace, unhurried and unbothered by the misfortunes or misdeeds of mere mortals. I curl my bare feet into the soft fur of her neck and feel a great weight lift from me. I leave behind my child and doing so leaves a wound in my heart but I believe that he is in safe hands and that my distance will protect him from Zaynab.

A soft glow appears; the rising dawn. The desert spirits whisper around me even as the birds wake. Did our queen, Tin Hinan, come this way once, long ago, on her white camel? Thiyya continues her long slow strides and I face the rising sun a free Tuareg woman, as I was born. My jewels sway with the rhythm of the riding. I hold my head high and then close my eyes to feel the first warmth of the sun touch my face.

I think of my son, of the power he will inherit and the gentleness with which I hope he will rule a peaceful kingdom. I pray for him. I pray that his father will recognise him and claim him for his own when it is safe to do so and that his life will be a happy one. When I open my eyes I see ahead of me the outlines of Amalu, Ekon and Adeola. Behind them stand many loaded camels and Amalu's slaves, ready for the trading routes that we will travel together.

As I draw closer Amalu comes towards me, as though he cannot bear to wait for me to reach them. Thiyya stops by him without my command and I look down on him. His eyes shine with love.

"Not dressed as a man?" he asks.

I shake my head. "I am a free woman," I say. "I have no need to hide."

He nods. "Ekon and Adeola are with us," he says, gesturing to where they stand.

"I set them free," I say.

"They would not leave you," he says. "They travel with us as friends."

"I come to you with nothing," I tell him.

He shakes his head and holds up his arms. "You are everything," he says.

I slip from Thiyya's back and feel his strong arms about me, claiming me for his own at last.

Historical Notes

I have tried to be authentic to the period and setting, incorporating as much of the history as possible, however this particular era has some large gaps in the sources available and so I have allowed myself some storytelling freedom. The idea for this story came from a trip to Morocco, where I loved the traditional jewellery and had the idea for a woman's story told through the individual pieces she gathers over a lifetime. I then began my research into Moroccan history and was fascinated by the Almoravid dynasty.

In 11th century Morocco Abu Bakr bin 'Umar and Yusuf bin Tashfin headed up a holy army, the *al-Mourabitoun*, starting a dynasty of rulers known later as the Almoravids (I have used this later name for simplicity), intent on bringing the country under Islamic rule. Up to this time Morocco, along with Tunisia and Algeria (collectively known as the Maghreb) was primarily a set of tribal Berber states with more or less strict adherence to Islam.

They were successful, taking the important city of Aghmat early on. Abu Bakr married the queen of the city, Zaynab, said to have been a very beautiful and clever woman known as 'the Magician'. When southern tribes rebelled Abu Bakr left both the foundling garrison city of Murakush (modern Marrakesh) and Zaynab to Yusuf (who married her) and went to deal with the tribes. When he returned Zaynab advised Yusuf on how to negotiate keeping his power. They came to an amicable agreement and Abu Bakr went back to the south, leaving Yusuf as commander of the whole army in all but name and Zaynab as his queen consort. My version of Zaynab's story is told in *None Such as She*, while her handmaid Hela's story is told in *The Cup*: a free novella which you can download from my website www. MelissaAddey.com.

Yusuf went on to conquer the whole of Morocco, plus parts of Tunisia and Algeria. When Muslim rulers in Spain asked for his aid he went to Spain and conquered almost all of Spain (this included fighting against El Cid). He died when he was very old. He had been a very religious man who disdained the riches of the world such as fine clothes or elaborate food, and was said to be quite a kindly person.

Although Zaynab is said to have borne Yusuf a lot of children and was most certainly his right hand in ruling the empire, he chose as his heir Ali, the son of a Christian slave woman, who was apparently a favoured wife, called Fadl-al-Husn, or 'Perfection of Beauty'. She could well have been Spanish (Andalusian) and thus would have originally had a Spanish name. I found this odd and I have invented Kella's story to account for this choice. In this series the Christian slave woman is named Isabella and her story is told in *Do Not Awaken Love*, the last of my Moroccan novels.

Ali became ruler when Yusuf died. A very religious man, not given to warfare, Ali held the empire for only part of his life before the Almoravid dynasty was toppled by the Almohads.

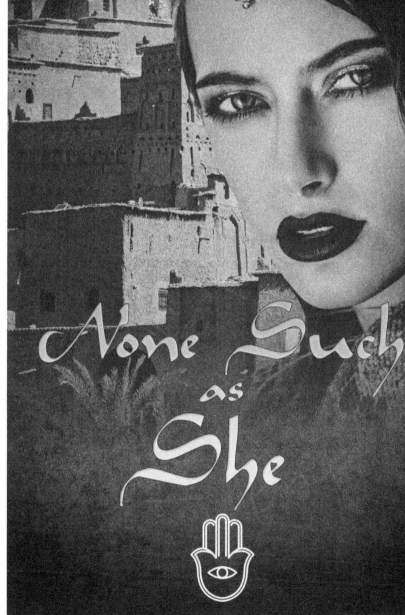

MELISSA ADDEY

None Such

as

She

None Such as She

Dedicated to Rachel Brice, dancer extraordinaire.

After her childhood in Tunisia, Zaynab mostly lived her life amongst the people of North Africa loosely called Berbers (preferred contemporary name, Amazigh). The Berbers belong to many tribes and have various names for themselves, including Tuareg. They are known for their blue indigo-dyed robes and beautiful silver jewellery.

Amongst these peoples it is traditionally the men, not women, who veil their faces.

In her time there was none such as she: none more beautiful or intelligent or witty ... she was married to Yusuf, who built Marrakech for her.

12th-century text Kitab al-Istibsar

Murakush (Marrakech), c. 1102

Walking pains me now. The distance to my rooms seems very great, each step jarring in my withered body.

Here and there I pass serving girls and slaves. They dip their heads in respect as I pass but I do not acknowledge them. I know as I move on that they make secret signs to themselves that they think I do not see. The slaves from the Dark Kingdom clutch at their amulets, hidden under their robes. The Christians make the sign of the cross and touch their crucifixes, amulets all the same. The others make their own gestures, murmur their own little spells of protection. They are afraid of me, as they have been these many years passed. They are so young they cannot even remember a time when I strode rather than shuffled, when my hair rippled down my back and my eyes were bright. But they have heard enough stories from the older servants, from whispers in the bright gardens and murmurs in the dark streets. They believe nonsense about me, believe that I command spirits and djinns.

The door to my rooms is protected by guards who spring forward to open it for me as I approach, heaving on the carved expanse of wood. Servants scatter as I enter and stand, heads bowed, awaiting my orders. When I tell them to leave they hurry to do so, for they have already heard the news, already know what has befallen me. The door swings shut behind them.

I trace the lines of my beloved maps with my fingertips. Every line fought for, every city's name grown great only because of my work and vision.

My legacy, turned to dust.

I open a carved chest that once belonged to Hela. My hands are stiff and pulling the stoppers from the tiny bottles I have chosen is hard.

The mixture smells foetid but I drink it all the same.

The city of Kairouan, Tunisia, c.1050

Daughter

THE SUN IS SINKING AND I am late back from the pools. My nursemaid Myriam is not her usual kindly self. She grabs me as soon as I come in and hustles me upstairs, gripping my arm in a painful way. I try to escape but she will not let me, hissing at me to be quiet and get into my bedroom, *immediately.*

"And wash that filthy mud off your legs!" she adds. "Where have you *been*?"

"The pools," I say as I am bundled, breathless, into my room. Myriam is already throwing open chests while two slave girls who have brought up large buckets of hot water are pouring them into a big basin.

Myriam barely hears me. "Faster!" she snaps at the slave girls and they flee the room with a pile of orders falling over their heads – more water, washing cloths, towels, robes, belts, hair pins. Myriam pulls my clothes off and flings them in a pile, then lifts me bodily into the basin. I stand up to my knees in water while Myriam scrubs me down and then shriek as she starts to brush my hair with none of her usual gentleness. She puts a hand over my mouth to stifle my cries. I squirm and try to bite her hand. This earns me a sharp smack on the legs. I stop shrieking and stand still, in dumbfounded pain. Myriam hardly ever smacks. I cannot even remember the last time she smacked me, but it must be whole years ago.

"What is happening, Myriam?" I ask, through tears of pain. She is still working on the knots in my long hair while the slave girls rush back and forth with everything she asked for. A yank on my head forces it to one side and I see that the robes being laid out for me are new, and the finest I have ever owned. They are very long, and more formal than I usually wear. They are entirely made of silk, a fabric more usually reserved in such quantities for my mother's clothes, and they are of many glorious colours. Myriam is arranging my hair very elegantly. I am going to look like a miniature version of my mother.

"Myriam?"

I try to get her attention but she does not seem willing to share any information with me. She is putting on her outer robes now, preparing to leave the house.

"Where are we going?"

"Engagement," she says without any elaboration.

Well of course I have been to engagements before, but never dressed like this. I would be well dressed, but not so elegantly and expensively. I run through all our family members trying to think who it might be that is getting married, for it must be someone important to us if we are going to all this trouble, but I have heard nothing about this and surely my gossiping aunts would have told me if something so exciting was happening in our own family?

There is no time to ponder this, for Myriam is rushing me back down the stairs. I am just opening my mouth to ask some more questions when I see my mother and father standing by the main door, about to depart. They are surrounded by servants.

My father Ibrahim looks like a prince. He is beautifully dressed and looks very handsome. I cannot help smiling at him, even though I am still confused. He catches sight of me and nods, stretches out his hands to me. I reach him and he holds me at arms' length to examine me.

"Very fine, Zaynab," he says. "The image of your mother."

I look towards my mother Djalila. She is always beautiful, but today she is stunning. Her robes are magnificent. If my father looks like a prince, she looks like a queen. I thought my new robes were grand, but she makes me look like a beggar girl. She is not smiling, however. Her face is pale and still. Beside her stands her handmaiden Hela, who rules our household in my mother's name.

"You are late," says Hela.

Myriam bows her head without speaking.

Hela ignores Myriam's contrite face and turns to the servants. "Ready?"

They all nod. It is only now that I look from one servant to the next and see what they are carrying.

A large jewellery box.

Dried fruits.

A live sheep.

An engagement cake.

I look again, unable to believe what I am seeing. Jewellery. Dried fruits.

The struggling sheep. The cake. These are the gifts that the groom takes to his intended bride on the day of their engagement.

My father is taking a second wife.

My mother has a beautiful mirror in her room. Sometimes when she is occupied elsewhere I snatch a peek at myself in it. My mother does not like anyone going into her room. Only two people are allowed: her personal maidservant Hela, who comes and goes at will. And my father, who makes his way to her rooms only rarely and with a slow tread.

When my mother is not in her room and I am sure no one will find me, I creep close to her mirror and peer at myself. I have long thick hair, although it is always tangled, for I twist and turn under Myriam's hands until she gives up and lets me escape. I have very large dark eyes, which Myriam praises and says are like my mother's. I am not sure she is right. My mother's eyes can gaze at you without blinking for whole minutes, whereas my eyes are always moving, seeking out curiosities and following movements around me. My mother is very still. I have never seen her run or move fast. The same is true for my aunts, but they are fat and like nothing better than to lie on their comfortable cushions and eat sweets and cakes, giggling and quivering with the latest gossip. They are my father's sisters and come often to visit, caressing their brother and praising him. They are polite to my mother but she does not join in with their sticky-fingered whispers. She ensures they have everything they need and then leaves them, retreating to her rooms and the songbirds who flutter in their ornate cages there. The aunts while away long afternoons on their visits, occasionally catching me as I run through our house. When they catch me they crush me to their warm, multicoloured breasts of velvet and silk. Hot roses and jasmine flowers pervade the air around them. They laugh and poke and ask questions, rewarding answers with kisses and tastes of honeyed treats, then let me race away, back to my own games.

The mirror reflects my mother's bedroom, a place of fine colours and rich scents, beautifully arranged objects, which I am not allowed to touch. So I content myself with observing them in the mirror, reaching out through the glass so that I leave each item exactly where I found it, for my mother would surely spot any small changes.

In her mirror I am a small scrawny girl of ten years, with scabbed knees and long dark hair, wide-open eyes and a too-large mouth. I am not yet grown to a woman, but Myriam swears it will not be long now. I do not care. I have no older sisters with whom to compare and find myself wanting. No brothers either. I am my parents' only child.

My father is a carpet merchant, and the carpets from his workshops are much prized. Kairouan is famous for its carpets, and my father's are the best in the city. His workshops are elaborate places, with beautiful intricate paper designs replicated in a thousand thousand tiny knots, tied by the deft hands of women, following the designs created by my laughing aunts. Some of the makers work at home, but many choose to work in my father's workshops where they can chatter amongst themselves as they work. His workshops are refined compared to those of the other crafts – the heavy beating of the copper, the stench of the tanneries, the wet muddy droplets and dust of the potteries. He is a busy man, so I see little of him. Sometimes when Myriam takes me on her shopping trips I visit his workshops where I can stroke the soft carpets as they grow on the looms, but I am not allowed to go to the dirtier workshops in the city.

Our house is large. We have a shaded courtyard filled with a gurgling fountain, flowers and trees. We have slaves, and some servants who carry out the more important household tasks, such as Myriam. It is Myriam who washes me but it is the slaves who heat and carry the heavy buckets of water to my room, they who clean the house, and do the chopping and stirring under the watchful eye of our cook, Hayfa. Our rooms have beautiful carved ceilings, our doors are painted and have marvellous thick handles and bolts in heavy beaten metal which I could not even draw until I was ten. We have great carved chests of perfumed woods in which to keep our belongings, and my father, although he is not a scholar himself, has many books. Sometimes he invites scholars from the great university to eat with us, and then they talk of many things until it is so late that I am falling asleep, and Myriam is summoned to carry me to bed. I am still small for my age and she is like a stocky little donkey, able to carry a great burden with no effort. She hoists me in her arms, whispering kind words so as not to waken me. She carries me to my soft bed and leaves me there till morning. Mostly she spends her time exclaiming in despair because I am always running about the city getting my costly robes dirty and sweaty from the heat and the dust. A girl from a good family like mine should not really be out on the streets.

But there is so much to see, for Kairouan is surely one of the greatest cities in the world! The surrounding lands are fertile and so there are grains, olives as well as great herds of sheep who provide wool, meat and milk. In the souks you can buy anything you want and on the big market days many hundreds of animals are slaughtered to feed the thousands of people who live here. Aside from its glorious carpets, Kairouan is known for its rose oil, which smells very sweet and rich. People say that if you marry a woman from Kairouan she will fill your house with roses and carpets, and it is true, for my mother smells wonderful and our house is full of beautiful soft carpets. Some carpet merchants use only the poorly designed or badly woven carpets for their own house, those that did not turn out as they were intended. My father says that is a poor economy, for when visitors and fine customers come to his house to be entertained they see extraordinary designs and marvel at their intricacy and quality. Then they eat and drink and gaze at my beautiful mother, who reclines in silence on finely-woven cushions in her gloriously coloured robes. The next day they buy many carpets from my father, finer and in greater quantities than they would have done had they not been so well entertained. I usually attend these dinners but the talk is often dull and the customers are old and smack their lips when they eat. Often I make my excuses after dinner and leave them to it. My mother watches me go. Occasionally I wonder if she would like to leave too, but if she is bored she never shows it.

Kairouan is also a very holy city. They say that Oqba found a golden cup in the sand here which he had lost many years before in the Zamzam well in Mecca, so perhaps there was a river flowing between Mecca and Kairouan. The water which comes up in the Bi'r Barouta well here is therefore holy, and if you drink enough of it you are exempted from the visit to Mecca which all good Muslims should undertake. The water is pulled up by a blindfolded camel that goes round and round all day. I watch it sometimes and wonder what it must think, on its endless wheel of walking, unable to see the daylight. Perhaps it is as well that it is blindfolded. If it realised that its journey would never end it might give up its life in despair.

Above all the rooftops towers the minaret of the great mosque. Inside the prayer hall are columns, very many of them. It is forbidden to count them or you will surely be blinded, but the street boys say there are four hundred and fourteen exactly. I have not counted them. Some of the street boys are blind in one eye or both, and it could be that they were the ones who counted the columns. I am not taking any chances. I love to see. Everywhere there are new things to see, especially in the souk. True, I often visit the souk with Myriam, but visiting it alone is different. I can run, I can get lost, I can visit parts of the souk where the shops get darker and smaller and the wares sold are more mysterious. I can stand and stare at the healers and their wares. There are teeth, snake skins, skulls of strange animals, bottles of every shape and size. The healers whisper that they can cure any illness, even ones I have never heard of but which the men and women who sit before them seem to be flustered by when they hear them mentioned. If I stare when I am with Myriam I am quickly dragged away as she tuts at me for my 'morbid fascinations'. Later I return alone to have my fill of staring, slipping out of the gate of my home when no-one is looking.

Although I come from a good family I find the other girls I am expected to spend my time with very dull. They only want to talk of their clothes, and their jewels, and whether their sisters will be married soon. The older ones whisper about boys they like and the younger ones beg to be told their secrets and follow them like unwanted pets, creeping a little closer every time, only to be pushed away when noticed.

I escape whenever I can and run through the city with the street children, who are quick, funny and clever. I take sweet cakes from our kitchen and share them with the greedy boys. Our cook marvels at how I can eat so many cakes and always be so bony, but she likes to feed me. She says our house does not have enough children for her to spoil, and what is the use of cooking for adults, who are too refined to say they enjoyed the food. She likes the way I beg her for treats and how greedily I bite into them. She heaps handfuls on me and I run into the streets and spread their honeyed stickiness across the whole city.

Sometimes we go beyond the city walls to the great pools, the reservoirs of the city. They feed the city so that no one goes without water. Even when there are droughts we can still visit the hammams and our fountains can still play, soothing our heat with their splashing.

The pools are deep. In the centre of the largest is a beautiful pavilion. In the summer evenings the fine men and women of Kairouan come down and sit inside it, enjoying the fresh breeze blown over the cooling water. During the day, though, it is our palace. We play at being great amirs, waving our hands regally at our servants. We take turns being servants or amirs. Those playing amirs think up ever more ridiculous tasks and those playing servants undertake them as badly as possible, moving stupidly slowly or doing the very opposite of what they have been told, so that we all shriek with laughter and even the 'amirs' snort and then hide their mouths so we do not see them losing their dignity. And when I return from my adventures, late as ever, Myriam despairs of me.

Especially today.

We are gradually joined by friends and family as we walk towards the mosque for the sunset prayers. I pretend to pray, but my head is spinning. My father is taking another wife! Who is she? I never heard anything being discussed. I berate myself for not spending more time with the gossiping aunts, who must have known all about these plans. No wonder my mother looks so still, so angry. But she must have given her permission or my father could not have taken another wife. I shudder at the very idea of suggesting such a course of action to my mother. My father must be a braver man than I realised. Who is she? Who is this woman who is brave enough to come into my mother's home and marry my father under her still, dark eyes? I am afraid for her, even though I do not know her name.

By the time prayers are finished and we have made our way outside the mosque there is a huge crowd. Word has spread of the engagement. More and more people join us as they emerge from other mosques or their houses as we stand there, waiting to go to the bride. The sheep, held tightly by two of our servants, has given up struggling and lies quietly on the ground, sadly contemplating its fate.

Now the crowd begins to move. Slowly we walk towards one of the quarters until we come to a door set into a high wall. The crowd is excited. My mother's face is rigid, without expression. My father is his usual reserved self, smiling wryly at some of the more ribald comments from the crowd and waving them away but I notice his left hand moving constantly, clenching and unclenching while his right hand reaches out to pat people's shoulders, to gently steer my mother through the crowded space.

My aunts are at the front of the crowd, and they start to pound on the door.

A laughing voice calls out. "Who is there?"

My aunts answer as one. "We have come to ask if you will give your daughter to be married to Ibrahim an-Nafzawi!"

The crowd cheers.

Of course there is much demurral before we are allowed in. It would not do for the bride's father to seem too eager. More calls, more responses, until finally the door is opened and we are welcomed inside. A great crowd streams in, myself and Myriam getting lost in it so that we fall back from our front-row positions and end up towards the back as we enter the courtyard.

It is a pretty place, not so grand as our own home, but still pleasing to the eye. It is cool and there is a small fountain that splashes merrily. There are fresh-scented trees which later will bear sweet fruits, although right now they are full of small boys who have climbed them to get a better view while the first surah of the Qur'an is recited over the engaged couple.

"In the name of Allah, Most Gracious, Most Merciful. Praise be to Allah The Cherisher and Sustainer of the Worlds; Most Gracious, Most Merciful; Master of the Day of Judgement. Thee do we worship and Thine aid we seek. Show us the straight way, The way of those on whom Thou has bestowed Thy Grace, those whose portion is not wrath, and who go not astray."

I have been craning my neck throughout this instead of paying attention, straining to see my father's new bride, earning myself several digs in the ribs from Myriam. I fail to spot them and now the crowd begins to depart, so we are buffeted here and there by the many moving bodies. I am regularly stopped by those leaving as they wish happiness and prosperity to all members of both families. Many women pinch my cheeks and smile, asking if I am happy with my new aunt. I can only smile and nod, the men patting my head as they pass, muttering blessings. I am hot, tired and hungry, for we have not yet eaten our evening meal. I am grumpy, too. Surely I should have seen this new aunt by now? Why am I at the back of the crowd?

At last the crowd begins to thin a little and I catch my first glimpse of Imen, my father's future wife. She is all curves and blushing smiles, with pink cheeks and bright eyes. She has tiny feet and hands, and stands well under my father's shoulder. I am about the same height and I am only ten. My mother is much taller than her. It is clear Imen is fond of good food and sweet things, and that one day she will attain the quivering mass of my aunties. I am sure my aunties have chosen her for this very reason. Her hair is long and shines silken in the sunset. Although she is shy now, I can see that she does not hold back from affection. She accepts with enthusiasm the many hugs and kisses and blessings as they fall all around her, and she looks truly happy. She even smiles at my mother. My mother looks away.

Our household prepares for the new bride. Rooms are set aside for her and the servants who will come with her. The house is in chaos as new carpets and cushions, drapes and a large bed are carried up to the rooms, which have been cleaned and repainted, their plaster carving and painted ceilings newly touched up. My mother keeps to her rooms, refusing to attend meals. Hela must carry all her meals to her and often they return uneaten. Meanwhile I try to find out more about my future aunt, and why she has come into our lives. The servants' whispers are, as always, most enlightening. I crouch in stairwells near the kitchens where I can hear our cook expounding her theories. Hayfa always has tall tales to tell, and the other servants act as her willing audience.

"*She* didn't give him a son, did she? What did she expect?"

She is always my mother when Hayfa or any of the other servants speak about our family. The other servants nod, their hands full of their appointed tasks but their minds mulling over the new turn of events which is causing all this extra work. The slaves whisper translations to one another of Hayfa's words. Some speak our tongue better than others, and they pass on her speculations to those slaves who have not yet learnt the subtleties of our language. Hayfa approves of this, as it increases her audience, and so she allows suitable pauses for her words to be fully understood. When she sees comprehension dawning on the slaves' faces she continues.

"A man has the right to expect a son," she says wisely. "And Allah knows the poor man has shown patience. One daughter she gave him, just the one child, and she is fully ten now, almost a woman. No sign of another child. That woman takes care of her bedding but I would say it is more than likely that she no longer has her courses."

That woman refers to Hela, my mother's handmaiden. Hela is the same age as my mother. She came with my mother when she was married to my father. I believe she served her family from when my mother was a girl. Hela is devoted to my mother. She takes her duties seriously and stands over her like a guard, always watching, always ready. If my mother is in a room there is a certainty that Hela is close by. You may not see her at first, but she will be there, ready to serve. Where my mother is tall and slender, beautiful and regal in her bearing, Hela is built like a man, with broad shoulders and a thick waist. Not fat, for she would never indulge so much in the pleasures of life to attain such a state, but strong as an ox. Her thick dark hair does not fall down her back as does my mother's, it is wrapped up in a plain dark cloth. When Hayfa talks about Hela she has more than once reminded her listeners that an ox is an excellent worker, loyal and strong, but that should it be badly treated it may well turn on those who torment it and kill them outright.

"And after all," she always finishes triumphantly, "who knows what an ox is thinking?"

This always leads to wise nods around the kitchen. The servants steer clear of Hela. She is not included in their whispers and giggles, she is obeyed without question as a senior servant, but she is not liked. Just as the servants are wary of my mother, so they are wary of Hela, for they know that she is my mother's eyes and ears and that Hela, to all intents and purposes, manages our household.

They approach Hela only when sickness or injury fall upon them. For she is a healer, it is well known. Her hands are sure and certain when a bone must be re-set and her face does not respond when her patients scream with pain as bone grates on bone as she finds its resting place. She knows the properties of many herbs and traders seek her out, coming to our house and asking for her by name to offer her far-flung remedies to add to her collection of tiny boxes and bottles, kept safe in her own room.

She is educated, and this make the other servants distrust her even more. "She *reads*, you know," they say, making faces at one another. "Like a *scholar*." Scholars are men of learning and wisdom, not serving-women.

My mother relies on her. She never has to ask for an item, only to stretch out her hand without even looking, for Hela will always be ready to drop it into her palm. When my mother retreats to her rooms Hela accompanies her, and only she is allowed to speak with her, to bring her food and clothing. The slaves leave water outside the door and it is taken inside by Hela, then left outside again when she has done with bathing my mother. She it is who goes on errands for my mother, walking swift and sure in the mazes of the souk, returning with little packages of this and that, secrets of which we know nothing. When my mother wishes to visit the hammam it is Hela who goes with her to the hot dark rooms to wash her, rub down her fine skin, massage her with delicate oils, comb through her long hair with rose-scented cleansers. I hear them talk to one another sometimes in my mother's rooms, their voices low and hard to overhear, for their words are indistinct. They do not raise their voices, only continue the slow steady murmuring that teases my sharp ears.

The rituals have been going on for days, even weeks by now. There have been meetings, parties, gifts, discussions and the painting of henna in intricate swirls. In just a few days Imen will leave her father's house and come to my father as his bride, her hair crowned in a golden headdress. She will be his new wife, my mother's sister, my aunt. The servants have their own views on this and Hayfa is holding forth again. The slaves' allotted tasks do not seem to be any closer to completion.

"The new one, Imen – she's here to provide a fine strapping boy. Maybe several. I had a look at her the other day when she was in the souk with her mother. A fine girl. Young. Wide hips. Plenty of fat on her." Hayfa outlines this figure with her hands in the air and nods her approval. "Imen will bear him many sons for sure." She lowers her voice slightly. "If *she* lets her."

"What do you mean?" one of the younger servants asks, her eyes wide. The others lean in. I come down two more steps, silently edging closer but still hidden.

Hayfa shakes her head slowly, as one who has seen all manner of things in this wicked world. "Do you think she will stand by and watch?" she asks. "You think she will open her arms and say, 'Oh, sister, welcome to my home. Bear my husband many sons with my blessing!'? Of course not. *I* would not be Imen for all the carpets in Kairouan."

"But what can she do?" This from one of the men.

Hayfa considers. "I don't know," she admits finally. This breaks her storytelling spell. "Back to work, now, all of you standing about here cluttering up my kitchen with your gossip and nonsense."

They begin to disperse. I get ready to make my getaway before any of them come up the stairs. But before I turn away I hear Hayfa as she mutters while scooping out oil from a jar close to me. I hold my breath and press my back against the wall. No-one else hears her but me, and later I will remember what she says and feel a cold river run through me.

"Allah knows I am a good and honest cook, but if I were Imen I would not eat what was laid before me in this house."

I turn and run up the stairs, past my mother's bedroom door and back to my own room.

Imen arrives at last, soft and blushing. She is kind to the servants, who love her at once. She gives few orders, always glancing towards my mother to get her tacit approval for even the most minor of requests. But the servants would find ways to obey her even if my mother withheld her consent, for who would not wish to please such a sweet little mistress, one whose voice of command is gentle and whose smile of thanks is radiant?

Our routine changes. My mother is now absent from most meals. The only meals she attends are the important ones, when there are guests. Then she descends, a princess amongst mere commoners, elegantly dressed, her beauty undimmed. Frequently on these occasions it seems that Imen is indisposed, and does not join us, leaving my mother and father to greet guests as they have always done, as though nothing had changed. But at breakfast it is Imen who sits by my father's side, who passes soft warm bread smeared with honey and butter, who pours tea and whose hair is somewhat dishevelled, her smile tender as my father wishes her a good day before he leaves the house.

At first I stay away from Imen, as my mother does. I think that my mother will be pleased if she comes to hear that I do not care for Imen, that she will see that I am her ally against this newcomer. But my mother stays in her rooms and I find it hard to avoid Imen. When I come to eat breakfast she is there, smiling, offering me sweet orange juice, fresh breads with honey. While I eat she pours herself more tea and stretches back on the cushions to enjoy the dappled sunlight of our courtyard.

"I have something for you, Zaynab," she says one morning.

I look up and see her pointing to a covered basket.

"Open it," she says, her eyes bright.

Inside the basket is a tiny tabby-brown kitten.

"It will need feeding with milk," she says. "It is still so young."

She shows me how to dip a little scrap of cloth into milk and drip it into the kitten's mouth, gives me some soft cloth from the chests in her room to line the basket and make a warm little nest for it. She has the servants bring fresh milk every day in a special container just for the kitten and giggles with me when it grows old enough to explore and is afraid of its own shadow or overbalances on our wall. My mother will not let me feed her songbirds, but Imen strokes my kitten and when I kneel by her side to hear it purr she strokes my hair too, and after a time I forget that I should be my mother's ally, for my mother does not smile whatever I do and Imen laughs so easily, it is easy to laugh with her.

My father has begun to smile when Imen is nearby. He seems happier, walking more slowly, speaking more kindly to the servants. His wrinkles, which were beginning to appear as the years went by, seem to be fading. Once as dusk descended I ran to his rooms to call him for the evening meal and found him buried under a pile of soft giggling silks, which turned out to be Imen, who blushed mightily when she saw me. My father only laughed and kissed her forehead, then rose and came with me to dinner. We had guests that night and Imen sent word that she was unwell and begged to be excused. My father accepted the sympathies of the guests with a charming smile while my mother, by his side as always when we have guests, said nothing.

Sometimes I see Imen drinking from a wooden cup, a faded reddish colour marked with worn carvings. I asked her once what it contained and she lowered her lashes a little and said that she hoped it would help her bear many brothers for me. Then she giggled and chased me round the courtyard with a long feather she had found from the storks who roost on the rooftops of Kairouan, seeking to pin me down and tickle me.

But the liquid in the cup must have worked its magic, for Imen smiles ever more broadly and now my father is very tender with her. Where before my mother ordered our food to her liking and Imen never presumed to countermand her orders, now my father has decreed that all food must be ordered by Imen. Everything must be to her tastes. My mother says nothing but bows her head and is seen even less, spending her days tending to her songbirds, whom I can hear tweeting. All our household now revolves around Imen. She giggles over all the fuss but enjoys her new status, basking in the petting from my aunts and the foods she craves. Sometimes she turns a little pale and clutches at her stomach, sometimes I even hear her retching, and servants hurry to her with clean cloths and fresh cool water, but the aunts only laugh kindly and say everyone must suffer so to bring forth a healthy child and he must be a boy to cause his mother such grief already. Then they offer Imen perfumed drinks to take away the sour taste of bile and fan her as she reclines on the soft cushions by their side. They amuse her with stories and the city's gossip and recite endless permutations of names that might suit my unborn brother. Imen still sips from the carved cup, but now it contains tonics for her baby's health, to make him grow strong within her ever-increasing belly.

"What shall you name him?" I ask.

Imen stretches out her bare toes in the dappled morning light of our garden and yawns. "I think your father has a name for him," she says, smiling. "He said he had kept it for many years for his first-born son."

I look down. "He will be pleased to have a son," I say.

Imen reaches out and pulls me to her. Her pale pink robes enfold me and her body's warmth spreads out from her to me. I tuck my feet under her cushions and lean my head against her.

"He will be grateful to have a kind grown-up daughter who can take good care of a baby brother," she says. "Think how much the baby will love you – a beautiful older sister to follow about and play games with. It is good for children to have brothers and sisters. When we are all old and wrinkled the two of you will be young and strong and will share your festive days together with your own families."

I cannot imagine pretty Imen being old and wrinkled but I smile anyway.

"Perhaps," offers Imen, "you might give a second name to your brother. What is your favourite name for a boy?"

To make her laugh I think up dreadful names, names that sound like they are only fit for a slave or a peasant boy. She laughs until she cries and then she gets the hiccups and I have to bring her water to sip to make them go away.

It is night and I am fully asleep when Myriam shakes me awake. At first she is in my dream, one of the street boys tugging at my sleeve as he shows me new hiding places in the souk's maze of streets. Then I am pulled from my dream and open my eyes in the darkness. I yelp, for Myriam's face, too close to mine and lit by a dim lamp, is like some terrifying djinn, one eye hidden altogether, the other bulging outwards. Then I am awake and puzzled. It is far too dark even for dawn prayers. The light dims as Myriam moves away from me and grabs a plain robe which she throws at me whilst struggling to unroll our prayer mats.

"Pray."

I hold the robe, sit up in bed. "What?"

"Pray!" Myriam hisses back.

She does not raise her voice as she usually would, nor ask me if I need my ears stretching like a donkey to hear her better. She has succeeded in unrolling the mats and is taking her place on one of them.

I climb awkwardly out of bed, pull the robe over my sleep-warmed naked body which is now beginning to tremble in the cool night air, then kneel beside her. "It's not dawn yet," I say crossly. "The call to prayer won't come for *hours*."

Myriam ignores me and begins to pray. I follow along with little grace and much mumbling. I stumble over words that ought to come smoothly, since I have been repeating them for many years and overbalance so that I knock my head too hard on the floor. The prayers seem to go on forever, far longer than usual. At last I see she intends to keep going all night and I stop, sitting back on my heels defiantly.

"I'm not praying anymore unless you tell me why we're praying in the middle of the night."

I think Myriam might ignore me, or yell at me. She does neither. She sits back on her heels and I see her face is streaked with tears. She sits still for a moment or two while the tears roll down her cheeks and then speaks, very low, as though afraid of being overheard. "Imen is ill."

I frown. "She looked well last night when we went to bed."

Myriam shakes her head. "She said she was indisposed."

I shrug. "She always says that when we have guests."

Myriam nods. "But she started to have pains. She thought it was the sickness again."

"I thought that was only at the beginning. She hasn't been sick for ages."

"Yes. She should have told one of us. We would have known something was wrong. She did not know the sickness should not come now. She had pains like knives in her belly." Myriam mumbles something else, which I don't catch.

"What?"

Myriam speaks a little louder. "Blood."

"*Blood*?" Even I know this is not a good sign.

Myriam nods again. "She started to bleed. Her maid got scared and called for help. The doctors are with her. Everyone is awake."

I turn my face towards the door and strain my ears. I have very good hearing, but if everyone is awake then the house seems unnaturally quiet – in the daytime you can barely hear a conversation for all the noise that goes on – clattering pots and pans, feet running up and down stairs, orders being shouted out. Now there is only silence. I look back at Myriam, frowning. "I can't hear anyone."

"They are all praying," she whispers, her face pale in the darkness.

I say nothing, but prostrate myself, the words suddenly coming to me, begging for His kindness, for His mercy, for any help He can offer to Imen as her crimson blood drains away in the darkness and my baby brother's life is lost.

As the cold pale light grows the streets awake. The dawn prayers are called and there is a brief lull before the bustle of the new day begins in earnest. Only our house is quiet. In the coming days we will find ourselves mourning twice over; for my brother who did not even have a name and for Imen, whose gentle nature was not strong enough to withstand the agony that gripped her, nor the tide of blood, which swept her away as though she was dust in the road.

Many, many months pass before our house seems normal again. My mother sits with us at all our meals again, and my father's hair is a little more grey. The rooms that were Imen's are not used for anything, their doors are kept shut and the dust is allowed to settle around the spiders, who rebuild their webs and await any foolish flies who mistake Imen's windows for a true entrance to our house. The flowers Imen had planted around her windows fade and wither, for no-one comes to water them.

I miss Imen. I miss her love of good food and her sleep-ruffled hair. I miss her perfumed robes in pale rippled colours, so different from my mother's dark magnificence. Most of all I miss her giggle, her embraces given without warning or reason, her delight in my father and his happiness with her. He is quiet again now, and I have not seen him smile for a long time.

I sit in a cushioned alcove in our courtyard and rip leaves into small shreds, following their marked-out pathways. There is no-one now to share these mornings with and I am bored.

My father is leaving the house, going to one of his workshops. As he leaves he crosses the path of Hela, who is carrying breakfast to my mother. They see each other and pause, then speak in low voices.

I lean forward to hear them. I am curious, I rarely see them speak to one another. My mother issues all commands to Hela and Hela barely speaks when others are present. My father and she do not pass their time conversing with one another.

"I have spoken with her father." I hear him say.

Hela shakes her head. It is a quick sharp movement, a direct refusal of whatever my father is proposing. A servant should not defy their master, my father would be within his rights to reprimand or even strike her. He does neither, only looks down at his hands.

"There will be only one," says Hela. "You must resign yourself."

"It is not only that," he replies. "It is..." but he does not finish his sentence, he seems unable to find the words.

Hela holds up one hand, the other still balancing my mother's breakfast, now going cold. "There will be no more new wives in this house," she says, and turns, walking away from him into the house, towards my mother's rooms.

My father stands still for a moment, looking down at the tiles of our courtyard. Then he makes his way out of the gates of our home, heading towards his workshops.

Sometimes I still go alone into the souks, but the street boys seem to have grown up all of a sudden. Many now work hard every day, fetching and carrying heavy loads. Some are apprenticed to their fathers or to a trade. By evening they are too tired to come to the great reservoirs and play at servants and amirs, and so I sit alone in the middle of the vast expanse of water and gaze over the side of the pavilion at my rippled reflection.

My face is becoming more like my mother's as time goes by, and I know that people say that I will be a great beauty like her. I gaze at my face in the water and hope that I will still look like a street girl – with untamed hair and a wide smile. But however often I look my hair grows ever faster and more silky, my eyes become wider and darker, my limbs longer and more graceful. I am becoming a woman.

Bride

I AM GROWN TO FULLY FIFTEEN now, and suitors seek my hand almost daily, or so it seems. Their families hope that my mother's beauty, if not her fertility, will have been passed down to me. I know that they whisper that I have all her beauty but that in addition I seem to have rosy cheeks and a warmer smile, that my grandmother on my father's side had more than one fine son and two lovely daughters and that perhaps, therefore, I will not only bring beauty but also bear many children, thus making my desirability complete.

I find it laughable that someone would want to marry me, for I feel like a child playing at dressing-up when I am paraded before would-be husbands or their emissaries. Each night when a guest is due for dinner with us I am dressed beautifully, my hair gleams and yet I am bound to tip over a drink or trip on the long brightly-coloured robes which now drape over every part of my body. I grow clumsy when I am shy, and it makes me shy to be stared at as though I were a delicious course laid at table. Sometimes I have to bite my lips to keep from giggling, and Myriam, who knows what I am thinking, will nudge me or shoot me a warning glance. When she does that I cast my eyes down, which must look delightfully demure to the visiting suitors, but in reality I am only trying not to laugh out loud.

I no longer sit in the reservoir pavilion at dusk, for it would be unseemly for an unmarried fifteen-year-old girl of a good family to wander the streets alone. It was tolerated, barely, when I was a child, but now neither my mother nor father will hear of it, and Myriam no longer makes excuses for me. She is too afraid of what would happen to her if my reputation were in any way damaged. So I can go out only when Myriam will accompany me, and she does not often do so. Besides, I grow weary of walking the streets when so many people watch me walk by and whisper my name to one another, murmuring my heritage, my beauty, my suitability for marriage. They speculate on my suitors, on which man will be chosen for me.

So most days I sit at home, alone and lonely. Sometimes I think I had better hurry up and get married. At least I might have someone to talk to.

It is boring. I am not allowed to cook, only to order the meals if I so wish, but if I venture to the kitchens it makes the servants nervous, for I am no longer a child to be hugged and spoiled with little cakes and tender meats, I am the young mistress of the house, second only to my mother. There are servants to do every possible task. Myriam only gossips about people I have no interest in. I play music and sing sometimes, or dance a little, but it is not much fun alone. All the little girls with whom I was encouraged to play as a child are no longer my friends after I ignored their company and favoured the street children for all those years, and anyway most of them have already been married off. My mother lives her own life with Hela, keeping to her rooms, waited on hand and foot. She emerges when her presence is required but otherwise ignores me entirely. My father is an older, sadder man now. He spends little time in our house except for the evening meals when we have guests, which, as always, are elaborate and elegant. No one ever speaks Imen's name and my memories of her have faded. From her short time in this house I remember only her laughter and the kitten she gave me, who is fat and slow now but still fond of being stroked and whose purr is still loud.

I pass the time watching the sun circle through the sky, being washed and dressed, attending fine meals, thinking up ever more elaborate dishes for the kitchen staff to attempt, watching the birds as they fly above our courtyard. In this last I am joined by the cat, who peers hopefully at them without the slightest chance of ever catching one.

I used to enjoy the heat and cleansing calm of the hammam and went there often to pass the time, but it has lost its charm now that my body is eyed up every time I disrobe. Gnarled old matchmakers sit in the dark corners and their eyes turn on me as soon as I enter, inspecting every part of me, from my hair to my toes. They note how much hair I have on my body, the size of my breasts, the length of my legs, the shape of my toes, the curve of my behind. I am aware that they think I am too thin, but other than that they concur that I have a fine body, well-proportioned and delicate for all my height. They mutter that I ought to eat more fatty meat and rich cakes, but they cannot say that I am not beautiful, and they admit that my mother is also slender and that therefore it may be something I cannot help – this is said in pitying tones, with much shaking of the head and pursed lips.

At first I used to stare in my own mirror and think about what I'd heard them say about me, wonder whether my breasts were the right size to please a future husband and whether I would bear sons easily, but having heard them discuss every other girl my age I know there is no pleasing them, there is always something they will find to tut over – one girl is too tall, another too short, I am too slender and another girl too fat. I have grown resigned to the knowledge that my naked body has been described to all their fellow matchmakers across the land, for their tongues do not lack speed even if their wrinkled old bodies creak and groan when they move from their warm dark corners. It is their descriptions that have brought the suitors to our table, night after night.

The suitors come in all shapes and sizes, and most importantly in all ages and degrees of wealth. There are the young eager ones, who blush more than I do and whose fathers accompany them, their lusting eyes wishing they were choosing a bride for themselves rather than for their sons. There are the wrinkled old ones, scrawny and with missing teeth or with red faces and fat bellies. These leer at me, eat too much and smack their lips. Some are old colleagues of my father's, who talk shop all during the meal, either barely glancing my way or else looking at me as they would at a fine carpet, expertly counting knots at a glance. When they look at me I see them counting up my assets – long silken hair, fine limbs, elegant features of the face, well-to-do family. Then they turn back to my father and the talks continue, bartering over prices – mine or the carpets, I am never quite sure. I am only another commodity, I suppose. For all the tales of great loves that Myriam is so fond of hearing from the storytellers in the marketplaces, I can't quite imagine any of these suitors inspiring any such feeling in me. There are a few rather touching ones, who have fallen in love – or lust – at first sight, and who return night after night, seeking to sway my father's opinion. They cannot take their gaze from my face, which grows wearisome when I want to bite hungrily into a piece of chicken or when something has become stuck in my teeth. I suffer them in silence and leave as soon as I can. In this way the poor love-stricken men see less of me than those who do not much care whom they marry, so long as the woman is attractive and of a good family.

They are all well off, of course, or they would not even attempt my hand. Even so, there are those who are sons of chiefs and amirs or indeed chiefs and amirs in their own right. The amirs, of course, do not come themselves. They send emissaries, wily men who look me up and down and mentally catalogue me alongside the other beauties they have seen on their travels to find the next queen of a grand city, the next wife for a rich and important ruler. They wonder how much favour I will bring them at a distant court if they bring me back to their lord.

The chiefs sometimes come themselves, unwilling to trust someone else's judgement. These are men who have fought for their chiefdoms, warriors, who trust no-one but their own sharp eyes and strong arms in battle. They are a little ill at ease in my father's house, full of rich carpets and fine foods. They are used to plainer fare and simple clothes, to sitting amongst men, not being joined for an elaborate dinner by women dressed in fine robes and jewels like my mother and me. Of course with my mother's past history the chiefs are often a little wary about my fertility. A son is everything to them, and if I should fail to provide one then all the beauty in the world would not be sufficient to entice them.

I could have been married a good year ago, for there have been plenty of suitors to choose from and many fine offers have been made. But my father delays my future marriage. He raises objections to the suitors, regarding their lineage, their wealth, their distance from our own city. And so the talks go on and on and yet more visitors come to our table. Word spreads, of course, that many have sought my hand and been turned away, and all this does is increase my value, my desirability. As time goes by only chiefs and amirs make their advances, their sons no longer deeming themselves worthy. The merchants, meanwhile, have long since fallen by the wayside, however rich they are. What at first seemed rather exciting – the idea of being wooed and married – has come to seem tedious and unlikely ever to actually happen.

Tonight my father has decided that for a change he will have an evening that does not feature a fawning suitor for my hand. He declares he is weary of the same conversations night after night. Myriam is happy, for she can go and visit her friends and not spend the evening beautifying me. Tonight my father has a customer for carpets. His name is Yusuf bin Ali, the chief of the Wurika and Aylana tribes, whose boundaries are close to the great city of Aghmat, very far to the South West. There he lives in a *ksar*, one of the fortified cities of the desert-dwellers. It is for his own home that he comes to buy carpets, but my father is keen to strike up a good trade with him, for it is known that he travels much and is a friend of many important men, including the amir of Aghmat and so if he should like my father's carpets it may well be that my father can expect patronage from the amir also.

I beg leave from the table. I, too, am weary of the grand banquets. I would like to be left alone, especially as this Yusuf has no interest in me – he has come to see carpets, not seek a bride. My father grants me permission to be absent. The servants can bring food to my rooms when I am hungry and I will have an evening to do as I please, an evening when I will not be stared at. I dress in my favourite robe, originally a stiff bright yellow silk for formal occasions, which over time has worn to a pale glow, soft and comfortable. I leave it loose. To be without jewels and heavy constricting belts is a relief. My hair falls free, untied and uncovered. My feet are bare. I lie on my bed playing with my cat, who enjoys sitting on me if I lie obediently still while she closes her eyes in happiness, gently kneading my stomach. Unlike other cats she remembers to sheath her claws and so the experience is a pleasant one and my robe is not pierced. I tickle her ears and sing to her, which is difficult when lying on your back with a heavy cat on your belly, but I try anyway and she purrs in sleepy contentment.

I awake in darkness and realise I must have slept for many hours. I had not realised how tired I was, nor how pleasant it is to sleep with a light stomach, albeit one topped with a heavy cat, rather than an uncomfortably full one. But now I am hungry and the house is quiet. The dinner must have finished some time ago and our guest will have gone away satisfied with his bartering and our generous table. Now everyone is asleep. If I creep quietly downstairs I will disturb no-one. In the kitchen there will be leftovers – fresh bread, olives, figs and butter. There may even be meat. My stomach grumbles. I set the cat aside. She keep her eyes shut and growls, annoyed at my having the audacity to move when she is still deep in slumber. I open the heavy wooden door of my room and make my way down the stairs.

In the kitchen I find everything I could wish for and prepare a plate of good food, my stomach making happy gurgles as it senses the smells around me. I dip into a large jar for fresh cool water and then decide to eat in our courtyard rather than upstairs. The night air is still warm and our courtyard is always a pleasant place, full of pale scented flowers in the darkness. My eyes have grown used to the night and I make my way to a low bench set into an alcove in the wall. I place the plate beside me, then eat hungrily. It feels good to sit here all alone and eat with real hunger rather than a false dainty refinement. My fingers get oily and I lick them clean and then continue to eat.

"What an appetite you have." The voice is a man's, low and amused.

I would scream but my mouth is full of bread and meat. I gulp and my throat hurts as the half-chewed food is forced down. I peer into the darkness. A shadow moves slightly in the alcove opposite me in the courtyard.

"If you come near me I will scream," I say. My voice trembles. I do not sound very threatening.

I hear a chuckle. I relax a little since the speaker has not yet moved from their bench. I consider running upstairs, but this would mean running past the man and I do not have the courage. I shrink back into the alcove.

"I would not dream of coming near the daughter of the house without her express permission."

"How do you know I am the daughter of the house?"

"Your robes sound like silk. You just helped yourself to food in the kitchens. If you were a servant girl you would be whipped if you were caught. Besides, a servant girl would not threaten a guest."

My shoulders drop with relief. I make my own deduction. "You are Yusuf bin Ali, my father's visitor."

I hear a slow, soft clap. "Very good."

"I thought you were only here for dinner."

"It got late. Your father is a kind host. He invited me to stay the night."

"On a bench in our courtyard?"

He laughs again. I am beginning to like his laughter, it is slow, as though he has all night to laugh. I do not often hear such laughter in our house. Besides, he is my father's guest, so he is not going to attack me after all. I am safe. "I bought many carpets. I think your father thought I was worth a room at least."

"Why are you not in it, then?"

"Too hot. I wanted some fresh night air as the day cooled."

We sit in silence for a while, on our opposite sides of the courtyard. When he speaks again I realise I have been waiting for him to do so. I like the way he speaks, unhurried, how I can hear his smile even in the dark. "Why did you not attend dinner?"

"I wanted a night without a banquet."

"Do you have so many fine meals then?"

"Yes."

"Always customers for your father's carpets?"

"No."

"What then?"

I am unwilling to tell him. It sounds like boasting. I mumble my words.

"What did you say?"

"Suitors."

"Suitors? Who for?"

"Me, of course," I say, a little indignantly. I did not want to boast but neither do I like his tone of surprise.

"How old are you?"

"Sixteen."

"Surely not."

"Why not?" I am put out, he sounds as though he thought I was merely a child to be entertained.

The shadows move. I hear him walk towards me. I should leave, of course, should not let a strange man approach me in the darkness, even if he is my father's guest, but I am curious. Why does he not believe I am sixteen? He comes closer and I move to one end of my bench. He comes close enough to be facing me were I standing and then stops, a tall form stood over me. I can smell him, a warm scent, of smoke and camels, a masculine smell tempered with a fleeting sweet perfume, something like orange blossoms. His robes seem to be dark. His face is mostly covered with a thick veil wrapped round his head, in the manner of tribesmen from the South. I can hear my own heart beating and my breathing seems very loud. I try to quiet it by breathing very lightly.

"You're very quiet," he says.

I breathe out more heavily, relieved that he cannot hear me breathing after all.

"Why are you sighing?" he asks.

I stop breathing altogether.

He sits down alongside me on the bench, although he is at the far end. If I were to reach out my hand I would just be able to touch him.

I tuck my hands into the sleeves of my robes and start to breathe again, but very quietly.

"So, these suitors," he says. He sounds as if he would like to laugh, as though he is talking to a child about a make-believe friend.

I feel myself stiffen with pride. "What about them?"

"Who are they?"

I will ensure he is impressed. He cannot fail to be. My suitors are the talk of Kairouan. "Amirs, mostly."

I hear him barely suppress a snort of laughter. "Really."

"Yes, really. Lots of them. They come practically every night, from all over the Maghreb. Asking for my hand." I know that I sound like a boastful child.

"How nice for you."

"Not really," I admit reluctantly.

"No? Why ever not? Lots of rich important men begging for your hand in marriage? I would have thought that was what every girl wanted."

"No."

"Why not?"

I struggle to explain. "They look at me… I have to dress up… they don't talk like…"

"Don't talk like what?"

"Like – like you." My face burns, I did not mean to say that at all. My toes clench.

His voice is softer, curious. He leans forward a little, trying to make out my features in the darkness. "Like me? How do I talk, then?"

"Properly."

"Properly?"

I squirm. But I have to explain now or he will think I am a mad babbling fool. Once I explain he will understand and I will not look like a fool. "You just – talk to me. Like a person. Like people who know me well. The suitors don't. They sit there and eat for hours, they talk to my father about boring things and sometimes they say polite things to my mother. They look at me as if I was a sweet cake but they don't talk to me. Just words that don't mean anything."

"Like what?"

"Like how gracious and beautiful I am."

He leans back, chuckling. "I'm sure you are."

I struggle on with my explanation. "No – not even as if they meant it. Just things you *say*, all formal and like a story. You know, 'the lady Zaynab, whose form is most lovely unto the eye and whose beauty must make the very birds of the air fly closer that they might see her better…' that sort of thing. They don't *mean* it. They just say it because you have to when you're asking for a girl's hand in marriage."

"Do you?"

"Yes."

He laughs out loud. "I shall remember that when I am next looking for a wife."

I laugh, but he suddenly stands up and I press back against the wall. He turns and walks away without another word. I want to follow him, want to say something else, although I am not sure what. A good-bye at least, it seems very rude for him to walk away without bidding me farewell. I get up too fast and my forgotten brass plate of half-eaten food crashes to the tiled floor. I gasp at the loudness of it and hear him chuckle as he goes up the stairs.

I stand all alone in the dark courtyard and breathe.

Myriam is grumpy and surprised when I wake her in the morning. It is usually she who wakes me, dragging me from my warm bed to say my prayers. Then I often return to my bed, asking for food to be brought to me, much to Myriam's disgust at my lazy ways. This morning I have already prepared our mats and as soon as prayers are over I run to my chests and pull out one of my finest robes, a rich pink silk with so much embroidery that it weighs as much as a heavy water jar. I normally object to wearing such clothes, complaining that they are too heavy and cumbersome, too formal for anything but a wedding perhaps. Now I insist on being washed, perfumed, and dressed not only in the robe but in all the additional items that go with it. Fine slippers, a heavy ornamental belt, a great deal of jewellery. I even kneel in front of my mirror and darken my eyes with kohl, put red stains on my lips and cheeks. I stand, satisfied, as Myriam holds up the mirror. I look much older than sixteen, and very beautiful, even I can see that. I turn this way and that, admiring myself, my cheeks growing pinker.

Myriam is perplexed. "Where are you going dressed like that?"

"Breakfast."

Myriam snorts. "Nobody dresses like that for breakfast. You look like you are going to a wedding." She considers my outfit for another moment. "In fact you look like you are the *bride*. You only need the gold headdress."

I smile a huge smile at her and walk slowly, gracefully, downstairs. This will show him. My clothes, bearing and beauty will show him that I am quite old enough to be married, that of *course* I have suitors clamouring for my hand. Last night he teased me as though I were a child, and then left without even having the manners to say goodbye. I am not a child, and now he will see this for himself. He will be obliged to behave better to me, more appropriately. He will have to notice that I am beautiful when I am dressed like this. The darkness was not my friend last night. I do not even know what he looks like, only how he laughs and the sound of his low voice.

My father is sat at a table in our courtyard, together with Yusuf bin Ali. I am relieved that my mother is not with them, she would only look at me with her unblinking eyes in a way that always makes me awkward and clumsy.

I stand for a moment and observe them before I make my presence known. I want to see this man who was so funny and interesting last night but who then walked away without even bidding me farewell. In the darkness he was only a shadow, a low, laughing voice and a scent that I would recognise anywhere if I smelt it again. Now I can see him by daylight.

He is tall, even sitting down he is taller than my father and I can see that he has long legs under his robes. His hair and eyes are very dark and he has strong thick brows. Much of his face is hidden, but his robes fall back from his arms as he raises a cup of tea to his lips and I see his forearms, which are thick with muscles. By his side lies a large sword, sheathed in a magnificent scabbard. He is a warrior, there can be no doubt about that. He must have fought for his chiefdom.

My father hears me coming and hears the servants ask me what I would like to eat. He has not yet seen me as I approach behind his back. Yusuf, however, can see me, for he sits facing my father. His eyes take in my appearance. I wait for his eyes to widen, for him to smile, as all my suitors, even the old and ugly ones, have always done. I am disappointed. He only raises his eyebrows, rises to his feet and bows politely. I might as well be an honoured and wrinkled old grandmother, hobbling to the table to suck toothlessly at some soft bread.

"It is an honour to meet the daughter of the house," he says without a trace of recognition or interest.

My father catches sight of me and looks surprised, but then waves me to a seat by him. "My daughter, Zaynab," he introduces me. "Very elegant, I am sure," he adds as he knits his brows at my clothes. He turns back to Yusuf. "Girls, you know, they do so like to dress up at their age." He pats my shoulder, not unkindly.

I am crushed. I sit at the table for another hour, eating a few mouthfuls and listening to my father and Yusuf discussing carpets – the patterns, knots, their transportation back to Yusuf's home. Payment, it seems, has already been dealt with. Yusuf pays no attention to me at all and I gradually lose my elegant posture and end up sitting slumped against cushions, stroking my lazy cat who is seeking comfort. When the time comes for Yusuf to leave I do not bother to stand up. He bows perfunctorily in my direction and leaves with my father for the workshops.

So he is gone. A rude man after all, certainly he seemed pleasant at first but his manners were very unrefined. I shall not have to see him again, so that is a good thing. I walk slowly back to my room and snap at Myriam to take off these hot heavy clothes, which she does without any expression on her face, for which I am grateful. I spend the rest of the day seeking out something to do and end up getting in all the servants' way as they try to complete their daily chores. Eventually I retire to my room and sit staring out at the sky until I fall asleep with boredom.

Tonight we have guests, not suitors but friends of my father's. There will be many of them, so I will be able to leave earlier. It would be rude to leave when there are just a few of us, but when we are many I can often sneak away. I do not wish to draw attention to myself when I escape so I discard almost all the robes Myriam offers, choosing the very plainest of my elegant robes, a dark blue silk, refuse most of my jewellery and present myself downstairs.

He is there. Yusuf. Talking and laughing with my father and his friends as though he has known them all for years. At ease, confident, full of charm and good humour. I keep well away from him, for the very sight of him makes me feel quite ill – why do I have to endure his presence again? He has behaved very rudely to me, so I will have nothing to do with him. Luckily he does not once look in my direction and I keep very close to my mother who eyes me with some surprise, for we do not generally spend much time together. But she tolerates me near her and when we have eaten and everyone has settled back to talk, replete with good food, I start to edge my way to the door. I creep outside and then breathe with relief and make my way up to my room. Inside I kick off my shoes, then decide to slip outside and sit by our fountain where it will be cooler.

"Was the company not to your liking?"

Yusuf is standing right outside my door. I yelp and leap backwards, slamming the door in his face. I lean against it, wondering what on earth he is doing. I can hear him laughing, not the low chuckle from the other night but a full belly-laugh. I open the door again in a temper. "Get away from my door! How dare you come near me again after your behaviour?"

He stops laughing and considers me carefully, as though surprised. "What behaviour?"

I am spluttering with indignation. The door opens wider as I enumerate his failings. "You made fun of me when we first met and then walked off without saying goodbye. Then you acted as though you'd never seen me before at the breakfast table and treated me like some old woman instead of..." Words fail me. "Well, anyway... and then you went off again really quite rudely, and then tonight, you barely looked at me."

He puts one hand on the doorframe and leans towards me. His face is close to mine and I breathe in his scent without realising it. His voice is low. "Did you want me to look at you?"

"No!" I say automatically, then stop. "I just..."

He looks at me and then reaches out one hand and cups my face very gently. "Lovely Zaynab," he says. His voice is so low that afterwards I am not sure that he really says what he does, although I cannot stop repeating it in my mind. "So very lovely. Do the birds really fly closer to the earth the better to see you?"

I do not know what to say or do except close my eyes that I might hear his words better. I feel his breath caress my cheek. Then there is silence. When I open my eyes again he is gone.

He comes again though, night after night, talking and laughing with my father, who enjoys his company. His trading in the city will be over soon but while he remains in Kairouan he is my father's guest, for my father will not hear of him going elsewhere in the evenings. Often he stays the night as well and I have to face him at breakfast. He is unfailingly courteous and charming to me, but he never again comes to the door of my bedroom, no matter how many times I try to tempt him by sneaking away in full sight of him as I did that night.

I burn for him. I had not known this was possible. I have liked boys, thought them brave or funny, clever or handsome, but I did not know one person could feel so much and not die. How to contain such feeling? I breathe and think of him. I sleep and dream of him. I spend some days in tears because he did not glance my way the night before, other days in ecstasy because he looked my way and smiled, because he passed me soft bread at breakfast and our fingers brushed together. I am being consumed by this man and he has barely touched me. I cannot even think of his doing so, for I become dizzy and have to lie on my bed, covering my face with my robes for shame.

The dark heat of the hammams is intolerable to me now, for I have heat running through me. I crave coolness. I dip my hands in our fountain, wipe my face with damp cloths ten times a day. I try to write a poem for him and burn my attempts, for they are laughable. I write him letters which I could never send for I have not the courage.

Myriam tuts and shakes her head. I cannot fool her for she knows me too well. I try to eat and leave all untouched. I grow thinner and Myriam mutters about no girl having ever been chosen as a bride who was so skinny. I try harder to eat, chewing and swallowing with disgust, feeling the food slip down me with nowhere to settle in my churning stomach.

When he enters the room I become very still, but every part of me knows where he is, even when my eyes remain fixed on another face. While I speak calmly of inconsequential things my mouth grows dry and I feel the heat flow through me as he moves into my field of vision. When he looks my way and does not even see me I move slightly to try and draw his eyes, a foolish gazelle drawing the gaze of the lion, longing for a crushing bite to drain my too-hot blood, to leave me cool and free of such emotion. When he leaves I make my excuses and leave also, that I might run up every step in our house to the roof and, panting, seek out his shape in the courtyard below as he goes to the rooms set aside for him. When he is out of my sight I often go to my room and fall asleep in exhaustion, a mere few hours of his presence too much to bear.

He is going home.

I will die, I know it. Although he spoke my name so low, although he called me lovely he has said nothing like that since then. He smiles occasionally, he attends all my father's gatherings but he does not spend his time with me. He does not speak with me even though I creep closer to the men as they talk and hope to be included in their conversations. When my father notices me he pats me gently and says a few words to me, but the men do not wish to talk with me. They admire my beauty but have no inclination to discuss their business with a girl.

He is heading back to his home, his tribe near to Aghmat, far to the

South West, many many days' journey away. I do not know how to bear it. I may never see him again and if I do I will be married, fat and old. I will have many children and he will glance my way but once and then turn away to speak with my even older husband who will smack his lips while he eats.

It is night-time and the guests are leaving. I am exhausted from crying half the day and sitting for hours through dull conversation. I see Yusuf leave the room and the tiredness takes away all my inhibitions. I follow him without muffling my steps, without disguising my presence from him. He does not turn his head, nor acknowledge my presence until we are outside his door. Then he turns to me and leans back against the heavy painted door. He smiles at me wearily. He looks older than he is, his eyes are soft with a pained tenderness. "Zaynab."

"Yusuf." We gaze at one another for many moments. He is about to speak but I hold up a hand to stop him. My heart does not race. My breath is even. I have to speak now or it will be too late. "Take me with you."

He raises his eyebrows but says nothing. I press on. "I love you. I want to be your wife."

His gaze is steady.

"Take me with you." I cannot help a pleading note entering my voice.

"You have your pick of any husband in the Maghreb. And you have a home here which you should not be so anxious to leave."

I frown at him. "This is not a happy home. The men I am offered as husbands disgust me."

"What makes you think I care for you?"

My face burns but I will not be dissuaded. "I love you. That is enough."

"Is it?"

"Yes."

"Even if I never love you?"

"I will love you. And that will be enough."

He looks at me and reaches out with great gentleness. His hand cups my cheek. "Oh, Zaynab," he says and if I were older, wiser, I would hear a great sorrow in his voice.

I close my eyes and listen for the words of love that are sure to follow. They come in a soft whisper.

"How wrong you are."

I open my eyes but he has slipped inside his room and I am left staring at the painted panels of flowers.

Myriam orders me to visit the hammam. I have not been for weeks, washing only in cold water at home. I do not wish to go. The dark fills my mind with sensual images, the heat is stifling, any touch on my skin, no matter from whom, is too intimate to bear. Myriam sets her lips firm and insists. I cannot argue, it is too much emotion on top of what I already feel. I go with her.

In the dim light she scrubs my body until I am sure I have no skin left, combs the knots from my dripping hair. She rubs me with perfumed oils as I complain about the heat and beg for us to return home. Only when she is all finished does she allow me to go to the coolest part of the room I can find and begins her own ablutions.

"I want to go home," I moan at her. "It's so *hot.* "

"You don't want to go home," says Myriam indistinctly from under a steady stream of hot water.

"I do," I insist.

"You need to stay here," says Myriam firmly as she rubs her skin with a rough cloth.

"Why?" I complain.

"Your father and Yusuf bin Ali need to speak and they do not need you wandering into the room."

I catch my breath. My heart flutters rather than beating as it should and I put one hand over it, for it feels very weak. "What are they talking about?"

Myriam finishes pouring water over herself and flicks back her wet hair. Her voice is flat. "He wants you for his wife."

I scream with joy. Every part of me is full of life, of happiness.

"Hush!" Myriam hurries over to silence me, nearly slipping on the wet floor. "What will people think?"

I escape her pinning arms and dance around the room, wet and happy. "He is asking for my hand? This very minute? *Now?*"

Myriam nods and starts to comb her hair. She does not seem very pleased.

"Aren't you happy for me?" I demand, sitting next to her again.

She looks doubtful. "I know you like him, Zaynab, but your father is not so sure about the marriage. You will live so far away. And you know so little about him."

Nothing can make me downcast. "I will be with him. I will learn all there is to know. I will be so happy, Myriam!"

Myriam rolls her eyes but this does not dampen me. I am carried away with my fantasies. I will be with Yusuf, and despite his protestations he will love me... my body grows flushed at the thought.

My father is overly formal when he tells me. I can barely stand still before him when I am summoned. Myriam stands behind me, having reminded me all the way to his rooms to behave with dignity.

"You are to be married, Zaynab. You will marry Yusuf bin Ali, chief of the Wurika and Aylana tribes close to the great city of Aghmat. Your mother and I have agreed that you may be married immediately, for your husband-to-be needs to return to his people and it has been decided that you will accompany him when he leaves here."

I am so happy that I do not even ask the obvious question and it is Myriam who asks it on my behalf.

"When is the marriage to take place?"

"In three days' time."

Myriam and I gasp together. This is unheard of. What about the rituals, the wooing, the prayers, the feasts? No-one gets married so fast. Myriam opens her mouth but my father is already speaking again and Myriam reluctantly closes it again.

"It is very fast of course but your husband-to-be leaves in four days and he insists that you should go with him. Fortunately all can be arranged for the ceremony and as for feasts and so on – " he waves his hand dismissively "– that can all happen at his home. You have many fine clothes and jewels and I will arrange that many more be made for you in the few days that we have left to us. Other things can be sent on. You will not go to him as a beggar."

Myriam and I open our mouths again but my father is still speaking, a frown on his face.

"I need to know that you desire this union, Zaynab. I will not force you into a marriage."

"Oh yes," I stammer, over-eager to agree. "Yes, I desire – I mean – I wish to be married to Yusuf."

He nods and then opens his mouth as though he were about to say something else, but then he shakes his head. "Very well," he says. "So be it."

With this he leaves the room, and Myriam and I are left dumbfounded, our two mouths still soundlessly shaping questions to the empty doorway.

In the days that follow all is strange to me. Servants rush to and fro, Myriam barely speaks to me except to tell me what I must do next, and all around us is chaos. My mother disappears entirely and it is Hela who commands what must be done, as usual. Clothes and jewels must be made. I stand before the mirror for only a moment in each outfit, barely turning this way and that before they are folded away in great chests, household goods and animals bartered for then readied for the long journey which we will undertake. One carpet after another is brought from my father's workshops and added to the pile of goods I will be taking with me to my new husband's home.

My husband! We have been married, but it has been so quick I do not even feel myself to be a wife and all the wild joy I felt at the news that I would marry this man who has consumed me has almost been thrown aside in all the hurry and the strangeness of the preparations. The words were spoken, the prayers said over our two bowed heads, mine heavy from the golden headpiece that every bride wears. There was even a feast, albeit a very minor one considering what it would have been like had the marriage not been so hasty.

I will not lie with him until we are in his home, so I am only a wife in name, not deed. I am almost grateful for this. No matter how much I wished for his touch I was afraid too, and all was done so fast I should have trembled had he come to me that night. But I am showered with good wishes and many young women of our city and their mothers smile at me most tenderly, for now I am married all those who once sought my hand may be inclined to look elsewhere.

The day of our departure has come. Prayers are said in almost-darkness and it is cold. I am wrapped in layers of clothes that I can gradually remove without losing any modesty as the sun grows hotter. Veils will cover my face from the heat of the day. There is a whole caravan of camels ready to take me and my possessions to my new home – along with those other animals that will come with us – sheep and goats, their lambs and kids bouncing along merrily for now although they will surely be weary by the time we reach our destination. As will we all. We will leave here now and join Yusuf's caravan near the outskirts of the city, before our long journey together begins.

And it is only now, after four days of madness, that I realise that I am leaving my father's home forever, and that I will live very, very far away. Only now that I look around me and realise that these familiar faces will be replaced by strangers and that I will be alone.

My mother is very pale. She kisses me and murmurs appropriate blessings, but she bites her lips repeatedly and steps back from me quickly.

Myriam is beside herself. It has been decided that I will not take servants, Yusuf will provide for me. My loving nursemaid weeps and weeps, her tears more than enough for a hundred mothers. We embrace tightly and my shoulders and cheeks are wet with tears, hers and mine.

She steps away only when my father approaches me, his face creased in a frown. "Are you truly happy, Zaynab? You have only to say the word and I will stop all of this."

I am crying but manage to smile. It comes out as more of a grimace but I need him to know that I am happy, despite appearances. "I am so happy to marry Yusuf, Father, but so sorry to leave you."

He nods and embraces me again, his voice warm against me. "Dearest Zaynab. Dearest daughter. I wish you a lifetime of happiness and no sorrows to blight your days. I know that you marry for love and I pray Allah brings you nothing but love in your life. And she will be gone one day, so have no fears."

I pull back to see his face, puzzled. "Who will be gone?"

He hushes me. "You are a beautiful girl. Young, warm-hearted. He has five healthy sons and now he will have you. In due course it will be as though they were your own sons and he will love you as you love him."

My many layers of clothes are too hot. I step away from him and remove my heavy outer robe, blindly letting it drop, saved from the dust only by a quick-witted servant. There is sweat springing up on my upper lip and under my eyes, running between my breasts and making my hands wet. I clench and open my hands hoping for the cold morning air to dry them. My throat, however, is already dry. When I speak my voice croaks. "Sons? He has a *wife*?"

My father opens his mouth to speak but already hands are lifting me onto a high wooden saddle, covered in soft cloths to make a comfortable seat. I keep my face turned towards my father, who stands in silence. I try to shape a question but my lips are too dry. The camels turn and we begin to move. Myriam's sobs grow louder and I look back to see my father and mother watching me as I leave.

Behind them, in the doorway of our house, Hela stands alone, a dark outline caught in the rays of the rising sun.

Concubine

MANY AND MANY HOURS OF travel go by, many and many days. The sun beats down by day, the cold nights make us shiver even in our thickest robes and the tents which are erected for us each night by the servants do little to protect us from either heat or cold. Yusuf travels far ahead of us with his men by his side. The servants are unknown to me, some speaking strange tongues, all belonging to a different land, a different household. I speak to no-one and no-one speaks to me.

I am grateful for the silence outside of me, for inside there are too many voices. I do not see the landscape change as we sway onwards, nor seek out new sights and sounds as we pass through foreign lands. My body is very still save for the movement of my camel and my face betrays no sign of my thoughts. This is how my mother always looked, still and straight, her face unmoving, her body elegant but always controlled. Did my mother also have these voices screaming in her head? I will never know now, for it is unlikely I will ever see her or any of my family again.

I want to ask her. I want to run up to her and scream into her face, to see if her eyes would blink, if she would step back. I would scream and scream until her dark eyes flickered and she looked away. I want to shake her and see her elegance and poise vanish into fear.

Why didn't anyone tell me before it was too late? Why didn't you tell me? Why? Why did no-one think I should know that he had another wife, one more senior than I, one who has five sons and will never be put aside for me to take her place? Why did you let me dream and love a man who had a wife of whom I knew nothing? Why?

My *why* is for everyone. In my mind as the hours pass I turn to each of them standing in our courtyard bidding me farewell. My mother, my father, Myriam, Hela, all of the servants. I see them step back from my screams. I see them cast down their gaze in shame before me. Of course many men have more than one wife, but not to know? To enter a house believing you are this man's only beloved and to find another woman standing there, her five sons gathered proudly around her? *Why?* As the miles go by I try to understand. Myriam and the servants, of course, may not have known, although they always seem to know everything. But my mother and father did know, and they did not tell me. Hela knows everything and she did not tell me. Yusuf did not tell me.

We pass the great city walls of Aghmat in the distance and continue towards the mountains, and it is only now I realise we have been travelling for more days than I thought, for we are nearing my new home. A narrow valley is our destination, greener than the hot deserts and scrubland around because of the river that runs through it, giving its name to both the valley and my husband's tribe. Here the mountains rise steep on either side of the river and any small patch of land that can be cultivated is set aside for food. The river is channelled here and there to wet the earth. The crops do not lack for water even if they must be hardy to grow so high. The sheep and goats are obliged to fend for themselves on the steeper rockier outcrops, with only bushes and rough grass for their food, although they are forever finding ways to try and sneak a little closer to the greener plants grown for their owners' benefit. If they are caught at their tricks they feel a stick across their haunches and bleat indignantly as they make their escape to higher ground.

Above the river, set high so as to avoid its fast and dangerous flooding in the winter, are the houses. Some are little groups of humble mud dwellings, their roofs thatched. Some, where the valley shape permits, form larger outlines. In the largest such space there are smaller houses surrounding a kasbah, a fortified castle, its moulded and decorated turrets towering above the simpler homes of the tribe. In the kasbah live those of importance, the chieftains, their families, their closest and most trusted men. Should danger come, as it so often does, from the nomads of the desert or refugees from tribal wars, those in the smaller houses would run here, their animals driven ahead of them, the heavy wooden doors then pushed closed by many hands, made to open only from inside. Here people and their animals can live for many days before hunger drives them out, and the turrets and rooftops allow for an advantage in warfare. This, then, is my husband's home, and now it is mine.

The kasbah towers above us as the camels make their final weary way up the hillside. The houses around it glow soft peach as the sun sets and their outlines offer a stepped silhouette following the shape of the valley sides. I look up towards the kasbah and see smiling faces at every window and on every rooftop leading to it. Their chieftain Yusuf bin Ali is home again after much time away, and every person feels some measure of relief that he is returned to protect them. Once they have looked at him their eyes run over the servants, all known to them of course, and at the many bundles of new goods that Yusuf has brought back with him. Then their eyes turn to me, the unknown woman in the caravan, dressed in fine robes, young and beautiful. The whispers run quickly from the base of the valley to its very summit, to the high turrets of the kasbah itself. It is clear what I am. A new wife for their chief. There are giggles between children, smiles between women and lecherous glances from the men at me behind Yusuf's back as we progress. The whispers all around me die to silence as we reach the kasbah and its great doors are flung open.

They stand in the doorway, five boys, little height difference between them. The eldest is perhaps only seven or eight, his cheeks round and pink as ripe figs, his smile full of delight at seeing his father. The youngest is only a baby, he cannot even stand alone but clings grinning to his oldest brother's robes. All of them come beaming towards Yusuf, who leaps down from his camel and embraces them one by one.

I scan the crowd from my place high on my camel. I see servants, soldiers, slaves and in the midst Yusuf and his sons. But I see no woman of high rank. Where is this wife who has won everlasting honour for having borne five sons in such quick succession?

One of Yusuf's men stands at my side and commands the camel to kneel. It does so with weary relief and I am lifted bodily from its back. I stagger a little, for I have been riding since daybreak. I am dizzy with fear.

Yusuf turns to me as I approach. The crowd's noise dims a little. He smiles at me. He is happy to be home, to be with his sons again. "Welcome Zaynab," he says. "Welcome to your home. These are your children now, as they are mine. Boys, welcome your new mother."

They make their welcomes to me, the eldest with a nervous but formal speech, the youngest with a grin that shows me his first tiny teeth, newly acquired.

I try to smile but I am watchful. Where is the mother of these children? It is dangerous to be enchanted by cubs when a mother is nearby and may rip you apart for passing on your scent to her offspring. But still there is no woman. Gently I greet each child. Then I am led through the gates and into my new home.

It is cool in my new rooms. The servants chatter excitedly to one another. They seem pleased by my presence, eager to welcome me. Yusuf and his sons have been ushered away, no doubt to visit his first wife, wherever she may be. Meanwhile I am brought fresh water to drink and for bathing, my belongings are unpacked at speed and distributed about my quarters. There is much admiration for my clothing, which is stupidly rich for my new life. My father's house was one of luxury and idleness. This is a community where there are farmers and warriors, where women work hard. Their clothes are of good quality but simple, of wool and sometimes linen in plain bold colours or stripes, not rich embroidered silks like mine. There are servants and slaves, but not as many as I am used to. They are more familiar, addressing me and smiling, trying to show me everything at once.

"Get out of the way, you fools, you're exhausting her."

The servants scatter and I see the woman who has entered. She is old, bent, but wiry and quick in her movements. She grins at me with a mouth missing many teeth and hustles the rest of the servants out of the room. She settles herself on my bed and pats it invitingly. I stumble slightly on my way across the room but recover and sit beside her. She smiles and puts one arm about me as though she has known me all her life.

"Cry if you like."

And I do. I do not speak, only sob against this stranger's shoulder, wetting her clothes, sniffling until I can cry no longer. She passes me water without removing her arm from me. I gulp it down and sit up, a little ashamed.

"S-sorry," I begin. "I – "

"Nonsense," she interrupts briskly. "What have you to be sorry for? You're only sixteen and you have been married off to a man who lives a very long way away from your home. You have travelled in the heat and you are tired. Too much for a child to bear."

I do not object to her calling me a child, for it is how I feel – a babe among strangers, disorientated and fearful, fretful for a familiar face.

She looks about the room. "Have you everything you need?"

I nod meekly.

"What do you need to know about this household that Yusuf has not already told you?"

I want to laugh. He told me nothing. He told me nothing at all and I did not ask. Because I was a fool. I begged him to marry him and swore that my love for him was enough. He took me at my word and brought me here and now I doubt my love is equal to this challenge.

I shake my head. I cannot even think where to begin. "Who are you?"

She smiles. "I am Yusuf's mother. My name is Khalila."

I am horrified. I try to move, to perform a gesture of respect to my mother-in-law but she only laughs and holds me tighter. She is strong for an old woman.

"No need for such things. I am too old to need them to feel important." I sit back in her embrace and we look at one another. She looks at my tear-stained face and asks very gently, "What do you know of Badra?'

This, then, is the unspoken name now made known to me.

"Is she..."

She nods. "Yusuf's first wife. Mother to his sons."

I shrug, eyes on the floor. I am not sure I want to hear anything about her, I am too afraid.

Khalila sighs but her tone is brisk, as though she means to tell me all quickly, with as little pain as possible. "She was lovely. Beautiful, light of heart, warm of smile. Yusuf loved her at first sight, he would see no other's face. But she refused him. She told him she did not love him, that her heart could not embrace him. But he would hear no refusal. He must have her. He swore his love would suffice for them both."

I turn my face back to her shoulder and feel the wetness of my spent tears. I cannot listen to this story, but Khalila continues. "So they were wed. Yusuf did all he could to make her love him as he loved her, for he was certain that her love would flow to him one day, if he could but make her happy. For her part she tried. She was fond of him and tender to him, but her love could not flow for him." She sighs again, as though this part is harder to tell. "A child came. And all rejoiced, Yusuf most of all. But after the child was born Badra's light heart and warm smile faltered. She grew sad. A sadness that would not leave her. The sun did not shine on her, food grew tasteless in her mouth, flowers lost their perfume. The years have gone by. She has birthed five sons, all healthy, all strong. She is honoured and loved like no other wife, but still her sadness has not left her, indeed it has grown greater with each child she has born. At last a physician said that she must bear no more children, for they do not delight her as they should a mother but instead make her eyes darker and her spirit heavier. Perhaps if she does not bear children for a time she will grow lighter of heart."

I pull away from her. "This is why he needs a new wife? To lie with rather than Badra, that she may not bear children?"

Khalila tightens her lips and nods.

A cold thought comes to me. "Am I to bear children also?"

She shakes her head slowly. "Yusuf has sworn not to hurt Badra's heart, for he loves her still. He will come to you when you will not fall with child. In this way he can satisfy his desires without risk of causing her greater grief."

I stare at her.

Gently she strokes my hair, with pity in her eyes. "He spoke with tenderness of you. He said you had a great sweetness in your eyes, that you laid your heart at his feet and he could not turn it away."

I shake my head and she gets up and softly leaves the room.

I lie back on the bed and stare up at the bare ceiling.

I have been taken as a concubine, nothing more.

I have been in my new home for three days when a servant comes to me and says that Yusuf will come to my room tonight. I thank him with grace and then give frantic orders for the preparation of my rooms, of myself. As the hours pass and evening grows closer my heart flutters still faster. This, after all, is why I am here, in this long narrow valley, perched on this hillside in my fortified rooms. I am here because this man took my heart in the darkness of my father's house, with only a few words. I am here because I am only sixteen and I fell in love for the first time with a man from another country, a man almost twice my age, a man who makes my body both hot and cold with nothing more than a glance. This is the man who is now my husband but with whom I have never yet lain. This is the man whose home I have tiptoed around, afraid to see his children's curious faces at every turning. I have kept to my rooms these past days, peering from my windows at the steeply-stacked houses below, unsure of my place in this new world. I feel Badra's shadow everywhere. I do not know how to proceed.

I long for tonight. Tonight I will welcome my husband to my bed and I will become his wife in more than name. His desire will raise my status within these walls and I will learn how I can claim my place in this new life. In years to come Badra may leave this world and he may grow to love me. Perhaps he will misjudge his visits to me and I will bear a child of my own.

I am clean and perfumed, dressed in my softest silks. My rooms, also, are clean and scented with incense, soft with fine carpets and wall hangings. They are warm and welcoming, as I am nervously trying to be. When Yusuf strides into my presence as the sun sinks and our mountain walls glow in the fading light I order food and drink and have to pitch my voice lower than I normally speak so that the tremor in my words will not be heard. When we are alone I shakingly pour water for our hands. We eat. Yusuf leans back, comfortable in his home, on my fine cushions, while I sit rigidly upright, afraid to spoil my fine clothes with creases or food dropped in ungraceful uneasiness.

"So it is true what they say," remarks Yusuf between mouthfuls.

"What do they say?" I ask.

I think 'they' must mean the servants, or worse, his sons. What might they say about me? That I stay in my rooms too much? Perhaps they think me rude or arrogant? In truth I am only very shy in this new world, but perhaps they do not see that, only note my absence and read into it something I do not intend. I look at him anxiously and wait to hear more. He takes a drink of sweet juice and grins at me.

"Why, that if you marry a girl from Kairouan she will fill your house with carpets and roses," he says, waving his hand at the soft patterned rugs and indicating the incense burner.

The breath I was holding in escapes in a laugh and he laughs with me. He offers me fruits and I take them from his hand. I am swept all over with love and desire. This is why I am here. I love Yusuf, and despite his first wife he must love me. Yes, he had another wife once, but she might as well be dead, for she does little else but sit in her rooms and gaze far away, or weep. He may mourn her spirit and he may have warned me he might not care for me, but he asked for me to be his wife and brought me here. I will live with him forever, loving, and in time, loved in turn. He moves closer to me, begins to disrobe me while he leads me to our bed. I, anxious to please, trembling with hope and fear, hold myself ready for whatever he may wish to do with me.

He looks at me, first at my too-fixed smile and then down to my meekly compliant body. He smiles and strokes my hair with tenderness, and then he reaches away from me, to where his clothes fell by the bedside, and pulls out two lengths of golden silk. He does not speak, but ties one round his eyes. With great care he ties the second piece about my own eyes.

In the darkness that has now descended on each of us he reaches out to my young, unknown body and holds his beloved wife Badra in his arms for the first time in more than a year. His strong voice breaks a little as he whispers gentle endearments that were never meant for my ears.

I see nothing. I feel only the man I love caressing me and with a moan I take him into me. The golden silk around my eyes hides my lover's face but in my mind I see Yusuf's eyes on mine. His face is filled with love, his arms wrapped tightly about my naked body. The endearments I hear whispered are for me and me alone. He is everything to me as I am everything to him.

His dark eyes are fixed on me as I cry out.

He comes and goes. He is away for long periods without telling me in advance, so that I am often wrong-footed when I inquire from the servants as to his whereabouts and

received a puzzled response that he has been away from us for many days and that he will not return for a month – did I not know? After a few such embarrassments I have learnt to hold my tongue. If he is here I embrace him, if he does not appear then I am silent and wait impatiently for his unknown return, keeping mostly to my rooms. I do not know how to be with his sons. I eat with them sometimes, stumble through their games and questions. I am awkward and do not know what my place is. It is easier to retreat to my rooms, where my servants wait on me without question, without the need for conversation. Slowly Yusuf's sons learn not to follow me, not to demand my presence. They forget about me.

Khalila does not forget about me. She tries to coax me out of my rooms. She takes me to see fresh fruits being grown, introduces me to the people of the tribe, who welcome me. They see in me a hope for Yusuf's future, a freshness and youth that has been missing in his life and which they hope will turn him away from Badra's misery. The servants care for her, but they know better than to expect thanks or a smile. They make sure she drinks enough water in the heat of the day, that she eats when the family eats. At night they make her bed and lay her gently in it. She does not resist, she eats and sleeps when told to but she takes no joy nor rest from either.

It is dusk on the day when I go to her. I follow a steep flight of stairs that wind to the roof. Inside a flower-carved door are her rooms. They are filled with flowers and fruits. The setting sun sheds its last rays on her face as she sits on her bed, facing the view to the valley below.

She is older than I, of course, but her skin is soft and her face sweet. Her hair is washed and combed and lies on her back in gentle ripples. Her clothes are good quality, woven in bright colours. She wears fine jewellery. I wince a little when I see the traditional gifts of love – the fine beads of engagement, the heavy bangles given for a wedding gift.

I stand awkward in the doorway. I feel as though I should not enter for she does not acknowledge me.

"I am Zaynab," I begin.

She does not answer, nor even blink at my voice, too loud in this quiet room.

"Sister," I try again, remembering that I must show respect to her, the elder and more senior wife.

There is no movement. I edge into the room and carefully sit beside her. I sit as she does, looking out towards the window, trying to see what she sees.

There is only a clear blue sky, paling now towards white as the sun's power fades. She does not look down towards the far valley where people tend to their crops and beasts. She does not look closer to the walls where her children play in the last light of day. She sits motionless and stares as blue becomes white and will soon become blackness.

I leave, and then return some days later, thinking perhaps to touch her shoulder, to sit in front of her so she may see my eyes and I hers. I come to the rooms at the very summit of the kasbah and stand in her doorway.

Yusuf is here. He lies with his back to me, facing her on their great bed, her face turned towards him so that I can see her from where I stand. He whispers soft words to her, caresses her shoulders and face with infinite love and tenderness. She lies immobile, does not respond, nor do her eyes flicker to meet mine as I stand shaking in the doorway.

I run back to my own rooms and weep.

I do not return to Badra's rooms again.

Yusuf has been gone a month this time and I am burning up for his touch. At least when it is dark and his skin is next to mine I can feel that he is mine and forget for a moment that he will be gone again by morning without a backward glance, with only the lengths of golden silk left on the floor of my chamber to remind me that he comes to me only to feel Badra's body in his arms.

I sit in front of my mirror and look at myself with rising impatience. I am sixteen years of age and nothing more than a concubine. So be it. If that is my role then I will be the best there is. I will not try to compete with his wife by having sons, for what more use of sons has Yusuf? I heard the whispers in the bathhouses, I know what herbs I must drink so that no life will take hold in my womb. I will take another road. I will learn such things as will bind Yusuf to me forever. I will leave him gasping for my presence. He will not go away again like this, leaving me here alone and idle, a living being only when he is nearby, a lifeless rock the rest of the time, merging perfectly with my rocky surroundings here on the hill-tops. He will not sit at table laughing with his sons while I wait alone in my room, hoping he will deign to reward my beauty with his presence in my bed. He will not lie by Badra's side and whisper to her while I wait in my rooms, unwanted for my too-fertile body. This is not the life I wish to live. I want to be desired, loved. I want to be a woman of importance in this household, not a mere adornment to its master.

I will make Yusuf love me. I call for my servant. She is taken aback by my request, but gold has its uses. She will never have seen so much gold in her own hand in all her life, and she never will again. This is her greatest chance to change her fortune, her station in life. She assures me that everything I wish will be done and that my request will go with her to her death.

The woman, when she arrives, is not as I expected. I thought I would be sent a woman so perfect in her beauty, so renowned in her skills, that men would run to her side and pay her whatever she asked. But when the door closes on the growing darkness outside and we are alone she removes her heavy robes and in the flickering lights of the lamps I see before me a brisk, stout woman. She is my own height, so taller than most, but her waist is thick and her features plain. Her long hair has many strands of grey in it. I am dissatisfied, and it shows on my face. I was going to welcome her, to ask for her help with humbleness. Now I step back from her rudely and sit on my bed, disappointed and embarrassed in equal measure. My servant girl deserves a beating for sending me this woman. What can she have to teach me? I may be unskilled but I am beautiful – and young. I am sixteen, this woman is my mother at least once over. I fold my arms and lift my chin to meet her eyes without comment. She will see that she has displeased me and she will leave.

She stands before me, her eyes on mine. Her heavy outer wraps lie at her feet, where she cast them off. Her robes are quite plain, dark and long, shapeless. I had thought such a woman would wear finer, more colourful apparel, something to draw the eye. But her eyes are warm and bright, as though she were truly happy to be here in this room, standing before a young girl who is sitting sulkily on her bed, not speaking. It is then that I notice she is moving, but only very slightly. I seek out the source of the movement, for she seemed very still only a moment before.

Her hips are barely moving. A tiny ripple from the folds of her robe is all I see, but it is so slight as to make me look harder, to catch her at it, to see how she can move and yet move so little. As I watch the movement becomes greater and her hips sway in ever increasing twin circles, the dark fabric around her accentuating and yet somehow hiding the rhythm. As I watch her hips her arms begin to rise past her thighs, up by her waist, catching my eyes and bringing them up towards her breasts, which are suddenly exposed as she undoes some secret fastening. My head jerks back at the sight of them, so quickly laid open to my eyes. They are larger than mine and not so pert, rounded and a softer brown than her arms. Her naked skin gleams with a patina of many years of soft creams and perfumes, warm water and caressing hands.

I draw my feet in towards me, sitting curled up now, shy and yet fascinated. I am not sure where to look. Of course she is nothing but a common whore, and so I am free to look where I choose, but still I find I am curled ever tighter, my face now resting on my knees. I am not quite ready to look at her eyes again, but I watch her dance, transfixed.

She is oblivious to me, it seems. She dances in silence but so intent is she that I can hear the rhythm she is following as though the room were filled with musicians. Her head rolls backs to shake out her long hair and she turns first one way and then another, sometimes with her back to me entirely. She moves now fast now slow, her arms languorous while her hips shake so fast it seems impossible. Then her hips slow down and sway in a curve that takes forever to move from one side to the other while her hands, quick and darting, draw attention to every part of herself, my eyes following them helplessly. In doing so she has drawn my eyes back to her face and her eyes, which I now dare to look at. When I do I see I was wrong. She was in no way oblivious to me. Indeed, I am the centre of her world.

Her eyes have never left mine. No matter where I was looking, her dark eyes have been fixed on me, no matter how she moved, even when she had her back to me her head has always turned back to look over her shoulder at me, a warm smile on her face, a smile that invites me to look where I will without fear or embarrassment. She has no false shame, no coyness. She loves every part of her body, she knows that she can dance like few women can even dream of dancing. She knows that for all her grey hair and her thick waist, her sturdy arms and broad hips, at this moment she is more beautiful than I will ever be.

I want to cry. What chance do I have? I will never prise Yusuf away from Badra. I have only my beauty, and that will fade away. I will always be the second wife, the pretty, useless adornment until that gift too leaves me and I will be truly useless. I may not even bear children even if I should drink other teas, which promise many sons. My mother bore only me, a girl. Other women pitied her behind her back. My father was saddened by his lack of sons. My head drops down to my knees, my eyes close and burn with tears.

I can still hear the woman dancing, her footsteps and skirts are still keeping to her rhythm. It does not falter but suddenly she is by my side. She has danced her way round my bed, and now her hands reach out and touch me. Startled, I look up and move slightly away from her, but she is smiling. She holds out her hands to me and invites me to dance with her. I shake my head. She will not accept my refusal, though, and turning her back on me she begins to shake her body whilst gradually arching her back until her whole body is curved backwards. Her eyes, upside down, meet mine and she invites me again. She grows comical in her entreaties, until I cannot help but laugh, although my nose is blocked and my eyes still sting with tears. I stumble off my bed and take her proffered hands. Reluctantly and ungracefully I begin to copy her movements. She does not speak, only helps me to improve, lifting her skirts to show me how my heels must lift when I sway so that my hips can move further and deeper in their endless curves back and forth. When she shakes her body forwards and back it ripples. When I shake mine it judders but she places her hands on me and makes the movement softer, slower. She indicates I should now remove my robes gradually, but I shake my head and refuse outright. She only smiles as one who has all the time in the world and we keep dancing, my feet learning new steps as my arms accentuate each movement of my hips and waist.

She stays with me for five days. I dance until I think my back will break, until my arms burn, my feet ache. My neck feels as though it will surely snap as I whirl it round to allow my hair to fly through the air like a great flock of birds. By the last day I dance naked, I dance like this silent woman dances. I hurt all over. I forget where I am, I forget everything except my dancing.

We never speak. Perhaps she cannot speak. Perhaps she does not speak my language. Perhaps she has no wish to speak. So we do not speak. We dance, we eat and drink, we sleep. Nothing more. I do not even know her name. We stay in my rooms, my servant girl brings food and then leaves again. I do not join the rest of the household, but they are used to my absences and do not remark on it.

On the last day we are practicing an intricate step, allowing me to move backwards and forwards, then side to side. My feet move gracefully in time to the beat only she and I can hear. My servant girl knocks and enters without waiting for my invitation. Another woman enters with her. The dancing woman and she nod at each other like old friends, then the dancing woman dons her heavy outer robes and leaves with my servant. She does not bid me farewell. She does not even look back at me. The servant girl closes the door and I stand bereft, my new friend and teacher gone. It is all done in a few moments. I turn from the door to the women who has just entered and see that she is already entirely at home. She has cast off her outer wraps and is now sitting on a cushion eating dried fruits from the platter on my low table. She has helped herself to the cooling tea from the pot.

I fumble for a robe to cover myself and after days of silence I find my voice. It croaks. "Who are you? What are you doing here?"

She takes no notice of me. She sips the tea and grimaces. "Call a servant," she says. "This tea is cold."

I stare at her.

Her voice is harsh, she speaks with a strange accent. She sounds like a common street woman. Her skin is wrinkled and coarse, dry with the years. Her back is crooked. Her fingers are twisted with age. She speaks as though I were her servant. I am too confused to respond. She raises her voice to a shout.

"GIRL!"

I flinch, but sure enough there are quick footsteps and my servant girl opens the door without knocking.

The woman nods approval at her speed. "This tea is cold. Hot tea, quickly. And food, plenty of food. I'm hungry."

The servant girl has the audacity to bow to her and, ignoring me, run back through the door, closing it behind her.

I sit on the bed. I need to be seated higher up than this woman. I have to find some way of regaining my status, which she seems to have stripped away from me in moments and with no effort. I settle myself and try to formulate a question that will identify who she is and what she is doing here since she ignored my initial question. My mouth moves slightly as I try to compose a sentence. I am about to speak when she interrupts me.

"How many positions do you know?"

"What?" I ask stupidly.

"Positions. For congress."

"Congress?"

She uses a very vulgar term for sexual intercourse, one used only by the crudest of the street boys.

I flinch.

"Oh, so you do know something, then?" She cackles and helps herself to more dried fruit, stuffing it into her mouth, cheeks bulging. She speaks with her mouth full. "Where'd you learn filth like that then, a lady like yourself?"

I gather myself. "Are you a whore?" I ask, haughtily. I mean to insult her, but she is not insulted so easily.

"Of course," she says. "Best there is."

I snort with laughter. I cannot help myself. She is an ugly old crone with appalling table manners and vulgar speech.

She raises her eyebrows and grins back at me. "Don't believe me?"

I shake my head.

She nods, still cheerful. "I'm the best there is. They may shut their eyes and dream of a sweet young beauty when they're with me, but they always come back. No-one knows as much as me."

I still look doubtful. We are interrupted by the servant girl, who has managed to prepare a ridiculous amount of food in a very short time. There are chunks of spiced meats, a thick soup, roasted vegetables, cakes dripping with honey, fresh and dried fruits and hot tea with yet more honey to add to it. She places it all on the table and the old crone flips a golden coin into her hand. I am shocked. How can she have so much money and dress so poorly? If she has money to throw about like that she could be living in a palace with her own servants. Perhaps she does.

The servant girl leaves and the old woman attacks the food as though she had not just eaten handfuls of dried fruits and drunk half a pot of tea. As she chews on a hunk of meat she looks up at me where I sit, still incredulous, staring at her. She rummages through her robes and throws something at me, which I try to catch but fumble and drop onto the bedcovers.

"Make yourself useful," she says. "I'm not planning on staying longer than I have to."

She belches loudly and selects another piece of meat. While she puts it in her mouth with one hand she pours tea with the other. I am impressed she can pour it accurately from such a height with barely a glance at it.

"Stop *staring*," she says. "Begin. I'm not here to teach you how to pour tea."

I scramble through the bedclothes and find the item she threw me. When I see it I nearly drop it again.

She sighs wearily. "You are *married*," she says. "Don't be such an innocent."

I gape first at her and then back at the item I am gingerly holding. I have never seen such a thing. It is a perfect replica of a man's organ, carved in ivory.

"Well?" she says. "*Begin.*"

"Begin what?" I ask, hardly wanting to hear her answer.

She rolls her eyes at me. "Now don't waste my time. I've got a lot to teach you and you need to learn fast. My time is worth a great deal of gold to some men." She laughs unpleasantly and loudly slurps her tea. She eyes me over the cup and then sets it down in a business-like manner. "In your mouth."

My eyes widen.

"Oh?" she says. "Indeed?" She sighs and settles herself comfortably on the cushions, adjusting them with small grunts until she is comfortable. "From the *very* beginning, then."

The days with the old crone are less than those with the dancing woman, but they are harder. I am made to practice until my jaw aches, and once she is happy with how I can manipulate the ivory toy then it is taken away from me without a word of praise and I am forced into many positions, both off and on my bed, an imaginary Yusuf above me, below me, behind me, to my side. She watches me critically and when she thinks I am not trying hard enough she will grab a limb and force it into a deeper pose, thinking nothing of my yelps of protest. She keeps up a disparaging running commentary on both my skills and those of other women that she knows, not least the dancing woman.

"What is the use of dancing if you cannot do what comes after? Dance all you wish, but once a man has come to your rooms he will hardly wish you to keep on dancing all night."

I nod meekly while attempting what feels like an impossible pose to hold for more than a breath. She makes me stay in the position for more than thirty breaths and shakes her head in annoyance when I collapse, sweating.

"And fine silks and jewels? What man has ever noticed such things except for a silk merchant or a gold trader? And they look at the cloth and the metal, not the woman underneath it all. Keep *still*, you useless girl. *Now* move."

When her time comes to leave me I am relieved but I am also grateful, and perhaps just a little sorry. I have grown used to her endless talking, her strictness, even her revolting table manners and snoring have become a comfort to me. I was not lonely, at least, while she was here. Now I am alone again. But at last I have new skills with which to draw Yusuf to me.

I await his return. When he comes I set aside the golden silks. He smiles at me and there are tears in his eyes as he gently replaces them about his own eyes, about my face.

I do not hold back. Every skill I have learnt is unleashed upon him, all at once.

When he cries out it is Badra's name on his lips.

What now for me? Am I to learn yet more skills? Is there anything new that I can learn even if it would make a difference? I sit alone in my rooms and see the future stretch out before me in my mirror, as I play out my part as concubine until my beauty fades. Perhaps I will mutter to myself as I tend flowers or birds, as old wives sometimes do who have proved childless, or form a great devotion to the days of fasting and praying. Then another girl will be brought here, shy on her camel, eyeing me up with pity, bringing dancers and whores here to teach her what she believes will draw Yusuf to her.

I move close to the mirror and place my hands on it. My breath clouds its surface so that my face becomes blurred. Who knows what the future holds? Perhaps there is another way. My heart leaps when I think about Yusuf and what might be of greater importance to him than nights of embraces. He is a chief. A powerful chief, beholden only to the amir of Aghmat. Might such a man not have greater ambitions? After all, many men marry to create those alliances and opportunities for advancement which take them from lowly leaders to great amirs. Yusuf is already married. His heart is Badra's. But if he could have a wife who would fan the burning coals of his ambition until they became a fire, sweeping all before it… might he then to turn to such a wife, a woman who might stand by his side in his future?

I choose my time carefully. I risk embarrassment by asking the servants many questions to ensure Yusuf will be at home. I make an announcement. I have a wish to know my new country better. Khalila is pleased with me. She thinks that at last I am emerging from my shell, that I will take part in the day-to-day life here. I say that I wish to visit the waterfalls that run close by to our valley. They are supposed to be a place of great importance, of strength and power. I order my servants to prepare my camel and food. As well as my own maidservants I take three male servants with me, chosen because they are strong but also ignorant and credulous. I set out with them, while Yusuf sits in council with his men and Badra sits silent in her rooms.

It takes us until the heat of the day is full upon us to reach the waterfalls, and they are indeed memorable. In a land that needs water, that cares for it and channels it, holds it and longs for it, this abundance of water, falling in multiple glimmering arcs, spilling on the rocks and earth, is a magnificent sight.

My servants prepare food and I eat. They eat a little way off from me and then I tell them that they may please themselves for a while. I say that I wish to sit quietly, that I have a headache coming on and my eyes cannot bear the bright light of the day. They arrange shade for me with blankets from the camels and then they move away from me, some of the men swimming, the women coyly pretending to turn their eyes away, paddling their toes daintily and shrieking when the men splash too close.

I prepare myself. My heart is beating fast. I mutter the words I have planned under my breath. I loosen my hair fastenings a little, such that they would easily fall out, take water from the water bags and sprinkle it over my brow. I am ready. I picture Yusuf in my mind, see myself by his side, his only beloved. In one quick movement, before I can think again, I bite down hard on my lower lip. The pain makes me cry out, and I do not smother the sound. As my servants turn I fall back, thrashing on the ground. My hair falls quickly from its poorly-placed pins and its thick darkness grows pale and dusty on the dry ground beneath my head. I taste salty blood in my mouth and wetness on my chin as my lip bleeds. I begin to pant as my servants rush to my side. They drown out my fast breaths with their panicked shouting at one another. Here is the new bride of their master, fallen into a fit, droplets of sweat on her brow, her body shaking in a frenzy, blood now spreading across her face as her hands flail. They are frightened. What if I die? How will they explain their negligence? Swimming, chattering, flirting, while their mistress, who had *told* them she felt unwell, falls into this state? They will be whipped for this, even if I recover. If I die... They try everything, they hold me down, try to pat my face clean with damp cloths. I can hear the women praying, hoping for some divine help.

I begin to moan, and this makes them even more scared. When words begin to escape me they lean in close, relieved that at least I am speaking. One of the men quiets the others and puts his ear close to my mouth. He listens, then draws back. I see his face from between my half-closed lashes. He has become pale. The others want to know what he heard. I save him the trouble of repeating it and speak again, louder and more clearly this time. They stare at me. I cry out my words one more time, this time so loudly that they fall back, letting go of my limbs. I arch my back.

"Zaynab!" My voice calls out my own name, echoing on the hills. "Zaynab! Lady to a mighty lord! Oh, happy man who calls Zaynab his bride! He shall be mighty indeed! Ruler of his own tribe, ruler of the Maghreb, ruler of lands beyond his own birth! Mighty is the husband of the lady Zaynab..."

My voice, so strong, fades away, and I fall still. My limbs lie loose and crooked upon the hot dusty ground.

I am quiet during the journey home, pale and lifeless in the litter they have assembled for me. The men carry me, the women urge them on, trot alongside me, applying cool cloths and trickling water between my torn lips whenever we pause.

I lie in my rooms for many days. I moan and clasp my head. At first I insist on darkness and cry out random words from my vision. Then, slowly, I begin to recover. Reluctantly I repeat my revelation to those that ask for it to be told to them again and again. The servants whisper, people of consequence in the tribe seek me out. I am becoming a person of importance. I am gracious with them. Soon I will be of importance in the eyes of Yusuf, and this is all that matters to me.

At first Yusuf does not come to me. I hear that he was summoned to the amir of Aghmat soon after my vision was known of, and I can imagine that the amir may want to hear of it for himself. On the day when Yusuf returns I dress in my finest silks and await his command. Perhaps he will come to me and tell me of his plans for our future together.

At last I am sent for and I go with joy in my heart. I am a little sorry for

Badra, for she will be swept aside now that Yusuf believes that I am his path to greatness. But she is already lost to this world. I cannot help the delight that makes my feet light as I walk with as much dignity as I can muster to his rooms, although I long to run to him as fast as I can, to arrive gasping for breath. I will be first in his heart now, as he is in mine. I will be his only love, his only wife.

When I enter his rooms Yusuf is surrounded by his advisors. I smile broadly at him, for this is how I dreamt it would be. I will no longer be a pretty concubine, hidden away amongst my carpets and cushions, incense and sweet juice drinks. I will be truly a wife, an equal at his side. Even his most trusted men will acknowledge my part in his future greatness. That is why they are gathered here.

But Yusuf's face is grave. I am surprised, but then I adjust my expression accordingly. Of course, he may have some difficult decisions to make now. He will have to set aside his wife, who has served him well. Her sons will also be set aside, for he will want to have sons with me: his heirs must come from me. But I am sure he will treat them with kindness, for he is a good man. Perhaps they will be minor leaders in the region. Now that he can see a glorious destiny prophesied for him he may well seek to establish an army of his own and look for opportunities to increase his own lands and powers. His men will be glad of this. And I will be by his side in all.

"Zaynab," he says, and his voice is so tender that my eyes fill with tears. I blink them back and look at him full in the face. Now is not the time for me to be a foolish girl. I must show him that I am a grown woman, that I could be his finest ally, his loyal and true wife, supporting him in all his endeavours.

"Zaynab, this vision that came to you."

I nod, eager.

"You must take it back. You must say it never happened, that you were mistaken."

I stare at him in amazement. "Indeed, my lord Yusuf," I say, my voice clear and strong. "It did indeed happen, I swear it by Allah. I saw true then and I speak true now." I know that I am lying to him, but he must believe me, he of all people must believe me. He must believe that by tying his destiny to me and me alone he will fulfil his true greatness. His men must believe it also. I tell myself that I am sure that Allah will forgive me, for He knows I am trying to be a good wife to Yusuf, which must count for something.

Yusuf looks at me for a long moment, and I see to my astonishment that he also has tears in his eyes. He speaks again, and his voice seems thick, as though the words hurt his throat as they emerge. "My lord, the amir of Aghmat, has heard of your vision."

Now I see what has happened. I misunderstood the amir's interest. He feels threatened. He may have challenged Yusuf to combat, or be demanding displays of loyalty, out of fear of Yusuf's possible future greatness. Yusuf is more than capable of fighting a battle. But he must believe in himself. He must believe in me, in my vision. I lift my head proudly. "My vision was true. My husband will be the greatest leader in the Maghreb and even further, to lands as yet unclaimed by our kings. This is the destiny of the man who calls himself my lord."

Yusuf nods and lowers his head. When he raises it again his eyes have cleared. His muscles are tight. He has come to a decision. I am proud of him. This is the beginning of our future together. "The amir of Aghmat also believes you have seen truly, Zaynab. He does not doubt your word. He believes that if he takes you as his queen then he will be the greatest leader in the Maghreb and beyond. And so he has commanded me to set you aside that he may take you as his wife. I cannot challenge his command. I am his vassal. You will no longer be my wife. And when the right time has passed you will go to Aghmat, as queen of that city. Until then you will live in my home but as my ruler. All care will be taken of you whilst you are in my protection, as befits your future status. I have promised that I will deliver you to the amir myself when the time comes."

He rises as I fall, standing above me as my costly silks cover the ground at his feet and my body shakes. My hands touch the cold floor and my eyes roll up to his face. He stands still and looks down into my eyes for a long, long moment. No-one in the room moves until Yusuf leaves the room. Then they all leave in haste, for my screams are unbearable, even to hardened warriors.

That night I seek out Yusuf in his own rooms, with servants busy at their tasks and a few of his men. When he sees me he stands and bows, as if I am already queen.

"Please dismiss your men and the servants," I say, my voice shaking. My eyes are bloodshot with crying.

"It would not be proper for me to be alone with you now," he says.

"Please," I say, more tears dripping fast down my face and onto the floor.

"I cannot," he says, his own voice grown thick. I can tell the servants are all ears and that his men are curious, even though they look elsewhere. But I have to speak. I stand very close to him.

"I lied," I whisper.

Yusuf stands. "You may leave us," he says.

The men and his servants hesitate, but the look on his face makes them obey without a further command. When we are alone I summon up all my courage.

"I lied," I say.

"Why?"

"I wanted to be important," I say. "I wanted to be more important than…" I do not say her name. I do not need to.

He closes his eyes for a minute, as though in pain. "I know," he says at last.

I gape at him. "What?"

"I tried to make you tell the truth," he says. "But you swore in front of everyone that it was true. Now it is too late. The Amir believed you. He is a man of great ambition, a man who believes that through you he will gain great power."

"Tell him I lied!" I say, clutching at his arm. "I do not care if they laugh at me!"

"It is too late now, Zaynab," he says. "He would not laugh at you. He would not believe you. He would think you were lying to stay with me. And if he did believe you then he would have us both put to death for seeking to deceive him, for making a fool of him."

"I would rather die than leave you," I sob.

He cups my face as he did that first time, his eyes full of tears. "Ah, Zaynab," he says tenderly. "I should never have brought you here. I have done nothing but make you unhappy. It was not my intention. I hoped your love would bring light into my life but instead I have brought darkness into yours."

And so there is nothing to be done. Yusuf stays away from me. My time goes by. There must be a period of time between one husband and the next of course, this is how it is done. It would be unseemly for the amir to take me to him at once as though I were some slave girl claimed as the spoils of battle. All must be done correctly if I am to be his respected queen, if my vision is to come true.

I pass the days sat on my bed, my eyes unfocused. I eat what is put in front of me, I drink when water is offered. I taste nothing. I hear nothing. I see nothing. When darkness comes I lie down and when it is light I sit up. I do not know if I sleep, perhaps I do. I cannot tell if I am awake or asleep. Either way I do not dream. There is only darkness inside me.

I know that sometimes Yusuf comes to the door of my room, that my servants hover behind him and whisper assurances that they tend to my needs, that I am washed and dressed each day, that I am fed and watered, that my bed is soft and warm. He nods, but he does not speak. I try not to look at him when he comes. There is nothing to say. Nothing can stop what is already decided. If the amir of Aghmat wants me as his queen, then it will be so. I have given my consent, as I am required to do, though it is given just as Yusuf's consent was given: our ruler has spoken and we cannot disobey. Already many of my possessions have been taken ahead of me to the palace. My rooms here grow bare as rooms there grow more elegant day by day. Already, I know, courtiers are preparing themselves for a new queen, shifting this way and that to curry favour, to take positions in my household of benefit to themselves and their families. Already the poets and singers are making ready to sing my praises – even if I were ugly or old, stupid or crippled, their songs and poems would wipe away my faults. How easy for them, then, when I am known to be a beauty and oh so young, without physical blemish. As for stupidity? They will have to wipe away that at least, for who can be so stupid as I? What woman, married to a kind husband whom she loves, with a silent and all-but-invisible co-wife, would be so stupid as I have been?

The day comes for my departure. I stand in my room as servants take the last of my belongings to the escort that waits below. One servant hurries by and I stop her. I reach into the basket she carries, items to be taken back to Khalila for household use and draw out the two lengths of golden silk. Slowly I turn them over in my hands and then I leave the room, my pace almost a shuffle.

I walk up the long steep flights of stairs and when I reach Badra's room I do not waver in the doorway. I look at her and see myself, sunk in a dark misery. I walk towards her and without pause I lay one length of golden silk on her lap. Then I turn and leave her to her silence and stillness.

Downstairs, at the great gates where I first saw Yusuf's sons, I am lifted into a carved saddle. The boys stare at me, clustered around Khalila. She tries to catch my eye but I stare at her as though I do not recognise her. Ahead, Yusuf gives a command and my mount turns, as do those of my escort. We begin our journey to Aghmat, Yusuf delivering me himself to my new husband, my new lord. I sit slumped, shoulders hunched over, my hands twisting the second length of golden silk.

I am only just seventeen and my destiny has changed. I am to leave the man I love to become queen to Luqut al-Maghrawi, the amir who rules over the great city of Aghmat. Its riches will be spread at my feet, the people will call my name and my every wish will be obeyed.

I think my heart will break.

Queen

*T*HE BIRD'S TALONS GRIP MY wrist so tightly I fear it will draw blood even through the thick leather of my glove. It looks this way and that, the wind ruffling its feathers, making it impatient. It shifts its feet and stares at me boldly, a challenge to my supposed authority over it. I whisper to calm it. There is as yet no prey in sight, it must contain its desire for freedom. I turn my horse a little and glance towards the falconer. His eyes scan the horizon and narrow at a glimpse of movement. His face is grown like that of his birds, I think, and stifle a smile. He nods and I lift my wrist in a quick swift movement, launching my falcon into the air. It sails away from us, strong wings beating, seeking out a trembled movement below.

"A good bird," says the falconer.

I nod. We wait, companionably silent together, watching the bird turn this way and that in the wind, feeling its way through the air currents holding it aloft.

He is one of the few servants who does not bow and scrape before me. He likes me because I enjoy this rare time outdoors; enjoy the soft feathers and hard eyes of his charges. He treats me with respect but does not fear to instruct me in how to manage my falcon.

One of my only pleasures here is falconry. There is a great festival in the spring for which many birds of prey are caught and trained. During the days of the feast itself many gather to see their feats in the air, their power and agility, their ferocity and courage. When the festival is over there comes the moment for which I long, every year of the last twelve years as the queen of Aghmat. At the end of their time in captivity most of the birds are released, to fly free once again. They take wing above the palace and leave us, never to be seen again. Each year I watch this moment, and then I withdraw to my rooms. Everyone thinks I am tired, for I am much in public demand during the festival, but when I reach my rooms I dismiss my servants and weep. I permit myself only this one moment of weakness, every year.

When I have finished weeping I stretch out my hand and Hela is there, unbidden, to pass me water to wet my dry throat. Then she will bathe me and put cold compresses of cooling herbs on my eyes, so that the redness will not be seen. I will come to dinner as a queen should, in fine clothes and jewels, my head high and a gracious smile on my face. No-one else witnesses this precious moment of weakness, only Hela.

I had only been queen for a year when word came of the fate of my childhood city of Kairouan. When the Zirids declared their conversion to Sunni by giving allegiance to Baghdad, the Fatimid Caliph sent as punishment great hordes of Arab tribes to invade. They burnt, they killed, they reduced buildings to rubble. They so utterly destroyed Kairouan that it was humbled in the dirt, a once proud city made nothing.

All of them perished. My father. My mother. Even loving Myriam. As for the street children with whom I used to play, now the men and women of that city, who knows who fell and who remained standing? Hela could not tell us.

She stood before us, her face grown old beyond her years, her body stooped, her clothes still streaked with ashes, smelling of smoke. The fall of Kairouan had taken her life away and left her a withered husk. She had come all this way to give me the news of my family. When my husband Luqut saw the way I shrank from her dark presence he at once appointed her my chief servant, as she had been to my mother. I did not argue. I had been married for only one year, yet I already knew the penalty I would pay should I defy him in any way. And so Hela came to be head of my household, my handmaiden as she was my mother's. And over the years I have grown used to her, her silent secret presence. I know my other servants are wary of her, just as the servants of my childhood home were. But they do not know what comfort it is to me to have one person who knows the truths of my life as queen, who does not exclaim or whisper but alters what she can and accepts what cannot be changed without sighing or wringing of hands. She makes me stronger than I could ever be alone.

That first night she came to me and dismissed the other servants. Already she had power over them, for they obeyed meekly. They brought all that she asked for, and then they left us alone.

She stood in the shadows and Luqut did not see her. She did not speak when she saw what he did to me. She had never been one for talking when it was unnecessary. When he left me a crumpled heap on the floor, then, only then, did she step out of the darkness and raise me up.

It still seemed strange to me that my family was dead. I did not weep, for I had suffered too much in the past year to weep, but my shoulders were stooped and my body was limp and unresisting in her hands. Had I not heard the news I would have been more uncomfortable in her presence. I remembered her strange forbidding presence from my childhood and how she had spoken of my father's second wife Imen. Her death had been sudden and unexpected and Hela's words at the time had frightened me, for they hinted at a dark hand behind gentle Imen's passing. I should have drawn away from her touch, but I stood still. I had never thought to see my family again, but still in my mind they had been alive, and now, suddenly, they were dead. It should not have made a difference, but it did.

I did not look down at myself, nor did I raise my head and look across the room at the carved mirror, which would have shown me what she now saw.

My body was covered in bruises. Not where they might show, of course. My neck and face, my hands and parts of my arms were made smooth and lustrous with fine creams and good food. My feet, also, were well shaped and delicate. But where my magnificent robes covered my body I was marked out in black and brown, yellow and purple. There were bruises that had almost healed and then had been marked again, so that there were layers of colours. And there were other marks.

Hela said nothing. She bathed me, standing close to each part of my body to stroke me with a warm wet cloth. As she did so she came even to my intimate parts, and she did not draw back at what she saw there.

When she had finished bathing me she went to a corner of the room. Here she had placed her two bags, both made of rough goat-hides. They were the bags of a poor serving woman, not a rich woman's favoured handmaid. She had never drawn unwanted attention to herself. From one she took several small pouches. Returning to me she extracted a few pots containing unguents, which she proceeded to smear on my body, different ones for different parts. Then she waved me to my bed, where I lay down. Hela stood over me. Gently, as though I were a child, she placed my covers over me, and then she looked down on me. Her voice was as deep as ever.

"How often does he come to you?"

I shrugged and closed my eyes. "When he wishes it. There is no pattern. Unless I have displeased him in some way. Then he will come until I have learnt my lesson."

"No child?"

I kept my eyes closed. "I know what to take to keep from having children."

"He does not wish for a child?"

"He has bastard children. He would think nothing of raising them up if he thought it would hurt me."

"Why does he want you then?"

I felt a tear creep from under my eyelid and make its way down my cheek. "For glory."

Hela was silent for a moment. "I heard about your vision. Every ambitious man in the Maghreb wanted you for a wife when they heard about it."

I did not reply but a tear made its way down my other cheek. I felt the wetness move down my neck.

"Do you often have visions?"

I did not reply, only lay there as the tears slipped down my face. Hela grew silent then and I heard her move softly away from me.

Life changed after Hela became my handmaiden. She ruled my household in my stead, lifting from me the burdens of managing servants, responding to supplicants, making arrangements for festivities and holy days. To me were left only the pleasant parts of being a queen – choosing fine clothes and furnishings, ordering the planting of gardens to delight me with colour and perfume, falconry, riding.

I was grateful for all of this of course, but it was one night that truly changed my life, only days after Hela came to me.

Luqut came to me and the servants fluttered round like shadowy moths as lamps were lit to make my bedchamber blaze with light. He needs to see to do his work.

I stood still and silent in the centre of my room. The servants did as they were bid. They did not stop to ponder the uses for the implements they laid out, nor count the bruises on my body as they stripped me bare. They had their orders, which had not changed since I had been brought here, and probably since before my time in this place. Those who disobeyed were likely to find out for themselves the meanings of these things.

I did not ponder them either. What would be the use? I thought of nothing else for months when I first came here, but after a year I was resigned. To protest would be to enhance his pleasure, to refuse would be to enhance my pain. I was better off imagining myself elsewhere, allowing my body to take the punishment that my mind could not withstand.

The first time, I screamed. I begged and cried for mercy. I tried to escape and found the doors barred. I had not known such cruelty existed, nor such men.

The second time I tried to avoid his sport by offering my own proficiency. Those skills I had learnt out of love and yearning for Yusuf I laid at the amir's feet to save myself. I hoped he might be enchanted and turn from his own path, but I was wrong. He laughed at my gentle offerings and continued along his own way, dragging me behind him, humbled in the midst of finery.

That first night Hela watched from the shadows. I do not know how he did not see her, but she has a way of melding with her surroundings. She saw it all. Not that this shamed me. I was beyond shame by then. Shame is for those who have been treated with tenderness.

Afterwards she did not commiserate with me, nor soothe me. She used her creams on me again and her touch was careful. That was all. But when the amir next announced his intention to visit my chambers, Hela dismissed the servants and made all preparations herself. She did everything without any mistakes, as though she had made such preparations all her life. Then she went to her own belongings and brought out her little pouches and a cup.

I stared. The lamps flickered and the cool breeze of the early night grew cold across my naked body. Reddish marks were etched into the worn wood. I found my voice although it came out as a croak.

"Where did you get that cup?"

Hela did not look up at me. She took pinches of substances, first from one pouch, then another, and combined them in the cup. Then she began to work them with a small silver pestle. The scraping noise made the hairs on my body raise.

"Is that Imen's cup?"

She shook her head. "It is mine. It has always been mine."

I shivered and wrapped my bare arms about my naked body as though their coldness might somehow warm me. "I have only ever seen it in Imen's hands."

She nodded.

"You gave it to her?"

"I gave her what was in it."

I felt my legs tremble. I tried to stop my voice from doing the same. I was feeling my way through a story whose ending I already knew. I was unsure whether I wanted to know where I would be taken, how much I truly wished to know. I tried again, hoping to hear that I was mistaken. "It put a child in her womb."

She nodded.

"And then…" I hesitated. She did not.

"Took it away again," she said. She stood and fetched water, a little of which she added to the cup.

I persisted, my teeth chattering. "The same mixture cannot have done both."

She looked up at me, frowned. "Of course not."

"So you gave her something that put life in her womb. And she was grateful to you. She thought you were helping her. Even though you were my mother's handmaiden."

She kept her eyes down. "Imen was a foolish girl. A trusting girl."

I turned away from her. A shadow moved opposite me and I gasped, then saw myself in the great mirror that dominates my chamber's wall, my body hunched with cold. I watched my face as she spoke behind me, her voice very low.

"She slipped away so fast there was no time for anyone to save her."

I whirled on her and cried out as I did so. "What is in that cup? What are you making? And for whom?"

She raised her face to me and her eyes did not flicker away from my fearful gaze. "I served your mother, body and soul, until she died. Now I will serve you until I die. You need not fear me. Only those who harm you need fear me."

I shook my head. "I forbid you to use that cup for anyone, Hela. I forbid it. He may harm me but I cannot kill someone. I cannot!"

She raised the cup. "Why would I kill him? Without him you would be in danger. How many other lords would seek to steal this city and the title of amir? How many men who heard of your vision would grasp this opportunity to take you as a bride?" She shook her head at me. "He made you queen of Aghmat. You have unimaginable privilege because of that position. You would be a fool to lose what you have for what you have to bear."

"You think what I bear is nothing? You who have seen?"

She raised the cup higher. "This will end your troubles."

"Without killing him?"

She nodded.

"How?"

She turned away, towards the door. "Trust me."

She left me then. Soon Luqut came for me. He had been at dinner. His eyes gleamed as he surveyed the room with all its apparatus and myself, standing alone in the midst of it, naked and defenceless. I bowed my head and braced myself for a long night of pain.

It lasted but a few moments.

No sooner had he begun than he was finished, his climax coming on him so suddenly, when he had barely touched my tender flesh with his instruments, that he was taken by surprise. He, who had always needed many hours to be satiated, was fulfilled so quickly that he gazed at me as though I might be expected to provide an answer to this mystery. But I only gazed back at him in silence and bewilderment, and he left me then.

He came often for a while, as though to wipe out that one time, but over and over again he was fulfilled with the merest touch, until he began to avoid me, seeking his pleasure elsewhere. I heard servants' whispers and once I heard a woman scream in another part of the palace, but I was tormented no longer. Hela's cup had done its work and I was free. True, I had to attend events with the him, maintain always the demeanour of a queen in public and still I had to endure his visits, but their intensity was so greatly diminished that I could feel once more that I was human rather than a beast.

That night was more than eleven years ago. I bore one year of marriage to Luqut alone, and these last years have been bearable only because of Hela. Without her I would surely have found a way to end my life, such as it is. My life is not happy now, but it is bearable. I survive. For what, I am not sure. In my secret heart I hope perhaps that Luqut will die. But this is an idle hope. He is older than I of course, but he has many years left to him. He is strong and healthy and he has me at his side. Zaynab, the promised consort of a great man, as foretold in a vision. What could bring him down?

This, then, is my life now. I am twenty-nine years old, and queen of Aghmat, have been so for over twelve years. I have no friends here, for my husband would not like that, nor can I take any servants save Hela into my confidence, for I know they may all be spies for my husband. I am childless, which might be shameful in another woman, but no-one cares about that. I was brought here for glory, not for childrearing, and certainly Aghmat basks in its glory.

It is a rich city. We are an important stop along the trade routes, and so we see the caravans come and go, swaying in and out of our gates from far away. Each trader might have a hundred or more camels, and their burdens comprise every wondrous thing that men might wish for, every good thing for which they are willing to pay. Rich cloths are spread out to catch the sun's rays. Wool and linen of course but also finer cloths, silks and those which have been decorated with shining discs of silver or twisted threads of gold. Delicate silken threads have been used for embroidering every manner of beauty upon the cloths –flowers and intricate patterns, even delicate script to spell out holy words.

There are sturdy iron utensils, plates or jugs of bright shining copper and twisted beaten precious metals studded with fine jewels, pearls and precious woods. More delicate than jewels is glass, heated and moulded in fantastical shapes, seeming lighter than air and yet safely holding water.

The smells of trade fill the air. The stench of camels and their long-travelled owners, the spices that enrich the foods cooked in the houses and at the market stalls, and the heady perfumes brought from far away to anoint the women of Aghmat. There is the dark smell of slaves too, unwashed, saddened and angry with their lot. I think I too would smell like this were my servants not forever washing and perfuming me to hide the smell of my sadness and anger.

There are sweets to tempt our tongues. Oranges, spices, sugar cane. Children beg for a little piece that they suck on all day long, chewing the soft spongy centre, strips of green fibre getting caught between their teeth. For the rich there is no need for such inconvenience. My own cooks will squeeze out all the sweetness and make rich dishes to tempt the amir and I.

The very best of all the goods are brought to me of course. I need not wander the hot markets, nor seek out one caravan or another, asking for favoured traders by name. When the best arrive, they come to the palace, where the quality of their goods are known and their faces are recognised. They do not enter my presence, they sit outside my chambers and wait for my favour to be made known to them by my servants. I can lie on a soft couch while goods from every part of the world are brought out and laid before me, I can dismiss or approve with a wave of my hand, a nod of my head. My husband is vain. He may dislike me and fear the rush that comes upon his manhood when he tries to touch me, but still my presence by his side, in his palace, promises great things for him and so I may have anything I want. We are to be denied nothing. He has the finest weapons, horses and women. I have the finest clothes, perfumes and furnishings. Our court eats the freshest and best foods, enjoys beautiful gardens and rooms bejewelled with coloured tiles in all directions, in patterns so complex they take experienced craftsmen months to create. Our court must be always magnificent so that the amir can be magnificent through its reflection.

Hela shops alone. When new traders arrive she will leave the brightly-lit palace rooms and go out into the dark streets. When she returns she will have replenished her stocks, carrying small bags of unknown items, which she will gradually use up over the coming months. The traders she uses do not come to the palace. They have perhaps four or five camels rather than over a hundred. They do not give their names, nor ask those of their best customers. There is no banter at their stall, nor much haggling. A simple nod, a few whispered words and gestures before coins and pouches swap hands. They know which cities to visit and their customers, like Hela, know where to find them when they arrive.

Later, servants will make their way to Hela's cool bright rooms, adjacent to mine, and whisper their fears and pains, and leave clutching cures. I watch as they come and go and recognise the servants of rich merchant's wives and courtiers amongst those who ask for her help. She is as much consulted as a noble physician. Sometimes she looks up from her whispered consultations and sees me watching her. Then she will look away. I would stop her, fearful of what happened to Imen, but I know that those in her care thrive and are cured, so I hold my tongue. Sometimes she tries to teach me her skills, but I have not learnt much. I know how to brew the drink that I take to keep from bearing a child to the amir, but I knew that before I came here. I can name a few cures for simple ills – for burns, for wounds, for fevers and to soothe coughs, colds. I mix things with so little precision that Hela takes the mortar and pestle away from me, will not allow me to make much beyond a simple tea for women's pains or a headache. She herself is meticulous in her measuring and weighing, in her mixing and brewing.

There are often visitors to our court, some from far away, some closer to home. Today Yusuf is at court and I am shaking.

He rarely comes to Aghmat. He used to come often when I was still his wife, but since I became queen his visits have grown fewer. I do not know why this is – if by command of my husband, or because of Badra, who still sits in her rooms and gazes at nothing as her sons grow into men. If it is by his own heart's wish then I do not know whether he does not wish to see me because I am a fool or because – and I am shaking even at the thought of this – because he longs for me and does not trust himself in my presence. Whatever his thoughts I know only that I lose my reason when he comes to court. I have maidservants who will pass me word of his coming in return for a little coin or trinkets. I pay more than they would ask for, for I must outbid my husband when it comes to paying for spies. When they come to me, pink-cheeked with whispers, I throw my chambers into disarray. I wear my finest clothes, my eyes are ringed with kohl. I come in state to the great chambers of the palace, in every way a great queen to those who behold me, in every way a foolish girl inside. Today he is at court and I am shaking still, even after twelve years away from his side. I have no-one else of whom to dream.

I sit carefully, the stiff silks folding around me as servants kneel before me to rearrange them more becomingly. They straighten and I try to appear at ease, as though I always look like this, as though every day I wear such formal clothing and sit in the state chambers of the palace rather than in my own rooms.

He enters and I catch my breath. As always he is dressed simply. He has little interest in finery and inwardly I curse myself. Why must I always appear before him so formally attired? Why does my nervousness at seeing him manifest itself in acting the part of a great queen rather than a young woman who was once his wife, whom he teased in the soft darkness?

But he, too, is formal with me. He sweeps a low bow, as he ought to his queen. "My lady Zaynab."

I incline my head, gracious, while the heat mounts in my cheeks. "Yusuf bin Ali. You are welcome to court."

He is seated and offered cool water to wash his hands, then sweet drinks and cakes, hot tea. He takes them with courtesy. "Is your husband the amir well?"

I hate it when he calls him this, 'your husband'. I want to cry out *he is*

not my husband, how can he be when I was your wife and you are still living?
He is not my husband, nor ever should have been! I am your wife, not his!

I bow my head. "The amir is well. He is gone hunting and will return this evening. He will be glad to see you."

This much is true. He loves to have Yusuf visit us. When he does I am required to attend the meal. I must sit by my husband's side and smile while he and Yusuf talk. I must accept choice morsels from my husband's jewelled fingers into my mouth and smile. If he kisses my hand or compliments me I must smile. I must always smile.

He does not stay long, and when he leaves I do not know when I shall see him again. It may be only the rise and fall of one moon, it may be several. Once it was from one blossoming of the almonds to another. That time I thought I might go mad.

I thought that as the years passed I would no longer feel the same towards him. I was wrong. At first I longed for him because I still loved him as his wife. I was alone at court and I longed for his gentle touch now that I knew how cruel my new husband could and would be for the rest of my married life. When Hela came I was freed from that torment but was rarely touched at all, which brought a new desire – to be held, to be loved. Now, after all these years, I hope that perhaps he still thinks of me as I do him, and that if I can wait long enough the amir might die. If he were dead, Yusuf could take me back as his wife. This time I would know what I had in him and in his first wife – I would be grateful for a gentle loving life, even if it were shared with the shadow of another woman. But time passes and the amir is still hale and hearty, while I grow older.

Hela, meanwhile, goes about her own business. There is no part of the palace she does not visit, no place into which she cannot find her way. I have been here for over twelve years and yet I barely leave my rooms or the state chambers save to attend some festivity or other. Sometimes I summon the falconer and we take my bird to fly. I do not explore Aghmat, merely use its riches to pass the long hours of my life. But Hela knows every part of this city. She knows where the armoury is, the stables. She knows the movements of the guards, the name of every servant, the tiny winding streets where the poor live and their miserable dwellings. She has entered the homes of the merchants and the metalworkers, the rich nobles and their servants. She is called on to be everywhere.

Today she is returned from one of her outings. The other servants make themselves scarce when Hela attends me. She makes them feel ill at ease, for she watches their every move as a cat watches a lizard. Sometimes she reads from great tomes as well, and this also makes them uncomfortable, for surely a maidservant should not pass her days studying like a scholar or a physician?

"What have you found today, Hela?" I ask her.

She is busy washing out little pots in a basin of water, rubbing each dry with a cloth and packing them away again in a carved chest. She keeps all her secrets in that chest now, after I told her that the old goat-bags were not befitting to the handmaiden of a queen. The chest is very plain. I offered her one of precious woods, carved with every kind of flower, but she refused.

She does not answer. She rarely engages in conversation. I throw a date at her, which she ignores. I am bored. I have no-one to talk to but her.

"What secrets do you know today that you did not know before, Hela? Sometimes I think you are planning to escape this place. You know where the stables are, the saddles. The names and watches of all the guards. Are you planning to run away?"

She does not answer, only keeps washing her little pots, changing the water after each one, pouring from big copper jugs into the basin, washing, then tipping the basin's contents into a large tub before refilling with clean water. She is methodical, exact, focused.

I yawn and roll back on the cushions. "*Talk* to me, Hela. There must be some gossip you can tell me. Who is having a scandalous affair? Who is seeking a husband? Who a wife? How are the crops? Tell me anything."

Her voice, when it comes, is so calm and steady that I barely take in what she is saying. "There is an army coming."

I sit up. "What?"

She tips the last of the water into the tub, then takes all her clean pots and puts them to one side in her chest, ready to be filled when a new trader comes to the city. She locks the chest, careful to put the key away in the folds of her robes.

I lean forward, my bare feet touching the cool floor. "Hela!"

She looks round at me as though my interest is unexpected. "What?"

"You said an *army* was coming!"

She nods and gets up, crosses the room, sits down and takes up a book. It is a medical book, I have tried to read it but I do not understand enough of it. I can see I will have to drag every small bit of information out of her. "Where is this army coming from?"

"The desert."

"The desert? There's no-one there. Only a few nomads and the traders."

She shakes her head, still trying to keep her focus on the book. "The Almoravids."

I sit back, disappointed. I had hoped for something of interest to happen. Anything to liven up my endless life here. A battle would at least bring news, glory to our army, tall tales for the men to boast of their prowess at the evening meals.

"Hela, the Almoravids came ten years back. You remember. They took a few places on the trade routes and then as soon as they crossed the mountains their leader got killed. They had to retreat. So much for their holy war."

But Hela has closed the book and is stubbornly shaking her head. "They have a new leader. Two in fact, for they say his second-in command is also a great warrior and a leader of men."

"What's his name?"

"The leader is Abu Bakr bin Umar. His second in command is his cousin, named Yusuf bin Tashfin."

She knows that the very name Yusuf, common as it is, makes my heart beat a little faster and gives me a look. I make a face at her. "They are still intent on their holy war? Have they not learnt anything?'

"Perhaps they have."

I shrug. "When they cross the mountains they will be defeated again."

Hela does not answer, only goes back to her book, and then a servant comes to tell us that I am required to attend dinner this evening, and the whole tedious business of washing, dressing, being perfumed and bedecked with jewels begins again.

There is a time where we hear no more news of the army. At first I tease Hela and tell her that if she had been imagining handsome warriors marching into her arms she was mistaken, and perhaps she dreamed them. But she takes no notice of me, only goes about her business every day as though nothing had changed. I forget about the Almoravids.

Today I am summoned to the state rooms. Luqut wishes me to be by his side during council. This is a frequent occurrence. I am there as a figurehead, a promise. With me by his side the amir can plan for greatness, for my very presence is a sign of future glory to come. His council of men plan for the future. Alliances are discussed, maps are consulted. Perhaps if they were to be linked to this lord or that amir... perhaps if they were to take a small town to add to Aghmat's existing vassals...

These conversations bore me. After years of this I know the names of every lord and vassal tribe in the Maghreb and have met most of them when they visit us to discuss possible unions. I could draw the maps with my eyes closed. I know who is to be trusted and who is deceitful, I know who has large armies and those leaders who for all their bluster have little in the way of real defences. The endless petty skirmishes and associations followed by disassociations weary me, for nothing significant ever seems to change. Leaders rise and fall, territories change hands. So it goes on.

I arrive, am greeted, settle myself by Luqut's side. I try to make myself comfortable even in my stiff silks and prepare to be bored once again. A servant pours tea for me and I sip it, my mind elsewhere until I hear the word 'Almoravids'. At once, I am all ears. No doubt they have crossed the mountains and been defeated. I will tease Hela with this news. Looking around the room I see there is a tension I had not noticed. Luqut has commanded a messenger to repeat the news he brought just this morning so that all may hear it for themselves. The man bows low to us all, flustered at being faced with so many great men as well as the unusual sight of a woman attending council.

"My lords – my lady," he stammers awkwardly.

He is unsure of where he should look, or to whom he should direct his bows. Luqut waves at him impatiently to proceed with less formality. The men lean forward.

"The Almoravids, under the command of Abu Bakr bin Umar, have crossed the Atlas Mountains and taken some small towns."

There are nods. This is not unexpected. This is what happened last time, and they were defeated. They will be on their way soon enough. The crossing of the mountains is no mean feat. It will have left them tired, vulnerable. They have no stronghold city in which to rest and recuperate. They must advance or flee, defeated. It makes them weak. They will be riding camels which are good for the desert but less fleet of foot now that they have reached more fertile plains.

"They have also taken Taroundannt."

There are gasps. Taroundannt is not much smaller than Aghmat. A pretty city, with mud-pink houses and white storks that nestle in its towers. It benefits from the shelter of the mountains and the rich fertile plain in which it sits, offering a large souk to those in the surrounding areas. Traders use it too, for it sits on the trade routes, as does Aghmat. If the Almoravids have taken it they are stronger than they were when they last crossed the mountains. Their leaders must be bolder, their men gathered in greater numbers. Now they have a stronghold. They can command food and water supplies, conscript men into their ranks. Their camels can be exchanged for horses if they wish. They are also commanding a city that sits on the trade route. They can confiscate gold and other merchandise with which to pay for their needs, raise a tax on merchants. Taroundannt changes the shape of this news. We are under threat. Aghmat is not so far away. It would be logical for them to attack our city next. Another rich city, another post on the trade route. A larger stronghold from which to create a capital should they wish. There will be a battle.

When the council is dismissed preparations begin. Fortifications must be made. Weapons must be assembled, as must be men. We will be ready when the army comes.

I tell Hela everything. While the other servants chatter and wring their hands Hela continues with her reading. She is unmoved by the news. I dismiss the other servants and move closer to her.

"Did you know about this?"

She says nothing but nods, keeping her eyes on the book.

"*How?* The messenger just arrived! He was brought straight to council!"

"I was with the amir."

"Why?"

She shrugs. She does not like being questioned.

"*Why*, Hela?"

"I was tending to a woman."

I turn my face away, thinking of the women in this palace who have paid for my freedom for more than eleven years with their own screams. But I cannot bring myself to look at Hela and order that she reverses her work, that Luqut should come to me again as he used to. I could not bear it.

I look at Hela and she looks back at me, sees my face. Sees that I will not give the order I should give if I were a good person, an honourable person. Nods.

I am ashamed. I have allowed Hela to take my pain and give it away elsewhere. I shake my head to rid it of my thoughts and return to the news.

"Are there truly many of them? They are stronger this time?"

She nods, eyes still on the page.

I move still closer and whisper. "Can they take Aghmat?"

She looks up at me, her dark eyes serious. Nods.

Three days go by and then word comes. The Almoravids have been seen. They are marching on Aghmat.

I climb to the topmost tower of the palace and look into the distance. I can see no army as yet, they are still too far off. By my side stands Hela. She does not scan the horizon. She looks at my face and then returns to my rooms. I follow her and sit down, watching to see what she will do next.

She looks at me and then speaks, abruptly, as though all her words have come at once. "They say their leader is a gentle man. Honourable. He has a wife, old of course, for he is old himself. But he has been a good husband to her these many years."

I nod, although I do not understand her meaning.

"If they are successful and take Aghmat it is likely you will be taken."

I look at her in horror. "As a prisoner of war?"

She shakes her head at my ignorance. "As a wife."

I frown. "They are not going to win, Hela. Luqut's forces are too great, his allies too many."

She ignores me and undoes the heavy locks of the wooden chest. She reaches in, takes out the carved red cup and holds it up.

Its worn surface glows in the rays of sunshine that enter the windows.

Widow

*H*E STANDS BEFORE ME IN the chilly dawn light. Luqut al-Maghrawi, amir of Aghmat. My husband. Magnificent in his armour, he towers over me. I will myself to stand still and not tremble. After all, we are surrounded by servants and his men. He does not have the tools of his secret desires to hand. He cannot hurt me.

"Give me your blessing, Zaynab," he says. "I fight for Aghmat and for glory. If I win I will take the city of Taroundannt from the Almoravids even as I crush them and send them back into the desert to weep. And I will be one step closer to the greatness which you yourself foresaw for me, your husband."

I nod. I swallow and find my voice. "May Allah bless you, husband," I say meekly. "May the battle be brief and your victory glorious in His eyes."

He smiles. "I will be victorious," he says loudly. Then he lowers his voice so that only I can hear. "When I return you and I will be alone together so that you may feel my might and taste my victory."

I lower my head in submission and he turns away, satisfied. As he reaches the doors a shape emerges from the shadows. It is Hela, and she bears the red cup. I watch as she approaches him, the very picture of submission, the faithful servant to her lord and master.

She speaks and her voice is low and soft. "My lord, I have prepared a drink to fortify you in battle."

Perhaps I hope that Luqut will refuse without my having to intervene. He barely knows Hela except as my handmaiden. If he refuses all will be well. I will not be obliged to cry out and warn him against the red cup.

But he takes the cup from her with a warm smile. "Thank you," he says. He speaks with courtesy.

I see him nod to one of the senior servants and they nod back. I have seen this gesture too many times not to know its meaning. Hela is to be given coins for her trouble. I frown. Why does Luqut trust her and pay her for her potions? Somewhere, at some time, I have missed something that has happened here in this palace. Somehow my husband trusts my handmaiden even though I know she has given him a potion which has made him unable to satisfy his dark needs with me. I knew she had escaped detection for this treasonous offence but it seems she has done more than just escape his eye. Somehow she has pleased him. Has she taken away his potency with me only to strengthen it with other women, the women who scream in distant rooms? Something in me knows this is true.

He lifts the cup.

I have one moment to choose. One chance to redeem myself. If I warn him now I will save his life. He will be victorious, I am sure, for he is on his own ground here, with a brave army at his command. He will return glorious. I will be at his mercy again, for I cannot continue to permit those other nameless women to take the screams from my mouth and place them in their own. If I speak now I will save his life and later save the pain of many women even if I pay with my own pain, my own life.

If I am silent...

If I am silent he will die today. I am sure of this. I do not know what is in Hela's red cup this time, but I know from her eyes that once he drinks from it he will die.

If I am silent he will die, and the women's screams will stop. If he is dead I will be a widow, and perhaps Yusuf will come to claim me for his own again. If I cry out...

I do not speak.

He drinks, gives the cup to Hela.

Raises his fist.

His men shout out a war cry and together they leave the chamber.

The red cup sits, empty, on the table by the door.

All is darkness.

I awake in my own rooms, on my own bed. The lamps are lit. Outside the windows is darkness. Hela sits in a corner by her chest, rearranging her little jars. I try to sit up in bed and she looks at me.

"Better if you lie still for a while. You fainted. I gave you something to help you sleep."

My heart begins to beat too fast, grasping at my breath. "Is there word yet from the battlefield?"

She puts down her work, turns fully to face me. "How long do you think you have slept?"

"A day? It was dawn when he left. It is dark now."

She shakes her head. "You have slept for three days and nights. The battle is over."

I leap out of the bed and run to the window. The city is very dark and quiet. There should be people in the streets in the evenings and even late into the nights, lamps in the houses. Aghmat is a large city, it does not rest, even at night. I can barely see the outlines of houses. I turn back to face Hela. She is standing right behind me. Our faces are so close I can feel her breath on my lips.

I cannot raise my voice above a whisper. "Where is Luqut?"

"The amir is dead."

My skin grows cold. Luqut, whatever he did to me, was a strong brave warrior. He had a large army. He knew his own land. To be defeated by a ragged band of fanatical believers from the desert... I see again the cup in his hand, the faded carvings, as he drank. "What happened?"

She speaks as a messenger to a king, no emotion, only the facts as they happened. "The amir was in the midst of battle when he grew dizzy and disorientated. His strength left him and he fell. The generals fought on, but they were lost without him. The army of Aghmat was overthrown. The Almoravids were stronger than anyone expected. They have many more men than before. Better weapons, better trained, commanded by powerful leaders. They took Aghmat yesterday. There is a curfew tonight. Their guards are everywhere. Their leaders are within the palace. Tonight they hold council. Tomorrow they will begin to establish themselves here so that they may reach out and grasp other lands. Much of the city is ruined though, they may choose another city to serve as their seat of power."

Everything is swept away. The city, Luqut, my status.

My status. "What am I, then?"

"A widow."

I am shaking. "A prisoner of war?" I know what happens to female prisoners of war, especially beautiful ones.

Hela smiles. She sees my thoughts before they are spoken. "It would be good if their leader were to be in need of a wife."

I shake my head.

Hela is serious. "It would be your best chance to stay safe. To be queen again. Marry their leader. Many have heard of Zaynab, the woman who will be wife to the man who conquers the Maghreb and more. Do you not think that is where their eyes turn now they have taken Aghmat so easily?"

My jaw moves without my command, my teeth strike one another and I cannot stop my whole body shaking. "T-there may be others who might ask for my hand..."

I can see Yusuf's face in my mind, hear his low laugh in the darkness of my family's courtyard all those years ago. Now, now he might claim me as his own again. Why does Hela not suggest him as a husband when she knows how I long for him?

A terrible thought strikes me. Hela sees the question forming before I speak my beloved's name. She shakes her head and grabs my waist tightly as I sink to the floor.

They are both gone. The husband who made me tremble and the husband for whom I still yearned. I am a widow twice over in one moment and worse, I am conscious of my precarious status. A widow is no-one. A prisoner of war who is a widow is less than no-one. She is in danger.

I am in danger.

But Hela seems unconcerned. It is coming close to dawn, a pale light begins to grow. Soon I will be able to see outside and then there will be little time left before I must face a new day and find out my new status.

"What will I do?"

"You are commanded to the council at first light, after prayers."

Hela is preparing my robes. She has chosen robes of state, magnificent, jewel-encrusted. A queen's robes.

I gesture to them. "You can't think I should wear those when I meet them. I am a supplicant to them. Not a queen. I am at their mercy."

Hela shakes her head. "You are the queen of Aghmat. You possess great riches. You are beautiful. It is foretold that your husband will conquer great lands. You have one chance to negotiate your position."

"How do I do that?"

She eyes me up as though she doubts my abilities. Her voice grows serious. "One chance, Zaynab. Their leader is a man named Abu Bakr bin Umar. He has only one wife, and she is not with him at present. Many of their wives were left behind when the army marched across the mountains. He is much older than you, but they say he is a kindly man – "

I interrupt her. "A kindly man who has just led a savage army of warriors to our gates and taken our city? A kindly man who has just killed my husband as well as the am – " I bite my tongue. I was about to say 'my husband as well as the amir' but I correct myself "– who has just killed my husband and one of our finest allies? You want me to marry this man?"

Hela shakes her head. "You need to think like a woman and not like a child, Zaynab."

I frown at this insult.

Hela ignores me. "You need to keep your wits about you. You must think about what is best for you, who your friends and enemies are, and then you must act to eliminate your enemies and bring your friends close to you."

I laugh. "Eliminate my enemies? You make me sound like a ruler of a great land, not a widow, not a prisoner of war!"

She shrugs. "It is how you should think. Everyone has enemies, opportunities for greatness, friends who can help them achieve their ambitions."

"Like you did for my mother when Imen came to my father's house?"

She does not recoil from the accusation. She bows her head and does not answer.

I have to know, have to ask one more question. "Like you did for me when the amir went into battle?"

She lifts up my glittering robes. "You need to get dressed. Abu Bakr needs to see a queen, not a supplicant. He must see in you a powerful ally, a symbol of his conquest. Not a widow, not a prisoner of war."

I allow her to begin dressing me. "I have nothing to offer him except my body and the empty promise of a false vision."

Hela sighs. "Forget about the amir. Forget about Yusuf. They are gone and you are alone. You have only me by your side. You need a powerful man to protect you. All women need this. You have one chance to secure him. You will go to him dressed as a queen. If he takes you as his wife he will have a beautiful woman in his bed, the promise of greatness in the future, a symbol of Aghmat fallen at his feet and the treasures of Aghmat at his disposal to pay for more men and more weapons. You are a prize and nothing more – a glittering prize which they can hold up to show their might. You need to be the legend that they can tell to their men and their enemies. But you will be safe if you do as I tell you."

And then she tells me what she has planned. What I must do.

I walk through the gardens and courtyards of the palace. Flowers bloom, fountains play in the sunshine that grows in strength and heat with every moment that passes as it approaches its zenith. All is peaceful. But if I turn my head as I walk I see glimpses through windows and gates to the city beyond.

It is ruined. There is rubble in the streets, broken pots and animals wandering without their masters. Many doors are splintered yet all are firmly closed. It seems the curfew goes on, or else the people are simply too afraid to walk the streets. I glimpse tall figures wrapped in thick blue robes carrying unsheathed swords. These are our new masters, the Almoravid soldiers. Their faces are mostly hidden although one or two catch the movement of my robes and glance towards me through gaps in the walls. They will know who I am, of course. Hela was right: my clothing, for now, is my protection. Any other woman would be shouted at, sent back to her house. The grandeur of my robes marks me out as the legendary Zaynab, until three days ago queen of Aghmat, now of as yet undetermined status.

I pass my servants, who serve new rulers now. Those I see are carrying food and drink, scurrying back and forth, cowed but knowing that, like myself, if they please these new masters they may yet keep their status. They see me pass but look away quickly, unsure what to do were I to command them – would obeying me be seen as a punishable offence under this new regime? Or if they refused to obey and then found my status unchanged – what then? Either way they risk punishment and so they avoid my gaze, hurrying onwards with their given tasks, hoping to avoid an error of judgement that might cost them dearly.

I come close to the great state chambers. There is only one guard, who bears a shield almost his own height and carries a sword. His robes are thick, dark and heavy, covering every part of his face but his eyes. He does not acknowledge me, only lets me past without hindrance.

I pause outside the door to the council room. I will have to face a room full of men now. Soldiers, the conquerors of this city, the murderers of the amir and of my long-lost husband. But I cannot accuse them, nor can I weep. I must hold my head high and charm them, make their leader believe that marrying me would enhance his status and ensure his claim to Aghmat is upheld. I lift my hand and steady my trembling, push the heavy door. It opens slowly and without sound.

The room is empty. The soft thick rugs on the floor and the bright glittering wall hangings have gone. There are no silk cushions on which to recline. The great jugs of shining copper and brass, which were used to hold many cups of sweet drinks and cool water for feasts and council meetings, have been taken away. It feels cold, as though the doors and windows have been open all night. The blue morning light enters the room, which is now decorated only with the white plaster carvings on the walls and the carvings on the doors. Below my feet the detailed tiles are still there, but they look strangely out of place now, overly gaudy in their newly-stripped surroundings.

I was expecting a room full of heavily armoured men, wrapped in their thick robes. Men ready to observe me, to pass judgement on me. There is no-one here.

"My lady Zaynab."

I nearly scream. I turn quickly and see a man framed in the doorway through which I have just come. He wears heavy robes, carries a shield and a sword. The guard I just passed.

"Who are you? And where is your leader?"

He rests his shield and sword against the doorway and pulls the door shut behind him as he enters the room. He discards his outer cloak and unwinds some, though not all, of the wool from his face so that I can see him better.

"I am Abu Bakr bin Umar, leader of the Almoravids. Praise be to Allah for His guidance, I am now also the new amir of Aghmat."

He is a short and stocky man, with a full beard as gray as his hair. He must be much older than I, perhaps as old as my father would have been by now were he still alive. He moves slowly, calmly, as though he has a great deal of time at his disposal. He does not stand in front of me, nor examine me as I feared he might. Instead he walks around the room, looking out into the courtyard with its sweet-scented gardens and splashing fountains.

"You have a very grand palace here, lady Zaynab."

"You have stripped it bare." It comes out too quickly, without my thinking. I bite on my lip, thinking that I must be silent. I must charm, not accuse.

He turns to me and smiles. He does not look angry. "It is not good to build up so much wealth, to live in splendour whilst others live in poverty. Allah says all men are equal – why then should some have so much and others have so little? A king should live as his people do."

I try to hold the words in but I cannot. How dare he come here and take my city, kill my people and then lecture me on how my life should or should not be lived? "Do you live as your men do?"

"I am happy in a simple tent, as they are. I pray with them, eat with them. We wear the same clothes." His mouth twists in a grin. "You thought I was a guard. You asked me where my leader was."

I blush and lift my shoulders in a gesture of resignation.

He grows serious. "And now? What is to become of you now?"

This is my moment. I should do as Hela told me.

I do nothing. I stand still. My life will change now, from one breath to the next. I tried once before to change the course of my life and it took me to a dark place. I allowed Hela to decide for me how to escape that place and that resulted only in the pain and death of others. I will let Allah decide now. I am unfit to make such choices. Let this man take my life into his own hands and make of it what he wills. His choices can be no worse than mine. His army has been given victory by Allah, who smiles on his endeavours. Perhaps if he chooses my life's path it will be smoother. I wait in silence.

He watches me for a moment and when he sees that I will not plead my case, that I will not choose to shape my destiny he comes closer to me.

"I have heard much about you," he says softly.

I risk a look at his face and see that he is smiling. He looks like a father speaking to a favoured child. He reaches out his hands and puts them on my shoulders and speaks directly to me.

"I have heard that you married a man who had a first wife. That you appeared unhappy in his household despite this husband having been your own choice, despite his first wife not treating you ill. It seemed that you could not find your place within that household." He pauses. "And then you had… a vision."

My eyes flicker and drop. I raise them again with difficulty and he nods as though I had confirmed something to him that he already knew.

"You had a vision that your husband would be the greatest in the Maghreb and beyond. And then something strange happened."

I chew at my lip.

"Instead of your husband keeping you by his side and reaching out for this promised greatness, as most men would have done, he divorced you, and gave you as queen to the amir of Aghmat."

His head tilts as he studies me. His voice is low and kind but his eyes miss nothing.

I squirm under his gaze.

"A man not known for his tenderness with women."

I feel tears well up but if I close my eyelids now they will surely fall on my cheeks. I open my eyes wider and meet his gaze, lifting my chin.

He steps away from me suddenly, paces down the room. His tone changes, becoming brisker. "Praise Allah for His mercy and favour, we have taken Taroundannt and Aghmat. Now we will reach out for more cities, more lands in His name. This is our intention. But we must have a place to call our own, a city that holds our strength as we march onwards. And we must have more men, more camels and horses, more weapons. And all must be fed. For this we need much gold."

He turns to face me and runs his hand through his grey hair. He looks older than he is, his mind on many things at once. He grins ruefully.

"So is this the time for me to be distracted by beautiful women, no matter what their promise of greatness? Why should I marry you, Zaynab? I know you need my protection but my men will whisper that I am allowing your beauty to blind me to the work there is ahead of us." He spreads his hands. "Give me a reason I can give my men, Zaynab. I am not an unkind man, I will be a gentle husband to you if that is what you need. But I cannot have my men wavering now. They have braved the desert and the mountains in the name of the most Almighty and I cannot let their faith turn to dust now that we are in the fertile plains."

It is the moment that Hela has prepared for me. It is this or no other. I turn and walk away from him, head held high. As I reach the door his voice catches me.

"Stop." His voice commands, it does not request.

I ignore him. I put both hands against the door and push, hard. It opens and the bright light of the morning blinds me.

Behind me I hear quick steps and a strong hand comes down on my shoulder. "I ordered you to stop. Stop."

He is angry now. He was kindly before but this man expects to be obeyed. I am no longer behaving as I ought. I turn to face him and before he can speak I take a strip of silk from my robes. It is golden, this silk, thickly woven. I take it and lift my hands behind his neck as though to embrace him. He steps back, surprised, but it is too late, I have blindfolded him. He makes to rip off the blindfold but I place my hands over his and lower my voice to a silken whisper, carried through the golden fabric to his ears.

"I will give you your answer, Abu Bakr, if you will trust me."

He hesitates. Trust the queen of a ruined captive city? Whose husband has been killed at his command? It is unwise, but his curiosity is roused. I know as soon as he hesitates that he will go with me, that he will step into the story I am telling him, take his place among the characters that I am bringing to life.

I take his hand. It is hard, calloused, and a little wrinkled. But strong and he clasps my hand with force. He must be a little afraid, I think. How long since he trusted someone like this, how long since he let himself be led somewhere unknown, at the whim of a woman?

We walk through the gardens, back the way I came a short while ago. Our robes brush against scented herbs and servants stare, but Abu Bakr does not know they see him, for he sees nothing. He walks gently, tentatively, but he does not stumble, for I guide him with care and he walks where I set his feet.

We do not speak. I had thought he would ask for answers, that he would demand our destination more than once, but he does not. We walk together, in the soft sunshine, hands clasped. We would look like lovers, were it not for the blindfold.

Hela is waiting, but as neither she nor I speak, and as her feet are shod with soft-soled sandals, Abu Bakr does not know another has joined us. If he thought about it he would think it was strange that we walk through doors that open with little effort on my part. But the world is strange to a newly-blinded man and he does not speak, does not acknowledge her presence.

We walk down stairs and through doors, then through winding passageways and down again. I am as lost as if I too were blindfolded, but Hela knows the way and I follow her as Abu Bakr follows me. When we come to a small door set in a rough mud wall Hela stops and indicates it. Then she turns and walks away. I want to call out to her, for I am afraid.

I do not call out. I push the small door and it opens a small crack. I have to push it harder to make it fully open and dust floats about us from the crumbling doorway.

We stoop to enter and when we are fully inside I close the door behind us. It is very dark now, and I keep one hand to the wall while the other clasps Abu Bakr tighter. He must know we are somewhere old and strange, for there is the smell of dust everywhere and it is very cold and silent. No perfume of sun-warmed flowers here, no trickling water. Only silence.

There is a soft glow but a few steps from us, and I lead him there. I push at the splintered wooden door, which opens silently, and I guide Abu Bakr through it ahead of me. Then I step through and close the door behind us. I swallow the gasp that rose to my lips as I entered. That would not be a part of the story I am telling.

I steady myself and then I speak. My voice is strong. It is the voice of the djinn in the tales told at night, commanding a mere mortal to behold a great wonder. Each word echoes.

"Remove your blindfold, Abu Bakr bin Umar."

His rough hands fumble with the fine silk and the blindfold drops to the floor. He makes to pick it up but stops. His eyes, so long denied the light, are glittering now as the room is reflected in them.

The walls are crumbling mud, the door is decaying wood. But the hundreds of lanterns which light the room are not there to light the walls or door. Their soft shining lights fall on the treasure held here.

There is gold and silver. There are rubies and pearls. There are gemstones of every hue, coins and ingots pouring out from chests, spilling onto the floor as though they were nothing but trinkets. They shine from every part of the room. The riches here are beyond any tale or conjuring of a djinn. They are boundless. Abu Bakr turns away from this sight and his eyes question me.

I speak again. "All that you see is yours. It is given from me to you, by the will of Allah. As he gave you Taroundannt and Aghmat, so he gives you as a wife Zaynab, whose husband will be blessed with greatness. Who will rule over the whole of the Maghreb. You need gold for your holy army. And Zaynab gives you this."

We gaze at one another and then he stoops. I think he will pick up a gem or a coin, for there are many scattered at our feet, but he does not. Instead he takes up the golden silk and hands it to me. I take it, and lift my arms around his neck once again. My robes fall back on my arms and my skin brushes his cheeks as I tie the silk around his eyes once again, and then he takes my hand.

As we leave I take one last look back at the room, at the many tiny mirrors, hidden here and there amongst the treasures, reflecting their glory a thousandfold to those who do not know how little wealth this room truly holds. Luqut was a spendthrift.

Afterwards it is easy. When we are far enough away from the room I remove the blindfold one more time. Our hands clasped, he returns me to my rooms in silence and there he leaves me with a courteous bow. Later I hear the whispers, here and there in the gardens and the streets.

"Abu Bakr is smitten with the lady Zaynab."

"She took him into an underground cavern full of treasures such as cannot be imagined."

"'All this is yours,' she told him."

"Now he is to take her as his wife and she will be queen once again, she who was a widow."

I am queen again and safe. Hela smiles and goes about the preparations for my wedding.

Even in this ruined city there must be a wedding. The people have been terrified, have lost loved ones, have seen their homes ruined but they must know that life goes on. That one thing, at least, has stayed the same in their newly-uncertain world. Zaynab is still queen of Aghmat. The people of the city cling to this one thought. If they ever doubted my vision, now they revere it. "It was foretold," they say. Now they believe it was His plan, that I was always meant for Abu Bakr's wife as the commander of this terrible army. My vision explains their suffering. It explains the new faith that has swept the city. Prayers are said with more conviction, there is more sobriety in dress, in behaviour. There is less dancing and flirting, more talk of war and conquest. The city that ran with water fountains and echoed with laughter now runs with the blood of animals to feed sacrifices and the army. It echoes with the beating of hammers on metal as new weapons are forged. The people of Aghmat can rail against the horrors they have seen or they can believe that this is His will, that a new era is coming and they will be placed at the centre of its power. They choose to believe.

I keep to my rooms. I look out of the palace only through the openings in walls; windows, small nooks and crannies, through the veils provided by elaborately worked gates. I cannot look the people of Aghmat in the eye. The servants know their place again and are reassured. I am queen, as always, and so palace life can resume, albeit with less grandeur.

How strange are these conquerors! Rough men, battle-scarred and pious all in one. They pray with a fevered devotion, all together, bodies swaying in rhythm. I have heard that Abu Bakr and his lieutenants pray with them, as common soldiers. Their clothes are lacking in any decoration. Made of thick coarse cloth, they cover their faces as do many of the men from local tribes, leaving them unknown, even to those of us who see them every day. They take no delight in the riches and comforts that are now available to them. They make little use of the servants, who grow idle. They do not call for rich foods prepared by our skilled cooks. They do not lie on the soft cushions of the palace state rooms. Instead every room is stripped bare and even foot soldiers lie there to sleep at night, on the bare cold tiles, wrapped in coarse blankets. Perhaps to them this is luxury enough after their former life. They were trained for war in the desert, in the burning days and freezing nights, with little in the way of food but camel meat and dates, perhaps rough barley bread. Now, associating past hardship with their victory, they do not seek out the luxuries of city living.

Many of the men are encamped around the city. There are guards, too, who control who may enter and leave the city. They do not seek to halt trade, but naturally each merchant must pay them for the privilege of passing through what is now their own territory. In this way their reserves of gold are growing, their plans for the future alongside their new wealth. They can command more men, more camels and horses, more weapons. The army grows stronger and better fed by the day. The men are rested now, they have eaten well if not lavishly. They have time to train, to sharpen and repair their weapons. Their steeds, also, are better fed on our rich plains and running rivers. This army can go on to far greater things than poor ruined Aghmat. Already I have heard whispers that they may build a city of their own. *Murakush,* they murmur, *land of God.* They want a city in His name, a city from which they can govern and show their might to the world, for what is more mighty than to raise up a city where there was none before? Most conquerors would have been happy to build a bigger, better palace here in Aghmat and live in grandeur, but Abu Bakr and his commanders have bigger eyes for greater things.

They meet in the state chambers, but I am no longer required to be present. I am left to my own devices and to women's work in preparing for the wedding.

Abu Bakr remains solicitous of me. He sends servants to ask if I have all I need, and occasionally he comes himself to my rooms. He does not enter, does not stay long. When he visits me I offer sweetmeats and tea in my courtyard, by the fountain. He refuses the stickiness of the freshly-made sweets but accepts tea and sits with me for a little while. We do not talk much, sometimes he asks me about the crops that grow in this region or tells me about new arrivals – more men, more horses and camels and where they will be located within or without the city. I answer his questions and nod when he tells me about his plans, but I do not question him. I do not ask about the much-murmured new city, nor about how far into the Maghreb he wishes to proceed, how far he wants his message to be taken, his men to march. I am almost afraid to hear the answer. To me it seems I am about to marry a man who will in truth rule all of the Maghreb and it makes me afraid. That my false vision as a young girl, created in the heat of passion for a man who is now dead should come to life frightens me, as though I had unleashed a djinn from its hiding place and made a pact with it. Now it whirls away from me and I stand helpless, watching its progress and unsure of its intentions towards me.

I think Abu Bakr is a good man, kindly and calm in his manner. I will be safe with him, of this I am sure, but I know that ours will not be a marriage of passion. He speaks to me once of his wife Aisha, and I hear a softness in his voice which I take for love.

"I have not seen her for a long time," he says.

I do not know how to reply but let him continue.

"She is my first wife, of course, but she is of my own age and has borne me fine children. She will understand that the marriage between you and me is not a threat to her, nor to what has been between us in the past."

I nod and smile but my eyes fill up with unexpected tears and I busy myself in serving more uneaten cakes, in calling a servant to bring fresh tea. My eyes clear so that I can look at him again.

"I will have nothing but respect and love for my older sister," I say, for I know such a speech is expected of me.

He smiles sadly at me, seeing the slight redness of my eyes. "You will meet her one day and see that she is worthy of such feelings," he says, "and she will care for you with gentleness, as she has cared for our children."

My heart feels heavy. In truth I already knew this was how it was, how it will always be, but to hear it from his lips makes my eyes sting. A child. This is how he sees me. How I will be to him. He will care for me – and perform his marital duties of course – but nonetheless I will not be a true wife to him. There will be no passion, no shared dreams. There might be children, old as he is, but I doubt he will visit me often enough for that. I am a duty, not a pleasure to him. He longs for the familiarity of his first wife, a woman who has been by his side for many years and who can read his mind, who knows all of his history and understands his secrets. To begin again with me – to tell me each and every part of his life… the thought must only weary him. In truth, why bother? What need is there to truly make me his wife in more than name? We are unlikely to spend much time together. He has much to do. His wife will join him eventually. Besides, if he is to conquer more of the Maghreb I may well be left behind. Battles are no place for women.

I try to make light of these thoughts.

"I hope you have many tales to tell me, Hela," I say to her.

She is immersed in plans. The wedding is not far away now, and although my clothes are prepared Hela has her mind on more than my appearance. The servants have been cleaning for days. The gardeners have received a telling-off because the flowers, coming to the end of their natural lives, look less than satisfying to her critical eye. New ones must be planted. The pools must be emptied and their tiles scrubbed, then filled again so that they glisten in the sunshine. The servants mutter behind her back but as usual no-one goes against Hela. They are afraid of her dark eyes, her bent back, her closeness to power.

"What tales?" she asks impatiently, her back still turned to me as she surveys the gardens. She has already chastised me for showing little or no interest in this wedding. She says I should think of nothing else, for not until I am married will I be truly queen again.

"Oh, gossip and fairy tales, Hela. I do not think my husband will be here much." I make my voice even lighter, amused. "Why, it will be as it was before they came. Just you and I in my rooms and a husband I never see!" I almost laugh at the end, but do not have enough breath as I find I suddenly need to swallow at the picture that is forming in my mind as I speak.

Hela turns and looks at me. I avoid her gaze. She sighs. "What gossip do you want to know?"

I shrug, clear my eyes, breathe again and lean back on my cushions. "Oh, I don't know. Tell me about my husband's council."

"Why?"

"It's where he spends all his time." I try not to sound like a whining child but I can see that Hela does not think I have succeeded.

She does not seem interested in the topic I have selected. "They all look the same under those veils. Rough manners. Smell of camel. No idea of how to dress – all that thick dark wool when they could wear anything they wanted. More interested in prayers and armoury than food or women."

I laugh and pour myself a sweet pomegranate drink. "See, you can be amusing when you want to be. Tell me more. Who is his right-hand man?"

She looks at me as if I were stupid. "Don't you know anything about them?"

"Not really. I only see Abu Bakr. The rest are always in the distance. They don't come to my quarters."

"His right-hand man is named Yusuf bin Tashfin."

Now that she says the name I remember it. The name Yusuf still makes me think of my first husband and my stomach clenches. I drink more pomegranate. I cannot mourn him forever. "Tell me about him, then."

Hela points out more unscrubbed tiles to a servant who sulkily returns to work.

"Makes Abu Bakr look like an unbeliever."

I choke on my drink and splutter with laughter. "No-one can be more holy than Abu Bakr!"

"*He* is. Prays all the time. Always looks disapproving about everything."

"Such as?"

"Pretty clothes. Women in pretty clothes. Festivities. Music. Dancing. Feasting. Any food that is not barley bread, camel meat, dates and water."

I laugh harder.

Hela waves her hand at the beautiful palace gardens. "Decorated palaces. Fountains. Jewellery. Anyone who doesn't pray, doesn't fast, doesn't do everything they ought to, when they ought to, how they ought to. He has no leniency, that's for certain."

"Is he a good fighter?"

"They say better than any man, better even than Abu Bakr. Trains harder and longer, rides for hours every day. Has no fear on the battlefield, doesn't seem to care whether he lives or dies – but it is always the other man who dies, never him. Fearsome."

"Is he married too?"

Hela nods. "Some tribal woman. Left her behind in some little village till he sends for her."

"Children?"

Hela shakes her head. "She lost a baby, they said. Kicked by a camel."

I picture her. An old tribeswoman like Abu Bakr's wife. A simple woman, surrounded by sands and camels. Left behind to await her husband Yusuf's summons or death, trusting only in Allah's will. Barren, probably, if he has no children by his age. No doubt these wives will arrive soon and I will be surrounded by toothless old women who look on me with pity, too young to share their huddled gossip, too old to have a chance of bearing many – if any – children. A not-woman, a child-queen, a figurehead and trophy of war. No more. I finish my drink and leave Hela to her scoldings, burrow into my bed and sleep.

The wedding is upon us. The day passes slowly but I am deaf to its sounds, seeing only images as time passes. The crowds. My jewels and heavy silken robes. Abu Bakr and all his men, as ever in their rough woollen robes without adornment. The prayers, rising and falling around me. The blessing. The feast afterwards. Simpler than it was for Luqut and me but still plates and plates of food, the rich meats and sticky sweetness of cakes, the fresh cooling drinks.

As the evening wears on I am brought back to my rooms where there are servants everywhere, lighting lanterns and candles until my bedchamber is ablaze with light. I stand amidst them all, unsure of what to do, how to be. I see myself in the great mirror and I seem small even though my robes take up twice the size of my real body. I try to stand straighter but this just seems to make me look wooden. I allow my shoulders to relax and watch my figure decrease in height.

At last Abu Bakr comes to me and our servants leave us. Even Hela makes her bows and disappears. We are alone.

I do all that I should. I welcome him with sweet drinks and delicate fruits, which he accepts even though I know they are not greatly to his taste.

"It is very bright in here," he says, smiling.

We make our way about the room, blowing on each tiny flame until the room grows dark, save for one lantern still lit by our bed.

I kneel before him to remove his shoes, rise again to help him disrobe. I struggle with the long wool wrap that he wears about his face and we smile at one another as at last his face is unveiled before me. I have not seen him fully unveiled before. His beard is thick and grey, his face broad and square-jawed. His eyes I know best, of course, a rich brown with many creases in the corners. His forehead, also, is much creased. Much of the skin on his face is paler than his hands and arms, since it is always covered from the sun's bright rays.

He in turn disrobes me. My rich silks fall to the ground and he looks over my body without shyness. He reaches out, but only strokes my shoulder, as though I were still fully dressed, before indicating the bed behind me. We make our separate ways to it and enter its luxurious covers. Once covered, we turn to face one another.

I am no fool. It has been a long time but I remember what will be expected of me now. I know, too, what I might offer in the way of delight to this man, but my courage fails me. His gaze is too tender, too much speaking of duty and care rather than desire or passion. I move closer to him and ensure our skin is touching, that my arms are neatly placed that he may embrace me with ease. I will be a good and dutiful wife, for what else can I offer? I had passion once and it was wasted by my foolishness. I have waited too long in fear and trembling for love to grow now for this man who thinks of me as a child to be cared for. But he is at least a kind man. I will be kind also. Our marriage may be one of convenience but perhaps it will also have tenderness. I have not had gentleness shown to me by a man for a long time. To be held gently will be something good in my life at last. Perhaps it will be a marriage more suited to two old people but that will suffice me. Perhaps he will not often come to my bed, but I will have some soft caresses and these will bring a longed-for warmth to my life.

Abu Bakr looks at me and cups my face in his hand. His gaze does not flicker from my face. "Now that we have a stronghold my wife Aisha will join us soon," he says.

I blink at his unexpected reference to her, but summon up the correct words. "I will be her respectful sister," I assure him.

He nods and strokes my face. I close my eyes. It has been a long time.

"Goodnight, Zaynab," he says gently, and turns his back to me. He blows out the candle and all is darkness.

I place one hand tentatively on his back. His skin is old, but the muscles underneath are still strong.

"Husband," I begin, tentatively.

"Goodnight, Zaynab," he repeats.

I withdraw my hand. "Goodnight, husband," I reply meekly.

I lie in the silent darkness.

I am a widow for a third time, in all but name.

Wife

1 KNOW THAT THE SERVANTS WHISPER. To have been married three times, even in such unusual circumstances as mine – it is not done. They watch me when I pass and their whispers are added to all the whispers of my life. I know that the story of my life grows with the telling, that I am becoming a character from a legend rather than a real person.

A young girl, her hand sought by so many. Who chose to travel across the Maghreb, far, far away from her home and her family, to her first husband, a man still grieving for his dead-but-still-living wife. A woman who had a great vision at the waterfalls and was demanded as queen by the amir of Aghmat. Encased in rich robes, yet barren. Whose city was destroyed and yet who cast a spell over the commander of the conquering army, showing him riches such as are only dreamed of in this life. Made queen again from the rubble of a ruined city, lifted once again to greatness. Her vision coming true at last as the army prepares for domination.

When I hear the whispers I want to roll my eyes, but more often than not I shiver. I was only a foolish girl who married a man I had a burning passion for without finding out about his own crazed passion for a woman no longer of this world. I tried everything I could to bind him to me and in desperation made up a mighty vision, which only led to me being given in tribute to a monster. A monster killed by a man who I then tricked with mirrors into marrying me, to save me from a dishonourable fate, only to find out that my marriage bed, yet again, was cursed. Where is the glory, the fated destiny of my growing legend here? There is no glory, there is no wondrous life, only a stumbling from one place to the next, from one error to another. I cannot seem to find my feet, to stand strong, reach out my hands and take a joyful life. When I reach out to grasp the pure gold of happiness it turns to sand between my fingers, blown away by a hot summer wind.

Abu Bakr does not dishonour my name. He comes to my bedchamber, he sleeps in my bed. The servants leave us each night, content that at last my destiny has been fulfilled. Here I am, Zaynab, married to a great leader, one whose mighty army grows stronger by the day, whose reach may well grasp the Maghreb and beyond as was foreseen. A man who lies with me each night, as is right between husband and wife. They even hope for a child, the more credulous amongst them, thinking that such a child would show Allah's approval for this marriage, set a seal upon our joint destinies.

They can keep hoping for all I care. I shake when I think of my life. I spoke of a vision and here it is, growing before me day by day. I do not know how to stop it and I am afraid. I am like the heroes of the old stories, who open up the great jars contained long-imprisoned djinns and find themselves with a towering giant before them of unimaginable power. They reach out their puny hands to try to push back the stopper but it is too late and the djinn they created is free to wreak whatever havoc it wishes, leaving our heroes to watch, helpless before their unwitting creation. I do not know where this destiny is leading me.

It does not take long before Abu Bakr discovers my true worth to him. He is a clever man and nothing escapes his quick eyes. I glance at a map of the Maghreb laid out on a table at which he has been sitting and he sees my eyebrows rise. It is but a moment, but he is a man who must be alert to all moments, be they large or small.

"You are surprised by something, Zaynab?"

I look up. "It is nothing," I say hastily. It is not a woman's place to judge military strategies.

He smiles. "Tell me what you saw."

I shrug awkwardly and make a vague gesture towards the map. "The amir of that city…" I stop.

"Yes?" He has come to stand by my side.

I back away slightly. "He is known to be in the pocket of that amir." I point to a different part of the map.

He narrows his eyes. "And?"

I shrug again.

"*And?*"

"You would do better to attack that city first. The other will bow down to you as soon as the first city falls. The amir is a coward. He will not fight. He will gladly become your vassal if you will allow him to stay in his current position of power. He is a man of letters and has no taste for war.

He will do whatever it takes to keep his scholarly life, so long as he does not need to fight." I am caught up in my thoughts now. The many, many hours of boredom spent in council as a figurehead for Luqut and his men are bearing fruit at last. I know every petty ruler and their strengths, interests, weaknesses. I know who is a fighter and who is a coward, whose favourite wife is sister to another chief, whose loyalties lie to one side or another. I point again and again. "This one, though, he is a fighter. You will need a strong army when you attack him. He needs to see all your might, all your power to realise that if he wishes to keep his honour he is better off making a treaty with you. If he thinks there is any chance of beating you in battle he will not stop fighting until he is dead and the ground strewn with the bodies of his men and yours. You will bear heavy losses if you do not overpower him quickly, for his men are as brave as he is. That one though – he is a fool. You can outwit him in battle, for his men are poorly trained. He is an idle man, too fond of eating and not fond enough of fighting. This one is old now, if you overpower him quickly by the time his son takes his throne you will be his masters and he will not question you." I look up. Abu Bakr is not watching my finger on the map. He is looking at my face. My eyes are bright, I am speaking quickly and with assurance.

"I did not know you were a military tactician, Zaynab," he says, grinning.

I try to back away from the table but he takes my hand and leads me forwards. He settles himself on the cushions by the table and gestures for me to do the same. We sit side by side, our heads close together, the map spread out in front of us, the names of rulers of every tribe and city laid out for us to consider.

"Tell me more," he says, and I do.

Now I attend council again, seated in honour by Abu Bakr's side. Perhaps I am not his true wife when we lie in our bed, but here I am his beloved. He praises my knowledge of the Maghreb to his men and although they are surprised they see quickly that he is right, my knowledge far surpasses theirs. They listen to me with interest as I share more and more information. As they file out that first day I see one of them gesture towards me and hear him mutter the name of Tin Hinan to another, who laughs. I smile. To be compared to a legendary warrior queen is no bad thing. My heart lifts.

The men leave the room while Abu Bakr and I stand looking down at the map we have been poring over. He is retracing various routes with his finger, considering first one plan, then another. I see a slight movement and look up to see one man still seated, at the end of the room from us. His dark robes and wrap cover most of his body and face. But his eyes are fixed on me.

Dark eyes, thick dark brows above them. The beginning of a sharp nose. Of the rest of his body I can see only his hands, which are hardened and calloused. He is playing with a dagger, this is the movement I saw.

We gaze at one another for a moment. I am curious, taking in what I can of him, face, hands, dagger, clothes. His gaze does not flicker. When I return to his eyes they are steady on mine.

Abu Bakr senses I am no longer following his muttered thoughts about the map and future conquests. He follows my gaze and smiles.

"Yusuf! I thought you had taken the men to training."

The name Yusuf has its customary effect on me, drawing up images of that first man whose voice teased me in the darkness. I clear away these thoughts. This, then is Yusuf bin Tashfin. In the crowd of dark-robed and veiled men it was hard to spot Abu Bakr's second-in-command. He did not take a place of honour, nor speak louder than the others, allowing each man to have his say.

Yusuf does not reply. He stays seated, draws the dagger from its scabbard and then slides it back in with a hissing sound of metal on metal.

Abu Bakr does not seem to take this as an insult. He looks down at the map and then back up at Yusuf. "Will our very own Tin Hinan bring us luck in our battles, do you suppose?" he says smiling and waving towards me.

Yusuf stands. It is done in one fluid movement, with none of the grunts or stiffness of the other men's movements after sitting in council while the sun moved across the sky. He stands in the doorway, black robes sweeping the floor and looks me in the eye. When he speaks his voice is low and soft, but his words are hard. "As I recall Tin Hinan fought back against her Muslim conquerors and killed many of their men. Are you sure you wish for another such woman to be your tactician? Are you sure she is on your side?"

I open my mouth to protest but he has left the room. I see a glimpse of his robes as he rounds a corner of the courtyard outside and is gone. I turn to Abu Bakr but he is laughing.

"Yusuf is a man of war," he says. "A fighter. A true warrior in body and spirit. Now look again at this map, Zaynab, and tell me where we can most easily build a stronghold. Aghmat is not truly ours, here we are only conquerors. I want a great new garrison which in time will be our seat of government."

I look down at the map and see only lines. In my mind I see the dark eyes filled with suspicion of me. I shake my head and look again. "There," I say. "Close to Aghmat that you may use this city to provision your garrison until it is of a size to fend for itself. On the plain so you may see enemies approaching, where the water runs from the mountains so you will not thirst."

Abu Bakr nods. "It will be a great city," he says with satisfaction. He gazes at the map and in his eyes I can see plans being drawn up for a garrison, a fortified stronghold, a place from which to conquer the Maghreb.

"I shall call it Murakush," he murmurs. "God's land."

I smile and take his arm as we walk out to the gardens.

The council meets more often now and I am always present. There are many plans to be discussed. Aghmat, a once-glorious city in its own right, will become a mere tributary stream to the new city that is being planned. Abu Bakr wants his Murakush to be a new beginning. He is so eager for it to be ready that he will not build it and then move there. He wants to be there as it is built, and for this reason we will all move to an empty spot on the great plain and begin the work. Men, women, children, slaves, animals, everyone. He does not care that we will all have to live in tents rather than our homes. Aghmat will still have some people left, mostly craftsmen and those who produce much of our food and livestock, but even I can see that they will not stay here long. Why hold a market in a decaying city? Soon enough the traders will come to the new encampment, then the craftsmen. It will not be long before Aghmat will be a city of spirits only. This new garrison, city of the future, Murakush, will drain away Aghmat's very lifeblood to feed its needs.

Now that Abu Bakr has found a common ground with me our life together is easier. He still keeps to the memory of his far-away wife, but we are closer, like beloved cousins. We sit on our bed, surrounded by maps, discussing plans well into the night. When we come to council by day we are as one, our thoughts clear, our minds united on actions to be taken. Abu Bakr's orders are given with the confidence of one who has considered all options, our glances to one another make it clear that we are in agreement. I do not have to speak much, for all can see that I am as much behind the orders given as he is. The men seem to take this as well as can be expected. They might be uncomfortable with a woman such as I were it not for their childhood memories of legends told about the warrior queen Tin Hinan, and also for my own vision. They cling to these two myths and in them they find strength and faith, believing that my place in this council is a sign of greater battles to be won, greater glory for their cause. They look as much to me as to Abu Bakr for confirmation. Their respect for me grows. I see it in their courtesy to me, their care in ensuring I am heard in council and their nods or bows in the courtyards of the palace when they come across me.

But Yusuf is not happy. I am a thorn in his side, a snake in his house. He sits as far from me as he can in council and glowers at me throughout.

"You should sit closer to me, you would not be able to see my face if it bothers you so. By sitting as far away as you can all you do is end up facing me for many hours, which I know is not to your liking."

We have arrived at the door to the council room together and are alone for a brief moment before we enter. I am laughing at him, for I know he does not like to be close to me and yet I am safe. I am the respected wife of his leader and even his loyal men have taken me into their hearts, ignoring his warnings about my possibly duplicitous nature.

He is ahead of me and puts one hand on the heavy door. When I speak he stops so suddenly that I almost step into him. He looks at me over his shoulder. "I sit where I can see you."

"So that you can keep an eye on me and my evil plotting behind your back?" I am laughing again.

His face darkens. "Yes," he says shortly, and pushes the door open.

We enter, take our usual places at opposite ends of the room and settle down to many more hours of gazing at one another as the talks go on, he balefully, I with laughter in my eyes which only serves to make him angrier.

My place by Abu Bakr's side is now kept only in council. His first wife Aisha arrives. He sent for her almost as soon as they arrived, and it has taken some time for her to make her way here. I await her with trepidation, afraid she will take more than I expect. I do not care if she takes Abu Bakr from my bed, for he has never touched me, but I am a little afraid for my place in his council.

The tall brown camel on which she sits has had an easy burden. Aisha is a withered leaf still golden in the sun. Small, wiry, her skin wrinkled, teeth missing here and there, her hands a little twisted and her shoulders hunched. But she has a warm smile and climbs down nimbly from her high seat, barely waiting for the unwilling camel to kneel. She comes straight towards me and enfolds me in a warm embrace, though she comes only up to my shoulder.

"A sister for me," she says, smiling.

I embrace her cautiously, feel her thin body and old bones, know as I do so that I may be younger, stronger, more beautiful but that I am not, never have been, a threat to her. She knows with one quick look that Abu Bakr has not lain with me as a true wife. She does not gloat about this, nor feel jealousy about my role in council, she accepts what she already knew and seeks to ease my humiliation – for each of us to acknowledge what the other brings.

"Our husband says you are his greatest strategist. He says with you to read the maps and Yusuf to lead the men there is nothing that cannot be done."

I cannot help laughing. No-one could be jealous of this little woman, only desire her as a friend and ally. She is too warm, too full of a quick bright strength that has come from many years as a beloved wife as well as her own self-reliance in being left without that husband for so long. "I do not think Yusuf would agree."

She grins back, her missing teeth making the grin bolder. "Abu Bakr said the two of you were not friends. He said anyone stepping between your gazes would be cut as by a dagger. But he also said you do not yet know one another's worth. Have you seen him fight yet?"

I shake my head.

She looks surprised. "Not even when they train?"

"I never watch them. I keep to my own apartments. Why would I want to watch them training?"

"It is a sight like no other. You should watch them one day."

I smile and call for hot tea and sweets. We sit together and talk of women's matters, our families and lineage, our rooms here at the palace. I offer her my rooms but she waves them aside. I take her to see other rooms nearby and she is content, calls for her servants to begin to unpack her belongings. I arrange for her to be bathed, give her fresh robes. She laughs at the fineness of my silks, asks for something simpler. It is Hela, unbidden, who steps forward with the bright striped woollens so much beloved of the desert dwellers. Aisha is pleased and when she returns from her ablutions she is restored. She asks to see the gardens, we climb up the walls that she may see the city from a height.

"It was beautiful," I say sadly, showing her the much-diminished glories of Aghmat. The signs of conquering are still much visible.

"It is still beautiful," she says gently. "But there will be new glories."

"Will there?"

She nods. "Abu Bakr does not fight for his own glory. He fights for Allah, and he fights for true faith. One day the wars will end."

We are interrupted, for Abu Bakr has been advised of her arrival. He comes across the gardens and takes her in his arms. I can only stand by and lower my eyes. After a few moments Abu Bakr turns to me.

"Zaynab, we will leave you now. Tomorrow I will see you in council." He smiles, his fatherly smile, and places one hand on my head, like a blessing.

I nod and smile at Aisha. I cannot even begrudge her this moment. When I saw how he looked at her and she at him I understood why he would not lie with me, no matter that she would have accepted it if he had. They are as one.

He begins to walk away. Aisha turns back to me and speaks softly. "Watch Yusuf," she says.

I raise my eyebrows.

She smiles at my incomprehension. "Watch him," she repeats. "Go to the walls when the men are training. Watch him fight."

She hurries to catch up with Abu Bakr as he reaches her rooms.

The doors close behind them and I am left alone in my courtyard.

I stand on the empty plain.

"It will be here."

I nod. "It is a good place," I say. I turn to look at Abu Bakr and we smile at one another.

"We will begin the move at once."

"Now?"

He nods, obliges my camel to kneel, helps me regain my seat and takes his own. On his command they both rise to their feet and we begin our journey back towards Aghmat, our escort of soldiers behind us. We have ridden since the dawn prayers and now we are in the heat of the day and it will be dark before we reach the city walls again. We have stood here for but a few moments and yet we know this is the right place. We have seen how the mountains will bring clear water to the planned city, how the earth underfoot is good and will support the animals who will need to graze to keep us fed. We will plant many trees – olives and almonds and dates will flourish here. By the time the city is fully built the trees will be bearing their fruits for the many mouths within its walls.

Now that Aisha is here I am more than ever Abu Bakr's child rather than his wife. I am a beloved daughter, favoured and treated almost as a son. I am a part of his plans, his strategies. He does not see me as a woman nor a wife. He does not see what robes I wear, nor how the sun touches my hair. He does not seek to touch my hand with his own when we walk together, only takes my finger and moves it to point at a different part of a map, the better to show me his thoughts on paper. He sees a clever mind, hears a quick tongue and treats me as he might one of his men.

I suppose I should be grateful I am excused training.

The day has come. We are going to Murakush. To an empty spot on a plain which we will fill with our tents and animals, our noise and plans for the future.

We look like dispossessed war captives rather than a conquering army about to build its stronghold. Battle-trained horses are loaded up like pack mules, hardened soldiers pack up belongings as though they were slaves. The slaves are worked almost to exhaustion. There is no time for good meals or fine clothes – we wear rough robes and slowly the palace empties of anyone and everyone of importance. A few soldiers are left behind to keep Aghmat safe but the army is on the move. Thousands of men, bright armour glinting here and there among their dark robes.

Many of the humble people come with us also. We have need of all – of women and children, of men and slaves. Even a garrison – for that is all Murakush is for now – needs bread, meat, vegetables, water, grains. Many hands are needed to feed many mouths. Craftsmen are needed to repair the armour of the soldiers and the saddles of horses and camels. Whole houses fall silent in a day and the streets are empty. Slowly, over many days, the procession away from Aghmat grows longer, while that empty spot on the plain begins to fill. Later there will be walls, buildings, a great city. For now, there are tents of all shapes and sizes. There is a great empty centre, which we leave for prayers since there is no mosque, for feasts and markets. Around it are placed the largest tents, those belonging to the people who command. Abu Bakr's tent is largest, for here is where we will hold council from now on. Our large cool palace rooms placed in gardens, tiled in a thousand bright colours, are very far away.

The work begins quickly. There are latrines to be dug. The shepherds must seek safe new pastures for their animals. Water must be brought. Already they are building the means to bring water to us without it being fetched jug by jug. There must be an acqueduct, and animals are brought to turn the wheels so that water will flow to us. It will be rough and ready for now, but later we can refine it, there will be a greater flow of water for the gardens that will be set aside to grow crops. For now, much of our food is preserved and brought from elsewhere. Abu Bakr's orders have been obeyed and the trade routes which pass through those cities they already hold are yielding a goodly source of taxes on the merchants who trade there and many goods are brought for our needs. Often we eat only coarse bread or couscous with dried dates and water. There is little time to prepare other foods. Sometimes there is fresh meat and it tastes better than all the great feasts I was used to in the palace at Aghmat.

"Not pining for your palace, lady Zaynab?" asks one of the men when he sees me emerge from my tent one day.

I am about to say that I miss it but other words come from my mouth. "It is a new life," I say. "But not a bad one."

The man seems surprised, no doubt expecting me to be fretting for my fine rooms, my cooling gardens, for a life of luxury such as I have been used to. He is right, of course. The tents are hot, there is little room inside them even though I have one of the larger ones. There is dust everywhere and chaos as more people arrive every day. Although I still have many servants and slaves to call my own they, too, are pressed into service to help set up the camp. There is new work to be done every day. Ovens have to be built that we may bake bread. Water still has to be fetched even if not from so far away. Cooking is not done in the big kitchens the slaves and servants were used to, but on campfires. Abu Bakr's men may be accustomed to desert life but the people of Aghmat have lived in cities for all their lives and their parents' lives before them, even their grandparents. This is a new, hard, life for them. They have come because they are needed and because as Aghmat empties it becomes clear that if they wish to rebuild their old lives they will need to be built here, in Murakush. Aghmat is a place of spirits now, each house gradually losing its living breathing inhabitants, being left for the winds to fill. There is still a souk, but it is becoming a desultory place, a quick stop-off for merchants before they come on to Murakush where their wares are wanted.

But I am happier here than I have been for many years. I do not live in fear. I am treated with respect by all and with kindness by my husband. I am wanted for my wits and my strategies, accepted by the men who matter most in this place. Even now there are tribes who are travelling here to meet with Abu Bakr, to see for themselves what manner of a man he is, how great an army he really has. When they arrive they are awestruck. Never have they seen so many men, so many camels and horses in one place. So many weapons. They are afraid at first but before they can become aggressive, as many men do when they are afraid, Abu Bakr's strong hand will be on their shoulder, a warm smile on his face. They are offered food and drink, taken to sit in council sessions, offered privileges if they will swear allegiance. They look about them and see that great things may be theirs if they agree, that their people will be slaughtered if they do not, and they agree. They leave Murakush with gifts and blessings, with safety in their hearts. They return home and as they do so they spread the word – Abu Bakr's army is not to be trifled with. It is better to be their friend than their foe. Then more leaders come to us, and so it goes on. We are fighting a war without bloodshed so far, in large part because of my knowledge. As the smaller leaders capitulate so the larger, stubborn ones are left without allies to call on.

There will still be fighting. I can see it coming when I look at the maps spread out before us. The leaders of the larger cities will not so easily roll over like trembling dogs. They will fight. But when they do they will find out what it is to fight the Almoravids, and they will suffer for their bravery.

Today Abu Bakr announces that he needs to focus on preparing his army for the next stages of conquest and so the rule of the camp's daily life is to be given to me. He has decreed that all who arrive in the camp must come to me first. I will direct where they are to set up their tents, where their animals are to graze, what work they are to be given. I have more slaves and servants given to me so that I may direct the camp's life with ease. When there are problems – when water is short or there must be a decision about grazing rights – I will be told and I must decide what is best for the camp. I am to be the ruler of my own garrison city. I am grateful for his trust and that of the men who agreed I should take on this role. Yusuf, of course, merely looks into my eyes and then away again. He does not agree, he does not disagree.

I smile at him as I leave the council. "We are both Abu Bakr's lieutenants now, Yusuf," I say, taunting him. I like to see him scowl at me. He is bad tempered and obstinate, still unwilling to acknowledge that I have been of great use to Abu Bakr's plans.

"You are a woman," he says, scowling as I had known he would.

"And you are a jealous man," I say, and move towards him to leave. He does not move, so I push my shoulder against his. He will not give way and I have to force my way out, our bodies hard against one another. I laugh as I go and feel his anger mounting behind me.

Days go by where I give out endless orders. The camp is at last beginning to come to some semblance of order although I can see that mine will never be a simple task. New people arrive daily – soldiers, slaves, animals, merchants. Families. All must be housed, all must be fed in a garrison that does not have all the facilities of a city. Those men who are not training are needed to dig trenches and build walls, for this city of tents must nevertheless be fortified. Houses will come later, safety is more important. Tents must be erected to some sort of pattern that people may walk easily and quickly between them and I find myself drawing up little maps to show paths between them. There are lavish tents made of fine leathers covered with rich embroideries and tents so tiny and grey with age they barely exist. My own tent is fairly small but Abu Bakr has told me I should have a new one made. I order a very large tent.

"What colour?" asks the man who is organising this for me.

I wave my hand impatiently. "Black, for all I care," I say. "I do not care about the colour, I care about the size. It must be large, taller than a man inside, do you understand? I am sick of being bent over double, all this crouching and stooping. It is uncomfortable. It will be a long time before I have a building in which my own airy rooms can be built. I refuse to be bent over like an old crone from now until then."

He nods and begins to walk away.

"And make it quickly!" I call after him. "My back is already aching!"

He laughs and promises that if it be Allah's will I may stand tall again very soon, very soon.

He is a man of his word. The tent is ready within ten days and it is gigantic. There are others more ornate but mine is the largest in the camp, as big as the council tent. It is a rich black all over, made with black cloth and skins and when I step inside I can not only stand at my full height but also lift my arms above my head. I am delighted. Abu Bakr laughs at me for my lavishness but I am happy. Hela is happy too. She makes up a bed for me and has my belongings brought to me. Meanwhile she takes over my old tent, which stands by the side of the new one and makes it her own, full of her chests of secrets.

The next day I wave aside all the usual demands on my time – the questions, demands, worries of hundreds of people who come daily. I appoint Hela in my place and watch in amusement as the crowd that always comes to ask me for decisions is changed into a crowd of those who seek her healing.

She looks over her shoulder at me as I walk away. "Where are you going?"

"To watch the men training,"

She turns back to the crowd, her hands already reaching for cures among her chests.

I speak with the foreman and he takes it upon himself to escort me to the first part of the walls to have been built, the part that looks out onto the training grounds. The men continue with the trenches and fortifying walls elsewhere, but at this part they are already built. There is much to-ing and fro-ing to find me something I can climb. One way or another, with many hands guiding me and the foreman holding his breath in terror at the thought of me falling and hurting myself, I am lifted up to the top of the wall, where I can sit, for the walls are broad enough for two large men to sit on, let alone my slender frame. I dismiss the foreman then and he backs away with many worries on his brow. I tell him I will call for him when I need to come back down. He nods but continues to worry and cast glances my way as he directs his men's work. Now that I am comfortably installed on the wall I can look out across the training ground.

Now I see what I did not see when they came to Aghmat, when I was taken by darkness. Here I sit on the fortified walls of a city, looking out to a conquering army. I have grown used by now to think of Abu Bakr, of Yusuf, of the army, as *my* army, *my* people, *my* plans for conquering. Now I look out and I see what others will soon see – a conquering army, the enemy, a fearful onslaught of weapons and men.

At first I struggle to form shapes within the sight before my eyes. Too many men to count – thousands had come to Aghmat but now there are tens of thousands. Camels and horses weave between the men, so that sometimes I almost see one being with a camel's body and a man's head, or the legs of a man with the head of a horse. Before they had used mostly camels, more suited to the desert and the mountains. Now horses arrive every day, for on the hard earth their hooves are swifter. All must be trained, just as the men must be. Many of the animals are fierce, fighting animals, not the docile slow beasts used for carrying women and goods. There is biting and kicking, neighs and grunts which the men must both temper and avoid.

Their weapons are everywhere. Within the camp I am used to seeing daggers on every belt, but here there are longer daggers, javelins, swords. There are shields that no common man could even lift, let alone fight behind. The hardened layers of skins shine in the light.

The men themselves I am better used to seeing around the camp. Seeing them all at once I am struck by their variety. They are of every size – the thin wiry short men, the tall loping men, the ones built like the very walls on which I am sitting. The ones who seem made of fat but whose size belies their strength. They are of many colours also. There are those so black that I can barely make out their features at this distance, those whose skin is honey-gold – they might have been even paler in their own lands but here the sun has made them its own. There are men who are so scarred by battles they might once have been of any hue. All glisten with sweat and all bear scars.

Now I begin to see individual shapes – where one man fights another, the better to learn their skills for the battlefield. My eyes move from one fighting pair to another. Sometimes they fight in larger groups. They fight with a strange mix of care and ferocity. They must truly fight if they are to be better fighters but they cannot harm one another for to do so gives greater strength to their enemies.

A shout goes up and is repeated. The men move at once and the shapes shift before me from little groups into tight, closed ranks. The foot soldiers are at the front, the mounted men behind – horses first, then camels, rising from the height of a man to twice that height. Seen like this the army is huge and terrifying. Too many men to conceive of defeating, so closely packed together that they look like one giant creature risen from dark dreams and made real.

They stand, immobile.

Then the drums begin. The beat is slow, the sound so deep it reverberates in my belly. I have heard it before, of course, but always when I was within the camp, with the chatter and noise of people and life around me, muffling its sound and making it nothing more than a distant thunderous rumble, which could be safely ignored. Sitting high on this wall the sound comes straight to me, strikes against me over and over again. The men begin to move, but no gaps appear between them. They are moving as one beast, forward, sideways, backwards. I know because I have heard that in battle they will not retreat, only advance, step after step, as slowly as is needed. In training, though, they must learn their part in this whole and to do so they must move in any direction without losing their connection, without allowing any gaps between them that could be exploited by the enemy.

In the sun's light their weapons shine and the drums add to the heat. The sound continues to beat within me. I feel myself growing dizzy and sick with it. I want to climb down from the wall but I am transfixed by the sight and though I feel ill I cannot look away, cannot raise my voice and call to the foreman who would be more than glad to see me return to the safety of my tent.

Then I see Yusuf. I had already spotted Abu Bakr earlier and smiled to myself to see him, sweating and grim faced, dealing strong blows to his sparring partner's sword. Persistent, serious, doggedly carrying out the moves needed to keep his arm strong and his lungs powerful. I saw him step back to watch the men as they made their formations, eyes squinting in the harsh light, seeking to spot any weaknesses, calling out to his lieutenants when he spotted mistakes or changes to be made.

Yusuf sits within the cavalry, close to the ramparts where I sit. His horse is huge and black, a fine animal that snorts and paws the ground. It would kick those surrounding it and gallop away were it not held tightly back by strong hands that know how to manage such a beast.

I have never seen him like this. His eyes are filled with a strange light. He is like a man seeing a vision before him, looking neither to left nor right but only ahead, no matter where the mass of men shifts to. Once I spot him I cannot look elsewhere, for the other men's faces are tired, or stern, or bloodthirsty, but Yusuf's is none of these. Now I know what Aisha meant when she said I should watch Yusuf, that he goes to war as though he can see Allah's hand urging him on.

Suddenly the drums stop. The formation shifts, then dissolves into its component parts. I blink and look about me in a daze. The foreman comes hurrying over. I allow him to help me down and return to the camp where I wave aside all food or drink and stumble onto my bed to sleep. My head pounds with the rhythm of the drums and only sleep can quiet it.

I cannot help myself. Every day, now, I go to the wall and call for the foreman to lift me up. Every day I watch while the men fight and train their horses. I wait for the moment when the beat of the drums begins, when I feel sick and dizzy yet cannot tear my eyes away. It is like a drug to me. I look always to Yusuf's face, for that light in his eyes which draws me. In council, later, I stare at him, searching for that light, wanting to see it close to, but it is not there as he talks, listens, agrees, disagrees. He catches me staring and as ever, glowers back at me.

The council is in an uproar. There are tribes to the South who have dared to raise their voices against us, who challenge our rule. We had thought the South well in hand, a safe place for us. But this new challenge threatens our hold on the trade routes and this spells danger. An army of this size must have access to the trade routes – to the taxes on merchants and traders, to the gold and slaves from the Dark Kingdom. These are what sustains us, what pays for weapons and food. There can be no rebellion. It must be crushed. Abu Bakr has decided he will take men and deal with this himself. No-one understands this. There are many who could be trusted to lead such a contingent. Yusuf, for one. Or the third-in command, also a fine warrior and a man of honour. But Abu Bakr will not listen. He has decided he will go himself and as Commander his word is law.

He holds up his hand and everyone falls silent. "I may be gone for much time," he says.

The men shift and look uncomfortable. This means he is about to appoint a leader in his absence. They are afraid he will pick a man who will make them build Murakush rather than go out and conquer new lands. These men are warriors, they lead warriors. They are tired of a peaceful life, it is dull to them. They are longing for action, for battles.

"Yusuf bin Tashfin will lead the army in my absence."

Uproar. There is much back-slapping and hugging. Yusuf is buffeted about by his men's proud congratulations. He finds time to bow his head to Abu Bakr. The council session finishes and the men whoop as they leave. They are pleased. Abu Bakr will flatten the rebellion and meantime they are left with Yusuf to lead them. He is a warrior, so there will be battles again. They all but run to the training grounds. Yusuf, Abu Bakr and I are left alone.

I turn to Abu Bakr. "What about me?" I ask, laughing. "Am I to be left with no husband?" I mean it as a joke – I will wait here just like any other wife for him to return, naturally – although I do not imagine Yusuf will want me in council. My life may change a little but I have enough to do with the camp and Abu Bakr will be back soon enough. A few rebel tribes are no match for his men. Meanwhile I have Aisha for a friend. I like her bright eyes and her matter-of-fact acceptance of the strange twists and turns of fate. I will try to learn from her.

Abu Bakr though, is not laughing. "I have thought about what is best for you, Zaynab," he says kindly.

I do not like his tone of voice. He sounds as though he has made a decision without my knowledge, a decision that will not be reversed. I fix my eyes on him and wait to hear what he has planned for me, which way my life is turning.

"The rebellion in the South is no minor matter," he begins. "I may be away for a very long time. This is why it was necessary to formally appoint Yusuf as the army's leader."

I nod. I know this. We have discussed every part of this rebellion. I might as well saddle up a horse and go there myself to quash it, for I know all that has been planned.

"I have decided that Aisha will accompany me."

I frown and open my mouth to object but he goes on before I can speak.

"We do not wish to be apart again for so long. She is used to a rough life, living in tents, as am I and all my men."

My mouth moves again to say that I, too, have learnt to live in tents of late – has he not noticed this? Once again I do not speak quickly enough.

"I believe that with your understanding of the strategies we are preparing for our future conquests you should remain here. You will be of great help to Yusuf in his new position – "

I cannot help it, I laugh out loud. I see Yusuf frown at me but really, does Abu Bakr think for one moment that Yusuf will accept my thoughts? He has made it very clear what he thinks of me. The light I search for in his eyes is reserved for the battleground alone: certainly it is not for me. He will do nothing but scowl until Abu Bakr returns.

Abu Bakr smiles ruefully but he is set in his decision now and no one can turn him. May Allah give me strength, I am surrounded by stubborn men.

"Neither of you know the worth of the other," he says. "But you will learn."

He stands up with a grunt and leaves the tent. Yusuf and I sit opposite one another for a few more moments. I wait for him to declare himself – to either concede that we will have to make the best of this unwished-for situation or to make a stand and tell me he will turn his back on me as soon as Abu Bakr leaves and that I will have no other reason to exist than to wait for my absent husband to return. He says nothing. I sigh and move onto my knees, so I may rise and leave the tent, when Abu Bakr reappears. Half-crouched in the doorway of the tent he addresses us both.

"I have been thinking. My absence may be long – perhaps more than a year. Zaynab should not be left here without the protection of a husband and therefore – "

I grin triumphantly at Yusuf. I will not be left here for him to crow over after all. I will go with Abu Bakr and Yusuf can think up his own strategies without me. If he can.

"– therefore I have decided that I will set Zaynab aside. After three months she may remarry and it is my wish, Yusuf, that you take her as your wife. In this way she will be protected and you will have a capable woman at your side. I will arrange for the divorce to take place as soon as possible."

He ducks out of the tent and leaves us again.

My grin freezes on my face. Yusuf's face is still, entirely without emotion. Slowly we each rise and leave the tent, one in one direction, one in another, in silence.

I try to object but Abu Bakr will have none of it. He is kind but he does not listen. No, I cannot go with him. No, I cannot wait for him for who knows how long. No, I cannot remain here unmarried. No, there is no-one more suitable for me to marry than Yusuf. The divorce takes only moments. I stand in my tent afterwards, speechless.

Hela is sitting by my bed, sewing. "He's younger, at least."

I turn to her, still agape from what has happened. "I don't want him! I don't care if he is younger than Abu Bakr!"

"You might have a real marriage," she offers matter-of-factly.

"Allah save me! You mean not only will he glower at me all day but he has to come to my bed as well?"

"You might have a child. Would you like one?"

"I am too old for that."

Hela sniffs. "Never too old," she says.

"Enough of your potions!" I lie on my bed and kick my heels in frustration. "Abu Bakr might not have lain with me but he was kind! He cared for me! He respected me! I sat in the council, I was honoured."

"You can still do that."

"With a man who hates me?'

Hela does not answer, only goes about her business leaving me to punch my cushions in a fury.

I sit on the wall and watch this man. In only a few months he will be my husband. If I thought that same light might shine in his eyes when he looked at me I might look forward to that event with more enthusiasm. As it is I shake my head and climb back down, return to my tent and bid a mournful farewell to Abu Bakr and Aisha as they leave.

Aisha is all smiles. "Be of good cheer, Zaynab," she whispers to me. "My husband has left you in his most trusted pair of hands. He would not see you unhappy."

"I am unhappy," I retort. "And I will miss you. So I am doubly unhappy." We embrace.

Abu Bakr comes to me. "I know you think I have wronged you, Zaynab," he says. "But you must trust my judgement."

I accept his embrace and do not argue. It is too late to argue now.

The camp feels strange, with tents missing here and there and a new leader in place. There is an unsettled feeling and I am more unsettled than anyone.

I cannot sleep tonight. I lie miserably awake, reliving every word or look Yusuf and I have exchanged. None have been kind or even courteous. He will be my fourth husband. I choke back a sobbing laugh. What is this torment of my life? How many more husbands am I to have? How many more marriages that are not true marriages? At least with Abu Bakr I felt safe and respected. The image of Luqut rises before me. What will it be like to have a cruel husband again when I had thought myself protected?

I rise. Outside all is dark and peaceful. From the tents come soft sounds of snoring, of lovemaking, of babies whimpering for milk.

I walk. Through the maze of tents, to the parts of the walls as yet unfinished, where there is still no need for gates. To one side of me, a high wall, to the other, nothing. By my feet remnants of clay, buckets of water, tools. I step past them all, walking until I am outside the camp, out on the plain where the animals graze. I can see them, those that cluster nearby, some eating, some lying peacefully chewing the cud. Those closest scatter as I walk by, those further away take no notice.

"Where do you think you are going?"

I almost scream as a man's rough hand grabs my arm. In the darkness I cannot see who it is but when he speaks again I know his voice.

"What are you doing out here?'

"Yusuf!"

"Well?" He has let go of my arm now and we stand facing one another, though neither of us can make out much more than a shape in the darkness.

"I needed to walk," I say. It sounds foolish.

"It is not safe," he says instantly.

I bristle. "Who are you to tell me what to do?"

I can hear the frown without even seeing it. "I am soon to be your husband."

"Perhaps. But you are not my husband now."

"No 'perhaps'. I might as well be your husband now."

Everything he says makes me want to challenge him. I draw myself up to my full height. When I do this we are the same height, for I am a tall woman.

"You will not be my husband until you lie with me," I say sharply, and turn to walk away.

He moves faster than I would have thought possible. He takes my arm and pulls me round to face him. He is stronger than I thought and I am a little scared at how easily he moves me with only one hand. With his other hand he pulls at the wrap around his face and then his lips are pressed to mine.

I struggle in terror, for this treatment reminds me of Luqut but then I feel his arms about me and although he is strong he is also gentle. He is not hurting me and his mouth is soft on mine. I have not been kissed upon the mouth for many years now. I stand still for a moment and then I tentatively place one hand on his arm before slowly returning his embrace. I am not as passionate as he at first, but I feel desire growing in me and I grow more bold. My embrace tightens.

He pulls away. We stand in the darkness, our breathing a little fast in the silence and then he walks away from me, back inside the camp. I cannot think quickly enough to follow, so I stand motionless in the cold air and breathe until my heart slows. Then I make my way back to my tent. I see his tent close by but I dare not even think of entering. My mind is confused with all that has happened tonight and sleep is long in coming.

In the bright daylight the darkness inside the council tent makes me blink.

I pause, for on stooping to enter I find that Yusuf is seated in Abu Bakr's place. My eyes flicker. Where should I sit? Abu Bakr welcomed me always to sit by his side, a place of honour and privilege. Side by side we could see the same things, confirm our thoughts with a quick glance to one another.

Now I am facing Yusuf and I do not know where he will want me to sit. Does he regret what passed between us last night? Will he ignore me? Will he refuse to let me sit in council, even? He had not wanted me to join the council in those early days and now that he leads this army it is his command that must be obeyed.

I brace myself, meet his gaze as steadily as I can.

He meets my eyes and then flickers them to one side. He gestures minutely with one hand to the empty place by his side. I am to sit in my usual place.

Carefully I lower myself to sit beside him. When I sat by Abu Bakr's side I never thought about how my body might touch his. I would lean across him or against him, the better to indicate maps. When I spoke my hands flew in quick gestures and if they brushed against him I did not draw back.

Now I sit very still. No part of my robes or body touches any part of Yusuf's. We both sit upright, our backs straight. We do not look to one another as Abu Bakr and I might do, laughing or challenging one another. We look to others in this confined space, we debate without turning our heads to see one another's eyes. Once we both look to the right, where one of the men is speaking, and I feel Yusuf's breath against my neck when, irritated with the point being made, he breathes out heavily. I feel the quick heat on my skin followed by the slow heat of my desire rising as my cheeks grow flushed. I shift my position, say loudly that this tent is stifling. I call for water, fresh air. The servants hurry to bring cups and to tie back larger parts of the tent's fabric that a breeze might be let in.

When the never-ending council session ends I am first on my feet, leaving the confined space before any of the men have slowly stretched to their full height. I go back to my own tent where the servants scatter before my snappish demands and finally leave me alone with the tent fully closed, cold water and cloths by my side, my body naked beneath a thin linen sheet.

I cannot sleep. I toss and turn, my body too hot as the sun rises above. Even as the evening cool descends I am too hot.

I have been a wife three times and three times I have been no wife at all. I am thirty-one years of age and I have been alone too long. I had resigned myself to a celibate life as wife to Abu Bakr, had been grateful for kindness since nothing else was offered to me. Now my fate has changed again and I have been given one more chance to feel love and desire for a man and to be loved and desired in turn. It has been a long time since I have wanted a man so badly. This time I will take him for my own and I will not share him.

Yusuf must be mine and mine alone.

Seductress

*1*T IS STILL DARK WHEN I awake. The call to prayer will come soon but for now all is silent. I sit for a few moments, drinking water that has been chilled by the night. Then I begin.

It is not long before Hela enters my tent. Her ears have always been sharp, you cannot stir, even in a tent ten paces from hers, without she will hear you. She stands just inside the doorway and observes me without speaking.

I ignore her. I am rifling through my great carved chests, throwing clothes and bed linen onto the floor. Down go my colourful silk robes, my intricately embroidered slippers, my shining veils, which are used to tie up my hair. I take whole chests; those studded with bright gems, and set them to one side, decanting their contents into plainer copies. I talk over my shoulder to Hela.

"After prayers you will find me the best carpenter and the best woodcarver in the camp. I want the best tailor of robes. I want the finest leatherworker. If the best are still tarrying in Aghmat you will send for them. Tell the traders when they come that I want fabrics, leathers and woods in black. It must be the finest, mind, none of their cheap stuff that washes to grey in three dips of water. Pure black. The traders of jewels you may turn away, for I want none of their merchandise. You are to take all of this – " I gesture at the piles of goods on the floor " – and give it to whomever has need of it."

I turn. Hela is standing over me in silence.

"Well?"

She speaks slowly, as though to an idiot. "He has to marry you whatever you are like. There is no need to change."

I come close to her so that she can see how my eyes shine in the thin light and feel my fevered breath on her cheek. "He is obliged to marry me. He is not obliged to desire me. Look at what happened with Abu Bakr."

She does not blink. Nothing intimidates her. "You think by moulding yourself to his image he will desire you?"

"He kissed me last night."

Hela nods as though this is not a surprise. "Exactly. So he desires you as you are now."

I shake my head. "I provoked him by speaking of lying together. He is a man. He is lonely here without a wife, without a woman. He is as good as my husband already, it might have been lust for any woman, not for me."

Hela's eyes roll. "And what are you moulding yourself into? What shape are you taking on now?"

I have lain awake for hours and even in my dreams I have fashioned this image. I pace back and forth within the tent as I speak – so great is my desire to make this a reality I cannot even keep still. "I will be everything he can desire. In council I will be his strategist. In the camp I will rule as his queen. Before his holy men I will be the most pious woman in the Maghreb. In our tent I will be the most desirable woman he has ever held."

"And what of his first wife?"

I shrug. "What is she to me? Or to him? If she was so precious to him he should have sent for her as quickly as Abu Bakr sent for Aisha."

Hela is picking up silks off the floor. "Why are you throwing these away?"

I kneel beside her to make the work faster, grabbing at items and stuffing them into one of the cast-off chests closest to the door of the tent.

"He wears plain dark robes and despises the riches of this world? So will I. Everything I wear will be black. I will have no embroidery, no bright gems."

Hela keeps packing in the silks. She pauses over a slipper, turning it this way and that. "Does he know that black silk is more costly than pink silk? Does he know that for leather slippers to be truly black they will have to come from a master leatherworker? You may dress all in black but your clothes will cost four-fold what they cost now."

I laugh and rest my head against her shoulder. "He is a man, Hela. What does he know of such things? If he wishes to see a pious woman who disdains finery then that is what he will see. And besides," I lower my voice, "when he holds me he must touch silk, not rough wool. He is still a man, for all his pious fervour."

She shakes her head and gathers up armfuls of my cast-off clothes. I see them later around the camp, worn by those women who can pay for such rich garments, worn by a queen.

"You are trying too hard to be loved," she says with sorrow.

"I have no choice," I retort. "He has sent for his first wife now, even if he left it late. I saw the escort leave the other day."

Hela turns back in the doorway. "The one who lost a baby to a camel kick?"

"Why, how many other wives does he have?"

She sighs at my bad temper. "Only one. She is probably old and barren, Zaynab," she says gently. "You will shine beside her."

"Like I did beside Aisha?"

She shrugs. "That was bad luck. A rare love."

I concentrate on what I am doing, taking out all my jewellery and piling it in a heap. I hold back nothing. "She will not arrive for many months. It is unlikely she will arrive before the wedding."

Hela smiles as she leaves me. "Then if you can draw him to you, your wedding night will be as you wish it to be, Zaynab," she says and ducks out of the tent.

I sit back on my heels and survey my changing tent. It is growing more sombre by the hour.

"If I can draw him to me," I murmur. "If."

Three months are long when you are burning up for a man's embrace but they are short when you must stoke a tiny spark within him until it is a raging fire. There is much I must do.

By now the camp is entirely mine to rule as I see fit. Now I order those things that will begin to make a city of it in due course. The walls move on apace, outside them I ensure that the first shoots of palm trees are nourished and kept safe from hungry animals. One day they will grow above our heads, providing shade and sweet fruits, for now, they must be protected. I designate an area to be set aside for a souk, for by now the traders would far rather come to us than to dwindling Aghmat. As the souk grows so grows our access to what we will need in the future – spices for better foods, incense for sweeter smells about us. I order fresh herbs to be grown and a slave woman takes on that job. I see her sometimes, a twisted figure of a woman limping back and forth watering her small green charges. As they grow she begins to sell them and soon trade at her stall is brisk. I am glad of it, for fresh foods have been lacking and dried dates with coarse grains and camel's milk are a poor diet. It is only now that we begin to eat more fresh meat as the flocks grow in the fertile plains, that we can use fresh herbs and taste the cleansing bitterness of green leaves rather than endless stored grains.

The people of the camp are grateful. They know they owe this change to me and I gain greater respect for it. They stop grumbling about this new life as they can see a new city beginning to take shape. It may still take many years but people will do much with a vision in their minds. A few still grumble that I have too much power but they are mostly men and their wives will hear none of it. They fear me a little, as all servants fear their masters, but they can see that I am right in my commands and so they are carried out to the letter.

There are strange looks at first for my new robes, but those who are ignorant think I am thus unadorned because to keep rich bright silks clean in this place is almost impossible, no matter how many servants and slaves you have at your disposal. Those who are pious see in me a new piety, a bending of my will to my husband-to-be's choice of garments and they nod approvingly. Only those who know fabrics and leathers smile when they see what I am wearing, for they know that no matter how unadorned I might be the clothes and slippers I wear now are those of a queen, as they have always been. Any fool with a few coins can buy cheap shining silks in a myriad of colours. Only a queen knows the value of quality and has the heavy gold coins to pay for it. In the council I see Yusuf's quick glance when I enter council in my new garb and his softened gaze. I know he never liked my opulent attire and when I continue to wear the same simple style day after day I see him look upon me with more favour. Gone are the disdainful stares when I would arrive with some fresh outrage of vivid silk held tight to my body with entwined belts of silver and gold. Now I am hidden under soft folds of black silk, which promises but does not deliver my true from. My hair falls loose and straight without shining silver veils or clasps to tame it, mostly it is only lightly covered with a black veil. Its softness brushes more than once against Yusuf's hand or arm in council and he does not draw back.

The robes have the added benefit that they accentuate my new-found public piety. Where once I prayed in my own tent now I pray ostentatiously in public. I pray when many are gathered, where the greatest gossips and the most pious pray. The gossips spread the word and the pious are pleased. I have no private moments of prayer now, all is done for show. My face is suffused with a holy fervour, my bows are so deep that were it not for Hela's precious unguents the skin of my forehead would grow calloused as it touches the rough ground over and over again. The holy men, who used to mutter in corners against me, finding it unwomanly for me to sit in council, are appeased. They talk of Yusuf's influence on me, of how their teachings are converting even those, who like me, enjoyed the riches of Aghmat in all their glory, showing little true belief. They believe that I have seen the error of my ways, that their pure interpretations of the faith have been heard. They tell Yusuf about these new changes and I see him glance at me when I arrive for prayers, a careful, considering glance. I do not return his gaze. I prostate myself and after a moment he does the same. Only once in these three months do the holy men falter in their new praise of me.

The man sits where he has been told to sit, despite his mortified protests. Slowly word carries through the camp. All make their way past my tent on one pretext or another. Even shepherds, who have no business being in camp at all, come from the fields and hills. No-one can resist the sight of which everyone is speaking. They stand a little way off, watching day after day as the curls of dense black wood fall to the ground. It is slow work, for the wood is harder than most.

Mostly our beds lie upon the ground and they are made of soft weavings with stuffing of one sort and another. The poorest sleep upon the earth with only a rug to keep the chill from entering their bones. The rich, of course, have grander beds, but even so they are made mostly of soft things – thick woollen blankets, fine silk cushions. The wood or metal that holds all of this softness is rarely of much interest. It may have a few carvings or be bent to better please the eye, but no-one has ever seen a bed like this one.

From the hard black wood begin to emerge flowers, and fruits. The children squat close to the wood and reach out a finger to touch them. Life-size and perfectly formed, were they not black and hard their little mouths might try to bite the perfect pomegranates and figs, their small noses sniff out the perfume of the roses and jasmine which twine about the legs of my bed, growing more beautiful by the day. When the carver begins his next stage of carving, however, these children are shooed away by their parents, and virtuous women blush as they walk by, their husbands glowering but then casting one quick backward glance as they walk on, unable to resist.

In the dark wood there are figures entwined and as the carving goes on, so their lusts grow stronger. There in the darkness are men and women whose bodies merge with one another in ecstasy. In the last days of its preparation the carver puts aside his sharp tools, takes up soft leathers and fats and begins to rub at his creations, bringing lustre to the writhing skin of the lovers. The women of the camp who have no children, whose business here is the pleasure of many soldiers are the only ones who dare comment now. They walk past with swaying hips and jangling jewellery, each claiming to have been the inspiration for the carver's work. They giggle amongst themselves and when a man walks by who looks more than once they call out and suggest he might like to taste such delights in soft flesh rather than in hard wood.

Hela watches me as I mix ingredients with pestle and mortar, a servant hovering by with hot water.

"What is that?"

"Nothing," I mutter, head down, arms aching with the grinding motion. The hot water is poured into the mortar and a deep intoxicating smell emerges.

"It is an aphrodisiac," says Hela without even inspecting the contents.

I do not reply.

"Who is it for?"

I continue grinding.

She sighs and gets up to leave. She pauses in the doorway. "You are not skilled with herbs, Zaynab. These drinks are for enhancing what is already there, not for forcing what is not."

I shake my head and keep grinding. "It is already there," I mutter to myself. "It *is*."

It is the heat I feel first, throwing off one cover after another until I lie naked on the bed. In the darkness with only the dying fire outside the bodies carved into the bed flicker and move, their movements lewd. I reach out to try to still them but find myself caressing them as though they might include me in their embrace. The silks of my bedcovers brush my feet where I kicked them away and I drag them back onto me, slipping them over my too hot and tender skin.

It is Hela who hears me moaning in the darkness and comes to me quickly, silently, muffling my mouth with a silk sheet while she searches around her for substances that will bring me back to myself. She pours cool water down my throat and dampens a cloth to pat me with but I turn towards her touch as to a lover, taking her hand and pressing it to my most intimate parts. She waits until I loosen her and then returns to her task, seeking to cool my fevered body and mind.

By morning I lie still and quiet. Only faint images of the night come to me. "What did I do? What did I say?"

Hela is mixing a new version of what I made. "You are not competent to mix such a drink. I should not have let you. I will do it myself now even though I think it should not be mixed at all."

"I wanted it for him. But I thought I should try it myself first."

"It was too strong. You were wild with passion."

I sit up eagerly. "I *want* him to be wild with passion."

Hela shakes her head. "If he had drunk this and been with a woman he would have hurt her. His passion would not have been contained. You can be passionate without being driven mad with lust."

I lean forward watching her closely. "But you will make it strong enough?"

She sighs. "I will increase it over time. Otherwise he will become desperate for a woman. He'll find a whore before your wedding if it is too strong."

I laugh. "He is too pious to use a whore."

"He has slaves."

"A good Muslim should not wed his slave," I recite piously.

"Who said he had to wed a slave to bed her?"

Well before the bed is entirely finished I am visited by one of Yusuf's religious advisors, who is appalled by the forms taking shape under the carver's hands.

"It is said," he begins with great firmness and keeping his eyes on me rather than the object in question, "that the angels will not enter the home of one who displays pictures or images such as…" he gestures rather weakly towards the offending carving, visible outside my tent.

I shake my head. I have been expecting this moment, I am ready. "It is *said* that when all souls are brought back to life those who have made images will be asked to breath life into them and if they cannot they will be cast aside for their presumption in taking the place of He who is greater than us all. That one should not make images of living beings for no mere mortal has the power to give them true life."

He nods, agreeing with what I am saying, but he looks doubtful. If I know all this, why am I proceeding with such shamelessness?

I stretch out my hand towards one of the finished parts of the bed. "They are not living beings," I say.

He frowns at me. I gesture back towards the carving and he reluctantly follows my hand's path to gaze at the blasphemous images. When he looks more closely a blush appears on his face but a frown begins to steal over his brow as well, for he can see that I have outwitted him. None of the men and women depicted have heads. There are no faces. Their heads are thrown back in ecstasy such that they cannot be seen or the carving, so detailed and accurate in every other way, so well planned, seems to be so large that where a head should come there the wood ends and when another figure begins the head must be imagined for it seems that the diligent carver has quite forgotten to place it there.

"But, but – " he splutters.

I smile meekly at him, my face the very image of a good and pious woman. "I would not dream of showing a living being in sculpture such as this. None of my figures may live, for where would their breath be since they have no mouths?"

He stares at me incredulously.

"Blessed is Allah and the teachings of His Prophet Mohammed," I say and he can only mumble a reply and retreat, confused.

I know the holy men argue amongst one another for days. By the time they have decided that the carvings are anyway a disgrace and should not be on public view it is too late. The bed is ready and has been taken into the privacy of my tent where it is assembled. But by now all of the camp knows that in my tent I now have a bed that is obscene, lustful, shameless. There is not a man in the camp who would not wish to lie in it with me, nor a woman who does not think of it and blush at the thought of Yusuf's power, his hard arms and dark eyes.

I make sure Yusuf drinks the potion Hela grudgingly prepares. I slip a little into his drink during council and see him grow flushed with anger over a disagreement, he who is always so calm. I mix it in his food and see him slip away in the early evening to his tent, where he lies restless. I hear him toss and turn late at night, standing quiet by his tent in the darkness. I hear him call out and moan in his sleep.

Traders from around the world provide bedding that shines like jewels within the darkness of the bed's embrace. There are blankets in wool so fine it is almost transparent. Sheets of delicate silk that slip over the skin like a lover's caress. Cushions of thickly woven silk embroidered with thread beaten from gold coins. In my tent now there is nothing of ostentation save this bed. There are large chests of perfumed black wood carved with only the most simple of designs. There are prayer mats displayed as though holy in their own right. All is black or the colour of sand. Only the reds, yellows and oranges of the bed burn like hot coals. The last of these covers arrives one day. It is a fine wool in a vivid orange with tiny discs of silver. I stand outside my tent and shake it out, turning the midday sky to a searing sunset. Through the colour I see a dark figure and when the cloth falls I see Yusuf before me.

"Yusuf," I say, bowing my head.

"Zaynab," he replies. He has little to say to me when we are outside of council. He bows his head to me and walks on but as he does so I see he glances slightly to one side, the better to glimpse the glowing bed through the open folds of my tent.

His long stride falters and I smile as I watch him go.

That night after mixing the potion, now stronger despite Hela's reluctance, into his food, I go back to the field outside the camp where I saw him that night and he is there again. I stand and watch him and he does not speak nor turn his head but when I turn to go he speaks. His voice is husky, I have not heard him speak like this before.

"That bed..."

I laugh softly. "There is nothing carved into it that I would not do when you are in my arms," I whisper. "Nothing."

He takes a deep breath and as he turns towards me I slip back behind the camp's wall and leave him alone.

The next morning a servant stands outside my tent, holding out a small pouch. Inside is a simple string of black beads and silver discs, the engagement necklace of his people. I wear it under my robes where it cannot be seen, the cold silver warming my skin.

There are small battles from time to time. Soon there will be greater ones but for now it is a matter of crushing small rebellions, challenging those tribal lands closest to Murakush, that its borders may grow piece by piece. When men return to us wounded it is Hela who provides their care. She walks from tent to tent, her healing salves and knowledgeable hands changing destinies. There are men who do not lose their limbs because of her care and men who lose limbs rather than lives. She is feared, for she has no gentleness in her manner or speech, but she is also revered. There is no wounded man who would refuse her ministrations. Meanwhile the stores in her tent grow every greater, with chests filled to brimming with bottles and measuring spoons, strange pouches and more mortars and pestles than any woman could use in a lifetime. The council can re-calculate their possible losses because of the knowledge that she is waiting in the camp.

"Perhaps Abu Bakr was right," Yusuf says as we leave the council tent.

"In what way?"

He looks across the camp, still growing larger but becoming more ordered under my guiding hand. It is no longer a random maze of tents, there are pathways which have been created, making it easier to move about. There are boundaries between what one day will be quarters.

"He said that if you were to read the maps and I was to lead the battles there was nothing that could not be done," he says.

I lift one hand to my neck, touch the tiny necklace given for our engagement and through that quick glimpse between the folds of my robes he can see that I have spared this one jewel from my purge of sober dressing. I do not reply and he does not speak again. We gaze, side by side, at the camp bustling around us and then we walk away from one another.

I have done everything I can to bring Yusuf to me with desire in his heart. I have thought of every thing that may make the warmth in him grow to a burning fire. When he turns his head in council he knows that by his side he has a woman who is shaped to his every desire. I am robed all in black, less adorned than a slave. I am pious in my speech and ruthless in my strategies. I rule the camp better than any man. He knows that in but a few days he will be my husband. When the words are spoken he knows he will come to me in the magnificent black tent which stands at the centre of this camp and lie with me in a bed of shameless desire. No man could hold the cool night air within him who has felt the flames of my desire lick at his skin for the past three months, growing hotter as our marriage day approaches. His blood has been heated with Hela's drink, day by day, drop by drop, growing stronger in its intensity as the marriage draws closer.

The words of the Holy Book are read out, the crowd murmurs and sacrifices are made. I stand in my black clothes, unadorned. One would think me a slave rather than a queen coming to be wed, were it not for the fineness of my delicate leather slippers, my rich silk robes. No jewels dress my hair or neck, nor jangle on my arms. I am still, and quiet. I stand as tall as Yusuf and looking at us the crowd murmurs again. They think we are alike, the two of us so still and dark, so sure of our rule. They see in us the truth of my false vision and they are content.

I am in ecstasy, for by my side is the man I desire and within a few words he will be my husband. His first wife has not yet arrived, her voice will not speak out against this union – or if it does, it will be too late. This all makes me happy but what brings me the greatest joy is Yusuf's hand on mine. His skin is burning up, his grip on me is tight. I slide my eyes to one side without moving my head and I see his gaze is fixed, not on the speaker of holy words, but on my lips. *I am desired,* I think, and a wave of happiness rushes through me. I have achieved what I had set out to do and only a few short hours hold me back from my reward.

I want to turn from that place as soon as the words are complete and run to my tent with Yusuf by my side. I want to feel his body on mine but it has been otherwise decided. It is still morning and there is a council to be held. After that, as dusk falls, there will be a great feast and then, only then, will I be satisfied at last. I watch him bow to me and turn to leave. I will not attend council today, for there is too much to do. I stand to watch him walk away and when he reaches the council tent I see a hesitation. He turns his head and looks to me, one glance, one quick look before he is gone. I let out my breath and turn to prepare for the feast.

There is food everywhere. Every slave has toiled for this day, every woman has brought her finest food to celebrate my wedding day. The ovens have been hot for many days and nights, blood has run freely as one animal after another has given up its life to feed this multitude. Now rich smells waft through the air and children cannot listen to the storytellers who are gathering, for their noses are filled with food and their mouths drip with hunger for all those good things now prepared with such abundance.

There is hot bread in great baskets and sweet cakes that drip with rosewater and honey. Cooking pots are filled to their brims with stews laden with every kind of spice. Pale golden with saffron, thick red with heat, the sumptuous brown of meat juices, carried with care to the central space where the feast will be held. The tents were moved back today, for fires the height of a man burned since dawn. Now their molten coals are ready to receive the whole bodies of camels, goats, sheep, cattle. The fat and herbs hiss and spit together to create a haze of taste in the air.

Rough rugs were laid out though those sitting are only the elderly and infirm for now, along with the children and the storytellers who are embroidering on my legend yet again. Those strong enough to be pressed into service have too much to do yet to sit and listen, but they joke and laugh as they go about their work. The women of pleasure are slowly emerging from their tents, hair oiled and curled, jewels tinkling, hips making a short journey a far more interesting one for those men who care to watch them pass. I watch and smile. Many men will lie with a woman tonight, and one of them will be Yusuf.

A little boy comes running towards me through the crowd. I stand still, heart beating, when I see his speed, how he darts like a fish round the many people, rushing to my side. It cannot be. It *cannot* be.

"Lady Zaynab!" He is panting with excitement as much as with the speed of his feet.

I grab at his hand and pull him into my tent where he gazes in awe at the surroundings, so different from his own family's humble tent, a ragged affair of worn colours and many mouths to feed.

"Speak quietly," I hiss at him. "What do you have to tell me?"

"She is here."

"*Now?*" No, not today, please not today. Let me have one night, one night where I am Yusuf's only wife, his only love.

He nods, eyes bright. He knows that this information is what I had asked him for, that coins will slip now from my hand to his and that his family's fortunes will change because of his quick feet and sharp eyes.

I struggle to smile, for no-one must gossip of how I looked when this woman arrived.

"She is my sister," I say, forcing a kindly tone. "And I have longed for her embrace."

"Allah be praised!" says the boy, aiming to please. "She is here for your wedding feast!"

My teeth clench so tightly together I think he will hear them grinding. I feel for coins and press them into his hand. He gapes at them, he will never even have seen some of these coins.

"How long?" I ask as he bows to me and makes for the door.

"An hour, no more, lady!" he assures me with a smile.

Hela shakes her head.

"You knew this moment would come," she says stubbornly.

"Yes," I hiss at her "But I did not know it would come on my wedding night."

She shrugs.

"You have been working on him for three months now," she says. "If he is not yours now, he never will be."

"His first wife is about to arrive," I say. "And if he goes to her tonight, my wedding night, I will die."

Hela is not impressed with my dramatic words. "You will not die," she says. "Besides, what kind of a man goes to his first wife on the wedding night of the second?"

"A man who has not seen his first wife for more than two years!"

"You will have to share him, Zaynab."

"Perhaps," I say. "But not tonight, Hela."

She sighs and gets out her mortar and pestle.

"Make it strong," I say.

She looks up, challenging me. "How strong?"

I look into her dark steady eyes. "Strong," I say. "Strong."

She hesitates, then opens a chest and pulls out the red cup.

I am shaking. My tent is too large. I long for a small place that will hold me in its warm embrace, not this mighty structure, which commands me to stand tall when all I want is to crouch, to curl up and brace myself for the unknown threat to come. I know that even now she is walking towards my tent. I sent Yusuf to prayers before our wedding feast knowing that while he prayed she would come to me.

I pray harder than any man or woman as the call to prayer echoes through the camp. My piety, though, is all for me. Let her be ugly, I pray. Let her be old. Let her be barren forever. Let her be stooped, stupid and too stunned by her new surroundings to take her rightful place in my world. Let me take Yusuf for myself over her reaching hands.

In the midst of my prayers a man's voice calls my name and I know that she has arrived. I think of the light in Yusuf's eyes, how it shines now when he looks at me, how his hand was hot on mine when we stood together to be married. I think of his growing desire and how tonight at last he will be mine. I stand tall and I walk to the door of my tent. Unseen to those outside Hela holds back the folds and I emerge.

In front of me is one of the guards sent to escort her here. He is following orders as he should, he has brought her here quickly and without taking her to Yusuf first as she no doubt will have begged him to do. She has already been betrayed. My eyes slide past his anxious face and at last I see Yusuf's first wife. Kella.

I keep my face still although I want to grimace. She is not old, as I had hoped. She is nowhere near Yusuf's age, indeed I would say she is younger than I, although she is weary with fear and travelling. She must have been almost a child when he married her, no older than when I married my first husband. Is this what Yusuf wants from a bride? A child-girl, barely rising past my shoulder? She should be rounded and pleasing to the eye but she is haggard with lack of food and water. She must have ridden day and night to come here so quickly and it has taken its toll on her. But underneath the worry and the exhaustion, the weight dropped too quickly from her breasts and face, she is pretty. A sweet face, a slender body but well formed. Bright robes, though dust-covered, wrap round her body. A young, pretty wife, heartbroken at the sight of me.

I have waited a heartbeat too long in silence. I know without looking that the escort is worried. I should have spoken by now. There is only one thing I can say in front of this man. I hold out my hands and smile at the child-wife.

"Sister," I say, and my heart shudders for the times I have spoken this word, the times it has brought me nothing but sorrow and another failed marriage.

She holds out her small travel-dirtied hands to me and dutifully repeats that untruthful word back to me. Her voice trembles as though on the brink of tears. I can only pray this means she is weak, that she will be easily swept aside so that nothing can stand between me and my last chance to be loved.

So begins my fourth wedding night.

Rival

*T*HE FIRES BURN BRIGHTLY, PLATE after plate of food is brought out. There are stories, music, much chatter and laughing. I sit in near-silence, so close to Yusuf I have to stop myself from reaching out to embrace him. He will come to me tonight.

He has no choice. The drug Hela mixed was stronger than she has ever made it. As we eat the wedding feast Kella sits in hopeless silence as each mouthful he takes makes his heart beat harder, his face turn ever more my way, his skin aching for my long-promised touch. She must have thought he would be glad to see her, and indeed he is solicitous, but she is a dish he has already tasted. I am new, and have been promised to him for so long that he can think of nothing else.

She sits on his other side, freshly robed. Under the dust that has been washed away her facial tattoos have emerged, claiming love and protection from her far-away people, who cannot see her present humiliation. Her hair is piled up in bright swathes of coloured cloth, her woollen striped reds and yellows are tied to accentuate every part of her slender body. Silver jewellery cascades from her. She should be glorious. Younger than I, bright and shining, while I am a childless woman growing older with every marriage.

But she looks like a colourful wild bird caught in a net, hopelessly seeking a way to escape while I sit freely, robed in my black rippling silks, back erect, surveying my domain, a sharp-eyed, cruel-taloned falcon to Yusuf's right hand. Perhaps before, in her desert tribe, she was ruler of her own domain, knew her own strengths. Here she is out of place, weakened, uncertain. There, Yusuf would have seen her bright spirit, her courage. To a man about to face an uncertain future these qualities may have drawn him. Here, where he feels safe in his conquests and dreams of more to come, he sees my power and it draws him more strongly. What can she offer when I have given him everything he might desire in a woman?

The feast drags on too long for my liking. I grow restless and at last, in a rare moment when Kella is not staring pitifully at him, I allow my hand to brush Yusuf's as I pass a dish. He turns as though burnt, with a quick low intake of breath, and meets my gaze. I lower my eyes but it is all the encouragement he needs. He stands and announces that we are retiring. This, of course, is met with cheers and whoops, with comments relating to my beauty, Yusuf's bravery in battle, the great bed awaiting us and other such ribaldry. Yusuf waves it all away, smiling, but his hand grips mine tightly as he leads me away. I look back for one second as we walk towards my tent and see Kella. Head down, her shoulders are hunched over as she sits in barely contained misery. I should feel sorry for her but I do not. It is the first time that I have been the woman more desired than my co-wife, the first time that I have longed to be in my husband's arms and known that he longs for me also. I cannot feel pity, for I am too happy.

He barely lets the folds of the tent close behind us, my foot is still outside the tent when he grabs me and throws me bodily onto the bed. I had thought to entice him further, to dance for him, to let him touch the figures on my bed, to then turn and touch my own warm body. I had thought I would slowly display my body, then let him discover my skills, taught to me so long ago, for another man in another time.

But he is wild with desire. He cannot pause for even a moment, grasping my silken robes and ripping them from me. I gasp, for I am afraid now. I know Hela made the drink strong tonight at my own request but now I doubt my choice. He is like a madman, tearing away all the fabric, leaving tatters of it on the floor and pulling at his own clothes. I would reach out, would try to stroke him gently to soothe his fire a little, to bring back some control, but I am pinned beneath him and he is moving too fast.

I think of my past husband, lord of Aghmat. I remember with fear his tortures and my body after a night in his rooms or mine. I try to remind myself that Yusuf is not intent on torturing me, indeed he holds me tightly and groans my name as might a gentler lover, but now he spreads my thighs and I brace myself for what is to come. I have not been touched by a man for many years now and I am afraid as though I were a new bride once more and not a woman lying with her fourth husband.

I have no choice but to try and tame him. He enters me too fast. I cry out in pain, but grip my legs around him and try to move in his rhythm. The tighter I hold him the faster he thrusts inside me and I cannot help but cry out with every stroke. But even as I cry out in pain and even as I feel his hands too tight on me, bruising my arms, my waist, my thighs, still as he groans I know I have a triumphant smile on my face although my teeth are clenched. This man would not look upon any other woman in this moment, he wants only me, he needs only my body and as he cries out I hold him tighter to me and feel his release.

He does not stop. He does not pause all night. Every time he is granted a release, a moment of sweetness in my arms so he begins again. He cannot stop, he is driven on and on by the potency of the drink. Sometimes he is gentle with me, whispers to me and kisses me, sometimes he forgets his soft caresses and once again I try to contain my cries. There are moments of sweetness for me too, when he is gentle enough and I can find my own rhythm and revel in his whispers, in his voice grown husky with love for me. But pain grows through the night, as parts of me that were made tender in his first passion are bruised and stretched again and again.

The days pass and despite the pain I cannot help but long for his presence.

"Too much," says Hela, as she smooths my bruises with her ointments. "You are mistaking pain for love. You have been twisted by Luqut and his ways."

"I never mistook what he did for love," I say.

"You think that love must be painful," she repeats. "You have known nothing else."

"My first marriage," I begin, although my voice dies away.

"A different kind of pain," says Hela. "Can you not trust that he loves you, that he will come to you without being gripped by a false desire?"

"It is not false!" I say too quickly.

She looks at me. "He would come anyway," she says. "I can make the drink lighter. Night by night. Then you will see that he comes out of true desire. And he will be gentler."

For a moment I am tempted. For a moment I contemplate giving her the order, imagine what it would be to have Yusuf come to me in gentleness. But I cannot give up the burning desire I see in him. I cannot give up being so badly wanted, no matter the physical pain. The feeling of being so greatly desired is something I cannot give up. I look away and Hela waits, but I stay silent and so the drink is made again and again.

One night I wait for him and he does not come. The drink waits, untouched. Restless, I pace about my own tent while time goes by, until I hear his voice close by. For a moment I feel a wave of relief, before I realise that he is not coming closer. I hear him laugh and I run to the door of the tent. In the darkness I see lights flickering in Kella's colourful tent and see his outline on its walls.

Hela refuses.

"You will take this to him," I snarl.

She shakes her head in silence.

"He must come to me," I say.

"It is too late," she tells me. "He is with her tonight. Let him be. You know he will return to you."

I shake my head and lift the cup.

"Be careful of what you do," says Hela.

"It will bring him back to me," I say.

"You cannot know what it will do," she says.

When I hold out the cup it takes everything I have to speak softly. My voice shakes a little and I can only hope that they think I am speaking from duty, one wife to another, a meek and obedient woman. I see her hesitant face and I return to my own tent and pray that she will not stop him from drinking it. I wait for him to come to me and instead I hear her cry out and I know that he has drunk the cup down to its very dregs and that his passion, his poisoned lust, has been unleashed upon her. I turn out every light in my tent and I kneel all night in the darkness, hearing their sounds, unable even to raise my hands to my ears. I do not want to hear and yet I must.

He comes back to me. I see that Kella no longer seeks him out. She keeps to herself. I know there will be bruises fading on her body. She is afraid of such passion, knows it for the sorcery that it is, knows herself unable to withstand it. And so I hold Yusuf to me again and endure the pain in order to feel myself desired. *What can she offer when I have given him everything he might desire in a woman?*

I am happy. I have defeated my rival. She stays away from me and from Yusuf. She seems well enough but she is no danger to me now, no threat.

Yusuf kisses me each morning, a lingering kiss that has him hesitating before he leaves my tent but I let him go, certain that he will return to me even as darkness falls. As he strides away I note with satisfaction that he does not even turn his head towards Kella's tent. Hela emerges from her own dwelling and comes towards me, her back warped from the night. She may be able to cure others but her own bones begin to grow old and it seems she will not or cannot treat her own suffering.

She stands on my threshold and I am about to gesture her inside when I hear retching. I turn my head and catch Kella as she staggers against her slave woman, her face white as she gags again, as she catches my gaze. *What can she offer when I have given him everything he might desire in a woman?*

A child.

Of course. There had to be something.

"You did it for my mother!"

Hela will not even look at me. I have to kneel before her, sink low and twist my face to make her see me. She turns away. Her shoulders are slumped, her hands tightly held in her lap. She looks old, defeated.

"You did it for my mother. Do it for me."

She tries to turn her face away. "I did nothing."

I pull her shoulder to make her look at me. "You took the life from Imen's womb!"

She shakes her head.

I will not let her forget. "Well who did, then? It was no accident. She was a healthy young woman. So who took the baby from her and left her to die in a river of blood?"

She answers but it is a mutter.

"Speak louder."

Hela looks away as though she cannot meet my eye. "I gave her a drink to put a child in her belly. I did it without your mother's knowledge. I thought if your father had a child from her he would no longer seek your mother's company, that she would be left alone to live her own life while Imen bore the sons he wished for."

"Why would my mother wish to be put aside?"

Hela shakes her head. "It does not matter now."

"Did you change your mind? Put a baby in her belly and then have a change of heart?"

Her voice is so low I have to lean towards her. She speaks cheek to cheek with me, the words coming straight to my ear, her eyes wandering elsewhere, back to the past we have shared. "Your mother tried to make a mixture that would take the baby from her and I stopped her, I told her she would kill Imen with the strength she had made. I tried to persuade her to leave Imen to bear children but she could not bear it. What she felt, it was so strong it tainted the cup. The next time Imen drank from it…" her voice grows thick with emotion, even after all this time. "I could not save her. You loved Imen. You would do to this girl what was done to her?"

I think of that night, how Myriam and I prayed in the darkness long before the dawn call to prayer. How the bright sun rose on Kairouan's walls as Imen's pale light left her. I think of my tears and the silence that descended on our house after she was gone, broken only years later when my first husband laughed low in the darkness of our courtyard. I think of Imen's fluttering pale silks, her giggles. I try to think of Imen with love but above the memory of her swelling belly I see the face of my new rival. My face darkens and I turn back to Hela's imploring gaze.

"Do it your way," I say. "Or I will do it mine."

Hela leaves my service for Kella's and I wait, impatient.

"Tell me what you need," I say when I see her. "Tell me what you need from your chests. I will have it brought to you. Whatever you need."

She turns away.

"Do you need the cup?" I ask, my voice low so that Kella will not hear me.

She shakes her head, makes a gesture as though to push the thought away. "I will do it my way," she tells me. "Do not interfere."

I watch and wait. All I can see is that Hela serves Kella well. She cooks for her, she cares for her as a devoted servant would. I feel fear grow in me, that Hela has turned against me and will protect the child growing within her until it is too late. But at last she comes to me one evening and her face tells me the news I have been waiting for.

"I will not forget what you have done for me," I tell her.

"Neither will I," she says and her voice cracks.

But I cannot dwell on what has been done in my name. I have a greater fear. Kella fell with child after one night with Yusuf. She is fertile.

"Give me a child," I say to Hela.

"That gift lies with Allah," she says, not looking at me.

"That gift lies with the cup," I say. "Give me a child."

"You have enough to do," she says. "There are rumours that Abu Bakr has subdued the Southern rebellions. What if he returns?"

"I need a child in my belly before she falls with child again," I say.

"Why must you always measure yourself against another woman?" asks Hela.

"You think no-one else does?" I ask. "You think if she bears Yusuf a son and I do not that everything else I do for him will count against a mewling babe? I could conquer the whole of the Maghreb for him and it would be forgotten against a son and heir."

"Spoken like a woman who longs to be a mother," says Hela.

I sigh. "Do it, Hela."

She does not speak but later she brings me the cup. My hands shake as I take it.

"What if I am barren?" I ask, my voice trembling.

"Is that what you are afraid of?" she asks.

"I have been married three times," I say.

She shrugs. "Were you expecting to bear a child to one of your previous husbands?" she asks.

"I am old," I say. "I am more than thirty and I have never yet born a child. She is barely twenty and she has fallen pregnant twice by Yusuf already."

"Drink," says Hela.

I drink and pray.

Hela sees my white face and nods.

"I am with child?" I gasp after I have vomited up everything I have eaten.

She nods again, her face unsmiling.

I beam. "I can tell Yusuf," I say.

"Wait," she counsels.

"Why?" I ask, touching my belly as though to ward off any ill luck.

"Too early to tell him," she says.

I shake my head and tell a servant to ask Yusuf to eat with me tonight. I send another servant to Kella's tent, inviting her also.

"Too soon," warns Hela, but I ignore her.

I have been unable to eat all day. Great waves of nausea roll over me, the smell of any food is disgusting to me. But I nod when the servants place great plates of food ready and swallow down the sharp bile that rises in my throat. When Yusuf comes and then Kella I welcome them with a smile. I pick at my food, trying to eat as little as possible, while they dine. When they are done and we have washed our hands I turn to Yusuf, a smile spreading on my face.

"Dearest husband," I say and my voice shakes a little. "I have been blessed."

I feel Kella shift next to me. I meet her gaze and smile, my words directed more to her than Yusuf. "I am with child," I say. "Allah has answered my prayers. Blessed is His kindness to this unworthy woman."

At once Yusuf's arms are about me. I am swept over with relief. I have beaten Kella. She has nothing to bring to Yusuf, I have given him everything.

But Kella is speaking and I pull away from Yusuf, unable to believe what I am hearing.

"I am also with child, blessed is Allah," she says brightly and I want to strike her. Instead I must exclaim, I must embrace her once she has emerged from Yusuf's arms. I put my arms stiffly about her, but as I am about to pull away I hear her whisper in my ear.

"My son will be born before yours."

If it were not for Yusuf by my side I would strike her. How is it that everything I do is thrown back to me, poisoned?

"Do it again!"

Hela shakes her head. She will not look at me but her voice is clear. "I will not."

"You did it the first time!"

"That was different."

"How, different?"

Hela fixes her dark eyes on me. "It was early that time. It is too late now."

I cannot stop myself pacing until she grabs me and forces me to sit down. Even so my legs pace, my feet tapping against the floor. "What can I do, then?"

Hela tries to soothe me. "Nothing. You must do nothing. You must rest and be well. You must think of your own child, not hers."

Seeing my angry face she tries to make me see it in a different light. "They will be born close together," she says. "They will be brothers." She sees a brightness in my eyes and mistakes it for happiness. "You see," she says, relieved, "it is a pleasing thought, no?"

I look at her and her smile fades.

"It is a race to be born," I say, my jaw stiffening.

"No," says Hela, trying to turn my thoughts.

"It is."

She reaches out for me. "A child comes when it is ready. A child born too soon is a child weakened."

I grasp her arm so hard I can feel my nails digging into her skin. She flinches.

"My son will be born first," I say. "You will make it so."

But I do not trust her, for Hela can be stubborn and I can see that she does not wish to bring the child early, that she will try to find ways to dissuade me. And so I ask here and there and find that the slave herb seller is a healer. She is from Al-Andalus but has lived here long enough to speak our language well enough.

I have her sent for when Hela is elsewhere.

She stands before me, her face still, as though she is adept at mastering her thoughts, at not allowing them to show to the outer world.

"You have knowledge of herbs? Of medicine?"

She nods.

I look her over. She limped when she entered the room, she stands a little crooked. I wonder whether she was born this way or whether something was done to her. Her face bears scars.

"Can you bring a child before its time?"

"Why would you wish to do that?"

"I have my reasons," I say.

She looks at me, her eyes settling on my robes where there should be fullness and there is not. "I would do nothing to harm a child," she says. She raises her eyes back to my gaze. "And nor would its mother," she adds.

"Leave me," I say.

I am so sick I think I will die.

"I cannot even hold down water," I tell Hela. "This baby will die within me."

She shakes her head. "The nausea will pass," she assures me.

"When?"

"Soon."

I watch Kella and see that she is well. She looks at me apprehensively if we pass, as well she might if she knew my thoughts towards her, but otherwise she is well. I see her eat without flinching, I see her touch her belly and know that beneath her robes it is beginning to change shape, that soon she will show. My own belly is flat, I am afraid that perhaps there is no child, that I am only sick, that I may die of something unknown.

"You are with child," Hela reassures me.

"How can you be sure?"

"I feel life within you," she says.

I make her touch me every morning, I press her hand to my belly and look fearfully into her face. Each morning she nods and I feel my shoulders drop with relief.

But the sickness begins to take its toll on me. "I feel as though I can barely stand."

"So rest," says Hela. "Rest. Leave Yusuf to rule. Rest and you will feel better."

"I cannot," I say. "Abu Bakr is returning."

She shrugs. "Let him return."

I shake my head. "Yusuf wishes to be Commander. The men are loyal to him. Abu Bakr is old, he does not have Yusuf's vision."

"Yusuf wishes to be Commander, or you wish it for him?"

"It is the same thing."

"If he challenges Abu Bakr for the leadership and fails, he will be executed for treason."

I nod.

"Still worth it?"

"I will not allow Yusuf's rule to come to an end. I will make him Commander."

"How?"

Yusuf is uncomfortable, he believes my plan may fail and he is all too aware of the consequences if it does. Besides, I am asking him to challenge his own cousin for leadership, his own kin. But I know that underneath his reluctance he desires what I desire.

"You are making your own prophecy come true," he half-jokes.

I think of the moment when I realised what I had done with my false vision, of my first husband's eyes the day he took me to Aghmat, the pain I had unwittingly put there. The pain that came after that. Something good must come from that pain. I tighten my lips. He needs the lie to give him resolve. It seems this lie is irresistible to men.

"It is my destiny," I say. "You are my husband and you will rule all of the Maghreb. But first you must deal with Abu Bakr."

The planning takes many days. Our only chance is to make enough of a show of strength to make it clear to Abu Bakr where the power now lies. Yet we cannot overtly threaten him. We must loudly offer honour and praise while silently warning what may happen if he does not accept what we want.

I inspect every part of the plan as it comes together. A personal guard for Yusuf, made up entirely of black-skinned warriors from the Dark Kingdom. I have them dressed in identical armour, their giant shields matching. The armourers work day and night to my command. Meanwhile the craftsmen build vast chests of carved wood and each is filled with treasures: weapons, silver, gold, robes of honour, jewellery, the finest skins and woven cloths. These are kept locked and ready. Meanwhile the carpenters are set to work, building the sections of a platform that can be quickly assembled.

"You are doing too much," says Hela.

"I am doing what has to be done," I tell her.

"You are not even eating," she says.

I look down at my robes. They are covered in dust. I know that they smell of sweat. My hands are bony, as is the rest of me. I still do not see any sign of my belly growing and yet I can swallow nothing but tiny sips of water and unleavened bread, one mouthful at a time. I stride by Yusuf's side so that all can see that we are as one and yet I think I may fall at any moment. Often my vision fills with a swirling darkness and I have to fight not to faint away.

"When will this sickness end?" I ask Hela.

She shakes her head. "There are women for whom it does not end until the baby is born," she admits reluctantly.

I gape at her. "I will die! Or the baby will."

"Most women survive," she says. "But it would be better if you rested, Zaynab."

"I will rest when this is over," I say.

"And when will that be?" she asks.

"I do not know," I say.

We wait.

When the children spot riders on the plain and soon after the sentries confirm that Abu Bakr's men are on their way, I give the signal and at once my plan is put into place. I watch as the platform is erected, the guard of honour takes its place, the great fires are lit and servants carry vast trays of food to be cooked.

"Be strong but kind," I whisper to Yusuf, and then I hurry to my own tent where Hela waits with fresh robes.

"Make me beautiful," I say.

"You said not to use makeup," she says. "You said Yusuf did not like it."

"I need it now," I say.

She uses rich creams and powders on my face, she tints my lips and cheeks.

"Drink this," she says and holds out the cup.

I turn it in my hands. "What is it?"

"It will give you energy," she says.

I drink it and leave her, almost running to the platform to take my place before Abu Bakr's advance guard arrives.

The platform has been covered with rich rugs, it is surrounded by Yusuf's guard of honour. Yusuf himself is already seated. He looks uncomfortable.

"Show that you are their Commander in all but name," I hiss.

"Abu Bakr," he begins.

"Is not with them. This is an advance party. He already knows that there may be a claim for leadership and he is not making his claim. He knows his time has come. These are your men. They will be loyal to you, if you can show them a ruler they can follow."

Crowds are flocking into the central square. I see Kella among them, her face turned up towards the platform in surprise. *How little you know of what must be done for a man like Yusuf*, I think. *You think bearing an heir is enough but that is worth nothing if his command is undermined.*

She is helped up onto the platform and takes up a place a little behind Yusuf and me. Now we see Abu Bakr's men arrive, a smallish party: a few high-ranking generals and then their officers, a handful of common men behind them.

They make their way through the crowd, then stand before the platform, their faces showing their shock. These are Yusuf's men, they have fought under his command for many years. When they left Murakush it was nothing but a city of tents, a garrison. Now they see city walls rising, the first buildings springing up. They see Yusuf sat side by side with a consort queen, surrounded by a fearsome personal guard. He looks like an amir.

I lift my chin as high as it will go and look down on the men. There is a silence. Then Yusuf stands.

"In the name of Allah, I welcome you back to Murakush, my brave and noble warriors."

I smile down on them as though they were each and every one my own beloved and see them swallow. Yusuf has spoken to them as if they are his men, not Abu Bakr's, while I, his beautiful queen, have welcomed them with warmth.

"Come, eat with us, my brothers, for you must be tired and hungry," continues Yusuf. He claps his hands and slaves step forwards with jugs of scented water. The men, dazed, allow their hands to be washed. The more senior join Yusuf and me on the platform while their common soldiers gather close by. Slaves bring huge platters of rich meats and fresh breads, spiced stews, piled-up fruits and other good things to eat and the men, unused to such food after many months away in harsh fighting conditions, eat heartily. Yusuf speaks with them as though they have returned from a mission he himself has commanded, praising their bravery and prowess without ever naming Abu Bakr. I watch as their shoulders relax, as they settle more comfortably, eat and drink well, smile at Yusuf and bow their heads to me. The common soldiers are given gold coins while their superiors are led to our own tent and offered gifts of honour. I stand by Yusuf. There is more than one man who glances at the lustfulness of my bed and blushes, whose eyes slip over my body in desire. They will remember the prophecy and believe they are witnessing it coming to pass at last.

"Now send back only a handful of the men," I tell Yusuf afterwards. "Only mid-ranked men and commoners may return to Abu Bakr to report back, and only a few of them. He must see that their numbers and loyalty are much diminished."

And so the smaller party of men returns to Abu Bakr and we wait again.

The messenger who arrives brings us good news. Abu Bakr agrees to our request to meet away from Murakush, at a place midway between here and the humbled Aghmat.

"He is no fool," I tell Yusuf. "He knows what is coming. We have only to play our part."

We ride out at dawn, Yusuf and I at the head of an army of several thousand. Just behind us, clearly visible, are the senior men Abu Bakr sent out. Also behind us somewhere is Kella, part of a group of people of importance: the tribal leaders who have sworn allegiance to Yusuf, generals. His guard surround us. Behind them, thousands upon thousands of men in full battle armour, a show of absolute power, of unbeatable strength.

"And if he has brought all of his army?" asks Yusuf. "You expect us to begin a battle? Cousin against cousin?"

"He will not have his army," I say.

"How do you know?"

I think back to Abu Bakr's kindly gruffness, his good nature, his growing weariness when more battles were spoken of. "He will be alone," I say.

I am right. On the plain is a tiny shelter, a simple thing made of a few poles and cloths. As we draw closer I can see less than twenty men around it, armoured but with their weapons sheathed. Beneath the shelter, protected from the heat, sits Abu Bakr himself. A little greyer, a little wearier, but otherwise the same. For a moment I think of his gentleness to me, how he treated me like a daughter, how he praised my intelligence and knowledge, gave me a voice in council. I think of calling off my plan, but we have gone too far now and anyway I can see that Abu Bakr is already resigned to what is about to happen.

We halt before him and there is a long silence. As his military subordinate and younger relative, Yusuf should dismount, should embrace Abu Bakr. Instead I make a tiny gesture and the guards step forward with the great chests of treasures. They unlock them, the turning metal keys loud in the silence. The lids are thrown back to display the treasures. It is the completion of our show of wealth and power, of transferred loyalty.

Abu Bakr looks out across the plain, filled with thousands of men in tight fighting formations. He looks at the chests of treasure and then, instead of looking at Yusuf, he looks at me. His eyes crinkle in a wry smile, an acknowledgement of what has happened and at whose command. Then he holds out a hand to Yusuf and speaks clearly, for all to hear.

"Will you join me, cousin?"

Yusuf waits just a moment longer, as I instructed him to. Then he dismounts and makes his way to Abu Bakr, sits down at his side. The men tighten their grips on their weapons but already Abu Bakr is speaking again. The words are smooth enough that I can tell he has already rehearsed them, knowing what was to come.

"My cousin Yusuf. My true brother before Allah. There can be no man more worthy than you to command this army of holy warriors and to undertake a holy war in the name of Allah."

I feel the tension lower, hear the tiny sound of every man loosening his grip on the hilt of his sword, magnified many thousands of times over. I meet Abu Bakr's gaze and he nods. I nod back, an acknowledgement of his good grace. He speaks again.

"I am a simple man, one who loves the desert, home of our families and seat of our power. I wish to return there with a small force of my own men. There we will continue our work, fighting back the rebel tribes and securing the trade routes for our own needs. Brother, I ask you to assume command in my name. I will return to the desert with all speed, for this is no longer my place."

Documents are to hand to be agreed on, already worded to my order. The transfer of power was over long before now. By the time Abu Bakr remounts his horse and gathers his men about him many of the soldiers have already been sent back, some with instructions from me. We turn our horses back towards Murakush, but not before Abu Bakr speaks with me.

"Aisha sends you her greetings."

I smile at the thought of her. "Send her mine," I say.

"Are you happy?" he asks.

I think of Kella's swelling belly. "I try to be," I say.

"You have a brilliant mind, Zaynab," he says. "You should have been a man, the world would have recognised your greatness."

"It still may," I say.

"I do not doubt it," he says. "I thought it before and I know it now."

"I have a warrior at my side," I say.

He smiles. "It is the superior warrior who wins without bloodshed," he says. "Goodbye, Zaynab."

"Goodbye," I say. Our hands touch for a moment before we turn away from each other. I look back over my shoulder before I join Yusuf at the head of the army again and see Abu Bakr's party, small on the vast plain, heading away from us.

I have won.

Murderess

*T*HE UNENDING SICKNESS OF MY pregnancy cripples me but my spirits lift at Yusuf's new status. Abu Bakr's name may remain on the gold coins but Yusuf is now leader of the Almoravids in all but name. And at last my belly swells and I feel life growing within me.

Now we can plan for greater conquests. The army is made vast by new recruits, each of them trained to Yusuf's standards. I watch them myself as they are drilled on the plain, over and over again. Money for armour comes from taxes levied on Jews and the merchants who follow the now secured and safer trading routes.

I think of what Abu Bakr said, that to win without bloodshed is the greater victory. The army is now so vast that I advise Yusuf to send out only a small part of it to Salé and the region quickly submits to his authority without fighting. They know that should they choose to fight, Yusuf will simply send the whole of the army and they will be utterly crushed. By offering their allegiance they will come under his protection, which is worth a great deal. Having seen the success of our strategy against Salé, it becomes our way forward. To each region, each leader, we offer a choice: submit to us, pledge allegiance and receive honour and protection, or face the might of an army the like of which has never been seen before. Meknes falls, its amir moving out of the city and setting up a humble settlement in the region, leaving the city open at Yusuf's command. It is an important win for us, for it is close to Fes, which may be harder to take. It will act as a provisioning ground for us, supporting any siege required.

While Yusuf builds the army, I build Murakush. I command the builders to work harder, faster, longer. The city's walls and ramparts are complete. Now they turn their attention to the homes and buildings that must rise within the walls. Bakeries, hammams, a mosque. The mosque is large although not large enough for Yusuf's liking, he will want a bigger one in due course. Homes spring up. First a large and imposing palace for Yusuf and me. He makes a face when he sees the plans for it.

"You are not in the desert now," I tell him. "You are the leader of the Almoravids and you will receive fallen amirs, new leaders who must pledge allegiance to you. They will not do so in a tent when they have come from a castle."

"I do not want splendour," he says.

"You need splendour," I retort.

And so the building is large, so that it can accommodate leaders and their entourages, the servants needed to offer feasts, the great chamber for council meetings. But it is simpler than many leaders would have created. I allow the craftsmen in but they must work to a difficult brief. Carved plasterwork yes, but only using calligraphy praising Allah. The paints and designs on the doors must be simple, none of the flourishes and elaborate designs they might usually offer for an amir. Carved chests for our belongings, but again they must be simple in design, although I have them made from perfumed woods, the better to care for our clothes and other belongings. The garden courtyard is lavishly planted but the pool is tiled with a simplicity that makes even the craftsmen look doubtful. But I am right, for the courtyard becomes one of Yusuf's favourite places, its simplicity and use of nature pleasing to him. Sometimes he even takes a blanket and sleeps there, as though remembering the old days when he slept by his men's side and ate only bread and meat.

He complains again when he sees the meals I order when we have visiting dignitaries staying.

"They are your honoured guests," I say. "You cannot feed them only bread, meat and dates. They are not your men on the training ground."

Reluctantly he allows me to order what is appropriate, although if we are alone then the servants know to bring only the simplest dishes.

Kella I place in her own house nearby. I do not want her too visible to Yusuf and by her face when I show her the new home I can see that she is relieved not to be too close to me. I eye up her swelling belly, larger than mine, with fear. I dare not ask when she is due, I am already afraid of what I will have to ask of Hela, of bringing my unborn child into the world too early, perhaps risking its life. So I have her placed elsewhere but tell Hela and two other servants to keep a watchful eye on her, to let me know if anything strange happens in her household, if she seems to be near her time.

Murakush grows under my hand. One tent and then another is taken down, our city of cloth becoming a city of mud bricks, rising higher each day.

The people of wealth commission tilework and pools, painted wood and beaten metals to adorn their homes. Craftsmen labour night and day, there is more work than they can keep up with. The last tents fade away as even the common soldiers and their families have their own homes built. Arches curve into shape, great gates are hung and painted or wrought in metal. Different quarters spring up: the armour-makers, the metalworkers who create jugs and platters, handles, hinges and locks, their great hammers beating, beating. The weavers' workshops turn out fine cloth and rugs, vast carpets to soften the newly-built homes. The leatherworkers, the vendors of street food, take up permanent positions rather than trading where they find themselves. Fresh fruits and vegetables are brought to the markets from the huge gardens growing up around Murakush, for a great city has need of many farmers to feed it. I have vast water tanks built, to save winter rains and melted ice from the mountains so that we will have water all year round and the gardens will be irrigated.

The people begin to grow proud of Murakush. They belong to a great city, they are no longer making do in a garrison camp. Now they crave finer clothes, better food. They wear perfumes and choose elaborate scabbards for their swords. Merchants seek out the city, it becomes a major point on the trade routes.

"You should be proud of what you have done," Hela says.

"There is still so much to do," I say.

She shakes her head. "You need to rest," she says. "You are coming into your final month."

I look down at my swollen belly, which sits oddly against my bony hands. Kella has grown plump, soft. Her cheeks are rounded, her hands have little dimples showing. She eats well and has not been sick since her very early days. I still struggle to keep food down.

"This baby has been grown on nothing but bread and water," I say fearfully.

"All will be well," says Hela. "But rest."

"I must attend council," I say.

In council we are entirely focused on Fes. It is a strange city, made up of two cities side by side but with a wall between them, with two amirs, one for each part. It will be like taking two cities at once. The first move has been made: we have sent and asked the amirs to submit with grace, to pledge allegiance and give their cities to us without a battle. Both have refused.

"There will be a siege," says Yusuf. Heads nod around the room.

I nod along with them. It is I who will provision the army, who must ensure Meknes will be ready to support the siege and act as a garrison for our men. The order to take Fes is no small matter to me. For a moment I envy Kella, no matter how much she has been put aside by Yusuf. She has nothing to do with her days but eat and rest, to feel her growing child within her and triumph in the knowledge that it is due before mine. Meanwhile I am racked with sickness and feel my body grow weak beneath its burden, yet I must continue, must plan strategies by Yusuf's side and carry out feats of military planning that would put a man to shame. If Fes falls it will not just be because Yusuf's men are strong, well trained and vast in their numbers. It will be because I moved thousands of men and animals there, because I ensured their weapons were fit for use. It will be I who feeds them, ensures there is water for the men and their mounts, that there are fresh troops ready to relieve them from our garrison in Meknes, that the armourers are ready to make repairs at night while the men fight by day. If Fes falls it will be I who will order the documents that will ensure peace, who will decide where and how the fallen amirs may live. I shake my head. She may have a son. But I will have many more. And if I can do her son harm, I will do it and I will not hold back. Every time I see that life grows in her womb I will find a way to take it from her. Before or after it is born, while I still live each one of her children will die. I will not be usurped by some nobody, some girl who thinks she is entitled to give Yusuf an heir when I have been everything to him, have been his right hand and a better strategic mind than his best generals. I will not have the baby of a foolish girl push my own children out of the way of inheriting Yusuf's kingdom, for it is a kingdom I have created alongside him, it is as much mine as it is his.

"Her shutters have not been opened today," reports a servant.

At once I am on my feet. Her time has come earlier than I thought. I have not had the time I needed.

"Leave her," says Hela from the back of the room.

I ignore her. Heavy with my own child I hurry to her home and catch the sound of a child's cry as I open the gate, although I cannot be certain where it comes from, whether Kella's own home or somewhere else. Inside the lanterns have not yet been lit, even though it is already dark. I make my way partly by feel inside the house, where a dim light draws me upstairs to Kella's rooms. My heart thuds, my weak legs ache at each step.

She lies alone, half-propped up on cushions, her face a little dazed. Her belly still protrudes, but not as it did before. At the sight of me in the doorway she startles and looks over my shoulder as though expecting someone else to join us. There is no baby.

"You have a son?" I ask. I cannot see a baby anywhere, I wonder whether one of her servants has taken it away, whether they knew I would come.

She does not answer, only stares up at me like a frightened animal.

"It is my own children who will follow Yusuf," I tell her, and I hear my voice tremble even though I meant to sound fierce, meant to intimidate her.

"Why do you hate me so much, Zaynab?" she asks, tears falling down her face. "I am nothing compared to you, yet you hate me and pursue me. You seek to do me harm at every possible opportunity. I have done nothing to you."

I look round the room again. I barely hear what she has said. She knows nothing of my life, this silly girl who wanted the freedom of the trade routes and ran away from her family to follow Yusuf and his army as though she were some lovesick fool, without a thought for what her future might hold, for what kind of mission Yusuf was embarking on. At her age I had already lost my first love and been thrown into the clutches of a monster.

"I am always second," I hear myself murmur.

"You are a queen," she whimpers. I want to laugh at her for thinking that being a queen must mean that I am happy, that my life must be good. Only a child thinks like this. And still I cannot see the baby. I think to search the house but then shake my head to myself. If there is a baby, I will find it soon enough.

"Before or after it is born, while I still live each one of your children will die," I threaten her and see her eyes widen. Now I know there is a child and it is alive. She cannot command her feelings well enough, they are visible all over her face.

"Get out," she says, her voice shaking in fear, while her eyes flit behind me again.

She lies. She claims that the baby died and Yusuf weeps with her.

"She is lying," I tell Hela. "That baby was alive when I went to her home."

"Did you see it?"

"No," I say.

"It might have died afterwards," she says.

I look at her.

"Forget the child," says Hela. "It is gone."

"Gone where?" I ask her and she does not reply.

"Find it," I tell her.

My own son must be destined for life as a warrior, for I gave instructions for the siege of Fes even as I birthed him, sending messages through gritted teeth to Yusuf with one servant and then another.

"The pain will be over soon," Hela tries to soothe me.

"It is never over," I say, panting. "It is one thing and then another, my whole life long."

I think I will split in two.

"Scream," says Hela, watching me.

My teeth are so tight together I think they will break, my jaw aches from my silence.

"Cry out, Zaynab," she says. "You cannot hold the pain inside."

But I do. I hold it until I am lost in darkness and when I awake there is a baby beside me.

"You have a son," says Hela.

He is tiny. I look down at him in silence. A fierce joy runs through me, a love so violent I am afraid to touch him in case I crush him.

"Hold him," says Hela.

I put out one hand and touch his face. At once he opens dark eyes and cries.

"Call a wet-nurse," I say.

Hela frowns. "You can feed him yourself, Zaynab," she says. "I will help you learn how."

I shake my head. "I cannot," I say. "I must attend council."

My son is named Abu Tahir al-Mu'izz and Murakush erupts in festivities for him, celebrating an heir for Yusuf, a sign of Allah's favour, surely. Why, I have been married three times before and have never born a child, I am old for childbearing and yet as soon as I wedded Yusuf I have been proven fertile after all. Abu Tahir is surrounded by nursemaids and an eager-to-please wetnurse, more servants and slaves are allocated to his service, whatever service a tiny baby has need of.

Hela shakes her head. "He only has need of a mother," she says.

"He must have everything," I tell her.

Council sits long hours and now the men begin to march North, joining the ever-growing garrison at Meknes, ready to take Fes.

I am regaining some strength, now that the nausea of the past nine months has left me. I eat hungrily, seeking to cover up the too-obvious bones of my hands, my neck and shoulders. When I look in a mirror I stand tall again, a women of power. I cannot help but feel a little sorry for Kella. She is nothing but a foolish girl who tried to take from me what was mine and now has lost everything.

Except that I catch sight of her one day and when I do I summon Hela.

"That is not a woman who has lost a child," I say. "Look at her. She is well fed, she smiles, she goes about her life as though all were well and yet she claims to have lost her son, her third child."

Hela says nothing.

"You will follow her, wherever she goes," I say. "That child is not dead. Find it." She makes to speak but I wave her away. "Find the child," I say.

The two amirs of Fes are given one more warning but they do not show wisdom, only stubbornness. The siege is about to begin.

"Have you found the child?" I ask Hela.

She shakes her head.

"It is somewhere in this city," I say. "I know it."

"Kella has not been anywhere near a baby," says Hela, holding Abu and half-singing to him. Her face lights up when she sees him.

I walk in the dark streets of the souk and ask for the merchants who will not flinch when I tell them what I need. I send Kella a ring set with a tiny box that contains a perfume, the use of which will kill her. If I cannot be certain of the babe, I will be certain of the mother. I will not have a baby hidden from me and then revealed as an heir who can topple my own children. I have the servant who delivers it to her claim it is a gift from Yusuf and she, the innocent, wears it with pride.

The siege begins.

Each day I await news. I sit in council or in my own rooms and I do not hear what goes on around me. I think only of the ever-beating war drums, how their endless rhythm makes the enemy uneasy at first, before they grow unable to think clearly, their ears and minds filled with the constant sound before they have even been engaged in battle. The soldiers and their families will look out from the walls of Fes and see an army the like of which has never been known before. They will swallow and wonder what it will be like to fight such an army, whose tight formations are so unlike anything they have encountered in previous local skirmishes.

The siege goes on day after day and while the armies of the amirs begin to diminish, our own stays strong in numbers. Now the people of Fes will beg their amirs to reconsider, for their fathers, brothers and husbands leave the safety of the walls to fight and do not return.

The drums beat on, I hear them in my mind even though they are in Fes. They are my waking pulse, my sleeping breath. I sit on the walls of the city and look out across the plain, think of our army, imagine the dark mass of our soldiers, slowly advancing on the men of Fes, crushing them.

"Lady Kella is in your rooms," a servant tells me.

I make my way to her, my feet swift. I am amazed she is still alive.

She looks drunk. Her eyes are unfocused, she moves her head this way and that as though she can hear something.

I sit above her on my bed, look down on her.

"What have you given me, Zaynab?" she asks, blinking at me as though she cannot see me clearly. "I thought the perfume was from Yusuf, but now I know it was from you. It does strange things to me, I see visions of terrible things and I hear things I do not wish to hear. My feet stumble and I feel that I might fly like a great bird if I were only to leap from my window. I talk and talk, telling all that is in my heart, no matter who is listening. I feel light, and then the colours grow so bright they hurt my eyes until I grow afraid." She talks too fast, then too slowly, too loud and then too soft as if she cannot hear her own voice, cannot control it.

"You are strong," I say. "I thought it would kill you."

She stares up at me. "Why do you hate me so much, Zaynab?" she asks, tears starting in her eyes.

I sigh. It is like speaking with a child. She cannot see beyond her own concerns. She is still speaking, not even waiting for an answer from me.

"I have not tried to fight you. I want only to help my husband succeed in his mission, to bear him children, to build a great country. Yet you treat me as your greatest enemy. What more can I give you? You have taken my husband. You have taken my children – one from my womb, one from my arms – "

I gasp and slide down from the bed so that our faces are suddenly barely a hand's breadth apart. My heart is pounding. I cannot believe she has let this slip.

"*Taken?*"

She tries to pull away from me, her eyes wide with the fear of what she has just revealed. "He is dead."

I shake my head. "You said I took him. He is *alive?*"

She tries to lie. She begs again for me to soften towards her. Her voice is nothing but an annoyance to me, her innocence enraging. And at last she says something of interest. She rises, unsteady on her feet.

"I am leaving, Zaynab. You have tried to poison me. No doubt you will try again. What do you want – my life in exchange for my son's?"

My heart is pounding. "I might consider such a bargain," I say.

I watch her walk away, clinging to walls as she goes. Behind me Hela enters.

"Watch her," I say.

Still we wait for a messenger from Fes.

"She is shopping," says Hela.

"What?"

"Kella," says Hela. "She is buying things in the souks."

"I do not care what she buys," I tell her. "What am I, a housewife? Do not bring me useless information."

"A saddle? Piles of household gifts? A sword?"

I frown. "For her own home?"

"Most has been sent away, back to her people's camp."

"Most?"

"She kept a racing saddle."

"She cannot be allowed to leave," I tell Hela. "I need to know where she is. She and her child."

"If she leaves she will no longer trouble you."

"Why?" I spit. "You think she will stay away forever, not return with a fully-grown son she can show to Yusuf and claim his place as heir?"

Hela shakes her head. "I do not think she will return, if she goes. I think she would leave to protect her son."

"I will not risk that," I tell her.

We look at each other.

"Command me," says Hela.

"You know what to do," I say.

"I want to hear you say it," says Hela. "I will not take a life on hints and whispers."

"Kill her," I say, the words out of my mouth so fast I am not even sure I have said them. They hang in the air between us.

She gazes at me as though she believes I will add something, as though I will countermand what I have said.

I hold her gaze. I hear footsteps running and a messenger stands before me, sweaty and dusty.

"Fes has fallen," he pants.

We are jubilant. There is feasting and celebrating throughout the city. Fes is now our stronghold in the North. Our army is unstoppable, we have conquered not one but two cities side by side. Now the great walls that separate them will be torn down and we will command one great city to rise from the ruins.

Yusuf and I sit late into the night, maps of the Maghreb spread out before us, our bodies slick with sweat from our coupling. With Fes falling, more and more leaders will submit to us without fighting, for they have been shown what it means to defy us. Yusuf's fingertips trace the contours of the regions that lie before us.

"The Mouluya valley," he murmurs.

"Tlemcen," I return.

He raises his eyebrows. "So far East?"

I shrug. "Why not? And further: Algiers."

He laughs. "You are unstoppable, Zaynab."

"I am," I say, curling my body back into his hands. "I am."

The dawn call to prayer comes and Yusuf leaves me in the half-light. I do not follow. I am lazy with relief at our plans coming to fruition. I lie in the tumble of blankets and listen to the world around me, the servants clattering about, the merchants in the alleyways. I have created a great city from nothing, from sand and tents. And I will create many more.

"She is gone."

I blink and struggle into a sitting position. Hela leans in my doorway as though unable to stand unsupported. Her face is white. In one hand she clutches something wrapped in a rag.

"Gone?" I repeat.

"Gone," she echoes.

"Dead?"

She shakes her head.

"I told you to kill her," I say.

"She broke the cup," she says, her voice shaking.

I frown. "What are you talking about?"

She lets go of the rag in her hand and two pieces of wood clatter out of it onto the floor, two halves of her carved cup. We both stare at it. I feel a sudden fear: what if the drink that drew Yusuf to me, that has kept him filled with desire for me, can no longer be made? What if it is not Hela's skills with plants but the cup itself that has done the work?

I swallow. "Did you poison her?"

"She spat it out."

"Did she swallow enough?"

"I do not know."

"And where is she now?"

"Gone," says Hela. "Her camel is gone. As has a man from her tribe, one of Yusuf's soldiers."

"She had a lover?" This, I had not expected.

Hela shrugs. Slowly she lets her body slide down the doorway until she is sat on the floor, her hands close to the cup's broken halves. She strokes one half, as though it is an injured pet, a dying creature. It makes my skin crawl.

"Does Yusuf know she is gone?" I ask.

She shakes her head.

"Do not tell him yet," I say.

I dress quickly and leave the room, brushing past Hela, who does not move.

I send out scouts in all directions but it is too late. Kella has gone, there is no trace of her. Her two slaves are also gone. Not much is known about the man when I enquire. He served in our army, he was from her tribe, perhaps they will return there although she cannot be so stupid. It is more likely that she believes we have made a pact: her disappearance for her child's safety. Perhaps she will return to the trading life she had before she met Yusuf.

I cannot keep the information from him for long. When he finds out that she has disappeared he, too, sends out scouts. I already know they will not find her but I stand by to comfort him. I remind him that her child died and that perhaps she has ended her life. I hold him when he weeps for her. But the days go by and then a month passes and he grows resigned, he no longer speaks of finding her. There is gossip of course but we weather it, it is nothing compared to our successes and I make sure my son's nursemaids show him off in public, that he is seen with Yusuf, a reminder that this is his heir, that I am his wife and queen.

I should feel relief. Kella is gone. I am Yusuf's queen, the mother of his heir. Our army cannot be stopped. If there is a baby, if Kella has actually left her child behind, then I cannot find it. Perhaps Kella wanted only for the baby to be safe, for if she is not here then how can the child ever be proved to be Yusuf's? A passing similarity of their features would not be sufficient. If there is no mother to claim its father, it will be one child among many hundreds, thousands in our kingdom. It cannot stake a claim. I should feel relief.

But Hela is sick. I think of the moment when she told me that the cup was broken and I think she has been sick from that moment onwards. Her skin has taken on a strange pallor, as though there is no blood beneath it. She no longer walks, she shuffles and she does not speak, only mumbles replies if she is asked a question or talks to herself when there is no-one nearby. The broken cup sits in her room, set into a niche in the wall as though it were something of beauty to be admired or something holy to be worshipped. When I visit her in her rooms, which she leaves less and less, I find her in half-darkness, the shutters closed. She sits on her bed, huddled in blankets as though she is permanently cold and she stares at the cup.

"Throw it away," I say, standing in the doorway. I do not want to enter the room, it feels heavy, as though it were full of something unseen.

She shakes her head.

"I will do it for you," I say, although I do not want to touch it. There is something about the cup that still seems alive, even though it is broken. I cannot but think about what it did to Luqut, how it took away his lust for me and then took his life when he went into battle. I think of the lust it stirred in Yusuf, a lust that has not yet faded. I owe the cup many things but I am still afraid of it. I think of Imen and Kella's lost children.

But Hela sits up at once, shaking her head. "Do not touch it."

"You are a healer in your own right," I tell her. "You do not need the cup." I am not sure this is true. I know she is a gifted healer and that she has her own powers, her skill for sensing the feelings of others, but still I am not certain how much of her power comes from her own abilities and how much from the cup. Her sickness frightens me, it is as though her life force has been broken along with the cup.

"Tell me what you need and I will have it made for you," I tell her. "Or a servant can bring your herbs here and you can make it yourself."

She shakes her head.

"You cannot die just because a cup breaks, Hela," I say, trying to sound light hearted. But my voice does not sound light. It trembles.

She does not answer.

"I command you," I say, trying a different approach. I make my voice hard. "You must rise up and serve me again, Hela. I have need of you."

"You are set upon your path," she says. "You can follow it alone now."

I feel a heavy weight settle in my belly. "I cannot manage alone," I say and my voice wavers more now, I can feel tears coming to my eyes.

"I have failed," she says.

"In what?" I ask.

"I swore to bring happiness to your family," she says and her head slumps down, she does not meet my gaze. "I failed."

"You served my mother," I say awkwardly.

"She was not happy," says Hela. "I tried but I failed. Then I looked to serve you, for I felt my obligation was not yet complete."

"Obligation?"

"And you are not happy," says Hela, ignoring me.

"I am Yusuf's wife and queen," I begin, then stop. "I have given him an heir," I add. "The army… our conquests…"

"You have spent your whole life desperate for love," says Hela from the darkness. "Desperate to be loved, to be the only object of a man's desire, to be his only thought, to be of supreme importance to him."

"Enough of this," I say. I do not like her voice, it sounds like a message from another world.

"It will kill you," she says. She sounds weary, each word an effort. Her breath rasps in and out and every time I think there may not be another breath. "This terrible need to be loved, Zaynab, it will kill you. It robs you of every moment of happiness you might otherwise claim."

"Enough," I say. "I will not listen to this, Hela."

I leave her but cannot settle to anything. I wander through the rooms of the building, I sit with my baby son, dandle him in my arms, ask questions of the servants to be certain he is being cared for. If I hear of anything in his treatment that is not right I have them whipped. He is too precious to me, the thought of anything happening to him fills me with dread. I take my place in council, but I cannot focus on what is being discussed. I send servants to Hela, offering food, drink, lanterns, healing herbs, blankets, whatever she has need of. She refuses them all. At last I return to her rooms. I can hear her breathing before I even reach her, the desperate sucking in of air and then its slow release. The room is dark, only faint streams of dusty light trickle through the closed shutters. There is a musky smell, as though something is decaying, rotting nearby. I stand by her bed.

"Finish this," says Hela. Her voice startles me.

"Finish what?" I ask although something in me already knows the answer.

"Release me from my vow," says Hela.

"I do not know what vow you made, but I release you from it," I say. "You have stood by my side, Hela. You have made me who I am today."

She sighs, as though my words are painful to her. "I know," she says. "I am sorry."

"I meant you have made me a queen, a wife. A mother," I say.

She shakes her head, a slow movement to one side and then the other.

I stand in the half-light and wait for her to speak again but she only continues to struggle for breath. Slowly I make my way to her side, sit on the edge of her bed, take her hand in mine. Her hands have always been sturdy. Now they have lost their strength and they feel like bones bound together with ragged skin, limp in my clasp.

"Release me," she says again, a croaking whisper.

"I do," I say. "I have."

Again the slow side-to-side shake of her head. "I cannot go," she says. "I have tried."

I swallow. "What can I do?"

Her spare hand feels about her until she finds a blanket. She tugs at the corner of it, pulls it until it touches my hand.

"No," I say.

"I cannot go," she says again. "Let me go."

She goes quickly. I do not have to hold the blanket for long, but when I pull it away again it is already wet from my tears. I wonder if she tasted them before she died, if my grief trickled through the warp and weft and touched her lips as the breath left her body.

I sit in council while the deaths are tallied. Fes has been crushed, thousands lost their lives, but we also lost men. Their names are listed so that they can be prayed for, so that the correct rituals can be carried out. I know that there are families in Fes who think of us as murderers, who curse Yusuf's name and would curse mine too if they knew my hand in their loss.

Back in my rooms I hold Hela's broken cup. It does not feel strange or powerful now, it feels like what it is: two broken pieces of wood, lifeless in my hands. Hela is the only person who saw the gaping emptiness within my outer perfection, the fear inside my utter control. She saw me for who I truly am.

Now she is gone. At my hand.

Spy

WITHOUT HELA AT MY SIDE I feel vulnerable. Now I must stand alone, must hold my power without her help.

I have feared for a while that my knowledge of the Maghreb and all its rulers, its secrets, deceits and counter-deceits, the certainty that the Almoravid council craves from me, would end. I have stretched out all I knew and of course I have learnt from them as they have learnt from me. But I feared the day would come when I would have nothing else to offer. Today I glimpse a different path to tread, and at once I realise its power, for it offers endless possibilities.

The man standing before me bows deeply and asks in a low voice if he may visit me in private. I wave him into my own bedchamber, call for servants to bring sweetmeats and cool drinks. His eyes widen when he sees the bed, of course, but I am used to that by now. He sits on the cushions laid out on the floor and we make ourselves comfortable. He has been in our council today, offering words from his lord, chief of a tribe to the North. A minor tribe, but one who wishes to stand at our side, one who fears a possible onslaught if he does not pledge allegiance to us.

"Your master is a wise man to become our ally," I say, trying to understand why he would want to delay his visit by idly talking with me rather than resting before his return to the North.

He nods. "Although…"

I sense he will not speak unless I make it easy for him.

"Although?"

"He can be… changeable."

I know this word when used in such circumstances. "Can I trust your lord's stated intentions and promises towards us?"

I ask it with great bluntness. The man blinks. Perhaps he thought more discretion would be used. He pauses and I lean forward. My perfume envelops him and he leans a little closer. He will tell his friends that he sat alone with the legendary Zaynab, queen of Aghmat, now queen of Murakush and Fes. They will not believe him but they will want to know more.

"I – I think perhaps you would be wise to put your trust in others before my lord," he says, stumbling over his words.

I put one hand on his and he trembles a little at my touch. "Can I put my trust in you?" I ask gently.

Now he cannot speak fast enough. "My lady – yes – yes, I would do anything to deserve…"

I am thinking as fast as I can. I lean forward a little more and place another hand over his. His hands are bound in mine now. "I would pay you well," I whisper. "And I would like to see you again – to hear from your own lips whatever news you have to bring me."

Just like that it is done. It is a matter of days before another man is ensnared by my hands and whispers, by my perfume which fills their senses. They cannot resist the idea of serving me, of being known by name to a woman whom the storytellers have already shaped into a legend.

Slowly I gather informants across the Maghreb. My two eyes become four, eight, sixteen, thirty-two, sixty-four… many hundreds. When I blink they blink, when I look to the right or left their eyes move with me. When I sleep they keep watch. Now I have information from across many lands.

Yusuf frowns when I begin to reveal changes to loyalties or successions, when I share the secrets of leaders, but when I am proved right time and again the men begin to lean towards me when I speak and Yusuf waits for my knowledge before choices are made, new allies approved. My power in the council is undimmed, indeed it grows stronger. I hear the storytellers call me 'the Magician' and claim that I speak with djinns to know all that I do. I laugh in private at such claims, but in public I let them think what they like. Let them fear me.

My son Abu Tahir grows. I see him take his first steps. I give him a little wooden sword of his own, I have a shield made for him, give him a drum and teach him the slow drumbeat of the battlefield. When Yusuf sees him pretending to be a soldier he laughs, but he is proud and I see that he grows closer to the boy because of his warlike nature. My only fear is that some harm will befall him. One child is not enough, for any child might grow sick and die and always I remember that Kella's child may be somewhere in Murakush. I must have more children, although the thought of it makes me want to weep. The endless sickness I endured weakened me so badly that to willingly undertake it again seems madness. Besides, I am growing older. I risk my life by birthing more children. I hope that perhaps, perhaps, the sickness will not come again, that the first time was the worst.

I am wrong. It seems I am fertile enough after all, for despite my age I fall with child again but the sickness is so great that I do not know how I will get through the pregnancy alive.

I send for one healer after another and all of them are useless. I am made to drink foul brews and wear meaningless amulets. They do nothing. I eat unleavened bread, one tiny fearful mouthful at a time, I sip water constantly, for I can only swallow a tiny amount at a time or risk losing everything I have eaten or drunk that day.

"Rest," says Yusuf, worried as my hands turn bony again and my skin grows pale from keeping indoors.

But I have spies who will speak only with me, I must sit in council. I must tend to my son. I must weave the endless warp and weft of Yusuf's kingdom.

I send for the herb-seller, the healer from Al-Andalus. She stands in my presence and waits for me to speak.

"I suffer with great sickness from this pregnancy," I tell her. "I have need of your healing powers."

"I do not have powers," she corrects me. "I only have knowledge of herbs and I pray to my God for His guidance."

I say nothing. I note her stubborn clinging to her own god, her Christian god. Much good he has done her, a scarred and crippled slave girl far from her homeland.

"What have you tried?" she asks.

I list various things: eating acrid things such as capers, *not* eating such things, avoiding chickpeas and other such legumes and rue, the use of fresh air, gentle walks, wool placed over my stomach. Various wines, diluted with one thing or another. The never-ending amulets.

She shakes her head when I have finished. "I will make you a syrup," she says. "Take it when you feel the sickness and at least twice a day even if you do not. Eat small meals and often."

"I can barely eat anything but unleavened bread," I say. "Everything else I vomit."

She shakes her head again. "I will send the syrup," she says.

"You must tell me what is in it," I say, suddenly wary. I do not like her stillness, her steady eyes that look me over as though she judges me.

"Pomegranate syrup with yarrow, stinging nettle, comfrey root, cinnamon, turmeric and bentonite clay," she says. Her tongue is quick as she names each ingredient. There is no hesitation, no subterfuge that I can see. There is nothing I have not heard of.

I nod. "Send it to me," I say.

The drink, when it arrives, has a sweet-sour taste to it, with a spicy warmth from the herbs. Luckily I cannot taste the clay. I sip it gingerly but it does not cause me to vomit and after a while I call for some food: the plainest couscous and white meat and find I am able to eat. It is the first real meal I have eaten since this child was conceived.

I send for her again and she stands before me.

"Did the drink work?" she asks.

"Yes," I say. I nod to a servant, who passes her a large pouch, heavy with money. "You will continue to send the drink throughout my pregnancy," I say. "You will be well paid for your service." I should say more perhaps, should be more fulsome, for I am overwhelmed with gratitude that she has taken away the gnawing hunger and the endless violent vomiting, that she has opened up the path for me to birth more children without suffering so badly each time. But her stillness, her dark eyes, her watching me does not make me feel close to her as I did with Hela.

She takes the money without gratitude, without bowing. "I can tell your servants how to prepare it," she says.

"No," I say. "I want you to prepare it."

She nods and steps away, making to leave.

"Wait," I say.

She pauses.

"You could work for me," I say. "My own handmaiden Hela has passed away and I have need of a healer in my service. Will you be my handmaiden?"

"No," she says simply.

I frown at the speed of her reply, she has not considered the proposal at all. "Why not?"

Her brown eyes fix steadily on mine. "I do not wish to serve you," she says. "I cannot serve a woman who has such darkness inside her." Without asking my permission, she turns and leaves the room.

I call for one of my spies. "Find out who she is," I demand. What I am really asking is, *who is she to speak to a queen as though she disdains her, disdains me?*

It is not long before they return with information. They tell me she is from the very Northern kingdoms of Spain, above Al-Andalus, even. That she is a devoted Christian, was a nun in a convent but got caught by a raiding party and sold as a slave to a rich man in Aghmat who, it seems, maimed her. Certainly she walks with a limp. She followed the army to Murakush, as did most of Aghmat's population, and set up her herb stall for a while, before some man set her up in a house of her own. No-one is sure of his name, he is one of the thousands of soldiers in our army.

I dress in the bright colours any woman here might wear, my long hair hidden under a wrap, my face overshadowed by a shawl. No-one would recognise me in such attire, even those who know me well would struggle to find my likeness at a distance.

The street where she lives is cramped, a hidden alleyway. The door is small: narrow and poorly painted. My knock sounds too loud and I look over my shoulder but there is no-one about. A servant's face appears in the half-open door. An ugly girl, one shoulder set too high, her skin coarse.

"Is this the home of the healer?" I ask.

The girl nods. "She's not here, though," she tells me.

I look beyond the girl. All I can see from here is a half-open door and a few plants in pots. Already I can feel my interest fading fast. Whoever keeps her here is no man of importance: some soldier whom she healed, perhaps, and was grateful enough to feel something for her, scarred as she is. He does not have much money or she would have better servants and be kept in better style. So she will not serve me? I do not care. She has given me a cure for what ails me and I have paid her well for it. It is enough. I would not want such a woman by my side all the time. She can make me the syrup when I ask for it. I do not even need to have her in my presence.

"It is not important," I say and turn away. Behind me I hear the door creak shut and think, so little does her man care for her that he does not even see to oiling it.

I see her from time to time, when she brings the syrup or in the streets. Occasionally I see her with a young child balanced on her hip. Perhaps she is too busy to serve me if she has a child of her own who must be cared for.

I do not have such a luxury. When my time comes and the pains grip me, I have no-one to cling to now that Hela is gone. There is no other woman I would summon and so I hold onto my own carved bed and birth a daughter, Fannu, all alone. I sigh when I see her, for although I would be glad enough of a daughter, I am always mindful that I must provide male heirs and so her birth forewarns me that I must endure another pregnancy. I know that some slave girl has given birth to a girl child named Tamima whom Yusuf has acknowledged as his own. I narrowed my lips when I heard of her but Yusuf still comes to me and I am still seated at his right hand. I am greater than the unnamed girl will ever be and she would not expect to become a wife. She would fear such a position, not crave it. So I look at Fannu and whisper to her that she will be a great queen one day, I will see her married to an amir, she will learn to rule as I have.

"Should I continue to follow the Spanish woman?" asks the spy.

I think about her and then shake my head. "She is not important," I tell him. "I have better things to think of."

He bows. "And the other slave girl?"

I shake my head. Yusuf may have rolled with some girl or other but she is no danger to me, he does not suggest her as a wife. "I am not interested in slave women who whelp bastard girls," I tell him. "Look beyond. I would know how Ibrahim the son of Abu Bakr fares."

It seems from what my spies report back to me that he seeks to challenge us again for leadership, in his father's name. I sigh at such stupidity, but I send gifts of honour and many fine words. My belly swells again and I provide a second son. I name him Abu Bakr, honouring our distant so-called Commander. Sure enough the boy-Ibrahim gives way at these meaningless honours and gifts, acknowledges Yusuf as amir, as his father will already have counselled. Such is the brashness of youth. It makes me feel even older than my years. But the power of my many eyes allows all such challenges to be swept away, for I know they will come our way before they are even spoken and can plan accordingly. I hear foolish tongues claim that I speak with djinns, that the spirits of the air tell me what is to come. I laugh at the very idea. People speak more loosely than any spirit, are easier to command than any djinn.

Mother

I AM GROWN TO BE THE mother of a great kingdom, of a future dynasty. Altogether I give Yusuf six sons and three daughters, more heirs to choose from than any man could need. Many of those years taste of the sour-spiced syrup from the Spanish healer to me, when I look back at them. The remedy saves me from the unending sickness I would otherwise suffer each time, for it seems I must always struggle to bring a child into this world. Two slave girls with whom Yusuf has brief dalliances provide one daughter and two sons between them, all of whom he acknowledges, treating them with care but keeping them well away from me. From time to time I wonder if there is still a ninth son, Ali, who was born first, but I hear nothing more of him, nor of Kella and as the many years pass I no longer fear for his re-emergence, nor hers. She is no doubt far away on some trading route with the man from her tribe. The child could be dead by now, many children die young. And if not, well, then his name is lost and there is no-one to speak it and make his claim.

We have come to the last of our battles, or so it seems. Yusuf sends his troops out to capture the Northern port of Tangier, from where Al-Andalus itself can be glimpsed across the sea. Its ruler Suqut fights for two days but then the sky grows dark and he dies as the sun hides its face in fear at Yusuf's coming. His spoilt son Diya' al-Dawla flees to Ceuta, a tiny outpost of land nearby, jutting into the sea and is promptly cut off from the Maghreb by our army. Meanwhile we take Algiers, just as we once dreamt of.

Poring over maps together Yusuf and I divide up the whole of the Maghreb into four great provinces, two in the North and two in the South. Each is placed under the command and care of a governor and every leader and tribal commander is brought to us to pledge loyalty.

We have created peace and prosperity, in a kingdom larger than was thought possible, a kingdom beyond what anyone could have dreamt of, with wealthy cities set as jewels within a crown across it. The tents of Murakush are long gone. Now it is a wealthy city. Fes is restored and grown ever greater. We command the trade routes, especially those of salt, slaves and gold. We have great riches at our disposal. I laugh when I think of the miserly treasure I once showed to Abu Bakr, enhancing it with mirrors in the darkness to hide its paltry amount. Now we could fill that storage room a hundred times over and still have gold to spare.

Yusuf, of course, still wishes to live as though we were in the desert. There are nights when he leaves my side and I find him the next morning lying in our courtyard gardens, wrapped only in a blanket, as though to turn away from all that he has at his command and return to the simple life he once led. At banquets for our allies he still waves away the rich spiced stews and honeyed sweets, eating only plain roast meats and bread, perhaps accepting some fruit. Our children sit with us, many of them grown tall now, our sons ready to take their places leading men into battle, our daughters beautiful, their hands already sought by suitors.

"There is not much for you to do," Yusuf jokes with our sons. "You have only a peaceful kingdom to govern. You will grow fat and soft like the Taifa kings of Al-Andalus."

Still, I ensure that all of our sons train with the soldiers and sit in council, so that they will learn to rule. Our eldest sons are given small regions to govern, so that they may see what it takes to lead our people. Our daughters will marry allies, to further strengthen our bonds. They are taught to read maps, to run a city. They take their places in council, for no-one will raise an eyebrow at a woman sitting in government, knowing what I have done for this kingdom. I will see to it myself that none of our children will be like the Taifa kings of Al-Andalus. Princelings only, each holding tiny regions of Al-Andalus and thinking themselves great rulers. If they had banded together they might have taken over all of Spain but they have grown fat and lazy living their lives of luxury. They squabble amongst themselves and therefore have ended up with the humiliation of paying tribute to the Christian king of the North, Alphonso.

"They do not follow Allah's way," says Yusuf, frowning when we hear news of them. "They cannot call themselves true Muslims when they tax their people so harshly."

"They are none of our business," I say. "They are fools. They have accomplished nothing but a comfortable life for themselves."

But a letter arrives from Al-Mu'tamid, the amir of Seville,.

"He did what?" I ask, appalled.

"Killed Alphonso's messenger," says the scribe who is reading the letter to our council.

Yusuf and I look at each other.

I shake my head. "Start from the beginning."

It seems that Al-Mu'tamid was late in paying the annual tribute demanded by the Christian king, Alphonso the Sixth.

"Alphonso most unjustly and violently demanded not only tribute but also the delivery of many strong castles in my region, in punishment for the delay in payment, blaming me with many untrue accusations," reads the scribe.

"And then Al-Mu'tamid killed Alphonso's messenger?" I ask again.

The scribe nods.

"And now he wants my help?" asks Yusuf, eyebrows raised.

"He asks that you, as one Muslim king to another, do advance in support of him and fight off these unreasonable demands by the Christian king. His scholars and other scholars of Al-Andalus agree that this is righteous."

Yusuf is silent for a while as the members of council murmur amongst themselves. "We need to take Ceuta," he reminds us at last. "It is the only part of the Maghreb not yet under our control. The late amir of Tlemcen's son still lives there, they say he lives a dissolute life. He is surrounded by our men but we cannot advance further for Ceuta juts into the sea and we have no sea-going ships."

I think of my spies, of the words they have brought from Al-Andalus, which until now seemed useless. But I listened to them anyway. One never knows when information will prove of use and now its time has come.

"Al-Mu'tamid is building a great ship," I say. "Tell him that we need it for Ceuta. Only then can we come to his aid."

Yusuf's eyes brighten. "Yes," he says. "Write to him and tell him that if Allah lets me take Ceuta, I will join him and gather my strength to attack the enemy with all my soul. But first we have need of his ship."

The ship towers above us, the men on board look like insects. It is like a fort rocking on the water, it cannot be resisted. The young amir of Ceuta, soft from his luxurious lifestyle, protected only by the sea, suddenly finds himself captured and put to death.

But now the kings of Al-Andalus send word that Alphonso has grown more aggressive. He comes to the region around Seville, on Muslim territory and ravages the land and people. He captures Toledo and the Muslim kings, frightened by this new move, ask Al-Mu'tamid to write again to us.

"Alphonso has come to us demanding pulpits, minarets, mihrabs and mosques, so that crosses may be erected in them and monks may run them."

The council members look appalled. I can see my sons tighten their grips on their swords, as though they are about to fight here and now.

"Allah has given us Ceuta," says Yusuf. "We will cross the sea and stand by our brothers. Pray with me. Oh Allah! If you know that my passage will be beneficial for the Muslims, then make it easy for me. If it is the opposite, then make it difficult for me so that I do not cross over."

"The Maghreb is quiet," I tell Yusuf. "You are free to do battle wherever you wish." I try not to smile at the eagerness of Yusuf and my sons to go into battle. They are trained soldiers, eager for combat. This kingdom we have created is too peaceful for the liking of warriors. I will remain behind, the Maghreb held safe in my able hands while our army supports the Muslim kings.

"Remember not to be too trusting," I remind them all before they depart. "The kings of Al-Andalus are weak men, their lifestyles have made them soft. They do not remember what it is to truly fight, nor are they always honest with one another. They have paid tribute for years to a Christian king whom they could have dispatched if they had banded together, instead they have bowed to him. He has been their lord and master all this time. They may have called on you but you are new to them and they may quickly return to their old lives and the tribute if the change is too hard for them. Be on your guard."

The crossing is blessed. The weather is perfect during the sailing and when Yusuf disembarks in Algeciras Al-Mu'tamid has sent splendid gifts, the inhabitants open their doors in welcome and the peasants of the region have been ordered to provide provisions. But Yusuf remembers my words and he has the men repair the crumbling walls and watchtowers of the city. After this they dig a deep trench around the city and fill it with weapons and provisions. He takes his best solders and creates a garrison to support any future military needs before he sets out for Seville.

"The amir Al-Mu'tamid embraced him and gave him many gifts," says the scribe.

"Gifts mean nothing," I say. "Did the other amirs join their forces with us, as they promised?"

The scribe looks back down at the letter. "The amirs of Seville, Granada and Badajoz joined forces with Yusuf."

I look down at the map laid out in front of me. "And the amir of Almeria?"

"He pleaded old age."

I snort. "He wants to wait and see what will happen before he commits himself," I say. "We will not forget his cowardice, nor his lack of loyalty."

"Yusuf wrote to Alphonso to offer mercy," reports the scribe.

I nod. This has always been our way, since we had an army large enough to command fear in the hearts of our enemies. We offer them the opportunity to avoid battles, to become our allies. "What did he offer?"

"He invited Alphonso to take one of three options. Convert to Islam, pay tribute, or fight."

"And?"

"Alphonso was filled with rage. He responded, saying: 'How can you send me such a letter when my father and I have imposed tribute on the people of your religion for the past eighty years. Advance towards me: it will not please me to meet you near a city which may protect you, for it will delay me from seizing you, killing you and assuaging my hatred of you.'"

I shrug. "A king who cannot control his temper," I say. "More fool him. He will find out what we are made of. He has only done battle with the kings there and they are not like us. He will realise it soon enough." I think that he has no idea what he is about to face. Our army is without equal, led by Yusuf who has more experience of battles than any man I know and supported by our sons, eager for glory. Our army is backed by a vast kingdom of huge wealth and power. While Yusuf heads up the army, I stand behind him with supplies, with more soldiers to call on.

Alphonso cannot win.

The two armies come together and as I predicted Alphonso is not ready for us. His camp is burned to the ground by a small party of our men while he is engaged with the rest of the army. Alphonso is grievously wounded in his knee and finds his troops enveloped by our own, a move the men have practiced time and again. He is forced to retreat.

Yusuf returns to us covered in glory but doubtful of how long this victory will last. "I have told the amirs that they must band together. It is their infighting and soft lives that has brought about their own ruin and weakness. They must unite, they must face Alphonso as one."

"And will they?"

He sighs. "I doubt it. Of course they swore to do so, but that was after a successful battle, when any man will swear to anything in his pride and exhilaration. It will be a different matter when they return to their palaces. They will go back to their old ways soon enough. And Alphonso has been lamed for life, he will not forget this humiliation."

"I too have news," I say. "Sad news. Your cousin, our Commander Abu Bakr, has died. He fell to a poisoned arrow in battle. A warrior to the end. "

Yusuf is sorrowful. "He was a good man," he says. "And he did great things for this kingdom."

"And kept his word to us," I say. "He did not go back on our agreement."

We praise his name and his deeds: the quelling of the tribes in the South, the re-opening of the salt route towards Aulil, the strengthening of the commercial trade routes. And above all, most recently, the conquest of Kumbi in Ghana, from where vast amounts of gold make their way to our mint, where dirhams are moulded and accepted as coinage not only across our own lands but far beyond, known for their quality.

Now it is Yusuf's name that is pressed into each coin at our mint. He is given a new title: Amir of the Muslims. His new title brings Al-Mu'tamid himself to our shores. He crosses the Strait and stands before us in council, full of words of praise and fine gifts. I do not trust him.

"We ask that you join us again, Yusuf," he says. "We will gather together as one under your command."

"As one?" I ask.

Al-Mu'tamid looks somewhat taken aback by my seat of honour in council but he knows better than to show it too much. "As one, oh Queen Zaynab," he says smiling. "I will even set aside my differences with Bin Rashiq of Murcia, who will join with us."

But of course the reality is not as smooth as the amir's words. Once the armies join together Bin Rashiq of Murcia tries to woo Yusuf with gifts so as to push out Al-Mu'tamid as our closest ally. In turn Al-Mu'tamid accuses him of favouring the Christians, which proves true. Bin Rashiq ends up loaded down with chains while his kingdom of Murcia is given to Seville, much to Al-Mu'tamid's pleasure. But the inhabitants of Murcia stubbornly refuse to provision the troops and at last Yusuf, disillusioned and weary of the infighting, returns to the Maghreb. At once Alphonso forces 'Abdullah of Granada to not only resume paying him tribute but also to sign a treaty declaring Granada against Yusuf and Seville.

Council is taken over with scholars, who argue that the amirs of Al-Andalus have been shown to be libertines and impious.

"They have corrupted their own people by their bad example and forgotten their religious duties," says one.

"And commanded illegal taxes, against the law of the Qu'ran," says another.

"I made it clear they were no longer to levy such taxes," says Yusuf.

"They have continued, regardless of what they agreed to when you saw them," I say. "They are nothing but liars."

"More than one is in alliance with Alphonso," reminds a scholar. "They prefer to bind themselves to a Christian king than their own Muslim brothers. It cannot be bourne."

Yusuf is wary. He dislikes the infighting, the disloyalties, the effort of trying to command poorly-trained troops, so different from his own. "How can I be certain this is the will of Allah?" he asks. "Perhaps it goes against His will. In which case I will not take action."

The eldest scholar stands. "We have sought assurance from the great scholars of Islam as far away as Egypt and Asia and all of them confirm our ruling on this matter. We take it on ourselves to answer for this action before Allah. If we are in error, we agree to pay the penalty for our conduct in the next world. We declare that you, Yusuf, Amir of the Muslims, are not responsible. But we firmly believe that if you leave the Andalusian kings in peace, they will deliver our country to the unbelievers and if that is the case, then you will have to render an account to Allah of your lack of action."

"Leave us," says Yusuf.

Alone, we sit tracing the contours of the map showing Al-Andalus, the kingdoms of the amirs, the kingdoms held by Alphonso.

"I am seventy years' old," says Yusuf. "I am too old for this."

I laugh. "You are still a greater warrior and leader than the amirs of Al-Andalus," I say. "They are like children. Squabbling and telling tales to their mothers."

"They are impossible to help," he says. "They go behind my back, they switch loyalty. I cannot trust their word, nor even their men in battle, for they are weak and poorly trained."

"Then do not help them," I say. "Command them. Rule over them."

"Do you not think the kingdom we have created is great enough?" he asks.

"Create an empire," I say.

"Go there without being summoned?"

"Yes," I say. "The fight is between you and Alphonso now. The petty kings must submit to you now, for they have been proven unfit to rule. Your greatest scholars have declared them so. Remember: do not trust them. Their lips speak honeyed words but they come only from the sweetmeats they fill their mouths with, not from their hearts."

Yusuf crosses the Strait again with his scholars' blessings but without being summoned. Once in Algeciras he leads his men towards Cordoba to begin a siege. As they pass Granada its king, 'Abdullah, meets with them and humbles himself before Yusuf, begging his pardon for displeasing him. But Yusuf is wise to their ways now. He replies that he has forgotten any grievance and invites him to enter his tent, where he will be honoured as an ally.

I sit in council and look down at 'Abdullah kneeling before me. I can barely keep from laughing.

"And so you entered the tent?"

"Yes," he mutters.

"And?"

"I was taken and bound in chains."

"You deserved it for your lying ways," I say. "Granada has been taken by Yusuf. Your people praised his name when he abolished all your unlawful taxes. They were not allowed by the Qu'ran. Are you not a good Muslim?"

He mutters something.

"You and your family have been sent to me in chains," I say. "And I am sending you to Aghmat. It is a poor city now, a humble city loyal only to Yusuf and me. You will live there for the rest of your days."

He looks at me with angry eyes as he is made to rise.

"You bow," I inform him. "You bow to me as your queen and you give thanks to Allah that I am merciful."

He has no choice but to do as I say.

Only a month passes before Yusuf sends me the king of Malaga, whom

I dispatch in a similar manner, to live out his days as a prisoner: a luxurious life, perhaps, but still a prisoner, watched and held at our will. I feel the vast power I wield as I dispose of these fallen kings and it gives me pleasure. Yusuf and I created a kingdom together. Now, we will create an empire.

Tarifa falls, then Cordoba's siege breaks when its inhabitants open the gates to us. Seville's fleet is burnt and Seville falls, swiftly followed by Almeria and Badajoz.

The once proud ruler of Seville, Al-Mu'tamid, kneels before me in council, sent here in chains like all the others.

"Welcome back to the Maghreb," I say. "You must regret the day you asked for Yusuf's help. You will not be leaving us again. You may join your old allies in Aghmat. Do not plot against us, for your life will not be spared a second time. Believe me when I say that you will be watched."

"Gracious Queen Zaynab," he begins, obsequiously.

"Go," I tell him. "I have no stomach for honeyed words, only loyalty and strong deeds, neither of which, it seems, you are capable of."

Yusuf leaves the army in the hands of his generals. Only Valencia is not yet fully ours and must be held. But the army struggles without Yusuf at its helm.

"Alphonso has a champion," says Yusuf. "A true warrior, by all accounts."

"What is his name?" I ask.

"Rodrigo Diaz de Vivas," he says. "They call him El Cid."

The infighting between the kings goes on, infuriating Yusuf. Behind our backs the ruler of Valencia, Al-Qadir, sends for El Cid to support him, pledging allegiance to Alphonso. But a Muslim judge lets our army into the city, causing Al-Qadir to flee, dressed as a woman along with his wives. They take shelter in a poor house but are found quickly enough and he is sentenced to death. The judge is made ruler but then double-crosses us, agreeing to pay tribute to El Cid, who agrees that he can be ruler if he will stand against us. Yusuf sends more troops but his general is poorly prepared and El Cid not only calls on Alphonso for help but makes a sortie at night when the men are unprepared.

"Why were they unprepared?" rages Yusuf, pacing the room.

I frown. "Continue," I say to the scribe reading us the report.

"El Cid pretended to retreat towards Valencia but hidden soldiers came out and attacked our camp," he reads. "El Cid took a great victory and claimed much booty."

There are many pages of explanations and justifications, apologies and humbling from the generals, none of which soothes Yusuf, especially when we receive word again and again about battles fought, all of which El Cid wins. "It is not acceptable," he declares. "Al-Andalus is ours except for Valencia and Valencia *will* be ours."

"You had better go yourself," I suggest and he nods.

"I will defeat this El Cid," he says. "He will fall before my sword."

I nod. I do not doubt it will be so.

"El Cid's son Diego was killed first," reads the scribe. "In the battle for Consuegra."

I think of Abu Tahir, of the grief I would feel if I saw my son fall in battle. "And El Cid himself?" I ask, already knowing the answer.

"Died shortly after," says the scribe.

Of a broken heart, I think. I had heard great things of this warrior but it seems he was not invincible after all, for Yusuf broke him.

Now that their hero is gone the spirit goes out of the Christians. Valencia falls to us. All of Al-Andalus is now Yusuf's. The Christian king Alphonso has been whipped like a dog, creeping back to his Northern lands, to face the cold and fury of his people, outraged that an old Moor has beaten them, that their attempt to claim back the lands of the past has failed. One set of Muslims or another, it is the same humiliation to them. At least with the old Taifa kings they received tribute and could fool themselves that they ruled over them. Now they cannot pretend. They huddle in the North and we claim the South as our own, our kingdom grown to an empire for our sons and daughters to rule over after us.

My eldest son Abu Tahir kneels before me and I touch his head in blessing. He is a fully-grown man now, scarred in battle, his body made hard by war. He has a gravity to him, he knows that one day he will follow Yusuf and become Amir of the Muslims.

"You must study Al-Andalus," I tell him. "We must know it as we know our own people, as well as we know the Maghreb."

"It is a rich land, full of good and beautiful things," he tells me. "Now it is ours."

"One day it will be yours," I tell him.

Crone

*1*N MY ROOMS I LIKE to study the maps I keep spread out, my mind wandering, as it often does now, back to the past. I am more than sixty years' old. I have aches and pains but I do not care about them, for I am at peace for the first time in my life. I can rest now. Our new-born empire is peaceful and prosperous. Whatever false vision I spoke and the men in my life believed in, none of us could have foreseen this moment of utter triumph. We hold an empire now, two lands spanning the sea. I wonder at it sometimes, that such a thing should come to pass and yet I know that every step towards such greatness has come about because of how Yusuf and I have worked together. He has led an army that made hardened warriors blench while I created first a rich and unified kingdom and then an empire from his conquered lands: managing a flourishing trade, the building of great cities, enacting good governance. We have done great things together, he and I. Our children will be worthy successors to us, for each of them has been raised to be the best: leaders, warriors, great queens. I once thought I would never find peace but here I am, an old woman, contented with the life she has made. I trace the lines of the maps once more, taking pleasure in their certainty for the future.

Yusuf stands in the doorway. He looks shaken.

"What is wrong?" I ask, unnerved. I have never seen him look like this. "Is there unrest? A rebellion?" I think quickly about who I must summon, which spies will be of greatest help to me, depending on what has happened. I think of where our troops are stationed, how fast they can be moved, what supplies they will need.

"I have found Ali," he says.

"Who?"

"Kella's son," Yusuf says.

I feel as though I have received a blow to the stomach. "His body?" I ask, reaching for hope.

"He is alive," says Yusuf.

"That cannot be true," I say. My heart is thudding. I have to sit on the edge of my bed.

"She gave him to a slave woman to bring up," Yusuf says.

I think of the two slave girls who have given Yusuf children but I have seen their offspring for myself and they were born years after Kella left here. "Is that what the woman claims?"

"She has proved it," he says.

"How?"

He holds up something in his hand. I have to peer at it. A necklace, the long silver beads of his people. He gave one to each of our children, saying it would make them tall and healthy. "Where did she get that?"

"Kella gave it to her, to make Ali's claim when the time was right."

I try to laugh, although it does not sound natural. "She could have got those from any jeweller."

He shakes his head. "Kella's name and mine are marked on the necklace," he says and shows me.

"A jeweller can be paid for such work," I say, but I know that he is not listening to me.

"He is my son," says Yusuf. "And he has lived close at hand for all these years." His voice trembles and he looks down at me. His eyes are filled with tears. "Did you know of this?"

I do not hesitate, not even for a breath. "No," I say. "I believed Kella's son was dead. She told us he was dead. Why would she lie to us? Why would she lie to you?"

Yusuf's face is full of distress. "She must have thought him threatened," he says.

"By whom?" I ask.

"I do not know," he says. "But now he is found, he is safe. I will have him declared my son."

I swallow. It is a bitter thing to accept. But so be it. The children of the slave girls have been acknowledged too but my own children have always been given pre-eminence over them. "I am sure he will be grateful for your generosity," I say. "Not all men would trust such a claim."

"I know it for the truth," says Yusuf.

He stands before us, this lost son of Kella and Yusuf. Ali. I look him over. He has a slender build, unlike my own sons, whose years upon years of training, first alongside and then in Yusuf's army, have made them large of shoulder, their muscles rippling. His eyes, as he looks about himself, are wide and trusting. The shape of them reminds me of his mother. This is a man who has not been lied to by supposed allies, who has not carried a sword on his hip all his life and a dagger hidden in his robes. He speaks with the scholars at the far end of the room earnestly, as though what they have to say is more important than what the generals and governors speak of.

Yusuf stands. "I ask the council to welcome my son, Ali. Child to my first wife Kella, now no longer with us."

The council chamber ripples with interest. They have heard such announcements before but those were babies, bastards born to slave girls. They were of little importance. This is a full-grown man born to Yusuf's first wife. Where has he been all this time? Next to me, my son Abu Tahir shifts, a little discomforted by this disclosure. I touch his shoulder gently and he settles again, resigned.

"The woman who raised him will vouch for his birth," continues Yusuf. He waves towards the doorway, where a woman stands, her face half-hidden from me. "Isabella, join us."

I blench at the sight of her, my hands clench without my knowledge. The Spanish healer stands before us, her eyes calm and steady, her head held high. One of our eldest and greatest scholars questions her.

"I swear that this man is Ali, son to Yusuf bin Tashfin and his wife Kella."

"Do you know where Kella is now?"

"I do not."

"Is she alive?"

"I do not know."

"How did you come to have this child in your care?"

"His mother summoned me as a midwife when she birthed him. He was born into my hands."

"Did she give him to you at once?"

"No. She came to me in great secrecy. She claimed that the boy's life was in danger, that he must be raised by another. She begged me to take him. I did so."

"From whom was he in danger?"

I wait for her to name me but she does not, she does not even glance my way although my breathing comes fast and shallow. I feel the room swirl about me and think I am about to faint but I dig my nails into the palms of my hands so hard that the pain brings me back to myself.

"Give me a name," insists the scholar.

"I cannot."

"Can you prove this story?"

She holds up the string of silver beads and says they were given to prove his lineage, she asks Yusuf if they are the same beads he gave to Kella and he agrees that they are. I try to calm my breathing as Yusuf and Ali stand side by side before the council and the council welcomes Ali as Yusuf's long-lost son and acknowledges Isabella's righteous behaviour in having kept him safe from harm all these years.

"Has the boy been raised a Christian?" worries the scholar.

Isabella shakes her head. "He has been raised in his father's religion. I thought it right," she adds.

There is a murmur of approval. Yusuf declares that Isabella and Ali must accompany him to our palace, where a banquet of welcome will be served. I stand, legs shaking beneath my robes and keep my face still as I approach Isabella. Ali has already turned to me and is bowing.

"Lady Zaynab," he says awkwardly. "I believe you knew my mother."

I look at him, see something of her in him, a distant echo of her innocence. "I did not know her well before she left," I say and watch his face turn crimson at the reminder that his mother ran away in the night, leaving him behind as though she cared nothing for him, as well as her legally wed husband Yusuf, to whom she owed her loyalty.

"Come," says Yusuf and he gestures to Ali to precede him out of the door. Then he turns to Isabella, one hand extended. "Join us," is all he says but as he speaks I feel a heavy weight settle in my belly. His hand takes hers with gentleness, pulling her closer to him so that their bodies touch as they move forwards together and the way he looks at her, the softness in his eyes…

"I beg you will excuse me," I say to Yusuf and then I leave, quickly, before he can frown and ask me where I am going.

"Mother?"

"Attend your father," I say to Abu Tahir and hurry away from him.

This time I do not disguise myself. I run through the streets, ignoring the surprised faces of those around me, the murmurs I leave behind, *lady Zaynab running as though the very djinns of the air were after her*. I make my way back to the tiny alleyway, the poorly painted gate. I have been here only once, so many years ago. This time I do not knock, I do not wait for the ugly serving girl to come at my summons. Instead I push hard against the fading paint. The door gives way to me, it opens with the same creaking protest and I step inside, slamming it behind me. Panting, I feel the great heat of the day turn cold as I turn on myself, slowly taking in what has been hidden from me all these years.

Behind the ill-painted, creaking door and the ill-favoured serving girl I once dismissed as unimportant lies a secret, a secret I would have seen many years ago had I looked beyond the narrow glimpse I caught over her shoulder, had I pushed at the door and opened it wide, stepped inside.

The courtyard in which I stand is large. The tiles stretching across the floor are brightly coloured and arranged in pleasing patterns. Above me stretch not two but three storeys, set out in carved woods and exquisite plasterwork. On each level I can see doors to hidden rooms, each painted by craftsmen. By my side a large and well-made fountain splashes cool water in the sun's bright rays. There are climbing plants and even a palm tree, which reaches up towards the clear blue sky. This hidden home is a small palace deliberately concealed behind an ugly exterior, a dwelling fit for any one of Yusuf's family members.

Fit even for a wife.

I sit alone, thinking of the many, many hundreds of pairs of eyes I claim as my spies. Men, of course, who serve their lords near and far but bring me word of their foibles, allowing me to be certain of their loyalties. Women, too, for women hear and see what men pass over. They know unspoken secrets as well as those passed off as mere gossip yet which contain a kernel of truth. I even claim children. They come and go, are forgotten when voices are lowered, see things left behind, understand far more than their elders would ever suspect or wish them to. I think of the hundreds of men and women whom I have had followed and watched.

I curse myself that I allowed Isabella's service to me during my pregnancies, the relief her remedy brought, to let her refusal to serve me go too easily. I know that had it been a spy who had reported to me I would have demanded more, that I would have required they enter Isabella's home and tell me every detail of what they saw. But because I took on the task myself, because I saw peeling paint and an ill-favoured serving girl I saw what I wanted to see and turned away, believing there was nothing else to be seen. Now I curse myself for that failure.

But most of all I think of Yusuf.

I have trusted few people in my life. I have had eyes watching so many people around me, yet I never thought to have them watch Yusuf. Certainly, when the slave girls were mentioned as mothers to his bastards I had them watched long enough to know that they were of no concern to me. But Yusuf himself I did not watch. And yet there is something between him and Isabella, I saw it at once, any fool would have spotted it. How long has it been going on? I try to tell myself it is only gratitude to the woman who raised his son to safety, but I am not stupid enough to believe my own soothing. She has been living in that house for many years, since Kella had been gone only a year or so. Did Yusuf know where his son was all this time? Has he been watching me to see if I will harm the child? Surely not. He was shaken to know Ali had been found and yet all this time he has known Isabella, has cared for her enough to give her such a house?

I wander Murakush for the rest of the day, not returning to the palace until I can be certain the banquet is complete and everyone has gone. I cannot face seeing Isabella sat at Yusuf's side, the looks between them. I had thought such fears long behind me, lost in my first marriages and yet here they are again, rearing up before me. Such love I felt and now it is swept away in lies and secrets. My stomach churns and from time to time tears well up in my eyes, I am carried on a swirling storm of emotions. I wander the streets without a plan, without a path before me.

But after a while the storm within me begins to subside. I look at the towering mosque, the bakeries, the hammams. I see the people going about their business, busy, proud of belonging to such a great city, I see the respect with which they greet me. *I have made this city,* I think. *I have made this kingdom what it is. I have made it even into an empire. My children will govern after me. Ali is nothing to me. If I should not have trusted Yusuf, so be it. I should not have trusted any man. But even he cannot take away what I have done, what has been achieved at my hand. My children will come after me. I will be known as the mother of this dynasty.*

When I see Yusuf the next morning I manage to hold my tongue about Isabella. She is a slave woman, not as important as the empire and dynasty we have created together. Ali may be Yusuf's son but he is clearly not suited even to take on such positions of power as our sons already have. He is a quiet, peaceable man, a man who enjoys study and the company of scholars.

Perhaps he can be a scholar and advise on matters of faith. Yusuf might be pleased to have a man of God for a son. But I must secure Abu Tahir's place.

"You should announce the name of your heir," I say. "An empire needs stability."

He nods. "You are right," he says. "It shall be done. I will announce it today, in council."

I feel the tension in me drain away. We are still a formidable partnership. My legacy is whole. I smile at him. "It is a great day," I say. "Praise be to Allah for all we have accomplished in His name."

When Yusuf leaves I summon Abu Tahir.

"I have asked Yusuf to name his heir," I tell him.

I see him glow with the knowledge. His day has come at last. "When?"

"Today."

Abu Tahir and I are the first to arrive in the council chambers. My other sons and daughters nod to us when they arrive. They know that today is a momentous occasion, that even as Abu Tahir's name is announced their own future status is assured, that they will swear fealty to him, stand by him throughout the years to come as our dynasty is known throughout the world. The empire we have created may well expand further through marriage or battle, giving each of them ever-greater opportunities for glory. The scholars and warriors, the governors and chieftains who make up our council and court bow with greater deference as they greet Abu Tahir and myself, acknowledging what is to come. The room rustles with excitement. I even manage to nod to Ali, sitting amongst my sons and daughters. I know that Isabella is also among us but I do not look for her. She is nothing to me. Today she will understand that no-one can take my place, for I have earned it a thousand times over. I have earned the name of heir for my son.

Yusuf stands. "Today I will declare my heir," he announces. "Now that I command an empire, it must have a named heir, that there can be no doubt over its future, nor any disruption when my time to leave this world comes."

I smile. I look to Abu Tahir, seated at my side, who nods to me, his hand on his sword hilt, the very image of a young amir. He is ready to stand, to bow his head to Yusuf's announcement, to speak words of fealty and power. I feel such pride in him. Whatever sadness my husbands have brought me in all these years, my son has been faithful to me, a blessing to me. He will be a great ruler one day, the head of a fearsome dynasty ready for glory.

All of us turn our faces towards Yusuf, waiting for Abu Tahir's name to be spoken.

"Ali will be my heir," says Yusuf.

I do not move. My eyes slide sideways. Abu Tahir's face has drained white. He does not look at me, will not meet my gaze. I watch as Ali stands before his father then kneels for his blessing, his mouth opening and closing as he acknowledges Yusuf's command and swears to rule over the empire as his successor. I cannot hear him, it is as though he is making a dumb show. I look around the council and catch the faces of those who are not quick-witted enough courtiers, who have not yet smiled and nodded, who have not yet hailed Ali. These look to me, waiting for me to speak, to protest. But I keep my face stonelike, there is nothing to be seen. Quickly their faces accept the news even as Abu Tahir leaves the council, his siblings' faces frozen in silent disbelief.

"There will be a ceremony of allegiance," says Yusuf. "Here and in Cordoba. Each governor will make a pledge of loyalty to Ali." He does not look at me.

One by one the council members leave the room, filing past me in silence. They dare not look at me, they dare not speak to me.

I find Abu Tahir in his rooms, seated before a mirror, his back to me. I see myself standing behind him, both our faces rigid with rage and grief. His features are mine. I see in him the man I would have been, powerful and strong, destined to be a ruler and yet cast aside on the whim of a man. I want to tell him that I understand, that the whole of my life I have felt as he does now.

"Did you know?" he asks me and his teeth are so tightly ground together I barely understand him when he speaks.

"No!" I say. "How can you think so?"

"You should have spoken for me."

I gape at him. "You cannot blame me! I did not know what Yusuf was about to say!"

He snorts as though he does not believe me. "You two are as one, everyone knows that."

"I did not even know Ali was alive," I say.

"What, you who know everything, even the future?" he says, his voice full of spite. "Do you not converse with djinns as everyone whispers, did you not have a great vision? Did your spirits not tell you this day would come?"

"Abu Tahir," I begin, but he stands and pushes past me to the door. I make to grasp his arm but he shoves me away from him and I find myself on the floor. Slowly I rise and see myself reflected in the mirror, all alone. For a long time I stand and stare at myself.

It seems the world cannot trust a woman who knows so much, who can hold a vision of the future in her bosom and bring it to fruition. Men look away when I meet their eye. Once they desired me because I was beautiful. Now they fear me because I am powerful, more powerful than any woman they have encountered in their lives and it makes them uncomfortable. Oh certainly, they still kneel to me, they still speak to me with courtesy, but the truth is they would rather I was not there. It humbles them to know a woman stands behind their leader and makes him stronger than he would be alone. Men do not like to be humbled. And even a great warrior like Yusuf would rather choose an heir for the sake of sentiment, for the long-lost memory of some old love or even for a new love than for the good of the empire. He will pass over my son, the son of a woman who has been the power behind his throne. Abu Tahir has been raised to be the amir after his father. He is a great warrior, a man of power and strength, a man raised in my own image as much as his father's. He is the man who should lead the Almoravid dynasty forwards and yet Yusuf has chosen what amounts to a boy, a man who has not yet been tried on the battlefields, who knows nothing of the empire we now hold, who has been raised by a Christian, of all things. For all I know she may have raised him as a traitor, he may join forces with Alphonso and restore Al-Andalus to a Christian rule, taking the Maghreb with it, reversing all we have done over decades in moments, should Yusuf die.

I am not sure how much time passes, only that the shadows of the sun have moved and still I gaze at myself in the mirror, unable to answer the questions in my mind. What am I, if I am not the founder of this dynasty? Have I created an empire from the dust only for my name to be forgotten, for my achievements to be gifted to another woman's son? Have I been punished by Allah for declaring a false vision all those years ago, a vision which has come true beyond anyone's wildest expectations? No, I do not believe that.

At last I stand up. I am done. I have spent my life forcing myself into one shape and then another: into every shape permitted to a woman and still it has not been enough. I have been a daughter, bride, concubine, queen, widow, wife, seductress, rival, murderess, spy, mother. Now I am a crone, an old and fearsome woman. I make my servants and spies tremble when they must be in the same room as me, for they are fools and believe everything they hear, that I speak with spirits and have visions of what is still to come. They do not, cannot, believe that a woman can shape her own life to achieve what she most desires. And I cannot believe that all my work has come to nothing.

I have been more than any woman is allowed to be. I should be remembered as an amir, as Commander, as Yusuf's right hand. Instead I will be remembered for my youthful beauty. They will make up stories about me and call me a magician. They will not see my network of spies, my insights, my endless hard work and military strategies, for they will not credit that to a woman, no, it must come from djinns and spirits.

At last I leave my son's rooms and walk down long corridors to my own chambers.

I am done.

Murakush c.1102

The taste is my mouth is beyond bitterness. I feel saliva drip down the side of my mouth, see it fall to the floor, a foaming wet whiteness.

There is a mirror in my room. I crawl towards it now, my silk robes brushing the floor, turning to rags beneath my knees. I cannot stand, my legs are too weak and my breathing too shallow.

My eyes are growing dim. Something cold touches me and I start back, then realise my face has touched the mirror, yet still I cannot see myself. I sit back on my heels, close my eyes and struggle for breath.

I reach out and place my palms on the cold hard mirror, bring my face close to its shining surface. I open my eyes wide and stare into its depths, seeking my reflection.

Daughter, bride, concubine, queen, widow, wife, seductress, rival, murderess, spy, mother. Crone.

I cannot see my face.

Historical Notes

It is both difficult and inspiring to write about someone when history does not give us much information to go on. Although she was famous in her era, the total information I could find on Zaynab amounted to little more than a couple of paragraphs. Zaynab was the daughter of a man named Ibrahim from Kairouan in Tunisia, a city known for its rose perfume and very fine carpets. She claimed to have had a vision that said her husband would rule all of the Maghreb (North Africa), at the time made up of many diverse tribal states. This drew a lot of attention and many important men sought her in marriage. However she ended up marrying Yusuf bin Ali, who was a chief, but only of a small tribe and a vassal to the amir (king) of Aghmat, which seems an oddly humble choice, especially as sources say she was a concubine (implying a first wife was already in place). There is no mention of Yusuf dying, instead it appears he then gave her up to Luqut, the amir of Aghmat, a wealthy city.

She was married to Luqut until the Almoravid army conquered Aghmat (and killed Luqut), when she was taken as a bride by their leader, Abu Bakr. It is said that she blindfolded Abu Bakr and took him to a cave filled with treasure, which she promised to him, then re-blindfolded him and took him back out again.

When Southern tribes started causing unrest, Abu Bakr gave the command of the army to his second-in command, Yusuf bin Tashfin, and divorced Zaynab (claiming that a rough desert life would not be suitable for her), giving her in marriage to Yusuf. In this way Zaynab managed to be married four times, an extraordinary thing for a woman in those times and somehow her initial prophecy came true, even though it took four marriages to happen, implying a certain amount of deliberate ambition. In my version of events, Zaynab naively makes up the vision to draw her first husband Yusuf closer to her, which backfires when Yusuf is then forced to give her up in marriage to his amir Luqut, ruler of Aghmat.

Zaynab became Yusuf bin Tashfin's right hand, acknowledged as a superb military tactician in her own right. She was highly important in negotiating the transfer of power from Abu Bakr to Yusuf. She is described in the quote I have used at the start of this novel: *In her time there was none such as she – none more beautiful or intelligent or witty ... she was married to Yusuf, who built Marrakech for her...* as well as texts saying that she spoke with djinns and spirits. She was nicknamed 'the Magician' for her negotiating skills. Having apparently had no children at all in her previous three marriages over many years, she then seemed to have quite a few children with Yusuf (the information is very piecemeal but Yusuf had several sons and possibly nine to eleven children altogether, a good amount of whom were Zayanb's).

There is no clarity on when or how Zaynab died.

The Almoravids conquered the whole of the Maghreb (North Africa) and most of Spain. But Yusuf's choice of heir, Ali, was a peaceful and religious man, not much inclined to fighting and his empire was eventually lost to the Almohad army.

I wanted to try and put some reasons behind some of the things I found odd about Zaynab's story. Why marry a not very important chief as a concubine when supposedly she could have anyone? Why move from Kairouan in Tunisia to the West of Morocco, a very long distance in those days? Why was she free to marry the king of Aghmat? How come she had visions about her own future as the wife of the man who would rule all of North Africa when this prophecy actually took an unheard-of four marriages to achieve? It also seemed very odd that she had no children at all despite three husbands and then had as many as ten with Yusuf bin Tashfin. Finally, considering Zaynab's undisputed beauty and intelligence, her status as Yusuf's right hand and that she had given him several children, as well as his own devout Muslim faith, it seemed very strange to me that Yusuf would choose as his heir Ali, the son of a Christian slave girl. It certainly made me wonder how Zaynab would have taken such a choice when she might reasonably have expected one of her own sons (the Almoravids did not use primogeniture) to inherit the empire. My series of books set around the Almoravids takes this strange choice and creates a possible narrative around it.

Yusuf's first wife, Kella, is fictional, although again it seems odd Yusuf would have had no wife at all until he was nearly fifty. Isabella is not fictional, she is the Christian slave girl mentioned in historical records, although information on her is even more limited, to little more than a sentence, and so I have created her life to suit my storytelling. It seemed to be important that she was a slave and that she was Christian, for this is almost all that has been recorded about her apart from her Arabic nickname, Perfection of Beauty. The child she raised seems to have been very ill suited in temperament for ruling a newly-created empire, being described as studious, pious, peace-loving and not a warrior.

What emerges in this novel, I hope, is the story of a very powerful woman in history, one who had an unusual life and who was credited with extraordinary influence at a time of great change, but whose own child was denied inheriting the empire which Zaynab was at least partly responsible for creating.

A note on names: the names of some of the men (especially Yusuf's sons) have been tricky to choose, especially where they are called Abu-something. This ought to mean 'father of' and would be a name they used as an adult, referencing their own son, but as there is no mention of their childhood names, it is all I can go on and I did not wish to make up names entirely. So I have simply stuck to their adult names. It is not clear who were the mothers of Yusuf's children, except for his eventual heir, so I have made the assumption that most were Zaynab's, but not all: since Yusuf clearly had at least one son by a slave I assumed there might have been a few more. A few of the sons and all of the daughters do not even have dates of birth, so the order in which the children were born could be wrong. I have used Murakush (land of God), the original name for Marrakech.

If you want to see the inspiration for Zaynab's bellydancing lessons in the Concubine chapter, find a video of Rachel Brice, a world-class belly dancer, whose artistry I hugely admire and to whom this book is respectfully dedicated. Her combination of sensuality and spectacular physical strength and control must take huge amounts of work to create something that looks both magical and effortless, and is a model for how I think of Zaynab.

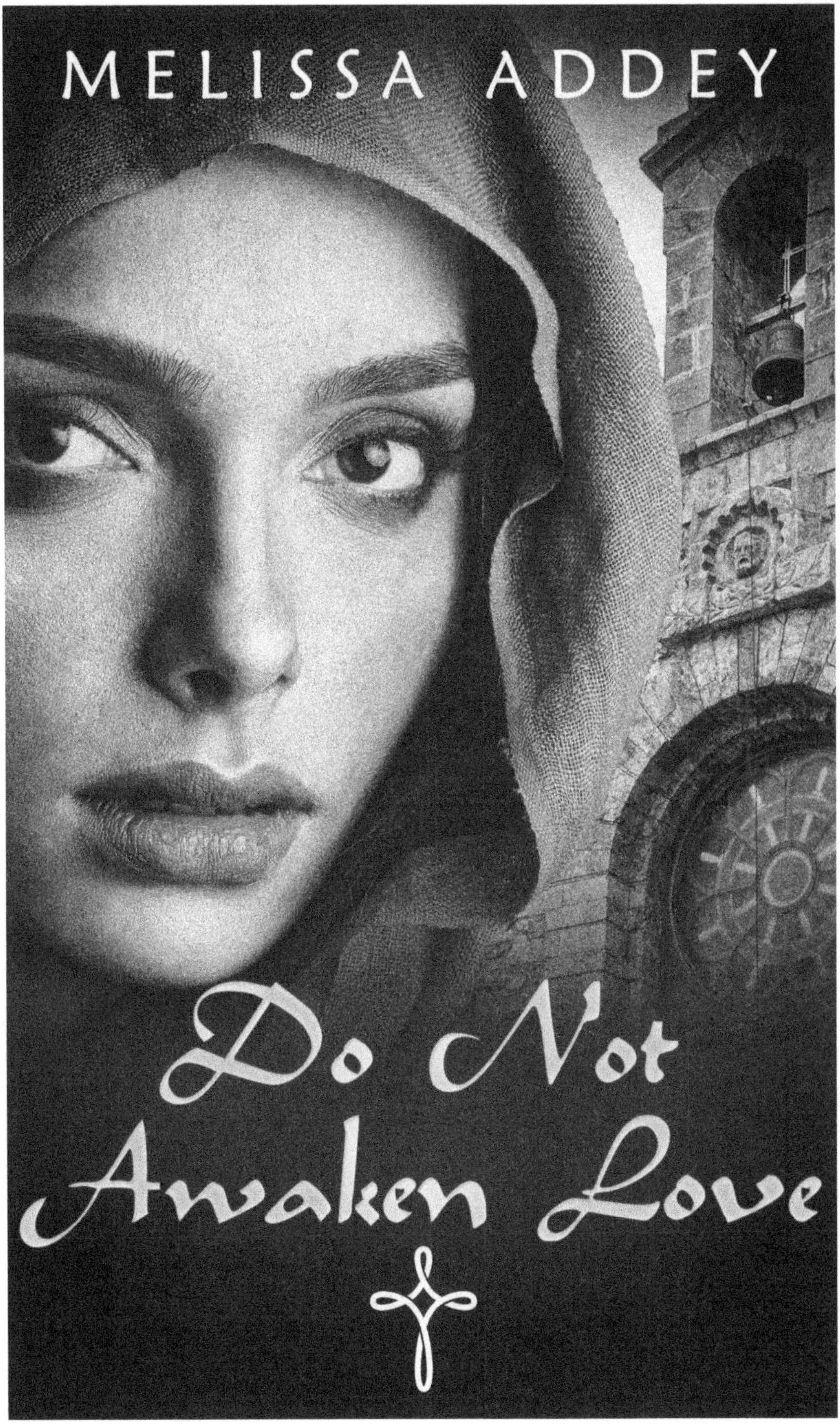
MELISSA ADDEY
Do Not
Awaken Love

Do Not
Awaken Love

For my daughter Isabelle, who is so full of love.

The Almoravids would have been what we call Berbers (preferred contemporary name, Amazigh). They belonged to many tribes and had various names for themselves, including Tuareg. They were known for their blue indigo-dyed robes and beautiful silver jewellery.

Amongst these people it was traditionally the men, not women, who veiled their faces.

Yusuf left his Muslim empire of North Africa and Spain to Ali, the son of a Christian slave girl nicknamed 'Perfection of Beauty.'

al-Bayān al-Mughrib
by Ibn Idhāri of Marrakech, approx. 1312
(Book of the Amazing Story of the History of the Kings of al-Andalus and Maghreb)

And now I will tell you of the news that came from beyond the sea, of Yusuf, that king, who was in Morocco. The King of Morocco was vexed with My Cid Don Rodrigo. "He has made himself strong in my lands," he said, "and he thanks no one for it but Jesus Christ!" The King of Morocco gathered up all his forces, fifty thousand men, all armed. He is going to Valencia to seek out My Cid Don Rodrigo!

The Poem of The Cid
(translated by Lesley Byrd Simpson)

I adjure you, O daughters of Jerusalem, do not stir up or awaken love...

Song of Solomon, 8:4

Galicia

(Northern Spain)

The Door, 1106

Who is this that cometh out of the wilderness?

Song of Solomon, 3:6

WE PASS BY THE APPLE *orchard, still there after all this time. I rein in my horse for a moment. On the breeze, the faint scent of the pink and white blossom comes to me. I wonder if Alberte's body was ever found amongst these trees. I make the sign of the cross, blessing him in his gentle goodness, his affinity with all God's creatures. I think that if it were harvest time I would dismount and pluck a fruit, bite into its sweetness, the taste that set me out on a journey I never asked for. But it is a different season now.*

Imari watches me for a few moments. "Do you wish to stop here?" he asks at last when I do not move on.

I shake my head. "No, thank you. I was only thinking."

He does not enquire further. Imari was never a man to question the thoughts of others.

We ride slowly, staying each night in a convent or monastery where we receive warm welcomes. They believe us pilgrims, returning home. I am not in a hurry. I know that once I enter the convent again, I will never leave and so this is the last time I will see the world. And the world is a beautiful place. I am glad to have seen it, to have known what it is to walk its ways before bidding it a final farewell.

It is mid-morning when I see, far away, the tall cream walls of the Convent of the Sacred Way. I glance at Imari, riding by my side. He catches the movement and nods to me, confirming that we are almost at our destination. I find my conversation has died away, preparing me for the silent life to which I am about to return. The fields and woods pass us by as the hours move on and when a farmer bids us a good day, I cannot find my tongue, only nod and smile.

The great door towers over me and I pause for a long moment. I think it must be time for the mid-afternoon prayer, None. *By the time* Vespers *comes, I will kneel among my sisters again after two decades of absence.*

"Do you wish me to knock?" asks Imari behind me.

I shake my head. I lift my wrinkled hand, take the great knocker, then let it fall. The deep sound reverberates around us. I look back over my shoulder. In the bright light of spring, I see Imari on horseback, a dark shadow in the sun's rays, fulfilling his last duty to a master who is now dead and gone.

When this door opens, we shall both be set free, returned to our former lives.

Before I was taken.

The Sacred Way, 1048

A garden inclosed is my sister.

Song of Solomon, 4:12

"SHE CAN WRITE A GOOD script," my mother says, trying not to sound boastful, aware of the sin of pride. But I know that in truth she is proud that I can write, it is a rare skill in a girl my age, from my background. "And I have taught her such healing herbs as I know, from my garden," she continues.

The Mother Superior nods. "What is your name, child?"

"Isabella, Reverend Mother," I say clearly, mindful of my mother's instructions on the way here to speak up and not whisper or shrink back.

"And how old are you?"

"Twelve," I say.

"And is it your wish to enter the Convent of the Sacred Way? To be a nun here, when you are older?"

"Yes," I say. "I have been promised here since I was born," I add, with a touch of the storyteller to my pronouncement. "My birth was a gift from Saint James himself."

The Mother Superior raises her eyebrows and my mother hurries to explain.

My mother was barren. There was not a saint on whose name she did not call in desperation for a child. The carvings on the beads of her rosary were worn away with her whispered prayers. At last, in despair, already past her fortieth year, she made the pilgrimage to Santiago de Compostela, walking barefoot for twenty days. She would have felt dread at being so far from her home and husband, for she was a meek woman, driven only by quiet desperation, not any bold sense of adventure.

There in the holy place she knelt, feet bleeding from her journey, and swore that should she have a child she would dedicate them to God, to be a nun or monk. Then she returned home, weary and having used up her last hope, for what else could she do, where else could she turn to beg for a child? When after three months she did not bleed, rather than laugh with joy she wept, for she believed her last chance had gone, and that old age was coming to claim her. Instead, it was a child that was coming, and true to her word, my mother promised me to this convent.

"The saint heard my prayers," says my mother. "And after his great gift to us, my husband agreed to move close to his shrine. We live by the road that the pilgrims take, we offer them water and food from our table daily. Isabella has helped me since she was a small child."

"What work does your husband do?"

"He is a bookseller and scribe," says my mother. "He writes letters for those who cannot write, he sells such books as his customers request. Books of learning, to scholars. Many are holy books," she adds, anxious to make a good impression. "He is a good Christian."

The Mother Superior is nodding, though I know that my mother could be charged with lying by omission. She is not mentioning that some of those holy books are sold to people of other faiths. My father has customers who are Jews and even, occasionally, Muslim scholars, although they are rarer, since the Muslim kingdoms, the *taifas*, are all to the South. The Mother Superior would not like to hear about these customers, just as my mother does not like them coming to my father.

"They are heathens," I hear her chastising my father. "Let them go elsewhere for their sacrilegious texts."

"They are scholars and men of learning," my father always replies, and she will huff and mutter to herself and insist that they visit discretely, she does not want people gossiping about us. When she has gone, my father will smile at me and say, "Books are a precious gift, Isabella. They teach us to see the world with new eyes."

"But what if they contain blasphemy?" I ask, a righteous child who has been raised knowing I will be a nun one day.

My father shakes his head when I say this. "It is men who speak blasphemy when they presume to speak for God," he says gently. "It is not blasphemy to seek to understand our fellow men, even if they speak of their God with a different name. For God is always God, no matter what name we poor mortals may give Him in our ignorance."

"He should not be called by any other name," I say, certain of the Church and my mother's teachings. "He is God. And it is blasphemy to call Him by any other name."

My father smiles at my certainty. "Not so very long ago, far south of Galicia, away in Al-Andalus, was a city called Cordoba, where men of learning lived side by side and spoke with one another of what they knew. They shared their understanding of God and they made great discoveries in medicine, in mathematics, in astronomy and other studies. And the women of that city were calligraphers and poets, teachers and lawyers and doctors. There were more than twenty schools, open to all so that any who wished to learn might enjoy the knowledge shared. There was a library with more than four hundred thousand books. It was a community of great scholars."

"And were they all Christians?" I ask, suspiciously.

"They were Christians and Jews and Muslims," says my father. "And they made a land of knowledge and culture the like of which has never been seen before. Or since," he adds, sadly. "Wars led to Al-Andalus being split into many small kingdoms. And now they bicker endlessly with each other, and so the great strides forward that were made are left to fade away."

"Well, I am glad we live in a Christian kingdom away from the heathen Moors," I say. "And I hope our king will one day conquer Al-Andalus, for the glory of God."

My father only nods, having heard my words coming from my mother's lips for many years. "Let us practice your calligraphy," he says. "It will stand you in good stead when you join the convent, for an educated woman will rise higher than one who has no learning."

"I seek only to serve God," I say. "It is not seemly to seek glory." But I bend my head to my studies anyway, for there is a little part of me that would like to be praised, who sometimes gives way to the sin of pride and imagines becoming a great Mother Superior or an Abbess, with a convent at my command, known for both my holy demeanour and brilliant mind.

The Mother Superior asks me to copy a verse from the Bible and nods at what I produce.

"Sister Rosa runs our infirmary and she is advancing in years now, she has need of an apprentice. The herbs and other ingredients she uses require a fair hand to label and as you say, Isabella has been taught the beginnings of the uses of herbs. If you do well, child, one day you will run the infirmary yourself, and there can be no greater service to God than to heal the sick that come to us. We care mostly for pilgrims," she explains to my mother, "as we are placed here, on the last part of the road to Santiago. I am sure she will do well with us. Say goodbye to your mother, Isabella."

My mother's eyes shine with tears. In part, of course, she is sorry to lose her only child, to bid me farewell, but at the same time she is fulfilling her promise to Saint James, she is seeing her long-ago pilgrimage come to its sacred conclusion. She is filled with a joyful pride that she, a woman from a lowly estate, has given a daughter to the Church who may one day run the infirmary of a large and important convent. "Thank you, Reverend Mother," she all but whispers. Her farewell to me is brisk and full of reminders of my sacred duty to obey the nuns in all things and to fulfil her promise to Saint James with reverence. I nod to everything she says, and then Sister Rosa comes to take me into the garden.

Sister Rosa is old, her skin is wrinkled and burnt brown by the sun as though she were a peasant, after all her years tending the garden to fill the still room and infirmary with remedies.

"We pray when we gather the herbs and we pray when we administer them," she wheezes, "for it is through our prayers that God acts to heal the sick. It is neither our own skills nor the roots and leaves we use, that heal. Both are only conduits for His powers."

"Yes, Sister," I murmur.

"You will learn from me all the properties and righteous uses of plants, including trees, as well as all those other things on which we can draw in our work. The elements and humours, of course, metals and stones, and also all those creatures whom God created for man's use: animals, fish, reptiles and birds. Naturally, you and I will focus on those that heal, but remember that healing comes also through everyday food, work and prayer, not just through the treating of an illness. It is part of our work to ensure that our sisters and visitors eat a health-giving diet. Meat, for example, should not be eaten too frequently, for it may inspire lust and that is incompatible with being a bride of Christ."

"Yes, Sister."

"Saint Benedict himself, when writing the Rule by which we live, said that caring for the sick was one of the instruments of good works. And so, you and I are blessed, Isabella, in that each and every day, we will be able to do good works through our humble tasks."

Sister Rosa, I will discover, talks a great deal, but she has kind eyes and a warm smile. The heady smell of sunwarmed lavender is all around me as we walk through the garden, the peaceful stillroom and the infirmary.

For nearly twenty years, this is my home.

The Apple Orchard

Let my beloved come into his garden, and eat his pleasant fruits.

Song of Solomon, 4:16

"ONCE AGAIN, YOU HAVE SHOWN yourself a true bride of Christ, Sister Juliana," says the Mother Superior as the pilgrim leaves us, bowing and promising that he will praise my name at every footstep from here to Santiago de Compostela, for without my knowledge of herbs he might well have died before ever reaching his holy destination.

I bow my head over the mortar and pestle. "I was only doing my duty," I say. "It is God's hand that cured him."

Mother Superior nods. "Indeed. But I have had to speak with some of the youngest sisters for their... *unnecessary* attention to that young man. I am afraid that in their youth and inexperience, they have been swayed by his name and fortune. As well as his looks," she adds, getting to the real cause for her concern. She sighs. "Temptation is everywhere, Sister."

"Yes, Reverend Mother," I say, carefully pouring the ground cinnamon into its container, its sweet smell scenting the air around us. The bark of the tree is very hot in nature and is good for banishing ill humours, therefore despite its expense I use it frequently to dose my sisters, that their humours may be good.

"And yet you were not led astray," says the Mother Superior with satisfaction. "It shows both your maturity and devotion to God and does you credit."

"Thank you, Reverend Mother," I say.

She looks around my stillroom, at all my remedies. The careful script marking each little bottle and jar, the cleanliness and order. "You are a credit to the name you took when you joined us," she adds.

I think of Saint Juliana, patron of the sick, a devoted Christian who refused to marry a pagan husband and was scarred for her disobedience. "I have not had to face her tribulations," I say. "I have been well treated here, Reverend Mother."

She pats my shoulder. "You have worked hard ever since you were a child and your skill with the sick is your reward, by which you serve God," she says. She stands for a moment but does not leave, gazing out of the window at my neat beds of herbs in the garden, as though turning something over in her mind. "I have a task for you," she says at last. "You are to leave the convent and travel beyond Santiago de Compostela, to the coast at A Lanzada, to collect a novice, a girl named Catalina. Her father is ill, and she cannot travel alone. You will be accompanied by Alberte."

"The stablehand? He does not have his full wits about him, Reverend Mother."

"He is obedient and strong," says the Mother Superior a little reproachfully. "We all have different gifts, given to us by God. You will also be accompanied by Sister Maria, so that there can be no impropriety in your travelling with a man."

"Yes, Reverend Mother," I say obediently, although privately I think that Sister Maria is a poor choice for a companion on a journey away from the convent. She is altogether too worldly for my liking, speaking often of life in the outside world as though it is something to be longed for, not grateful to be set apart from.

"I am entrusting you with this task because of your dedication to our convent," says the Mother Superior. "I know that you will not be swayed in your faith by seeing the world outside our walls, that you will provide an example to our novice as she journeys here, to view entering our convent as a homecoming, rather than a loss of her childhood freedom."

I stand a little straighter. "Yes, Reverend Mother," I say.

"It is so exciting to be out in the world!" says Sister Maria on the morning when we set out.

I watch Alberte hoist her up into the saddle. Being both short and plump she is unable to mount alone. Her horse is skittish and once she is seated, Alberte bows his head to the mare's muzzle and whispers to her, stroking her neck to calm the beast.

"It is an honour to bring home a young soul who is destined for the spiritual life," I say.

Sister Maria beams at me as Alberte adjusts her stirrups. "I am sure our Reverend Mother has seen great qualities of devotion in you," she says without jealousy. "Perhaps she sees a future for you as a Mother Superior yourself and this journey is a mark of her favour."

I put a foot in my stirrup and lift myself into the saddle in one move. "You should not say such things, for I have no expectations," I say. "The service I give in the infirmary is all that I desire." I know that this is not quite true and note that I will need to do penance for the little burst of pride her words gave me, the thought that this journey, if well carried out, might lead to possible future elevation within our community.

Sister Maria is not in the least abashed. She readjusts her habit so that it falls more gracefully from her high seat. "Bless you, Alberte," she says, looking down at the stablehand with an undiminished smile. "You have an affinity with horses, they listen to you. The Lord has given you a gift." She is always free and easy with her compliments to those about her. I suppose she means well, although she may not realise that such comments can lead to the sin of pride in others.

"We must make a start," I say to them both. "We cannot waste time."

I feel a little anxious as we make our way through the gates of the convent and out into the open farmland that surrounds us. I have not left these walls except for brief walks to forage for plants since I came here as a child, excepting very occasionally to tend to a local noblewoman. To look back and see the convent recede into the distance is unnerving. Alberte's expression is mostly blank, although he murmurs to his horse from time to time and I note that he watches the birds as they fly past. He is a good-natured lad, I suppose, it is not his fault that he was born with a simple mind. He works hard and is obedient enough. Sister Maria, of course, cannot be relied upon to maintain an appropriate silence.

"The crops are doing well this year," she announces to no-one in particular. "I believe we will be able to give thanks for a generous harvest."

As I recall Sister Maria came to us from farming stock, so it is no wonder she interests herself in such matters. I do not reply, hoping that she will recollect in due course that we should obey the rule of silence, since there is no need to speak. My hopes are not met.

"Good morning!" she cries when we pass a farmer and his children in a wagon, on their way to work in the fields.

"Good morning, Sisters," he returns politely. "I wish you a pleasant journey."

I bow my head but do not answer, while Sister Maria beams down at his children. "May the Lord bless you," she says as they trundle slowly by. She twists her head to watch them. "Ah, Sister Juliana," she says. "I know we are blessed to live a holy life, but I do sometimes think that it would have been a great joy to bear children."

"There is no greater joy than to serve God," I remind her a little sharply, but she does not look in the least humbled.

"There is joy in all walks of life," she says. "For God is in our hearts, whatever work we turn our hands to."

"Perhaps we may think on that blessing in silence," I say and at last Sister Maria stills her tongue for a little while.

With Alberte's orders to stick to a brisk but dignified pace, we reach the outskirts of Santiago de Compostela itself in three days, riding alongside pilgrims making their way to the holy shrine. I have to remind Sister Maria on an irritatingly frequent basis to restrict her conversation with those whom we pass. We sleep each night in welcoming houses of God, so that we can be assured of safety and of being watched over by a holy presence, in silence and comfort. I feel a small pang on the fourth day that we cannot visit the great city and pray in the cathedral, but it will only slow us down. There are still two more days' journey to go and so we pass by the city walls in the distance and continue on our journey, following the River Ulla down its southern side as it widens out into the Arousa Estuary.

"The sea!" exclaims Sister Maria.

"God be praised," I say. "We are almost at our destination."

"I have never been to the sea," says Sister Maria, almost standing in her stirrups to look farther ahead, shading her eyes.

"We are not here to sightsee," I tell her, but she and Alberte pay no attention, exclaiming together over every little thing they notice as we reach the coastline and the small village of A Lanzada. The sound of the waves lapping, the white-gold sand and the deep blue shade of the sea all catch their attention and it is left entirely to me to seek out the right household.

"I thought it would be bigger," says Alberte, looking a little forlorn at the sight of the huddled houses along the shoreline. Seagulls scream overhead. I have only ever seen them rarely, when the weather at sea is bad and they come inland to screech in the convent's fields.

"It is not the size of the village that matters to us, but that it chooses to give up one of its daughters to our holy life," I remind him.

"Is that the hermitage?" asks Sister Maria.

A rocky outcrop jutting into the sea from the shoreline holds a tiny building, like a miniature church, with a large tower to one side.

"Yes," I say. "We will give thanks there for our peaceful journey here and again when we leave with the girl, that we may have a safe journey home."

"What is the tower for?" wonders Sister Maria.

I do not answer her, for a boy has run up to greet us.

"Have you come for Catalina?"

I look down into his wide eyes. "I am Sister Juliana of the Convent of the Sacred Way," I tell him. "I and my Sister Maria here have come to take Catalina home."

The boy looks puzzled. "This is her home," he says.

"She has been promised as a bride of Christ," I say. "Her true home is at the convent now."

He only stares at me.

"Where is her father's house?" I ask.

He points, then runs alongside us as we make our way to the largest house in the village, where a woman is already standing waiting for us. Word of strangers spreads fast in a small village.

Catalina's father is a merchant of middling means. He is a chandler, supplying ropes and other such necessities to ships both large and small, although his trade is mostly with the smaller fishermen and merchants, not ocean-going craft or grand vessels. He finds himself in ill health, suffering from a growth in his stomach which is likely to kill him soon, for there is no cure. Therefore, he has been taking care of his affairs, including marrying off various sons and daughters who are old enough. He has a houseful of daughters, hence the dedication of Catalina to our convent.

The girl is thirteen years old. She looks nervous at the sight of me. I think of myself at her age, almost twenty years ago, although since I had been told I would come to the holy orders since I was a baby, I think I was more prepared.

"My dear girl," says Sister Maria, enfolding her in an unnecessary embrace. "We are so glad to see you! It is a great honour to have been chosen to journey here and bring you home to our convent. I am sure you will be happy there and you will become ordained one day yourself, praise be to God."

Catalina gives a weak smile, but she is brave enough when bidding goodbye to her family the next morning. Our departure is delayed by her mother insisting on us all eating a final and overly lavish breakfast together and her father fussing too much over ensuring her stirrups are well-set for her legs. She has very little in the way of belongings, but of course she will not need anything personal at the convent. Her brothers and sisters and what appears to be half the village have come to bid her farewell, which delays us still further. Catalina's lower lip trembles a little when her mother weeps while blessing her, but that is natural enough and shows a good heart and a familial devotion which I am sure will in due course become a devotion to the convent. She mounts the horse that Alberte has brought for her by herself and lifts one hand to her family. I see a little tear fall but I look away so that she need not be ashamed of her moment of weakness.

"We will pray at the hermitage for a safe journey home," I say.

We ride down to the shoreline and then walk past the tall tower to the tiny chapel. It is smaller than our refectory inside, but all places of worship bring me a sense of peace and we pray together, the three of us, while Alberte waits on the beach with the horses. When we emerge, he is staring open-mouthed at the way the waves rush onto the sand and then pull away again. Catalina, perhaps out of nerves, chatters incessantly.

"The tower was built as a lookout against the Norsemen," she informs us. "They use the estuary to sail upriver and come closer to Santiago de Compostela on their raiding parties."

"The Norsemen's raids were long ago," I point out.

She shakes her head. "They still go on now," she says, "just more rarely. They try to take women and children, to sell them for slaves."

Alberte and Sister Maria stare at her, fascinated.

"We need to begin our journey," I say. "It is already late."

We mount again and turn the horses inland, ready to journey home.

"Will you miss living by the sea?" asks Sister Maria.

Catalina looks back over her shoulder at the sea, sparkling in the midmorning sun. "Yes," she admits. "There is so much to see, it changes every day. And they say it has healing properties."

"What kind of properties?" I ask.

"Women who are barren go down to the hermitage once a year at midnight for the Ritual of the Nine Waves," she says. "Once a woman has undressed and been washed in nine waves by the light of the moon, she will have children for sure."

"That is a pagan belief and practice," I say sharply. "I will not hear of such nonsense, nor should you repeat it." I hope the girl will not gossip all the way home; she is worse than Sister Maria. "We will not speak for the rest of the journey unless it is necessary," I tell her. "It is best to grow used to the rule of silence as quickly as possible, so that it will come to seem natural to you."

She nods, chastised. I give her a small smile of approval for showing her agreement and obedience without speaking.

Our late departure means that the midday sun burns down on us while we are still progressing along the banks of the estuary, passing small farms as we go. To our right, we pass a large apple orchard, the very first apples turning shining red. The sweetly tart fruits of early summer come as a welcome relief after the bitter greens and heavy chestnut flour of the winter. The breeze rustles through the branches and birds sing. It is a place of great peace, reminding me of my herb garden at the convent. I have missed the garden, even in these few days away from it, the silence and the scent, the mastery of my own little kingdom.

"May we rest, Sister Juliana?" asks Sister Maria.

I consider for a moment. We should ride on, but the sun is at its zenith and the rustling leaves and faint scent of apples calls to me. "Very well," I concede. "We will rest a little while. The shade will be cooling."

Sister Maria slides ungracefully down from her horse, landing with a solid thud on her small feet. Her round face is beaming. "May we taste the fruits?"

"No," I say sharply. "They are not ours to pick, Sister. You should know better."

But Sister Maria is already holding a red apple in her hand. "A windfall," she says. "A gift of God to the needy."

"You are hardly in need, Sister," I say, looking with disapproval at her ample girth.

Sister Maria is not listening, of course, she is hunting for other windfalls in the long grass. She finds and offers one to Alberte, then another to Catalina, who looks to me for guidance. I am glad to see her hesitation; it speaks of humility and reverence for one's elders and superiors. "You may accept," I say. It would be a waste of God's bounty to let the windfall fruit rot in the field, after all. Alberte is sharing his apple with his horse, the foolish boy. When Sister Maria holds out a fruit to me, I hesitate but then take it with care, wiping a little mud off the red peel. Apples are easily digested by persons in good health, even when eaten raw, and the first apples of the season have a crisp sweetness that is pleasing to the palate. A little further down the slope is an old tree stump shaded by a young tree and I make my way to it, leaving the others behind. I sit down and look out over the fields, then lift my hand to my mouth. I bite, feel the sharp-sweet flesh crunch beneath my teeth and even as I do so, Catalina screams somewhere behind me.

I twist on my seat and look round, expecting the girl to have perhaps disturbed a snake in the long grass, but instead I am faced with Alberte, who is staggering towards me, his face ashen, eye wide, his neck ending in a scarlet slash from which blood is pouring. Even as I rise, he falls, so that behind him I can see Sister Maria struggling in the arms of a man and Catalina running back towards the road, pursued by another man. I open my mouth to cry out and a rough hand comes over my mouth, my left arm is pinned back so hard I think for a moment my shoulder is about to dislocate. I struggle and try to bite the hand and it is taken away for a moment, only to strike me so hard the world grows dark.

Something wakes me. My shoulders ache and my stomach hurts, for all my weight is pushed onto it, I am lying draped over something moving, my head hanging down, longer grass stems touching my face. I open my mouth and vomit spews from it, filling my mouth and nose with the sweet-bitter-sharp taste of apple mixed with bile. My head feels cold even in the sunlight and it takes me a moment to realise that the men who took me have removed my coif, wimple and veil, so that my shaven scalp is exposed to the air. My hands are tied behind my back, I have been thrown over a saddle and when I try to move, I realise I have also been bound to it, for I cannot slide down from the horse. Now I realise that I have also been stripped of my habit, I am now wearing only my shift and my shoes. In terror, I think that I have been violated, that our captors have defiled our bodies, but there is no pain between my legs.

I twist my head to the right and see a horse being ridden ahead of me, the high leather boots of a man, nothing more. I twist my head the other way and see more horses behind me: the first bearing the shaven and unconscious head of Sister Maria, the one behind that the long dark locks of Catalina, whose face is turned towards mine, her eyes open in mute terror.

I meet her gaze but only shake my head at her not to make a noise, for if we do, we may be struck again, or our mouths bound up. Beyond Catalina's horse, I can only make out the legs of two, perhaps three, horses and more leather boots. I cannot see the faces of the riders.

We are no longer on the road. Instead, the horses pick their way through fields, keeping to the rough overgrown borders or through wooded areas so that my face is scratched by shrubs and low-hanging branches. I keep my eyes shut, for there is not much to see and I am afraid of brambles. But my mind is racing. One word keeps coming back to me. *Rus*. As a child, my father told me of the Norsemen, whom the Arabs called Rus. They sailed great ships and raided our coastlines, kidnapping men and women, taking them as slaves for themselves or selling them to the Maghreb, across the sea south of Al-Andalus, in the lands of the Muslims. The worst of their attacks took place long before our time, but as Catalina told us, there are still the odd raids, brutal and quick, taking unwary women and children for slaves. I think of the moment of temptation to which I succumbed: the shade, the ripe fruit, the fresh scent of apples in the warm air and curse myself. Poor half-witted Alberte is already dead for my sin and the fate of Sister Maria and Catalina is my burden to carry now, for I cannot think how we might escape. Eyes still closed, I pray for help to Our Lady, though the pain in my shoulders and the ache in my head tells me that my prayers may go unanswered, that my temptation to stray from the path I had been commanded to follow is about to be punished more severely than I could have imagined.

The horses stop in a heavily wooded area, but I can hear the sea again, the rush of waves on the shore not far away and guess that we are somewhere back close to A Lanzada. I think of the watchtower by the hermitage and hope that someone is watching, that they will spot something amiss and come to our aid. It is full daylight, surely a Norse ship would be spotted at once?

But the men have other ideas. They yank us down from the horses, I hear the muffled yelps from Sister Maria and Catalina as they fall to the ground, their bound hands meaning they are unable to break their falls. When my turn comes, I try to brace myself, but it makes no difference, I am half-pulled, half-thrown into the shrubby undergrowth and left to lie there. I dare not move, expecting the men to force themselves on us, but instead I hear them move a few steps away, speaking to one another in a guttural tongue, their voices unafraid, one even laughs. I cannot see them, but I hear them sit down and then faintly smell food that they are eating, bread and apples, no doubt picked from the same orchard where they took us. I can hear them crunching, smell again the faint sweet fresh smell. I look carefully about me without moving. I can see Sister Maria's feet and some of Catalina's long hair. I can hear Catalina crying softly.

Time goes by. Occasionally I move a little, only to stop my limbs from going numb. I dare not draw attention by moving a great deal. The men continue to talk between themselves as though they were merely passing the time together in idleness. I hear one snore when he snoozes for a while. They are unhurried, unconcerned at being found out. They must know this place well, know that they are fully concealed. They are waiting for something, but I am not sure what. I see Sister Maria wriggle violently once and one of the men throws an apple core at her with a command, no doubt to be still and silent, then laughs.

They have been waiting for darkness.

The sun sinks. I cannot see it, but I feel the cool breeze of the evening, see the shadows fade and change to dusk. We have been here for many hours. My mouth is dry with the desire for water, for I have not drunk since late morning. At last one of the men squats near each of us and lets us drink from a waterbag. It is not enough to fully sate my thirst but the few gulps I am allowed are desperately welcome.

They wait a little longer, as dusk turns to night. I think of the watching tower and wonder if it has a light in it, how far out to sea that light might shine. I pray to Our Lady of the Lanzada, the hermitage in which we knelt only this morning, where we asked for a safe journey home. I pray for a miracle.

I am thrown back over my horse, my stomach pressed hard against the saddle, I hear the other two women served in the same manner before the Norsemen begin to lead us further through the woods and then out into an open space, I think we must be on a clifftop overlooking the sea, for I hear the waves closer than ever and beyond the ground I can only make out an empty nothingness of darkness. The stars shine brightly, but the moon is only a tiny crescent, I cannot make out any details by its pale glow. I twist my head this way and that, trying to make out anything, anything at all, the tiny lights of the village or even of a single house. One of the men cuffs my bare scalp and hisses something at me, no doubt an order to be still. I kick out at him and he cuffs me harder. I hang loose again, my face half against the hard leather saddle, half on the horse's warm flank.

This time, when we are pulled down, we land in soft sand, then are yanked to our feet and made to trudge through it, my feet slipping and sliding as the sand yields to my steps. I and my captor are leading the others closer to the sea. Twice I nearly fall, but the man behind me jerks me back to my feet, pulling my arm so hard it hurts.

When cold water washes over my feet I step back, but the Norseman has other ideas. He forces me forwards. I struggle, for a moment unreasonably fearing that he intends to drown me, which would be easy enough. If I were to fall now, knee-deep in water, my hands bound, I would drown in moments. I am pushed forwards again into the shallows of the sea, feel the wetness cover my feet, my ankles, my calves and the cold embrace of my shift as it becomes soaked, clinging to my thighs and waist. Now I see a moving shape close to us and realise there is a small rowing boat bobbing up and down. I am all but thrown into it, then pushed to take a seat on a rough wooden plank that serves as a bench. In the darkness, I make out the other men, Sister Maria and Catalina joining us. The boat rocks wildly and I want to clutch at the side but cannot. I wonder what is to become of the horses and wonder if perhaps these men have an accomplice here by the shore, a traitorous Galician who is well paid for his silence, trading the lives of good Christians for valuable horseflesh.

Two of the men take up oars and now there is the fast sound of wood against water and the boat begins to move across the waves. Far off along the shore, at last, I glimpse a cluster of tiny lights which may well be A Lanzada, but they are too far away to hear our screams, even were we able to scream.

I twist my head in the darkness and see a faint light in the endless dark waters. The men are rowing towards it. I feel a cold shudder pass through me, certain that a larger boat, a ship, is waiting for us, out there on the waves, showing only enough light to guide us towards it.

We draw closer and closer to the dim light. One of the men in our boat lets out a sudden call and at once, more lights appear ahead of us, illuminating what has been waiting all this time.

The ship fills my heart with fear. Its carved prow is surmounted with the head of a beast and it rocks slowly back and forth on the water as though it is alive. The lights now shining from it should reassure me, but they do not, they only tell me that these men, out here in the deep waters of the sea, are no longer afraid of being caught, that it is too late for the miraculous rescue I prayed for.

Each of us is tightly held by the men in the little boat and passed up to the many disembodied hands reaching over the sides of the ship. Lifted over the waters beneath us, we are then thrown onto the deck. I fall poorly, hitting one elbow so that pain shoots up my arm. I yelp in pain. A hand pulls me to my feet, a lantern is lifted. I come face to face with a man, his face a hand's breadth from mine.

His eyes are pale blue, like an early morning sky, a colour I have never seen before. His hair is dark yellow, long and coarse, pulled back from his head into a rough plait as though he were a peasant woman, though this is no woman. He towers over me, his shoulders massive and bare under a sleeveless leather jerkin, his muscled arms and even his neck marked with dark blue designs, shapes and whorls I do not know the meaning of. He pulls the gag from my mouth and then says something loudly into my face, but I do not know what he is saying. I turn my face to one side, and he slaps at me to look back at him. He repeats the words, but I only stare at him. He shrugs and drags me towards Sister Maria and Catalina, who are already sitting, their hands tied behind their backs, their tear-streaked faces turned towards me, eyes fixed on me as I stumble my way behind the man. Their captors have left them, gone to join the rest of the crew.

Suddenly I am fighting, hitting and biting, kicking and screaming, not words but only screeching fear. My composure has gone from me. My thoughts of caring for Sister Maria and Catalina are gone, at this moment I care only for myself and my safety, my ability to escape the man holding me prisoner.

But every bit of my strength and desperation is nothing to this man. He half-laughs, then pushes me so that I stagger backwards landing hard on my behind, almost in the laps of Sister Maria and Catalina, their bodies softening the blow.

"Sister Juliana," whispers Sister Maria, but I do not know what she was planning to say, for the man reaches over and gives her a hard slap to the face, so that she cries out and then hangs her head low, tears dripping from her face in silence. Catalina flinches and her shoulders shake with the effort of keeping her own sobs silent. I sit in silence, though no tears fall from my eyes. My mind goes over and over the moment when Sister Maria asked me if we might rest a while. I think of my hesitation, my agreement. I wonder, if I had said no and kept riding, would we be safe within the walls of the convent that would have hosted us tonight? Or would the Norsemen have taken us anyway? Were they on the road behind us, or hiding in the orchard? Had they already marked us as their victims, was our fate already written, or was there a moment when the wheel of destiny turned? Was it the moment when I reached out my hand for the sharp-sweet scarlet flesh and gave myself over to the pleasures of the world?

Above us, the beast-ship's head towers over us. I see its open mouth, the carved teeth within, a scarlet-painted tongue rippling out.

"Do not fight them," I whisper quickly. "They will only hurt you."

All around the ship orders are given and shouts come in response. I consider screaming for help but know already that it is too late for that now, we are far from the shore and I saw no other ships or even little boats. There is a heavy falling sound above our heads and craning upwards I catch sight of the bottom of a vast dark sail unfurling above us.

The Slave Block

They took away my veil.

Song of Solomon 5:7

*T*HROUGHOUT THAT NIGHT OUR PROGRESS is marked only by the occasional splash of oars, mostly by the billowing sound of the sail above us. The men do not talk much between themselves. The rise and fall of the sea makes me sick to my stomach and I hear Catalina retching over and over again, smell the bitter bile of her vomit, which in turn has me gagging until my stomach voids again. I taste, amidst the bitterness, the last sweet hint of apple and think of Eve's mouth, whether she could still taste the sweetness of the forbidden fruit on her tongue even as she stumbled out of the Garden of Eden. Perhaps she could. It would have been a bitter reproach, for all its sweetness.

At some time in the night, exhausted from all that has gone before, I begin to doze. I am awoken by a splash and the shouts of the men. There is a lot of noise and a torch is lit, but I cannot see much beyond the vomit-spattered deck. But shortly afterwards I am lifted up and carried over a man's shoulder as though I were a sack of grain, to a different part of the ship. I feel my bonds first loosened and then fastened to something. I seem to be tied to a heavy weight of some kind. I feel Catalina placed close by me, but I am so tired that the ensuing darkness calls to me again and I fall asleep not long after.

The half-light of early dawn wakes me. At last I can see. I look about me, see Catalina asleep at my feet, her long ropes bound to a metal ring set into the deck, as are mine. Above us is a small awning of heavy red silk, pulled low over us like a tiny shelter, so that I can hardly see out of the sides.

But Sister Maria is not with us.

Panicked, I try to stand but cannot, for the rope is not long enough. Instead, I kneel and try to scan the boat deck, wriggling to the edge of the awning and poking my head out. The light dazzles me.

I can see a few men on the deck. Two stand by the prow, one by the mast, a handful lie wrapped in rough blankets, sleeping. The oars are stacked by the sides, waiting for use. The ship rises and falls with the waves, but the motion is calmer than I feared. From low down, I cannot see a shoreline. There is no sign of Sister Maria.

"Sister Maria!" I call out.

The men at the prow turn to look at me and then look back at the sea, uninterested. I can hear them talking to one another, there is a brief laugh, then silence.

"Sister Maria!" I call more loudly, my voice higher than I would like, wavering.

Catalina's eyes open suddenly, she jerks awake and struggles briefly against her bonds as though having forgotten what happened, before recalling where she is and what has gone before now. Seeing me, she begins to cry. "Sister Juliana," she gulps, "what will become of us? Will the convent send men to bring us home?"

Poor innocent. She has little knowledge of the world. No doubt she has heard heroic stories of knights rescuing their ladies, of noble men setting the world to rights. She does not know, has not thought, as I have done, that the convent may never even hear word of our whereabouts. Alberte's body may not be found, our horses may be sold to some disreputable dealer, our Mother Superior may believe that we have run away, or she may guess that bandits or Norsemen have robbed, raped, killed or kidnapped us, but certainly there is nothing she can do about it. The Norsemen have taken us onto the high seas without a soul seeing us and I am certain their destination is either their own homelands far to the north, or the Maghreb, to the south. I squint at the rising sun in the east. It is on my left. We are sailing south.

"Catalina," I say.

She continues to sob, but looks up at me.

"It is likely that we are sailing to the south of Al-Andalus, most likely to the Maghreb," I tell her. "We are to be sold as slaves to the Muslims."

She lets out a little cry and one of the men turns. Seeing us still bound, he looks away again.

"Catalina, if it is Al-Andalus and we are separated, then if you can ever run away, head north, back to Galicia."

"And the Maghreb?" she asks.

I have no answer. Already what I have suggested to her is absurd, that a thirteen-year-old girl might escape her captors and travel safely from Al-Andalus to Galicia, but it is all the hope I can offer her. I wanted to give her something to cling to. But from the Maghreb? Who knows where we might be sold to? How would we escape and travel over the sea even to reach Al-Andalus?

"You must pray," I tell her at last. I do not know what else to tell her.

"For rescue?" she asks.

How can I tell her she will not be rescued? How can I tell her, looking at her long black hair and fine features, her large black eyes now rimmed red with tears, that she is a beautiful young girl, that she is likely to be sold to a rich man as a bedfellow, a whore?

"You must pray to the Virgin Mary for her guidance and protection," I say at last.

Catalina begins to mumble. "Hail Mary, Full of Grace, the Lord is with thee. Blessed art thou among women…"

I look about me, still fearful for Sister Maria. Where has she been taken? Has she been hurt, or taken by one of the men to… to…? I hardly dare think what I fear. But the deck is mostly uncovered, surely she should be visible to me. I twist my head this way and that and finally I open my mouth and scream her name as loud as I can. "Sister Maria!" I only want to hear her answer me once, if she can, just to know that she is here, with us.

I open my mouth to scream again and am cuffed sharply round the head. A Norseman has come close to us and he is scowling.

"Silentium," he says in oddly accented Latin, *silence*.

"Please," I say, kneeling up, staring up into his strange blue eyes, replying in Latin, hopeful that we can speak together. "Please. Where is Sister Maria?"

He stares at me. I had thought perhaps he spoke Latin well, but it appears he does not.

I point at Catalina, at myself, at an invisible Sister Maria. "Where?"

He makes a gesture at the green-blue waves. "Transulto." Then he walks away, joining the men by the prow.

I stare at the man and then at the sea. I think through what I said, the exact words, the exact gestures I made for him to understand me. I think of his answer, *leapt*, of the gesture, the exact direction to which he indicated.

I think through our brief exchange over and over again trying to find a different possible explanation.

There is none.

Sister Maria, in the night, jumped overboard and drowned.

That was the cause of the splash and shouts I heard in the night and the reason why Catalina and I were lifted to the middle of the ship and bound to the deck, so that we could not do the same. Fat little Sister Maria, too much in love with the outside world for my liking, who wished she might have had children of her own, who spoke cheerfully and too long with everyone she met, who ate greedily of nature's bounty, chose to die rather than face what might come and in so doing, has committed a mortal sin.

Catalina has not understood the conversation I had with the Norseman. She is still quietly sobbing and repeating Hail Marys; she has not reacted to the news. Perhaps she thinks Sister Maria is tied up somewhere behind us, perhaps she thinks she has been taken elsewhere on the ship. I sit in silence as the sun rises in the sky and listen to Catalina's whispered prayers. I do not speak again until night falls. In the darkness, after repeated questions, I have to tell Catalina what has become of Sister Maria, then listen to her weeping for the rest of the night.

I lose track of time, but the ship rises and falls on the water for one day after another, perhaps seven in all, perhaps ten, I cannot be sure. We are kept under the little shelter, the height of it meaning we cannot stand, only lie or sit. They change our bonds, so that we are tied around the waist with our hands free, this so that we can use a pail to relieve ourselves. The Norsemen care enough for us as cargo that they give us water and a little food during the voyage, enough to keep us alive but not enough to stop our endless thirst, our endless hunger. At night we have our hands bound again, they are not willing to risk the loss of another valuable commodity. We see daylight and darkness come and go but rarely see anything beyond our tiny red shelter: not the sea, nor the ship, nor the men, except for one or two who empty our pail of waste or throw food into our laps. But there comes a day when we make land, I can hear the men shout and I prepare myself to know to what shore we have come.

Our little awning is suddenly unfastened, rolled up and put away. Catalina and I shrink back, newly made afraid of the outside world, knowing our destiny is about to take on an as yet unknown shape.

Where our departure was secret and solitary, the Norsemen's beast-ship lying dark on the sea, hidden from any who might hinder their ungodly work, our arrival is its very opposite. The ship comes closer and closer to the shore, the great red sail now taken down, our progress made by the oarsmen aboard. The long neck and head of our beast glides past small fishing boats. The men aboard them are darker-skinned than we are, burnt browner still by the sun. They wear long robes in bright colours, some have their heads wrapped with cloths, a few even have their faces fully veiled with only their eyes visible. They watch our boat with interest but not with fear. I believe they know the Norsemen and their business here. These are the docks of a large city, beyond the quayside lie mud-coloured ramparts and rooftops, with high towers dotted here and there amongst them. Released from our crouched shelter, the sun beats down on us so hard that it makes my head swim.

"Where are we?" whispers Catalina beside me.

I shake my head. The Maghreb, I believe, but I do not know what port. There is the smell of rotting fish, of dung, of sweat. I feel my stomach roll and hope I will not disgrace myself by vomiting again. The Norsemen busy themselves with securing the ship alongside the dock, the oars now put away. The yellow-haired man comes towards us and with a quick movement unties us from the metal fastenings. I stand, unsteady, but already I am being pushed towards the edge of the ship with Catalina. One of the Norsemen has jumped ashore and now he places a rough plank between the ship and the dockside, which we both stagger across, followed by the yellow-haired man. Having my feet on the ground again makes tears start to my eyes, despite the circumstances. The Norseman pushes at me to walk forwards and I do so, Catalina clinging to my arm. There are men everywhere and there are few who do not leer at Catalina and I as we pass, our heads uncovered and dressed only in our by now filthy linen shifts.

"What is that?" whispers Catalina, cringing back against me.

A strange beast lumbers past us, its body like a horse but one spawned by the devil, warped in its nature. It is hairy, with a misshapen hump on its back and legs that look as though they were put on backwards, ending in soft cloven feet tipped with wide blunt claws.

"A camel," I say, having seen a picture of one once, an illustration in a book. I had thought it fanciful then but now I see that the artist was correct. They are everywhere across the docks, being laden with goods or unburdened. I see one or two horses also, a few mules and donkeys, but it is clear that the chief beast in use here is the camel. They make strange groaning noises when they are told to rise or sit, and both Catalina and I give them as wide a berth as we can when we pass by a group of them.

All around us, men shout and labour. But as we disembark a strange sound fills the air, a wailing, an unearthly cry emanating from the rooftops and on a sudden most of the men stop their work and kneel in the dust, all facing in the same direction. They hold their hands before their faces and bow their heads towards the dirt, again and again.

"What are they doing?" asks Catalina, wide-eyed at the spectacle.

"Praying," I say tightly. "It is not true prayer of course," I add, mindful that I am still all Catalina has in the way of spiritual guidance. "How can it be? Out here in the open, without even being in a sacred space nor with a holy man to direct the prayers. It is what passes for prayer amongst these people. They are Muslims, heathens."

She nods, cowed. The prayer seems to have finished, for the men rise and go about their business. The Norseman pushes us forwards, towards a low building at the back of the dockyard. We stagger towards it, our feet made unsteady by the heat, by fear, by the hard ground that does not rock beneath us.

There is an ill-painted door on which the Norseman hammers with his fist. It opens quickly, a short ugly man nodding when he sees us, as though we are expected. He waves us in, and we follow him into darkness and then into a dusty courtyard. A fat well-dressed man is sat under an awning and he gestures to our captor when he sees him, greets him as though they are old friends. The Norseman speaks with him for a few moments, then gestures towards us. The fat man shows little interest, only nods to his servant, the short man, who pushes me towards a door at one end of the courtyard. For a moment, ridiculously, I want to run to the Norseman from whom we are being taken. He is the only person who knows where we came from, who could, if he wished, takes us back to that same place, to the apple orchard where he and his men killed Alberte and took us women. If he leaves us, if we never see him again, how would anyone here ever take us home again? But the short man pushes me again and I know that there is nothing I can do to avoid the fate that has already been laid upon me, the fate I first glimpsed when I saw Alberte stumbling towards me, already half-dead.

Whether I ever see the Norseman again or not, makes no difference. I walk towards the door and the man opens it and pushes me through the doorway.

The room is mostly empty, apart from some old rags and a little straw. In a corner is a large vessel, perhaps for water. In another corner is a covered pail and from the smell in the room I can only imagine that it has already been used for bodily functions. The floor is made of bare tiles, dirty and chipped. There are thick iron links set into the walls, such as might be used to tie up a horse, were they outside. In here, they are no doubt used to tie up people. The door bangs shut behind us. I hear a lock turn and Catalina and I are alone for the first time since we first met. She begins to weep at once, clinging to me as a child might to its mother. I pat her stiffly. She will need to be stronger than this, will need to put her faith in God rather than in a fallible human such as myself.

"What will we do? Oh, what will we do?" she begs me.

"I do not know," I say, trying to sound as though there is no reason to wail. "First, we must drink." I make my way over to the vessel and am glad to see that I was right, it is half-filled with water. Just behind it lies a wooden cup, badly split but which I use to scoop up some of the water. I taste it cautiously and although it is not fresh or cold, at least it does not taste foul. I make Catalina drink three full cups and although her shrunken stomach makes her gag briefly at the sudden filling, still, she does not vomit, and I drink deeply myself. There is a window, which lets in light, but it has bars across it, and I do not trouble myself with checking whether they are solid. It is clear to me that we are in a room in which many unfortunates such as ourselves have been before. This is a room made for captives. For slaves.

Catalina has slumped to the floor. She looks up at me, her face white, her eyes rimmed with red, tears still falling. "If we could only speak their language," she whimpers. "My father is not very rich, but he would pay a goodly sum if he knew we were here. Would the convent pay for our release?"

I shake my head. "Your father will believe you to be safely at the convent by now," I say. "And the convent..." I stop. I wonder what they will think of me, if they will think that harm has befallen our little group, or whether they will think that we were tempted by the world, that we ran away. I hope that the Mother Superior will not think such a thing of us, that she will realise that something must have occurred. But even if she does... "No-one will know what has become of us," I say simply. "We have travelled too far, and the Norsemen made sure not to be seen. There is no way home."

Catalina bursts into noisy sobs and I hear her cry out for her mother. I gaze out of the window, but I can see nothing but a sky so blue it makes my eyes sting.

Later that day a squat serving woman opens the door and indicates we should follow her. We are taken outside, to a walled yard with pecking chickens scratching in the dirt and a tethered goat that bleats incessantly. There is a small tiled area on which the serving woman gestures that I should stand, then she tugs at my shift and makes a movement to show I should remove it. I shake my head. She pulls from her pocket a sharp knife and holds it up. I am unsure whether she means to threaten me or indicate that she will cut the shift, but I comply, lifting the shift over my head. She takes it from me and turns away. I have not been naked before another person since I was a child and my mother washed me. In the convent we bathed rarely, instead washing ourselves with a cloth and a basin of water. If we bathed it was done quickly and we kept our shifts on, so that we should not think on our mortal flesh. I have barely seen my own naked body as a grown woman. I stand naked in the hot sun, wondering on what saint I could possibly call that would not turn away in horror at what has become of me, a woman whose life should be devoted to holy service, an anointed bride of Christ, standing shamelessly naked in the open air.

The woman returns with two pails of water and some small rags and indicates that we should wash, which I do gladly, for I am still spattered with vomit and mud, seawater and urine. When I am clean, I use what is left of the water to wash my shift, placing it back on my body dripping wet but at least cleaner than it was. Catalina follows my example, her still half-formed body hunched and miserable. Afterwards, we are led back a different way and shown into a different room, this one far larger and already filled. Later I count more than sixty people, men, women and children. Most are dark skinned, the odd few here and there are lighter skinned. There are women weeping, clutching their children to them, knowing, no doubt, that they are to be separated. The women whisper to their older children, tears running down their faces, no doubt aware these are their last words to them. Beside them stand or squat their menfolk, faces closed up, one hand on their women's shoulders, their fingers digging deep into the flesh for one last touch, one last chance to make their feelings known. A few men and women stand or sit alone, friendless and without even the comfort of a desperate familiar touch. Their faces are closed in bitterness.

A young, light-skinned woman gestures to an empty space beside her. I nod to her with as much dignity and courtesy as I can manage, and she manages a small smile and a nod in return. Catalina and I lower ourselves to the floor by her. She says something that I do not understand. I shake my head.

"I do not speak your language," I say in Latin.

"My name is Rachel," she replies, her Latin passable.

"I am Sister Juliana," I tell her, relief at speaking flooding my voice. "This is Catalina."

"'Sister'?"

"I am a nun," I say. "Catalina was to be a novice in our convent."

"Where was your convent?"

"In Galicia."

Her eyes widen. "What are you doing here?"

"Where is here?" I ask, suddenly aware I still do not know.

"Tangier," she says.

I feel the heaviness in my belly from the confirmation that I was right. We are in the Maghreb. "We were kidnapped. Brought here by Norsemen," I say. "You?"

"The same, but from Al-Andalus," she says. "I lived by the sea on the Southern coast. I could see the shores of the Maghreb from my home. I never thought I would cross the sea to come here."

I move closer and kneel by her, untie her hands from the tight leather strips that have been used to bind her. I chafe at her wrists which are badly marked from the ties and she smiles at me.

"Thank you," she says. "You are very kind."

I look her over. Her colouring is similar to mine, she has a Biblical name. "Are you a Christian?" I ask.

She shakes her head, hesitates for a moment. "I am a Jew."

I sit back. I had thought I was speaking with a woman of my own faith. I am among heathens twice over. I see that she understands my disapproval and reluctance to converse with her further, for she does not speak to me again that night. Sleep is impossible, it is a night of weeping in the darkness, one sob leading to another echoing around the stifling room, the stench of bodily waste growing stronger.

When morning comes the merchant and his servant return, accompanied by the Norseman. Judging by his colourful robes and the thick gold bracelet he wears, the merchant is well-off. No doubt trading in slaves has made him good money over the years.

The slave merchant looks the three of us over. He speaks with the Norseman.

"What language are they speaking? Do you understand them?" Catalina asks Rachel, who is paying attention to them.

She nods. "Arabic, although the accents are hard to follow. I know it from my own land, from Al-Andalus. It sounds different here."

"What is he saying?" Catalina asks Rachel. I frown at Catalina to hold her tongue, but she does not look at me and I, too, wish to know what is said, although I do not wish to speak with the Jewess.

She looks uncomfortable but speaks in a whisper. "He says your hair is very fine and that you are very beautiful."

I feel a cold shudder go through me. I can already sense Catalina's fate and it is one of such depravity that I do not know how to erase it from my mind.

The merchant is looking at me and shaking his head. He jabbers at the Norseman and the Norseman replies with something that makes the merchant laugh.

"What did he say?" asks Catalina again.

Rachel shakes her head.

"Tell me," she insists.

"He said Sister Juliana is… not beautiful. Or young," she says, looking away.

He said I am ugly and old, I think to myself, guessing from her awkwardness that the merchant did not mince his words.

"Why did he laugh?"

"I would rather not say," she whispers.

"Please," says Catalina. "Perhaps it will help us."

"He asked why she had no hair, he said it makes her ugly. The Norseman said she is a holy woman, that she must be an untouched virgin even if she is old. He said her hair will grow soon enough and that virginity is worth a better price than hair." Rachel's cheeks are scarlet.

I look away, gaze at the painful blue sky.

Catalina yelps with pain. I look to see that the merchant has pulled her to her feet by her hair, she twists in his clutches so she can look to me.

"Help me!" she screams.

"Our Lady will protect you," I say loudly, as she struggles with the merchant.

"Our Lady has forgotten me!" she cries.

I do not reprimand her in her hour of need, it is natural that she should have doubts, even Our Lady's holy son doubted His father in His own hour of need. Instead, I pray out loud, so that she will hear holy words even as she is taken from us. "Hail Mary, full of grace, the Lord is with thee; blessed art thou amongst women, and blessed is the fruit of thy womb."

"Help me!" she screams again as they reach the door, but the merchant's servant has lifted her bodily and she cannot escape him, he carries her from the room and out of our sight. He returns swiftly for a girl so dark-skinned her skin seems to have glints of blue and another with pink-white skin and hair the colour of saffron. My heart sinks, for it is clear the three girls have been specially selected, being young and beautiful, perhaps for a harem, for I have heard of such places.

Beside me, Rachel is weeping. "Poor child," she says, turning to me and trying to embrace me. "To be violated…"

"What is done to her body will not dishonour her soul as long as she stays true to her faith," I say, extracting myself from her arms. "She will be a martyr to our faith. These heathens will go to hell for what they have done."

Rachel stares at me as though I am mad, but I ignore her. I cannot expect a Jewess to understand. Instead I pray for Catalina's soul, that it will rise above the treatment her body may receive. I pray for my own sin in failing to bring her home safely to the convent, this girl-child entrusted to my care whom I have failed to protect.

The slave merchant's servant returns after a little while and this time he takes Rachel.

"I will pray for you," she says to me as she is dragged from the room. I do not answer her. I am not sure I want the prayers of a Jewess, nor whether it would be right for me to pray for her.

There is a delay of perhaps some hours, but then the door opens, revealing the merchant's assistant with several armed men. There are commands given. Although I have no-one to tell me what is happening, it soon becomes clear that we are all to leave this room, to follow the assistant and his guards. The women begin to wail, their voices chiming and clashing together. One woman crawls on her knees to the merchant's assistant and clutches at his feet, speaking quickly. She opens her robe to show him her breasts, perhaps promising him the use of her body if he will not take away her children, but he only pushes her away with his foot and gestures to the armed men to accompany us. A few of the men are bound, but we women and the children are not. Where would we run to? We would be caught and beaten in moments, for we do not know the city, nor any people here, there would be no door to hide behind, no protection we might seek. The children cling to their mothers and fathers in desperate fear, they would not run even if their parents urged them to. We pass through the narrow streets, this sorry trail of men, women and children, bound to meet our fate.

Our walk is brief, we come to an open area, a large public square. There are stalls around the edges, many dozens of them. We are led to an empty space, facing the centre of the square, behind a small wooden platform.

The heat is like nothing I have ever felt before. I have grown used to the cool stone corridors of the convent, the shaded corners of the garden even in summer. Although it is autumn, still the sun rages down on us. I can feel my pale skin prickle and burn in the heat and see even the dark-skinned children shrink under its rays, their mothers trying to shield them from the worst of the heat by holding out their own arms to cover their children's heads, taking the burning into their own skins rather than let it hurt their offspring.

A crowd begins to gather at the sight of us and now the merchant steps forwards. He is dressed in bright red and yellow robes, no doubt the better to be seen and he speaks at length, gesturing towards us, a beaming smile on his face as he enumerates our qualities as future slaves. He holds up a woman's long hair, he pats the muscles of the largest, strongest men, he exposes the breasts and thighs of the best-looking women. He pushes the older children forwards, showing their teeth and height, their potential to grow and serve for many years to come. I watch him and see only the Devil himself, his forked tongue calling come buy, come buy, to the watching crowd.

The bidding, when it begins, is brisk enough. The merchant knows his business, he has spoken long enough for the crowd to have already made their choices. The strongest, tallest men go quickly and the wails of their womenfolk as they are led away make me shudder. The children go quickly also, their mothers screaming as they are dragged away, tears running down their terrified faces, slapped and kicked for struggling against their new owners in their efforts to run back to their mothers. Now the women go, the most beautiful first, shaking as they reach their new masters, then the mothers, who follow their bidders without question, their bodies already broken by their hearts, shuffling as though only half living. I wonder how many of them will even live for long, such is their pain.

Now the merchant indicates me and speaks quickly, pointing to my shaven head and laughing as he makes some bawdy joke, at which the crowd titters. One man calls out something and the crowd laughs harder. I wait, silent. The merchant brushes my arm, perhaps to draw attention to my pale skin, although it is more pink than white just now, burnt by the sun. I have no doubt that he has already mentioned my provenance, suggested that I must be a virgin, since I have been a holy woman until now. I think that only a beast of a man would even find pleasure in the idea of defiling a woman dedicated to God, even the God of another. But now two men are bidding for me, one a sallow-skinned man who looks ill, the other a fat man in richly made robes, who quickly outbids the other. The merchant is delighted, for all that he said I was old and ugly, he has sold me to a wealthy man for a price with which he seems pleased. He pushes me forwards and I find myself eye to eye with the fat man. I am almost as tall as he, despite being only of average height myself. He grins at the sight of me, reaches out and runs his hand over my bare scalp, letting his fingers linger over it. I stiffen at his touch, but he has already turned away. I think for a moment that I could run while his back is turned but suddenly realise that he is not alone, he has an armed man beside him, a black skinned bodyguard who now grips my elbow and steers me through the crowd after my new owner. I think of Catalina as she was taken from me, her face full of misery. I doubt I will ever see her again and I dread to think what will happen to a girl as young as she is, as beautiful. I know that she can only expect to be defiled, to be used as a plaything by a heathen Moor. I wonder what possible sin she can have committed in her short life, to be punished like this by God. For myself, I know that I have been punished because of my temptation in the apple orchard, for my arrogance in believing that I was above the worldly desires such as gluttony, that I could travel safely out into the world and not be ensnared by all it could offer. I thought myself better than my sisters because I did not have my head turned by a handsome young nobleman in my care, believed I might be destined for a senior role within the convent and yet the temptation of a crisp sweet fruit on a tree turned my head, even as it did Eve in the Garden. I know that all of my life I will hold Catalina's face in my mind, knowing that I and I alone brought her to this place. I should have brought her safely home to our holy house, even as I was taken there by my mother, who would have died rather than see me here now, her daughter in a land of heathen Moors, torn from her holy devotions.

I should have trodden in the footsteps of the saints.

Instead, I am now a slave.

I am put in a tiny locked room for the night, given a flat bread and some kind of bean stew, too heavily spiced with cumin, but I eat it in great gulping mouthfuls, not having eaten hot food for many days now. I have plentiful water, too, and I drink as much as I can hold, afraid of what the future may hold. I have been given a small length of cloth, which I wrap around my head to protect it further from the burning sun. I wish I had some salve, for I can tell that the delicate skin of my head has been sunburnt, but all I can do is put cold water on it and hope the wrap will allow it to heal. Covering my scalp gives me some small comfort. I wait for a summons, for my new owner to call for me, but nothing and no one comes, and I fall asleep, huddled on the floor, my dreams full of an endless screaming by the women and children sold today. I do not know if I, too, scream in my sleep, but no-one would care even if I did.

I am woken before dawn, stumble my way behind the man who brought me here. It is colder than I expected outside, and I shiver, standing in my shift and bare feet. All around us echoes, over and over again, the strange, warbling call echoing from the rooftops. I think it must be a call to prayer, for I see shadows here and there, kneeling in the dirt. The bodyguard, though, does not pray. He pulls me forwards and from the darkness emerge five more men, their skins so black I had not noticed them in the half light. Behind them come more than twenty camels, a few loaded up, many without burdens, but instead saddled for riding. I shrink back from the men, but the bodyguard pushes me forwards and one of the men takes my wrist. His grip is not hard, but his hand is large, and I do not doubt that if I were to fight or flee, I would not get very far.

He says something and suddenly I am in the air and then find myself sat on the back of a camel, the wide saddle spreading my legs in an obscene manner. I try to find a better way of seating, but this saddle is not made for riding sideways and my shift is not made for riding astride. The men watch me as I struggle and there are a few chuckles that make my skin feel colder than the grey light. At last something lands on me, a crumpled robe such as I have seen people here wearing, which I gratefully pull over my shift, covering my shame.

Within moments the men are also mounted. The lead bodyguard makes a clicking sound with his mouth and the camels begin to move. I clutch at the neck of my own mount, but have been given no reins, there is only the broad saddle made of cloth to hang on to. The camel's gait is slow, swaying, but it is not difficult to remain seated, even for a novice rider such as I. I am sat higher than I would be on a horse, there can be no question of slipping to the ground and trying to escape. My hands and feet are free, but I am bound to go wherever these men intend to take me. I find my lips trembling as I whisper a prayer for safety. I do not know where the man is who bought me, I know only that he owns me. I do not know my destination; I know only that I am to make another journey.

Days and days and days pass. I do not know how many, and by the time I have thought of counting them, too many have passed to remember. The heat here is unlike anything I have ever felt before. It is dry, so dry that sometimes I feel as though my lungs cannot draw breath, as though all the moisture has been sucked from my mouth and nose. I drink water when it is given to me, greedily, desperately. It does not taste like the pure cool water of the convent, kept in stone jars. This water tastes of goatskin, it is warm and fetid, but I drink it anyway. I am more grateful than ever that I was given the robe I wear, which covers most of my skin, for I would have been burnt beyond repair otherwise, my skin being pale and unused to long periods of time in the sun. My hair has begun to grow back. I touch it in wonder in the early mornings, when I retie my headwrap. It is a soft downy fuzz, like a new-born baby, like a cat or dog. I stroke it at night and wonder how soon I will be able to cut it again, shave it back to the skin as it should be.

I grow used to the endless swaying walk of the camels, they are a different kind of beast to a horse, having neither their skittishness nor their elegance. They are bad-tempered and slow, groaning in protest when they are made to sit and stand. I suppose I should be grateful that I am allowed to ride them at all, for to walk this distance each day in this heat would kill me. I do not know where we are going, I do not know how far away our destination is. I know only that the landscape through which we travel is so different to the one I am used to that it feels as though I am in a dream, or some fantastical tale told by a storyteller. If I were one amongst many slaves, I would assume that I was being taken elsewhere, to be traded onwards. But I am the only one. I try to ask the men with whom I travel where we're going, who they are, but they speak only what I suppose is Arabic and I do not understand their gestures.

One thing I give grateful thanks for each night, however, is that my body has not yet been sullied. I have not been dishonoured. I know from what Rachel said that my virginity was seen as a valuable commodity, which explains why the Norsemen did not touch me, as I expected them to. I can only suppose that these men, with whom I travel, have been instructed not to tarnish me, for they leave me alone, only touching me to help me gain my seat or leave it each day. I give thanks to Our Lady for this, for in her purity she has protected mine. I do not know how long this protection will last, nor for whom my virginity is intended, for I cannot help but think that if it has been respected so far, it is not because of my faith, but rather because I am the property of one man. I do not know if the man is the one who walked around me in the marketplace, whose fingers crawled across my bare scalp, or whether he was only choosing me for another.

At night I watch the sky and the stars, knowing that we are travelling south-west, further and further from my home. By day, I sway endlessly on my mount and wonder whether this journey will continue to the ends of the earth. Much of the land here is like a desert, reminding me of passages from the Bible, of Jesus' time in the wilderness, of His fasting and prayer, of the Devil's temptations and His refusals to be tempted. I think that perhaps I, too, should fast, but when I am offered hard bread and sweet dates, I am too afraid of possible future deprivations to refuse. I eat what is given to me, I drink as much water as I can. Whatever is to come, I must be prepared for it.

The dread in my heart is lifted only by a few tiny moments each day, when I recognise some plant or tree. The olive trees at first, for they are large and easy to recognise. But later on, smaller plants come to my attention. I see wild thyme and smell it as we trample over it along tiny paths and the smell gives me courage, for it signals to me that, even in this strange new land, in this unknown world, in what is to be my unwilling new life, there are things I know. That my knowledge has sailed here with me, is travelling with me even as we make our way through desert dunes and treacherous mountain paths. And all the time I am learning things about this new world. I see chattering monkeys for the first time, which I have only ever seen before in paintings, see date palms up close, look across desert sands.

I grow accustomed to the camels and their ways, sometimes pat my own mount, who huffs and nuzzles my hand, the only touch of kindness I can expect.

Once or twice we stop on the outskirts of the city, and on those days, we eat better food. I eat hot stews, flavoured in ways I have never thought of, but with plants which I recognise. I taste cumin, which I had previously used mixed with flour and egg yolk, baked in a hot oven and given to patients to avoid nausea in their intestines. Here, it is being used for flavour only. I smell rose water and wonder if they use it for cramps, as I would have done. There is much use of cinnamon and fennel, both of which bring heat, and I wonder at their use in a country already so hot. After the first days, I felt the fear inside me lessen a little, for the men surrounding me at least seemed to bear me no ill will nor to have evil intentions towards me. They are even, perhaps, slaves, as I am, doing only what they have been told to do, bound to the same invisible and unknown master.

One morning there is much chatter amongst the men, and one of them even turns to me, smiling broadly.

"Aghmat," he says.

I frown and shake my head.

"Aghmat," he says again, very clearly and carefully, as though this is a word I should know.

I shake my head again and he turns away, disappointed, his companions only shrugging their shoulders. I wonder what the word means, whether it is our destination, or his name perhaps, although he did not gesture to himself. There is nothing I can do but wait.

Later that day, on the horizon, we see the outline of the city. It is a large city, as large as the city the Norsemen sold me into.

The man who spoke to me earlier turns in his saddle and points to the horizon. "Aghmat," he says, with insistence.

It is the name of the city, then, I suppose. And, since no one has bothered to tell me the name of any other of our destinations along this route, I can only suppose it to be our final destination. I feel my belly clench, wondering what fate has in store for me in this place, this Aghmat. I say the name over and over quietly to myself, my tongue struggling with the sound, this, my first word in the language I will no doubt have to learn to speak, if I am to be kept here. It has a guttural sound, like the rest of their tongue, like a patient bringing up phlegm from congested lungs.

Aghmat is a large city. The walls, when we reach them, tower high above us and from the many traders coming and going through the main gates, I can see that it is also wealthy. Only a large and wealthy city has need of so many merchants visiting it along the trade routes. There are gold merchants surrounded by guards, silk merchants whose wares must be packed with care, merchants whose trade includes herbs and spices, for I can smell them in their camels' packs as we pass close by. And there are all the smaller local traders, mostly farmers, bringing fruit and vegetables, livestock and the other goods needed to feed a city of this size.

The men know their way, they guide the camels down one street after another, until we come to a narrow street, where three of the men remove any camels without burdens and walk away with them. Meanwhile the rest of the men and I, along with the six camels that carry packs, make our way further down the narrow street and one of the men hammers at a large gate set into the wall, which is opened promptly. There is what sounds like jovial banter between the men and the person opening the door, a woman's voice.

The camels have their burdens removed and passed from man to man until they disappear through the open gate and into whatever space lies beyond. I wait, high on my camel, uncertain if I, too, am to be passed through this gate.

It seems I am to be unpacked. The camel is ordered to kneel, and I hold on tightly as it lowers itself to the ground. I have already learnt that camels possess no grace when preparing for dismount. I dismount and stand up, grateful to be on my feet again, although my knees are weak, having sat in the same place for many hours.

Now I see the woman. It is her voice I heard speaking with the men, but now that she sees me, her chattering stops. She looks me over, from my wrapped head to my bare feet, sliding over my crumpled robe. I look her over in turn. She has very black skin and tightly curled hair, cut short. She wears a faded yellow robe. But it is her height that is most noticeable. She is a dwarf. I have not seen many in my lifetime. There was one, when I was a child, servant to a local noble. He was a man. And there was another, once, on a pilgrimage, who stayed overnight in our convent. I have never seen a female dwarf. She carries herself with confidence, as though she is a person of some standing in the household, approaching me with frank curiosity. She points at me and asks a question and when the men answer her face falls a little. She looks at me and smiles, as though she pities me.

"Aisha," she says, indicating herself to me.

I keep my face still. I do not know her well enough to respond and I do not know what she has been told to make her look at me with pity. Whatever it is, I will find out for myself before I return her smile.

She says other things, but I do not understand her, do not respond. She falls silent.

I stand still in the narrow street but when she gestures me to enter the doorway, I do so, following her slightly lurching, waddling, gait.

The house is built on three storeys around a courtyard, which is planted like a garden. There are trees, reaching high into the sky, and a fountain with splashing water. The whole of the floor is made up of tiny tiles, repeating over and over again a starred pattern in green and white. This is a house of extraordinary decoration. Everywhere are carved wooden doors, brightened with paint and featuring many artistic flourishes, such as fruits and flowers. Each of the storeys above us has an open walkway, like a balcony, around it. From the uppermost walkway, the faces of four women look down on us, curious and silent. This must be the house of my new master, whoever he is. I am, suddenly, more afraid than I have ever been, more afraid even than when the Norsemen took us and I thought that someone might rescue us before we reached the coast. Now I know that this is my destination, that someone is waiting for me in this house and I am so afraid that I forget to pray.

I turn and run.

I hear shouts behind me as I run out of the gate into the alleyway and then as fast as I can down first one street and then another, tiny narrow alleyways, with high walls on either side, closed gates and doors everywhere, no place to hide, no place to duck down and hope that my captors will pass me. No, they are close behind me, shouting. I burst out into a wider street but now my appearance and the shouts of the men behind me only draw more attention to my flight. I feel a sudden cramp in my leg, my limbs unused to movement after all these days sat atop a camel. The cramp is so hard that I stumble and fall and as soon as I do so I feel a hand on my leg and know that my attempt at escape was futile, laughable.

They pull me back to the house, dragging me along. I do not try to turn and run again, that would be useless. But I resist, being taken back the same way I have come step-by-step, my reluctance clear. When they get me back to the same doorway, I feel a hand between my shoulder blades before I am roughly shoved, falling forwards into the courtyard space again, landing this time on my hands and knees. I look up and meet the gaze of the dwarf, who shakes her head and looks at the man who brought me back. They talk between themselves and at last she nods, as though reluctantly. I find myself forced to my feet and pushed down a small walkway and through a door. Ahead are stairs, heading downwards. I baulk but am pushed forwards in no uncertain terms and make my way down the steps, which are shallow. At the bottom of the steps is a door. The man with me pushes it open.

It is a small room and bare, it smells of stale air, having no window, only the door. I hesitate but I am pushed forwards again and hear the door crash behind me. The door, I now see, is made of a plain wood, no painted flourishes here. In the centre, rather than a window, or plain wood, it has a small open space, fitted with bars, through which a small amount of light comes, although when I edge close to it and look out there is hardly anything to see, only the corridor I have just walked down. This room is a form of prison, there is no doubt about that. And I, in it, am a prisoner. The thought ought to frighten me, but there is something about the room, so silent, so empty, so without luxuries, that somehow reminds me of the convent. Slowly, I kneel, feel the cold stone floor against my legs, my palms touching one another, and the words come unbidden, Our Fathers followed by Hail Marys, each prayer turning my prison into a holy sanctuary.

Some time passes before they bring me a pot for my bodily needs, a water jar and dipper. I am given bread and a rough stew of some sort of beans mixed with vegetables, heavily spiced. I eat all of it. Later, as the light fades from the door, it opens briefly, and a rough woollen blanket is thrown towards me. Perhaps God has reached out his hand and blessed me, reminded me of my vows by meeting my simplest needs and putting me in this silent space.

This idea at least stops me thinking of the obvious question: what sort of a house needs a prison?

The House of Women

Fair as the moon…

Song of Solomon 6:10

I AM NOT SURE HOW MANY days I have been in the room. I have almost grown used to the silence, the small dark space, the unending prayers I offer up, having nothing else to do and no way of knowing what the outside world holds for my future. I almost begin to think of myself as an anchorite, locked up forever to pray for the world's sins, this tiny room my reclusory. Perhaps it is a life I could grow used to, although I would miss my garden, miss tending both plants and people.

But I am only fooling myself with such ideas. Instead, after a handful of days, the door opens and rather than a quick silhouette appearing to bring me food and dispose of my waste, it stays open and I have to adjust my blinded eyes to the light streaming in, until I can see who has come for me.

There are two women. One is the black-skinned dwarf, behind her a sturdy older woman, wrinkled with age. Behind the both of them towers a strange looking woman, taller than any I have ever seen before, her heavy shape lowering over the dwarf, making both of their heights more extreme through contrast.

The dwarf gestures that I should follow her. I shake my head. She shrugs and points to the tall woman, who takes a step forward, hands held in menacing fists.

I hold up my hands in submission. "I will come," I say, my voice cracking from disuse.

I allow myself to be led through the doorway and along a narrow corridor. At the end of it is a fantastically painted door, bright colours swirled around a heavy metal handle. The giantess steps forwards and pushes the door open. We follow.

The room is dimly lit and hot, so hot that I gasp. The air is thick with moisture, my lungs feel as though I am drowning with every breath I take. I am reminded of the steam I would make my convent sisters breath in if they were afflicted with hoarseness and coughs. The giantess lingers in the doorway for a moment but now that we are inside the room the dwarf waves her away and she closes the door behind her, leaving the room with even less light. She has barely gone when the older woman has lifted my robe and shift over my head. I clutch at them, but I am too late. Now I am entirely naked, standing before the women. I hunch my shoulders and try to cover my nakedness with my hands, mortified. I am about to speak, to request something to cover my modesty with, when a wave of hot water crashes over my head, overwhelms me, fills my half-open mouth. I bend over double with the shock, coughing and spluttering as I seek to clear my lungs. But another wave comes, then another. It takes me this long to realise that the older woman is throwing pail after pail of what feels like near-boiling water over me. Even when I stand and turn to face her, my hands extended in front of me to make her stop, she does not cease. She must throw more than eight pails of water at me before she stops, so that in the end I give up, eyes and mouth shut, trying only to remain upright in the face of her onslaught. I fail and sink to my knees.

At once she stops, but the dwarf, standing behind me, quickly has her hands on my head, rubbing vigorously across my scalp and then continuing over the whole of my body, much to my shame. The sensation of hands against my bare flesh is shocking to me and at first, I push her away, but at last I realise that she will not be stopped, that I can succumb or fight but the end result will be the same. The substance in her hands is a slippery kind of black soap, which has a strong smell, reminding me of olive oil when it is first pressed, the sharp fresh smell of the crushed fruit like fresh-cut grass at haying time. She rubs this all over me and then takes a small rough cloth and proceeds to scrub me with it, so fiercely that I can see my own skin peeling away, the new skin beneath it scarlet with the heat and her rough treatment.

I feel faint. The heat, the drowning sensation of my lungs, the excess of sensation across my untouched body. I stagger and the women catch me, then lower me to the floor, murmuring to one another. I feel something hard scrape against my skull and realise they are shaving my head of what little hair had grown back. I am happy for this, at least, to be done, it feels like the only familiar thing that has happened to me since I was taken. When they are done, I lie on the warm wet floor tiles and hope that they have finished.

They have not. Now they crouch by my side and suddenly there is a ripping pain moving across my leg. I shriek but the older woman holds me down. I try to raise my head and see the dwarf doing something strange with a thread in her mouth and hands, moving back and forth across my leg. It takes me a moment to realise that she is, with her thread, somehow pulling out all the hairs on my legs. My head spins again and I have to lower it back to the hard floor. I lie there, held by one woman while the other pulls out every hair on my legs. When she has finished, I feel my shoulders slump in relief as the pain stops, before, to my horror, she begins the same work on my most intimate parts. The pain is indescribable. I scream aloud and at once, a rough warm hand presses down over my mouth as the pain continues.

Then comes cold water, thrown over my prone and shaking body. They roll me onto my stomach so that they can throw more cold water, then hoist me to my feet and rub a scented oil over every part of me, which I believe contains rose perfume in it. They wrap me in a large cloth, which I clutch at. I stare at them, seeking an answer for their behaviour in their faces, but they are busy with their work. Now they lead me out of the darkness through the doorway and upstairs into an enclosed courtyard, with a bright blue sky above it. I do not even think that I am half-naked except for the cloth, for I am still shaking with the cold, or perhaps with my own fear.

We pass quickly through the tiled sunny courtyard. I am in such shock from my treatment that I can barely see properly, only enough to stop myself falling as we ascend more stairs and find ourselves on the upper level, looking down on the courtyard. A door opens to my right and I am pushed into it.

The room is large. After my prison and the bathing room downstairs, it is so bright that I blink as I look around it. There are long drapes at the window, through which I can see rooftops beyond, yellow-brown layers of different heights.

A push on my shoulder leads me to sit. I look down and see that I am sitting on the edge of a large bed, covered with bright blankets. My bare feet rest on soft rugs. The room contains little else other than a large chest in carved wood.

The dwarf opens and then rummages in the chest, removing several garments in bright silks, scarlet and orange trimmed in tiny discs of beaten silver. She holds them out but I only stare at her as though my wits have left me and so she stands before me and begins to dress me as though I were a small child, tugging at my limbs, pulling me upright, pushing me back down onto the bed. The silks feel very strange, touching yet not touching, warming instantly to my skin as they slip over me. One foot and then another is pushed into a yellow leather slipper and then after consultation with her older companion, a long piece of yellow silk is wrapped tightly about my head. The feel of it, the knowledge that my bare scalp is once again modestly covered, as it should be, brings tears suddenly spilling down my cheeks. The dwarf reaches out and wipes them away, making a grimace as she does so, whether a smile or a reproach I am uncertain. The older woman dabs something on me and a strong smell of rose perfume fills the air.

The headwrap brings me such comfort I barely realise what the dwarf is now doing to my face, working with a little tray of pots and a pointed wooden stick. She rubs and pokes, then there is a sudden sharp pain through one earlobe and, before I can think, another in the other earlobe. I yelp, but she and the older woman only shrug me away. When I touch my lobes, I feel a hard, dangling, circle and look down in disbelief at blood on my fingertips. They have pierced my ears.

Warily I look beyond my bloodied fingers. Down at my waist, now encircled with a thick silken belt dangling with larger silver discs. There is no mirror here, but I am horribly aware that I have been dressed as some kind of rich man's fancy, in bright silks and chiming jewellery. I touch my lips and see that there is a red paint on them, rub my eyes and see blackness on my knuckles. The women tut at my actions and take pains to tidy up the damage I have done to the make-up they had applied to my face. I slap at their hands, wipe my mouth against the silk sleeves I am wearing and note with satisfaction that the red smear will stain the orange silk. I will not be painted like a whore, paraded in gauzy silks as though I were suggesting to a man what might lie beneath them.

But the older woman has grown tired of my antics. From her pocket she holds up leather thongs. Her words are a stream of gibberish, but her face makes it clear that she is threatening me with being imprisoned again in the tiny room downstairs, with my hands being bound. I stop trying to remove the paint and allow the dwarf to repair whatever damage I have done to their handiwork. The older woman nods when it is done and then the two of them simply walk out of the door, leaving me alone. I think for a moment that I could run out of the door, but I can hear a heavy lock turning and know that I am still a prisoner, however I am dressed. I make my way to the large window and look down, onto a narrow street below. I take a sheet from the bed and think to tie it, to let myself down, but then I see a guard standing below the window and know that if I do so I will swiftly find myself caught and brought back to the tiny room downstairs.

I kneel and pray. I cannot formulate any kind of meaningful thoughts and so instead I only repeat the Hail Mary over and over again, the prayer I learnt when I was only a child, from my mother. In the midst of this I open my eyes and see the bed. A dread cold comes over me, an understanding of what lies ahead. I have been bought as a slave and now, in a rich man's house, have been dressed in silks and jewels, have been washed and perfumed and painted... only a fool would not understand what is to become of me. I think of the narrow street below and wonder, if I leapt, whether I would break my neck and so join Maria in her mortal sin, or whether I would only be crippled. Behind me, the door opens, and at last I see my master.

I was right. It is the man from the slave market, the fat man who turned me around and touched my head, who laughed as he spoke with the trader of slaves. He is almost as round as he is tall, indeed he stands shorter than I, and has to look up to me, which he does not seem to care about. He lets out a laugh when he sees me, as though I am of amusement to him. He walks around me and then says something which I do not understand. I do not speak. I simply stand still and wait. He pulls at my head wrap, so that it falls to the ground and once again my scalp is exposed. He rubs his hand over the skin, grinning broadly, saying something like "Kamra", which I do not understand. Even his touch on my skin is a violation, I shudder against it. My heart is beating so hard I think I may die; I think that perhaps its speed will cause me great pain in my chest and that I will fall to the floor and die.

But this does not happen. What does happen is that the merchant places one fat hand, thick with golden rings, over my breast and squeezes it hard. I step backwards, unable to help myself. He slaps me round the head, and places his hand on my other breast, while a second reaches round to fondle my buttocks. The silk I am wearing does nothing to protect me, it is too fine, too delicate. I shake my head and step backwards again and again, quickly find myself pressed up against a wall, at which he laughs, and slips his hand between my legs. I turn my head and bite the arm closest to me, the one whose hand is currently touching my neck. He yelps and I take advantage of his surprise to climb across the bed away from him, but he grabs my ankle and with surprising strength pulls me towards him, belly down. He kneels on one of my legs, so that I cannot move, his great weight bearing down on me so that I think my leg bone may snap. I cannot move, can only struggle, face down, as he places one hand over the silken trousers I am wearing and rips them downwards, a tearing sound exposing my buttocks. I scream, but he only laughs and slaps me across the buttocks, as though I were a wicked child. He is speaking throughout, but none of the words mean anything to me, only that he sounds happy enough, even as he attempts to defile me.

And for one moment, one tiny moment, he releases my leg and I am across the bed and crumpled to the floor, jumping up again and clutching at the drapes around the window shutters, which have been closed, the light streaming through them, tinting the room yellow-red. He shouts behind me, but I have already made up my mind without even thinking about it, even as I fumble with the drapes and pull open the shutters. I do not climb, I simply lean forwards, tipping the whole of my bodyweight towards the street below, hoping for a quick death. It is an unholy death of course, but it is better than what is to come if I stay in this room.

There is one fleeting moment when I am free, when only the air can touch me. Then there is a thud that reverberates through me and the *crack* sound as my thigh bone snaps as I hit the hard-cobbled street below. Then pain, only pain, such pain. I scream because I cannot do anything else, because the pain bursts out of my mouth. Above me I hear shouting, look up to see the merchant's angry red face, before darkness descends over me.

When I open my eyes, I am in a darkened room, and too hot. It takes a moment before I realise I am in the kitchen of the house, that over me are standing the dwarf and the older woman, a moment before the pain comes back in such terrible waves that I cry out again and again, putting my hand over my own mouth to stop my cries and failing. The dwarf is weeping, holding my other hand and tentatively dabbing at my face with something cold. It hurts every time she touches me, which I do not understand, as nothing has happened to my face. I am close to the open cooking fire, it is this that is making me too hot, I am sure of it. I look down at my thigh, I can see the unnatural crookedness of it, the flesh failing to hide the fault within. I look around me, hoping that a physician has been sent for, although inside I know full well that this is not the case. I have defied my master, I have not subjected myself to his evil desires, I leapt into the air rather than be touched by him, I have broken his property.

I try to push the dwarf away, but as soon as she stops dabbing the cold cloth onto my face heat rages through it. I try to touch my face, to touch the heat and the resulting pain is so bad that I whimper. Something has been done to my face. I look at the dwarf, gesture to my face, my eyes asking the question I have no words for. She shakes her head, looking at me with fear, but the older woman, standing behind her, has understood me and knows that I will find out, sooner or later. She walks away and returns shortly holding up a little mirror. It is very small, and the image is blurred, but one look in it reflects back to me what has happened.

I have been branded, burned, over and over again across my face, welts of red raised flesh, blisters already forming. I know that no remedy I may use, no unguent, will ever entirely remove such scars. My leg is broken, my face is forever scarred.

An irate shout comes from the courtyard. I cower, recognising my master's voice. But the older woman shakes her head quickly. He is not calling for me, he is calling for someone else, he is done with me. This scarring, this raging heat in my face, is his punishment, inflicted whilst I was in the darkness of pain, unaware of what was happening. So be it. I will be scarred, there is nothing I can do. But my leg... my leg fills me with fear. It must be set. I know how to do it, but once bound I must stay still for many, many days, months even. I do not know if I will be allowed this, and even if I am, whether it will heal straight or crooked. I look up at the older woman and then down at my leg, gesture to it as tears flow down my cheeks. She nods, a serious nod, filled with understanding of the gravity of my injury. She grimaces at the danger of it, the likelihood that it will not heal well. But then she points to a corner of the kitchen, she indicates sitting there, points to vegetables and a knife. She is suggesting that I may stay here, in her kitchen, for I believe her to be the cook here. She is suggesting I could be given little tasks to do, in the hopes that staying still will aid my recovery. I bow my head to her, still weeping, and reach for her hands. I kiss each of them, giving thanks to God out loud that there is someone here who will protect me as much as her position in this household allows. She can tell, perhaps, from my weeping and the seriousness of my tone, that I am blessing her, and she nods, places one of her hands over her heart in return.

The dwarf points to herself and says "Aisha," then points to the older woman.

"Maadah," she says and the cook nods, then points at me in turn. She does not wait for me to say my own name, instead she says "Kamra".

I do the best I can. I ask, with gestures, for what I need. Maadah brings me strips of cloth, that my leg may be tightly bound, alongside a few short pieces of wood. With her help, and Aisha's, we bind my leg as tightly and straight as possible. They cut away my ripped silken apparel and to my relief I am given a plain loose robe in a faded green, which is far too big for me and therefore falls comfortably over my awkwardly straight leg. I know that I must drink the root of cornflower, but I do not know how to ask for it. I make gestures to ask for writing implements. It takes a day before Aisha can lay her hands on ink and a sheet of something which I think is vellum at first, although it is not quite like it. At any rate, I can draw on it and I do my best to draw a cornflower, indicating that the petals should be blue by touching Maadah's robe, which is of a similar colour. I draw the little dangling purple flowers of comfrey also, known as knitbone, for its ability to do just that. Aisha nods at this, and takes away my drawing, I think she goes to the market with it to show to a seller of such remedies and sure enough returns with roots and leaves which I recognise. I embrace her as best I can, so grateful am I for her help. I drink the cornflower root daily, wrap comfrey around my leg and meanwhile Maadah smears some kind of mixture on my face, which eases the burns. I try to smell it, to find out what is in it, but I am not sure I recognise all the ingredients, some of them may be local to here. After several days Maadah nods approvingly at my face and tries to show me the progress of my burns in the mirror, but I only shake my head and look away. It is vanity to be more concerned with my face than with my ability to walk in the future. I am a bride of Christ, and Christ looks only at our hearts. He does not concern Himself with a woman's good looks or otherwise.

Time passes. I live all of my life in the kitchen. Early on, we find a way that I may relieve myself, with much pain and difficulty, but Maadah and Aisha do not shy away from such crude matters, only helping me when needed and disposing of my bodily waste without comment. A corner of the kitchen becomes mine, they place a sack stuffed with straw under me and give me a blanket to lie under at night. I know that my legs will grow wasted if I do not use them, so I try to move a little each day, even from my sitting position, half-crawling across the kitchen floor, folding and straightening the good leg.

    I try to make myself useful. I peel and chop vegetables, butcher meats, grind spices and herbs for the meals. I learn one dish after another, until

Maadah nods and smiles at my efforts in making them myself, without her input. I learn to roll tiny grains until they are made into something called *couscous*, to be buttered and salted, then topped with the thick stews they like to eat here. Once or twice I suggest, by pointing, a different spice or herb and Maadah nods, acknowledging that my choices are good. By night, I sleep by the last embers of the fire, wrapped in my blanket, and wake to find a little basin of water and a cloth laid out for me by Aisha so that I may keep myself clean.

I do not see my master, for which I am grateful. Day by day I learn new words, now that I can hear Aisha's chatter and Maadah's responses all day, alongside the other women who visit the kitchen. I begin by pointing to each herb and spice, for I know what they are, and to know their name in this new language is a comfort to me. Then I point to other things: the fire, the wood, a pot, water. Slowly, slowly, my leg heals, slowly, slowly, I learn to speak. Finally, the day comes when I can stand, leaning heavily on two sturdy sticks Aisha has found and brought to me. I look down. My work was not perfect, the leg is twisted. I will always limp. But I am standing, I am walking again, and I give thanks for this, grateful that God has not entirely deserted me, even here.

I work harder to learn the language. Aisha laughs at me when I speak, for she says my accent makes their words sound strange, but at least I begin to understand those around me and make myself understood in turn. Once I can ask questions and comprehend the answers to some degree an endless stream of them falls from my lips. I ask about the city, about the country, about our master.

"We sit on the trade routes," she explains, "that is what has brought the Master riches."

"What does the Master trade in?"

She makes a face, as she always does when he is mentioned. "Gold," she says curtly. "He trades with the Dark Kingdoms, to the south. He used to trade in slaves, but then he found that gold was easier. Gold does not die if you mistreat it," she adds.

I nod. This makes sense of our master's riches: the silk robes, the dark-skinned and heavily armed bodyguards he surrounds himself with on his journeys, this large and elegant house.

"Caravans come and go from Aghmat all the time," she tells me. "They are vast, you will have seen them on your journey here."

I nod. Traders can have more than a hundred camels, I have learnt. The caravans go on and on into the distance, and because they all follow the same trade routes, one caravan will often join in close with another, for there is safety in numbers, from bandits and other dangers. When crossing the deserts, there is the danger of getting lost and so many of the caravans follow one another.

"What other traders are there?" I ask.

"Oh, all kinds. Cloth: wool and linen of course, but also silks, and those that have been decorated are worth a great deal, the merchants who trade in them are rich. The cloth destined for the nobles will have been decorated with embroidery, or silver – they like to put little silver discs on some clothes, or twisted threads of gold. And there is jewellery of course, made with silver, or gold. Some of it is very fine, it is embedded with pearls or precious gems and woods. Have you seen ebony? It is black as night, black like a coal. And prized, of course."

I continue my work, but Aisha has sat back on her heels, with a dreamy expression on her face.

"Imagine being a queen," she says, a faraway smile on her face. "Imagine sitting on a throne while the best merchants bring you their wares. You could choose any jewellery you wanted, you could have glass cups and the best rose perfume. You wouldn't just chew on a stick of sugarcane, or peel an orange yourself, you'd have cooks, to make all kinds of delicacies and sweetmeats." She puffs out her cheeks and blows out a sigh. "Well, I suppose I can dream of such a day," she adds, laughing. "There is no chance Maadah will make such things for us, she's a good cook but not fancy."

"Are there many traders in spices?" I ask. "And in the ingredients for healing?"

"There are plenty," she says. "Although some seem a little frightening."

"Frightening?"

"Such things they have! Skulls from snakes and creatures pickled in jars, as though they were radishes. And teeth, so many teeth! They pull them right out of your head, if they hurt."

I nod, my tongue creeping over my own teeth, which thankfully I still have all of. Sister Rosa was always insistent on cleaning them with salt and a little stick, although she also kept a good supply of cloves for toothache and had a sturdy pair of pliers for pulling out any teeth that had gone rotten. Her own teeth were healthier than most, so I followed her example.

"Why am I called Kamra?" I ask her. "What does it mean?"

"Moon," she says.

"Why did the Master call me that?" I ask. "He could have called me anything."

She looks awkward. "It is just a name," she says.

"But why that name?" I persist.

She gestures vaguely towards me, at my head. "He said your head was like the moon," she half mutters.

I frown and then think about what she has said. My clean-shaven scalp, when he first saw me, the skin on my head whiter than white from the many years' protection from the sun, the lack of hair. It is a cruel nickname then, a name he chose to refer to the distinctive thing about me. The name was both accurate and intended as a jest, a jeering. My white scalp earned me the name of moon. I think for a moment of telling Aisha what my real name is, or at least one of them, but then I think that this name is good enough. It is a reminder of who I really am, that my scalp should have remained shaven, it has something of my past to it and is easy enough to pronounce, amidst these other words that I find so difficult. So, I remain Kamra, not challenging the name.

"Why did he buy me? He obviously did not think me beautiful. And there were beautiful women on the slave block, he could have bought them." I think of Catalina.

Aisha sits back on her heels from scrubbing the tiled floor. "The Master often brings women home from his travels," she says. "He likes them to look different."

"Different?"

"Different colours, different sizes, different ages. He says he likes variety," she adds, grimacing. "He has had many women in the rooms upstairs," she adds. "Old women, girls not yet past childhood, even one or two men."

I am appalled by such depravity but Aisha only shrugs. They have all grown used to their master's ways by now, know that they must bow their heads and ensure he is happy when he is here, that it is not their place to refuse him anything. He travels a great deal, Aisha tells me, so that much of the time the household is relatively ungoverned, for there is no mistress. "There was one, once, but after she had borne him two sons she died, and he never replaced her. He preferred to hire nursemaids for his sons and take his own pleasures where he wished. His sons are now grown men, both traders of Aghmat in their own rights, one deals in silks, one in gemstones. We do not often see them; they have their own households."

"Why would he choose me?"

"He said you were a religious woman, he had never seen one for sale before, he would have found that interesting."

I shake my head at the kind of man who would even think that. "Where are the other women?" I ask.

"Most are sold on, if they are worth selling. One ran away. A few of us he could not sell on, so we are still here."

I stop what I am doing and think about what she has said. By now I know that the household is made up of six women: myself, elderly Maadah, tiny Aisha, a very young girl named Ranya, barely out of childhood, who stays in the shadows of giantess Dalia. And Faiza, whose skin is mottled, half brown and half white, in patches like a leopard. And now I see what we are. A household of discarded playthings, a house of women who are too odd to be resold, kept only to carry out domestic chores, ready for the Master's rare visits.

Aisha watches me at my work. When she sees me pause when watering a plant to touch its leaves and smell it, she brings me a little potted plant of my own, though I have no idea where she got it from. It is mint, the mint they use here in their tea, which they drink copious amounts of, laced with honey. I take it in my hands and look at her. She indicates that it is mine, and reluctantly I nod my head to her and give her something approaching a smile. She beams back at me as though I have embraced her and she must say something to Maadah, who then seeks me out.

"You know plants?" she says.

"Yes," says Aisha, standing beside her.

"Be quiet," she says. She looks more directly at me, shapes her words carefully and clearly. "You know plants?"

"Yes," I say without adding anything more.

She nods her head, as though confirming what Aisha has told her. She asks something else, but I do not understand.

I shake my head.

"Can you heal sick people?" she asks.

I nod my head.

She calls for young Ranya, who has a bad cough. She makes her stand in front of me and then asks her to cough, which she does, a thick hacking sound. Maadah looks at me. "Can you help?" she asks.

I turn away from her and walk to where the lavender flowers are growing. I pick a few, then make my way to the kitchen, where I take honey and water and mix all of them into a little pot, which I set on the fire. Maadah, Aisha and Ranya watch me, curious. When the mixture has bubbled for a little while I pour it carefully into a cup, straining out the flowers as I do so. I hand the cup to Ranya and say, in my awkward accent, "Drink this, every day. It will drive out the stuffiness in your chest." Privately, I also think that it will drive out malign spirits and that perhaps this girl, who has been through such hardships here, may suffer from them also.

I make the mixture every day for four days and by the fourth day Ranya is smiling at me, and Maadah nods her head as she can hear for herself that the cough is abating, becoming lighter.

Now I have a function in the household. I am given the care of all the plants in the courtyard, and I rearrange them to my liking, placing the ones who enjoy the sun in the centre and those that prefer a cooler, shadier location at the edges, where they are sheltered from the blazing rays of the midday sun. The various members of the household come to me with their ailments and Maadah lets me have a pestle and mortar of my own, along with a few other little implements and pots that I may use when creating my remedies. When I ask for ingredients that I do not grow myself in the courtyard, at first she tries to give instructions to Aisha, who shops in the market for the household. But after a little while this becomes difficult, I cannot adequately explain everything I need. And so one day I am given leave to go with Aisha to the marketplace and told that I may select my own herbs and other ingredients.

I am nervous. Since the first day I arrived in Aghmat, I have not left this house, its courtyard, its walls. I have looked out over the rooftops, and seen the wide stretch of the city, but I have never ventured outside of the closed courtyard gate. But now I want to see more of this world in which I live, and so, tentatively, I follow Aisha out. I remember the narrow street in which I am standing, the street that brought me here and where I tried to run away. As we walk on, I see the narrow side street where I tried to jump from the window and fell. I will remember that street forever, I think bitterly. I will limp forever because of that one moment, my leg twisted and broken, the pain of it and the knowledge that it saved only my chastity. It did not release me from slavery, it did not return me home. I wonder briefly if the price I paid was too high, but by now we are joining the main street towards the market square and my thoughts are distracted by the world around us.

The marketplace is very large. Aghmat is a rich city and it displays its riches here, in a wide-open square, entirely surrounded by market stalls, and further behind it, dark warrens, tiny side streets making up the maze of further shops. There is a large mosque, where the people of the city pray. The stalls and shops offer everything one might wish for. From luxurious carpets, laid out on vast racks to show their beauty, down to tiny vials of rose perfume, so rich and sweet a scent that it makes your head spin. There are food stalls where merchants call their wares, offering stuffed dates, roasted meats, fresh breads, tiny sweetmeats and juices freshly squeezed to take away the day's heat. I can hear the metalworkers, the constant clang-clang-clang of their work, metal against metal as spoons and jugs and platters are created in their burnished hands. No doubt there are other metalworkers, those who make weapons, but they are needed less than daily utensils. Everywhere we walk our paths are blocked by beasts of burden, camels, mules, donkeys, horses, carrying everything from water jars to fruits and vegetables, even struggling livestock bound for slaughter. We have to start and stop with every step, allowing the traders to make their way towards stalls and the souks through narrow streets, pausing at the houses of well-known customers. There is every kind of person here. Little children run past us, shrieking as they play games, occasionally I spot one clasping stolen fruit or sweetmeats, a stallholder raising their voice behind them in indignation. There are old traders, sucking on pipes, swilling back sweet teas as they call out to passers-by, inviting them to look more closely at their goods: carpets, blankets, woven hangings. They promise shade and tea in return for a customer's attention.

There are those who make other kinds of promises. Whilst most of the women here dress in long robes, with little flesh on show, the colours of their fabrics bright but not gaudy, there are other women. These wear golden beads strung into their hair, their lips are painted bright shades of red, their arms are full of jangling bangles which they make sure to shake as they move, their robes, while long, seem somehow to offer glimpses of an arm, a leg, to gape open for a tantalising glimpse of their necklines. They laugh and joke amongst themselves, they call out to the men who pass by, something about sweetness, about honey, although they have nothing for sale but themselves.

There are jewellers, leather workers, and a slave trading block, which I move away from as soon as I recognise what it is, as though the trader might suddenly grab me and sell me onwards.

Aisha winks at me and puts one finger to her lips, indicating a secret, before using a small coin to pay for fresh oranges, cut and sprinkled with cinnamon and rosewater. After we have enjoyed their sweet taste, she busies herself buying fresh butter and cheese. She points to a lamb and a pair of chickens and they are slaughtered for us there and then, the blood spilling on the ground while a blessing of sorts is spoken over them. Behind the butcher sits an old man, his father perhaps, now too old for such a violent trade, whittling away at a wooden spoon he is creating. He nods and smiles to me and says something, but I do not understand and so I only nod and move away, once the meat has been parcelled up for us. Our baskets have grown heavy by the time we reach a small store to which Aisha nods and points, smiling.

And here at last are all the remedies which I have been lacking. Cumin and fennel seeds, cinnamon and ginger, pepper and rose. There is Java pepper and black hellebore, fenugreek and fern. I find dried hops and fresh sage, caperberries and dill. There is mallow and mustard, poppy and plantain, as well as thistle. I touch wormwood and clover, henbane and horseradish. Aisha laughs. I look at her and she indicates my own face and makes a face indicating extreme happiness, a ludicrous grin. I cannot help but laugh a little, knowing full well that she caught me smiling at the sight of these ingredients, so well-known to me. I touch one or two of the ingredients and raise my eyebrows at her, asking permission to buy them. I do not know what Maadah has told her, what I am allowed. But Aisha nods at everything I touch, she waves her hands to indicate more, that I must not be stinted. Maadah is being generous, now that she knows that I have healing skills, she seems determined to make use of them. I return to the house with one tiny packet after another spilling from my basket and Maadah smiles, well pleased. I beg some little jars from her and set up a shelf within the kitchen in which to store my remedies and ingredients. Seeing what I am doing she even clears a second shelf when it becomes obvious that my collection will not fit on one shelf alone.

I grow so busy with my remedies that I half begin to think myself at home. I do not just treat the household, for Maadah begins to spread word of my skills further afield, her friends and neighbours arriving at our gate and being shown to me, my name being called as soon as they appear. They are grateful to me, these slaves and other servants, they bring me little gifts when they are cured, perhaps a little bunch of dates still on the branch, a fistful of olives, such gifts as one slave can offer to another. When a woman brings a new-born child who seems to have difficulty breathing, and I cure it, she returns to ask for my name, that she may give the child the same. It is a girl, and Aisha, understanding the woman, tells her the name by which I am known, Kamra. The woman is happy with the name and goes away clutching her baby daughter to her.

I do not forget my prayers. Even though I live among these people, learn their language and eat their food, even though I have accepted a name in their own tongue, still I keep to my own prayers. I try to find a quiet place in which to pray each day, I try to follow, as best I can, the correct prayers for the right part of the day. And I turn my face away when the servants of the household pray in turn, preferring not to see their heathen practice. I look away from their devotions and continue to work even as I see them put away their work and obey the call to prayer that rings out across the rooftops of Aghmat five times each day. It would be all too easy to feel the need to be one of them, to convert so as to be accepted. It is not a temptation I intend to give into. For their part, they watch me pray at first with curiosity and later with disinterest, as they grow used to it.

The Master does not visit often. He travels various trade routes, making connections, seeking out those rich enough to need his gold. And perhaps he travels so that he may visit more than one slave market, so that he may look for those women who are strange, different, who give him the thrill of the new. When he does return home, our household is on high alert. We women shrink back from his presence, afraid that his time away will have tarnished us with new, will have reminded him of our difference and what he sought in us. We scurry to do as we are bid, we hurry to please him in any other way than the purpose for which we were bought. The house is immaculate, each room is luxurious and perfectly clean, we serve meals full of exotic and exquisitely made delicacies, for which we scour the market even as he scours markets for other pleasures. We arrange for dancing girls, for musicians, for jugglers and other such entertainers, in the hopes that they will draw his attention away from us. No matter what happens, when he is in the house, his attention must be drawn away from us. It is an unspoken pact between us, each woman protecting the others in any way she can. When he is in residence, his sons also visit, and they, too must be warded off. They have straying hands, each of us has felt their fingers on our arm, our legs, our behind, caressing and poking, pinching or lightly slapping. Each of us knows not to stand too close, to move gracefully away, to offer something else to keep their prying hands busy: a hot drink, sweetmeats, fresh fruits, anything but ourselves. When their father is gone, the sons do not seem to visit us, for which I am grateful. No doubt they have their own households to torment. I wonder what their wives make of them, these men who seek elsewhere. Perhaps they are grateful to be left alone.

And of course, the inevitable day comes, when a new girl is delivered to this household. There is no mistaking what she has been chosen for, her skin is a warm golden colour, but it is the bulk of her that draws the eye. The flesh of her body ripples when she moves, her breasts are larger than any woman I have ever seen, her vast behind balancing them perfectly. Her triple chins set off a rounded face with high fat cheeks tinged with pink and large black eyes, a rosebud mouth too small for the rest of her. She arrives, as I did, with a commotion in the street, the heavy battering of our gate and when it is opened there she is, sat atop a camel, eyes wide and frightened. She is pulled down from the camel's saddle and lands ungracefully, clutching the beast as though it is her only friend. It probably has been, for the past few days. Aisha exchanges glances with me and I nod, I understand what she is here for. She stumbles forwards, shuffling ungracefully as she seeks to regain her balance after so long astride the camel's swaying gait.

She does not fight so is not locked away in the room downstairs. She does not jump from the open window as I did. We wash and dress her, she sleeps obediently where we tell her to, and when the Master arrives, a few days later, we can see from her face and the slump of her shoulders that she knows full well what is to come. She submits. In silence, for we hear no screams. The Master, it seems, is pleased enough with her, for he gives her a necklace and when he leaves, orders that she be sold on, he is tired of her now, she is no longer a novelty. But it seems she is not that easy to sell and so she re-joins us, returns to our house of women and tells us her name, Nilah, bringing our total to seven. And we, this household, await the next woman to arrive, the next novelty that has caught our master's eye. There is a slave girl in Aghmat whom I have seen once or twice, for she is easy to spot in a crowd. Her hair is the colour of saffron, her skin extraordinarily pale, her eyes are blue like cornflowers. I am quite certain that once, however long ago, she made up part of our household. I wonder if this is my new destiny. If I am to live in a household of strange sisters, welcoming one novice after another to be fed to our Master and then discarded, as I lost Catalina whom I should have delivered safely home to the convent. I wonder if I will ever forget Catalina, if I will ever see her again to beg her forgiveness.

I avoid the Master's straying hands several times and as the seasons change, I begin almost to feel myself safe.

There is a festival once a year here, where birds of prey are displayed and then some are set free. The Master is away and so I stand with the other women in the crowd and watch the birds as their leather anklets are unclipped or cut loose and they are thrown forwards into the sky, the way they circle above their masters before realising that they are free, that they need not return to the commands they have been trained to but instead may return to the forests and deserts whence they came, to seek out their long-lost mates and their favourite hunting grounds. They test the air and feel the wind turn their wings towards freedom, away from the minarets and rooftops that have so long held them captive. We watch as they leave the city's sky, turning from large to small, then disappearing altogether from sight. I hear Nilah sigh to herself.

"Let's go home," I say.

Aisha clutches my arm. "Do you not want to see Zaynab?"

"Who is Zaynab?" I ask.

She widens her eyes at my ignorance. "The queen of Aghmat," she tells me. "She is the most beautiful woman in the world, so they say."

I shrug.

"Come with me," she says. "The procession of the nobles will pass by the main street on their way back to the palace and we will see her."

"Haven't you seen her before, if she is the queen?" I ask. I have little interest in seeing the procession, nor a woman who is no doubt vain as well as being a heathen.

"She does not often go out in public," says Aisha, still tugging at me. "Come on!"

I follow, dragging my feet, hoping that we will miss the procession after all. But when we reach the main street there are big crowds lining the road on both sides, eager to see King Luqut as well as Queen Zaynab.

"She had a vision," breathes Aisha.

"Who?"

"Zaynab. She said she would marry the man who would rule all of the Maghreb."

"Is that why Luqut wanted to marry her?" I ask.

"Yes. He made her divorce her first husband so he could have her for himself."

I am appalled. "He took her from her lawful husband?"

"Yes," says Aisha, with all the gusto of one telling a fantastical tale. "She was only a girl and married to a man she loved, but because of her vision, Luqut took her for himself. They say she screamed when she was told. But now she is the queen of Aghmat and Luqut says that with her by his side there can be no doubt that her vision will come true."

I am about to ask more questions but there are shouts and cheers from our right and Aisha grips my arm, pulling me forward so that we will see better. Already we can see the fine horses of the royal guards who are leading the procession. Behind them, I can see two riders, a man and a woman.

"There they are!" whispers Aisha in excitement.

The two riders come abreast of us and I see an older man, broad of shoulder, his face turning this way and that to acknowledge the crowd with a confident smile, a man certain of acclaim. Closer to us is the queen, Zaynab. The procession slows, as guards ahead clear the crowds out of the way and so I see her for longer than I might otherwise have done.

She is far younger than her husband, she is probably a few years younger than I am. Her face does not turn this way and that. Instead she looks straight ahead, her eyes unwavering, as though she were a statue. She is certainly beautiful, and I note the absurd lavishness of her clothing and jewels, rich silks tumbling all around her, ropes of gemstones and heavy gold weighing her down. But I have to concede that perhaps to suppose her vain may be a mistake. She does not look as though she is revelling in her beauty, in the opulence of her clothing and heavy gold headdress. She looks unhappy. It makes me sad to look at her. I wonder whether we share the same pain, this queen and I, a slave. Torn from our vows, she from her husband, I from God's own son, forced to live another life at another's whim.

"I have had enough," I say to Aisha, and I turn for home, away from Queen Zaynab's sad face.

The Beat of Drums

Terrible as an army with banners.

Song of Solomon 6:4

1 AM LAYING OUT HERBS ON the airy rooftop to dry them, turning each bundle, each leaf and flower every day under a shaded awning, to avoid them turning musty. The awning shelters them from the too-hot sun which would diminish their powers. I hear footsteps and panting, and Aisha joins me. She drags me away from my chores, to the edge of the rooftop.

"They say an army is coming," she says, pointing beyond Aghmat's city walls.

I look out at the empty plain and then back at Aisha. "An army? What do you mean, an army?"

"The Almoravids!"

"Who are they?"

"Desert warriors," breathes Aisha. "From the south."

"Should we be afraid?"

"They tried to cross the mountains before, years ago, but they failed. But now they say there are more of them, and that they have a greater leader, named Abu Bakr."

"If they failed before, it is likely they will fail again," I say, exasperated with Aisha's gossiping. "I have work to do."

But it is not long before fear spreads in the city. The Almoravids have succeeded in crossing the mountains. It seems that their new leader Abu Bakr is indeed a strong man, and word has it that his second-in-command, a man named Yusuf, is also a redoubtable warrior and leader of men. Their army has taken Taroundant, a strong city, a city almost as big as Aghmat.

Suddenly armed men are everywhere in the streets. The Amir's army prepares for battle, we see guards and soldiers in the streets, we hear of their preparations, the armourers in the markets deafen passers-by with their hammering, sharpening swords and fashioning spears.

"King Luqut will beat them," says Aisha, with certainty.

"How can you be sure?" I ask. "Everyone says they are stronger this time."

"He had better beat them," says Aisha, looking less certain. "No woman will be safe if an army conquers this city."

I think that anyway, no woman is safe in our own household, considering the Master's behaviour. I want to say that I will take my chances with a new army, although I know that this is nonsense. A conquering army, soldiers, will certainly be worse than a single man.

"Well, there is nothing we can do," I say. "It is God's will what will happen."

"Allah be praised," says Aisha. "I give thanks that we have a strong Amir, he will protect us."

We hear whispers, rumours, gossip, nonsense. But at last there comes a day when the nonsense becomes truth. The Amir and his army are heading out to fight the Almoravids. He is a fearsome warrior, this land is his, he knows it well. He has a strong army, there is no reason why he should lose the coming battle. Still, I find myself whispering prayers under my breath as I work, praying for this heathen king to defeat the coming army. I should not care what happens to him, but certainly if he loses, I and all of this household, this city, will be at risk.

The city withdraws into itself. People retreat to their houses, close their shops, the market falls silent. We gather on the rooftops, straining our eyes to look out over the plain to see anything, though we can see nothing. The army rides out at dawn. Aisha and I buy food at the market, as always, but there are only a few stalls open. The main shops are shuttered, the merchants are hurrying either back to their own homes or to places of safety, herding their animals with brisk shouts. One by one the gates set into the high city walls close, pushed to by guards who stand waiting, hoping to welcome our army back into the safety of the city, once they have defeated the Almoravids.

Darkness falls. The Master is still away on a trading trip and we are unsure whether this is of benefit to us or not. For once, perhaps, we would have liked to have had a man in the house. If, God forbid, Luqut is defeated, what will a conquering army do to a houseful of unprotected women? We stay inside, keeping only a couple of lanterns with us, but first one and then another of us hears a sound, looks to the others to see if they, too, can hear it. It is a low sound, so far away that it is hard to hear it. We can only feel it, as though it were a heartbeat. It comes again and again and again, like a heartbeat indeed. We look from one to another and when it becomes clear that all of us can hear it, we make our way up the stairs, moving towards the windows, which we dare not open, looking upwards to the stairs which would take us to the rooftops, which we dare not ascend. It is a beat. It comes regularly, repetitively, so deep that it sounds in our bellies and our feet rather than in our ears.

"What can it be?" whimpers Dalia, shoulders hunched, making her smaller than usual.

"Drums," says Aisha in a whisper.

"Drums?"

"The Almoravids carry drums in battle," she says. "They will drum all night and all through the battle, however long it lasts."

They do. The beat continues, coming closer and closer, until it feels as though even the city walls must be reverberating. In the darkness of the night, Aisha and I open a shuttered window one tiny crack and hear the sound come louder.

"They must be just outside the city walls," I say, horrified.

"The Amir must have retreated," says Aisha, squatting on the ground. She sits in grim silence for a little while. "If they storm the city, we must find a way out of here," she says.

"There is no way out," I say. "If a conquering army enters the city, we are all dead. Or worse," I add.

She nods and is silent for a while longer. "We could dress as men," she says.

"Then they will sever our heads from our bodies," I say.

One by one, the other women of the household find us, seeking us from room to room. When they do find us, they huddle on the floor, robes wrapped around cold feet, in terrified silence occasionally broken by small whispers to one another.

The drums continue all night. When dawn breaks, there is no call to prayer, its absence deafening. Still the drumbeat goes on. The city walls have not yet been breached, but the drums are so close that we know that Luqut's army must be failing, that the men of Aghmat, the husbands and sons, fathers and brothers the city sent out to battle, are being killed, one by one. We relieve ourselves in a pot and carry it at night down to the courtyard. We take furniture from other rooms and push it against the door of the room in which we are huddled. The seven of us wait, certain of a hammering at the gate below, certain that the door of this room will be shattered open, to reveal the Almoravids, these unknown and powerful desert warriors. We do not even know what they look like, although Maadah says that she has heard that they wear only dark robes, carry shields almost as big as themselves and that all the men veil their faces. Although there are plenty of local men who veil their faces, somehow the thought of conquerors whose faces we cannot even see is more frightening than if they were to show themselves.

In the end it takes three days and three nights. By the third day, the city walls are breached. We hear running and shouts, screams of people dying, both men and women. We hear things being broken, whether by the city people throwing things such as pots to protect themselves or deliberate damage being caused by the conquering army. It is clear that we are overrun, that our army has lost, and that we are now in the hands of the Almoravids. We no longer dare to leave the room in which we have locked ourselves. We relieve ourselves in a pot which has a lid, but as the hours go by without emptying it, the room begins to smell fetid from the waste of our bodies and our stale breath, tainted with our growing fear.

Sometime in the late afternoon, the room grown hot, our bellies crying out with hunger, our mouths dry with thirst, we hear shouts from the streets. Not shouts of panic, as we heard before, but rather announcements, orders. We stand close to the shuttered window and hear, over and over again, that there is a curfew being placed over the whole city. No one is to leave their houses after darkness, on pain of death.

"Will we be safe tonight, do you think?" asks Maadah. "Can we leave the room once darkness falls?"

None of us are sure. On the one hand, perhaps the curfew means that our conquerors will leave us alone, so long as we obey their rule. On the other hand, perhaps they wish for all of us to be shuttered in our houses so that they may visit each house in turn, take what they want, rape and loot at will. Perhaps it is convenient for all of us to be immured within our walls. Perhaps they wish to burn us to death.

But night comes and the streets are silent. After much whispered debate,

Aisha and I push open the shuttered window and look down into the street below, holding ourselves back a little, afraid of being seen. In the dark night, there is little light in which to see anything, but there is a dark shadow at the end of the street, holding a tall spear. It stays motionless, even when we watch it for some time, and at last we can only surmise that it is an Almoravid guard, that there are guards set all over the city tonight to ensure curfew is being respected. The open shutter allows in some fresh cold air, which all of us gulp in greedily, taking turns to stand close to the window, tiptoeing across the floor to exchange places.

The moon is fully high in the sky before we dare to leave the room. It takes all of us to lift the furniture fully off the ground before we can move it, to minimise the sounds we make. At last we edge the door open, creep out onto the balcony and look down into the courtyard below. There is no one there, the gate is still closed, as we left it. It seems that the curfew is indeed a peaceful one.

We tiptoe down the stairs, bare feet on cold tiles and creep into the kitchen, where we gulp cold water and share stale bread, dried dates, handfuls of nuts. We cram our fasting bellies with as much food as we can, not knowing what tomorrow will bring. We empty our waste, clean ourselves a little. We are free to sit in the courtyard of course, but we find ourselves retreating back to the room we have spent the past few days in, it feels like a place of safety. We pull blankets and rugs over ourselves and sleep fitfully, every little creak or too-loud snore jolting us awake in fear.

Dawn brings the sound we have not heard for three days, the call to prayer has been reinstated. We can only assume that the Almoravids have ordered the holy men of the city to take up their usual routines. The women pray and for once, I do not turn away or find something else to do. I kneel and clasp my hands, pray alongside them, only with my own words. I am not sure what to pray for, only that we be spared whatever harm the Almoravids intend to do to us.

Once again, loud voices from the street tell us that we are free to go about our daily business. The Almoravids now rule the city, we are told, but mean us no harm, if we treat them as our new masters. The night-time curfew will stay in place, otherwise, our lives may go on as they did before.

"As if we could go about our daily business as though nothing is happened," sniffs Maadah.

"We should at least eat and bathe," says Aisha, ever practical. "We cannot know what will happen from one day to the next. If we are safe within these walls, then let us make the most of it for now."

We spend the day in silence, as though I were back in the convent. There is nothing to say, nor anything much to do. We eat, we bathe, we sit in the quiet courtyard and listen, our ears ever ready for sound, our feet ever ready to run.

While there is still light, before the curfew takes place, I gesture to Aisha and point to the stairs leading to the roof. The others shake their heads, but she nods and together we climbed the stairs, reaching the rooftops step-by-step, crouched down in fear.

We are almost surprised to see the city's rooftops still there, as though nothing has happened. But that is not quite true. We can see a part of the city walls that is damaged, we can see fires here and there, sullen smoke still rising after the flames have been put out. The streets are too quiet, the odd animal wanders, lost without a master, harnesses trailing. We see two bodies, lying in the street at the back of the house, daggers still in hand and no one come to collect them, men too eager to protect their city when it was already too late to do so. I cross myself and utter words of blessing, wondering if they are any use to a Muslim, although Aisha nods at what I am doing and mutters some words of her own.

"You are safe then," comes a hiss.

We jump and clutch at each other, but it is only a woman from the next house, on the rooftop of her own house, barely a jump away.

"Thanks be to Allah, we are safe," says Aisha. "And you?"

The woman gives a quick nod. "My husband was fighting," she says. "But he escaped, came back here. Allah be praised."

"Has he been injured?" I ask.

"No, praise be," she says. "But he said it was terrible."

"What happened? asks Aisha.

"He said that they had barely left the city walls when the amir became confused, as though ill, that his sword arm grew weak. He fell almost at once. The generals soon afterwards, they lost their courage with Luqut gone. He said the Almoravids were like no army he has ever seen, and his father fought them last time, he saw them as a boy. He said that they have changed beyond recognition. He said they arrange themselves into line upon line, stretching to the horizon. They beat their drums without stopping, hour after hour, day after day as the men advance. They do not stop, they do not break rank, they only advance, one step at a time, side-by-side, no gaps between them. He said the drums made our men feel dizzy and sick, that they could find no gap in the lines through which to attack. The Almoravids would not retreat, only advance so slowly it seemed imperceptible and then our soldiers found themselves backed up against the city walls and it was too late. They must die or submit. Many men died, until it became clear that the only thing left to do was surrender. The remaining nobles and officers laid down their weapons and told the men to do the same. My husband said he was filled with shame, but what else could he do? He knew he would not return to me and to his children if he did not. The nobles swore loyalty to Abu Bakr and ordered the city gates to be opened, so that the city might not be further damaged. The army was too terrible, there was no chance of winning, they were lucky to escape with only a third of the men killed. There will be families grieving all over Aghmat, but at least some men have been saved."

There is a heavy hammering at the outer gate, the sound we have been waiting for. We look to one another, even look to the woman as though we might leap to safety, from one rooftop to another, but it is too far for me, let alone Aisha.

"Hide," says the woman and retreats into the safety of her own house.

Aisha and I make our way back down the stairs, cautious, slow, before Aisha suddenly clutches my arm.

"It is the Master!" she says.

I stare at her, but her ears are better than mine, more accustomed to his voice, for she is right, I can hear him now.

"Open this accursed gate or I will have you all strangled!"

We run down the second flight of stairs, across the courtyard, pull back the gate to see the Master with six of his bodyguards, all of them pale with fear, pushing too hard to get through the tight gateway.

"I should have you all beaten," he blusters. "What is the meaning of this, barricading the gate against me, eh?"

"We were afraid of the Almoravids, Master," cringes Aisha, ducking out of the way of his flailing hands as he attempts to strike us. I am not so quick, he ends up half-smacking my cheek, a glancing blow that hardly satisfies him.

"Well close it again now we are in!" he yells at his bodyguards, who move quickly to do his bidding. I hear fear in the Master's voice now, feel it in his shouts and blows. He is unnerved by what has happened to this city in his absence, what it may mean for him, for his business, his family.

We women are commanded to bring water to wash, food at once, no matter that we have few supplies. Later his two sons arrive, slipping through the streets with hooded robes borrowed from servants rather than their usual finery.

We all, even the Master, peep from closed windows, watching the dark shadows patrolling the streets, tall men, their faces fully veiled, long spears and vast shields held at their sides. We hear the clatter of horses' hooves and brace ourselves for what is to come.

The Master, and no doubt others from amongst the richest merchants, have been summoned to visit the amir's palace, now the stronghold of our conquerors. He sets out alone, without the safety and comfort of his bodyguards. We wait for his return.

He returns shaking, his usual arrogant demeanour broken. It seems the conquerors have stripped the palace of its decorations and finery. We huddle in the corners of the courtyard and staircases, eavesdrop on him speaking with his sons.

"They claim to disdain luxury," he says. "Their leader looks like a common soldier. You would not be able to tell him from his men."

"What did they want with you?" asks one of his sons.

"They want gold," says the Master, shoulders drooping. "They want more gold than can be imagined."

"For what?"

"For men, for armour, for horses. For a kingdom. They intend to control all the trade routes; they will tax us to get what they need."

The three men sit in silence for a while, digesting the news, trying to foresee their future in all of this. On the one hand, as merchants, their trade is needed. On the other hand, there is a risk that they will be taxed so harshly that their trading will barely be worthwhile. They cannot tell yet, they can only wait and discover how these, their new masters, will treat them. They are cowed by the news, wary of their futures, afraid to put a foot wrong, not knowing how this new regime will treat any failure to comply. I have never seen the Master so shrunken, so defeated.

The hammering we were afraid of comes again and this time at night. The Master is dragged from his bed by the dark-robed men, spluttering and cursing them as he goes, leaving us alone, untouched, the house unstripped of its goods. It seems he tried to hide the extent of his wealth from our new rulers, that he did not pay what was promised and they, in turn, have shown that they will not be defied. We are uncertain whether he has been killed, but it seems likely when he does not return. Our household falls empty and silent. We wait to know our fate, expecting one of his sons to take his place, to command us. But they do not come. Eventually we hear whispers that they, too, defied the Almoravids and paid the price.

We stay indoors for several more days, too afraid to venture out, too afraid to believe the Almoravids when they say the citizens of Aghmat should go about our business. The fountain brings water to the house, so that we may drink and bathe, the kitchen has enough dried foodstuffs that we can eat, albeit plain fare. None of us desires fresh fruit and vegetables enough to risk going into the unknown new world outside our gate.

The rooftops become our source of knowledge, of gossip, rumours and whispers. The men and women of the city gather on the rooftops before the curfew comes each day, exchanging sources of knowledge which may or may not be true.

The new regime allows us to leave the house by day, although the curfew by night still stands. At last the day comes when Aisha and I must leave the house, for we are without food and no one else in the household dares to venture out. We wrap ourselves in winter cloaks, as though the heavy cloth might somehow protect us. Clutching a basket, we creep out of the main gate and into the narrow street. There should be children running, the clip clop of mules and donkeys, the huffing of camels. But the city is quiet, our neighbours still afraid to venture out if they can avoid it.

"Let's go back," begs Aisha.

"We need food," I remind her. "And we are allowed to go to market, so long as we do not defy the curfew." Even so, I hold her hand tightly in mine as we come to the end of our street and make our way onto the wider road that leads to the market.

There are people about, here and there, although they walk quickly and quietly. The men do not look about them, the women walk with their heads down. No one chatters or stops to greet one another. They go about their business quickly. Not all the market stalls that should be open are trading, only a few, here and there, those of which people have most need. There is a stall selling vegetables and we make our way there and, in half whispers, make our purchases, not even daring to gossip. Next to them is a dried goods stall, and we purchase dried fruit, lentils, chickpeas. I find myself buying more than is necessary, more than we would usually buy, so that we will not need to venture out again in a hurry. There is no meat for sale today, no spices, nor fresh cheese and butter. We will have to make do without.

We turn to leave and suddenly see our first Almoravid up close. A tall man, wrapped in a long dark cloak, a spear in one hand, a sword at his belt. His face is fully veiled, I can see only his eyes, and only his eyes follow our movement. He does not move, only watches as we pass and then turns his attention back to the rest of the market square, no doubt searching for any signs of unrest. But this is a cowed city, a city that has recognised its defeat. The days pass and there is no sign of disobedience, no sign of reprisals. The merchants who escaped punishments pay the heavy taxes demanded of them and are grateful they are not higher. The people begin to go out and about again, quietly at first and then more boldly, until the city chatters again and it is as though nothing had ever happened.

But there are stories emerging, which Aisha, of course, quickly finds out about.

"Queen Zaynab is to marry Abu Bakr!" she says.

Maadah stops what she's doing, and all the women gather together to relish this gossip.

"Is this one of your nonsense stories, again, Aisha?" I ask.

"It is the truth!" she says. "May Allah strike me down if it is not true!"

"She is marrying him?" I say.

"Yes! They say that she met with him, and took him, blindfolded – "

"Aisha," I say warningly.

"I swear! She took him blindfolded to a secret place, where she showed him untold riches. Gems and gold beyond counting. 'All this is yours,' she told him, and now they are to be married. She will be the queen of the Almoravids. And they wish to create a new city."

"Not very loyal," comments Maadah.

I think of the only time I have seen Queen Zaynab, how beautiful she was, but also how unhappy she looked. I am not sure that she felt much loyalty towards Luqut, who took her from her first husband when she was still a young bride. Perhaps she hopes for a better marriage with Abu Bakr.

Perhaps showing him whatever riches Luqut had in his treasury is her way of securing her future.

Aisha's news is proven to be correct. Zaynab marries Abu Bakr with great pomp and ceremony and the people of our city repeat again the story of her vision, that she would marry the man who would rule the Maghreb.

"Her vision has come true. It was foretold that she would be wife to the man who would rule all of the Maghreb."

"It was not Luqut's destiny to rule. It was the Almoravids, her vision is coming true at last."

"How ridiculous," I say, when I hear this. "Did her vision require her to marry three times before it came true?"

"It was foretold," says the stallholder, speaking with conviction while weighing out barley.

I roll my eyes. I do not believe in Zaynab's so-called vision, it seems too convenient to me. Too much like convincing a conquering warlord to spare her life and treat her with dignity rather than take her as a common prisoner of war or indeed simply end her life. She has protected herself by creating a legend.

A young girl, her hand sought by so many. Who chose to travel across the Maghreb, far, far away from her home and her family, to her first husband. A woman who had a great vision and was demanded as queen by the Amir of Aghmat. Whose city was destroyed and yet who cast a spell over the commander of the conquering army, showing him riches such as are only dreamed of in this life. Made queen again from the rubble of a ruined city, lifted once again to greatness. Her vision coming true at last as the army prepares for domination.

The people begin to think that perhaps their amir's fall was destined, that Allah always meant for the Almoravids to take over this city, that he guided them to this place, to marry their queen, and fulfil her holy vision. No doubt this idea is welcomed and encouraged by the Almoravids. I do not know what to think. But I give thanks to God that this army has not yet brought harm to myself and the other women of our household, as we once feared. We are not sure how long we will be left alone in this household, or even if the small amount of money we have will last us more than a month or two, but for now, at least, what we were afraid of has not befallen us.

A new piety sweeps the city. The people dress with more sobriety, dance and flirt less, sacrifice more animals and say their prayers with renewed conviction. It is a way to survive, I suppose, to believe that what has happened, the suffering caused by losing so many men of the city, was intended. That Aghmat, rather than being humiliated, is part of a grander plan, one approved by Allah, who has guided the Almoravids this far. The people choose to believe this. The metalworkers set to making new weapons, the merchants feed and clothe their conquerors, although the Almoravids take little pleasure in the riches and comforts that a city like this one might offer them. They seem to disdain the luxuries of the world to a degree that surprises. We hear that every room of the palace has been stripped bare, that generals and common foot soldiers alike lie on the bare floors, wrapped in coarse blankets to sleep, that the servants grow idle, not called upon to provide rich foods and sweet drinks, massages and bathing that were required by the former amir. Now they need only bake bread and roast plain meets, serve dried dates without adornment and pour cold water to drink. I wonder whether Queen Zaynab approves this new austerity in her life, or whether she is still served as she once was.

Perhaps for the first time since I came here, our household relaxes. The conquerors have shown no interest in us. The Master and his sons, who made all of us nervous, are gone. Apparently, we have been forgotten. We eat, we pray, we sleep. We clean the house and ourselves, we speak of small matters. I gather leaves and roots from the plants in the courtyard and make remedies for such minor ailments as afflict us or our neighbours, which we barter for vegetables and grains to eke out our food stores, which are running low.

I begin to think that I have somehow found myself in a new convent, peopled with this strange array of women collected by our late master. I wonder, even, if I might convert them, if somehow this household might become a nunnery, under my guidance. It seems unlikely, for all of them cling to their own faith, as I do to mine and who could imagine a nunnery here of all places? And yet the rhythm of the day seems familiar to me, and it brings me an unexpected peace. There are days when I hope this time will last for ever, that no one will come to disturb this fragile peace we have somehow made between us in this uncertain time.

But it seems God has other plans for me.

I am watering the plants in the courtyard, squatting down to remove dead flowers and leaves, touching the earth in each pot to see if it is dry or damp, when a shadow falls over me. I look up, expecting Maadah or some other known person and find myself at the feet of an Almoravid soldier. I freeze, waiting for a blow or worse, but the man only stands there, looking down on me.

"Stand," he says. His voice is calm, unhurried, unconcerned.

I let go of the pot of water and slowly, slowly stand before him, his dark eyes staying steady on mine. We are very close, there is less than a hand's breadth between us. I wait. To be grabbed, to be forced in some way.

But instead he takes a step backwards, away from me, as though he, too, finds the closeness disconcerting, although his eyes do not leave mine. "You are a member of this household?" he asks.

"Yes," I say. I do not say anything more. When it becomes clear that I am not about to speak again without prompting, he speaks.

"You are a slave?"

"Yes," I say.

"How many others are here?"

I tell him. He nods.

"Gather them."

I step away from him and walk slowly away, aware of having my back to him, of not knowing what he's doing when I cannot see him. I make my way to the kitchen, and whisper to Maadah. Her face drains white. One by one, we gather together the other women and make our way back into the courtyard.

The Almoravid is standing where I left him, he has barely moved. We stand before him, leaving a fearful distance between us.

"Are you all women here?" he asks.

I nod.

"I am Yusuf bin Tashfin," he says. "I will be your new master and you will be my new household."

Nobody speaks. We stand in silence.

"Show me to a bedroom," he says. "And bring me water and bread."

Maadah finds her voice first. "I am the cook here. Shall I make a meal, Master?" she asks, her voice a little shaky.

He shakes his head. "Just water and bread," he repeats.

She nods, and scuttles away, followed by the rest of the household, none of whom wish to lead this man, our new master, anywhere.

"You," he says, addressing me.

"Yes, Master," I say.

"A bedroom," he says.

I turn my back on him and walk away, hear his footsteps behind me across the courtyard and up the stairs, trying not to tremble at the thought that, once we reach a bedroom, he may well choose to have his sport with me. I wonder which room to take him to, but decide that, if he is our new master, then he must be taken to the master's bedchamber. I open the door, and step back, hoping he will not drag me in with him. But he only walks through the doorway and looks around the room. "Very well," he says. "You may bring me the bread and water when it is ready."

"Yes, Master," I say, quickly shutting the door and running down the stairs to the relative safety of the kitchen. The other women are huddled there, their faces afraid.

Maadah's hands shake when she passes me the tray to carry upstairs. "Be careful," she says.

I nod and take the tray.

"He is their second in command," breathes Aisha. "Why would he come alone?"

I stop halfway to the door. "What do you mean," I ask, "their second-in-command?"

"Yusuf bin Tashfin," she says, repeating the name he gave. "He is Abu Bakr's second-in-command."

"He can't be," I object. "Why would he not have men with him?" I think of our amir and his nobles, even our late Master, how they would go nowhere without an entourage of guards, lesser nobles, bodyguards, servants, slaves.

"Never mind that now," hisses Maadah. "Take that food up to him." The tray she has given me contains fresh-baked bread from this morning, cool water in a jug with a cup ready to fill, dates and slices of fresh orange, as well as little cakes.

"He didn't ask for all this," I say.

"If he is our new master," says Maadah, "then it's our business to please him. And the way to please a man is to fill his belly."

I shake my head and hurry away from her, across the courtyard and back up the stairs, until I reach his door. I want to leave the tray here, do not want to face him again, but I know that I must. I tap gently on the door.

"Come," I hear.

Tentatively, I open the door.

In the brief time I have been gone, he has managed to transform the room. He has removed the silken drapes, the bright blankets, decorative objects. The bed has been stripped bare, only a yellow blanket remains, the plainest of them all, woven in wool. The rest of the room's hangings and covers have been piled in a corner, as though they were rags for washing. His sword has been left on the floor beside the bed, where he now lies, a dark figure in this light room.

"You may leave the food there," he says, indicating the low table by the bed.

I do so. He looks at the tray, eyebrows raised. "You may tell the cook that when I ask for bread and water, I mean bread and water," he says. He sounds amused. "There is no need to try and impress me," he adds. "Only to obey me."

I nod my head in silence. I stand, waiting for further orders, while he props himself up on one arm and pours himself a cup of water, which he drinks quickly, then fills again.

"You needn't hover there," he tells me. "I will call for you if I want something. I need to sleep."

I move towards the door.

"Wait," he says.

I stop.

"What is your name?" he asks.

I hesitate. "Kamra," I say at last.

His eyes travel over me, from my crooked leg and the limp he has already seen, up to my face and the scars it bears. "Kamra? Where are you from?"

"Galicia," I say.

He frowns. "Kamra is not a Galician name. What was your name before you were taken as a slave?"

I do not speak. Am I to give this man the name I was born with? Or the name I took as a nun? Neither seems right, neither seems suited to this world in which I find myself. "You may call me whatever you wish," I say.

"Stubbornness is not usually a desirable trait in a slave," he says. There is something teasing about his tone, as though he finds this conversation amusing. It raises my hackles.

"You may call me whatever you wish," I say again.

He nods, but still does not use any name. "You may go now," he says.

Now a new life begins for all of us. We are relieved not to have been left destitute and certainly now we are protected, but we struggle to adapt to his ways, at first. Our new master eats bread and water, a little meat. He sleeps like the dead, I can hear him softly snoring sometimes, if I pass by his bedchamber. He has the house stripped bare of all superfluous decorations, telling me, when I ask what to do with them, to give them to the poor, the needy. I stand, with my hands full of silks and precious trinkets and stare at him.

"There are no poor and needy in Aghmat?" he asks me, amused again.

"Every city has poor and needy people," I say.

"Then seek them out," he says and turns away, wrapping the yellow blanket about him and preparing to sleep.

Somehow, I become his personal servant. It is to me he gives his orders, barely speaking to the rest of the household. It is I who have to repeat his commands to Maadah, who feels underused, to the other women, who regard me with uncertainty at first, as though I am making up the odd orders he gives. Sometimes he does not even sleep in his bedchamber. I find him in the courtyard, in the early hours, saying the dawn prayers. He kneels amidst my plant pots, a rough mat on the tiled floor beneath him. The first time I see him like this, I stand silently watching him. It takes me a little while to think who he reminds me of and when I realise, I shake my head. Surely, I am mistaken. He reminds me of the Mother Superior in the convent, so long ago, in my other life. She had a way of praying that seemed truly holy, as though she could hear God's voice speaking to her while she was on her knees, her eyes uplifted, her face filled with a kind of joy. It seems strange to see the same joy in the face of a man, a Muslim, a heathen praying to a god who does not exist. The strangeness of it draws me somehow, and from then on when I see him at prayer, I pause to watch him, hidden in the shadows. I do not think he sees me, until the morning when he addresses me as he stands.

"You do not pray?" he asks me, without turning his head towards me, near the kitchen doorway.

I am silent for a moment, before I realise that he has indeed seen me, and is speaking to me. "No," I say.

"Why not?"

"I am a Christian," I say stiffly.

"He turns to look at me more directly. "Even Christians pray," he says.

"I pray in my room," I say.

"You could convert," he says.

I am so shocked I do not say anything, and he suddenly laughs out loud, the first time I've heard him do so. "I see your faith is more important to you than I thought," he says. "I meant no disrespect."

I say nothing.

"My apologies," he says again, more seriously. "You are a woman of faith, then?"

"I am a nun," I tell him.

He looks up, his hands busy making the mat into a neat roll. "You are a slave," he reminds me.

"I am a nun," I repeat. "I have not renounced my vows."

"How did a nun end up as a slave in Aghmat?" he asks, stepping closer to me.

"The Norsemen took me," I say.

"From a holy place?" he asks, frowning.

I shake my head. "I was on a journey," I say.

"Alone?"

I shake my head. I am not about to describe what happened to me, to us, to this man.

He nods, grave now. "I am sorry," he says simply, handing me the mat to be put away. Then he turns and leaves, the gate closing behind him.

Aisha has more news. I swear the girl is nothing but a gossip sometimes. Although I have to admit her gossip often brings us valuable information.

"We are to leave Aghmat," she says.

"Leave?"

"Yes. The Almoravids want to build a new capital city. It is to be on the plain and they will call it *Murakush*, land of God."

"But there's nothing there," objects Maadah. "Where are we to live?"

"Tents," says Aisha.

"Tents?" echoes Maadah. "Don't be ridiculous, girl."

"Well they don't care, do they?" says Aisha. "Look at the Master, sleeping on the floor in the courtyard when he could be in a silken bed."

"I'm not living in a tent, and that's an end to it," says Maadah.

But we find out soon enough that Aisha is right. A new city is to be built, a fortified garrison city, where the army will be based. But a city cannot be built without food, water, labourers, and their families.

"Gather the household," Yusuf says to me. When we are all grouped before him in the courtyard, he looks at our expectant faces. "Aghmat is finished as a city," he says. "It will become smaller and less important once Murakush is built. Henceforth I will need only two slaves to serve me." His finger briefly indicates Aisha and me. "The rest of you will be given to new masters." He looks at the other women's worried faces. "I will choose your new masters myself," he adds. "And I will do so with care."

The women choose to stay in Aghmat. By now it is their city. They cannot believe that its glory will fade as Yusuf suggests. They cannot ally themselves to this invisible city, this *Murakush* that exists in name only, as a thought, an idea. They need walls and streets, they need the stalls of the traders they have frequented, they need one another. Yusuf tells us that this house, and the women, will be given to an older officer in his army, one who wishes to take up a quieter administrative position in charge of Aghmat, while the army continues on its way to greater conquests. "He is a good man," he says. "He will treat you well. He has a wife and family; he is not one to mistreat nor take advantage of his slaves."

He surprises us by setting Maadah free.

"I think perhaps you have served as a slave long enough," he says, looking at her wrinkled face. "I have agreed a paid position for you here, as a cook. I am sure your cooking is better than I have allowed it to be."

She kneels at his feet and blesses him, promises to pray for him and for his glory in coming battles.

"So, I am left with only two slaves," he says, looking at Aisha and me. "I daresay that will be enough. I am a man of few needs."

The two of us stare at each other, wondering what our new life will be like.

The army is sent ahead, Aisha and I are told to join Yusuf in a few days' time. In the meantime, we are charged with clearing the house, giving anything not yet donated to the poor to them now. The officer will bring his own family goods to fill the house, we are told.

"What do we do with your plants?" asks Aisha.

"I don't know," I confess. I hate to leave them behind, but I am a slave, they are not mine. It is not for me to request that they come with us, to a strange and rough new life.

But Aisha is bolder. She goes to Yusuf and tells him, rather than asks him, that I must keep my herbs, that they are important.

"I told him he may well have need of a slave who is also a healer," she says to me, her face beaming when he gives permission to take the plants with us, and gives her coins so that she can hire a man and his beasts to carry them. "He says it is your business to find water for them, the new city will not have a proper irrigation system for a long time," she adds. "He says you may have to work hard to carry enough for them."

We all cry when it is time to leave. Maadah, Dalia, Ranya, Faiza and Nilah stand in the narrow street, watching as Aisha and I climb awkwardly onto two old mules, followed by several more loaded down with crates of plants. Their owner looks surprised at the cargo he is to carry, but he knows we serve the second-in command of the new rulers and so he only nods brusquely, clicks his tongue to start the beasts walking, ignoring our endless waving and last words called out to one another.

When we reach the plain after a jolting ride, I forget to dismount, astonished at the sight before us. It is a city of tents, laid out as though around a central square, with streets marked out between them. There are huge tents, fit for a large family, there are smaller tents. Then there are tents so tiny they seem to be made of nothing more than a blanket and some poles. All around the edge of this cloth city are soldiers, currently engaged in digging, building, carrying, lifting. Water must be brought from nearby, there must be places to relieve ourselves, there must be firmly trodden paths so that traders may visit this sudden city that has appeared almost overnight. No trader worth the name would miss the opportunity to serve such an army.

I had never realised the true scale of Yusuf's troops, there are thousands, tens of thousands of men of every hue and size, both battle-scarred and still fresh, creating this new garrison camp for their leaders to call home.

"Come," Aisha exhorts me. "We must find Yusuf's tent."

I could have described his tent before even seeing it, it is as plain as he is. A dirty brown in colour, ragged at the edges, yet large enough to comfortably hold the three of us. I hesitate a little at the idea that we will sleep so close to him, fearing perhaps that his demeanour so far may not hold true for ever. But I swallow my fears, unpack the plants, which I place around the borders of the tent's outer walls as though creating a tiny garden in circular form, and busy myself, with Aisha's help, in making the interior comfortable. We find a source of water, order large water jars to keep our supply cool, create a little campfire outside where we can cook evening meals. We have brought some basic provisions, but we will need to find traders. We walk around the camp, finding our way in this new home.

There are people here from all over the Maghreb and beyond. I see men and women with hair the colour of the yellow Norsemen, who make me nervous despite myself. I see men with skin so black they all but disappear into their black robes. I even see a woman with hair like fire, who knows full well the value of her scarcity. She has decked herself out with cheap jewellery and robes which leave nothing to be imagined. I turn my face away.

It turns out to be easy enough to find stallholders, even if their stalls are no longer as elaborate or permanent as they might have been in Aghmat. Here, they make do with displaying their goods in woven baskets on the ground, squatting beside them in the open space at the centre of the tents. It does not take long for vendors of food to arrive when there is an army to feed. There is need of grain, legumes, meat, vegetables and fruit. Yusuf has been generous with the money we are given to care for him, considering how basic his own tastes are. We buy what we have need of and carry it back towards his tent.

In the centre of the camp, not far away from Yusuf's, stands a tent like no other. Larger than any family tent, it looks newly made and is black, a deep strong black. It towers over the other tents, a tall man could stand within it and keep his head high, indeed, raise his arms above his head.

"Queen Zaynab's tent," whispers Aisha as we pass it. "She had it built specially."

"Why does she not share Abu Bakr's tent?" I ask.

Aisha shrugs. "He is used to a rough life," she says. "She is used to a palace."

I wonder if we will see her, but the only person standing nearby is an older woman, with dark eyes, who watches us pass, her gaze lingering on the plants around Yusuf's tent.

"Who is she?" I ask.

"Hela," whispers Aisha. "Queen Zaynab's handmaiden."

"Why is she staring at the plants?"

"They say she is a healer," says Aisha. "Like you. Perhaps you could work together."

We have reached Yusuf's tent with our purchases. "I doubt it," I say, looking back at the woman's dark eyes, her unsmiling face even when she meets my eye. "Besides, I am not a healer. I am a slave."

I begin to wish I was indeed able to practice as a healer, for Yusuf certainly does not keep us busy enough. He has no need of two slaves, for he barely eats anything requiring much work. We bake flatbreads and sometimes roast a little meat; he will eat a few dates or nuts and consider it a meal. He drinks water, there is no need to prepare fresh juices. Aisha and I eat well enough, indeed sometimes I think we eat better than our master. We keep the tent clean and fresh; we wash his clothes when he gives them to us, we water the plants and watch the world go by.

But after a little while a change comes over Aisha. She spends time on the outer edges of the city of tents, watching the soldiers practice their war skills. She dresses with more care; she offers to do all the purchases from the market. At last I ask her what is going on and she confesses.

"He is such a man," she breathes. "So kind. So strong. He says he will buy my freedom."

I think that Yusuf will refuse, but to my amazement it turns out that Aisha has caught the eye of one of his bodyguards, a special troop of men, all from the Dark Kingdom, chosen to match one another in height and breadth, in their black skin. Deliberately clad in matching armour, they make a fearsome force around Yusuf when he is in battle. Imari is a man who would dwarf a woman twice Aisha's height. When Yusuf hears of his desire to marry Aisha, he gives Aisha her freedom as a wedding gift. Suddenly she is a free woman with a husband, all within a few days. I gather herbs for her, herbs that will bring her the child that she so dearly wishes for and tell her how to prepare them. I embrace her and watch her as she says her vows, as she is promised to this man forever.

"I am going nowhere, though," she tells me. "Else how will you know all the camp gossip?"

"It is a sin to gossip," I say. "But I will miss you."

"You will see me every day," she promises and she is true enough to her word, not a day passes but she comes to see me, even if only briefly, and I am glad not to have lost her altogether, I have come to think of her as a good friend.

"I am not sure there is a need for another slave," says Yusuf to me after a few days. He has finished his evening prayers and is sharpening his sword, sat on his blankets on the floor of the tent. He still does not wish for a bed. "I have you, you are enough."

I am not sure how to answer. I am uncertain of properness surrounding the two of us sharing this tent, alone together. I only bow my head in agreement with his decision and wait to see what will happen.

What happens is nothing, at first. Things go on as they did before. But slowly a new intimacy grows between us. Where before, Aisha and I would sit together sewing, weaving, cooking or only speaking together, now I am alone and Yusuf begins to talk to me, in the evenings.

"Tell me about the convent you lived in," he says one evening.

I stiffen a little. I cannot imagine what a Muslim would want to know about living in a convent. I mention a few of the prayers, the readings that our Mother Superior would relate during evening mealtimes, but he waves this aside.

"I mean daily life," he says.

And so instead I talk of the sparrows who nested in a crumbling wall in the garden, the herbs I planted and cared for. The cool stillroom where I prepared and stored remedies, the pilgrims who came and went and the stories they told us of the outside world. I tell him about Sister Rosa, the wheezing old nun who taught me everything I know and who died in my arms, all the remedies she had taught me useless at that last moment. How she looked at me and smiled, as I busily ground some new attempt at a cure, how she reached out from her bed and took my hand away from the pestle and told me that it was time to stop, that she was ready to leave. I feel my voice grow choked as I describe this and stop speaking.

"She was right," he says, keeping his eyes steady on me. "There is a time to stay and fight, and there is a time to leave. And it is Allah Himself who must tell us which is which, for we are not always wise enough to know for ourselves."

I nod and wait for my eyes to clear. "My name was Sister Juliana in the convent," I tell him.

"And before that? As a child?"

I hesitate, then speak my Christian name, the name my mother and father gave me. "Isabella."

He nods gravely at what I have shared.

"Tell me more," he says. "Tell me of happy times."

I tell him of spring, the plants leaping back into life, of summer, when the cool chapel walls were a blessing sheltering us from the heat of the day. Of autumn, when we gave thanks for a good harvest and kept our hands busy with preserving. And harsh winters, when we were warmed by the sense of sisterhood, of community.

He begins to tell me things about himself. He tells me of his life as a child, roaming the sweeping desert dunes far to the south. He tells me of joining forces with his cousin Abu Bakr and their realisation of what might be, when they succeeded where others had failed and took Aghmat.

"You do not have a wife?" I ask, wondering at my boldness in asking.

"I do," he says, chuckling as though this is an amusement to him.

"Where is she?" I ask.

"On the other side of the mountains," he says. "She will come here soon enough, but I would want a more comfortable life ready for her. She is very young, and I was afraid to bring her with me whilst there was a chance that I would fall in battle. I would not want anything bad to happen to her."

"Who is she?" I ask, surprised by him describing a young woman.

"A runaway," he says, chuckling again. "A girl from my own people, who lived a strange life as a child, dressed as a boy of all things, trading along the routes with her father and brothers. They tried to make her settle down and learn women's skills, but she would have none of it. She dressed as a man again and followed my army."

I stare at him. "How did you find out?"

He laughs out loud at the memory. "Oh, I saw her at once. I waited to see how long she would follow us, but when she'd been with us a whole day and night, I had to find out why."

"Was she badly treated at home?"

"No, she was treated well enough. But she had a spirit for adventure that could not be contained." He looks away, thinking about her, his eyes warm at the thought. "I liked her spirit; I liked her desire for adventure. And I thought she would be safer with me than if she ran away again alone. I thought she might make a good wife when we founded a new kingdom. I married her then and there."

I try to reconcile this severe leader with a man who finds a runaway girl amusing and takes her as a bride without further thought. "When will she come?" I ask, thinking that it will be strange to have a mistress instead of just a master.

"I will wait a little longer to send for her," he says. "There is much to do here, and I want to be able to give her some attention when she does arrive."

I want to ask what will become of me when she arrives, but I assume that I will be given a little tent close by and will serve both of them. I wonder what she will be like, this woman from his tribal lands, this wayward adventurer who sought out a life of war and travel, of excitement, when I tried so hard to avoid such things, safe in my convent. And yet somehow, we will have arrived in the same place, at the same time, finding ourselves living in a city of cloth that will one day turn into a city of towering rooftops, if Yusuf and Abu Bakr have their way.

City of Cloth

The flowers appear on the earth...

Song of Solomon 2:12

*T*HE CAMP CONTINUES TO GROW, as more soldiers join the army and their families, if they have them, follow them. More and more tents continue to be erected, on the outskirts of the tents already here. This strange cloth city grows day by day.

"I think you must be bored," says Yusuf to me one night.

"Why do you say that?" I ask.

"Your garden of plants is growing," he says. "It is almost a field."

"Does it bother you?" I ask.

"Not at all, why should it?" he asks. "They are useful, both for our meals," he gestures at the food I have laid out, rich with herbs and seasonings, "and for healing, in battle. One never knows when one may need such skills."

"Do you wish me to move them?"

"I think perhaps you need a bigger space," he says, still eating.

"We would not use all the herbs I could grow in a larger space," I say.

"You may sell them, if you wish," he says. "This is still a new city, there is need for fresh grown food."

"Sell them?"

He shrugs. "You may keep the money," he says. "Use it as you wish," he adds.

I stare at him, but he is drinking a cup of water, and then he leaves me, muttering something about needing to speak with Abu Bakr.

I take him at his word. I find a small piece of land on the outskirts of the camp and claim it for my own, murmuring Yusuf's name to the only person who queries what I am doing. It has an immediate effect. I move many of my plants to the space and let them grow more vigorously, especially the mint, which grows wild and rampant, popping up here and there where least expected in vibrant clumps. Even though I must haul water to keep the plants green, I grow so fond of my little garden that sometimes I forget the passing of time and have to run back to Yusuf's tent to prepare a meal. The plants grow well and soon I can make up little bunches of parsley, coriander, sage, cumin, fennel tops and other herbs and vegetables. Yusuf was right, the people of our cloth city long for freshness. The traders come often but they bring food that can be stored, not the bright green tendrils that bring flavour and freshness to a dish. The women reach out eagerly for what I can give them, and my bundles of herbs are used up every day well before the midday sun strikes. With the first coins I begin to accumulate, I buy a hoe, so that I can work the ground more easily. The rest of the money, I put into a little stitched bag, kept under my blanket. I do not know what it is for, yet, whether I might one day be able to buy my freedom, or whether that will never be allowed. Aisha comes to watch me at work sometimes, helps me to thin out seedlings. One day she tells me, her smile lighting up her face, that she is with child. I embrace her, truly happy for my friend.

Occasionally I see a beggar woman making her way around the camp, her feet bare, her long dark hair dirty and lank. Despite her appearance, I think she is still young, perhaps barely twenty. Sometimes she is given a little work to do by a trader or one of the women, perhaps carrying water or washing clothes and I see that she does it well, she is a hard worker but somehow has found herself here, lost and alone, with no one to protect her. I notice she has no shoes and give her a coin so that she can buy simple shoes to protect her feet from the rough ground.

"May God bless you," she says.

Her accent is odd. "What is your name?" I ask.

"Rebecca," she says.

"Are you a Christian?" I ask.

She shakes her head.

"A Jew?" I ask, a little disappointed.

"I was born and raised Jewish, in Al-Andalus," she says, looking away. "But I fell in love with a Muslim when I was very young, and my family disowned me when we married. I was his second wife and his first wife hated me. When my husband died, she threw me out of the house and my family would not take me back, they said I was dead to them." She swallows. "I offered myself as a slave, for I had no way to make a living. Then my master sold me to a man in the Maghreb and I ended up here. He died, so I suppose I am free, but still, I have no way to make a living. The camp allows me to scrape by, there is always someone who needs willing hands."

I nod. Once I might have turned away, knowing her for a Jewess, but she has been turned away from often enough already in her young life. There can be no harm in showing her a little charity, I decide. I give her the odd bunch of herbs or greens and she always thanks and blesses me. The law states a Jew cannot live in the city, they may trade here but must sleep beyond the city walls, so those Jews who do trade here often live at a little distance from Murakush and travel here each day to work. Rebecca, I find out, sleeps just beyond the encampment.

The tent flaps are yanked aside so hard that I hear one of them rip at the top. I look up in consternation, as Yusuf storms into the tent. He does not sit down in his usual place, only stands, fuming, in the middle of the tent. I had been seated, sewing. Now I am uncertain whether to stand or not, he looks so angry that I am a little afraid to come any closer to him. Staying low to the ground seems safer.

"Is all well?" I venture, finally.

"No," he snaps.

He does not offer anything else and I do not enquire further. I have never seen him so angry, he has never been so abrupt with me. I continue my work, keeping a cautious eye on him, my stitches growing erratic with my lack of attention. Some time goes by before I dare to look up at him directly again. He's still standing, staring at the tent walls, what I can see of his face somewhat flushed, his brows lowered.

"Tea," he orders, in a manner he has never spoken to me before.

I stand, see to the fire outside, bring water to the boil and make tea. When I return, a cup in my hands, he is now seated, arms wrapped around his knees, his brows lowered. He takes the tea without a word of thanks and I retreat to my place and my sewing.

"It is madness!" he suddenly exclaims, startling me a little, for I had expected him to remain quiet.

"What is?" I venture carefully.

"Abu Bakr has decided to quell the rebels in the south himself, instead of sending one of the generals. It is absurd and unnecessary!"

I nod, not daring to speak. Then I think that he requires more comfort than this. "It does seem strange," I say. "Surely there is no need for him to go himself?"

"Exactly! It is madness!"

He goes back to brooding for a while and I continue sewing, unpicking most of the stitches I have made since he entered the tent and starting again. Although Yusuf is right, in that it seems odd that Abu Bakr himself should need to go to the south to quell what is, by all accounts, a fairly minor rebellion, I cannot help but wonder why Yusuf is so angry about it. Perhaps he wished to go himself, though I have never heard him talk about any interest in going south. His focus always seems to be on conquering more of the Maghreb rather than any southern kingdoms. "Did you wish to go yourself?" I ask, finally.

"Of course not! Neither of us should go. An officer can go, a minor general. There is no need to take such a step."

"And he will not listen to reason?" I ask.

"Oh, he has lost his mind," spits Yusuf. "There is no reasoning with him."

I am surprised at both his insulting tone and words. Yusuf is usually very loyal to Abu Bakr; he speaks of him only in the highest tones of praise and respect. For some reason, this choice by Abu Bakr has riled him.

"And who is to manage the army while he is gone?" I ask finally, wondering if perhaps Abu Bakr has gone so far as to overlook Yusuf and give this role to a more minor general, which would certainly explain Yusuf's current behaviour, although it seems a very unlikely proposition: Yusuf is known to all as Abu Bakr's right-hand man, he would be the only possible choice of leader in Abu Bakr's absence.

"I am, of course," says Yusuf. There is a pause. "With the she-bitch at my side," he adds in a half mutter.

"What?" I think I have misheard him, it is not like Yusuf to speak disrespectfully of a woman and besides I have no idea who he is talking about.

"Abu Bakr, in his infinite wisdom, has decided to divorce Zaynab."

I stare at him.

"And he wishes me to marry her."

It takes me a while to find my voice. "But – but you have a wife," I manage at last.

He shrugs. "He wishes me to take another. Zaynab. Of all people."

"Why?"

"He says Zaynab is not fit for a rough life in tents in the middle of the desert."

"But she has been living in a tent all this time," I object weakly. "And she does not complain of it, does she?"

"How would I know what she complains of? She is not my wife. Yet," he adds grimly.

"But your first wife…"

He gestures impatiently. "That is not the issue. I may take more than one wife. And Kella will just have to accept it when she arrives. That is not the point. I would never have chosen Zaynab. Never. She is untrustworthy."

"I thought she pleased Abu Bakr," I say. "I heard she was allowed to sit in Council, that she had knowledge of the Maghreb, of the politics between the tribes."

"Abu Bakr killed her husband," snarls Yusuf. "Who is not to say she is biding her time, tricking us, waiting for Abu Bakr to trust her and then follow her lead into a trap?"

I think of her face, riding alongside her husband the amir, the sadness in it, the unhappiness. "Did she love Luqut?" I ask.

"How should I know? All I know is, our army defeated his, she was taken as a prisoner of war, and then managed to worm her way into marrying Abu Bakr, thus becoming our queen. I don't trust her. She is like a cat, landing on her feet after a fall."

I realise something about myself, something which I can only regard as a sin. That I am pleased that Yusuf does not wish to marry Zaynab, when whether he marries or not should be of no regard to me. I am finding myself pleased that he does not desire her, that he does not love her. I am pleased that he is reluctant to take her as a wife, that he has so far not even summoned his first wife. I know that this is a sin on my part, that there is something in me that wishes Yusuf to remain, to all intents and purposes, unwed. That for now, for these past months, I have been the only woman in his life, in his tent, by his bed. I have enjoyed the intimacy of our evening conversations. I bow my head to my sewing, resolving to no longer take part in this conversation, to pray on my sins and ask for God's forgiveness later, when Yusuf is gone. We sit in silence for some time before he speaks again.

"And he has the audacity to tell me that we will be an excellent team together, she and I! He said something ridiculous about her reading the maps and me leading the men, that together we would be unstoppable. I have no desire to be allied to that woman."

"You could refuse," I say and immediately bite my tongue. Why am I trying to encourage Yusuf not to marry Zaynab? There is no reason why he should not marry her, if his leader so wishes it and believes that together they would make a good match. Abu Bakr, after all, has been married to Zaynab for these past months and must know her better than any of us. If he admires her and believes her a suitable match for Yusuf, then who am I to speak for or against her? It should be no concern of mine, and yet the words keep coming out of my mouth. "You could say that you do not wish to marry her, that she should marry someone else."

"My leader commands it," he says, but I can still hear the anger in his voice at the path he is being set on.

He leaves the tent then, and I do not see him for the rest of the day. As soon as he leaves, I kneel and spend many hours in prayer, asking forgiveness for the feelings springing up in me, the absurd jealousy over Zaynab. I ask for greater guidance, to be set on a righteous path, to be reminded daily of my vows.

He returns later on but is still restless during the evening meal, which he eats angrily, stuffing the food into his face, with no remark on whether it is good or not, nor any conversation. I realise that I have grown used to our evenings together, talking about this and that, about nothing in particular, perhaps the day's events. Now we sit in tense silence and I am not sure if there is any topic I can broach that will put him in a better mood.

"Is the army's training going well?" I ask at last. Usually, talk of his men and their training puts him in a good mood, he will talk for hours about this or that training strategy, about which men seem to be proving themselves as possible future leaders, the most reliable warriors. Now he only grunts.

I return to silence. If this, his favourite topic, has only brought out of him a grunt, then I am wasting my time trying to think of any other conversation.

After dinner, he sits hunched, his face stuck in a scowl. I tidy the tent, clean away the food, and still he sits there.

"Perhaps a walk in the night air will refresh you after your difficult day," I say at last. It is all I can do not to tell him to stop being so sulky, as though he were a small child. At any rate, he nods, then gets up and leaves. I hope that he will come back in a better mood.

He is gone a long time. I lie down to sleep, but sleep will not come. I lie first on one side and then the other, neither of which feels comfortable. I try to think of calming things, such as listing the names of herbs, or the uses for one root or another. But this does not work. At last I give up, and lie awake, wondering where Yusuf is, for he has been gone a long time.

Sometime very late, he returns. And instead of taking to his bed, he kneels and prays. I have never seen him do this before, so late at night. I wonder whether I have always been asleep when he has prayed at this time, but I doubt it. There is something still preying on his mind.

Both of us sleep poorly that night. I hear him toss and turn even as I lie sleepless till the dawn. The notion of a marriage to Zaynab seems to have deeply affected him. Something in me, a voice I do not wish to answer, nor hear, asks whether in fact, despite his protestations, he already has feelings for her.

"Marry Yusuf? That would be her fourth marriage!" exclaims Aisha, as we make our way round the market together. "First she was a concubine, they say she married for love. Then after her vision, Luqut took her as his queen. Then Abu Bakr after she was their prisoner of war and now, he intends to turn her over to Yusuf? I have never heard of a woman being married so many times."

"Is she pleased, do you think?" I ask. The thought of Zaynab desiring Yusuf still unsettles me, despite my prayers.

"Who knows? I would have thought she would be grateful of a younger husband than Abu Bakr, at any rate," says Aisha. "He is old enough to be her grandfather. Perhaps they will make a good team," she adds, turning her attention to the vegetables she is purchasing, prodding them to see if they are fresh. "Yusuf will be the leader of our army while Abu Bakr is away, and she is a great beauty, whatever her character is like. Perhaps she will bear some children."

The thought of children only brings to mind what must be done to create them, and I shy away from the thought, hastily smelling one fruit after another, touching more items than I need to, confused and failing to select what I need to buy. "Surely not," I say. "She has been married three times and borne none. She must be barren." The thought gives me comfort and I chastise myself for it. My list of penances is growing longer by the moment.

"Perhaps she has never been married to the right man," says Aisha with a broad wink.

"Don't be vulgar," I say.

But it seems that Zaynab does indeed intend for Yusuf to desire her, not merely marry her to please his leader.

"Have you seen what she is doing?" asks Aisha, standing in the doorway of the tent.

I look up at her, framed in the light, her belly broadening before her. "Who?"

"Zaynab."

"What about her?"

"Have you *seen* it?"

"Seen what?"

"You have to see it for yourself," says Aisha, half giggling. "Come with me," she adds, holding out her hand.

"I am busy," I say.

"Not busy enough to miss seeing this," says Aisha firmly.

She will not accept my refusal. I get up and follow her, expecting some foolishness, uncomfortable with seeking out Zaynab.

Outside of Zaynab's vast black tent there is a little crowd gathered, mostly made up of children, two known prostitutes and a couple of young men, who seem to be blushing furiously.

"Look!" hisses Aisha, as we approach.

There is a carpenter at work, on a wooden bed. The bed is very large, and the man is currently carving its headboard. I frown at what I'm seeing, then take a step backwards. Beside me, Aisha giggles.

The bed is obscene. The man is carving a series of images, of couples consorting. There is no detail left to the imagination. The bodies writhe together as though alive, the most intimate parts of male and female bodies rising out of the wood as though desiring to be touched. I turn my face away, and one of the prostitutes laughs.

"I told you!" says Aisha, still giggling.

I walk away, my feet too fast for my head, which is still whirling. I nearly trip twice. "What is she thinking, making something like that?"

"Oh, I think she is thinking that if she is to marry him, she must make Yusuf a little more interested in her," says Aisha.

"He has been commanded to marry her," I say, my voice sharp. "She does not need to woo him, as though she were a harlot. It has been arranged; it is a marriage of convenience."

"It may be convenient for Abu Bakr," says Aisha. "But I think our queen wants there to be more than just convenience in her marriage bed."

I look down at her and she gives me a broad wink. I look away and continue walking, aware that Aisha can barely keep up with my pace, and not caring. I am tired of her prattling.

"She has changed the way she dresses, too," comments Aisha, panting a little behind me.

"What are you talking about?"

"Oh, have you not seen her since the marriage was announced?"

"No."

"She has got rid of all her jewellery. And all her bright silks. And her face is no longer painted. Not that that makes much difference," Aisha adds generously. "I've never seen a woman so beautiful, even without paint."

I think of how Zaynab usually dresses, the vibrant silks draped becomingly about her, the heavy strings of gems, the golden headdresses. Her painted lips, her dark-ringed eyes. "What is she wearing, then?" I ask, slowing down despite myself.

"Black," says Aisha.

I stop and turn to look at her. "Black?"

Aisha nods, catching her breath. "Black all over. Clothes, shoes. No jewellery. Of course," she adds, smirking slightly, "it's still the best silk and leather money can buy. She is hardly dressed in rags. But I'd say she had an eye to pleasing Yusuf, he's the one that doesn't like ostentation, Abu Bakr never complained about how she was dressed."

Again, something in me turns over at the thought of Zaynab deliberately wooing Yusuf, shaping herself to his desires, seeking to please him. "You always did like to gossip," I say. "What do we care how she dresses?"

Aisha put her head on one side, regarding me without answering.

"Well?"

"He is your master," she reminds me. "When he marries her, she will be your mistress. I thought you would like to know how she is treating this marriage."

I give an exaggerated shrug. "I am a slave," I say, my tone bitter. "I have no say in who my master marries, nor who my mistress is. I certainly have no views on whether their marriage will be a good one or not. It has been commanded, so it will be."

Aisha nods, but it is as though she is nodding herself, rather than at my words, as though she has confirmed something she thought about me.

"What?" I snap at her.

She smiles more broadly. "Perhaps Yusuf might let you serve elsewhere, when he marries her," she says. "If you do not wish to serve her."

"I doubt I will be given the choice."

"There are always choices," says Aisha. "It is just that we do not always know what we wish for."

"I do not know what you are talking about," I say. "And now I must tend the plants."

"Your plants are always a good refuge," says Aisha. "I will bid you farewell then, until we next speak."

"Farewell," I say, already turning my shoulders to her. I do not know why I spend so much time with her, she is nothing but a busybody.

The Cup of Love

Jealousy... the coals thereof are coals of fire,
which hath a most vehement flame.

Song of Solomon 8:6

I AM PREPARING YUSUF'S FOOD WHEN the tent darkens. I look up and see Hela, Zaynab's handmaid, standing in the doorway, blocking the light.

"My mistress sends a drink for your master, to be taken with his evening meal," she says. Her voice is deep for a woman.

"What drink?" I ask, standing to face her.

"This," she says, holding out a wooden cup. It is worn, perhaps it used to be red once but much of the colour has been rubbed away with time.

I don't reach out for it. "He only drinks water. What is it?" I repeat.

Her mouth twists a little, as though she is suppressing a smile. "Ah yes," she says. "You are trained in herbs. Perhaps you can tell what it is for yourself."

I reach out and take the cup. For a brief moment I hear what I think is a sigh, feel a heat within me, rising upwards. I would let go of the cup, but Hela has already released it, it would fall and break if I did so. She is watching me closely. I smell the contents, then set the cup against my lips.

"Careful," she says.

I allow the liquid only to touch my tongue.

Hela watches me. "Well?" she asks.

I frown. "Houseleek? Cow parsnip? Lady's Mantle?"

Hela smiles. "And more."

I hold the cup back out to her. "These inflame lust," I say.

"Indeed," she says.

"My master has no need of this remedy," I say.

Her eyebrows raise up. "Is that so? Are you speaking from experience?"

I can feel heat rush to my cheeks. "I have taken holy vows of chastity," I say.

She nods. "So I understand. Then you will hardly object if my lady wishes your lord to drink this before their marriage. It can be no concern of yours, what goes on between them."

"Take it away," I say.

She shakes her head. "Give it to him each day when I bring it," she says. "I will know whether he has drunk it or not. If you do not give it to him, I will. And I will make it stronger. Tell him it is from Zaynab and he will drink it."

I want to refuse, but I am afraid of both Hela and Zaynab. Of what they could do to me, if they wished. I am a slave, they could get rid of me in an instant, on no pretext at all. I think that perhaps if I give this lust-inducing drink to Yusuf myself I could also lessen its powers. "Very well," I say, reluctantly.

Hela smiles a slow smile that makes my skin cold. "Thank you," she says. "I will bring it each day until the wedding takes place, less than three months from now. You will return the cup to me each night." She pauses, as though waiting for me to say something else, but I stay silent. "Do not interfere with what you do not understand," she adds, her face grave.

"I know herbs as well as you," I say boldly.

"You are a gifted healer," she says. "I know this. But there are other things you do not understand."

"Such as?" I challenge.

"Why I serve Zaynab. Why Zaynab desires your master. What the…" she pauses, looking at the cup I am holding, then swallows, as though suddenly afraid. "…What the drink may do if you interfere with it," she finishes.

"I have agreed to what you want me to do," I say. "You may go."

She does so without speaking further and I am left holding the cup at arm's length. Yusuf will be back soon and in an effort to diminish the power of what Hela has made I add plantain, which can cool a man's lust, to a syrup of pomegranates and dates I already possess. I wonder, as I do so, why Zaynab wishes to increase Yusuf's lust. It can only be because she does not believe he actually desires her. I find some comfort in this. One cannot simply increase a man's lust for a woman he does not already desire, love philtres are only nonsense, as Zaynab will no doubt discover for herself.

I am about to pour away half of the cup's contents and add my own mixture to refill it, when I hear footsteps and, fearing Yusuf's approach, I hold the cup to my lips and drink half of its contents myself, then hastily stir in the syrup. The drink will be warm rather than cool, but I cannot help that.

I give Yusuf the cup. I tell him it is from Zaynab and hope he will refuse it but instead he takes it without question and I watch him drain it, although he makes a face at the excessive sweetness and follows it with water while I hurry to serve his evening meal.

Night comes and I cannot sleep. I try to say my prayers, to still my mind and yet all that comes to mind are my over-keen senses. I can hear Yusuf turn first one way and then the other in his bed, can hear his breath as it rises and falls, smell the scent of him in these close quarters. Images run through my mind, of Yusuf when he laughs, of how his eyes, which seem so dark on first sight, hold within them tiny glints of golden brown next to darker tones, which are only noticed in the sunlight. How his eyes crease at the corners when he is amused, how his mouth, which I have never seen, hidden as it always is under a veil, must curve when he smiles. The glimpses I have had of an ankle, a calf, of his forearms, which are sinewy with muscles, when he reaches out to me to take food or drink. My mind will not let go of these images; it will not let me sleep. In my mouth I can taste the drink that was in the cup and I wonder, if Yusuf's lips were set against mine, if our mouths would taste the same. I turn away in my bed, clasp my hands together even as I lie under the blankets and pray for God's help in setting such sinful thoughts aside. But God is not listening. I wonder whether He has stopped listening to me forever or whether, if I were to somehow atone, if He would make His voice heard again, find a way to set my feet back on a righteous path.

I am trying so hard to pray that I am startled when I hear Yusuf rise from his bed in the darkness. I think that he may be going outside to relieve himself but instead there is a long silent pause. I am about to turn over and see what he is doing when I hear him move again and then feel his hand on my hair. I freeze. Yusuf has never touched me, never allowed more than a finger to brush mine by accident if I pass him a dish of food. Now his hand is on my hair and he is stroking my cheek. My heart is beating so hard I think he must hear it. And then, just when I think that I cannot pretend to be asleep, I hear him curse under his breath and his touch is gone from me. I hear the tent flaps draw apart and when I roll over, he is gone into the night.

In the morning, when there is a cool breeze and Yusuf has left the tent, I try to pray. I kneel, I fold my hands together. I try to pray, and nothing comes. Nothing that would be acceptable to God. All that comes, unbidden, are images in my mind and sensations across my body. I close my eyes so tightly I see stars; I clasp my hands so fervently my knuckles turn white. And yet all I feel is Yusuf's touch on my hair and cheek, and all I see are his eyes. When I take deep breaths, trying to still my beating heart, all I smell is his scent, too well-known to me. I stay on my knees as the sun rises and sets, and still I cannot pray. Still I feel his hand upon me, I smell his scent. And then I smell something else. Something that reminds me of myself, the smell of herbs and roots that lingers around a healer.

"You must not drink from the cup."

I nearly scream. I open my eyes and stumble backwards, ending up on my behind, looking up at Hela, who is standing in my room, without my having heard her enter. She regards me with her large dark eyes, her emotionless face. I clamber awkwardly to my feet, so that I may face her. "What are you doing here?"

"You must not drink from the cup. It is not intended for you."

"I know that you are trying to drug my master," I say, trying to regain my dignity.

"Do not interfere. The drink is a matter between my mistress and your master."

"How can it be a matter between my master and your mistress, if my master does not know what he is being asked to drink?"

"He desires her. The drink will only enhance what is there already. As you already know."

"I know only that you have made a love potion for my master, that you intend to make him drink it every day, without his knowing."

"And I know that you drank from it," she says.

"How would you know that?"

"I know."

"How?"

She does not answer. Instead, she reaches out her hand and touches mine, only for a moment, her fingers cool. She nods, as though this has told her something, as though I have spoken to her.

"What?" I ask.

"You burn for him," she says. She speaks as though what she has said is of no consequence, as though it were simply a statement of fact.

"I have taken a vow of chastity," I say. But even as I speak, I can feel the heat in my cheeks.

"Then stop drinking from the cup," she says. "You are only making your own life harder; your vows will be impossible to keep if you continue to drink from it."

"You think you are so gifted with herbs?"

She shakes her head. "I am warning you," she says. "Take heed of what I say."

"Or what?" I ask, trying to sound bold. "What will you do to me?"

Her eyebrows go up. "I? I will do nothing. You are doing it to yourself."

"Doing what?"

"Building up lust within yourself for a man who is not yours, for a man whose company you have forsworn. You say you have taken vows of chastity. The cup will make you break them, if you continue to drink from it."

"Why do you keep saying 'the cup' will make me lust for him?" I ask. "It is what you have put in the cup that might lead me astray."

"If you say so," she says. There is a heaviness to her voice, a weariness. "I am only warning you not to drink from it. Let Yusuf desire Zaynab. They can be no harm in it. They are betrothed, they are to be married, they may as well desire one another. Why would you seek otherwise?"

She has asked the question I cannot answer, of course. There is no reason why I should drink from the cup, no reason I should not let Yusuf drink from it, since I know full well what it contains and what its intended purpose is.

I look away. "I do not wish my master to be drugged," I say.

"It only enhances what is already there," she says. "You might want to think on that."

"Meaning what?"

"Meaning that you feel what you feel for your master already," she says. "The cup did not put that feeling there. It has only forced you to acknowledge that it exists. Stop drinking from it. Go back to your prayers. Keep your distance from Yusuf. In time, the feelings will fade. If you let them."

"Leave me," I say.

"Do not touch the cup again," she says.

"Is that a threat?" I ask.

"It is a warning," she says. She has already turned away from me, is already out of the door before I can think how to reply.

I stand, uncertain for a moment, then kneel again, my hands tight together, my eyes closed. I mumble a prayer by rote, without meaning, without any feeling attached to it, knowing as I do so that it is meaningless to pray like this.

That night the cup is brought for Yusuf again, this time by a servant. I do not touch it, I turn my face away and pretend not to have seen it. I tell myself that this is my choice, that I have not been influenced by Hela. Which I know is a lie. I keep away from Yusuf, I try to be busy elsewhere when he is nearby, I avoid our conversations in the evenings, claiming to be busy, to be tired. I hear him toss and turn at night as I lie awake, forcing myself to stay where I am rather than reach out to him. I may have stopped drinking from the cup, but I have to admit to myself, to no-one else, that Hela was right in what she said. The cup only enhances what was already there.

"My marriage will take place soon," Yusuf says suddenly one evening.

I try not to look at him, continue stirring the stew I am making. I want to tell him that 'soon' is precisely ten days away, that I know the number of days till the day of his marriage at all times, that if a stranger were to stop me in the street and ask me, I could tell him not just the days but the very hours until the ceremony that will bind Yusuf and Zaynab together. I am like a candle, burning down to the appointed time, knowing darkness is coming soon. I only nod, staying silent.

"You already know I am a man of simple needs," he says. He sounds awkward, his words circuitous coming from a man who usually speaks his mind plainly and without decoration.

I look up at him briefly, nod to show I am listening.

"Some small buildings have already been built," he says. "Soon there will be many more." He pauses, as though I should comment, as though he has made himself clear already.

I say nothing.

"I have arranged for you to have a small house," he says, looking down at his sword, which he is unnecessarily polishing. "It is nothing elaborate, only a room in a little courtyard, but you will be safe there and can live as you wish."

I stare at him. "Live as I wish?"

He shrugs. "Tend your plants, pray, whatever makes you happy." He swallows, turns the sword over in his lap, begins polishing the other side. "I would like you to be happy."

I want to reach out. I want to touch his face, pull aside his veil so that I may see what is hidden from me. I want to thank him and at the same time, I want to refuse. He is pushing me away; he is giving me a home so that he can go to Zaynab unimpeded. It is a hugely generous gesture towards a slave, and yet it fills me with anguish. I do not want to serve Zaynab, but I cannot bear to be separated from Yusuf. I say nothing, I do not know what to say, and what I do want to say is impossible.

"I have told Imari where it is, Aisha can take you there tomorrow. If you need help to move your plants, Imari can arrange it."

I should say something. I should express gratitude. Instead, I spoon out the stew into a bowl and pass it to him, in silence.

Aisha does not comment. For once, she is silent. She stands in the doorway of the tent and nods to me. Behind her are two men with mules, ready to load up my plants and follow behind us. I stand and follow her, walking through the city of tents, towards one of the small areas where building has already begun. She pushes open a little gate in a high wall, showing me into a tiny courtyard, off of which are two rooms. One is a tiny kitchen, in which I can just about turn around. The other is a larger plain room, without any hint of decoration.

Aisha watches the men unloading the plants, scattering them haphazardly around the courtyard space. "Useless," she comments. "You will have to rearrange them all when they've gone."

I nod.

"Well at least I can visit you here and not in Zaynab's tent," she says. "I wasn't looking forward to that."

I nod.

"Will you be all right?" she asks.

"Yes," I say. "Yusuf has been very generous."

"But is it what you wanted?" she asks. She does not meet my eye, she looks away, as though to allow me the freedom to answer without having to meet her gaze.

"I am a nun and a slave," I say. "I am sworn to obedience twice over. My own desires are not important."

"It depends how strong they are," says Aisha, still looking away. "The stronger they are, the harder it is to contain them."

She leaves me then, and I spend the rest of the day rearranging the plants to my satisfaction. The sun is almost setting when I look up to see Yusuf standing in the gateway.

"I am sorry," I say, springing to my feet. "I will prepare dinner at once."

He looks amused. "I have not come to chastise you," he says. "I came to see if all was well here." He walks around the courtyard, sticks his head into the tiny kitchen and then the room next door to it. "Bare enough for you?" he asks, teasing.

"I am more grateful than I can say," I say. I try to keep my voice and words formal, but I am aware that my eyes are welling up with tears. "But I am sorry to no longer serve you."

"You will see me again," he says. "I am still your master; you cannot rid yourself of me that easily. You have served me well and you may be of use to me in the future. Having a healer to hand is no bad thing, when you must go into battle."

My heart lurches at the thought of him in battle. "I am sure Zaynab's healer is very accomplished," I say.

"I'm sure she is," he says. "But sometimes one would rather have one's own healer." He pauses. "I hope you will be happy here," he says.

"I am so grateful," I repeat. "I am sure I will be happy here. But..."

"But what?" he asks.

"I will miss our conversations," I say, stumbling over the words, feeling myself flush.

He looks around the tiny courtyard, gestures to the plants and a rough block of building stone left discarded. "I may have need of a quiet place, sometimes, where I can sit peacefully and talk to someone about small matters," he says. "It is tiring to speak only of great matters."

"I will be here," I say. I look away, I cannot meet his gaze, but the words still come. "I will be here whenever you wish to come."

He takes a step closer to me, pauses as though uncertain of his own movements, then lifts one hand and lightly strokes my cheek, his fingers brushing over my scars. Then, suddenly, he turns and in a moment is gone, the gate closing behind him with a shudder.

I let out the breath I did not know I was holding.

Preparations have been going on in the camp for many days, but today they reached their zenith. From before dawn, great piles of wood were assembled, ready for fires later. Women rose earlier than usual to knead bread and have it at the bakeries to be cooked in time. Yesterday the blood of hundreds of animals spilled across the earth, today they will be roasted, served on great platters to the whole of the camp.

Today is Yusuf's wedding. Today, he will marry Zaynab.

I wake and listen to the call to prayer. I wonder whether I could simply stay here all day, and see nothing of the ceremony, nothing of the feasting that will go on later. But Aisha is already at my door.

"Are you coming?" she asks and there is nothing I can say that would be acceptable. I only nod and follow her.

In the absence of a mosque, the ceremony is held in the open air, in the central space amongst this city of tents and half made buildings. Zaynab is dressed as plainly as though she were a slave, her robes all in black, her shoes black, her long black hair falling down over her shoulders. She is bereft of jewellery, although there is a tiny glint of something around her neck, half hidden by her robes, perhaps a very small necklace, although I cannot see it well. A contract has been drawn up, which is signed after Yusuf, before the crowd, asks for Zaynab's hand in marriage, having already presented many gifts to her. Both of them declare their acceptance three times. From where I am standing, I can barely hear their voices, only see how their eyes never leave one another, how Yusuf's hand trembles as he offers Zaynab a date to eat and receives one from her, the sharing of sweetness a wish for their marriage. They stand together while prayers are read over the pair of them, from the first surah of the Qu'ran.

"In the name of Allah, Most Gracious, Most Merciful. Praise be to Allah The Cherisher and Sustainer of the Worlds; Most Gracious, Most Merciful; Master of the Day of Judgement. Thee do we worship and Thine aid we seek. Show us the straight way, The way of those on whom Thou has bestowed Thy Grace, those whose portion is not wrath, and who go not astray."

This first prayer, which can be heard above the crowd, since the officiant has a carrying voice and is determined to be heard, is followed by many and varied blessings over the couple, everything from wishes for them to bear children to having a peaceful household. I tug at Aisha, wishing to leave. After all, the marriage is done now, these are only niceties, and I cannot find it in my heart to echo these blessings.

"Oh Allah," intones the officiant, "Bless this couple with faith, love and happiness in this world and the Next. Oh Allah, You are the Loving and the Merciful. Put love and mercy in the hearts of this couple for each other. Our Creator, strengthen the hearts of the bride and groom with faith, and let them increase in their love and commitment to You through their bond. Oh Lord of the Universe, all power is with You. Let this couple's marriage become a beautiful example to other couples. My God, protect this couple from the misguidance and planning of Shaytan. Help them resist his call to break their bond. Oh Allah, bless this couple with children who will be a source of happiness and joy to them and the world."

I slip my hand from Aisha's grasp and turn and walk away, unable to listen any longer. It is difficult to make my way through the crowd and the words of blessing continue to reach me, even as I struggle to leave the ceremony behind me and return to the barren peacefulness of my own empty room.

"Oh Allah, unite the couple and their families in faith and love. Oh Lord, You are the Just. Let this couple live their lives being fair and just to each other. Oh Forgiver, bless this couple with the strength to forgive each other's shortcomings. Oh Allah, give them the loving relationship which Muhammad and Aisha had. May Allah be pleased with them."

By the time I have left the crowd, I am almost running, making my way through the little mazes between the tents and outwards to where the first buildings lie, past stone and mud, wooden planks and half-erected scaffolding. I push open the gate to my own home, ignore my plants and make my way into the dark recess of the kitchen, the only space I can bear right now.

I kneel in the gloom and ask God to relieve me of the thoughts I am having, to take away the pain I should not even acknowledge, nor be feeling. The commander of our army is marrying a queen. It should not, must not, be of any matter to me. And yet it is.

Here in the darkness, here all alone, I acknowledge to myself and to God that I love Yusuf, that I desire him as a man, that I am jealous of Zaynab. That, watching them just now, all I wished for was to stand in Zaynab's place. To take Yusuf's hands in mine, to place the sweet date in his mouth, to know that tonight, when the ceremonies, the celebrations and the feasting are all complete, Yusuf will make his way, not to the great black tent and Zaynab's lustful bed but to my empty room, in this quiet part of the city, and take me in his arms.

Aisha seeks me out later, finding me amidst my plants, tending to them one by one in an effort to still my mind.

"Yusuf's first wife arrived, but too late to stop the ceremony, even if she could have done."

I stare up at her. "What?"

"His wife arrived!"

"Kella?"

"How do you know her name?"

"He mentioned her," I say, thinking of how Yusuf described an adventurous young girl, seeking freedom, willing to risk joining an army, dressed as a man.

"Well she is here now, and she is miserable."

I think of my own feelings, watching Yusuf take Zaynab's hands in his, and feel nothing but a common sorrow with this unknown woman. "She did not arrive in time for the ceremony."

"No," says Aisha, squatting down and beginning to deadhead a chamomile plant. "She arrived only a little time ago, and was taken straight to Zaynab, no doubt against her wishes."

"What does she look like?" I ask.

"Miserable," repeats Aisha. "Young. Much younger than Zaynab. But not as beautiful."

I nod, continue watering a few of the drier plants.

"You don't look so happy yourself," says Aisha.

I say nothing. I keep my head down, but unbidden tears roll down my cheeks, attempting to water the plants.

"I know you care for him," says Aisha softly.

"I have no right to care for him," I say.

"We none of us choose who to care for," says Aisha.

"I have taken vows," I say.

"Vows are hard to keep," says Aisha.

"My temptation has been taken from me," I say.

"Has it?" she asks. "Temptation does not need to stand by our side to make itself felt."

"Then the path before me will be hard," I say.

The House of Secrets

Turn away thine eyes from me...

Song of Solomon 6:5

Lᴛʜᴏᴜɢʜ I ᴛʀʏ ᴛᴏ ᴋᴇᴇᴘ away from the main market square, eventually I see Yusuf's first wife for myself. Aisha was right, she is very young, younger than myself and Zaynab. She ought to outshine Zaynab, but she does not. When I see her, her skin looks very pale and she seems either ill or very tired. Or perhaps she is just unhappy, I think. Perhaps the sight of Yusuf with another woman, this unexpected queen holding the position Kella might have thought to take, is too much for her. She dresses in the bright colours that come from her tribe in the desert, but instead of illuminating her face, they only drain away its colour. She looks small and pale, tired and meek. I struggle to recognise the woman Yusuf described: an adventurer, someone bold enough to seek a life of freedom and to take it even when the odds were against her. All I see is defeat, in the slump of her shoulders, in her dull skin, in her eyes which do not look up and about but down at her feet. I tell myself that this is not my business, that how Yusuf chooses to manage the relationship between his first and second wife is not for me to either judge or even think about. He does not visit me, he has left me to my own devices. I should leave him to his.

I keep the little house bare, austere, trying to emulate the life I once led. I use the money I make selling herbs, not for fine robes or elaborate meals, for they are only worldly affectations. Instead I save them and buy writing implements. Here, what I first mistook for a strange kind of parchment is something called paper, made from beating rags or waste fibres from plants. It is thinner and finer than parchment and is in use everywhere, even by small traders. I resolve to spend my time writing down all the remedies I can recall, how to make them and store them, their uses and counter uses. I use my best script, I take a long time over each letter, each word. There is little to fill my days with, I may as well do the best work I can. I think that perhaps if I can remember all of the remedies I was taught, I will at least have made use of these days, created something that might be used by myself and others. I continue to grow herbs, to sell them.

"Are you well?" asks Aisha.

"Yes," I say. I always say this, I do not tell her that I am lonely. I see less of her than I would like to, now that she has her own household and her first baby has been born, a son, on whom Imari dotes. I see Yusuf mostly at a distance. And as I have no one else in this city, so I remain lonely.

"Zaynab has given her handmaiden Hela to Kella, as a servant," says Aisha.

"Why?" I cannot imagine why she would do this, it is clear that Hela is no mere servant to Zaynab. She is her personal healer, her confidante, why would she so easily hand her over to Kella?

Aisha shrugs. "Who knows?"

I walk through the market on a route that passes Kella's tent. I try to give the impression of looking elsewhere, but my eyes slide towards the sight of Hela standing outside the tent, cooking. I have never seen her cook before, I am surprised to see her doing it. Whatever she is making, it is heavily scented with parsley, I can smell it even at this distance. I hope, for Kella's sake, that she is not with child. Parsley in such great quantities would not be beneficial to an early pregnancy. But the thought of Kella being with child only makes me think of Yusuf lying with her, and I try to turn my thoughts elsewhere. She is his wife, he may lie with her if he so chooses, although I am aware that the rumours say that he does not, as he should, split his time evenly between the two of them, but rather favours Zaynab. I chastise myself for my interest in his affairs and turn my face away, focusing only on the purchases that I must make.

But my attempt at disinterest is about to be challenged.

The day is hotter than usual, and I am sweating. I wipe my forehead and under my eyes, my upper lip, then crouch down to take a drink of water from the pail I have beneath my stall.

"I need parsley."

I stand and find Kella standing before me. Her bright clothing is making her face look even whiter than it is, she looks ill and also as though she has not been much outside. She stands, waiting.

I fumble with the herbs but collect myself and pick up a large bunch of parsley, which I hand to her.

She shakes her head. "More."

I add another bunch and then another before she nods. She holds out payment, but her hand is shaking. I think of the rumours that she was with child. I think of the food I saw Hela prepare, how I thought then that it contained too much parsley. I look at her shaking hand and have a sudden intuition that she already knows, that she is not seeking to buy herbs from me but instead to have confirmed what she has already guessed. "Do not eat too much."

She looks at me as though she has waited for these words. In coming here and buying the herbs she has asked me a question, which I am now answering. "Why not?" she asks, and her voice shakes just as her hands do.

I want to make her sit down, for I am afraid she will faint. But her waiting eyes are fixed on me, there is a fear in them that frightens me.

"Parsley can take away life from within the womb," I say.

Her shaking hand falls, the coins she had brought as payment bouncing and striking the wooden surface of my stall even as she drops the parsley into the choking dust of the path. I step forward but she is already walking away, her feet shuffling as though she cannot even lift them, such is the weight of the burden she carries, the knowledge I have just given her. Something dark has been done to her, of this I am certain. I can prove nothing. But if I had to seek out that darkness, I know that I would find it in the great dark tent that sits in the centre of this rising city. I would find blackness seeping from Zaynab's heart and through Hela's hands. I am fearful for Kella, even though I barely know her. And I wonder if even Yusuf is safe by Zaynab's side.

I have begun to add my own remedies to the fresh herbs I sell, little jars of ointments or packets of dried leaves. People tell me of their ailments, and I help them if I can, sometimes asking them to return another day so that I can bring what is needed.

It is early in the morning and I finish dealing with one customer, then see that Kella has returned to my stall. She chooses dried nettles and then looks at me doubtfully. I nod and add red clover and the leaves of raspberries.

"For a child," I say, and she nods without replying, her eyes filling with tears.

I want to say more but I do not know her well enough, cannot warn her to be more careful, but then I suppose she knows this already. I watch her walk away and say a small prayer for her. Perhaps Our Lady will look kindly on this woman who seeks only to bear a child to her husband. I hope that if she does so, her marriage with Yusuf will be strengthened and Zaynab's power over him will be lessened. I hope that if he is happy with these two wives I will be taught a lesson in humility, return to my own chaste life and think no more of him.

I hoe the field, water the plants, pick the herbs, sell them. I write down my remedies, creating a stack of paper that grows day by day. I pray. I eat, I sleep. My loneliness grows. This pale imitation of the life I once led, that I am now trying to recreate, does not come with the same sense of contentment and peace that I had then, it has neither the community of my sisters around me nor the calm of knowing that my path lies bright before me, clear and well-trodden. I feel adrift, uncertain of what I am doing, clinging to the remnants of a past that cannot be replicated here. I ask for a carpenter to carve a wooden cross to hang on my wall and he does so, for money overrides faith, it seems. I hoped its presence on my bare wall would bring me comfort, but it feels more like a reminder that I am very far from home.

There is a knocking at my gate when darkness has already fallen and I open it cautiously, to see the face of the Jewess, Rebecca, her cheeks streaked with tears, her hands bloodied.

"What has happened?" I ask.

"I was attacked," she says, in a half whisper, looking over her shoulder. "I was – I was violated."

I pull her inside and tend to her, giving her the means to clean herself and then bandaging her hands. "How did this happen?"

"I fought them," she says, looking down at her hands. "But they had a knife and all I did was cut myself."

"Who was it?" I ask.

"I do not know," she says. "It was dark, there were two men. They came upon me from behind, and even when I fought them, I could not see their faces well enough." She is still trembling from the ordeal, wiping away tears as they continue to fall.

"I can give you something," I say.

"What sort of thing?" she asks.

"To stop a child from growing in your womb," I say.

She shakes her head. "I have cleaned myself," she says, under her breath.

"Are you certain?" I ask. "It might be better if you took something."

"No, thank you," she says.

I think she is foolish, but I can hardly force her. I give her bread and dried fruit and she eats both hungrily. I give her more to take away with her, along with a blanket. I think for a moment of offering her shelter in my house, but I am not sure that she would accept, nor whether it would be right for me to share a house with a Jewess. Besides, the law says she must not live within the city walls. I believe that she was taken by force, as she says, but I do not know enough of her not to be certain that she did not in some way encourage such an advance, if she is a woman of loose morals. If she were, I most certainly could not have her near me.

She leaves me, sobbing her thanks, clutching the blankets and food to her. I spend much of my night unable to sleep, wondering at the daily dangers she faces and what might come to me, too, as an unprotected woman in this city. Yes, I am Yusuf's slave, but few would know that by now, as I rarely see him.

Murakush swirls with rumours. Abu Bakr is returning, having subdued the unrest in the South. He has sent messengers to announce his imminent arrival. In his absence, Yusuf has been commander of the army, has married Zaynab, and is beloved by both the army and the people of this new, growing, city. If Abu Bakr returns, is he to take back the leadership he left in Yusuf's hands? And if so, what is to become of Yusuf? Must he step down? The people are unsettled, they are afraid of a fight for leadership. I think of how Yusuf always spoke of Abu Bakr, with loyalty and family love, and I cannot imagine them fighting one another, yet neither can I imagine Yusuf stepping down. But if he were to challenge Abu Bakr for leadership and fail, he could face execution for treason.

The response to Abu Bakr's imminent arrival is twofold. The messengers bearing the news, high-ranking officials and soldiers, are greeted as old friends, at a vast feast over which Yusuf and Zaynab preside, held in the central square. They are fed and entertained, then taken into Zaynab's own tent and offered gifts of honour. After this, the more important men are kept within Murakush, by Yusuf's side, whilst the mid-ranked men and common soldiers return to Abu Bakr to report back and issue an invitation to meet. He will see from this that their numbers and loyalty have been diminished, that Yusuf has already issued a silent warning. And sure enough, Abu Bakr agrees to meet away from Murakush, at a place closer to the humbled Aghmat, as though echoing his own possible future status.

The party that rides out to meet Abu Bakr is vast. At its head are Yusuf and Zaynab, side-by-side, powerful consorts, surrounded by Yusuf's personal guards, including Imari. They wear identical armour, carry giant matching shields, their black skin forming a dark shadow around the two leaders. Behind them are carried vast chests, made in carved wood. Each is filled with treasures: silver, gold and jewellery, skins and fine cloths as well as robes of honour, and of course weapons, always treasured by warriors. Behind this offering, this all-but-bribe, ride several thousand soldiers of the army, men in full battle armour, a show of military strength and power, of leadership already held, which will not be released without a struggle.

I do not ride out with the party of course, I wait with the commoners of the city to know our fate, powerless to influence it. I try to return to my own home, to tend my plants and pray as I should, but I find it impossible. I find myself pacing the tiny courtyard, until I can bear it no longer and make my way to the central square, eager for news. Little children balance on the growing city walls, looking out across the plains for a sighting of our army returning, their keen eyes ready to spot who leads it. The midday sun burns down on us, yet none of us take shelter, nor eat. There is talk, rumours. The general consensus seems to be that Zaynab is behind this show of strength, not wishing her husband to be demoted. That it is she, rather than Yusuf, who has masterminded this meeting. I find a part of the city walls onto which I can climb, make my way up it and sit, on its broad top, looking out over the plain with the children. Aisha finds me there, and, unwillingly, I climb back down and join her, wishing that I could stay in still silence, my eyes desperately searching the horizon for a glimpse of Yusuf.

"Imari thinks that Abu Bakr will not fight," Aisha says, stroking her belly, which is growing again. She is hopeful for a daughter. She must be fearful for Imari's safety, placed as he is close to Yusuf, in the front line of any fighting that might occur. If anything goes wrong with this plan, this child may end up fatherless, before it is even born.

"I am sure everything will be peaceful," I say, trying to sound reassuring. I'm aware that my own hands tremble if they are not laid firmly in my lap, I clasp them together so as not to give away my nerves, not to make Aisha more worried than she already is.

"Kella is with child," says Aisha.

"I am glad," I say. I mean it. I am sorry for Yusuf's first wife, who has found herself usurped by a woman who has no qualms when it comes to getting what she wants. "Can you warn her against Hela?" I say. "She should not allow her to serve her, she should stay in her own home and only allow her own servants to care for her."

"I think she has realised that for herself," says Aisha. "She has barely been seen out of her house, and her belly already has a curve to it, perhaps she is far enough along that it would be hard to harm the child."

I say nothing, but I think that if Zaynab and Hela were prepared to take a child from Kella's womb, there is no knowing what they would do once a child is already born. I hope that Kella shows a stronger mettle than she has done so far, now that she knows what may be done to her.

"Still no sign?" asks Aisha, anxiously peering upwards to the top of the wall where the small children sit, shading their eyes from the sun, peering into the distance.

They shake their heads.

We wait. And wait. The sun is low in the sky when a shout alerts us that the army has been spotted, and it is not long before it is confirmed that Yusuf and Zaynab are still riding at the head of it. There are screams of excitement and celebration, cheering and applauding as they make their way back into the city, where a raised platform has been built and a feast is ready to be eaten. Zaynab, who recently appeared pale and tired, now seems to glow, her cheeks pink, her eyes dark ringed with kohl, something she has not worn for some time. Both of Yusuf's wives are present for the festivities, although Kella seats herself quietly to one side of the platform, while Zaynab reclines magnificently in the centre of the stage and lowers a hand to her belly, deliberately stroking the black silk enrobing her, showing off a tiny curve. Beside me, I hear Aisha gasp before the whole square erupts with celebration, cheering Zaynab's unexpected fertility at this most auspicious moment. I chastise myself silently for the sudden bitter thoughts that perhaps she is only faking a pregnancy. Deliberately, I bow my head and praise God for Yusuf's triumph and bless his future children. I watch as Yusuf speaks to the crowd, presents both his wives with magnificent pendant necklaces, offers gifts of honour to his generals. I see his happiness and pride, and am certain he does not think of me once, does not even search for my face in the crowd, unlike Imari, who, as soon as he is released from service, rushes to Aisha's side and greets her with great tenderness, the two of them beaming at each other with love and relief. I see their bond and have to acknowledge to myself that Yusuf shares just such a bond with Zaynab, that she is the right mate for him, a consort queen to an ambitious warlord, matching his power and ambition with her own. It would be best if I recalled who I really am: a discarded slave, property of a master who has forgotten me.

I increase my efforts to live as I once did. I have enough money to last me some time, so I cease trading in herbs. The market of Murakush has grown large enough by now that there are plenty of traders who can offer fresh fruits, vegetables and herbs. There is no need for my work to continue. I give over the little field to a family in need and retreat ever more into my own little world, seeking to know nothing of Yusuf's family life. I try to follow the timing of daily prayers as I would have done in the convent, I stop eating the food that they prepare here and instead eat as much as possible as I would have done at home in Galicia. I stay within the four walls of my tiny home, except when I must go to buy food. I wrap my hair tightly with a plain white cloth and seek out only dull colours for my robes.

I see Rebecca in the street, begging for alms. I look at her body and see that it has changed, she catches my eye and looks away, ashamed perhaps or sorry that she did not take my advice. She is with child and I cannot imagine how she will face life on the streets with a baby in her arms. I tell myself that I must keep away from those I have known, they only distract me from the life I should be leading. I have strayed too far already from the path I should have followed.

A month passes and Aisha is brought to bed with a child, a baby girl whom she and Imari welcome into the world with joy. I visit her, exclaim over the baby, stroke her little face and hold her hand in mine, but Aisha's new arrival means that I see her even less as she has two little ones now and she does not realise how much I have retreated from life here. I miss her, but I think it is as well that she does not see me as I am now, for she would only try to change my mind, and I can think of no other way in which to continue my life here, except to mimic that which came before. Let the months pass, I think, let time pass as quickly as possible. Let the seasons change from one into another, let this new life become the only life I can imagine.

I am at prayer when a dark-skinned slave woman finds me.

"Healer," she says, indicating me.

I nod and wait.

"Need help," she says. "My mistress."

"What is wrong with her?" I ask.

"Baby," says the woman.

"She is in labour?" I ask.

She nods.

"What is your name?" I ask.

"Adeola," she says.

I gather a few things and follow her. When I see the shuttered house she has brought me to I step back, shaking my head. It is Kella's house.

"Please," says the slave.

I shake my head again. "I cannot serve this woman." I say. "You must tell your master, her husband."

But Adeola looks alarmed at this idea. "No!" she says quickly. "Secret."

I think that it is no secret that Kella is with child, it is common knowledge. But she is in labour too soon, and she is Yusuf's wife, this is a woman who should have the very best physicians attending her. But then I think of Kella's visits to my stall, the green parsley she let fall into the dust when I told her the damage it could do, had already done, to her. I swallow and gesture to the slave woman to lead me into the house.

Inside it is very dark, for all the windows are shuttered, and there seems to be only one other servant, a male slave, dark-skinned like Adeola. She tells me he is named Ekon. By the way she greets him and touches his arm they are, perhaps, a couple. They hurry me to a bedroom, where I find Kella on her knees, panting and clutching at her covers as a wave of pain overwhelms her. I stare at her, shocked. Yusuf's wife, left alone to bear a child come too early? How is this possible?

"Why do you not have a midwife with you?" I ask.

"There is no-one I trust," she says, gasping at the pain. "Zaynab..." she does not finish the sentence, but I nod. Her words confirm my thoughts, I do not need to hear more. I kneel beside her, pull open my little bag of remedies.

"What is your name?" she asks.

I hesitate. "Isabella," I say at last. She will have heard my hesitation, will know that I am in some way lying, but it is the only name I feel able to give her. And anyway, for now I have more important things to worry about. "Your child comes too soon." I say, without even examining her. Everyone in the camp knows that Zaynab's child will be born first and Zaynab is not yet at her full term.

But Kella shakes her head, awash in another wave of pain.

I give her my hands to hold, which she grips tightly. As the pain dies away, she sighs in relief.

"Not early?"

She shakes her head again.

"Zaynab…" I begin.

She continues shaking her head.

I nod to myself. "So." Zaynab has lied, then, I think, perhaps saw that Kella was with child and claimed the same. I wonder whether she is truly with child now, or only pretending, still. Or whether her handmaiden Hela has done something, used her skills and whatever powers she has to bring about a child for her mistress.

I do not question Kella further. I examine her carefully. Certainly her belly is very large and she seems well enough in herself.

She looks up at me hopefully. "I think it will be born very soon," she says. "I have been in pain for a long time."

I try not to smile. I have attended births over the years, both for noblewomen who wanted to be attended by the sisters of the convent to feel adequately protected at a difficult birth and occasionally for the local peasant women, although most of them gave birth with little fuss and ceremony. First babies are always the hardest and come the slowest. Kella does not know this, of course. But it is best to be honest. "You have not yet felt pain," I say simply. "And your baby will not be born for a long time yet."

She stares at me in horror.

I try to make Kella comfortable as the hours pass. She is healthy, the baby is well placed. There is little I can do but allow her to grip my hands when the pain comes, to offer her sips of tea that will help her body to open up, made from the dried leaves of the raspberry plant. Adeola fans her as the heat of the day grows and Ekon brings cool water and food, though she is not hungry. I force her to walk about the room, for this will help the baby to come.

At last I examine her and see that she is ready, that the baby will come soon. I dismiss Ekon and help Kella onto her knees, Adeola helping to hold her up. I place my hands ready and feel a hard skull pressed against my fingertips, urge her to push again and feel the sudden movement of the child's head as it emerges, followed by the whole body, a slippery rush and a small cry. I look at Kella's exhausted face as she falls back on her bed.

"A son," I tell her, cutting the cord that lies between them with a sharp knife and tying it tightly. I give the child to her, her fingers slipping on his wet skin, her face lit up with awe at him.

Adeola and I busy ourselves with cleaning the bed and the room. I massage Kella's belly to release the afterbirth, which comes away whole, filling me with relief.

Kella is laughing out loud, full of joy at her son and I cannot help but smile. I take him from her briefly, to wrap him warmly while Adeola washes Kella and covers her. The baby nuzzles at me and I touch his silken skin, look down on him. His face is all Yusuf's, it is like seeing him as a babe and a great tenderness rises up in me. I give the boy back to Kella. A baby is a sweet thing, I think to myself, a gift of God, though I know that it is the dark eyes and wide eyebrows that have touched my heart, the rounded earlobes of his father that I should not even have noticed. I will pray later, I think, to give thanks for this child's safe arrival but also to ask forgiveness for the desire I felt to hold him a little longer.

I call for Ekon to bring food and water and to make a strong golden broth that the local women drink after their births, to which I have added garlic, thyme and mint to warm Kella. Adeola insists on bringing two raw eggs, a common food for new mothers here, although I warn her that these are too cold in nature and harmful to the intestine, but she is stubborn and places them on a dish anyway. I sigh and think that I will tell Kella not to eat them. I show her how to feed the child and he learns quickly, impatient to be fed.

"You shall be called Ali," I hear Kella say in a half-whisper, touching his dark tufts of hair. "As your father wished. You are his first son, and you will be much loved."

I wonder what Zaynab will say when she sees this child, but Adeola suddenly pushes past me, gives Kella the broth and takes the child from her. He lets out a grumbling snort, but she is already indicating that Kella must drink the broth.

"The eggs," I begin but Adeola pulls me hard by the hand to another room. I follow her, wondering at her behaviour but even as we reach the room, I see a figure at the end of the corridor, entering Kella's bedchamber. Zaynab. I would know her walk anywhere.

"Leave now," says Adeola in a hissed whisper.

"The baby?" I ask.

She nods, clutching him to her, pushes me towards the door.

I look up and down the corridor but Zaynab must still be with Kella. I wonder what she will say, what she will do when she realises that Kella has birthed a child but cannot see it anywhere. I think for a moment that I could take the baby with me but then I think it is better if I simply slip away. I must not meddle between Yusuf's wives. I find a way to leave the house without passing Kella's room and hurry through the darkening streets. I am certain that no-one has seen me, and I know that both Kella and the baby are well. I have done my duty. Even so, when I reach my own home, I find myself praying for the child's safety.

I am already in bed when I hear a soft knocking at the gate. I ignore it, thinking it may be meant for my neighbours, it is such a quiet sound. But the sound comes again. I throw a robe over my head and make my way to the gate

"Who is there?" I ask. There is no answer. I pull the gate open a little and see Kella standing in the dark street, alone, clutching what can only be her baby to her. I stare at her. "Is the baby ill?" I ask and then, stupidly, "Do you bleed?" although if she were bleeding, she would never have made it to my home.

She shakes her head. "May I enter?" she asks, not answering me.

I step back so that she can move past me into the courtyard. I look behind her, almost expecting armed guards, but there is no one there. I close the gate and follow her into my tiny home. She is standing in the centre of the room, looking about her. I am aware of how bare, how plain, the room must seem to her, how strange, with its cross on the wall and my stack of paper, the calligraphy of another land.

"Kella?"

She turns to face me, frowning.

"Why are you here?" I ask.

She takes a deep breath, swallows, as though she cannot say something that must be said. "I want you to take my son."

I stare at her, unable to believe what she has just said. "Why?"

"Zaynab… threatened him."

"You could go to your husband."

She only shakes her head as though what I have suggested is not even worth considering.

I think of Zaynab and think that perhaps she is right, although I am also angry with Yusuf for not protecting this girl from the power of Zaynab, for not seeing the imbalance and seeking to redress it, as he should.

"Will you take him?" she asks. Her voice shakes, I can see tears welling up in her eyes.

I look at the tiny shock of dark hair emerging from the bundle in her arms, am about to reach out. But I am unsure. "For how long?"

"Forever," she says.

I step back. "Forever? Where will you be?"

She shakes her head. "I do not know," she says. "I may have to leave this place to ensure Ali is safe. But I cannot visit him, cannot see him again, or Zaynab will know I am his mother."

"She came to your house."

"She did not see him," she says. "I will say he is dead." Even the thought of it makes her arms tighten round the baby and he stirs in her arms, lets out a tiny cry but then settles again.

"And his father?" I think of telling Yusuf his son has died, what pain that would cause.

She swallows again. "He will know him when he is old enough."

"How?"

She fumbles one-handed in her robes and pulls out a string of silver beads. They are shaped like slender tubes half a finger long, marked with tiny designs. "Yusuf gave me these for our child. He will recognise them when he sees them again. You must keep them safe for Ali when he is old enough to make himself known, when he is a man."

I stand silently.

"Will you take him?" she asks again.

"I must pray," I say abruptly.

I turn away from Kella and kneel below the cross. I know she is watching me, but my hands are shaking, my stomach is roiling. Perhaps she thinks that I am unwilling to take the baby, that I want no part of this falsehood, that I will not allow lies to be told over his birth, his ancestry.

She is wrong.

I want this baby desperately.

I am lonely here and yet bound by my vows. The person to whom I gave my heart I cannot have, yet here is his son, alike to him in every way, his tiny face a copy of his father, of Yusuf. I want this child more than anything I have ever desired. I want to have him for my own, to feel close to his father, to pretend, in my sinful soul, that there is something between us, that his child might have been my child, our child.

I try to pray but the words do not come, not even of prayers I know by rote. I should be asking for the strength to refuse this child, and yet I cannot form the prayer to ask for His guidance. Rather I find myself imagining holding the baby again, as I did when he was born into my hands, of clasping his tiny warm body close to mine, of looking into his dark eyes and knowing that I am holding Yusuf's son.

At last I give up. I know exactly what I am doing and why, I know that I am sinning because of my desire for a man, because of my loneliness here. I cross myself even as I commit this sin and rise, turn back to Kella. Even now I might refuse, might do what is right.

"I will take him," I say and now it is too late. "I will keep him safe until he is grown to be a man and I will bear witness to your husband that he is your child and his." My voice is shaking, my arms tremble as I hold them out to receive the child, every part of me aching with desire.

She tries to move, tries to hold him out to me but her whole body convulses in sobs. She rocks him in her arms, her face buried against his skin and I see a desire that matches mine, a pain like nothing I can imagine. I wait, but I can see that she will not, cannot, let him go. That if I do not take him from her, she will be unable to give him to me. I reach out and take him from her very gently, my hands cradling him, trying to show Kella with my every tiny movement how much I will love him. She lets out a low moan of pain, tears falling so fast down her face that the floor is covered with tiny drops of her grief. Ali begins to cry and at once her hands reach out for him, but I shake my head.

"You must go now," I say. "Or you will be found out."

She backs away from me and then turns. I hear her footsteps in the darkness of the tiny courtyard and the heavy thud of the gate.

Ali begins to cry, and I realise suddenly that he will need feeding, milk. How could I not have thought of this before? For a moment I think I will take him back, run after Kella and return him, to deal with Zaynab as she sees fit, without involving me in her rivalries and struggles. But I have given my word, and I do not know what may become of this baby, Ali, if I do not care for him. If I return him, will I hear that he has died, and know that I am to blame? No, I have given my word, and now I must face the consequences. I try to rock him, but he is displeased with my awkward efforts. He cries more loudly.

I think of the beggar woman Rebecca, her belly swelling day by day and wonder whether her time has come and if she could be persuaded, for a little money, to feed another mouth. I rock Ali in my arms, his warm body struggling against mine, dissatisfied with his treatment. Already, I have failed him. I grab a cloak, one-handed, marvelling at the difficulty of holding a baby and doing anything else at the same time. Clutching him to me, still wailing, I make my way through the night, out to the city walls. I slip through a gate and then follow the edge of the walls, nervous at being outside the safety of the city. But I do not walk far before I see a shape huddled against the wall. I crouch down beside her, noting as I do so that her shape has changed, the broad belly she held before her has gone, and now there is only an empty pouch.

"Rebecca," I say, shaking her shoulder. "Rebecca, wake up."

She stirs, mutters something and returns to her sleep, pulling the worn cover I once gave her over her head. But I cannot let her escape me so easily.

"Rebecca, I have need of you."

It is not my voice but Ali's whimpering that she responds to. Slowly, she pulls away the cover over her head and stares up at him, eyes narrowed.

"Jacob?" she says, in a whisper. "Jacob, is that you?"

I squat down next to her. "His name is Ali," I say. "What happened to your baby?"

She keeps her gaze on Ali. "Jacob?" she asks, one more time.

"Ali," I repeat.

She looks away then, unhappy, disappointed.

"Did your baby die?" I ask. "Or was he taken?"

She shakes her head. "Died," she says dully, without emotion, as though all her feeling has already been drained from her.

"When?" I ask.

"Don't know," she says. She shakes her head, as though trying to remember, although her life has little need of dates. "Three days?"

I do not know if what I am about to suggest is cruelty in its highest form or a kindness. Perhaps it is both. "Can you feed this child?" I ask. "He has no mother," I add.

"Where is she?"

I shake my head. I have to know what lie to tell, from now until forever. "She died in childbirth," I say. "I promised to care for him. Can you feed him? I have no one else to ask. I can pay you."

"I – I don't know," she says, but her eyes are fixed on him again.

"I will pay you," I say again. "You can live with me, there is food and a warm bed, I have a little money."

"What if my milk does not come?"

"It will come," I say with certainty, although I am not as sure as I sound.

She does not look at me. She looks at Ali. "Yes," she says at last, and reaches out to touch the little tuft of black hair he has on his head. "Yes."

We make our way back through the streets, back to my home. By the time we reach the gate, Ali is screaming, his lungs belying his size. As soon as we are inside, I find her a seat and thrust him into Rebecca's arms. "Feed him," I say.

They fumble together, the two of them, she uncertain of what to do and he certain of what he wants, frustrated at the inability to get it immediately. I try to help, but only get in the way. Suddenly she gasps and he is silent, and I realise that he has found what he sought.

"He is sucking," she says.

"God be praised," I say, my voice weak with relief. "I will make you a tea, it will help your milk."

I make her fenugreek tea, preparing a large pot of it and giving it to her every hour that night, waking her from where she sleeps on my bed. I do not sleep. I hold Ali in my arms and rock him throughout the night, while thinking of all I must do when the morning comes. I watch her sleep huddled in my blankets, watch Ali sleep in my arms, and give him to her two or three times that night when he wishes to feed again. When he sleeps, near dawn, I make bread and more tea, prepare nuts and stewed fruit and a broth to strengthen Rebecca. When she wakes, I feed her until she can eat no more, give her a basin of warm water with which to wash herself, and my spare robe to dress in, so that she is clean. When she is clothed and fed, I give her Ali again and tell her I am going out.

I walk through the marketplace and buy things I have never bought before, spending much of the money I have. I buy more food, cloth to sew new robes for Rebecca and myself and to use for swaddling bands. I buy plates and cups, more fenugreek seeds than Rebecca will ever be able to drink, another blanket. I ask for a carpenter to come and build a second bed, a second chair. My household has tripled in one strange night. By the time I reach home, I find Rebecca asleep, with Ali contented by her side.

I take a blanket from the bed, wrap myself in it and sleep on the floor, so tired I cannot even think, nor feel the hard tiles beneath my body.

When I awake Rebecca is feeding Ali and we sit together, for a little while, not speaking, only looking at him, the two of us wondering how our life has changed so fast and so unexpectedly.

"What will your master say?" Rebecca asks me.

"I do not know," I say. "He is a kind man. I will tell him the baby is yours but that I have agreed to help you care for him." I do not say what I am thinking, which is, what will Kella say to Yusuf? Will she claim the child died in childbirth? Will she even stay strong enough to tell such a lie, to not break down in his arms and tell him everything that happened, leading him back to me and my part in all of this. I shake my head. What lies will I have to tell him? What will he say when he sees this child? And what if – what if he recognises his own son?

I take Ali, now half asleep, from Rebecca and stare into his face. He is the very image of Yusuf. I cannot imagine how anyone could look at him and not see the resemblance. But perhaps, I think, it is only I who sees this, because I have gazed at Yusuf's face once too often, have let my eyes linger on every part of him that I can see, and thought of him daily. Perhaps it is only my eyes that wish to see his countenance in this baby.

The sun is sinking when I hear the gate open and look out to see Yusuf standing in the courtyard. His eyes are rimmed red. He comes to the doorway, and looks at Rebecca, frowning.

"She's a beggar girl," I say, too quickly. "She had a baby and nowhere to live. I have taken her in, for now."

He looks at Rebecca, and the tiny dark head of Ali. I freeze, waiting for him to ask to see the baby, to look into his face. But he only nods and makes a gesture of dismissal. Rebecca quickly stands and leaves the room with Ali, murmuring something about a walk. I look into Yusuf's face, to see if I am about to be unmasked, called a liar and worse. Yusuf takes a few steps forwards, so that he is standing in front of me, closer than he has ever been. I swallow and look up into his face, seeing again the red rims of his eyes, realising that he has been crying.

"My son Ali is dead," he says, and suddenly he sinks to his knees before me, puts his face against my belly and weeps.

I do not speak. I find my hands on his head, pushing back the veil that has always hidden his face from me, letting its folds of cloth slip down onto his shoulders as he sobs against me, his shoulders shaking so hard that I think I may fall over. I brace my legs against his grief and run my hands through his dark hair, that I have never seen before, let alone touched.

He looks up at me, and I see his face in its entirety for the first time since I have known him. The skin below his eyes is very pale, protected from sunlight and drained by grief, his dark eyes, the only part of him I know, now flooded with tears. I stare back at him, my own eyes filled with tears as I think of the pain he is being unnecessarily caused.

I open my mouth to tell him it is not true, that his child lives and is safe in Rebecca's arms as she paces the narrow street outside, that he is a strong baby and will outlive us both. But I cannot. I have sworn otherwise, and I am afraid for this child, for the lies surrounding him and the power of Zaynab's jealousy. I am afraid of what Hela might do to serve her mistress, I am afraid that she has powers greater than mine, that she is no common healer and that she serves the darkness in Zaynab's heart without question. I have to look into Yusuf's eyes, raw with grief, and lie to him.

"I am so sorry," I say, and my voice shakes. "I am so sorry."

"He was my first son," says Yusuf, the words gulped and choked in his mouth.

I cannot bear to meet his gaze and so I pull his head towards me, pull him tight against my belly and my thighs, against my most secret parts and feel his warmth and strength against me. I am swept all over with a desire so strong it frightens me more than the lies I have told. I know now that I have told myself greater lies than I would have thought possible, that those lies and these new ones I am telling will have to live together, side-by-side, for the rest of my life. I wonder what I have become, what kind of a nun I could possibly claim to be, who lusts for this man, this heathen man, who holds a baby in her arms and tells lies about his birth to his own father's face. I am committing sins such as I never dreamed of, teetering on the edge of the abyss, the devil himself calling my name in ever more seductive tones. And I know that it would take so little, so very, very little, to take one more step and fall.

"What is the woman's name?" asks Yusuf at last, sitting back on his heels, his head bowed low. His voice is still hoarse.

"A beggar girl," I repeat. "Her name is Rebecca."

"The Jewess?" he asks.

I stare at him in surprise. "Is there nothing you do not know?" I ask.

He stands, face still unveiled, looks down at me and shakes his head. "I look about me. I listen."

I nod in silence. I wonder if he will insist that Rebecca must leave Murakush, that she may not live within the city walls, as is the law.

"You must keep her here," he says. "There has been enough sadness for one day. I am glad at least one person has been made happy today, has been cared for. I will send you money, enough for both of you to live well."

"Thank you," I say. "I will ask her to name the baby Ali, in honour of your son," I say, knowing that I am casting myself ever deeper into dishonesty.

He bows his head as though acknowledging this offer. "I will find you a bigger house," he says. "I must go now, Kella has need of me." His hands are swift. Suddenly the dark veil is wrapped around his face again and once again I can see only his eyes. I try to think of something to say, but he has already gone.

It is a long time before I see Yusuf again, although he sends me money, as he promised, far more than Rebecca and I have need of. He also sends a tiny ivory rattle for Ali, a grand gift for the supposed child of a beggar. I wonder sadly whether he bought it in anticipation of Ali's birth and am comforted that if so, at least it has reached its intended recipient.

Murakush celebrates, for Zaynab gives birth to another son for Yusuf, this child named Abu Tahir al-Mu'izz. Zaynab's legend grows greater, her prophecy seems more accurate than ever. For she was barren for three marriages and now, at an age when many women might have stopped bearing children, she has given Yusuf a son and heir. His younger first wife has lost her son at birth, so it has been given out, but Zaynab has succeeded where her younger rival has failed. Zaynab's son is surrounded by servants and slaves, as though a tiny baby has need of much. When I catch glimpses of Zaynab I see that she is recovering well from her pregnancy, filling back out again after the nausea rumoured to plague her, standing tall and powerful once again.

It is she who will prepare everything that is needed to support Yusuf's army as it marches against Fes, a twin city, whose two amirs have been given due warning to surrender, which they have ignored and for which they will pay a heavy price. The troops march north, and I can only pray for Yusuf's safety, hoping that Ali will not lose the father he does not even know is his.

At first, I care for Ali's needs with brisk efficiency. He is kept clean and well fed, I keep a note of when he feeds and when he sleeps. Rebecca, I see, pours the love intended for her lost child into Ali, sometimes she weeps when she is rocking him, but she also smiles and murmurs to him, sings to him, strokes his hair. But I begin to find my own care of him growing softer, caught up in his wide-eyed gaze and the scent of him. He holds my finger in his whole fist one day and I sit with him for more than an hour in the warm sunshine, unwilling to move lest he let go again.

I do not see much of Kella, catch sight of her briefly sometimes in the market crowds, but it is a rare thing. I wonder whether she sometimes sees Ali with Rebecca or me and hope that she knows he is cared for. I wish that she could see him at night, curled by either my own or Rebecca's side, his chubby little hands held in ours, the loving embraces he wakes to each day. I knew that I desired this baby, and so it proves. He is showered with love, both by Rebecca who has lost her own child and by me, attempting to fill the emptiness in my heart made by his father. Our days revolve around him and I already know that if Kella were ever to demand him back, I would struggle to give him away, even to his own mother.

I wake to shouts in the streets, hurry to the windows, afraid of what such commotion means, but see smiles on people's faces, hear chants of celebration. Fes has fallen. Yusuf now holds an important city in the north. Any amirs across the breadth of the Maghreb whom he has not yet conquered must tremble in their shoes today, knowing their time will come soon. A few, lying close to Fes, surrender immediately, bowing to the inevitable moment when Yusuf will claim their territories. Better to be his tributes and allies and keep their lands than suffer the consequences of defying him. Rebecca and I are grateful for his success, for our continued safety and prosperity.

"Yusuf's first wife seems happy for a woman who has so recently lost her child," says Aisha. She has taken to visiting me each day, her own baby girl and Ali lying side by side on a mat beside us, gurgling, beginning to wave their arms and legs about, occasionally succeeding in rolling over for a different view of the world. Her older son toddles about the courtyard, poking at my plants and attempting to befriend the neighbour's cat, who has until now considered my tiny courtyard a good place to rest peacefully in the sun. Rebecca sits with us, sewing. There is a peaceful feeling to these days, a comfort in seeing these small children explore the world around them, their desires so simple, so easy to grant.

"In what way?" I ask, my ears pricking up at the mention of Kella. I have never confided in Aisha about Ali's parentage, although when she first saw him, she cast me a look which suggested that she did not quite believe my story of him being Rebecca's child.

"I saw her in the marketplace," says Aisha. "Shopping for more goods than she can possibly have need of, laughing and bartering with the traders as though she had no cares in the world."

I ponder this. I wonder if Kella intends to leave, and shudder at the idea that she might return for Ali, take him with her somewhere else.

That night I wrap myself in a heavy cloak and leave Ali with Rebecca, making my way through the streets until I reach Kella's house. I stand outside it in the darkness, wondering whether to make myself known to her, to ask her how she does. But I am not brave enough, I fear she will ask for Ali's return. I return several nights in a row. Each night I turn away, always uncertain whether my own questions will prove our joint undoing.

On the fifth night, I am about to turn away when I see a side gate open. A cloaked figure leaves the house. It is Kella, I am sure of it. I step forward to speak with her, but there is something about the way she moves, hurried and secretive, that makes me stand back in the dark and let her go her own way, wherever that is. I hear a tiny *chink*, as of something metal striking the ground and see her head turn, but she does not stop, only walks swiftly away in the direction of the stables where Yusuf's personal steeds are kept. When she has gone, I retrace her steps and see something on the ground, the tiny glint of metal I heard fall. I pick up the object and retreat to a street corner where a lantern bobs. In the flickering light I see a tiny necklace, the shape of which, I know, is a betrothal necklace amongst Kella's people, a simple thing for such a weighty promise, made up of tiny black beads interspersed with silver, and dangling triangles. It must be the betrothal necklace Yusuf gave her when he took her as his bride. It lies in my hand, tiny, insignificant, yet loaded with the past. I am certain from her behaviour that Kella is leaving Murakush, but I do not raise the alarm, nor chase after her. She knows better than I what risks Ali may face in his life and she is taking steps to mitigate them. I trust her judgement and besides, I am relieved that she is not taking Ali away. My oath to her still stands, indeed it is strengthened by her absence.

I place the tiny necklace in a little casket in my own room, which already contains the string of silver beads she gave me with which to prove Ali's parentage. Perhaps, should the day ever come when such proof is needed, this necklace will only strengthen his claim on Yusuf.

News spreads fast that Yusuf's first wife has disappeared. Scouts are sent everywhere, but there is no word of her, it is as though the desert has swallowed her up without a trace. There are rumours and gossip everywhere. It seems she left with a man from her own tribe, perhaps a childhood sweetheart. That she left with slaves whom she had already set free. That her favourite camel from when she was a child has also disappeared from Yusuf's stables. Ludicrously, there are rumours that Zaynab spoke with the djinns of the desert, who magicked Kella away.

I await a visit from Yusuf, dreading the lies that I must tell, but he does not seek me out. This news has come at a time when he must plan for military success, it is too easy for Zaynab to claim to have searched for her everywhere and failed. Myself, I doubt she looked very hard. Zaynab never wanted Kella here, it is surprising enough that she did not kill her off in person. There are rumours of that as well of course, spoken more quietly in darker corners, for everyone knew that Zaynab was jealous of Kella being Yusuf's first wife. I choose to believe that Kella, adventurous as Yusuf described her, ever seeking a life of freedom, thought it best to seek out the life she longed to lead and in so doing lend protection to her son. I pray that she is safe and happy, but I also allow myself to look at Ali sleeping and pray that I may keep him with me and bring him safely to manhood, that I may know the joys of motherhood through him, however selfish that may be.

Aisha comes to me, her face doubtful at the message she is bringing. "The Queen's handmaid Hela is ill. She has asked to see you," she says. "Do you wish me to make your excuses?" she adds, as though to protect me.

"I will see her if she has asked for me," I say. I follow Aisha back to the palace where Yusuf and Zaynab live, noting the shuttered empty house nearby that used to be Kella's, still sitting empty without her. It would seem Yusuf has not yet given up hope of seeing her again.

Aisha knows her way through the palace, so that I do not need to risk meeting Zaynab. She leaves me outside a room with a pattern of flowers painted over it. I nod to her, then slip inside.

The room is very dark, I stand for a moment blinking, trying to adjust my eyes to the gloom.

"You came," says a voice. I barely recognise her, her already deep voice now rasps, wheezes with the effort of speaking.

I think of Sister Rosa, of her last days and swallow.

"You do not need to be afraid," she says. "I will not harm you." She pauses for a moment. "Nor die in your presence, if that is what you are afraid of."

"How did you know?" I ask.

"I felt it," she sighs. "Do you not know what I can do by now, Isabella?"

"I do not know all you can do," I say, unnerved by the sound of my childhood name in her mouth. "Nor would I wish to."

"So certain of yourself," she says, almost sounding amused. "After all this time, after all you have been through, still so certain of yourself, of your religion, your vows, your holiness."

"I can only pray for holiness," I say. "I have never felt so far from God."

"Surely that depends on how you define being close to God?"

I do not wish to speak with her of such matters. "You sent for me," I say. "What do you want?"

"Learn from me," she says. "Open up your life, do not close it down to nothing. You help no one that way. Your skills as a healer are valuable, use them for a greater good, learn more."

"I have been an apprentice and a healer for more than twenty years," I say. "I doubt I have much more to learn."

Her laugh turns into a coughing fit. When she has finished, she breathes heavily for a few moments. "You know almost nothing," she says. "Have you studied the medicine that we practice here? That is practised across the Muslim world?"

"No," I say. "It can hardly be that different."

She closes her eyes, as though what I am saying is exhausting. "You have no idea," she says. "I have seen your herbals. They are laughable. There is so much more medical knowledge of which you are unaware."

"Such as?"

"So much," she repeats, but she begins to cough again.

I stand waiting. When she has recovered herself, she looks me over again, her breath still coming with difficulty.

"I know how you feel for Yusuf," she says. "How you still burn for him."

I say nothing.

"He is drawn to you," she says, as though it were an insignificant thing to say.

I feel my heart beat harder, swallow at the rush of heat in my cheeks.

"Oh, did you not know that?" she says. "Of course he is. I was surprised when he did not bed you before the marriage with Zaynab. The drink I gave him… It was intended to increase his desire for Zaynab. Which it did, of course, she is a hard woman to resist. But it almost went the other way. I could see him watching you. I could see his desire growing for you, I had not realised before, that he already cared for you, that it would take so little to turn that into love."

I think of the night when Yusuf knelt by my bed, how his hand brushed my cheek. "I must go," I say.

"Take my advice before you do that," she says.

"Why should I trust you?"

"I have nothing to lose now," she says. "I am dying."

"You serve Zaynab," I say. "And that makes me distrust you."

"A fair enough assumption," she says. "But you know nothing of my own story. And I do not have the time to tell you. Only that my choices have not always been right. Neither in the past, nor more recently. I will only tell you this. That there is more to healing than you know, and that a woman like you, gifted with such skills, should know of it. And as for Yusuf…" She sighs. "Try to put him aside in your mind. He is as drawn to you as you are to him, but Zaynab is a dangerous enemy. And besides, he needs her by his side, she is everything a leader needs to create a kingdom."

"You serve her," I say. "It is you who makes her dangerous."

"I serve her for my own reasons," she says. "Do not cross her, with or without me when I am gone. She has a past of her own and it has made her ruthless."

"Is that all your advice?" I ask.

She is silent, as though thinking. "Love can be found in many ways," she says at last. "And hidden in many guises."

"I doubt you know what love is," I say.

"Do you?" she asks.

"I am a Christian," I say. "I seek to follow God's teachings on love."

"And what have you learned so far?" she asks.

I do not answer.

"Sometimes we have to learn for ourselves," she says. "Not everything can be taught." She struggles with her breathing for a few moments, I stand and watch her, uncertain of whether to help her, although when I step forwards, she waves me away. "You may go now," she says.

The brightness outside her darkroom makes me blink, I stand, pondering her words. I wonder what Zaynab will do without Hela by her side, whether she will grow more or less ruthless. Is it Zaynab, who gives dark orders to Hela, or Hela who carries out Zaynab's wishes no matter what it takes? If Hela dies, no doubt we will all find out soon enough.

Aisha is waiting at the foot of the stairs.

"What did she say?" she asks.

"She was confused," I say. "I believe she is dying."

Within two days I am proved right, word spreads that Hela has died. Zaynab has lost her handmaid even as she has gained Fes.

We begin to shape our days a little more, to know what and when we should eat, when Ali will want to suckle and when he will want to sleep. He is an easy child, content, and I marvel at this, after such an entrance to the world. We prepare a little food for him, so that he may taste fruits and grains, he explores them, wide-eyed. He chuckles at the smallest things, from a bird landing nearby to the sound of a spoon banging on a cup and Rebecca and I end up giggling at his antics.

It is not Yusuf who comes to tell me that I have a new house, but one of his men.

"Follow me," he says, briskly.

I look back at Rebecca, nod to her and hurry after him, wondering what is going on.

"The Commander says you're to have a new house," says the man as we walk. "He says you're his healer."

I can hear doubt in his voice but do not correct him. The man does not care, anyway, if his commander has a slave woman as a mistress, as he no doubt thinks of me. Plenty of men of importance have slave girls here and there, hidden away in houses or even kept in their homes, whether their wives like it or not. Yusuf has already had two wives, a slave woman added to the list is hardly a surprise.

We walk down a narrow street a few moments' walk from where I now live, then come to a stop outside a poorly painted orange door, set into a high wall, newly built. The shabby door is an odd contrast to the newness of the wall. I think that this house may be bigger than where I am now but that it will be as simple. But I am mistaken. The creaking gate hides a secret. Inside is a courtyard, tiled in glorious colours, a fountain at its centre. The house is two storeys high, and there are ten rooms in all, including a spacious kitchen and its own bathing room, a ludicrous extravagance of a house. It is fit not just for a mistress, but for a wife.

I walk from room to room when the man has left, wondering what Yusuf means by giving me this house. I am a slave, not even his mistress, and yet he has given me a house worthy of a wife. I think again of the creaking gate and the way it conceals what this house truly is. I know that Yusuf, for all his love of Zaynab, is aware that I need protection from her, that she must not know of my existence. I know this without being told, without him saying a word. The peeling paint of the orange gate tells me this even as I walk from room to room and look down into the beautiful courtyard.

When Rebecca sees the house, her mouth stays open and I catch her looking more than once at me, her eyes full of questions that she does not speak aloud. I do not try to answer them, for I do not know what the answers are.

The man who brought me here left me with a leather pouch that contains more money than Yusuf has ever given me before.

I fill the courtyard with my plants and with a tree. I give Rebecca a bedchamber of her own and set aside a room for when Ali is older. Besides my own bedchamber, I now have a room in which I may write and pray, a room sparse and simple enough to make me believe I am back in the convent. Rebecca ignores this monastic impulse and hangs bright covers and drapes in all the other rooms. Water splashes in the fountain, we fill the house with Ali's contented gurgles and our shared laughter at his antics, with the good smells of cooking and my drying herbs.

I set aside a bedchamber for Yusuf, should he ever wish to stay here, and even as I do so I know, as Hela said, that I would rather this room did not exist, that he should come to my bedchamber instead. But that is a step too far into the darkness that calls to me, louder every day.

The Chest of Books

Blow upon my garden, that the spices thereof may flow out.

Song of Solomon 4:16

ALI IS GROWING. HE LEARNS to walk. Rebecca and I clap our hands and rejoice, although now nothing is sacred. Not my plants, from which he rips leaves and flowers, threatening to stuff them into his ever-eager mouth. I have to remove those which are poisonous if misused and keep them on a high wooden shelf in the courtyard, specially built to withstand his interest. He splashes water from the courtyard fountain everywhere and slips and slides as a result, wailing when he hurts himself and rushing to one or the other of us for comfort. He enjoys walking through the market, pointing to everything he sees to hear its sound, to taste or smell whatever it has to offer. I tell him the names of my plants and he repeats them back to me, stumbling over the longer names.

He calls both Rebecca and me 'Mother' and we accept his naming, although officially we always say that he is Rebecca's son to anyone that asks, we brush away further questions by saying only that she was in difficulties and that I offered to help her raise him.

I sometimes see Zaynab's son, Ali's brother, in the markets with his nursemaids. I marvel at how similar the two boys look. I wonder that Yusuf cannot see it, but perhaps men do not look so closely.

The first time Yusuf visits us in the new house he walks round the rooms, nodding at Rebecca's bright and inviting decoration of each room, at the domestic warmth she has brought. His mouth twists a little when he sees his own bedchamber. "I will only end up sleeping in the courtyard, as you well know," he says. "Where is your room?"

I feel heat in my cheeks. I show him my own bedchamber, strewn with little signs of Ali's presence, such as the ivory rattle Yusuf sent for him.

"Do you not have a prayer room?" he asks. "I thought you would."

I lead him next door to the bare room I work in. A table and chair set under my wooden cross. A pile of paper, ink, pens, the pages of the herbal I am trying to complete.

He lets out a snort of laughter. "Exactly as I pictured it," he says, as though satisfied.

"I cannot tell you how grateful I am," I begin, but he cuts me off.

"It is nothing," he says. "How is the child?"

I lead him back to the courtyard where Rebecca is waiting with cakes and fruits, tea and Ali, who is eager to taste the unexpected treats.

"A fine boy," says Yusuf, patting Ali on the head as he waddles unsteadily towards him.

"He grows well," I say.

"Suckled by a Jewess and cared for by a Christian," he says, chuckling.

Fathered by a Muslim, I want to say, but I do not. I watch Yusuf lift Ali and dip his toes in the fountain's clear bubbling water, hear Ali's shrieks of glee, and Yusuf's deep chuckle. I wonder what it would be like, to be Ali's mother, to sit by Yusuf in the sunshine and feel such love.

A man comes to me with a carved chest. It is plain, unscented. When I lift the lid, it is full of books. I stare at it in amazement.

"Who is this from?" I ask.

"The Queen's handmaid," he says. "Hela."

"She is dead," I say.

"Yes," he says. "She sent the chest to a scholar before she died. There was a note to say that it should be sent to you, once she had gone."

"To me? What did it say?"

The man shrugs. "Send these books to the healer who used to be a nun," he says.

I can hardly argue that there must be many such women. Clearly, Hela intended me to have these books. I look down at them. They are huge tomes, very many of them. "There was nothing else in the message?" I ask.

The man shakes his head and leaves.

I look through the books. I cannot read any of them, but the illustrations are exquisite, in many colours, like the holy books in our convent. Some concern medical matters, for I can see illustrations of herbs, of people's bodies. Some seem to be about astronomy, mathematics, and other scholarly subjects. I wish that I could read them.

But Hela has even thought of this. The next day, an elderly man presents himself at my home. "I am here to teach you to read and write," he says.

"I can read and write," I say. "And who are you?"

"You cannot read and write in Arabic," he says. "I was paid to teach you."

"By whom?"

"A woman named Hela," he says. "She paid me a goodly sum, she said that I was not to leave you until you could read and write in Arabic."

I hesitate. I am not sure that I want gifts like these from Hela, from beyond the grave. I wonder why she thought of me so much, when our paths crossed so little. I wonder if somehow, with her strange powers, she knew something of what happened with Kella. Is this gift a curse? A blessing? A trick? But I think of the tomes of learning held in the chest which has been placed in my work room, of the knowledge held within them to which I would dearly like access. I nod and step back to let the man enter.

So begins a period of learning for me, such as I have not undertaken since I was a girl with my father and then under Sister Rosa's care in the stillroom and sickroom of the convent. I am as an ignorant child, learning once again the letters and sounds of a language, turning meaningless symbols into knowledge, shaping clumsy letters and sighing over my lessons. The letters I have known until now are useless to me, these new shapes bear no resemblance to them. I must even learn to write in a different direction, to read right to left rather than left to right. I no longer possess the flowing script of an educated woman, instead I know, by comparing my efforts with my tutor's hand, that my script is awkward, inelegant. My fingers grow ink stained and I spend money on more and more new paper so that I may practice longer and harder. Rebecca watches me in surprise but shakes her head when I offer to teach her in turn. And slowly, slowly, the books that Hela left me begin to open their pages to me, begin to share what they contain.

And such knowledge as I prided myself in having, such knowledge as I thought the Christian scholars held, is swept away by what I find. These books are the works of Muslim scholars, who themselves have drawn on past scholars from across the world and far back in time. Their knowledge surpasses all that I have ever read. I find myself staring in amazement at the books on medicine, on their depth and detail, on the knowledge that has been kept from me, a Christian woman who believed herself educated. And for what? Only because of my faith. I find myself thinking on my father, and his words, which my mother dismissed but which I now recognise as the truth, as containing wisdom. I think of the times he talked of in Cordoba, long ago, when scholars of all faiths came together and shared knowledge, wisdom, such books as these. They did not allow their faith to create a barrier, they looked beyond it and waded into a pool of shared knowledge, adding to it through their time together, their shared discussions. The more I read, the more I wish my father was still alive, so that I could return to him and ask for more.

In particular I study medicine, finding volumes from *The Complete Book of the Medical Art* and more from a scholar and physician named Bin Sina, whose work is called *A Canon of Medicine*. I stare, fascinated, at illustrations of anatomy. I learn of the importance of the six 'non-naturals,' which are the surrounding air, food and drink, sleeping and waking, exercise and rest, retention and evacuation and the mental state of the patient. I learn that to maintain good health all of these must be balanced. There is mention of being able to inoculate a person against illness such as smallpox, through introducing a tiny amount of the disease into them, which leaves me stupefied. My education in healing, of which I was so proud, feels childish, like the work of a new apprentice when I set it against this vast collection of knowledge.

I grow hungry for what has been denied to me all this time. I seek out the booksellers, the scholars' libraries, and I purchase or borrow whatever they can give me, adding book after book to those already in my possession. I read of geology and chemistry, of mathematics and philosophy. My tutor holds up his hands and says that he has nothing more to teach me, that my script has grown smooth and my reading fluent. He invites me to join him, at the school where he teaches, that I may learn more. But I am always wary of being too visible, and so I refuse. But I pay him myself, now that he has fulfilled his work for Hela. I ask him to come and read to me, to discuss with me the ideas that I have found in these works. I feel that I have been set free from my bonds as a slave, now that my mind may wander wherever it wishes.

I wonder if Hela read all these books, I assume she must have done.

Was she so knowledgeable then, so gifted in medical work? And what of her other powers, which I still believe she held? Were they there from birth or did she find them in these books? Perhaps she sought answers for what she could do in these tomes and did not find it. I wonder if she was afraid of her own abilities, if she found them too much to bear. I wish she could have exercised them for the common good rather than in service of Zaynab. And I think that perhaps I could use what she has given me to help others more than I have done so far.

I look about me when I walk through the city and when I see a girl, sitting begging for alms, instead of passing by or giving her a small coin, I bring her back to the house, and offer her work as my servant, which she gladly accepts. She is an ill-favoured girl, being hunched in one shoulder, her back bent forwards and to one side, as well as having a twisted mouth from birth. I use ointments on her and teach her exercises to stretch and relieve the aches she feels from her twisted back. There is nothing I can do for her looks, but now that she is fed and dressed well, has a safe warm bed to sleep in at night and a household to be part of, her face seems prettier, for she smiles more often, and her gaze brightens. She was born to a slave woman who died, and her master, seeing no possibility of selling her and disliking her looks, cast her out into the street. Her name is Fatima, name of the daughter of the Prophet Muhammad and considered here a virtuous woman to be emulated, as women of my own faith might emulate a saint. She proves to be a hard worker and of a cheerful disposition, once she comes to trust me and to believe that she will stay with us, that she will not be cast out again. She watches me when I work with plants and begins to ask their names and uses, which I gladly share with her. I think that in this way she might learn a useful skill which she may use throughout her life and perhaps even have as a source of income, should she ever leave us. I tell her that she may have been born of a slave, but if her master abandoned her, she should consider herself a free woman. And as such, that she may create her own life and make it a happy one, despite her base origins.

A servant bangs on the gate and Rebecca comes to me, her face anxious, to tell me that I am summoned to Zaynab.

"Why?" I ask, trying to ignore the drop in my stomach. Why should

Zaynab summon me? How does she even know I exist? Does she know, has she found out about, Ali?

The servant shrugs. "The order was to bring you to her. At once," he says.

"I will come in a moment," I say, trying not to let my voice shake. I pull Rebecca to a corner with me. "You know what to do if anyone comes here, if I do not return?" I ask her.

She nods. "Hide Ali, take him elsewhere if needs be. If anything happens to you, seek Yusuf's protection."

I look beyond her to where Ali plays in the sunlight, dipping water from the fountain into a little pail and back again, immersed in the games small children play. I want to embrace him, in case this is the last time I see him, but I do not want to startle him or frighten him, nor do I want to draw attention to him if the servant has not seen him. I raise my hand a little, make the sign of the cross over him and slip through the gate.

I follow the man through the streets to Zaynab's rooms, the grandest within the palace that has been built for Yusuf. Servants are everywhere, the courtyard and rooms are large, although I can see Yusuf's restraining hand on the decorations that have been used. The plasterwork contains only calligraphy praising Allah, the courtyard relies on plants rather than overly-elaborate tilework, even the many guards and servants we pass are plainly dressed, considering they serve an amir and his queen.

Guards stand at the entrance to Zaynab's rooms. At a nod from the servant they spring apart and allow us entry.

The room into which I am shown is very large. A rich powerful perfume fills the air, the perfume of a queen. Most of the room is taken up with a bed, on which Zaynab is sitting, looking down at maps spread out across her lap. Zaynab's bed. I recognise the carvings. Now it is draped with every kind of silken coverlet, with blankets of such fine wool they are more like gauze, all in reds and golds, yellows and oranges, as though it were aflame. The lustful carvings are polished so well that they seem to glow with life. This is the bed in which Zaynab lies with Yusuf. I swallow. It should not bother me, and yet it does.

Zaynab has looked up from her maps and is watching me. My heart is beating fast, but I stand in silence. Whatever accusations she makes, whatever she knows, I will only refuse to speak until the end, will deny all knowledge of Ali's birth and even of his very existence. It is all I can do.

"I suffer with great sickness from this pregnancy," Zaynab says. "I have need of your healing powers."

I wonder if this is a trick, if she intends to somehow catch me out, but I am not sure how, I am not sure what trap she is laying. "I do not have powers," I say at last, as it becomes clear that she is waiting for an answer. "I only have knowledge of herbs and I pray to my God for His guidance." It comes out more sharply than I intended, I sound as though I am defying her.

She stares at me in silence and I wonder whether in fact I have misjudged this meeting, whether she is indeed asking only for my help. I know that Zaynab suffers greatly from nausea with her pregnancies, everyone knows this and now that Hela is dead perhaps she is truly only asking for herbs that will help her. Certainly, she is very thin and pale, her beauty watered-down.

"What have you tried?" I ask cautiously.

She lists various remedies: eating acrid things such as capers, *not* eating such things, avoiding rue and all legumes especially chickpeas, the use of fresh air, gentle walks, wool placed over her stomach. Various wines, either diluted or added to. A range of amulets.

The relief I feel at her listing such commonplace remedies makes me light-headed. I shake my head a little to try and dispel the feeling. "I will make you a syrup," I say, hoping that by promising this I can quickly leave her presence. "Take it when you feel the sickness and at least twice a day even if you do not. Eat small meals and often."

"I can barely eat anything but unleavened bread," she says pitifully. Her voice sounds as thin as she is. "Everything else I vomit."

I shake my head again. I do not want to feel pity for this woman. "I will send the syrup," I say, already beginning to move towards the door, eager to leave.

"You must tell me what is in it," she says sharply, as though she is suddenly distrustful of me, having sought my help.

"Pomegranate syrup with yarrow, stinging nettle, comfrey root, cinnamon, turmeric and bentonite clay," I say. The list comes quickly, I have made the remedy so many times, for one woman or another who had called on the convent for our help, even for ladies of the local nobility. It is an effective remedy; I have never not known it work.

She nods slowly, as though my quick recital has comforted her. "Send it to me," she says.

Rebecca nearly cries when I return. "I was afraid you would not come back," she says, embracing me.

Ali has barely noticed my absence, he has moved on to water the plants, using a battered old ladle I gave him, dripping most of the water all over the tiles of the courtyard. He beams at me when he sees me and continues his task, earnestly over-soaking each plant.

I gather the ingredients I need and mix a syrup for Zaynab, take it to the palace gates and give it to one of her servants.

A few days pass and I am summoned again. I wonder whether this is the moment when a trap will spring but now the guards bow when they see me and Zaynab looks up as soon as I enter the room.

"Did the drink work?" I ask.

"Yes," she says. There is a little more colour to her cheeks. She nods to a servant, who hands me a large leather pouch. It is weighty with coins. I grasp it, dumbfounded.

"You will continue to send the drink throughout my pregnancy," she says. "You will be well paid for your service."

The leather pouch sits heavy in my hands. I should bow, perhaps, should thank her, but I am too shocked at what has happened, at finding myself somehow serving a woman whom I despise, a woman I believe to be a handmaiden of the devil. Am I, too, serving the devil, through my healing skills? "I can tell your servants how to prepare it," I say, trying to sever the bond she is creating between us.

"No," she says. "I want you to prepare it."

I nod and step away, hoping to leave as quickly as possible. I dare not refuse to make the syrup, nor her payment, but I wish to leave her presence.

"Wait," she says.

I stop and wait. Is this the moment when she reveals all of this has been a pretence, that she knows everything?

"You could work for me," she says. "My own handmaiden Hela has passed away and I have need of a healer in my service. Will you be my handmaiden?"

"No," I say instantly.

She frowns. "Why not?"

The words spill from my mouth, as though they have been waiting to be said, as though a higher power has taken over my body. "I do not wish to serve you," I say. "I cannot serve a woman who has such darkness inside her."

Without asking her permission, I turn and leave the room, walk through her palace and back to my own home, all the way fearing a hand on my shoulder, all the while burning as though an invisible light is inside of me. This, I think, this is how Our Lord felt when he refused the devil's temptations, when He looked out over all the kingdoms that he might command and refused such earthly wiles, holding true to His given purpose. I cannot even speak with Rebecca when I return home, only tell her that I must pray. I spend all night on my knees and when dawn comes, I wake to find I have fallen asleep at prayer, that Rebecca has draped me with a woollen blanket while Fatima makes breakfast for Ali. My knees cramp when I try to stand but for now, it seems, we are safe.

Ali is a scholar in the making. He finds my paper and a pen and spills ink everywhere but manages to form a clumsy letter and I, enchanted, begin to teach him his letters and numbers. He loves them. He draws the shapes in water in the summer, in sand, in the mud of winter. He sits himself by my side, like a little scholar and attends to his studies.

Rebecca finds him a little kitten and he is careful and soft with it, a gentle soul. I think of his mother's adventurous spirit and Yusuf's leadership, but I do not see it in him. I see a scholar and a kind heart, a child who loves lullabies and stories, embraces and soft words. I think perhaps, as he is Yusuf's son, that he should be taught the skills of war, that he should have a dagger and a shield and think himself a soldier. But I cannot bring myself to do this, to harden his little heart against the outside world. Instead, I read to him the legends of his own world and recite the stories from mine. I take him to the market square, where we sit in rapturous silence and listen to the storyteller peddle his wares. Ali likes to imagine that he is a great king, with a queen who tells him such stories as Scheherazade once told her lord, although I cannot imagine him being so unkind as to behead any previous wives. His eyes grow round with the tales of Sinbad, of the forty thieves, of adventures and heroes, monsters and good-for-nothings populating a city like his own. He examines large oil jars in case he should find thieves hiding there, waves his hand to command doors to open and reveal their hidden treasure. I hold him to me when he will keep still long enough to let me and smell his hair, the perfume of innocence and happiness.

The scholar who taught me suggests that I might like to work alongside physicians, in the first hospital that is being built in Marrakech. But I am afraid of drawing too much attention to myself, as I surely would working alongside physicians, a woman from another country. Instead I look about me, at the over-large house Yusuf has given me. I see Rebecca's smiling face and listen to Fatima's cheerful singing as she goes about her chores. I look at my plants and remedies and make up my mind.

"I wish to care for the sick," I tell Rebecca. "Here, in this house. We could work to heal the sick, and to help those who have nothing, as Fatima had nothing."

"Nor did I," Rebecca reminds me, "I would do anything to repay my debt to you."

"You did that long ago," I say. "You saved Ali's life; he would have died without your milk. There is no debt to repay to me, but we could do much good here, this house is too big, even for the four of us."

And so we make changes to our household. I set aside a room to be an infirmary, and another to be my stillroom. I find a beggar boy to fetch and carry and find a young girl to join our household as a servant, while Fatima becomes my assistant. I let it be known that I will use my healing skills for anyone who needs them. My days grow busy, preparing and using remedies, looking to use my newfound knowledge as well as my existing skills on those who come to us for help. Since I have already engaged the services of a tutor for Ali, I offer the opportunity to learn to read and write to any who wish to attend, and so there is always a little group of slaves, children and women who cannot attend a formal school but can spare a little time to learn alongside Ali.

"You are privileged," I tell him, "and so it is meet that you should share that privilege with those whose lives are harder than yours." He straightens with pride at the thought, offering, even though he is a little child, to help others in their quest for knowledge. He will show them how to form a letter, tongue between his lips as he shapes them, frowning in concentration. His little finger traces across the Qu'ran while he speaks its words aloud for the benefit of those still learning. He is a born scholar, with a scholar's desire to share what he knows.

Rebecca, meanwhile, is absent for much of several days and when I ask her where she went she whispers that a Jewish trader invited her to his home, outside of Murakush, to celebrate Passover, knowing her to be of his faith.

"I told him I had been disowned by my family," she says. "I did not want to lie to him, but he said we are far from Al-Andalus here and there are so few of our faith, we must stick together."

There is something lighter about her, a brightness in her eyes and I am not surprised when a few months later a man presents himself at our house and asks to speak with me. He is named Daniel and he asks if he may marry Rebecca.

"Gladly, if you will love and protect her," I tell him. "But she is so much a part of my life. Can she still work with me?"

He is happy with this arrangement and so Rebecca marries back into her faith, a homecoming for her after all these years being cast out. I see a new confidence grow in her, a sense of belonging rather than the pitiful gratitude of the early years together. She seems an equal with me now and although she leaves our house each afternoon to travel home with her husband, she spends most of each day with us. Ali, of course, latches on to Daniel and asks him all manner of questions about the Jewish faith, even attends one or two prayer meetings to observe their rituals. He is insatiable in his desire for knowledge, with an open-mindedness that continues to amaze and humble me.

I do not often see Yusuf but having work to keep me busy each and every day, having a household that is full of need and noise fills the silence and emptiness within me, lessens a little the longing for what I cannot have. I think sometimes of Hela, of her gift to me of knowledge, and whether she meant for it so that I might use my healing skills, or whether she thought it might help to lessen my desire for Yusuf, I do not know. I know nothing of her past. I know only that she saw something in me that needed help and gave it in the only way she knew how. When I make my daily devotions, I pray for her soul, wherever she may be.

City of Light

Until the day break, and the shadows flee away...

Song of Solomon 4:6

W HEN I LOOK AT ALI now, standing taller than Rebecca and me, I wonder where these past years have gone. He is not yet a man, but I can no longer call him a child. He has grown up with no father, with two mothers, in a household full of the sick and impoverished and he is wiser than I was at his age.

"Your son is an excellent scholar," says his tutor proudly. "He has a great feeling for the Qur'an, for its nuances. He has a great understanding both of religion and the law."

"I am glad to hear it," I say, although I feel again the familiar uncertainty. Am I doing the right thing, raising him as a Muslim when it is quite possible that Yusuf will never know he is his son, when perhaps he will only have me for a mother? It draws attention to us, for I am known as a Christian, and people will wonder why I am raising a child in my care as a Muslim. But I know that if the day comes when I may return him safely to Yusuf as his son, I cannot have raised him against his father's wishes.

I do not tell him much about my own life before I came here, only that I was a religious woman, in a religious house in my own country, but I was brought here and became Yusuf's slave. I tell him that I have been well treated, that I owe Yusuf a great deal, and he, hero-worshipping Yusuf as he already does, adds this to his list of glories and behaves ever more as a son to him. He waits for him to return from campaigns, hangs upon his every word, and takes every opportunity to show, his face a little flushed with pride, how his studies have progressed. He writes a beautiful script in Arabic, my own, by comparison, having come later to it in life, is not as fine. I teach him to read and write my own letters and he attends to them with great care, begs for the use of all my books in both languages and spends many hours a day reading them. His Latin is good, although his accent betrays our location, but still he would not disgrace any gathering of scholars. I think sometimes of my father, and how he would have been proud to have a scholar in his family, how he would have showered him with books, introduced him to the scholars who visited his shop. He would have praised his fine hand and his turn of phrase when he writes or speaks. I miss my father. My mother, of course, would be utterly appalled at what I have done. She would turn away in horror at the very idea of me being a slave to a Muslim master. That I would choose for a child I was raising to become a Muslim and not a Christian, would be beyond her understanding.

"Tell me again how you pray," Ali says. He is eager to learn, it does not matter what. He has been taught to pray as a Muslim, but he continues to ask all manner of questions of Rebecca and Daniel about the Jewish faith, listening wide-eyed to stories from her childhood, of the rituals of their family life. He follows me when I go to my room to pray and watches me earnestly, confused by the silence of my prayers.

"But what are you saying inside your head?" he asks.

I repeat my prayers for him out loud, they sound strange in this place, for I have not spoken them aloud for many years now. He learns them quickly, learns the Hail Mary and Our Father. When I mention in passing that we used to sing, he asks me to sing again and I do so, my voice faltering without my sisters all around me. He tries to copy me, although he is not a gifted singer. I think of our choir mistress, that she would wince at the way he sings, as she used to when I was a child before she improved my performance with endless repetition and practice. It feels strange to have another person to pray with, for Ali will willingly pray with me as well as with the other scholars and people of the city in the mosque.

"I have never met someone like you," I tell him, honestly. "You remind me of the people of Cordoba, about whom my father used to speak."

"Tell me again about Cordoba," he begs.

And so I tell him about Cordoba, trying to remember everything my father told me, while I refused to pay proper attention. I wish I had listened more closely now, for Ali's face lights up at what I describe.

"Yes!" he says, enthused. "It does not matter what name we give to God. In matters only that we share his wisdom and the blessing of knowledge he has given us, whatever name we in our mortal ignorance have given him."

I have such pride in him that I sometimes wonder if it is sinful, but I cannot help it. I show him all the books Hela gave me and he reads them avidly, sits up at night to discuss what he has read with me.

Rebecca and Daniel have been blessed with two children, both of whom I brought into the world. Her son is named Samuel, her daughter she asked me to name and I called her Rachel, for another Jewess long ago who tried to befriend me. Now that she has little children to care for again and Ali is older, she comes less frequently to the house, but I still see her every few days and she, Aisha and I are often together, working and talking together as we help those who come for healing and learning. Aisha has learnt to read and write and now she passes on what she has learnt to the little children who come, sitting patiently by their side as they gain in confidence.

Yusuf visits us often. His eyebrows have grown grey. He has secured the Maghreb now, he need no longer go to war, he may rest and reap the rewards of his courage and faith, as befits an older man. Usually of an evening, between training with the army and returning to his palace, he will slip in through the gate to our courtyard, as twilight falls and most of my patients have left for the day. Those who are truly sick, who must stay in our infirmary for a night or more, are by now asleep, cared for by earnest Fatima, who has become an accomplished healer in her own right. Yusuf squats amongst my potted plants. Always disdaining of luxury, he will wave away chairs and even soft rugs. He accepts cold water to wash his face and hands, plain bread, which I have baked for him late in the day, so that it will be fresh when he needs it. A handful of dates, a few scraps of roast meat if there are leftovers, this is all he wants. I bring him cold water and sit with him. Sometimes we will spend all of his visit in silence, listening to the fountain play, watching as the first stars come out. Then he will rise and leave, with a smile for me and a wave and nothing more. On other days, he will talk to me of something he has seen that day, of a bird, a plant, a child in the street. He does not talk of military strategy, of plans for conquest, of amirs surrendering to his growing power. The whole of the Maghreb is now under his control. It is divided up into four great provinces, two in the north and two in the south, each under the control of a governor appointed by Yusuf, every tribal commander pledging loyalty to the kingdom. His generals have little left to do, although he still commands a vast army. I know of his conquests from others, never from himself. Long gone are the days when Murakush was a city of tents. The city walls rise high, surrounded by palm trees. There is water in the public fountains and the houses of the well-to-do, the whole city fully built at last, including a great mosque at its centre. Yusuf owns Fes and the northern port of Tangier, he controls the trade routes, including all trade in salt, slaves and gold.

On some evenings, Ali finds and joins us, his face all alight with hero worship. Yusuf is always kind to him, always welcoming. He will question him on his studies, and then listen as Ali recites from the Qu'ran. Ali asks him about matters of law and taxation regarding how the kingdom is run. Yusuf answers him honestly, explaining even minor details in great depth. Illiterate himself, he seems to relish Ali's learning. The better his tutors say he does, the higher quality tuition Yusuf purchases for him, calling on great scholars of the city to spend time with Ali, sharing their knowledge and their debates with him.

"He has a learned mind," he repeats often. "There will be a place in my Council for him when he is grown to manhood. A leader must have wise counsel from those about him, and young eyes see what old minds have forgotten."

Ali glows at such praise, bends ever more earnestly to his studies. The warmth of their relationship pleases me, although always, there is something in me that worries when they are together, that the moment of discovery will come when I least expect it.

I see Zaynab's children at a distance, over the years. For each pregnancy, I must make and send to her the syrup, each time I am amply rewarded, the gold I receive then used to heal or teach, while I try not to think of Yusuf lying in her arms. One after another they are born, six sons and three daughters, and all of them are prepared for a future in her footsteps or those of Yusuf. The boys are warlike, they follow the army out to the plain and copy their every movement, they carry miniature swords and drums, they are trained to become warriors of the future. Her daughters are dressed as befits princesses, they are shown maps of their parents' empire and sit in Council from when they can barely speak, future consorts to great lords and rulers, every one of them. Zaynab herself grows older but never less than beautiful, her eyes dark with power and the knowledge that she has achieved great things. If Yusuf were to die, she could rule this kingdom alone, for she has done as much as he to create it.

Twice in those years, I hear from Aisha that Yusuf has also fathered a child with a slave, a boy and a girl born to one woman, one boy born to the other. I see that he acknowledges these children, that they take their place alongside their legitimate siblings, as though there were no difference between them. But I see also that their mothers are not accorded the status of a wife, they are kept secret and hidden away, as I am. At first, their existence wounds me, makes me feel that I am one of many, perhaps dozens of slave girls and their offspring hidden all over Murakush and beyond. But I see no more children born to such women, and so it seems that they were little more than dalliances, the children acknowledged, the women left behind, though no doubt Yusuf, being a generous man, will have provided for them. I do not speak to him of them, ask no questions, just as I rarely mention Zaynab. Instead I speak of new knowledge found in my books, of what I have tried and whether it has worked, whether it is time to pick this or that petal or leaf, of the birds who have made a nest on the corner of our rooftop and wash in our fountain at dawn.

From the way Yusuf talks to Ali, I make the mistake of thinking that he is content, that now that his kingdom is complete and peaceful under him, he seeks no further conquest, no further adventure. But I am wrong. It is hard to tame a warlord, a warrior-made-king.

It seems that there is trouble in Al-Andalus. Divided into princeling *taifa* states, each a tiny region, ruled over by Muslim kings, it seems they have forgotten the shining days of Cordoba and instead squabble amongst themselves, grown lazy while living lives of luxury. They might have worked together, to create a kingdom, an army strong enough to defeat Alphonso the Sixth, the Christian king of the North, but they prefer to continue in their comfortable lives and pay him tribute. But now the Amir of Seville, Al-Mu'tamid, having been late in paying the annual tribute demanded by Alphonso, has tried the king's patience too far. Alphonso demands not only tribute but recompense for the delay, insisting on the delivery of many strong castles in Seville's region. Rather than negotiate, the Amir of Seville kills Alphonso's messenger and then, worried by what he has done, writes to Yusuf, as one Muslim king to another, asking for his support against the Christian king. He claims that the scholars of Al-Andalus agree that this is righteous.

"But Yusuf has no seagoing ships," I point out to Aisha, when she tells me this.

"He has demanded a ship from the Amir," says Aisha. "The Amir of Ceuta, on our northern coast, has yet to be conquered, but with a ship

Yusuf will defeat him in no time. If he can do so, he has promised his aid to Al-Andalus."

I had thought my years of praying for Yusuf's safety were over. It seems they are to begin again. I think that I should perhaps be praying for Alphonso, but that thought comes and goes in an instant. Galicia was too long ago, I cannot summon the desire to support a Christian king I know nothing of, against a man who sits amongst my plants in the twilight, eats food prepared by my hands and talks to me of nesting birds. I hope that Yusuf will support the taifa states only as long as is necessary for them to form a stronger alliance of their own, to fight their own battles against Alphonso and let Yusuf return safely home to Murakush. To me.

Shadows in the Alleys

The watchmen that go about the city found me...

Song of Solomon 3:3

IF I THOUGHT THAT YUSUF's time in Al-Andalus would be brief, now I learn my mistake. The taifa kings cannot be relied upon, Yusuf leads them to one victory after another, and yet still they squabble amongst themselves, turn traitor on each other and on him, showing loyalty to Alphonso when they think to gain from him, returning to Yusuf when they need his help. Yusuf is not a man to accept disloyalty. The scholars of the Council are in agreement: the amirs of Al-Andalus have been shown to be impious libertines who care only for their own comforts and luxuries, corrupting their own people with their poor example and commanding illegal taxes, expressly forbidden by the Qu'ran.

After some debate, Yusuf agrees on a new strategy. He will embark once again for Al-Andalus, but this time he will ignore the lying ways of the taifa kings. He will fight his own war against Alphonso, and he is determined to win. If he does, he will be able to claim the whole of Al-Andalus for himself and his kingdom will become an empire.

I am making my way home from the market when I realise I am being followed. I take first one street and then another, circling my house, unwilling to lead the man, whoever he may be, into my world. At last, in a narrow alleyway one street away from my home, I turn to face him. He is dressed like a local, but his skin is fairer than most and when he speaks, I swallow. His accent is like mine; I hear in it the notes of my childhood.

"May I speak with you?" he says.

"You are already speaking with me," I say, wanting to hear him speak again, so that I can be certain of what I heard, so that I can hear again a voice from my past.

"I would like to speak with you in private," says the man. He does not move forwards; he does not sound threatening.

"How do I know I can trust you?" I ask.

"I have not harmed you," he says. "I have known who you are for some time and have brought no harm to you or your household."

"My household?"

"A child, I believe," he says. "And a handmaiden for many years, or companion, whatever she is. A Jewess."

"Why would you need to know about me?" I ask.

"I am from Galicia, like yourself."

"And what is that to me?" I ask.

"I could return you to your home," he says. "The Convent of the Sacred Way, was it not?"

I have not heard its name for so long and yet in his mouth, I am suddenly there, in the silent cloisters, in the peace of my stillroom, tending to the sick along the pilgrims' route, surrounded by my sisters in God, my fellow brides of Christ. The scent of my plants rises up before me in the garden that I tended for so many years.

"How do you know its name?"

"That hardly matters," he says. "But it is your home, and I have the means to return you there."

"How?"

"In return for something," he says.

Of course. There is always a price to be paid. "What do you want from me?" I ask.

"Not much," he says. "May I enter your house?"

I take him away from curious gazes. I take him to an empty room, unwilling even to show him my study, wanting to share as little as possible with this man, this stranger, this person who knows so much about me. I do not offer him a seat; I do not offer him refreshment. I only take him to the room and turn to face him.

"What do you want from me?" I repeat.

"I believe you could do my master a great service," he says.

"And who is your master?" I ask.

"Rodrigo del Díaz," he says.

"I do not know this man," I say.

"He is a great warrior in our homeland," says the man. "But now he must face a vast and powerful army from a foreign land. He has need of knowledge."

"What army?" I ask, knowing the answer already.

"The Almoravids," he says. "Yusuf bin Tashfin intends to come against my master. And I believe you are in a position to find out when, and how, and other such knowledge as may benefit my master."

"Yusuf bin Tashfin is my master," I point out. "It would seem our masters are set against one another."

"Perhaps we could share a master," says the man.

"Meaning?"

"My master would gladly become your master," says the man. "And would set you free in return for your service, would return you to your home at the convent, with a goodly sum of money to benefit your holy community."

"You cannot promise such a thing," I say.

"I can," says the man. "It would not be impossible to take you away from here, to the sea, to have you set sail on a ship and be returned to our homeland. It can be arranged. For a price."

"And what do you want to know?" I ask.

"Timings. Numbers of men. Locations."

"I know nothing of these things. These are not things my master discusses with me."

"But you could ask."

"Then he would be suspicious."

"I am sure a woman of your learning could find a way."

"What makes you think I am disloyal to my master?"

"You are a slave," he reminds me, "and a slave has little loyalty to a master who has not set them free."

"He has given me a great deal," I say. "He has treated me well."

"But you are still a slave," he says. "Or are you more to him than that?"

"That is not your business," I say.

"Is the child yours?" he asks.

"He belongs to the Jewess," I say.

"Does he?" says the man.

"Yes," I say.

"I wonder," says the man. "I wonder if I should look into his parentage."

I stand in silence before him.

He waits, then nods his head. "You are not as eager to return to the convent as I expected," he says. "I thought your vows were sacred."

"I think you should leave now," I say.

"Of course," he says, and bows to me in the style of our country, which looks odd in the local robes he affects. "But think on what I have said. If you need to find me, you may tell the storyteller in the marketplace and he will know where to seek me out."

"Leave," I say.

"Think on it carefully," he says, walking down the stairs, his voice drifting back to me. "Think on where your loyalties lie, Sister Juliana."

I spend the rest of the day at prayer, shaken by the man's visit, by his knowledge of my life before here, by the offer he has made, even the use of my old name. I could leave here. I know that Yusuf would tell me enough that I could please the man's master, that I could ask questions carefully, without arousing his suspicion. I know that I could gather what has been asked for, and be stolen away from here in the night, travel far away before Yusuf finds out, sail across the sea and return to the convent, return to the life I once led. I believe what the man offers, I know that such knowledge as he has asked for would be of sufficient value that it would be worth his while to honour his promise to me in return. And have I not longed for the convent, all these years? I could leave here, with Ali in Rebecca's loving hands. I am sure he would be safe enough. I could leave here, and sail away from the past years, from all my sins and failings, from all the temptations this world has offered me and have my slate wiped clean. Begin again, anew, ask for forgiveness and receive absolution, for was I not sinned against? Was I not taken by force and kept without my will by heathens? I would be welcomed back with open arms; of this I am certain. Years have passed, but my sisters will have remembered me, prayed for me, hoped that I might one day return, whilst grieving for my loss. They will have thought me dead. If I returned, I would be a holy miracle, proof of God's will and blessing.

It would be so easy. But I cannot.

Ali hugs me goodnight and I bid Rebecca farewell for the day as she returns to Daniel, before retreating to my prayer room.

And I lie to myself, as always. I know full well what keeps me here, and it is neither Aisha nor Rebecca, who now have their own families, nor Fatima, now a healer and grown woman. In part it is Ali of course, although I know that he would be cared for in my absence. But it is my own heart that I think of, not the hearts of others. It is my own treacherous desire for Yusuf, and the knowledge that he is not just my master but my beloved, that means I cannot leave this place while he still lives, nor can I ever choose what I long for.

And now that I know this, why do I not give in? Why do I not choose the life I long for, choose Yusuf? Perhaps I cannot let go of the vows I once made, perhaps I am too much of a coward to knowingly pit myself against Zaynab, knowing what she is capable of, what I might have to face. Or perhaps I am too afraid to open my heart more than a crack, that I cannot face what emotions I might feel, if I were to love Yusuf as I long to.

The next day I go to the market square and watch the storyteller. I wonder if I could touch his arm and ask him under my breath where the man from Galicia is, to send him a message that the woman he spoke with wishes to speak with him again. But I do not. So now I know where my loyalties lie. I am going against my own homeland, my own king and his chosen warrior. The man they call El Cid will not be my hero, will not be the man whose armies and banners I cheer on. Instead I send against my own countryman another man, a veiled warrior who carries my heart by his side. I have forsworn my own people and cast in my lot with the heathen army that seeks to vanquish them, an army whose God is not my God.

Who am I then, who am I if I have forsworn my vows and the God to whom I made them? I kneel to pray but cannot find the answer.

Yusuf does not hold back. The King of Granada is taken and bound in chains, then sent across the sea to Zaynab, who decrees that he will henceforth live in Aghmat, now only a humble outpost. He is followed in less than a month by the King of Malaga, then the King of Seville. Zaynab must be enjoying her power over these foreign rulers, who must kneel to a woman and show gratitude for having their life spared. Valencia holds out the longest, but Rodrigo Del Diaz, known as El Cid, does not last long once his own son falls in battle. He dies shortly afterwards, broken by his son's demise and Yusuf's strength. And with this hero gone, the Christian armies lose their spirit. They huddle in the North, Al-Andalus is now wholly in Yusuf's hands. His kingdom has become an empire.

I hear from Aisha that Yusuf is due to return from Al-Andalus and my heart leaps. I try to pretend that I want the house cleaned from top to bottom out of the desire for cleanliness and order, but I know it is not true. I make Ali recite to me from his studies, I stand over him to see how smooth his handwriting is. I find myself stitching new robes for all of our household, in fine new wools and bright colours. I look down at what I'm stitching for myself, a golden yellow, so much unlike how I used to dress that I wonder for a moment if I should wear my customary grey or brown. But the colour mirrors what is in my heart, a lightening, a gladdening. I keep stitching.

The day that Yusuf returns to Murakush I feel giddy, I can settle to nothing. At last Rebecca says that she will take Ali out, that she needs to buy fruits in the marketplace. I agree that they may go, reminding myself that Yusuf will not visit us today, he has barely returned and will have much to do. He will not think of us for many days, I am certain of it.

It is a quiet day, Fatima tends to one or two patients upstairs, but most of the house is silent. I sit by the fountain in the empty courtyard and look into the water below, see my rippled reflection. Slowly I untie my hair wrap and look at how long and dark my hair has grown in these years. I should shave it of course, should return to the pale scalp that earned me the cruel name of moon, but I have not done so and I know, running my hands through its thickness, that I will not do so in the future. I see many strands of grey, and wonder whether, if I were to wash it with rosemary and walnut shells, whether I might reverse the greying, return my hair to the darkness of my youth. I reach out to rub a nearby sprig of rosemary between my fingertips, pluck it and hold it close to my nose, the smell overwhelming. Such vanity.

"There you are. With your plants, of course, as always."

I leap to my feet and take several steps towards Yusuf before I come to a sudden halt, holding myself back from throwing myself into his arms. I cannot do such a thing, but for one moment it was all I thought of.

"Have you changed your mind about greeting me?" he asks, closing the gap between us and coming to a halt so close in front of me that I take a step backwards.

I breathe in to answer and smell his scent, the rough smell of camel and sweat, but beneath that the smell of his own body, which I know too well. I breathe out again, unable to answer.

"You need not step away from me," he says, and his voice has grown deeper and quieter. He lifts his arm and to my astonishment runs his fingers through my hair. "I have never seen your hair unbound," he says.

"It is supposed to be veiled, like your face," I say, my voice shaking.

He takes his hand away from my head and instead pulls at his face veil, dropping it to the floor beside him, so that we stand face to face, the paleness of the skin beneath his eyes still startling to me. He has aged, these past years of fighting have been hard on a man already advanced in years. I feel myself trembling, think to kneel and collect my own head wrap, to pin it fiercely about myself and turn away from this intimacy. But I do not. I stand and gaze into his eyes in silence, until his hand reaches out again and this time touches my cheek.

"I have found a name for you," he says.

I jerk out a laugh. "After all these years without one that pleased you?"

"It is a name that suits you," he says.

I can think of nothing but his fingers on my skin. I have to blink, have to focus on what he has said. "And what is this name?"

"Fadl al-Hasan," he says.

I frown, then give a forced laugh. "Perfection of Beauty? I am hardly perfect."

He does not smile. His finger slips over the skin of my cheek, over my scars at the side of my face, usually hidden under my headwrap. "I think a better meaning is 'More than Perfection,'" he says softly, and I feel my skin turn to goose flesh, my cheeks grow flushed beneath his touch. "You are more than perfect."

I do not know how to respond to this intimacy from Yusuf. "You have changed," I say, my voice still shaking. "You have not spoken like this to me before."

"I missed you," he says simply.

"How did you have time to miss me?"

"I told you before. I miss speaking to someone of the small things."

"You have achieved great things while you were away," I say.

"Perhaps it is time to achieve something else," he says.

I should step away. I should make some light-hearted jest, to break the moment.

"It seems I must rule two lands now," he says. "But I have only one queen. Perhaps I should have another."

I say nothing.

"If each queen had her own land to rule over," he continues, his voice very low, "there could surely be no rivalry."

"Jealousy does not arise over lands," I say, my own voice barely above a whisper. "It arises when it is a heart that must be shared."

"You could rule as my queen over Al-Andalus," he says. "I will divide my time between there and here."

"I have no desire to rule over a kingdom," I say.

"Do you desire anything else that is in my power to give?" he asks.

I breathe in. The scent of him, standing so close to me, is almost too much to bear. "Do not ask that question," I say finally. "I cannot bring myself to answer it."

"And if I continue to ask?"

"I beg you not to," I say, and the effort it is costing me, to stand so close to him yet not touch him, to speak without accepting what he is offering, grows too much.

I turn and run away from him, make my way up the staircase and into my own bedchamber. I kneel by the window and look up at the bright sky above me, breathe deeply, wipe tears from my eyes.

Near to my hand is the small carved box in which I keep my most precious items, such few things as I have. I take it and turn around so that I am sitting on the floor, knees pulled up, the casket in my hands.

Falling Silver Beads

Let him kiss me with the kisses of his mouth.

Song of Solomon, 1:2

I TRY TO BREATHE SLOWLY, OPEN the casket to soothe myself with its familiar contents. I pull out the ivory rattle that Yusuf gave to Ali when he was a baby. I shake it and smile, replace it in the casket. There is a tiny cross that Rebecca gave to me when she married Daniel. My fingers touch the betrothal necklace I picked up from the ground when Kella left Murakush. I pull it out and look at it more closely, it has been years since I held it. It is a simple thing, little black beads interspersed with silver triangles, marked with symbols from her people, which mean nothing to me.

"Where did you get that from?" Yusuf has followed me, he is standing in the doorway, frowning. He has replaced his veil, I can only see his eyes and brows.

"It is nothing," I say quickly, replacing the necklace in the casket. My fingers are on the lid, ready to close it. My breath, which had begun to slow, comes faster again.

"Show me it."

His tone tells me I cannot disobey. Slowly, I reach back into the casket and hold up the little necklace.

He crosses the room and takes it. His fingers are shaking. He turns the necklace over in his hands, looks for something I cannot see and then stares down at me. "Where did you get this?"

"I – I found it." I feel vulnerable, sitting so low down, but I do not have the courage to stand and face him. I try to look away, but it is not a good enough answer. When I look up again his gaze is still on me, the hand that holds the necklace still shaking.

He is waiting.

"I found it after Kella left," I say. It is clear to me that he knows to whom it belongs, although I have seen other such necklaces. There is something about it that has identified it to him as Kella's and there is no use denying where it comes from.

"Where is she?"

"I do not know," I say honestly. "Truly, I would tell you if I knew."

"You found it where?"

"Outside her home."

"What were you doing there?"

"I – I saw her leave."

He stares at me in disbelief. "You knew she was leaving, and you did not call for me? You did not tell me afterwards where she had gone?"

"I did not know where she was going," I say.

"You did not try to stop her?"

I hesitate. "She was afraid of Zaynab," I say at last. "She had to leave."

"No harm would have come to her," says Yusuf, and his eyes have grown angry. "She was under my protection. Zaynab would not have harmed her."

"If you say so," I say.

"What is your meaning?" he asks, his voice tight.

"She set Hela to serve her and Hela saw to it that she lost a child." I say, standing up. He comes very close to me, looks into my face as though to seek the truth in my eyes. I meet his gaze without flinching, without looking away.

"Why did she leave?" he asks. "She could have come to me for protection."

I shake my head. "I do not know," I say. "I do not know all that was in her mind."

"What else do you keep in that casket?" he asks.

I feel the blood drain from my face, then rush back, my neck and cheeks hot. "Nothing," I say.

"You will forgive me, but I do not believe you," he says. "Give it to me."

"It is mine," I say.

He holds up the little necklace, the tiny silver triangles dangling. "But this was mine," he says. "It was mine and I gave it to Kella. It was not yours to keep, all these years. Show me the casket."

This is the moment then, the moment as I have thought of all the years that I have raised Ali. This is the moment when all I have done will come to light. I hold out the casket, my hands shaking so hard that the lid rattles, my knees suddenly weak. I try to steady my breathing. Yusuf takes it, his eyes never leaving my face.

"What is it?" he asks. He looks concerned now, he does not even look at the casket that he holds, he looks only into my eyes.

I shake my head. "Open it," I say.

He looks down at the tiny casket, lifts the lid and pulls out the tiny rattle he once gave Ali, looks at me.

"The beads," I say, my voice almost a whisper.

He looks down again, frowns, then returns the rattle to the casket and instead lifts out the long string of silver beads. He holds them closer, looks at the engravings on each and suddenly the casket drops from his other hand, hits the floor with a shattered thud, lies broken on the tiles beneath our feet. Neither of us look at it.

"What is the meaning of this?" he asks. "Why do you have the beads I gave to Kella for our son? He died at birth."

I try to speak, but my mouth is so dry it will not even open. I try to wet my lips, finally manage to open them and whisper. "He... did not die."

He stares at me. "What?"

I try again, speak a little louder. "He did not die," I say. "He lives."

"She took him away with her?"

I shake my head.

"How would you know whether he is alive or dead?"

"She gave him to me," I say.

He says nothing, only gazes at me for a long moment. "*Gave* him to you?"

"To protect him," I say. "From Zaynab. Kella was afraid of her. She gave Ali to me and left, so that Zaynab would leave him alone."

"She gave Ali, my son, to you?"

"Yes," I say.

"And he lives?"

"Yes," I say.

He is silent. "The child you have raised all these years," he says at last, "and whom you have called Ali, he is..."

"He is your son," I say, and the relief of saying it, after all this time, brings tears pouring down my cheeks so suddenly that they surprise me. I put a hand up to wipe them away and Yusuf takes me by the wrist, pulls me close to him, so close that our bodies touch.

"Swear," he says, and I am almost afraid of him for a moment, his voice is so hard, his grip on my wrist so tight that it is painful.

"I swear," I say.

We stare at each other. His grip on my wrist does not lessen.

"I swear," I say, my voice stronger now. "Your wife Kella gave me her son, your son Ali, to raise, to protect from Zaynab. She left this place and you to protect Ali. She gave me those beads to prove his lineage. I watched her leave and saw the necklace fall. I have kept them all these years. And I have raised Ali, as I promised Kella I would do."

"You have raised my son?"

"Yes," I say.

"He is the child I have seen all these years? Now a man?"

"Yes," I say. He is repeating himself but I can see belief beginning to dawn in his face.

He lets go of my wrist. Slowly, he kneels before me. I look down on him, uncertain of what he is doing. He takes the hem of my robe in his hands and kisses it. When he looks up at me, his eyes are overflowing with tears. "You have performed a greater service than I could ever have asked of you," he says.

"I swore I would care for him," I say, my tears falling down onto his veil. "I brought him into this world and now I deliver him back into your hands."

He makes me tell him everything, every time that my path crossed with Kella, everything she said, however small. It should be difficult, after all this time, but such were the events of that time that they are emblazoned on my mind. I tell him of Ali's birth and of Kella's visit to my home, of her desperate request and my promise to her. I explain how Rebecca came into our lives, and he blesses her name, laughing through his tears.

"I must see him," he says suddenly, as though the idea has only just occurred to him. "I must tell him everything."

"He knows nothing," I say. "Tell him gently, it will be a shock to him. He thinks of Rebecca and me as his mothers. He knows nothing of Kella. But he will be proud to be your son," I add.

Yusuf is beside himself. He cannot wait to speak with Ali, he paces impatiently about the house until he returns from his studies. I find myself growing nervous. The son I had is about to be lost to me, he will no longer call me mother. I find the tears welling up in me and force them back down.

I am not his mother, I remind myself, he has a mother of his own and a father, whose identity he is about to learn. My promise is fulfilled, I have protected him all these years and I am about to deliver him safely to his father.

When Ali does come home, Yusuf's face is flushed with joy. I watch from the upper storey as he takes Ali's arm and pulls him towards the fountain, the two of them sat side-by-side on the tiled edge, Yusuf's voice is low, his words rapid. I keep my eyes on Ali's face and watch it turn from puzzlement to wonder. He looks up at me, searching for my confirmation of what he's being told and when I nod, his shoulders shake, and Yusuf takes him in his arms.

"I must go," says Yusuf to me, after some time has passed. "I will return tomorrow," he adds, looking at Ali, whose face is both lit up with the wonderment of what has happened and blotched with his tears.

When he has gone, I stand awkwardly, waiting to hear what Ali has to say to me, but when he comes to me, he kneels at my feet and looks up into my face. "You are still my mother," he says. "For you and Rebecca are the only mothers I have ever known."

"I can tell you about your mother if you wish," I say.

"I would like to hear about the woman who gave me life," he says. "But I cannot call her mother. You are my mother."

I sit with him and tell him all I can about Kella, about her life before she met Yusuf, about the moment when she threw in her lot with him, and how she came to leave this place. I try not to accuse Zaynab, for I cannot risk Ali taking offence against her. A young man might foolishly swear vengeance on such a woman, should he know the true story between her and his mother. Instead I say only that Zaynab was fiercely jealous, that Kella did not wish for Ali to grow up with such rivalry around him and that she was unhappy herself, unable to live alongside Yusuf as she would have wished. That she made her way to a different life, that I know a good man went with her, along with loyal servants. Throughout, I tell him how much she loved him, how distraught she was on the black night when she brought him to me and begged for my help. I show him the string of silver beads, I show him the engagement necklace Yusuf gave her, and he holds them as though they were holy relics. Some of his questions I do not have the answers to but again and again he embraces me and thanks me, calls me mother. Our tears mingle and that night I retire to bed, exhausted from the emotions of two decades released in one afternoon.

The days that follow are filled with even more emotion. Rebecca hears what has happened and spends time with Ali, telling him her own story. Yusuf returns daily, speaking with Ali and embracing him constantly. He kneels to me every time he sees me, thanking me over and over again for what I have done, offering me anything, anything I desire, to which I shake my head and insist he stands. But then the arguments begin.

"Council will be held," Yusuf tells me while Ali is absent. "I will name Ali as my son. Once he has been accepted, I will name him my heir."

I feel myself grow cold. "You cannot," I say, too quickly.

"Why?"

I want to say Zaynab's name, but I dare not, even here, alone with him. "Ali has not been raised to be your heir," I say. "He has been raised to be a man of peace, not a man of war. Your empire is still so new, it will need a warrior to hold it."

But Yusuf only beams. "I have created an empire," he says. "Now it needs a man of peace to rule it, to create a land of plenty, a land filled with knowledge and goodwill amongst my people."

"He – " I begin.

"I have known him all his life," says Yusuf, interrupting me, still delighted. "He has been taught by the finest scholars, he is a man of knowledge, a man of the law. There is not one scholar who could argue with his knowledge of our religion and the law."

"He knows nothing of military strategy," I say.

"He has an army at his disposal," says Yusuf, unperturbed. "He has experienced generals at his command. His brothers, my other sons, will guide him in these matters."

"One of his brothers will expect to inherit your throne," I say. "They will be angry at being passed over. Why should they help him?"

"The choice of heir lies in my hands," says Yusuf. "Ali is my first son and the son of my first wife. And he has been raised by you," he adds softly.

I cannot help myself. "Zaynab – " I begin.

"The decision is mine to take," says Yusuf and from his tone I know it is useless to argue any further. I am greatly fearful for Ali's safety once Zaynab knows of his existence, but there is nothing I can do to change Yusuf's mind and Ali himself glows when he is told what is to come. He looks into the future and sees himself following in the footsteps of Yusuf, leading the empire into an era of peace and tranquillity, of stability.

"It will be like Cordoba," he says to me, his eyes alight with joy. "It will be everything you said Cordoba once was, but greater. Muslims, Christians, and Jews sharing knowledge, an empire the like of which has never been seen before."

I want to believe it is possible, that the vision he has for the future can come true, but at the same time I curse myself for having told Ali stories of the past that may be impossible to emulate. Cordoba's glory did not last long. I wish that I could consult with my own father, to ask him how Cordoba came to be and whether it is possible for this boy, this man, whom I think of as my son, to make such a time come alive again. I think that if anyone can manage it, this child, son of a Muslim, raised by a Christian, suckled by a Jewess, could be the one to do it, but I am afraid for him.

"I will pray that you are successful," I say. "I will pray every day of my life that your empire shines greater than Cordoba.

"We will go there together, you and I," he says enthusiastically. "We will pray together in Cordoba that its light may shine out across this new empire again."

I can only embrace him and nod, can only pray for his success and that he escapes Zaynab's wrath.

"Council has been summoned," Yusuf tells me. He has come to my house early; the dawn prayer was less than an hour ago. "You will attend with Ali," he tells me.

"There is no need for me to attend," I say quickly. "Ali is your son, I am not even his mother," I add, forswearing my child in an instant, for the chance to avoid being in the same room as Zaynab when she hears this news.

"Zaynab was calm enough," says Yusuf, knowing full well why I refuse to go.

"I do not believe that," I say. "Does she know that you are about to name him your heir?"

"No," he says. His tone is set, stubborn.

"Then I will not be there when you tell her," I say. "How do you think she will react? She surely expects her own son to succeed you."

"It is my choice," repeats Yusuf. I give a tiny sigh and he frowns.. "Surely you want Ali, the child you have raised, to succeed me?"

"It will be as you wish," I say.

"Yes, it will," he says, and sweeps from the room. "You will attend with Ali," he calls over his shoulder as he leaves.

I have no choice. Guards are sent to accompany us. Ali, dressed in his best robes, is glowing, although his demeanour changes a little as we come close to the Council chambers set within the palace. I can see him growing nervous and reach out a hand to touch his shoulder as Yusuf comes to greet him with open arms, gesturing to me to follow them into the chambers. I stand in the doorway, half hidden from the room, watching as Ali steps into the space. I look beyond him, to Yusuf's other sons, most born to Zaynab, two to slave women I do not know the names of. They are so very different from Ali. All of them have broad shoulders, their forearms ripple with muscles. These are men of war; they have been trained by the best warriors in Yusuf's army. They may have completed some studies, but they have not been held to their books day after day. Instead they have learned to fight, to command, to face the enemy in battle and ride out with courage in their hearts. They carry swords on their hips, daggers in their belts. Zaynab's eldest son, Abu Tahir, sits next to her and he looks every inch a future amir, the man everyone expects to succeed Yusuf. I swallow. Will he step aside and let Ali rule? Or will he seek him out in some deserted backstreet and end my son's life with a single stroke of the sword his hand is resting on?

Ali has joined the scholars, who are seated at the far end of the room, speaking with them, his back turned to the generals and governors that make up the rest of the room.

Yusuf stands and I brace myself.

"I ask the council to welcome my son, Ali. Child to my first wife Kella, now no longer with us."

There is a murmur, a ripple of interest. The council members turn their heads, stare at Ali with curiosity. He stands, a little pale, but with his head held high, looking to Yusuf for his confidence.

"The woman who raised him will vouch for his birth," says Yusuf. He gestures to me. "Isabella, join us."

I step forwards, my stomach churning, vomit rising in my throat. One of the scholars is rising, no doubt to question me. I look towards Zaynab and see her face has grown white, her hands are clenched into fists at her side.

The scholar is old, one of Yusuf's most important advisers. He begins to question me. I try to give my answers in a clear voice, without trembling.

"I swear that this man is Ali, son to Yusuf bin Tashfin and his wife Kella."

"Do you know where Kella is now?"

"I do not."

"Is she alive?"

"I do not know."

"How did you come to have this child in your care?"

Zaynab leans forwards, her dark eyes darker still in her white face.

"His mother summoned me as a midwife when she birthed him. He was born into my hands."

"Did she give him to you at once?"

"No. She came to me in great secrecy later that night. She claimed that the boy's life was in danger, that he must be raised by another. She begged me to take him. I did so." I swallow, trying to stop the tears that are welling in my eyes at the thought of that night, that request, that choice.

"From whom was he in danger?"

I do not let my eyes flicker towards her. I know that she is watching me. I know that she is waiting to hear her own name, preparing herself to fight. I shake my head.

"Give me a name," the old man insists. I can feel the tightness in the chamber, can hear the Council members waiting.

"I cannot."

There is a pause, while the scholar and the rest of the Council wait to see if I will relent, if there is any value to be had in continuing to press me for a name that I appear unwilling to give. Certainly, they know there is a name, but for now they have more pressing matters.

"Can you prove this story?"

I pull the string of silver beads from my robes and explain that Kella gave them to me to prove Ali's lineage. I look to Yusuf and ask if they are the same beads that he gave to his first wife and he agrees that they are. He adds that he confirms my story, that he believes the truth of what I say, that he himself accepts Ali as his son, his firstborn son.

The council cannot gainsay a father's word, nor the evidence I have provided. Besides, they do not need this proof. Ali may look like a scholar rather than a warrior, but no one could doubt him for Yusuf's son, the eyes are the same, even the way he turns his head from one side to another is the same. There is no argument. Only the elderly scholar wonders worriedly whether Ali, under my influence, has been raised a Christian, but I shake my head and tell them that he has been raised a Muslim, in deference to his lineage. There is a murmur of approval and the scholar himself presses my hand and declares me a blessed woman for having protected Ali all these years and having delivered him back to his father. The rest of the Council welcomes Ali as Yusuf's son and I feel my shoulders drop with relief. Even Zaynab gives a long slow nod, her face stony, but the nod has been given.

"There will be a banquet of welcome for my son," declares Yusuf. "You will all accompany us to give thanks and celebrate on this joyful day."

I try to steady myself at the thought of sitting at the same table as Zaynab. She is already approaching me.

Ali turns to her and bows deeply. "Lady Zaynab," he says, "I believe you knew my mother."

She looks him over and her eyes do not flicker, her mouth does not curve into a smile. "I did not know her well before she left," she says. Her smile comes as she watches Ali's face flush at the deliberate reminder that his mother abandoned him. I want to step forward, but I remind myself that if all she is going to do is make pointed barbs about his mother, then he is still safe.

"Come," says Yusuf, gesturing to Ali to precede him out of the door. As Ali does so, Yusuf turns to me, ignoring Zaynab, who is waiting for his hand. Instead, he extends his hand to me. "Join us," he says, his voice soft, pulling me towards him with his fingertips, my body brushing against his as we move forwards together. I should look behind me. I should be wary, but I cannot help it. I look up at Yusuf and he looks down at me with infinite tenderness. For one moment I am his queen and we are celebrating our son. Zaynab is far away and we can be happy. Behind me, I hear her voice say something, very low, but then she brushes past us and moves away, followed by her son Abu Tahir, whom she waves away as though he were unimportant. She is not headed towards the palace, rather back into some other part of the city. But I am swept away in this moment of happiness and I do not watch to see where she goes. She does not attend the banquet, and because I have Ali with me, I do not wonder where she has gone, I am only grateful that I do not have to sit near her, that I can celebrate with a full heart. No doubt, she cannot bear to attend such a celebration, and for this I do not blame her. She will hide

away in her rooms and emerge later, when I have gone, and Ali is no longer
being toasted.

We are sent a messenger the very next day. Yusuf does not wish to wait. He
will announce his heir today, in the Council chambers. Again, we set out,
again I am overcome with nerves but have to smile for Ali, have to nod at his
happy talk of what is to come. When we arrive, Ali is seated amongst Yusuf's
sons and daughters, as is now his right. He takes his place happily and his
half siblings nod graciously, well versed enough in court etiquette to know
that it would be unseemly to scowl and turn their faces away, especially
when Yusuf's eyes are upon them.

Abu Tahir has not yet joined his siblings. Instead he stands with Zaynab
while the council members arrive, and I feel myself grow cold as I see all
of them, scholars, warriors, governors, major and minor officials, bowing
deeply to the pair of them. It is clear that the Council expects Abu Tahir to
be named as Yusuf's heir today. I take a seat far at the back of the chamber,
afraid of what is to come. I wonder if fighting will break out, or whether
Yusuf's authority will keep them all in check.

Yusuf himself looks excited, rejuvenated. When he stands, the Council
falls silent and everyone leans forward, their faces beaming, expectant, their
eyes half on Yusuf, half on Abu Tahir. Zaynab, sat by her son, lifts her
chin high, waiting for the moment that will acknowledge everything she has
done for this empire.

Yusuf stands. "Today I will declare my heir," he says, loudly and clearly.
"Now that I command an empire, it must have a named heir, so that there
can be no doubt over its future, nor any disruption nor disputation when
my time to leave this world comes."

Zaynab is openly smiling. Her beauty is still exquisite despite her
advancing years, she is every inch a queen.

"Ali will be my heir," says Yusuf.

There is utter silence. Mouths open, eyes widen. Abu Tahir's face drains
white, his hand tightens on the hilt of his sword.

Quickly, the Council members gather themselves. They nod and smile,
they make comments to indicate that they knew this all along, that they
accept Yusuf's word. There is movement and chatter, there are loud voices.

Zaynab stays absolutely still. She is frozen, made of stone. She does
not speak to her son; she does not look at Yusuf. She stares only ahead, as

Ali kneels for his father's blessing, makes a speech about loyalty and peace, turns to greet the most senior Council members who offer him their fealty. His half siblings reluctantly swear the same, even Abu Tahir, unable to do otherwise under his father's watchful eyes, although he then strides from the council chambers, hand still on his sword, people hastily making way for him. Through all of this, Zaynab sits still, her face empty of emotion.

"There will be a ceremony of allegiance," says Yusuf. "Here and in Cordoba. Each governor will make a pledge of loyalty to Ali."

I know that this location has already been agreed upon with Ali, who thinks of Cordoba as a sort of holy land, a city that encompasses a past that he wishes to resurrect. Yusuf and Ali embrace, then leave the room, as do all the Council members. I join them, trying to hide in the crowd, aware that all of us are filing past Zaynab as though she were not there, pretending not to see her upright body, her set face, waiting for us to leave so that she can release the rage and grief inside of her. I hardly dare look at her, but when I do, I see that her eyes do not even follow any of us, she looks only straight ahead, as though seeing something we do not, perhaps her empire crumbling.

Aisha comes to my house, her face white.

"What is it?" I ask. "Has something happened to Ali? To Yusuf?"

"Let me in," she says in a half whisper.

I stand aside, and she pushes past me, pulling her hood back from her face as she does so. She refuses to speak until we are fully inside the house, sitting at my table.

"Well?"

"Zaynab is dead."

"That is not possible," I say. "I saw her yesterday. She was well. I saw her at the naming ceremony for Ali." I stop speaking, aware of what I have just said, of where I saw her, of what had happened. I meet Aisha's gaze. "Did she – " I cannot complete the sentence, do not want to complete the thought.

"They think so," whispers Aisha, as though we were surrounded by listeners. "They found her with a cup in her hand."

I think at once of Hela's cup, but that broke long ago, this would have been another cup, nothing magic about it, but containing something that ended Zaynab's life. She would have known what to make, she would have known what to put together, which ingredients to mix. The mixture would have smelt strong and unpleasant, even fetid, but she would have drunk it anyway, she would have set the cup to her lips and swallowed, knowing full well what she did. I shiver, knowing that she did this, took this action, because of Ali, because of Yusuf's choice to make him his heir, and I know that he did this in part because he loves me. It is a choice of emotion and love, not the choice he should have made. I know full well that Zaynab's son would have been a better choice, he has been raised as a warrior, has been raised as a future ruler. I think of Zaynab's face as Yusuf spoke the words that crowned Ali as his successor. I was too grateful for her absence to wonder where she had gone, to think of how she felt, having her empire given to a child she had long thought dead, son of the mother she managed to get rid of, raised by a woman whose relationship with Yusuf she never knew existed. But she knew before she died, I would swear to it. She knew in the very moment that Yusuf touched my arm, in the deepness and softness of his voice when he spoke to me. She was a clever woman; she could not fail to see. I sit in silence while Aisha stares at me.

"I must pray," I say.

She sits beside me. I do not know if she, too, prays, or whether she only thinks on what has happened. I try to pray, but the words do not come. I try to empty my heart and have God's word fill it, but nothing comes. There is only an emptiness and below that, so deep below, so far down that I should not acknowledge it even to myself, there is relief and gladness. I am free. I am safe. The woman I have feared all these years is gone. The boy I think of as my son is Yusuf's heir. And Yusuf... Yusuf is now mine alone, should I wish to claim him. I rise from my knees. Aisha follows me back to the table, and we sit again in silence.

"What will you do now?" she asks.

I shake my head. "I do not know," I say.

In the days that follow, my prayers for Zaynab come unbidden. I try to forgive her sins, though I am not sure that I do so fully, but I pray for her soul and I pray that what she and Yusuf created together, this great empire, may endure without her. I cannot but acknowledge that she was a great ruler, for all her savage jealousy and the cruelties she inflicted on others. I know that if I had been by Yusuf's side, his empire would have failed. I think of the three of us: of Kella, who gave Yusuf a son but could not withstand Zaynab, of Zaynab herself, a great and terrifying queen who created an empire. And myself? I have not been a mother, yet I have mothered Ali. I am nothing to Yusuf and yet I know he is everything to me and that I am held in his heart. I have played no part in creating this empire, yet I have raised the man who will rule it one day. I wonder at the strangeness of my life here. I have saved one abandoned woman and raised a desperate woman's child, I have loved a man and know I am loved in return, I have made a Jewess and a Muslim my closest friends. And yet, I am still a virgin untouched, a bride of Christ, my vows are still upheld. I wonder at God's ways, at his intentions for me. I wonder if the whole of my life since touching that red fruit so long ago has been one long punishment or an endless gift. Was I cast out of the Garden of Eden or sent out on a holy pilgrimage? I do not know, even after all these years I still cannot tell.

I do not see Zaynab's body before she is buried. She had grown old, but her beauty was legendary, it remained undimmed by time. Servants and slaves cowered away from her, thinking her powerful beyond this world. They claimed she spoke with djinns and other such nonsense, though I did not believe that. I believe, instead, that she was a woman who knew how to make others talk, divulging secrets they would not entrust to anyone else.

I think back to the first time I saw her, riding past in the streets of Aghmat, queen to a powerful amir, more beautiful than any woman I had ever seen, loaded down with gemstones and rich silks. She had everything, and yet her face was that of a truly unhappy woman. I believe she found a better match in Yusuf, although it burns my heart to think of it. She was his equal, the right woman to have led his empire with him side-by-side. However she ensnared him, I have to admit that she was a peerless queen for him. My own feelings for Yusuf are my own sin, my own temptation. She was free to marry, and she saw in him everything I did and more. She was right to claim him for her own, even though I have hated her for it all these years and tried to deny what I felt for her: jealousy, pure and simple. I am honest enough to admit it, now.

"I will send you home, should you wish it," says Yusuf.

I stare at him.

"I have had the documents drawn up," he says. He pushes paper towards me, and I look down at it, words appearing out of a blur: my own name, the word freedom, his name at the bottom.

I look up at him. Do not speak. My belly feels as though it is weighed down, I sense a rising nausea.

"You are a free woman," he says. "I have granted you a sum of money, to do with as you please."

I look back down at the document, see what has been granted to me. It is a vast quantity of gold, a sum for a princess, a queen. I raise my eyes to meet his.

"If you wish to return to the convent," he says, "I have appointed Imari to take you. He has been paid a goodly sum to carry out this task whenever you should wish to go, be it now or after my death. I have made enquiries; he has maps and all the needed directions to return you to the place you came from. You have only to call on him and it will be done."

"You are sending me away?" It comes out of my mouth so fast I blink.

For the first time in this conversation, he looks amused. "I would never do that," he says. "As you know full well. I would rather ask you to be my queen, but I believe the answer would be no."

I stare at him.

"Well? Will you be my queen?"

Slowly, I shake my head.

"Why?"

"For the same reason as always," I say, and a tear trickles down my cheek.

He nods. "As I thought. So, given that you will not accept what I would like to offer, I thought I would offer something else. What you long for."

"I long for you," I say.

"But what you long for, you will not accept."

I nod. I no longer deny it.

"So, will you accept my other offer?"

"I cannot leave," I say. "I cannot."

"What holds you here?"

"You know what holds me here."

"I would like to hear it from you."

"Ali."

He waits.

"And you."

"If I were to die?"

"I would go."

"And Ali?"

"A grown man does not need a mother following him about," I say.

He nods. "Will you move into the palace with me?"

I shake my head.

He snorts with laughter. "So stubborn."

"Too weak," I say, serious.

"Weak?"

"I am not stupid enough to bring temptation so close to me every day," I say.

"I wish you would," he says.

There is a short time of peace, of sunlit afternoons when Yusuf visits me and we do not have to be hidden from the world, when Ali sits by us, his face lit up with love for the both of us. We talk of the small things, as we always did, sometimes we even walk through Murakush's streets together in the bright dawns and shining twilights. The city of cloth is long gone now, replaced by the towering minarets and sturdy city walls of an empire's capital. Yusuf's pace is slow now but there is no hurry to be anywhere. We eat fresh oranges together and I open my mouth to Yusuf as he feeds me dates, their rich sweetness unable to match my happiness. A golden time.

The call I have so long dreaded comes at night. There is a beating on my gate, and I do not even enquire of the veiled guard why he has come. I throw a warm wrap over my robe and follow him through the narrow streets until we reach the palace gates, where guards spring apart to let me pass, my status here well known.

The room is lit with dozens of lanterns, their flames flickering around Yusuf's bed, his guards and senior officers lining the walls, his sons kneeling by him. Ali stands when he sees me, comes to me and kisses my hands. Yusuf's eyes are closed.

"Is he – " I begin, but already my eyes have seen the rise and fall of his chest and my question is answered.

"It will not be long now, my lady," says the attending physician. I notice his deference, his knowledge of who I am.

Yusuf's eyes open, slowly, as though the action costs him an effort. He must already have heard my voice, for his gaze is already on me. "Clear the room," he says.

"My lord – " begins one of the generals.

"My heir is already named. You have no further need of me," he says, with a trace of humour. "Clear the room."

They do so, reluctantly, beginning with the lesser officials and guards, then his sons, even Ali at the end.

I stand at the foot of his bed, the two of us alone.

"Well, I have managed to make you enter my bedchamber," he says, half smiling. "It has only taken me two decades or so."

I smile, although the tears are already flowing.

"Oh, come now," he says. "A slave kept as a concubine must make herself pleasant to her master. You must smile, at the very least."

I swallow. "You forget," I retort, trying to laugh. "I am no longer a slave. And I was never a concubine, not even to my last master."

"Indeed, how could I forget? I have never heard of any woman leaping from a window to avoid becoming a concubine."

"Then taking two decades to enter your bedchamber should hardly be surprising, by comparison."

He holds out his hand to me and I walk around the side of the bed and sit on a stool beside him. I take his hand in mine. It is surprisingly warm, dry, as wiry as ever.

"Everything is taken care of," he says. "You know where Imari is, you will be given an army escort if it is required, there will be a ship ready to take you at your command back across the seas. Unless you prefer to travel by land. Al-Andalus is under our command now; you may travel however you wish."

I say nothing.

"Will you go home?" he asks.

"I am not sure where home is," I say.

"For a rich woman, home can be wherever she chooses," he says, smiling.

I nod.

"A woman as rich as you will be made an Abbess," he says ruefully. "Perhaps those of faith should not be swayed by money, but they usually are."

"A woman who has lived among Muslims? A woman who has raised a child? Who is rumoured to be the concubine of the heathen warlord who killed El Cid?"

"Gold is a wonderful thing for creating memory loss," he says. "As a healer you should know that."

"As a healer I should cure memory loss, not create it," I say.

"Sometimes forgetting the past is a form of healing," he says. "You can forget everything that has happened and return to your life in the convent."

I laugh out loud. "There is not enough gold in the world to forget all that has happened to me," I tell him.

We sit in silence for a little while, then I kneel by his bedside and clasp my hands together.

"What are you doing?"

"Praying for your soul," I say.

"To which god?" he asks, his voice full of laughter.

"It does not matter," I say. "Be quiet and let me pray."

When I have finished, I stand and look down on him, at the dark eyes, thick brows, the sharp nose. I put my hand to his face and pull away his veil, so that I can see his lips.

"Are you afraid you will forget my face?" he asks. He is teasing but his eyes grow serious when he sees the look on my face, how I hold his gaze.

Slowly, I bend down, close my eyes and feel our faces touch, forehead to forehead, nose to nose. I breathe in his breath and he breathes in mine. Our lips meet, one moment of temptation given into, all the past years of longing and desire distilled into this one touch, this one moment. When I straighten up, I keep my eyes on him a moment longer and then I turn and leave the room. The corridor is full of men, who part before me as I leave Yusuf's palace for the last time and make my way home, where I kneel by the fountain and weep until a messenger comes to tell me that Yusuf is gone. When he does, I send a message of my own to Imari.

I spend the days before my departure comforting Ali, who mourns his father but thrills with the thought of ruling an empire.

"Don't go," he begs me.

"I have to return home, to fulfil my vows," I tell him. "And you are a grown man, you have no need of me. You will be a great ruler."

"I am – afraid," he admits.

"There is no shame in fear," I tell him. "Rule by your heart. Be good to your people. They deserve peace after all these years of war."

He is excited by this thought, nodding keenly.

"And Rebecca is still here," I say. "She is your mother as much as I."

"I have had three mothers," he says earnestly. "And I will honour each of you."

"You have been a blessing in all our lives," I say and embrace him again and again, thinking of Kella and how she found it impossible to let go of him, how she clung just a little longer to the feel and scent of him.

Rebecca weeps and begs me not to go, but I hold her tightly.

"Ali is close by, you have your children, your husband," I say.

"My life has changed beyond recognition, thanks to you," she says.

"Thanks to your good heart," I remind her.

"I never thought the pain of life's path would bring me to call a Christian my sister," she says, wiping her tears and mine with a corner of her robe.

I have to laugh. "Nor I a Jewess," I say. "But you are indeed my sister."

"And I?" says Aisha.

"Both my sisters, God be praised," I say.

"I will not ask which god," says Aisha. "That much at least I have learnt from you."

We laugh through our tears, the three of us embracing while Imari waits with our camels.

"Send him home safe to me," says Aisha.

"You know I will," I say.

"Do not forget us," calls Rebecca, watching me mount an irate camel who will be my steed until we reach the sea.

"I cannot forget my sisters," I call back, steadying myself in the saddle and pulling my robe about me against the morning chill.

I look back only once, see their hands raised in farewell. I raise my own hand so that they can see it, hold it aloft until I know I am no longer in their sight, then use it to wipe my eyes of the tears that will not stop falling.

The journey I make now, retracing the steps of long ago, is entirely different. Escorts of soldiers follow us from encampment to encampment, in every city I am treated as a guest of honour, lavishly fed and bedded, bowed and scraped to by the nobles and warriors that make up each city's rulers. I am almost grateful for the quiet days, when Imari and I travel mostly alone, when our food is something simple, bread and dates eaten under the shade of a tree. I watch the landscape change, watch the mountains fade away and the coast approach.

When we reach the docks, I stand for some time in the market square, watching a slave auction being prepared. I allow the merchant, a different one now, to make his opening speech, to display all his wares, before I step out of the crowd and speak with him, my lips close to his ear, his eyes wide and startled. He stands by as every slave sees their names written out in my own hand, the gold passed over to buy their freedom and the coins in heavy leather pouches they each receive so that they may make their way in the world as free men and women, their children safe by their sides. I know more slaves will come tomorrow and tomorrow and tomorrow, but at least today's slaves are free. I hope that amongst them is a girl like Catalina, now destined for something better than a rich man's plaything.

Imari watches me with a strange half smile. "If someone had bought your freedom when you were sold," he says, curious, "would you have been grateful not to have lived the life that came after you were bought?"

I smile back. "There are not many slaves whose lives beyond today would have brought them what my life here has brought me," I say.

He nods at the truth of what I say and goes about finding a ship we can board, an easy task. There is no shortage of captains willing to be paid in gold for a simple voyage with a small cargo.

I do not know where in the dark waters Sister Maria died. I do not know which part of the sea received her body, nor where her spirit went. But when the stars are bright above us on our last night of sailing, I throw dried rose petals onto the waves beneath us and hope that my too-late tribute reaches her in some form. I think of her ready smile and her love for the world in all its forms, her kindness to others and her fear of what might happen to her when we were taken, how the darkness of our future must have been too much to bear. I think of what it must have taken for her to look into a different kind of darkness below and how cold the water must have been around her as she died. We took such different paths, she and I, each of which might be condemned, and by each of which we might have been blessed.

It is dawn when we land, still half-dark. I am not bound. I am not pushed, or pulled, lifted without my permission. Strong hands hold mine with courtesy, I am lifted gently and with all due care and respect for both my age and status, into a little boat which will take us to the shore. Again, I am lifted and now my feet touch the soil of Galicia. I bend down to touch it, lift the sand and let it run through my fingertips. I am home.

We brought two horses with us and they are helped to swim to shore. Imari sees me comfortable in the saddle, I am given the reins to my steed. We look out to sea to see the ship already setting sail.

We ride the short distance along the coast to A Lanzada. I think of Catalina's family still living close by but there is no news I could give them that would bring them happiness. Instead I make my way to the hermitage while Imari waits on the beach with the horses.

The tiny chapel is very quiet. I have not been in a Christian church for two decades and it is both familiar and strange to me. I touch the pews, make my way to the altar and kneel.

I pray for Catalina, wherever she may be. She would be in her mid-thirties by now, as I was when we were taken. I hope that she has made some kind of life for herself in the Maghreb, that her destiny turned out better than I feared, as mine did.

I give thanks for my own safe return, the miracle I prayed for all those years ago now accomplished. I feel I have been sent on a pilgrimage of sorts and now I give thanks for the wisdom received, for the kindness I have been shown along the way.

When I return to the beach, I stand for a moment looking out to sea, watching the waves rippling against the sand. I wonder if the barren women of the area still make their way here once a year and stand in the moonlight while nine waves wash over them. I say a small prayer that those who do will be blessed with the children they so long for.

"Are you ready, my lady?"

I hesitate. Am I ready? Am I ready, to return to a world I had thought lost to me forever? But this is the moment I have thought about for years, it is a sign of God's blessing on me that he has brought me home. "Yes," I say, my voice so quiet that Imari has to tilt his head to look at my face, for he has not heard me. I nod and he nods in return. He helps me back into the saddle and then mounts his own horse. I take the reins in my hands, take a deep breath, and dig in my heels. The convent is only a few days' ride away, even at a leisurely pace.

Day of Judgement, Galicia, 1106

Set me as a seal upon thine heart.

Song of Solomon 8:6

I HEAR FOOTSTEPS COMING TO THE *heavy wooden door, and fastenings being undone. I know that I will be welcomed here, that the fortune which Yusuf left to me will elevate me to a place of honour in a short space of time. I may even end my days as a Mother Superior, for memories are short and money speaks, even within holy walls.*

I will miss my son. For he will always be my son, no matter that I pray in a convent and he in a mosque. For me, Ali will always be the baby whose hand took my finger and whose smile changed my heart.

This is a place where I can end my days in peace. I will not be stolen nor bought; I will fear neither man nor war. Here I will be able to rest, to speak with my God in the last years left to me, live without looking over my shoulder for watching eyes.

I could have wished for a different path of course, for a simple life, to have remained all my years in this protected place. I would have been spared fear and humiliation, pain and persecution. Had I lived here I would not have had to raise a son in another's faith, nor have loved and been loved by a man who could never be my husband. But I know now that I would have been a lesser woman.

I look back over my shoulder for the last time. Imari waits, patient as always, to make certain that I have entered the great door, returned to a place of safety.

"You will care for my sister," I call to him, my voice breaking a little.
"And love her," he replies, placing one hand over his heart.
I nod and turn back to the door as it opens.

When I stand before my God on the great Day of Judgement there are those who will charge me with having abandoned my calling, indeed my faith. They will accuse me of lusting after a heathen Moor and forgetting my holy vows, with raising a child to rule an empire whose people are set against my own, with consorting with both a Jewess and a Muslim as though they were my sisters in Christ. They will ask what I did with my life, to atone for such sins.

I will look my God full in His terrible face and I will say, "Lord, I learned to love."

And He will understand.

Historical Notes

In 11th century Morocco Abu Bakr bin 'Umar and Yusuf bin Tashfin headed up a holy army, the al-Mourabitoun, known later as the Almoravids (I have used this name for simplicity), intent on bringing the country under Islamic rule. Up to this time Morocco, along with Tunisia and Algeria (collectively known as the Maghreb) was primarily a set of tribal Berber states with more or less strict adherence to Islam.

They were successful, taking the important city of Aghmat early on. Abu Bakr married the queen of the city, Zaynab, said to have been a very beautiful and clever woman known as 'the Magician'. When southern tribes rebelled, Abu Bakr left both the foundling garrison city of Murakush (modern Marrakesh) and Zaynab to Yusuf (who married her) and went to deal with the tribes. When he returned, Zaynab advised Yusuf on how to negotiate keeping his power. They came to an amicable agreement and Abu Bakr went back to the south, leaving Yusuf as commander of the whole army in all but name and Zaynab as his queen consort.

Yusuf went on to conquer the whole of Morocco, plus parts of Tunisia and Algeria. When Muslim rulers in Al-Andalus (Andalusia) asked for his aid, he went to help them, but they could not maintain loyalty to each other or him, so he ended up taking all of their small kingdoms for himself (this included fighting against and defeating El Cid). He died when he was very old. He had been a very religious man who disdained the riches of the world such as fine clothes or elaborate food and was said to be quite a kindly person.

From the very beginning of my research into Yusuf bin Tashfin and the Almoravids, one fact surprised and confused me. Yusuf was married to Zaynab, who apparently was very much a co-leader and a trusted right-hand woman, creating an empire alongside him. She also, it seems, bore him quite a few children. Considering Zaynab's undisputed beauty and intelligence, her status as Yusuf's right hand and that she had given him several children, as well as his own devout Muslim faith, it seemed very strange to me that

Yusuf would choose as his heir a child named Ali, "the son of a Christian slave girl." It certainly made me wonder how Zaynab would have taken such a choice when she might reasonably have expected one of her own sons (the Almoravids did not use primogeniture) to inherit the empire. My series of books set around the Almoravids takes this strange choice and creates a possible narrative around it.

This era has a lot of missing information, so while Zaynab's historical record has a few paragraphs of information (some of it rather vague), the woman on whom I have based Isabella has even less information. It seemed to be important to historians of the time that she was a slave and that she was Christian, for this is almost all that has been recorded about her apart from a possible name, Kamra (moon) and nickname, Perfection of Beauty.

Ali seems to have been very ill suited in temperament for ruling a newly created empire, being described as studious, pious, peace-loving and not a warrior, which effectively led to him rapidly losing the empire his father had created to the Almohad dynasty. Given that primogeniture was not being used (so that, one presumes, a ruler could choose the most appropriate child to inherit) this choice seems very odd and suggests perhaps more of an emotional choice than a logical one. He treated both Jews and Christians better than previous rulers, with the number of Christians present in the Maghreb hugely increasing under his rule.

I thought that the "Christian slave girl" could well have been Spanish, given the Viking raids of the era. Her original name is Isabella because I like the name (this book is dedicated to my daughter Isabelle) and I then gave her the religious name Sister Juliana because I needed an early saint and chose the name from a list. It made me laugh to then realise that Saint Juliana was actually a martyr because she refused to marry a pagan husband and was scarred as punishment, thus beautifully echoing the plot I had already written… one of those strange coincidences that happens when you write historical fiction.

I chose to create a character who began with a very strong Christian faith which could come into conflict with people of other faiths she would encounter. I had read about the golden age of Al-Andalus, some time before the era of this novel, where Muslim, Christian and Jewish scholars had achieved a peaceful, fantastically knowledgeable and creative society with the city of Cordoba at its centre (there is a lovely documentary on this era called *Cities of Light*). I really wanted Isabella's character to move from a perhaps overly prescriptive understanding of faith into experiencing people of other faiths as friends and loved ones and receiving a lesson in 'love' (in both the romantic and wider sense) through those experiences. Isabella moves from a rather rigid and small world (emotionally, mentally and physically) into a bigger space and understanding. Although Isabella chooses to return to her convent at the end, she does so with a deeper understanding of the world and a greater ability to love people for who they are. The last few sentences of the book, where Isabella thinks about what people may accuse her of on the Day of Judgement (and God's wiser and kinder understanding of what she has experienced) were with me from the very beginning of planning this novel. They sum up my desire for Isabella's experiences to be both life – and faith – changing and I hope I have done the concept justice.

Isabella's fictional Benedictine 'Convent of the Sacred Way' is set in Galicia (North-West Spain) along the pilgrimage route to Santiago de Compostela, which was already a major pilgrimage destination by the eleventh century. The place where she is kidnapped, A Lanzada, is right on the coast, where there was both a watchtower against the Vikings and a hermitage at the time. The Vikings were known to use the Arousa Estuary to bring their ships close to Santiago de Compostela, hence the watchtower.

The Vikings conducted a lot of raids across Spain including Northern Spain/Galicia. They were referred to as Norsemen by the Galicians. They kidnapped people and mostly sold them as slaves to North Africa. Although there were far less raids at this time than in the previous two centuries, they still continued. If you'd like to see *Draken Harald Hafagre*, the world's largest replica Viking ship, just look it up on www.drakenhh.com, it's an amazing sight and was very useful to me in my research, although the footage of it sailing on the open sea made me feel pretty seasick!

Yusuf's first wife, Kella, is fictional, although it seems odd Yusuf would have had no wife at all until he was nearly fifty. Her story is told in *A String of Silver Beads*.

Zaynab was Yusuf bin Tashfin's queen and right hand, acknowledged as a superb military tactician. She was highly important in negotiating the transfer of power from Abu Bakr to Yusuf. She is described as follows: *In her time there was none such as she – none more beautiful or intelligent or witty ... she was married to Yusuf, who built Marrakech for her.* There is no clarity on when or how Zaynab died. Her story, including her extraordinary total of four marriages, is told in *None Such as She* and her fictional handmaid Hela's story is told in *The Cup,* a free novella which you can download from my website www.MelissaAddey.com.

Bin Sina would be Ibn Sina or Avicenna (I use bin rather than ibn in my books to help with pronunciation), the father of modern medicine, a Persian scholar and physician. The Islamic world was far ahead of the Western world in medicine at this time, having drawn on multiple sources including Graeco-Roman, Indian and Chinese medical knowledge and traditions, in a way that Western medicine had not. His book was not used in the West until the 13th century, when it set the medical standard for centuries.

A note on names: the names of some of the men (especially Yusuf's sons) were tricky to choose, especially where they are called Abu-something. This ought to mean 'father of' and would be a name they used as an adult, referencing their own son, but as there is no mention of their childhood names, it is all I can go on and I did not wish to make up names entirely. Therefore, I have simply stuck to their adult names.

It is not clear who were the mothers of Yusuf's children, so I have proceeded on the basis that most but not all were Zaynab's, since Yusuf had at least one son by a slave.

I have used Murakush (land of God), the original name for Marrakech.

Have you read The Forbidden City series?

18th century China. All girls aged thirteen to sixteen had to attend the Imperial Daughters' Draft, so that the Emperor could have the first choice of every woman in his empire as a possible concubine. This award-winning series follows the interlinked lives of four real women who entered the Forbidden City and whose lives were changed forever.

Your Free Book

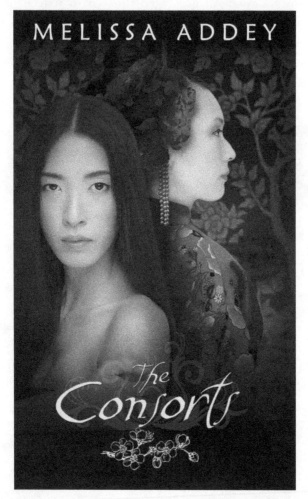

China, 1700s. Lady Qing has spent the past seven years languishing inside the high red walls of the Forbidden City. Classed as an Honoured Lady, a lowly-ranked concubine, Qing is neglected by the Emperor, passed over for more ambitious women. But when a new concubine, Lady Ying, arrives, Qing's world is turned upside down. As the highest position at court becomes available and every woman fights for status, Qing finds love for the first time in her life… if Lady Ula Nara, the most ambitious woman at court, will allow her a taste of happiness.

Download your free copy on your local Amazon

Interview with Melissa Addey

Where do you get your ideas from?

I call it the 'footnotes of history,' usually a brief mention in a history or travel book that attracts my attention. For the Moroccan series, it was a paragraph on the symbolism and beauty of Berber jewellery in a Lonely Planet guide to Morocco. I read it and then thought how wonderful it would be to have a book focused on a Moroccan woman, in which each chapter was symbolised by a piece of jewellery she is given to mark a certain point in her life and the story. This became *A String of Silver Beads*. For the Chinese series set in the Forbidden City, it was mention of the legend of the 'fragrant concubine' in a travelogue written about China. The legend had two such very different versions that it intrigued me and the more I read up on it, the more curious I became. That became *The Fragrant Concubine* and once I had read up on the Qing court I found more and more characters whose stories I wanted to tell. For my Ancient Rome series I found myself wondering who the 'backstage team' were at the Colosseum and then realised hardly anything had been written about them even though a building on that scale producing that many Games must have had a permanent team. The gaps in the historical record are gold dust to a writer.

What comes first, the plot or the characters?

Usually the kernel of an idea or a very vague person. Then comes some early research, where characters begin to emerge, both from the historical record and those I would like to explore or those who seem to be blatantly missing from the record. The plot comes much later, a part of it may be imposed upon me, like historical events, but part of it is made up of the things I would like my characters to experience within those historical events.

How do you come up with the titles to your books?

Some of them are easy. *The Fragrant Concubine* could only ever have been called that. The Moroccan series I struggled with. It was originally going to be called Desert Jewel (*A String of Silver Beads*), Desert Flower (the meaning of Zaynab's name, now *None Such as She*) and Desert Slave (*Do Not Awaken Love*). I prefer the current names. For the Roman series, I wanted to work through the four elements and reflect that in the names. So book 1 is fire (*From the Ashes*), book 2 is water (*Beneath the Waves*), book 3 is earth (*On Bloodied Ground*) and book 4 is air (*The Flight of Birds*). Choosing titles is a lot of fun, especially when you hit on the right one, it feels like recognising it rather than inventing it.

Describe your writing space

I have a little room heavily lined with books to one side, with a large desk and also a bike-desk which allows me to dictate some of my work whilst cycling, otherwise I don't think I'd get any exercise at all! I have a collection of funny little cacti and house leeks on my windowsill and a marketing planner on my right, which allows me to see when new books are due for publication, festivals I'm speaking at, etc. In front of me is a beautiful picture of a pelican with its wing up, it looks like an otherworldly being and I love it. Behind me is an old letterpress drawer, now painted in black and gold, which holds lots of little bits that I find interesting, from a genuine tiny Roman statuette which I bought when I started the Roman series, little pebbles I have found over the years and a lovely carved wooden representation of a walnut I bought in China. They're mostly small items that I find curious or inspiring.

Does writing sad scenes ever make you cry?

Not at the time, for an emotional scene I'm just very caught up in writing it. But when I read them back, yes, they make me cry. I hope that's a good sign, that the writing has managed to draw emotion out of me. I always wonder if my readers cry at the same points that I do.

Who is your favourite character?

I quite like the 'baddies'! Because I spend a lot of time thinking about them, wondering what would make them be that way. I liked writing Ula Nara's story in *The Cold Palace* and I found Zaynab very intriguing. I've had readers say they didn't like the way she behaved, but I think if she were a man one would barely notice what she did. And she co-created an empire, she was an extraordinary woman. And I thought, how would she feel about her empire being given to another woman's child? The mystery of that strange choice of heir was the foundation of the whole Moroccan series. I also liked

Hela, in *The Cup*, I think vows at that time would have been very sacred, and I wondered what kind of vow a very young girl would make: probably something too dramatic and impossible to actually fulfil. I also tried hard, in that book, to keep the balance between: is the cup itself magical or is it just Hela's own powers alongside her interpretation of events?

Do you write listening to music? If so, what kind?
Oh yes! When I'm writing the actual story, I try to listen to music from that culture and or era, depending what's available. Some of it takes some getting used to. I found Chinese music difficult at first, but grew to like it over the years that I wrote the series. Moroccan music, I found easier from the start. Ancient Roman music has been a little harder to trace and I'm still getting used to it. Listening to music appropriate to the story is hugely helpful when you come back to a piece of writing and need to remember the feel of it.

Why did you choose certain times and places as your settings?
The Chinese series had to be that time and place because of the fragrant concubine herself. So that set the era for me, and I mostly kept within a couple of decades of that. For the Moroccan series, I travelled back through Moroccan history to find an era that spoke to me. When I came across the Almoravids and in particular Yusuf bin Tashfin I felt that this was a very strong setting. Not only was it the moment when the whole of North Africa came together as one, but Yusuf then went on to conquer Spain as well, he was the leader of the army that conquered El Cid. Then I realised he had a powerful queen by his side, and found Zaynab an interesting person. And finally, his choice of heir made me very curious. For the Roman series, it was all about the Colosseum, and I wanted to begin right at the beginning. I had to go and look up when the Colosseum was inaugurated and when I found that it was 80AD and that Pompeii had been devastated by Vesuvius just before that, in 79AD, I thought that was a very strong time and place to begin the story I wanted to tell.

What is the best part of your working day?
Probably settling down in the office with music, a cup of coffee and a very long to-do list, when you still think you're going to get it all done. I'm a great one for to-do lists and set myself impossibly long ones.

How many plot ideas are waiting to be written? Can you tell us about one?

Oh, so many! I try not to think about them as it can be distracting. I have some very strong and clear in my mind, others aren't quite in focus yet, but have a little element that intrigues me. Right now I'm focused on the Roman series so that's very exciting because I can finally start the research and the writing, having thought about it for quite some time beforehand while I was still trying to finish the Moroccan series and the Chinese series. After that... I don't know yet, I choose the idea that seems most vivid to me at the time when I have availability. One day there will definitely be a series set in New Orleans, because I love it as a location and it has so much history to choose from. I have a lot of random history books in my collection that remind me of ideas I've had. Maybe something in Victorian times too, it was such a strange era, so old-fashioned in some ways and yet so full of ideas and stories that have shaped us now.

Who is your favourite author and why?

I'm very lucky to have three authors whose books I enjoy immensely and who regularly write a book a year, which all seem to come out just before my birthday in October, it's very kind of them. They are Philippa Gregory, who writes wonderful historical fiction: I've learned a lot from her writing style and in particular enjoyed the books where she views the same events and characters from another angle in another book, something I've done with both my Moroccan and Chinese series. I love Stephen King because his storytelling is superb, especially about ordinary people living ordinary lives, he somehow makes it compelling. I wish he didn't write horror though, it scares the living daylights out of me. I don't read any other horror writer or watch any horror films. But I keep coming back to Stephen King because of his storytelling. I wonder if I could persuade him to write a light-hearted romance?! My third author is Terry Pratchett and every year since he died, I still miss there not being a book from him. I cried when the last book was delivered. But I take pleasure in re-reading the books he wrote, they are an extraordinary legacy.

What book is currently on your bedside table?

Um... when you say *book*... there's at least six on my bedside table at any one time. They range from historical fiction, to research books, to books I'm reading for my book club that's been going for more than a decade, sometimes children's books that I'm reading to my children at bedtime. And then there's more than thirty stacked up in my office, waiting to be transferred to the bedside table… and I keep buying them and people keep giving them to me! There are so many books to read in the world and I'm never going to read them all, which has been a genuine sadness to me ever since I was a child.

What is your favourite book?

The Grapes of Wrath by John Steinbeck. It manages to be both devastatingly sad when it looks at the big picture and, at times, hilariously funny about the minutiae of daily life. I don't know how he did it. And when you look at the history of the Great Depression, which to him was current affairs, it is crushingly awful. I think you can look at a lot of his other books and see glimpses of *The Grapes of Wrath* and somehow it all comes together in that book. I read some articles he wrote for newspapers at the time and you can feel the rage building up in him about how terrible life was for the migrant workers.

What was your favourite book as a child?

Well I did play a game centred around the main family in *The Grapes of Wrath* as a child, which sounds peculiar, but they were very strongly drawn characters. I also loved Italo Calvino's folktales, which came in a giant tome. There's a picture of me reading it, having to balance the book on my knees because it's so heavy. I loved mythology from all parts of the world and read voraciously, the main difficulty was having enough new books since I got through them so fast. I think all the reading I did built up my imagination: all that mythology, all those stories, created a lot of worlds to inhabit. I used to play by myself quite a lot and pretend to be everything from Odysseus sailing home to an Egyptian goddess: I think talking to yourself and pretending to be other people is good practice for being a writer one day.

Share something your readers wouldn't know about you

I was home educated, so I never went to school! I've done a lot of dance classes over the years, from flamenco to Kathak, Bollywood to salsa, dancing is something I love to do and I enjoyed giving Zaynab a dance lesson in *None Such as She*.

What research trips have you been on?

I've been on a trip for each one of my series so far. I visited Morocco with my husband, where I got the original idea for the Moroccan series from. It was wonderful to see the landscape, ride camels, and eat the local food. For China, my family and I spent two weeks in Beijing, visiting key locations. The Forbidden City and The Garden of Perfect Brightness were just extraordinary, the city like a maze of endless corridors and doors, the garden like a countryside Venice, they were both beautiful. For Rome, I visited the Colosseum and was able to go underground, where the backstage team would have worked. It was highly evocative, it must have been very dark down there and they have replica lifts to show you how the gladiators and beasts would have been lifted into the arena, appearing through concealed trapdoors. I've made videos of my research trips, which you can see on my website and my You Tube channel. It's not so much about looking at a particular building or location, it's about the feelings it triggers in you, what it tastes and smells and feels like. It's a very sensory experience.

Does writing energise or exhaust you?

Thinking about writing, like plotting and doing the research, energises me a lot. Writing energises me to some degree, it depends how much I'm doing a day. I've taken part in NaNoWriMo a couple of times (an online writing challenge, National Novel Writing Month requires authors to write 50,000 words in one month) and by the end of the month I can barely speak, let alone write, it's like all the brainpower's been used up.

What was the best money you ever spent as an author?

Getting my own business card with 'writer' on it. It made me believe that I was really, truly, a writer.

What would you choose as your daemon (an animal representing your spirit, from Philip Pullman's books)?

My favourite description of myself was by my father, who said he'd never seen anybody get so much done while giving the impression of lying on the sofa all day. So maybe a cosy soft sloth (I love sloths) who secretly turns into a cheetah when there's work to do.

What do you owe the real people on whom you base your characters?

I owe them good quality research, to find out everything I can about them.

Where the historical record has gaps, then I owe myself and my readers a good story, one which I hope reflects the character and their life. Sometimes my characters, although they are a real person, contain composite elements of other people in the same situation, mostly lost to history. For example, with Ula Nara in *The Cold Palace*, perhaps she didn't have a childhood sweetheart, but I imagine a lot of the girls chosen as concubines between the age of thirteen and sixteen did in fact have someone they were in love with and were taken away from. There wasn't enough information to explain why she 'went mad,' so I spent a lot of time thinking about all the aspects of the Forbidden City that might cause someone distress and depression. There were a lot of them. So perhaps they weren't all correct, but I'm sure many of them contributed to her state of mind and the state of mind of many concubines over the centuries. And I hope that any book I write makes the reader go and check out the history for themselves, that's the best thing I can give to the people from the past.

How do you do your research and how long does it take?
Maybe 3 to 6 months at the start, followed by little bits of additional research as I write. I always start from a position of absolute ignorance, so I have to learn everything, which I find very exciting. I start with children's reference books because they tell you what people ate for breakfast, what underwear they wore and how the toilets worked. That's really important to me. Then I start building up my knowledge as I realise what I need to know and start to make lists of what I need. My book collection grows pretty vast during a series, and I build up TV documentaries and pages and pages of notes and articles as well. I go on research trips and also do more hands-on research, like making food from that era or lighting an oil lamp. Sometimes it's only by doing something that you realise a minor detail. I once watched a gladiatorial combat by a re-enactment group on real sand and suddenly realised that the oil and sweat on the bodies of the gladiators would mean the sand would stick to them. No book tells you that. Books for grown-ups tend to focus on the large-scale politics, the grand sweep of history. But I need to know what my characters do when they wake up in the morning, how they eat, what they wear, what kind of bed they sleep in and the work they do. It's fascinating, I love doing research.

Do you work from research notes when you write?
Not really. By the time I've done all my research a lot of it is embedded: I

know what clothes they wear and the food they eat, I know the shape of the story, so I only have to look up the odd detail.

How do you select character names?

Some names are on the historical record, like Zaynab. Quite often I have to make a decision on how to use the names on record. The concubines in the Forbidden City only had their clan names recorded. Rather than make names up for them, I used these clan names as their first names. A lot of the Moroccan names involved the word Abu at the start, which means 'father of' and would refer to their sons, but I used them as they were even when the characters were children because their childhood names were lost to us. Sometimes the names are available but completely unusable for my purposes. The Kangxi Emperor had thirty-five sons, all of whose names began with Yong. This would have made things impossible for my readers. So, I chose to focus on only a few of the sons and used their princely titles instead. When I am free to choose, I will gather names that I think are appropriate to that culture and era and choose from them. Partly based on the sound of the name, partly on what the names mean. Sometimes I have to take into account other names in the book, it doesn't help the reader if everybody's names begin with the same letter, for example. Many traditional female Berber names begin with a T, and I had to pick my way through them so as not to cause confusion. The Roman naming system is very complicated, I'm still grappling with understanding it!

Do you read your reviews?

Yes, every one. There is nothing more special than reading that someone missed their bus stop or stayed up late to read just another chapter of your book, it makes me so happy. Occasionally the reviews aren't as good, but I take on board the comments if I can, for future books. I'm always grateful to any reader who takes the time to share their thoughts on my books, it helps my stories find new readers and that's a precious gift to a writer.

Do you hide any secrets in your books that only a few people would spot?

They're not really secrets, but I notice that many animals and my own pets have made an appearance over the years. Thiyya, the white camel in *A String of Silver Beads*, came about because of my research trip to Morocco, where I rode camels and really liked their rather grumpy characters. In *The Cold*

Palace, my mother laughed when she read the description of the two dogs in the snow in the first chapter, they were based on two small pet dogs of our own, one who used to tunnel through the snow and the other who used to leap through it like a dolphin. There's also a kitten who belongs to the fragrant concubine, who fights snakes, and that was based on a cat we had, whose fights with snakes were absolutely terrifying to us as children. The cat won every time, though.

What is the most difficult part of the writing process?
Moving from the first draft to the final draft. It's your last chance to make sure you said what you wanted to say, that the readers will receive the story you wanted to tell.

How do you choose covers?
I spend a lot of time looking at the woman who is to appear on the front cover. It's strange how you can see pictures that theoretically are fine, but the person just doesn't look the way you imagined them. When I find the right person, I get very excited.

Do you have any advice for new writers?
Your writing naturally gets better the more you write. So write lots. And it draws on what you read, so read lots: it helps your unconscious mind understand storytelling structure. Tell the stories you want to tell, don't try to follow trends, you'll never keep up.

Current and forthcoming books include:

Historical Fiction
China
The Consorts (free on Amazon)
The Fragrant Concubine
The Garden of Perfect Brightness
The Cold Palace

Morocco
The Cup (free on my website)
A String of Silver Beads
None Such as She
Do Not Awaken Love

Ancient Rome
From the Ashes
Beneath the Waves
On Bloodied Ground
The Flight of Birds

Picture Books for Children
Kameko and the Monkey-King

Non-Fiction
The Storytelling Entrepreneur
Merchandise for Authors
The Happy Commuter
100 Things to Do while Breastfeeding

Biography

I mainly write historical fiction and have completed two series: The Moroccan Empire, set in 11th century Morocco and Spain and The Forbidden City, set in 18th century China. My next series will focus on the 'backstage team' of the Colosseum (Flavian Amphitheatre) set in 80AD in ancient Rome. For more information, visit my website www.melissaaddey.com

I was the 2016 Leverhulme Trust Writer in Residence at the British Library and winner of the 2019 Novel London award. I have a PhD in Creative Writing from the University of Surrey. I enjoy teaching and run regular writing workshops at the British Library and at writing festivals.

I live in London with my husband and two children.

CPSIA information can be obtained
at www.ICGtesting.com
Printed in the USA
LVHW042250160822
726102LV00001B/105

9 781910 940761